Acclaim for

FLAS

'Cleverly crafted crime story from an exciting new writer . . . frightening . . . gutsy' – *Daily Mail*

'Frissons of psychological terror . . . Sonora is a lively and sympathetic addition to the ranks of fictional female coppery' – *The Times*

'A powerful original book . . . Like all the best thrillers, *Flashpoint* leaves you uneasily aware of shadows, especially those that start at your own feet' – Reginald Hill

Acclaim for Lynn Hightower

EYESHOT

'Suspenseful and psychologically sound, with a fierce, frazzled quality to the writing which gives it edge and credibility. With her second novel, Hightower gives notice she's here to stay. Astonishingly good' –
Philip Oakes in the *Literary Review*

'Hightower has invented a heroine who is both flawed and likeable, and she knows how to keep the psychological pressure turned up high' – *Sunday Telegraph*

Acclaim for Lynn Hightower

NO GOOD DEED

'Genuinely fresh and exciting' – Observer

'A cracking tale told at a stunning pace . . . the characterisation is great, the suspects are 10 a dollar and the dialogue worth a million' – Frances Fyfield, *The Mail on Sunday*

'Sharp, shocking and shamelessly satisfying' – Val McDermid, *Manchester Evening News*

THE DEBT COLLECTOR

'Authentic and satisfying' – *Publishing News*

'Well-written and satisfyingly plotted. Best of all is Sonora herself – a feisty babe who packs a red lipstick along with her gun' *The Times*

'Suspenseful and psychologically sound, with a fierce, frazzled quality to the writing which gives it edge and credibility. Astonishingly good' – *Literary Review*

By Lynn Hightower

Flashpoint
Eyeshot
No Good Deed
The Debt Collector

About the author

Lynn Hightower was born in Chattanooga, Tennessee and graduated in journalism from the University of Kentucky. She now lives in LA where she works full time writing fiction. She loves canoeing and horseback riding, and is witty after two glasses of wine. She is the author of four highly acclaimed Sonora Blair novels, all available in paperback from New English Library.

Flashpoint
Eyeshot

Lynn Hightower

NEW ENGLISH LIBRARY
Hodder & Stoughton

Flashpoint: Copyright © 1995 Lynn Hightower
Eyeshot: Copyright © 1996 Lynn Hightower

The right of Lynn Hightower to be identified as the Author of
the Work has been asserted by her in accordance with the
Copyright, Designs and Patents Act 1988.

Flashpoint first published in Great Britain in 1995
by Hodder and Stoughton
Eyeshot first published in Great Britain in 1996
by Hodder and Stoughton
A division of Hodder Headline

This edition first published in 2000 in Great Britain
by Hodder and Stoughton
A division of Hodder Headline

A New English Library Paperback

10 9 8 7 6 5 4 3 2 1

All rights reserved. No part of this publication may be
reproduced, stored in a retrieval system, or transmitted,
in any form or by any means without the prior written
permission of the publisher, nor be otherwise circulated
in any form of binding or cover other than that in which
it is published and without a similar condition being
imposed on the subsequent purchaser.

All characters in this publication are fictitious and any resemblance to
real persons, living or dead, is purely coincidental.

ISBN 0 340 79405 4

Printed and bound in Great Britain by
Clays Ltd, St Ives plc

Hodder and Stoughton
A division of Hodder Headline
338 Euston Road
London NW1 3BH

Dedication

For Matt Bialer, world's best agent.

Acknowledgements

I had a lot of help on this one.

My thanks to Michael Miller, primary school teacher, for sharing insight and experience, and whose perception and wit made for an entertaining interview.

I was made very welcome by the Homicide and Crime Scene Units of the Cincinnati Police Department. My thanks to Police Specialist Mike O'Brien, who went out of his way to help and answer my questions, and to Police Specialist Jim Murray, Police Specialist Diane Arnold, Community Services Police Specialist Kim Moreno, and Police Chief Michael Snowden.

My sincere thanks to Detective Maria Neal, of the Lexington Police Department's Bureau of Investigation. She went out of her way to answer my questions and share insight and expertise.

My thanks to Dr. George Nichols, of the Louisville coroner's office, for putting up with my fascination with and questions about his work. I did appreciate your time and trouble.

To Detective David A. Green, of the Jefferson County Police Department's Arson Unit, even if you did say you'd be keeping an eye on me. And to Arson Investigator Gary Nolan.

To my favorite lawyer, Jim Lyon, who never tires of my constant questions, scenarios, and what-ifs.

To another favorite lawyer, C. William Swinford, who was kind to me, and represented me well.

To talented artist and good pal Steve Sawyer, for insight, discussions, and good coffee.

To Anthony Smallwood, world's best dancer, who helped Sonora with her two-step.

To Ron Balcom, of Balcom Investigative Services, for early research and last minute questions.

To my good buddy and fellow mystery writer, Taylor McCafferty, who is always up for forensic 'girltalk,' and a trip to the morgue on our way to lunch. My phone bills are your fault.

To Carolyn Marino, my terrific editor, whose judgement and instinct are always dead on, and who is a pleasure to work with.

My thanks to Allstate agent Rebecca Turner, Jonathan Edwards, Jonathan Amherst, and Physician's Assistant Lynn Hanna, who always wants to know if I'm mad at anybody before she gives me technical details on anything medical and violent.

And to my agent Matt Bialer, who told me to write this book, and didn't let up till I got it right.

FLASHPOINT

Flashpoint: the temperature at which vapour from a flammable substance will ignite.

World Book Dictionary, V.1

Chapter One

Sonora was not asleep when the call came in. She was curled sideways, a blanket over her head, vaguely aware of the wind blowing the phone cables in tandem against the back wall of the house. She caught the bedside phone on the second ring, thinking it was going to be a bad one. This time of night, people meant business.

'Homicide. Blair.'

'Blair, you always answer your phone like you're at work?'

'Only when it's you, Sergeant. Anyway, Sam's on call, not me.' She rubbed the back of her neck. Her head ached.

There was a pause. 'You're catching it together. It's a nasty one, Sonora. Guy burned up in his car.'

Sonora turned on the bedside lamp. The bulb flared and went out. 'Sounds like insurance fraud getting out of hand. Why not let arson catch it?'

'Arson called us. Vic, name of Daniels, Mark, handcuffed to the steering wheel of his car, and doused with accelerant.'

Sonora winced. 'Sounds pointed. Where?'

'Mt. Airy Forest. Couple miles in, be a uniform there to direct. Delarosa's headed out to the scene now, EAT four-fifty.'

Sonora looked at her watch. Four-twenty AM.

'Vic's still alive, unconscious, but he may come to, and if so, it might not be for long. He's over at University, which is where I want you. See if he comes around any, maybe even get a death bed statement. Could be a gay thing, you know? Those are the usual ones in the park, week nights this time of year. Get him to spill who done it. Any luck, we can clear the books by morning.'

'It is morning.'

'Do it right, Blair.'

Sonora dressed quickly – sliding on a pair of black cotton trousers that satisfied the dress code, barely. She ran a pick through the tangles of her hair, took a glance in the mirror, and gave up. Too curly, too slept on. Definitely a bad hair day. She gathered the ends back and slipped them through a black velvet band. Her eyes were dark shadowed and red rimmed. She wished she had a moment for the miracle of makeup, but if Daniels was just hanging on, she didn't have time. And he wasn't likely to complain.

She turned on the hall light and peeped in at the kids. Both sleeping soundly. She maneuvered through the maze of laundry, clean and dirty, filed on the floor in an obscure system only her son understood. He was sleeping at the wrong end of the bed, a booklet on *ADVANCED DUNGEONS AND DRAGONS* splayed on the pillow.

'Tim?'

His eyes flickered open, then closed. Asleep, he looked younger than thirteen, fine black hair cropped short.

'Come on, Tim, wake up.'

He sat up suddenly, eyes wide and confused.

'Got to go to work, hon, sorry. I'll leave you locked up, but keep an ear out for your sister, okay?'

He nodded, blinking painfully, too young and too tired to be wakened in the middle of the night.

'What time is it?' he said.

'After four. You got a while to sleep. Be sure and get up with the alarm. You'll have to get Heather off to school.'

''kay. Be careful, Mom. Load your gun.' He slumped

back down on the bed, turning his back on the bright shaft of light from the hallway.

Sonora left his door open and went to her daughter's bedroom. An explosion of nude Barbie dolls, some of them headless, littered the dingy yellow carpet. Sonora made her way to the bed, noting the neat pile of clothes and shoes carefully laid out in the stuffed animal bin. It was September, just a few weeks into the school year, and the excitement of first grade had yet to wear off.

A reddish-blond dog groaned and lifted his head from the pillow where he'd been sleeping next to the tiny, black-haired girl. He was a big dog, three legged, thick fur coat, wise brown eyes.

Sonora patted his head. 'Guard, Clampett.'

The dog wagged his tail. Sonora noticed three cotton hair holders beside her daughter's lavender tennis shoes. That meant braids, only Mommy wouldn't be around to fix them.

Sonora grimaced. 'Thank you, I *will* have some guilt with my homicide.'

She kissed her daughter's soft plump cheek, double checked the house locks and alarms, and left.

It was raining again, softly now, the windshield wipers doing a second-rate job. Sonora squinted through the fogged windshield and winced at the glare of headlights on the rain-slick road. Her night vision wasn't what it should be.

University Hospital was nestled amid scaffolding, piles of dirt, stacks of lumber. Health care, at least, was booming. Sonora passed a sign that said Mesner Construction.

The emergency entrance was brightly lit, two ambulances parked under the overhang, a smattering of patrol cars in the circle drive. The parking structure was dark. Sonora scraped by the ambulances and parked on the side of the road. She reached into the glove compartment for a flowered tie that didn't exactly match her shirt, but at least didn't clash, slid the loosely knotted loop over her head, and tucked the back band under the collar of her tailored shirt. The blazer lying on the back seat was wrinkled, but Sonora decided it would pass. She locked her car.

Inside, the air was thick with the smell of hospital and damp cops, both overlaid with a tangible odor of smoke. The muted crackle and mutter of too many police radios was punctuated by the ding of very slow elevators. An ambulance crew was bringing a stretcher through, and Sonora stepped sideways, moving away from the path of a medic holding an IV packet. A trail of blood droplets marked their route.

Sonora's vision blurred and she stopped for a minute to rub her eyes.

'Specialist Blair?'

The patrolman at her elbow couldn't have been more than twenty-two or twenty-three. His uniform was stained with sweat and soot.

'I'm Finch. Captain Burke said I should check in with you. I responded to the scene right after Kyle. He's burned pretty bad.'

'Kyle?'

'Kyle Minner, Officer Minner. He got there just before I did.'

Sonora put a hand on his arm. 'You see anybody? Hear a car pull away?'

The patrolman swallowed. 'Don't know. It was . . . the guy was screaming and his hair was burning. I didn't see anything but him.'

'Okay, you did good. You hurt?'

'No ma'am.'

'How bad's Minner?'

Finch swallowed. 'I don't know.'

'I'll ask after him and let you know. What can you tell me about the vic? Daniels, right?'

'Car's registered to a Keaton Daniels, victim is his brother, Mark. College student, twenty-two years old, lives in Kentucky. Up for a visit. Evidently borrowed his brother's car.'

'So what happened?'

'Dispatch got an anonymous call from somebody in the park. Said something funny was going on. I thought it was teenagers parking or something. By the time I got there it was burning good. The guy was screaming, sounding, God, unreal. Minner was working at that park station, typing up a report, so he's like a minute away. So he's there ahead of me, grabbing the door handle of the car. He jerks his hands back and the skin comes right off 'em. Then he reaches in through the driver's window and grabs the guy, and starts pulling him out. But it . . . he . . . Minner yells something about handcuffs. He told me before the ambulance came, this guy Daniels was handcuffed to the steering wheel. Anyway, Officer Minner disengages Daniels from the cuffs— '

'*Disengages* Daniels from the cuffs?'

Finches' eyes seemed glittery. 'Guys hands are almost burned off. It's like he snagged for a minute, then slid right on through.'

Sonora squinted her eyes.

'It was the only way, the only chance of getting him out of there. So he's burning, Minner's burning, they're rolling. I've got my jacket on, so I throw it over the both of them and smother the flames.'

'You sure you're okay?'

'Just singed my eyebrows a little. Minner's really hurt. And the vic, Daniels, he's charred.'

'Did you ride over with them in the ambulance?'

'Yes ma'am.'

'He say anything?'

'He was out. But he was screaming when I got there. Sounded like "key" or something.'

'Key?'

Finch shrugged.

'That's all?'

The patrolman nodded.

'You did good,' Sonora told him. 'You want to go home?'

'I'd like to stay around and see how Kyle's doing. I'm also supposed to tell you that O'Connor brought in Daniels' next of kin. The brother.' Minner inclined his head toward a man who stood in the shadows of the hallway, watching them.

Sonora had an impression of height, solid presence, a face pale under heavy five o'clock shadow.

'Anybody talked to a doctor?'

'Guy came out of emergency and talked to the brother.'

'Hear what he said?'

'Just that they were very concerned with Mark's condition, and were doing all they could.'

'Shit. Daniels won't make it then. They're already hanging the crepe.'

'Ma'am?'

'Never mind. Get somebody to take the brother a cup of coffee, looks like he could use it. Have one yourself.' Sonora headed past the plastic couches and went through the swing doors into emergency.

Chapter Two

Inside the ER, the lights were bright enough to be energizing. Sonora spotted a black woman in blue cotton pants and top, hospital issue, her hair back in a cap, feet encased in plastic booties.

'Gracie! Just the woman I want.'

'You here about the burn guy?' Gracie took Sonora's arm and pulled her out of the way of a technician rolling an IV pole.

'How's he doing?'

Gracie pointed to a cubicle, white curtains billowing with movement. 'They called Farrow over from Shriners. Should be here any minute, but even that may be too late. ET gave him thiosulfate to detox, but his blood gases are the worst. He's on the respirator – he won't be talking to you.'

'Yes or no questions?'

Gracie narrowed her eyes. 'He's conscious. Give it a try.'

She led Sonora past a man pushing a steel cart that seemed to be extraordinarily heavy. They went in from the side, where the curtains split. Sonora frowned. The ER doctor was Malden. Malden didn't like her.

'Okay?' she asked.

He gave her barely a glance, but didn't say no. She hung over Gracie's shoulder.

Mark Daniels was conscious, which, Sonora thought, as they worked him over, was her good luck and his bad. She saw death in his eyes. She was vaguely aware of the doctors and technicians, hands busy as they invaded Daniels with the nightmare of medical technology. The air was thick with the smell of smoke and the sound of jargon – hypovolemic shock, Ringer's solution, central venous pressure. Someone was gauging the extent of the burns – eighteen percent, anterior trunk – the tally continued. Hypothermia, body temp 78 degrees. Cardiac arrhythmia. Auscultate the lungs.

Daniels' scalp was white and hairless, with a look of pliability that contrasted with the charred and inelastic surface of his chest, arms and neck. His face was ravaged, the lips melted and smeared. One eye was black-socketed and the right ear had the crumpled look of charred foil.

Nothing left of the right hand. Sonora saw the whiteness of bone. The left hand had a blackened lump of flesh at the end, like an infant's curled fist.

Sonora turned on her recorder. 'Mr. Daniels, I'm Specialist Sonora Blair, Cincinnati Police.'

He moved his head. She said it again, and connected suddenly with the good eye. He focused on her face, and Sonora had the odd sensation that she and Daniels were worlds away from the doctors, the technicians, the bright, intrusive lights.

'I'm going to ask you some questions about your assailant. Mr. Daniels? Shake your head yes or no. Okay? You with me here?'

He nodded his head, smearing stickiness on the white sheet. The thick tube of the respirator parted the melted lips, expanded and deflated the scorched lungs.

'Did . . . do you know your assailant?'

Daniels did not respond, but his eyes were locked with hers. He was thinking. He nodded, finally.

'Had you known him long?'

Daniels shook his head.

'Not long?'

He shook his head. Kept shaking it.

'Met him tonight?'

Nodded his head, then turned it from side to side. Sonora wondered if he was connecting. But the awareness was there, in the eyes. Something he was trying to tell her. She frowned, thought about it.

Ground zero, she thought. 'Man or woman. Mr. Daniels was your assailant a man?'

The head shake. Vigorous. Not a man.

Wife, Sonora thought. Ex-wife. Girlfriend.

'Your assailant was a woman?'

Sonora stepped to one side, out of the doctor's way. But she caught his response. 'Witness indicates the assailant was a woman,' she said for the benefit of the recorder. 'Someone you know?'

Back to that again. No.

'Wife?' No. 'Girlfriend?' No. 'Just pick her up tonight?'

That was it. A stranger.

He was fading on her. 'Young?' she asked. 'Under thirty?'

He focused again, aware and intent, in spite of the chaos of the ER, the sensory overload. Sonora had a sudden strong feeling that he wanted her to touch him.

She was afraid to. Afraid she would cause pain, infection, the wrath of the doctors.

Sonora tried to remember the rest of her questions. Daniels watched her, his eyes large and lidless. The fire had stripped him to almost embryonic form.

Sonora laid two fingers on the blackened flesh of his arm and thought she saw some kind of acknowledgement in his eyes. Likely her imagination.

Questions, she thought. Get this man's killer.

'Young?' she asked again. 'Under thirty?'

He hesitated. Nodded.

'Black?'

No.

'White?'

Yes.
'Prostitute?'
Hesitation. No.
Young. White. Not a prostitute. Maybe.
'Black hair?'
No.
'Blonde?'
Yes. Definite.
'Eyes,' Sonora said. 'Blue?'
He was going on her.
'Brown?'
Something about him changed. An alarm went off, the doctor shouted clear. Sonora stepped away from the table, and ducked out from under the white curtains. She knew without looking that the EKG monitor would be flat.

Chapter Three

Officer Finch stood in a hushed circle of uniformed cops, telling and retelling his story, answering questions. Sonora paused, but kept walking. Talking would be therapeutic, at least, and Finch was young to be wracking up nightmares. They seemed to be hiring them right out of the nursery.

There'd be no playing it close on this one. The cops wouldn't talk to civilians, but the hospital people would. They were the worst, even ahead of lawyers. Putting something in a medical record was worse than telling Oprah and Phil, though not as bad as faxing Geraldo.

'Specialist Blair!'

Sonora glanced sideways. Channel 81's Tracy Vandemeer moved close, trailed by cameras. No other press around. At the crime scene, Sonora thought. It was where she wanted to be. She waved a repressive hand at the camera.

'Tracy, you're way too early here. Not before makeup, please.'

Tracy Vandemeer blinked. She herself had had ample time, though less reason, to do her own makeup. She wore a crisp red blouse, silk, and a high waisted lycra skirt that could only be worn by a woman who was a stranger to childbirth and chocolate.

'Specialist Blair, can you give us the identity of the— '

'Come on, Tracy, you know better. We'll have the release out in a few hours. Any questions have to go through my sergeant.'

Vandemeer smiled. 'Come on, Sonora. I've got deadlines.'

'Going to interrupt the farm report with a special bulletin?'

Vandemeer's smile faded and Sonora remembered a beat too late that Tracy had started out on the six AM broadcast, covering burley and corn crops.

'For that remark, Sonora, we'll be filming you from your bad side.'

'What? Me walking in and out of the ER is news?'

'It is if you don't give me anything else.'

'Homicide cop forgets to brush hair. Don't forget to call CNN.'

Tracy Vandemeer let the microphone relax, eyes roving, surveying the huddle of cops in the corner. Sonora took advantage of the lapse of attention to move away. Vandemeer would have no luck with the boys' club.

Sonora scanned the room, looking for hospital security. Saw the brother, shoulder against the wall in the hallway. It struck her that hers was the last face Mark Daniels had seen.

Daniels took a sip from a cup of coffee, his free hand jammed deeply into the pocket of his coat. Moisture glistened on the navy blue raincoat that hung open and unbuttoned, the cloth belt trailing the floor. Behind him, a door stood open. The sign on the door said FAMILY CONSULTATION/CHAPLAIN.

Sonora looked him over carefully as she drew close, checking for tears in the white dress shirt, soot on the shoes and beige khakis. She took a breath, wondering if he'd reek of smoke. He didn't. But she wished he'd lose the raincoat. No telling what might be under it.

Sonora smiled and put on the mom-voice. 'Your coat's wet. Probably ought to get it off.'

The man's eyes were glazed, but they focused on her suddenly, intensely. He had a raw, pained look she knew only too well. It was a look that begged for a miracle, for peace of heart. It was a look she saw in her dreams.

'Your coat?'

He took it off slowly and draped it over his arm. The white cotton shirt was wrinkled but clean. If this guy was involved with the killing he'd had time to change clothes.

No stone unturned, Sonora thought. She held out a hand.

'Specialist Sonora Blair, Cincinnati Police Department.'

He met her eyes steadily and took her hand, holding tightly. He had brown eyes and he looked intelligent, younger than she had first supposed. He had black hair, thick and curly.

'Keaton Daniels.'

Keaton, Sonora thought. Key? Mark had been screaming 'key' when Officer Minner had pulled him from the burning car.

'How is Mark?'

His voice was deep, shadowed with fear. He still had her hand, though she didn't think he realized it. The automatic doors swooshed opened, and Sonora glanced over her shoulder.

Another news team, idling in the restricted lane out front, a guy in blue jeans and an old army jacket arguing with a uniform.

Sonora guided Daniels into the consultation room.

Inside was an oasis of worn green carpet, a brown vinyl loveseat, and a well-padded easy chair. Sonora steered Daniels into the chair, for her money, the best seat in the house for comfort and a moment of peace.

'Sit down, Mr. Daniels. Be back in a minute.'

She slipped into the hallway and motioned to a uniform, checking his name tag.

'O'Connor? Looks like you got plenty of help out here.' She waved a hand toward the lobby. 'Channel 26 just arrived in their action Pinto, and there's never just one ant at the picnic. Keep them *in* the waiting room. I don't want anybody sneaking into the ER. Tracy and her bunch are okay, but watch the cameraman from 26. See that guy over there in the suit? Norris Weber, hospital security. Used to be one of us, retired. Coordinate with him. Victim's brother is in the consultation room – I don't want him bothered. Got all that?'

'Yes ma'am.'

'Thank God for you.'

Sonora headed back toward the ER to double check with Gracie. It would be unkind to break the bad news to Keaton Daniels, if his brother had been revived.

The door to the consultation room was shut. Sonora paused to put a fresh tape in her recorder, then pushed the door open gently.

Keaton Daniels sat on the edge of the easy chair. He'd put the raincoat back on, though it was hot in the tiny room.

'Mr. Daniels?'

'Yes?' His look managed to be both wary and stunned.

'Sorry, didn't mean to leave you quite so long.'

'How's Mark? Any chance of me getting to see him?'

The vinyl loveseat made squeaking noises as Sonora sat down. Her knees touched Daniels' and she moved to one side. She checked his left hand. Wedding band.

'Is there someone I can call to be with you? Your wife?'

Keaton Daniels looked away suddenly, his eyes on the floor. 'No, thank you.'

'A friend maybe?'

Keaton looked at her. 'My wife and I are separated. I can call a friend later.'

Sonora nodded, and leaned toward him.

'Are you a detective?' he asked suddenly.

'Yes.'

'I thought my brother was in a car accident. You – when you introduced yourself, you said specialist.'

'Specialist is the current jargon – a union thing. I'm a homicide detective, Mr. Daniels. They call me for any suspicious dea . . . circumstances.'

He swallowed. 'Suspicious— '

'I'm very sorry to have to tell you that your brother Mark is dead.'

He had known it was coming, but still he was stunned. His shoulders sagged, and he cleared his throat. He fought it, but the tears would come. Sonora knew it. He knew it.

'Tell me.' The words were an effort. He caught his lip between his teeth. 'Tell me what happened.'

'We're still trying to piece it together. The police and the fire department were dispatched to a burning vehicle. Your brother was inside. We think the fire was deliberately set.'

Keaton Daniels looked at her. A peculiar, puzzled look. The tears came, coursing down his rough, unshaven cheeks, his eyes going puffy and red.

Sonora touched his hand. 'Would you like some time? Can I call that friend?'

He shook his head slowly, and Sonora was reminded of Mark Daniels' white sluglike head trailing fluid across the sheet. She wondered what he'd looked like before – if he'd been handsome, like his brother.

'I need to ask you a few quick questions, the sooner the better. But if you need— '

'Go ahead.'

'You're sure?'

'Go ahead.'

A moment passed. Sonora fiddled with the recorder.

'Mr. Daniels, did you talk to Mark today? See him today?'

He clutched the knees of his pants. 'Yes. He's up visiting. We had supper. Then he dropped me off, and went back out.'

'Any idea where he went?'

'A place called Cujos. Cujos Cafe-Bar.'

'Up in the Mt. Adams area?'

'Yes.'

Sonora nodded. 'I know it. You didn't go with him?'

'I had to get some things put together for work. A lot of cutting and pasting stuff. Not hard, but time consuming. I offered to let Mark help me with it but he was . . . bored. And I was going to go to bed early anyway. I teach. I'm a teacher. So we had some supper and he decided to go on to Cujos and get a beer or something.'

'By himself?'

'Yes.'

'In your car?'

'He came up with a friend, someone from school. He's a student at the University of Kentucky. The friend dropped him off, and I was going to drive him home on the weekend. We were going to stop and see our mother.' He looked at the floor, then back up to Sonora. 'I need to call her, or should I wait till morning? Let her sleep?'

'Call her tonight. Otherwise she'll feel slighted. Unless – is she unwell?'

'Not exactly.'

Sonora was mildly interested, made a mental note to pursue it. 'This bar, this Cujos. Is it more a bar or more a cafe?'

'More bar.'

'You go there yourself?'

'Sometimes. For a while I was going there a lot. Then I stopped.'

'I'm not sure I follow.'

Daniels grimaced. 'My wife and I are separated. For a while, I was going out a lot at night. Bars and stuff. Cujos a lot. But that gets old. Plus, I really had to buckle down to my work. Hard to face the kids with a hangover every morning. Not to mention the expense, on a teacher's salary.'

'What age do you teach?'

'I teach a primary program. Grades one and two.'

'Elementary school?'

Her surprise annoyed him. 'That's where they teach grades one and two.'

Sonora let it pass. 'Where'd you go for dinner?'

'LaRosa's. We split a pizza.'

'Beer at dinner?'

Daniels narrowed his eyes. 'I had a Sprite. Mark had Dr. Pepper.'

'Any chance Mark was meeting up with some friends?'

'I don't think so. He didn't know anybody here.'

'How about the one that dropped him off?'

'On his way to Dayton, far as I know.'

'His? Male?'

'Yeah. Caldwell, Carter Caldwell.' He rubbed a hand over his jaw. 'Look, I don't understand this. Did something happen at the bar?'

'Mr. Daniels, at this point I just don't know. I know it sounds trite, but does you brother have any enemies? Bad enemies?'

'Enemies? Mark? He's a college kid, Detective. And a nice one. No drugs, no steroids. He liked to party— '

'Drink a lot?'

He shrugged. 'It's a stage. A lot of kids go through it.'

Sonora nodded, keeping her face noncommittal, notching possible alcohol problem in her mind.

'He was just a kid.' The tears flowed freely now. 'Twenty-two. He was too young and too sweet to have enemies.'

'Lot of girlfriends?'

'He has a girlfriend in Lexington. They've been steady now for two years.'

'She the only one?'

'Pretty much. Lots of friend girls, if you see what I mean. But not to date.'

'Popular?' Sonora asked.

Keaton Daniels nodded.

'Have you ever known him to pick up a girl in a bar?'

'No.'

'Come on, think about it.'

'I don't think so. Not here, in a strange town. He was twenty-two. And young for his age.'

'Your brother ever talked about going to a prostitute? Maybe joked about it? Asked your advice?'

The tears dried. Daniels sat forward in his seat.

'Just what's going on here?'

Sonora leaned back. 'Mr. Daniels, your brother was murdered tonight. I have to cover every angle, every possibility. Help me out on it.'

'How could he burn up in the car? Did it wreck or something? Was he unconscious?'

'Like I said, Mr. Daniels, we're still— '

'For God's sake, Detective.' His grip on her arm was firm to the point of being painful. He stood up and leaned over her, hands clenching the arms of the loveseat. 'What exactly did they . . . whoever this was. What did they do to him?'

'Mr.— '

'*Please*. Tell me something.'

She stood up, forcing him backward. He stayed close, his face no more than an inch from hers. Not going to give ground.

'Mr. Daniels, sit down, okay?'

She could smell the powdery scent of his bath soap, the coffee on his breath. They stayed eye to eye for a long moment.

'Please sit down, Mr. Daniels. I'll tell you everything that I can. I have a brother, okay?'

He sat back down, coat tightening across the broad shoulders.

Sonora sat across from him, laid a hand on his arm, felt him tremble. 'I don't have the details, I haven't been to the scene. Mark was found in your car in Mt. Airy Forest, handcuffed to the steering wheel. He'd been deliberately doused with accelerant and set on fire.'

'Sweet Jesus God.'
'Put your head between your knees.'
'I don't— '
'Humor me. Please.'

He resisted, just for a moment, then let her guide his head down.

Good going, Blair, she thought. Please explain to the sergeant how you managed to kill off the victim's brother.

'Okay?'

'Yeah, okay.'

He sat up slowly, leaned back in his seat. She looked at his face, chalk white.

'I need some time.'

'Of course.'

'Can I . . . Can I go home, to my wife's? For a while?'

'I'll have someone drive you.'

'Thanks.'

'Stay put. I'll get— '

Daniels got up slowly, hand against the wall for support.

'Steady,' Sonora said, and took his arm.

Chapter Four

It was daylight when Sonora left the hospital. The sky was still grimy but the rain had stopped. She was driving too fast and the tires on her Nissan sprayed water. She tapped the brakes as the car picked up speed moving down the steep hill. Sonora was vaguely aware she'd just squeaked through on a yellow light.

In her mind, she saw Mark Daniels, under the harsh lights and torturous ministrations of the ER.

It was foggy, and Sonora snapped on the headlights. Her radio sputtered the usual comforting background of static. She was never quite alone. She glanced at her watch, thinking that the kids would be waking up now, getting ready for school.

She turned right onto Colerain. A dark wall of trees lined the left-hand side of the road – Mt. Airy Forest. Sonora noted pedestrian entrances, street lights on Colerain, none in the forest. She passed St. Anthony's shrine. The main entrance to the forest was blocked by police cars. Sonora showed her ID and was waved past. The narrow two-lane road had dried in patches, giving the asphalt a speckled look.

Three wooden signs, the bottom one crooked, let her know that the speed limit was twenty-five, wheeled vehicles were restricted to paved road, and park hours were from six AM to ten PM. She was cautioned to watch for bicycles, warned not to park off the roadway, informed that the dog leash law was enforced.

Have fun, kids, Sonora thought.

She passed a battered trailer that was labeled TOOL SHED. The trees here were black oak, birch and beech. She saw a sign for Oak Ridge Lodge and knew she was getting close.

The Crime Scene Unit's van was half on the grass, half on the road. The guys – wearing blue jumpsuits, POLICE stenciled on the back, heavy fire boots on their feet – were giving it the once over. She parked behind the bronze department-issue Ford Taurus that she shared with her partner, fished in the glove compartment for new cassette tapes, notebook, investigation reports.

She liked to approach the scene on foot. Move in and focus. She wandered past the fire chief's wagon, the patrol cars. She thought of Mark Daniels. Why had he come out here? It was a long way from Cujos and trendy Mt. Adams. A longer way from Kentucky.

She put a new tape in the recorder as she walked, crumpling the cellophane wrapper and stuffing it into her jacket pocket.

How had the killer left the scene? On foot? Had she planned it well enough to have a car waiting? Did she have an accomplice? Where did she get the accelerant? What kind of woman handcuffed a twenty-two-year-old boy to a steering wheel and lit a match?

The CS technicians were well into the work, and Sonora, usually an hour ahead of the van, had the depressed feeling of someone who's missed the party.

She counted heads. Sergeant. Coroner. A lot of uniforms.

'Sonora?'

She climbed indelicately over the band of yellow tape, and headed for a broad-shouldered, solidly built man with dark, fine brown hair, side-parted, that fell into his eyes. The eyes were blue, with crinkles around the edges, caused in equal parts by laughter and worry. His complexion was swarthy, and he had a boyish look about him. People always thought he was younger than he was, and women tried to feed him.

He was the kind of guy who watched football games, the kind of guy you'd call if you heard a noise late at night – breathtakingly normal, in a world full of nuts. He and Sonora had been partners for five years.

'Hey, Sam.'

''Bout time you got out here, girl.'

'You smell like smoke.'

'You look like hell. How is he?'

Sonora grimaced.

'Dead, huh?'

She nodded. 'Twenty-two-year-old college kid from Kentucky. Your neck of the woods. Probably one of your cousins. You're all related down there, aren't you?'

'He talk to you?'

'Had to do it around a respirator. Yes or no questions.'

Sam nodded. Looking grim.

'Killer was a woman,' Sonora said.

'*No* shit?'

'Blonde, I think brown eyes, but he died on me there, so I'm not sure. Young, between twenty-five and thirty.'

'Prostitute?'

'Said not. If I got this straight, he met her last night. Probably in a bar. The brother said he was on his way to Cujos when they split.'

Sam frowned. 'Why'd they separate?'

'Brother had to go to work early.'

'Cujos, huh?'

'Place in Mt. Adams.'

'La de dah.'

'Hey. Not every bar has to be full of cowboys.'

'Don't let your brother hear you say that.'

Sonora gave him a half smile.

'Here, Mickey, give her the grand tour.'

A short man, arms thickly muscled, came out from under the blackened hood of the car. Sonora looked in the side window at the gutted interior of what used to be a Cutlass.

'Rolling fire trap, otherwise known as an automobile.' Mickey wore a blue jacket that said ARSON on the back, heavy fire boots on his feet.

Sonora took a speculative sniff. 'Know what the accelerant was?'

'Gasoline. We'll test it again in the lab. I got a sample.' He pointed to a charred piece of fabric under the gas pedal that had been peeled up, exposing ridges in the metal of the floorboard. 'Had some liquid accumulate, in the grooves there, so we can back it in court. Fire burned hot, and the explosion busted the windshield front and back.'

'Explosion?'

'Sure. Gasoline, right? Fire melted the glass. But everything inside's plastic, which means petroleum, which means inferno. Pretty good roast.'

'God. Is that what I smell?'

Sam said, 'Burnt flesh. Pretty distinctive.'

Sonora thought of the frozen sirloin tip in her freezer at home. Maybe it would stay there awhile.

Mickey moved to the front of the car, walking like it hurt. He'd been a fireman on the hose until he'd fallen in a hole fighting a fire after dark, slipping the disc in his back. Most of the firemen Sonora knew didn't get hurt fighting the fires, they just creamed their backs lugging equipment, or falling down in the dark.

Mickey pointed under the hood. His gloves were thick, soot stained.

'I double checked the fuel pump, carburetor, wiring. Pretty clear.'

Sonora wondered what was clear.

'Fan belt's burned, we got melted lead from the radiator.'

He looked up at her. 'I see under the hood fascinates you not.'

'It all fascinates me,' Sonora said.

'Don't take it personal. She looks grumpy because her tummy hurts,' Sam said.

Mickey rubbed his eye with the back of his arm. 'Still plenty of gas in the tank.'

'Didn't it burn in the fire?' Sonora said.

Sam grinned. 'I said the same thing.'

'Gasoline isn't all that flammable,' Mickey said. 'It's a stupid thing to set fires with. Volatile. Got to get the oxygen mix right and it can blow up in your face. Most of the arsonists I've seen who use gasoline usually blow themselves to pieces. On the other hand, you can throw a match in a puddle of gasoline and get nothing. There's better things to use.'

'Thanks for the tip,' Sonora said.

'Fire didn't really get to the tank. And unlike what you see on TV, the tank isn't necessarily going to explode. 'Less you're driving a Pinto or being filmed by NBC.'

'You think the killer could have used the gas in the tank to start the fire?'

'I'm saying it's a good possibility. Plenty of gas there. And thing is, we got melted plastic on the ground right by the gas tank. I'm thinking tubing for a siphon.'

Sonora looked at Sam.

Mickey waved a hand. 'Tell you what else. We got residue inside and ash outside of some kind of rope or clothesline.'

'Tell me you've got a knot.'

Sam shook his head. 'We don't got a knot.'

'Looks like he used it as a wick, lit it from outside the car, had it tied somewhere on the driver's side—'

'Tied to Daniels,' Sam said.

Mickey nodded. 'Makes sense.' He pointed to the melted

steering wheel. 'Fire started there. See the bulb in the overhead light?'

Sonora looked up. The bulb was miraculously intact. The bottom had melted to a point that aimed toward the driver's side. She stared at it a long moment, but Mickey was impatient, directing her attention to the mangled springs on the driver's side of the car.

'Point of origin. Burned the longest and hottest right there. See that?'

Two gnarled, fused loops of metal hung from the wadded steering wheel.

'Handcuffs, carbonized now.'

Sonora bit her lip. Thought of Mark Daniels' hands turned to ash, the gnarled infant fist, the white of bone.

'You sure enough to prove it to a jury?'

'Easy. You come to the scene and see what is. I see what was.'

'Everything on video?'

'S-O-P.'

Sonora looked at the mess of ash and foam in the front of the car. 'Too bad you guys always fuck up the scene.'

'Yeah, firefighters are such bastards. Think their job is to put the fire out.'

Sam put a cigarette in his mouth, studying the inside of the car with a quiet focus that worked wonders in the interrogation room as well as on women.

Sonora folded her arms, faced Mickey. 'By the way. You've been saying he. It's she.'

Mickey looked at her. 'A *woman* did this?'

'Surprised, huh?'

He shrugged. 'As I think about it, no. I been married long enough.'

Sam took the unlit cigarette from his mouth and rolled it between thick, callused fingers.

'Don't smoke in my crime scene,' Sonora said.

'*Your* crime scene? I haven't lit it, Sonora, I'm just

tasting the tobacco. There's the sergeant, looks like you're wanted, girl.'

'Wait a second. Terry?'

A woman in a jump suit came out of the brush, about a hundred yards from the car. She had long black hair, carelessly tied back, broad cheekbones that bespoke American Indian descent. She wore black-rimmed cat glasses, and moved in the kind of preoccupied absentminded fog that Sonora associated with college professors with research grants.

She looked at Sonora and blinked. 'Footprint.'

Sonora felt a twinge of excitement at the base of her spine. 'You have a footprint?'

Terry pushed her glasses up on her nose, leaving a streak of dirt on her forehead. 'Small though. A woman in high heels. Which is odd, out here in the woods. Was there anybody with this guy?'

'His killer,' Sonora said.

Chapter Five

Around the department they called Sergeant Crick the bulldog.

He crooked his finger at Sonora, crossed ham-like arms across a barrel chest – a Buddha with attitude. He leaned against his dark blue Dodge Aries, department issue, and he didn't look happy. He was built like a boxer gone to fat, his face seamy, red, and unpleasant enough that there was speculation that early in his career he'd been hit full in the face with a shovel. Rumor had it he worked in his church nursery whenever he had a Sunday free. People were known to wonder if he scared the babies.

Loosen your tie, Sonora thought. Your disposition will improve.

'Tell me you got a deathbed ID, Blair.' Crick's voice was deep, as expected from the look of him, surprisingly pleasant when he made the effort. In his off time, he sang in a barber shop quartet.

Sonora leaned against Sam. 'Killer was a woman, Caucasian, blonde hair, maybe brown eyes. Young, twenty-five to thirty. Someone Daniels met tonight. He was last seen heading to a bar called Cujos, according to his brother. The brother owns the car, by the way.'

'Has the brother's car, but the brother doesn't go with him? I don't like that.'

Sam stepped backward in mock surprise. 'Come on now, Sergeant. I've known guys that would kill their brother, but not if it meant trashing their car.'

Sonora continued, 'Terry has a footprint. Setting it in moulage as we speak.'

'Good.' Crick scratched the end of his nose. 'Cujos, huh? Stupid name for a bar.'

'Yes sir.'

'Delarosa?'

Sam straightened. 'Victim was handcuffed, naked, to the steering wheel of the car.'

'You sure he was naked?'

'The guys that pulled him out thought so. And I asked Mickey. No sign of burned fabric stuck to the seat. No belt buckle, grommets or burned rubber from shoes. I don't know where this guy's clothes are, but it doesn't look like they're in the car.'

'Interesting. Go on.'

'Fragments of rope or clothesline outside the car. Mickey thinks she tied him up, looped the rope or whatever through the steering wheel and around Daniels, then stood outside the car and got it going. Looks like the accelerant was gasoline – it's possible she got it from the tank of the car. He also said he found a small melted lump he thinks is a key. A small key.'

'Safe deposit box? Locker?'

Sam shrugged. 'Anything's possible.'

'Find the car keys?' Crick asked.

'Nothing yet. But the car is still full of hot spots and slush. So they may be there, just not in the obvious place.'

Sonora looked at Sam. 'She's not going to leave the keys in the ignition with him in the driver's seat. Even handcuffed, he might be able to get the engine going or something.'

Sam nodded. 'Anyway, she cuffs him to the wheel, ties the rope around his waist. Douses him with gasoline. The rope is about six feet out of the car, which is where she is, otherwise she's going to blow herself up. Windows are open, plenty of oxygen. She lights the end of the rope, so Daniels gets to sit in there and watch that fire coming at him. Then, boom, the car bursts into flame.'

Sonora scratched her chin. 'The footprint is small. Woman wearing high heels. So where did she go, in shoes like that? How fast could she move?'

'Maybe she changed them,' Sam said.

Sonora nodded. 'I wonder if her car was parked here. We need to search the park, do a neighborhood canvas.'

Crick was nodding. 'I've got uniforms in the woods and officers coming in.'

'Any witnesses?'

'Not a one. The call that came in was anonymous, guy used the pay phone at the front entrance.'

'Man or woman?' Sonora asked.

'Man.' Crick looked at her, then at Sam, and pulled the lobe of his ear. 'We'll get you manpower on this. I'll cover the canvas here. Get out to that bar, the two of you. Likely Daniels picked her up there.'

Sonora pursed her lips. 'Yeah, right. Next you'll be telling me he wore his jeans too tight, and had his shirt unbuttoned to his waist.'

'What's that supposed to mean?'

'Who picked up who, Sergeant? She's got handcuffs, rope, and, for my money, a getaway car. We're not talking date rape and revenge are we? This woman was looking for trouble. This woman was hunting *him*.'

Sonora winced. The ulcer said hello with a pain that was a little like hunger pangs, with an overlay of just pangs.

She looked at Sam. 'Leave my car here and you drive.'

Sam reached into his jacket pocket, pulled out an envelope of Red Man, and stuffed a wad of loose tobacco into his cheek.

'You look deformed when you do that. Like there's a tumor on your cheek.'

Sam shifted sideways in the driver's seat, dove back into

the jacket pocket, and came up with a crumpled cylinder of paper and cellophane that had pictures of tiny strawberries on the front. He pitched the packet into Sonora's lap.

'Feed your ulcer.'

'The less I eat the worse I feel, but the worse I feel the less I want.'

'You lost me there.' Sam started the car, did a U-turn, headed out of the park.

Sonora unpeeled the wrapper, stripped the dried fruit off the plastic and rolled it into a tube. 'Since when did you start eating fruit rollups?'

'I keep them for Annie, she loves 'em. Trying to see if I can get her to pick up a little weight.'

'I thought she'd added a pound or two, last time I saw her. That was what, two weeks ago?'

Sam didn't smile, but there was warmth in his eyes, as if he appreciated the effort. Annie at seven was small for her age, and thin enough to break her daddy's heart. She'd been diagnosed with leukemia a month after she'd started kindergarten, about the time Sam had been headfirst in a special investigation he only told Sonora about on stakeouts, or after several drinks. He hadn't played ball with somebody special, and he was going to have to like his rating exactly where it was. He'd never see another promotion. If Crick hadn't gone to bat for him, he'd have lost his job.

'So how is Annie?'

'Tires too easily. Shel's worried and so am I. She's dropping weight she can't afford, and her white blood count is up.' Sam spit tobacco out the window. 'No little girl should have circles under her eyes like Annie does.'

Sonora studied her partner, seeing new lines on the tired face. The last two years had been rough ones – trying to hold onto his job and his little girl.

'She's cranky as hell.'

'Annie? Or Shel?'

'Both. Eat your roll-up.'

Sonora wadded what was left of fruit, corn syrup, and mysterious chemicals into a chewy red ball. Sam eased the car to a stop, waiting at a red light, staring moodily out the window.

'Killer's a woman, huh?'

'Yeah, and it isn't her first time,' Sonora said.

Sam spit tobacco out the window, a stream of dirty brown juice. 'The patrol car must have just missed her. I wonder if they saw anything.'

'I talked to the guy who got there second. He didn't see anything but the fire. And the first guy – Minner. He was trying to pull Mark Daniels out of the car. But it's worth checking. He was still unconscious when I left the hospital.'

Sam looked at her. 'What do you mean, this isn't her first time? The killer?'

'Well planned, perfectly executed.'

'We just haven't poked in the holes.'

'So far so good, okay? Pretty bold, pretty efficient. We're not talking virgin killer, we're talking pro.'

'Like a hit?'

'Idiot. No, not like a hit. Like loving care. Like somebody who's enjoying what they do.'

'Like some kind of psychopathic serial killer.'

'Gosh no, I think some normal person burned Daniels up.'

'You said a woman.'

'Women can be serial killers.'

'Why sure, Sonora, I bet your mama raised you up to be anything you want. There are still about as many women serial killers as there are women CEOs.'

'You think there's some kind of glass ceiling for murderers? I'm putting it out on the system, Sam. See if there's been something similar, another jurisdiction.'

'I say we look at the brother and the wife.'

'No wife, but a girlfriend. The brother, no. I don't think so.'

'Okay, Sonora, consider the girlfriend. Or a prostitute. Think S & M, going a little too far.'

'I'll say. You know what worries me?'

'I know three things that worry you. Car repairs, college tuition, and orthodontists.'

'Those terrify me, I'm talking worry. About the case. I'd like it if Mickey found some melted lump and said car keys.'

'He might.'

'She took the clothes, she'd probably take the keys. Which means Keaton Daniels' keys. Car keys. Probably house keys.'

'What can she tell from a key?'

'She could have grabbed the car registration.'

'You might let the brother know.'

'I might at that. While I'm at it, I can warn him to leave the tight jeans at home and keep his shirt buttoned up.'

'I'm trying to remember if you were this bitchy before the ulcer.'

Chapter Six

They were halfway to Mt. Adams when Sonora's cellular phone rang.

'Bet Heather missed the bus,' she muttered. 'Hello? Hi, Shelly. You, Sam, your wife.'

He held his hand out.

Sonora glanced out the window. Wondered why two teenagers were walking so close behind an old man with a briefcase, and not in school. The man turned, suddenly, and told the kids to catch up.

Sam tromped the accelerator jerkily, then hit the brakes, barely pausing at a stop sign. 'No, Shelly, I wish I could, but we caught ourselves a hot one. Can you put her on?' His shoulders were tense, his voice tired. Someone honked; he didn't seem to notice. 'I see. I'm sorry. Tell her I love her and do what you can. She'll get through it.'

Sam handed Sonora the phone, and she pressed the end button because he always forgot to.

'What is it?' Sonora said.

'Doctor wants Annie back in for some tests and she's having hysterics. Blood work, needles, et cetera.'

'Sorry, Sam.'

'Shoot, last week when we drove by the hospital on the way to take her to see a movie? Honest to God, she threw up in the truck, just from the bad associations.'

Sonora looked out the window. 'You better go.'

'No chance.'

'I'll cover, Sam.'

'You've covered enough. We don't be careful, girl, we'll both be out of a job.'

Sonora chewed her lip. They'd been walking a fine line, the last eighteen months.

'Look, Sam, I want to talk to the brother before I go to the bar anyway. Get a picture of Mark, get a line on the girlfriend. You go to the hospital with Annie and get her settled in. She calms down the minute you walk in the room, you know that. Even if you have to leave her later, you go with her through that door.'

'I don't know.'

He did know, and she resented, just a little, having to do the old familiar nurture talk, but only just a little.

'Come on, Sam, Mark Daniels is dead, he'll keep. I'll drop you off at the house, and you can meet me later at Cujos.'

'Thanks, Sonora.'

'Yeah, yeah.'

Keaton Daniels hadn't answered his door when Sonora tried the Mt. Adams address, which was when she remembered he'd said something about his wife. She flipped through her notes. The other side of town, naturally.

She checked her machine on the way, got a message from Tim that Heather had gotten off to school okay and he was on his way. She worried about him, walking alone so early in the morning. Part of the daily ritual, that worry. In the afternoon, she would worry until the two of them made it home.

The mailbox said Mr. & Mrs. K. Daniels and there was a *For Sale* sign out front. Getting serious about the divorce, Sonora thought, if their house was on the block. There was no swing set in the backyard, no toys on the porch, no Halloween decorations in the window. No children. Just as well, if things weren't working out.

The house was small, a tiny three-bedroom ranch on a

postage stamp yard, much like her own house and not without charm. A lush fern hung in a basket by the front door, and a white wicker rocker sat on the tiny concrete porch. Sonora figured the rocker and the fern had a pre-stolen/vandalized life span of about six weeks.

The living room curtains were a gossamer film of fine white lace – lovely, but giving no privacy at all. The blinds in the bedrooms were tightly closed and the porch light was on.

Sonora rang the doorbell.

For a lonely moment nothing happened. She was debating ringing it again when she heard the snap of a deadbolt being released. The door made a cracking noise and swung open.

Sonora was surprised more often than not at how little outward change there was in people in trouble. You had to look carefully, sometimes, to see the signs. Keaton Daniels was showing the signs.

His shirt tail was out and he still wore the khakis – wrinkled now, like he'd slept in them. Thick white socks sagged and bunched around his ankles. He hadn't shaved. The slight childish fullness in his cheeks, which Sonora had found rather sweet, had somehow hollowed and sagged, making him seem older. All of thirty, perhaps.

He ran a hand through thick black hair, the kind of hair that looked good, even messy. Men were often lucky that way.

'I woke you up,' Sonora said.

'No, no.' He rubbed the back of his neck.

Sonora did not envy him the months ahead. She'd been there herself, when Zack died, dealing with the grief of her children. Heather had been just a toddler, and Tim had turned very quiet, asking, from time to time, why she did not cry, and if she really missed his daddy.

Sonora touched Keaton Daniels' shoulder. 'I'm sorry,

sleep's the best thing for you right now, and I hate to disturb you. But it's pretty urgent that we talk.'

'Come in, please. Sit down.'

He moved a rumpled blanket to one side of the couch and sat while she took the rattan rocking chair. He clasped his hands, letting them hang heavily between his knees. He seemed dulled, somehow. Muted.

'Mr. Daniels, I'm very sorry about the death of your brother.' She always said the words, and they always seemed inadequate. People appreciated it more often than not.

Daniels nodded, and his eyes reddened. Sonora wondered what he was like in real life, regretting, more than usual, that she had to meet him under harsh circumstances. It was the way she always met people.

Once in a while someone kept in touch, cards and such. Usually the parents of murdered children, grateful if they'd been shown tact, more grateful if the killer had been caught.

Daniels rubbed his face. 'Look, I bet you could use a cup of coffee.'

Sonora studied him. Not from Ohio, then, but somewhere farther south, though it didn't show up in his speech patterns. Otherwise he'd have said *I* need a cup of coffee. She had a sense of time slipping away, but knew from experience it was better not to hurry these interviews.

Daniels kicked over one of his shoes – tennis shoes, high tops, white with a grey swoosh. It knocked into a pile of other shoes – one more with a grey swoosh, a pair with red, and an odd one out, solid white. Sonora was reminded that Heather's shoes were getting tight, and that Tim would fight for Nikes, and promptly ruin them on the first muddy day. She saw Daniels watching her.

'Got enough tennies?' she asked.

He stretched. 'You have kids?'

'Two.'

'So you know that even in elementary school, they're very

brand conscious. If Mr. Daniels wears Reeboks, everybody wants Reeboks, and the kid with Nikes feels bad. Last year I taught at a different school, one in the city. A lot of my kids didn't get breakfast in the morning, their moms couldn't go out and buy brand name stuff. One kid in particular was catching hell from the others because his were from Kmart, so I went out and got a pair from Kmart. Next thing you know, half the class has shoes from Kmart. From then on, I started wearing about every brand there is. But I always start with Kmart.'

'I think you're very kind. And I wish you taught my son.'

Daniels smiled. 'Let me get you that coffee.'

Sonora leaned back in the rocking chair and closed her eyes. The bubble of a coffee maker starting up drifted comfortably in from the kitchen, the warm smell of coffee a comfort. Sonora let her head roll sideways, thinking how peaceful the Daniels' household was – no ringing phones, no arguing children, no hair-pulling chorus of video game theme songs, playing over and over again.

She wondered if Tim had helped Heather get the tangles out of her hair, and if her daughter had felt bad about not having Mom there to plait her hair into braids.

She caught herself, just before she drifted off to sleep, and was properly wide-eyed and alert when Keaton Daniels came back in the room. The flowered porcelain coffee cups looked delicate in his large hands.

'You look tired, Detective.'

'Not at all,' she said. He surprised her. Crime victims rarely noticed much beyond their own pain. She took a sip from her cup and gave him a second look.

He had gathered himself together, there in the kitchen. She was aware of a physical self-confidence, a maleness that made her wish it wasn't a bad hair day. And he was looking back at her in a steady way that made her nervous. She had the sudden urge to go sit beside him on the couch.

She knew certain male cops who would do exactly that if the witness was attractive and female.

Sonora scooted to the edge of the rocking chair. 'Mr. Daniels — '

'Keaton.'

'Keaton. Let's get this over with.'

His voice went dull. 'What do you want to know?'

'The last time you saw your brother. He dropped you off at your apartment and headed for Cujos Cafe-Bar.'

'Right.'

'What time was that?'

'About eight-thirty. Quarter to nine.'

'You never saw Mark after he left for Cujos? He didn't call or anything?'

'No. The phone rang once, but whoever it was hung up.'

Sonora frowned. 'You hear any background noises?'

'Yeah, there was some noise. People talking, like at a mall or — '

'Or a bar?'

He frowned. 'Could be. But if it had been Mark he would have said something. He wouldn't just call and listen.'

'You think he got cut off? Think back now, give me the whole thing. What were you doing?'

'I was on the floor in the living room, doing some cutouts and stuff. Catching the tail end of somebody or other on the comedy channel.' He squinted his eyes and looked up at the ceiling. 'So the phone rang and I said hello. And got nothing. But there were background noises from the line, so I thought maybe I didn't hear what they said. I turned the television down and said hello again. Then whoever it was hung up. Not Mark, because he wouldn't just breathe at me. Besides, I've been getting calls like this a while now, where they listen and hang up.'

'How often?'

'Every few days. Two or three times a month. Depends.'

'How long's this been going on?'

He glanced toward the bedrooms, where his wife was likely still asleep. 'Last few months, mainly at the townhouse. I'm subletting it from a friend who's in Germany on business. I figured it was kids or something.'

'Any reason to think your brother might have gone somewhere else after Cujos? Pub crawl kind of thing?'

'It's possible. Mark was restless and outgoing. He talked to people, made friends.'

'Girl friends?'

Daniels narrowed his eyes. 'You keep going back to that. You really think he picked up some girl?'

'His killer was a woman, Mr. Daniels. She had to come from somewhere.'

'That was why you asked me about prostitutes? Look, Mark wasn't some kind of sleazy jerk, Specialist Blair. He had a girlfriend in Lexington and they were committed. They were thinking about moving in together. Talking about getting married.'

'Were they engaged?'

'Nothing official. Mark talked about it, but he was only twenty-two. And her parents wanted her to wait till she was out of school.'

'Wise,' Sonora said absently. 'Okay, look, I'm going to ask you a question that's going to seem a little offensive. Get over it fast, think hard, and be very honest.'

Daniels pulled his bottom lip and frowned at her.

'Was your brother into any kind of unusual sexual practices? He have a lot of bruises, you know, more often than would seem average?'

'You have a nasty turn of mind, don't you?'

'Hazard of the profession, and I do have to ask. Your brother is still the victim here, I haven't forgotten that.'

He leaned back on the couch. 'It's not like I know everything 'bout my brother's sex life. You have a brother, you know what I mean. But I never saw any sign of anything

... anything like what you're saying. He didn't go to tough bars. He didn't date girls who wore lots of mascara and black leather and a leash around their neck. He read *Gentlemen's Quarterly* and *Playboy*.'

'For the articles.'

'For the foldouts. And he always bought the swimsuit issue of *Sports Illustrated*. I'd say my brother's reading material was pretty much normal, for a healthy American male.'

'American as apple pie.'

Daniels smiled at her, just a little one.

'What's as American as apple pie?'

Sonora hadn't heard the woman come in – the carpet had muted the sound of her high, spiky heels. She was the kind of female Sonora had always envied – naturally thin, brown eyes, thick, shiny auburn hair. The kind of woman for whom makeup was optional, who got the part in the school play.

Daniels stood up. 'Ashley. This is Police Specialist Sonora Blair. she's investigating Mark's . . . Mark's death.'

Sonora stood up and offered a hand. Ashley Daniels was dressed up – soft rose business suit, white stockings, high heels that Sonora knew she herself wouldn't last in for more than an hour.

She shook Sonora's hand firmly, then bent close to Keaton, trailing perfume and kissing him gently on the cheek. 'You all right, Keat?'

He patted her shoulder. 'Yeah.'

'I need to go down to the booth just a few minutes. I have to pick up a couple of files, make one or two calls, and then I'll be right back. Will you be okay?'

'I'm headed home anyway.'

'You sure?'

He nodded.

Sonora felt their awkwardness. Sort of married. Sort of not.

Ashley Daniels' voice turned cool. 'There's that car again. I hope it's somebody interested in the house.' She walked across the room, shifted the curtains to one side.

Sonora set her coffee cup on the end table and went to the window. 'What car?'

Ashley Daniels looked at her over one shoulder. 'Gone. Why?'

Sonora looked out at the street. Pavement, new sidewalk, baby grass on vulnerable, emerging lawns. No cars.

Ashley looked at Keaton. 'You want the rental car delivered here or at your place?'

'Here, I guess. Can you get it for me this morning?'

'Done. And I'll have your check in three days. There are some advantages to having an Allstate agent in the family.' Ashley smiled at Sonora, pulled a business card from her blazer pocket. 'I work out of a booth at Tri-County Mall. If you ever want a rate estimate, give me a call. Mostly I handle property and casualty – car insurance, homeowners. Life when I'm lucky.'

Sonora nodded, pocketed the card, watched Ashley Daniels go into the kitchen, heels clacking. She heard a garage door.

'Where were we?' Keaton said.

'You were telling me what kind of magazines your brother read.'

'More interesting than the ones I get. *Weekly Reader. Highlights For Children*.'

'For the foldout.'

'They have some great ones where you connect the dots.'

Sonora tilted her head to one side. 'Mr. Daniels, one thing I want to bring up. Our arson investigator couldn't find your brother's keys.'

'The car keys?'

'Yeah. What keys were on the ring?'

'Keys to this house. Keys to my apartment. My car and

Ashley's car, and my desk at school. They must have burned up.'

'Even so, he should have been able to find them. Melted, carbonized, they'd still be there.'

'And he'd be able to tell?'

'Reads fires scenes like you read *Highlights For Children*. It's possible the killer kept them.'

'You think it's something to worry about?'

She opened her arms. 'I'm not saying go overboard, but I don't like the killer having keys to your house. Just to be on the safe side, why don't you change your locks?'

'She won't know where I live, anyway.'

'Was there a registration in your car?'

'Yeah, sure.'

'There you go.'

'You really think — '

'I think it's a good precaution. Do it, why don't you? Getting robbed is no fun.'

'You think she'd rob my apartment?'

She thought robbery might be the least of his worries, but she didn't point it out. 'It's best to take precautions. Change your locks, Mr. Daniels.'

Chapter Seven

The only picture of Mark that Keaton Daniels had handy was a wedding picture he'd removed from a gilt-edged frame. Sonora had been reluctant to take it. The pose showed Keaton, sturdy and serious, with Mark on one side, and Ashley, radiant and beautiful, on the other. Mark looked young and smug, his elbow on Keaton's shoulder.

They did not look particularly alike, these brothers. Mark had light brown hair, fine and straight. His face was thin, chin pointed. His build was wiry in contrast to his brother's more solid mass. His eyes were blue.

Not a case of mistaken identity.

A closed sign hung in the window of Cujos Cafe-Bar, but the front door was unlocked. Sonora saw no sign of Sam, and didn't feel like waiting on the doorstep. She thought of Annie, tiny in a hospital bed. She would try to take Heather over for a visit.

The cafe was warm inside, divided into two main sections. The first was a bar, the second a small dining room with a nonsmoking sign over the frame.

The bar itself was beautiful but battered, the rich teak wood scuffed and gouged. The brass plate along the bottom needed polishing. The bar stools were high, but they had backs and armrests. Comfortable, Sonora thought, settling in. She studied the array of bottles grouped under the mirror that ran along the back.

The sight of so much alcohol so early in the morning

offended the ulcer, and Sonora checked her jacket pocket for a Mylanta tablet. She was frowning at an empty foil packet when she heard soft footsteps, and looked up to see a woman, short and stout like a fireplug, walk in from the dining room.

'Ma'am, I'm sorry, we don't open till noon.'

'Yeah, I figured there might be a reason the chairs were stacked up on the tables. Plus the closed sign was kind of a tip off.' Sonora opened the leather case that housed her ID, waited patiently while the woman looked the badge over carefully. The days when you could flash ID and not break stride were long gone.

'Detective Bear?'

'Blair,' Sonora said.

'Sorry, I don't have my reading glasses. What can I help you with?' The woman moved behind the counter, heading for a coffee pot. She'd have to stand on a stool to tend bar. 'Get you a cup?'

The ulcer had segued neatly from ache to nausea and Sonora grimaced. 'No thanks.' She heard a car engine, and spotted a pickup pulling up by the curb out front. Sam. She took the recorder out of her purse and laid it on the bartop.

'You work here, Ms. . . . ?'

'Anders. Celia Anders. I'm day manager.'

The bell over the front door jingled and Sam came into the bar. Sonora waved.

'Ms. Anders, this is my partner, Detective Delarosa.'

He nodded. Celia Anders smiled at him. She liked him, Sonora could tell, though all he'd done was walk through the door. Sonora looked at Sam in mild irritation.

'Ms. Anders, did you work last night?' Sonora asked.

Celia Anders looked at the recorder. 'No, I'm *day* manager. I go home at seven.'

'Who was here?'

'Let's see. Usually Ronnie seats people in the restaurant

part. And Chita tends bar. They own the place. Ronnie Knapp and Chita Childers.'

'Either of them around?' Sam asked.

'They're in the kitchen. At least, Chita was.'

'We'd like to talk to them,' Sonora said.

'What's this all about?'

Sonora smiled.

'Okay then,' Celia Anders said. 'I'll get 'em.'

Sonora glanced at her watch. Both Tim and Heather should be snug in school. Provided, of course, Heather's bus hadn't wrecked or been hijacked by terrorists, and some middle-aged man in a raincoat hadn't forced Tim into his nondescript brown car. Sonora sighed and Sam looked at her. He had an air of distraction that let her know he was upset. Annie was no doubt having a rough morning.

'Okay?'

He put a hand on her shoulder and squeezed. 'We got her settled.'

Sonora heard muted female voices, then a tall woman with a pure vanilla complexion and frizzy red-gold hair walked in, followed by Celia Anders. They looked remarkable, walking together, one tall, thin and confident, the other short and squat, shoulders hunched together as if she expected to be hit.

'Hi, I'm Chita Childers.'

Her voice was thin and she'd sing soprano. Her eyes were blue and her hair was long, pulled up on the sides with a silver and turquoise barette. She wore jeans and a Bengals tee shirt.

'I'm Sonora Blair, this is Sam Delarosa, Cincinnati police.'

'What did you want to see me about?' She looked over her shoulder. 'Ronnie!'

'I'm in the bathroom.' The voice was muted, male, irritable.

Sonora put the wedding picture on the counter.

'Do you recognize this man?'

Chita Childers squinted and stared down at the picture. 'Yeah, this one. He's here all the time.'

She stabbed a long skinny finger at Keaton Daniels. Her nails were long and coated with maroon polish. Glued in the corner of each squared-off nail was a tiny zircon, glinting like a diamond.

'*This* guy?'

'Yeah.'

'Was he in last night?'

Childers squeezed her eyes shut and tilted her head upward to aid her memory. So all the thoughts in the top of her head could slide into her brain, Sonora thought.

'No, I don't think so. He hasn't been in that much lately. For a while, he was here two or three nights a week. But.' She opened her eyes. 'Not last night.'

'What about the other one?'

'The woman?'

'Either.'

'The woman, I don't know. She's a type. Ronnie might remember.'

'And the guy?' Sonora pointed to Mark Daniels.

From somewhere close came the sound of a flushing toilet, the noise of running water, a door opening, closing. A man in his mid to late thirties, slender, thinning brown hair and a mustache, came in from the dining room. He stopped in the doorway.

'Oh.'

'Police Specialists Blair and Delarosa,' Sonora said. 'Didn't mean to catch you at a bad time.'

Knapp's cheeks went dusky red. Sam coughed and cleared his throat.

Knapp extended a hand to Sonora and gave her a firm, damp handshake. He glanced at Celia. 'We're out of paper towels in the bathroom, by the way.'

Sonora wiped her hands on the back of her jacket, and settled back down on the stool.

Sam scooted the picture across the bar. 'Mr. Knapp, did any of these people come in last night?'

Knapp picked up the picture and studied it. 'Last night, hmmm. That one didn't.'

Sonora rubbed her stomach. 'Which one?'

Knapp flipped the picture around and pointed to Keaton Daniels. 'This one. He used to come in a lot, but I haven't seen him lately. The other guy was here, though.'

'You sure?'

'Yeah. Talking to the blonde.'

Sonora felt rather than saw Sam tensing. She kept her voice casual. 'What blonde?'

'Just some girl.'

'She a regular?'

'Been in a few times.'

'What blonde is this?' Chita Childers asked.

'You've seen her. Kind of little. Delicate, sort of. Never smiles.'

'How long did she talk to this guy?' Sonora pointed to Mark's picture.

'A while.'

'Do you remember how long?'

'Not really.'

'An hour?'

'Maybe not that long.'

'Just a few minutes? Half an hour?'

'Longer than half an hour. Like maybe forty-five minutes. Like that. They had a drink together. She drinks Bud from the bottle.'

'What was he drinking?'

'Draft beer. Bourbon chaser.'

'Did they leave together?'

'No.'

'Who left first?'

'Don't know.'

'About what time?'

'Jeez, I really don't know. Before eleven.'

Chita Childers edged forward, and Celia Anders had to step backward. 'She must have left before he did, then. 'Cause this guy stayed late.'

'How late?' Sam said.

'Almost midnight. I thought he'd be around to close us down.'

Sam smiled at Celia Anders, then turned his attention to Chita Childers. Sonora leaned into the back of the stool.

'And the blonde had left by then?' Sam asked.

'Yeah.'

'He talk to anyone else?'

Chita shrugged. 'He talked to lots of people. He talked to me. How come? He in some kind of trouble?'

'He's dead.'

'Dead? Killed?'

'Burned to death in his car.'

'*That* guy? I heard that on the news this morning.' She gripped the edge of the bar, eyes wide. 'Oh God, and I just talked to him. He was so young, too. I actually carded him. The news said somebody burned him *alive*.'

Ronnie Knapp sat down on a stool, turning it so he faced Sonora. 'You think maybe this blonde saw the killer?'

Sonora kept her voice careful. 'It's possible. Right now we're trying to reconstruct Daniels' last hours. This blonde woman – you didn't overhear a name, by any chance?'

Ronnie and Chita both frowned. Chita's tongue came out – more help with concentration. Then she shook her head.

Sonora looked at Ronnie. 'You?'

'No.'

'How'd she pay? Cash? Credit card?'

He shook his head. 'I don't remember.'

'She tip?'

'Uh, yeah.'

'Stingy? Generous?'

'Kind of in the middle.'

'Cash or on credit?'

'Cash.'

'All right. Gather up all your credit receipts for last night, and make copies. In fact, we'll need copies of everything that's come in over the last, say, six weeks.'

Ronnie nodded glumly.

Sonora smiled. 'We appreciate your cooperation, Mr. Knapp. It would help us a lot if you'd bring the receipts down to our office today, and make a formal statement. We'll make an appointment for you to get with our artist on a sketch of this blonde. We're on the fifth floor of the Board of Elections building, 825 Broadway. Public parking lot a block away. Just tell the man in the booth out front what you're there for, and he'll tell you where to go.'

Ronnie and Chita acquired the glazed and wary look of people who suddenly found themselves in the middle of a murder investigation.

'As soon as possible,' Sonora said.

'What if she comes back in?' Celia Anders had been left out and didn't like it.

Sonora took a card from her jacket pocket.

'She comes back in, call me, any time. If I'm not there, be sure and explain to the detective who answers the phone, don't just leave a message. Here, this is my home number.' Sonora scrawled on the back of the card with a pen. 'Any of you see her again, don't approach her, just give me a call.'

'Out of earshot,' Celia said.

Sam grinned at her.

'There a pay phone here?' Sonora asked.

Celia pointed down a dark hallway to the left of the bar. 'Right between the bathrooms.'

'Works okay?'

Ronnie nodded.

'Get pretty noisy in here last night? You have a crowd?'

'Not bad for a week night. We offer twofers from four to seven and that brings people in on their way home from work.'

Sonora looked at Ronnie. 'Tell me everything you remember about the blonde.'

Ronnie closed his eyes and his brow furrowed. 'She was real blonde.'

'Real blonde? Like me?'

He opened his eyes. 'Lighter.'

Sonora sighed. 'Look dyed?'

'Not really, but it's hard to tell sometimes. It didn't have that fakey, cotton candy look to it. It was very light. Kind of collar length and turned under. Very . . . kind of . . . ethereal.'

Chita Childers made a rude noise. 'Ethereal? It was dyed, if it's the one I'm thinking of.'

'Eyes?' Sonora asked.

'Brown. Big brown eyes. Kind of . . . funny.'

'How could she have funny eyes?' Chita said.

Sonora clenched her fist, let it go. Smiled at Chita Childers and looked back at Ronnie.

'Brown eyes,' Ronnie said.

'Blue,' Chita chimed in. They glared at each other.

'Maybe she changed them. With contacts.' Celia Anders looked pleased.

Sonora glanced at Sam. The old witness shuffle.

Ronnie scratched his chin and looked at Sonora. 'She's very small. Shorter even than you.'

'Wow,' Sam said. 'Pretty short, huh?'

Ronnie grinned. 'She looked kind of, I don't know, fragile? But she never smiled. Oh, and her lips were scarred. Like she bit them a lot.'

'She talk to a lot of guys? Flirt a lot?'

'Not with me. I thought she seemed kind of shy. I

remember being surprised she was talking to that guy. In the picture.'

'She was dressed to kill,' Chita said. 'Short black jean skirt, and cowboy boots, and a bodysuit. Lots of makeup and long earrings.'

Ronnie nodded. 'Yeah. She had on a short skirt. I noticed that.'

Chita sounded deceptively sweet. 'She's come in before, dressed like that. I've seen her talking to the other one.'

Sonora turned the picture around, her fingertips grazing the features of Keaton Daniels. 'The other one? This one?'

'Yeah, him.'

'The woman in the picture. The bride here. You ever see her come in?'

Chita frowned and shook her head. 'Not that I remember.'

Sonora passed the picture to Ronnie.

'No. Her I would remember.'

'I just bet you would,' Chita muttered, and was politely ignored. Ronnie handed the picture to Sonora, but Celia Anders intercepted it and gave it a good look. Sonora thought of sticky fingerprints. It was high time for copies.

Sam pulled his ear. 'Did Mark Daniels or the blonde use the phone? Ask for change, maybe?'

Negative. Blank looks. The witness fairy wasn't going to come.

Sonora climbed down from the stool, took her purse with her, found a quarter to call her answering machine and check out the phone. She listened. No emergencies. And the pay phone worked. She pulled out her notebook and jotted down the number. They could pull records from the phone company. She wanted to know if Keaton Daniels had been called from the bar.

Chapter Eight

Sonora went into the Board of Elections building and took the elevator to the fifth floor, to Homicide. There were non-smoking signs in three places, one of them over a metal ashtray. Crimestoppers wanted posters were pinned neatly on a bulletin board. There were no coats in the coat rack out front. There never were.

A woman sat in the glass booth doing a crossword puzzle, and Sonora waved. The door on the left led to the Crime Scene Unit, the other to Homicide. Both warned against entry without proper police escort.

Sonora veered right, walked past the worn down interview rooms, smelling fresh coffee. The box outside the door of the brass's office was full of soda cans. Homicide recycled. As always, she glanced at the poster board that listed homicides for the year, solved and unsolved. Most of the unsolved were drug drive-bys. Hard as hell to track and prove, and the only satisfaction was in knowing that the shooter had a good chance of showing up on the board as a victim sometime in the next few months.

Mark Daniels was the latest entry.

Everyone was in, and the energy level was high. A lot of people on the phones, and Sonora getting speculative looks. Daniels was a real whodunit, and the other detectives were being pulled off their cases to run down leads.

This one would be a headliner.

The message light on her phone was lit and blinking. Her desk, piled with forms, files, a Rolodex, an evidence bag, and a half-filled can of Coke, was placed in the center of the room, butted up to Sam's. Every desk had a plastic-wrapped teddy bear on top – some new program or other. A grant for every cop to carry a stuffed animal to give to children trapped in the crossfire of adults who screwed up. Sonora tossed her purse underneath the desk, and kicked it where it would be out of range of the wheels of her chair.

Her phone rang just as she settled into her chair. 'Homicide, Sonora Blair.'

'Can I please speak to one of the detectives?'

'You're speaking to one.'

'You're not the secretary?'

'No, I'm not the secretary.'

Sonora heard a laugh, looked over her shoulder at Gruber.

He grinned. 'They want a real cop, I'm available.'

Sonora put a hand over the phone. 'Make yourself useful, honey, and get me a cup of coffee.'

Gruber looked her up and down in a way guaranteed to annoy. He had bedroom eyes, a perpetual slump to his shoulders, a swarthy complexion and New Jersey manners that offended some people and attracted young women.

Sonora focused on the voice on the other end of the phone. 'I'm sorry?'

'You know that guy that burned up?'

Sonora frowned and picked up a pen. 'What guy is that?'

'The one in the news. They didn't give his name. But I think I better explain to you the situation with my brother-in-law, make of it what you will.'

Not much, Sonora thought. She made a face, took useless notes. No stone unturned.

'Another nut,' she said, hanging up the phone.

'You attract 'em,' Gruber said. ''Member when we took you out trawling? You pulled in the weirdest nut cases, even for a hooker detail.'

Sonora nodded. She'd hated and resented the prostitution detail, and had been unable to refrain from giving prospective johns the copper's eyefuck. Only one or two had been inexperienced or desperate or intrigued enough to try and do business. Sonora had been pulled off the streets after two weeks.

'I always wondered if you screwed up on purpose, you know? To get off that detail.'

Sonora smiled. 'Keep wondering, Gruber.'

'Molliter didn't think so, but I figured maybe you did.'

'Where is old Molliter these days? He quit and become a television evangelist?'

'Working personal crime since last Christmas.'

'*Molliter?*'

Gruber folded his arms and cocked his head sideways. 'Can't you just hear him lecturing the rape victims on provocative clothing and those jiggly walks?'

Sonora bit her lip. Actually, she could.

Gruber shrugged. 'Yeah, well. Bad choice. They had to pull him out of vice, he was trying to save souls. Didn't really fit in down there, if you know what I mean.'

Sonora draped her jacket over the back of her chair. Thought about coffee, thought about ulcers, decided against the one she had some choice about. The message light on her machine was still blinking. She settled into her chair and pushed the button.

One informant looking for a handout, a terse one from Chas, who was feeling neglected, a coroner's assistant about the suicide she hadn't liked. There was a message from one of the mothers from Heather's class reminding her to send cupcakes for day after tomorrow – (shit, Sonora thought) – and the one from Tim, letting her know that Heather had gotten on the bus okay, he was on his way, and *yes* he had his keys.

Sonora took out a scratch pad, roughing out the description she would put out on the NCIC. Early days yet, but this one looked like a repeater, and she wasn't asking permission. Under key points, she put homicide involving white female, victim white male, burned to death in car. She chewed the end of her pen.

She felt a large hand on her shoulder, and a familiar presence by her side. 'Sonora, girl, that pen taste good, or you didn't get any breakfast?'

Gruber waved a hand. 'It's an oral thing. What she needs . . .' He caught the expression on Sonora's face. Trailed off.

'Wise,' she told him.

She swiveled her chair and looked at her partner, and flashed back to a night four years ago, before she really knew Sam's wife, Shelly, and, hell, she'd decided not to feel guilty about that anymore. Sometimes she looked at Sam and still felt the urge. Something about Gruber put thoughts like that in her head.

'Crick wants us,' Sam said.

The brass had their own office, more desks butted together, phones, files. Crick was at the computer when Sam and Sonora walked in, and he looked irritable. He did not get along with the department terminals, which were inferior to the setup he had at home. He was often overheard making rude comments about archaic software.

Loosen your tie, Sonora thought. Your disposition will improve. Someday she would say it out loud.

'Sit down, Blair. Delarosa.' Crick rolled his chair backward. Sam took two chairs from behind empty desks, straddled one, aimed the other at Sonora. She stopped it with her foot. 'God, the two of you. Just sit.'

Sonora glanced at Sam, and wondered if he was thinking what she was thinking. Were they caught? Were they going to get fired?

'How are you doing on that suicide?' Crick said.

Slow, Sonora thought. Way behind. She cleared her throat. 'Family went squirrelly over the autopsy, Sergeant.

We're moving them along easy, trying to keep things from boiling over.'

Crick stuck a finger under his collar and scratched his neck. 'Drop the bullshit, Blair.'

She crossed her legs, resting a foot on her knee. 'I don't like it. There's a large insurance policy involved, just barely past the two-year limit on suicide. Coroner can't find anything definite, but we're waiting for test results. We can fly by the grand jury, but if we go to trial, their forensic whores will take us apart.'

'How'd the coroner sign it off?'

'I'm pressuring, but he's probably going to rule it suicide.'

'Drop it, then.'

'Lot of money at stake.'

'Let the insurance company worry about it. I can tell you now or the DA can tell you later.'

'Yes sir.'

'What else you working on?'

'Crenshaw baby. Stabbing on Ryker Street, looks like a drug burn. And we got that burning bed, Meredith.'

'You sure the wife did it?'

'No doubt in my mind,' Sam said.

'No doubt the husband deserved it.'

Sam wagged a finger. 'You got to get off this "I hate men" kick, Sonora. Not all guys are like your dead husband.'

They had this conversation two or three times a month, and Sonora went on with her lines. 'Yeah, *they're* breathing. So why is it, Sam, if a woman calls a spade a spade, or a jerk a jerk, she gets labeled a manhater?'

Crick waved a hand. 'Enough already, you guys are worse than my kids. Give your files to Nelson, and sit up and pay attention here. Coffee?'

'Sure,' Sam said. Sonora nodded and looked at Sam. He winked, but he was worried. There were budget cutbacks again this year. They'd seen some pretty good people get screwed.

Maybe they were being transferred somewhere awful.

Crick poured them both a cup from a pot that sat amid stacks of computer printouts. Sonora was aware of a tiny, annoying buzz coming from the timer that turned the pot on every morning at seven-fifty. It was the wrong kind of timer, not made to handle the load, and had melted down twice. Fire hazard, Sonora thought. She was seeing them everywhere, all of a sudden.

Sonora took a big sip of coffee, tasting nothing. Crick sat back down. His chair squeaked. He squinted his eyes.

'You feeling okay, Blair? You don't look too good.'

'What am I, Miss America? I been up all night looking for a killer who set a twenty-two-year-old kid on fire. How would you look?'

'My wife says I always look the same, no matter what.'

Can't argue with that, Sonora thought.

Crick leaned back in his chair. 'This Daniels thing is going to be a big deal. Heinous crime, innocent kid. It's all over the news, we been getting calls like you wouldn't believe. There's a lot of leads to follow and a lot of coordinating to do with the arson guys.' He pointed a thick finger. 'You caught it, you're the lead detectives. You got to know everything that goes down. Every witness statement, every tiny piece of evidence, you know the drill. We're going to task force this thing. We'll pull in twelve detectives from district, plus our own people. You're even going to get your own computer.'

Sam whistled.

'We'll meet every morning to hand out lead cards, then everybody goes out. We meet up again the end of the day. Couple of guys from arson will be in on this, Lieutenant Abalone and I will handle the press. Any information we hand out, we'll clear through the task force. Kick it around first. We can use the media on this, maybe push a few buttons with this headcase we got here. Run a description, if we get a good one.

'Nobody's taking anything away from you, you understand. I'm just pulling in some help, organizing everything all around you, so you two super cops can bring me this bitch's head on a stick.'

Sonora took a breath. They weren't being fired. She could still pay the mortgage. Her children were safe.

Crick's phone rang. 'Yeah. She's here.' He looked at Sonora. 'You got a call. Keaton Daniels. Wants to talk specifically to you.'

'I'll take it at my desk.'

The light on line four was blinking red when Sonora sat down. She picked up the stuffed bear and tossed it on Sam's desk.

'Specialist Blair,' she said, propping her chin on the shoulder piece. 'Mr. Daniels?'

'Yeah, hi. I thought I should let you know. I've had an odd phone call.'

He sounded confident. A woman, Sonora thought, would have been defensive, would have apologized for bothering her, and would have made five disclaimers about how it was probably nothing. At least men didn't have to be coaxed and reassured.

'Tell me about it.'

Sam had come out of Crick's office and was examining the bear on his desk. He glanced at Sonora out of the corner of his eye.

'She said—'

'She?' Sonora asked.

'It was a woman. She asked me about Mark.'

Sonora sat forward in her chair and picked up a pen. 'Start at the beginning, Keaton, and tell me the exact words, as well as you can remember.'

He paused. Sonora pictured him, concentrating, gathering his thoughts.

'She called me . . . I guess an hour ago.'

Sonora checked her watch. Made a note on the scratch pad.

'I said hello. And there was a long silence. I was about to hang up, then she said she wanted to check on me, and see how I was doing. I thought at first it might be Ashley, my wife. I even thought for a minute it might be you. So I said I was shaky, and kind of numb. And she made a noise, you know, a sympathy thing.'

'Sarcastic?' Sonora asked.

'It didn't strike me that way.'

'Go on.'

Sonora saw that Sam was watching her, intent on her end of the conversation, waiting her out with a patience that always amazed her. Mr. Stakeout.

Daniels cleared his throat. 'She said . . . how did she put it? She said, it's a terrible thing, to lose a brother. Were you . . . no. She said you'uns. Were you'uns real close?'

'You'uns,' Sonora muttered.

'And I said . . . I didn't answer her. It dawned on me that I didn't know who this was. But I still had the feeling that it was a friend or something, because she knew about Mark. So I said, I'm sorry, who is this?

'And she said someone who's interested. Then she asked if I was thinking much about how he died. Was it terrible for me? Was I missing him, had I thought about the funeral? So then I thought maybe she was a reporter or something. I was going to hang up, but it made me mad. I thought she was out of line, and that I should get her name and her newspaper, or whatever, so I asked her again who it was.'

Sonora gave him a moment. 'What did she say?'

'She said . . . she said Mark was brave.'

The nib of Sonora's pen tore through the paper on the notepad. She listened to Keaton Daniels, breathing on the other end of the line. She flipped the notepaper up, exposing a clean sheet.

What is it? Sam mouthed. Gruber had picked up on the tension. Sonora could feel him edging close behind her.

'Mr. Daniels, I don't guess you've had a chance to change the locks on your doors?'

'No.'

'Why don't you get on to that right away?'

'It was her, then, wasn't it?'

Sonora pursed her lips, measuring her words. 'It's a possibility. It's also possible, likely even, that it was some crank, some sick puppy out there getting a nasty little vicarious thrill.'

Sam raised an eyebrow at her.

'We haven't released your brother's name to the press,' Sonora continued. 'But something like this – the gossip mill churns pretty fast. The hospital people will talk. The reporters know the ID from the car license. Forgive me, but your wife may have talked about it to the wrong person at work.' How well are the two of you getting along, Sonora wondered.

'I don't think it was a reporter. And it wasn't my wife, I'd know it.'

Jumped right on that one, Sonora thought. She'd seen divorcing parties do worse.

Keaton's voice thickened. 'There's something else.'

'Yes?'

'After she said that about Mark. That he was brave. She said . . . will you be?'

Chapter Nine

Mark Daniels' roommate had said the apartment was in the Chevy Chase area, next to the University of Kentucky campus. The Taurus inched down Rose Street, and Sam squinted as he strained to avoid the knots of university students who seemed oddly oblivious to traffic. Sonora glanced at the sheet of directions.

'Take a right at the intersection. I can't read your writing here, Sam. Eunice?' She glanced at a street sign. 'Euclid. Turn here.' She noticed a Hardees and a Baskin Robbins and decided she was hungry. 'Here,' she said, looking up. 'No. Casa Galvan, that's the Mex restaurant he mentioned. Turn around, we've gone too far.'

It was a part of the city that mixed campus, old residential, and commercial. Mark's apartment was in a pinkish red brick building with a black, wrought iron fire escape down one side. Sam parked the car a long block away, tucking the Taurus between a pickup and an ancient Kharmen Ghia.

Sonora shut the passenger door softly. 'Well, Sam, Lexington is one town where your pickup would blend.'

Sam gave her a look. 'Yeah, and who do you call when you need a load of firewood?'

Sonora grinned and Sam waved her ahead, always the gentleman. The pebbled sidewalk in front of Mark Daniels' apartment building had cracked and buckled. The lawn was sparse, equal parts Crab, Dandelion, and Bluegrass.

Sonora paused on the front walk and looked at the windows. No one was stirring. The mix of sagging venetian blinds, cheap threadbare curtains, and woven shades – one open, one closed – gave the building a bedraggled look of neglect. People slept here. They didn't stay long.

Sonora checked her watch. Just after seven. Sam caught her look.

'Yeah, well. Be sure to find people home, this time of day. Plus the roommate has an eight o'clock class.'

Sonora thought of her own university days. 'Doesn't mean he actually goes. I can't believe you got me up at five to drive down here.'

She wondered if the killer had stalked Mark Daniels, if she'd known him from Adam. Was this a random hit? A well-planned hit, random victim? Why did Keaton Daniels come up every time she looked for Mark?

The linoleum in the apartment hallway was peeling up in the corner and overlaid with muddy footprints. The mud was reddish brown – most of the prints showed the webwork of rubber soles. Big feet, too. A lot of size tens and elevens, one that looked bigger. Mostly guys, Sonora decided. Lexington had evidently had its share of rain. Their footsteps were muffled by a hideous, raisin-colored runner.

'Sam, what color was the mud in the park?'

'Grey-black, Sherlock.'

Sonora was out of breath by the time they passed the second floor. 'What's the kid's name?'

'Brian Winthrop. Age twenty-three.'

'Ever notice we never talk to people who live on the first floor?'

'It's a well known phenomenon. Always the third floor people who get into trouble.'

'Is he going to say you'uns too?'

Sam gave her a sour look.

'Hey, I only meant to be offensive.'

Sonora scooted to the door ahead of him and knocked, thinking how much time she spent on doorsteps, wishing she could somehow convert it to time spent with her kids, or better still, sleeping. She crooked her finger at Sam, and he dipped his head to listen.

'The guy *I* want to talk to is the one who called it in. You think there's any chance he'll get back to us?'

'Shit, no. He's in Mt. Airy Forest on a week night, after dark, in the rain. Who do you know who goes to the park under those circumstances?'

'Gays.'

'Closet gays. He did his civic duty and called 911. I don't look for him to buy any more trouble.'

A dead bolt clicked, and the door cracked open just slightly, then stuck. The thin wood bowed inward and Sonora heard a muted mutter.

'Yes?'

Mark's roommate was a tall boy, and thin; shoulders bumpy, hip bones jutting, Adam's apple prominent. His head seemed overlarge for his body. His hair was dark brown and wavy, and a bad barber had given him a poor haircut too long ago. His skin showed blemishes here and there, nothing major, and he was of an age to shave daily, though he hadn't. Sonora wondered if he was into the stubble look, or trying to grow a beard.

Sam showed his ID. 'Specialists Delarosa and Blair, Cincinnati Police Department, about Mark Daniels. We talked last night?'

Sonora tried not to yawn. 'Can we come in?'

'Inside. That would . . . yeah, in the room, that would be to say, for the best.' Winthrop nodded vigorously and stepped back.

Sonora scratched her cheek and looked at Sam. He raised one eyebrow, and motioned her ahead.

The room smelled like fried fish and tartar sauce. The rug was worn, mustard colored, with a rusty looking stain under the window.

Bloodstain? Sonora wondered. Always a copper.

A card table sagged under the clutter of books, papers,

and pizza cartons. A set of barbells and weights sat in the corner. Along the wall behind the couch was an IBM PS/2, a modem beneath a phone, and a Hewlett Packard laser printer. The computer screen was lit, the background a searing blue. A miniature cartoon man in a green suit with an orange vest did back flips to the tune of a ditty that set Sonora's teeth on edge.

Winthrop flung an arm toward the living room. 'Place to sit. Here. If you'd like. Of course, you might not, but probably you would.'

Sam sat in the middle of the couch and reached into his coat pocket for his recorder. Sonora took a worn arm chair that had a Salvation Army look. The chair sank beneath her, a wayward spring the only thing keeping her off the floor. She scooted forward, balanced on the edge, and studied Winthrop.

'Brian, how long were you and Mark roommates?'

'You . . . we were friends a lot of, well, knowing. I could tell you but remembering is one thing, but it is more than years.'

Sonora wondered if Winthrop was sincerely unable to communicate, playing it smart, or terrified of police. Sam met her gaze, raised his right shoulder slightly. Big help.

It could never be easy.

Sonora tried again. 'So you've known Mark several years?'

Winthrop made an obvious effort. 'Three. That would be as roommates. Ten as known friends. Longer really.'

For the first time in her life, Sonora missed the sneering streetwise punks who were sometimes irritating, sometimes chilling, but at least able to communicate, often in lyrical, if obscene, rap.

'So you've roomed with Mark for the last three years?'

Winthrop nodded vigorously.

He seemed bright enough. She detected a working mind behind the intelligence of the gaze, and a look of panic to go with the sheen of sweat on the forehead. He could have had something to do with Mark's killing, but she didn't think so. Her instinct told her the panic was due to sheer social nervousness, and she supposed that if she talked the way Winthrop did, she'd be nervous too.

She thought of her brother, going through school with his speech impediment, teased, imitated, retreating every afternoon to his room.

Winthrop cleared his throat loudly. Impossible not to root for him in his intense effort to organize his thoughts into speech. And that was the problem, she decided. Some kind of mental stuttering.

She grimaced, turning it into a smile. 'Did Mark date around a lot? Was he pretty popular with girls?'

'No, but they all, to say, that's because you know Sandra. But they would if he wouldn't.'

'Sandra's his girlfriend, right?'

Winthrop nodded.

'Did he date anyone else?'

'Well I don't. Not to my . . . my own understanding, I couldn't say always know ever. But he, as far as I would know, and I didn't ever see it.'

'He didn't as far as you know?'

She was beginning to get the hang of talking to this guy – very like communicating with a two-year-old. Grab the gist, double check the results, and resist the urge to drop to your knees and beg him to just *say* it.

She led him through the routine patiently, getting a lead on Mark's favorite bars (three or four, Lynagh's in particular); favorite restaurants (the Mex place, Casa Galvan, and Jozo's Cajun); what he studied (social work) and what bothered him (the job market, AIDS, final exams). There were no surprises – an average male college student in his early twenties.

He loved Sandra, he partied on Friday and Saturday, spent Sunday afternoons playing pickup basketball, and studied weeknights after work. He worked evenings, but had recently been 'let go' by new management. Nothing major there, just something of a personality clash with the new guy. Winthrop suspected Mark had been fired because the new owners didn't want to pay more than minimum wage. They were letting a lot of the regulars go and putting in new people. Mark hadn't been the only one out the door.

Sonora shifted on the uncomfortable rim of the armchair, wishing she'd beat Sam to the couch.

'Okay, Brian, there's something I want you to think about. Did Mark get any odd phone calls – anything unusual, maybe someone calling and hanging up?'

'The phone now that's a . . . its . . . I might not. Because you never know if he'd say in particular, though he might, you know. He might.' Spittle spewed from lips that were thick, chapped and dry. Sonora shifted to one side so that Sam was in the direct line of fire.

'Anything you're sure about? Any calls you took, any calls Mark mentioned?'

'I don't. No. Usually, Mark would— '

'Mark answered the phone?'

Winthrop nodded. Sonora nodded too. Made perfect sense.

'Did he seem upset over anything? Ever mention he thought somebody might be watching him?'

Winthrop's blank look answered that one.

Sonora's back was aching and the computer-generated song made her grind her teeth. She wondered what sin she had committed to deserve this witness.

'Brian, Specialist Delarosa and I need to take a look at Mark's room, go through his things. Any objection? Good. While we're looking, I'd like you to write down everything you remember that happened the last day you saw Mark. I'm interested in everything, all the routine stuff, and of course, anything unusual.'

Winthrop nodded.

Sonora stood up. She had more questions, but not in a chair with a spring coming up, and not with a computer game chanting in the background.

Chapter Ten

Sonora looked at Mark Daniels' bedroom, thinking that she wouldn't call him neat.

Likely he'd left for Cincinnati in a hurry, but the signs were there of someone always in a hurry on the way to somewhere else. A large mound in the corner would probably prove to be a chair. Clothes were piled on the floor, and the bed had an ingrained unmade look Sonora recognized. Likely it was pulled together on special occasions only.

A Gameboy sat on the edge of a cheap metal desk. Sam picked it up, and Sonora took it away from him.

'Gosh, Mom.'

They gravitated to their 'own' parts of the room, a pattern and rhythm set by countless shared homicide investigations. Sonora gathered a stack of CDs.

'New Age shit and rap.' Sonora stacked them in a dust-grimed corner. The desk drawers were crammed to the limit and she had to work to get them open. 'Just once, I'd like the DB to be a neat freak. Like those victims you always see on TV? Bank statements neatly filed, a journal with— '

Sam looked up. 'You found a journal?'

'No, I'm talking about TV.'

He coughed. 'At least on TV they change the sheets.'

'I hope I never get murdered. I wouldn't want you and Gruber tossing my house.'

'Better clean it up, Sonora, you're just the kind of female

who does get murdered. Which reminds me, Chas called me up last night.'

'Chas called *you*?' Sonora sorted carefully through the top middle drawer, finding it touchingly similar to her own son's clutter. A collection of bottlecaps – she wondered why guys collected bottle caps – several superballs of various colors, baseball cards, a half-eaten Butterfinger candy bar that had gone white around the edges. 'This chocolate actually tempts me, Sam. I must be further gone than I thought.'

'I've seen you pick M&Ms up off the floor.'

She started on another drawer, sorting through an eclectic collection of tiny screwdrivers, wrenches, stray nuts and bolts. 'What did Chas want? Ah. A bank statement. Looks depressingly like mine.'

'No money?'

'When he gets it, he spends it.'

'Bar hopping is expensive.'

'I vaguely remember, back from the days when my life was fun.'

Sam looked at her and smiled. 'That would be before children?'

'Like everything else pleasant.' She looked at him covertly, saw the shadow that crossed his face, realized he was wondering if his daughter would get a chance to grow up. Time to quit making stupid parent jokes.

Sam finished with the mattress and under the bed and was methodically going through the pockets of Daniels' discarded clothing.

'Anything?' she asked.

'Trojans be the brand of choice. At least two in every pocket.'

'I like Ramses myself. I wonder if Sandra's on the pill.'

Sam nodded. 'That would let you know if he was looking.'

'Or if it's a true like a commitment of a— '

'Shhh, Winthrop'll hear you.' Sam moved across the

room and closed the door. He picked a shirt up off the floor.

'You going through the underwear, too?'

'I'm not that dedicated.'

Sonora opened another drawer. 'Jesus, this guy's still reading comic books. What a baby.'

'I read comic books. Hey, the X-Men. And by the way, Chas wanted to know why you weren't returning his calls. Playing hard to get, girl?'

Sonora found a packet of pictures. The negatives fell to the floor and she bent over and picked them up.

'I never get the reason for these stupid strips of negatives. Nobody ever really uses them, they're just there to fall out and be irritating.'

'I use them.'

'You do not either.' Sonora began sorting. The pictures had been developed on the two-fer plan, so she got to see everything twice.

'I thought you liked Chas,' Sam said.

'He's okay for Friday nights, but now he's talking marriage.'

'Let me be the first to congratulate you, girl.'

Sonora scooted backward in her chair. 'Marriage, Sam, is for men and sweet young things in their twenties. I'm happy as I go.'

'You have an ulcer.'

'I'm happy all around this ulcer.'

'So live with him.'

'My washing machine won't take another person.'

Sam looked at her over his shoulder. 'You know, Sonora, just because your dear departed was a son of a bitch— '

'I know, I know. Doesn't mean all men are sons of bitches. I'd marry you, Sam, if you changed your socks more often.'

Sam tossed a shirt in a pile and sat on the edge of the bed. 'Last year you said you were lonely.'

'Last year I didn't know I had it so good.'

'No, now, something happened. Three months ago you were over the moon about this guy.'

'Yeah, well. He did a funny thing with the car.'

'What kind of funny thing?'

'It . . . I'm embarrassed, okay?'

'No it's not okay. This is me, remember? You got me worried here, girl, what thing?'

'It just made me realize. I mean, if I didn't know better, I'd think I was dating my dead husband all over again.'

'Run, girl,' Sam said, giving her a look.

Sonora grinned. 'Run screaming.'

A toilet flushed in the apartment next door, and a door slammed in the hallway.

Sonora opened another envelope of pictures. 'So this is Sandra.'

'You're changing the subject on me.'

'Can't get anything past you, can I, Sam?'

He stood by Sonora's elbow. 'She doesn't look old enough to have a boyfriend.'

'My six-year-old has a boyfriend.'

Sandra looked impossibly young, plumpish, brown hair overpermed. She stood next to Mark, giving him a look of intense adoration that could only be mustered by a very young woman.

Sam took the picture and squinted. 'There goes our number one suspect. You can't tell me *she* handcuffed him to a steering wheel and set him on fire.'

'Glued him to a pedestal, maybe.'

'What?'

'I'm agreeing with you.'

Sam turned the picture sideways. 'You ever look at Chas like that?'

'I don't have to, he does it with mirrors.'

'Is it police work, Sonora, or were you born mean? I mean, this thing with the car, whatever it was, maybe you're making too much of it. Maybe Chas was under pressure or something.'

'Shut up, Sam, before you annoy me.'

Sonora turned her back on him, flipped through another stack of pictures. Lots of friends, lots of parties, a few of the same faces again and again. One of Winthrop straining at the barbells. A lot of the three of them – Daniels, Sandra, and Winthrop. Winthrop looked happy in these, Mark, tolerant, Sandra, enduring. If Winthrop had been murdered, Sandra would be up at the top of the list of suspects.

Sonora selected two or three shots, set them aside, and opened an old cigar-style school box. MARK DANIELS had been printed across the top in purple magic marker by a childish, sloppy hand. Inside were more bottlecaps, fantasy miniatures, gum ball machine playing cards, and more pictures.

These were older, various sizes and camera types, a collection from the past. Sonora picked them up and thumbed through.

The brothers had been close – at least when they were younger. Mark was the mug, making faces and devil horns behind his big brother's head; never serious, but somehow never quite comfortable in the eye of the camera. Keaton self-confident, solid masculine build contrasting with his brother's gangly boy's body.

A number of shots caught Keaton behind a fishing pole, looking relaxed and happy. Mark was always pictured displaying a nice-sized, dripping fish, Keaton ever without a trophy. How was it she knew that Keaton had caught those fish?

Keaton Daniels was very much on her mind. His footprints were everywhere – natural, perhaps, he was Mark's brother. Sonora wondered if Keaton would go back to his wife in the midst of his crisis.

As the thought occurred, she ran across a picture of Keaton Daniels asleep, his back to a tree, muscles slack, fishing pole loose in his hands. The shot was recent, likely taken by Mark. She placed it on top of the pile she had set aside, then changed her mind, and slipped it into her jacket pocket.

Sam stretched, then scratched the back of his neck. 'What do you think?'

'I think he was a typical kid, young for his age, and on the verge of getting engaged before he had any business being married. I don't see him inspiring a killing like this. I don't see him stirring that mature kind of rage.'

'Just one of those random, drive-by, handcuff 'em and douse 'em with gasoline killings.'

'No, Sam, this killer stalked her victim. She just took advantage of a small and unexpected opportunity.'

'Such as?'

'Such as Mark. The little brother.'

'The little brother? So you're saying— '

'Yeah. Of her intended victim. Keaton Daniels.'

Chapter Eleven

It was late when Sonora and Sam made it into Lynagh's to ask about Mark Daniels and a mysterious blonde. The Metropolitan Blues Allstars were playing and the air was thick with cigarette smoke and the smell of beer. The music was dark and bluesy – beautifully executed and way too loud for conversation.

Sam staked out a tiny table for two in the back left corner, the only empty seats left in the house. The Allstars packed 'em in, even on weeknights.

Sonora watched the crowd – a mix, spanning the college and thirty-something generation. A noisy group of men and women in chinos and plaid shirts sat at a long table in the middle of the room, generating enormous activity at the bar. The women watched the dance floor wistfully; the men pretended not to notice.

'. . . no, she said put on your clothes and go home.'
'. . . burned the canoe, instead of the . . .'
'. . . pounding him till he pays . . .'
'. . . oh no, the judge is a total nutcase.'

Lawyers, Sonora decided.

'Sonora, you want a Coke or something?' Sam was shouting in her ear.

She shook her head, then focused on the kids at the tables in front, wondering if any of them knew Mark. One of the girls looked familiar – long brown hair past her waist. Sonora pulled the snapshots she'd taken from Mark Daniels' desk. This girl was in one.

Sonora tracked her, watching to see who she talked to, eyeing the kids she hung out with. Mark was supposedly a regular – maybe this was his crowd. She nudged Sam and he saluted her with his Dr. Pepper. She took the glass out of his hands, drank deeply, and winced. Her children drank Dr. Pepper too. She wondered why.

Sonora showed Sam the picture, then nodded her head toward the girl on the dance floor. Sam nodded and stuck a wad of tobacco in his cheek. Sonora suddenly remembered that she was supposed to deliver thirty cupcakes to her daughter's primary class the next morning.

She crooked her finger and Sam leaned close. She pointed to her watch. '*Time*. I'll go talk to the girlfriend. You stay here and see what you can get with that bunch up front, particularly the girl. I'll pick you up on my way back.'

'Which girl again? The redhead?'

'In your dreams. That one over there. Hair to her feet and fingernails.'

'Figures.'

Sonora stopped in the ladies room – cramped, dark, and overheated; gouged linoleum and paper towels lining the floor. There was a pay phone, and she checked on the kids – safe at grandma's – and the machine at the office.

Two messages – one from Chas, and one odd one. Sonora frowned, dialed the work number again, fast forwarded through Chas, and listened hard.

'Hello there, girlfriend. You'uns get around, don't you? Recognize my voice? I bet not. Don't worry, girl, I'll call back.'

Sonora ran a thumb up and down the coin slot. You'uns. The woman who had called Keaton had said you'uns. This was no blast from the past, no playful old college buddy, blowing through town. No threats, no challenges, a friendly woman in a good mood.

This was the killer calling in.

Chapter Twelve

Sandra Corliss lived with her parents on Trevillian Street in a small tri-level house that would have been new about the year Mark Daniels was born. Trees were few and far between and the street had an unadorned look of bitter age. The cars parked in the driveways were old V-8s that had good pickup, touched up paint jobs, and the solid build of tanks. Good safe family cars. Being Kentucky, there was the usual sprinkling of pickups.

The hazy glow from the street lights showed the Corliss house backed up to a park, the backyard sloping toward a wide expanse of open meadow. A large, above-ground pool squatted at the end of the driveway. The front porch light was on.

Sonora parked the Taurus in front of the house, locked the doors, and walked up the asphalt drive. She cut sideways across the lawn and bumped a ceramic 'yard boy'. The paint was peeling away from the statue's right eye, giving him an aura that was both shabby and grotesque.

Sonora rang the doorbell twice. The television noises stopped abruptly, and the front curtain, heavy and blue, twitched at the edge. The front door was pulled open, creating a momentary suction that rattled the storm door.

Sandra Corliss's father was a large man, with broad stooped shoulders. His brown corduroy shirt strained at the belly. His hair was sparse, still fair, blond eyebrows thick. He held the sports section of the newspaper loose by his side. He looked tired.

'Mr. Corliss? I'm Specialist Blair, Cincinnati Police. Excuse me for disturbing you so late. I spoke with Mrs. Corliss yesterday?' She held out her ID.

'Sure, come in.' He took a furtive glance at the identification, as if he felt the inspection was impolite. Sonora saw that he was wearing worn brown slippers.

A motley collection of shoes, various sizes, was lined neatly on a mat near the front door. The wall to wall carpet was pale blue, very thick, and in mint condition.

Sonora wondered if this was one of those households where everyone took off their shoes to preserve the carpet. She was uncomfortably aware that the heel had worn through in her left sock, and she pretended not to notice when Corliss glanced at her feet. Police officers did not take off their shoes on duty. No doubt there was a regulation.

'Sandra's in her room,' Corliss said.

Sonora wondered if he expected her to fetch the child herself.

'Perry, who's this?' A woman in an emerald green sweat suit came in from the kitchen. She was carefully made up with frosty blue eye shadow and heavy eyebrow pencil, and her hair had been securely sprayed in place. The woman's knuckles were coarse and red.

Sonora extended a hand. 'I'm Sonora Blair, Cincinnati Police Department. We talked yesterday?'

Mrs. Corliss nodded firmly. 'Yes, of course.' Her voice dropped to a whisper. 'Sandra is very upset. She's in her room.'

'Sit down, Detective.' Sandra's father led her to the couch.

Sonora's ears were still ringing from the music in the bar, and she knew she reeked of cigarette smoke. She felt bad, suddenly, one of the inexplicable waves of illness she was getting lately. It felt good to sit down.

Corliss settled in a gold velveteen recliner. A picture of a Spanish galleon in storm-tossed seas hung from the wall over his head. An open jar of peanuts sat on a floor lamp that also had a built-in table, imitation marble. The lampshade still wore the plastic slipcover put on at the factory. Corliss sat on the edge of the recliner, tucked the newspaper on the seat behind him, and let his heavy, coarse hands hang between his knees. Sonora wondered what he did for a living.

'Sandra's been real upset,' he told her. 'We all have.'

Sonora nodded. 'How long had your daughter been dating Mark Daniels?'

'Two . . . no, three years. We were expecting them to get engaged some time down the road.' He noted the look on her face. 'Me and Sandra made an agreement when I took on extra time to pay for her college. She's not even supposed to think about getting married till after she graduates. Sandra's real smart. Her mama and I agreed she's got to finish school, not quit and put somebody's else's boy through.'

'I think you are very wise, Mr. Corliss.'

He nodded. He agreed.

'What's her major?'

'Computer science, though her mom's got her taking secretarial courses. That way she'll always have something to fall back on.'

'You could get her a couch,' Sonora muttered.

Corliss frowned. 'A couch?'

To fall back on, Sonora thought. A door opened and closed and she heard the soft tread of slippered feet on thick carpet.

The girl was heavy-hipped and fleshy in blue jeans and a pink sweatshirt with kittens on the front. Her hair was neatly flipped under and she wore no makeup. Sonora had seen junior high school girls with a more worldly air. Sandra was like Mark, who had baseball cards and bottle caps in his desk drawer. She probably had stuffed animals on her bed, and would live at home till she graduated.

Sandra kept her eyes downcast, her mother a force at

her back. She took soft tiny steps and came all the way to the couch to shake Sonora's hand.

Mrs. Corliss stood at the edge of the kitchen. 'Unless you need us, her daddy and I will be in here.'

Mr. Corliss looked startled to find himself relegated to the kitchen, but obediently stood up.

'That will be fine,' Sonora said, well aware they would be listening in. She took out her notebook, and inserted a blank tape in the recorder. She could see that Sandra had been doing a lot of crying, and was likely on the verge again. True love, she told her cynical self.

'How long have you and Mark been dating?' Sonora asked. Always start with something easy.

'Two years and two months.'

'Two years and two months,' Sonora repeated softly. She had the feeling that Sandra would be able to reel off hours, days, and minutes.

Sandra swallowed heavily and tucked her chin to her chest, reminding Sonora of her own little girl. Remember the cupcakes, she thought.

Sandra lifted her head and gave Sonora a look of pain-laced eagerness she often got from victims. Still new with their grief, still in denial, they looked to her to bring order to the chaotic abyss of violent crime.

What I bring, Sonora thought, is more pain. She looked at Sandra steadily, knowing the question would bring tears. She was used to tears.

'Talk to me about Mark, Sandra. Tell me all about him.' She hit the button on her recorder. Sandra would be inhibited at first, but in a few minutes she would forget it was there.

Sandra cleared her throat. 'Mark was smart. He was nice. He was fun.'

Sonora liked the look of intelligence in the girl's eyes. She leaned sideways against the couch and braced herself for a sanitized description of a boy Sandra would mold into the kind of sainthood engendered by sudden, bitter death.

'He liked animals, and basketball, and walking in the rain.'

Sonora's smile was friendly. 'He *liked* walking in the rain?'

Sandra squinched her eyes together. 'Sort of.' She twisted the ends of her sweatshirt. 'Mainly, I guess he didn't like fooling with umbrellas.'

Here we go, Sonora thought. The terrible truth.

'What else can you tell me about him?'

'Well, I guess Mark thought Keat hung the moon. Their dad died when Mark was in high school. He had a heart attack. And Mark is very . . . he really looked up to Keaton. Keaton's the kind of brother you look up to. Not like mine.' She grimaced.

'Were Mark and Keaton competitive?'

Sandra pulled her bottom lip. 'Only a little. Keaton always tried to build Mark up, you know? Make him look good, talk guy stuff, go to basketball games. But Keaton is always good at everything, and people just like him. Women like him.' She seemed puzzled by women who would prefer Keaton over Mark. 'So sometimes I think Mark was a little . . . oh, I don't know.'

'Out to prove himself?'

'Yeah, like that. But it wasn't tense or anything. Not like they were rivals.'

'Mark have a lot of friends?'

'Gosh, yes. He liked goofing. Like he liked going out, and playing jokes on his friends. He'd talk to just anybody.'

Talked to one body too many, Sonora thought.

'Was he in a fraternity?' she asked.

Sandra shook her head. 'He really had a thing against them. See, he's got this friend, this roommate, they've known each other from junior high school. And the roommate is one of those, you know, he— '

'Brian Winthrop? I've met him.'

'Oh, so you know. They both went out for rush, but nobody wanted Brian, so Mark said the heck with the whole thing. Keaton hadn't been in a fraternity either, because he worked all the time, to make sure there would be money for Mark too. I mean, Mark's the kind of guy you imagine in a frat house, he fits in with the guys and likes all the company and goings on. But he wouldn't, because of Brian.'

It showed character, Sonora thought. Mark was taking shape. Keaton's admiring little brother, Sandra's courteous fun-loving boyfriend, Brian's staunch friend.

He was brave, the mystery woman had said over the phone. Had Keaton been talking to the killer?

Sandra's mother leaned into the room, feet still in the kitchen, not *officially* interrupting, but ever mindful of being the hostess.

'Can I get you something to drink, Detective Blair? Some coffee, or maybe a pop? I got Diet Sprite, Diet Orange, and Coke Classic.'

'A Coke sounds really nice,' Sonora said.

Mrs. Corliss looked at her daughter. 'Sandra, you want a Diet Sprite?'

'No, Mama.'

The sound of ice being dropped into glasses was distracting. The small rapport between Sonora and Sandra faded.

The drinks came on a tray with a plate of cookies – homemade and high in fat. Sonora took a sip of Coke. It did not sit well.

Sandra ignored the cookies and took a tiny sip of the Sprite that had been delivered with the attitude that mama knows best. She grimaced, and set her glass down with a gesture that dripped rejection.

Grief indeed, Sonora thought.

'Everything tastes like sawdust. Mama's been on me to eat since it happened, but food makes me choke.'

Sonora had been much the same when Zack was killed

– food like ashes in her mouth. She'd also wanted to make passionate love to all of the men that she liked. She decided not to share this with Sandra.

'She's just worried about you. Mothers look after their children by feeding them.'

Sandra nodded, eyes glazing over.

'What did your mother think of Mark?' Sonora asked.

'She was crazy about him, she was always inviting him to dinner. He ate like a field hand, and she liked that. He could eat and eat and not gain an ounce.'

'How irritating.' Sonora picked up a cookie.

Sandra nodded vigorously. She picked up a cookie. A tear spilled down her cheek. Sonora could not help but think of her own daughter, of Heather's steady intelligent eyes behind round lenses, the way she would blink if you looked her eye to eye, and push the glasses back on her nose. She hoped never to have to talk a child of hers through something like this. Mr. and Mrs. Corliss were not going to have an easy year.

Mark had been a practical joker, never cruel, but constant, always up for a laugh. And never at the expense of Brian, who made an easy target. Sonora listened closely, head bent, hearing the edge that hardened Sandra's voice whenever Winthrop's name came up.

Sonora probed gently, but got no hint of jealousy, other than of Winthrop. If Mark had been looking past her, Sandra hadn't known. Sonora wondered what kind of story Sam was getting from the brunette at the bar.

'Sandra, did Mark say anything about strange phone calls? Or maybe someone he met who was . . . peculiar?'

Sandra frowned. 'No, not that I know of. And he would have told me, I'm sure.'

'Did he seem worried or subdued?'

'He was upset about losing his job. He thought they were unfair, and it hurt his feelings.'

Sonora nodded.

'But he was pretty much over it. I think Keaton gave him some money to kind of tide him over, and he had some saved. He was doing okay. He has . . . he had a real heavy load this semester, so Keaton told him to wait on another job till after finals, then put in a lot of hours as Christmas help. So he was okay. He had more time even, and it took a lot off him. That was why he was up seeing Keaton. Cause Keat was kind of down, and Mark wasn't tied to work, so he could go.'

Sonora leaned back against the couch. 'What was his brother down about?'

'Him and his wife are having problems. They've been separated for a while, and Keaton was trying to make up his mind if he should go back to her.'

'What did Mark think he should do?'

'There was some kind of problem about the schools where Keaton taught. He took the inner city ones, by request, and she pushed him into going to a nice one in the suburbs, and he wasn't happy. But he didn't seem so happy *without* her. He was lonely, going to bars a lot. I know Mark was worried. He'd have to be to cut class to go up there.'

'Do you know Keaton's wife?'

'Ashley? I've met her a few times. She works a lot.'

'Mark make any new friends lately? Say in the last month or two?'

'A couple new guys he was playing basketball with. Mainly pick-up games.'

Sonora reached into her briefcase. 'I want you to look at this sketch, and tell me if this woman looks at all familiar.'

Sandra took the sketch, turned it to one side, studied it carefully. Sonora watched her and felt disappointed. The blank look on the girl's face seemed genuine.

'It's just a sketch, it's not dead on,' Sonora said. 'Does it remind you of anyone at all?'

Sandra shook her head. 'Nope. Who is she?'

Sonora was aware of irony. 'Could be a witness. We just want to talk to her.'

Chapter Thirteen

The parking lot at Lynagh's had emptied by the time Sonora got back to pick up Sam. She noticed a Mini-Mart next door, remembered she needed mix for Heather's cupcakes. Her ears were still ringing from earlier in the bar, so she didn't hear the pickup truck pull up.

A young guy with longish hair and a sun-bronzed neck leaned out the window and grinned. Sonora did not catch what he said, but the sexual hostility was thick and the three men in the front seat laughed.

Sonora went into the grocery. Instinct led her to the aisle where chocolate was sold brazenly out on a shelf like any other uncontrolled and unregulated substance. She heard a masculine snicker and saw, from the corner of her eye, that the three guys from the pickup had followed her in. She was aware of pain in her stomach – the ulcer was dependable, if nothing else. Her face felt hot. She was tired, and not in a good frame of mind for this kind of stuff.

The one who had shouted at her, Bronze Neck, ripped into a carton of cigarettes and extracted two cellophane-wrapped packets. His fingers were thick, oil-stained. He nudged the guy next to him – overalls and a red neckerchief tied around the top of his head.

The third one had a crewcut and a space between his front teeth. He stuck the tip of his tongue through the gap. '*My* oh *my*.'

Sonora moved away, thinking she would not be sorry to

see these three handcuffed to their pickup and set on fire. She found an aisle that looked promising, passed Apple Jacks, pancake syrup – Aunt Jemima, juice boxes. She heard laughter, saw the men huddled at the end of the aisle. They headed toward her, balancing potato chips, snack cakes, beer and cigarettes.

The diet alone would kill them, Sonora thought. Just not soon enough.

Neckerchief walked close, jeans almost but not quite grazing her legs.

Sonora stayed put. Wondered what they'd do next. Her heart was pounding, which annoyed her. She did not give ground. They turned and went by again, shark passes.

Boys will be boys. Sonora paid for the cake mix, hands unsteady while she dug for change.

They were out front when Sonora left the store – short attention spans focused on a fresh victim.

She supposed that to certain Neanderthal-thinking juries, the girl could be dismissed as looking for trouble. She was anywhere from fourteen to twenty-four. Makeup was like that.

Hers had been put on with a heavy hand, black eye liner making the face look pale and harsh. The line of blemishes across the forehead and clustered on the chin were caked with foundation and pressed powder. Her hips were slim, jeans tiny, fashionably torn at the knee. The hair was carefully volumized with scoops of gel, and the small pointed breasts were loose under the tee shirt.

The girl was smiling, but it was an embarrassed smile, ingratiating, please-just-leave-me-alone.

One of the men had her arm.

'Come on, jailbait.'

Sonora winced. It was a term that always put a bad taste in her mouth.

'... not safe for a girl looks like you do.' It was Neckerchief talking. 'Hop on in the truck, honey, and we'll take you home.'

The girl pulled away. 'No thanks. My mom's coming.'

'Your mom?' Crewcut swished a toothpick to the other side of his mouth with a tobacco-stained tongue. 'Let's ride around a while 'fore she gets here. How 'bout that? That sound good?'

'Please,' the girl said. Neckerchief still had her arm and she tried to pull away. Her laugh was nervous but polite. 'Really, don't.'

'*Don't, stop, don't, stop.*' Bronze Neck talking. The men laughed, circled in closer.

'I got to go now,' the girl said softly.

Sonora wondered if her mom was really coming, if there was a mom, what this kid was doing out so late on a school night, how old she really was.

Neckerchief's grip tightened and the girl winced. 'Where you want to go, now, honey? We'll see you get home right and tight.'

This last brought the laughter out from all of them, and Neckerchief pulled the girl toward the truck.

Sonora unzipped her purse, hand resting on the Baretta with a light but joyous touch. The threat was tangible, and she gave herself permission to get involved.

'I really don't like you guys.' It was the first thing that came to mind. The girl looked up, startled, still smiling. Sonora was not smiling.

Bronze Neck laughed, but Crewcut was frowning. Something about her seemed to disturb him. One mark for intelligence.

'I think I want an apology.' Sounded good, Sonora thought, wondering what she should do with these guys. Arresting them would be incredibly time consuming, and on what charge? Menacing? They'd be back on the streets before the paperwork was done. And this wasn't her town.

'What you give me if I do?'

Sonora looked over her shoulder. It was late. That was always the way – nobody around.

'Looking for help, honey?'

Sonora took the gun out of her purse, took careful aim.

Crewcut took a step backward. 'Aw shit. We were just fooling around.'

'Say you're sorry,' Sonora said.

'No way.'

'Okay, fine. But get in your truck, and get out of my face. You too, Neckerchief Head.'

'Bitch.'

Later, when she went over the incident in her mind, she could not remember making the conscious decision to shoot. But the gun went off in her hand, and the man's face went dead white, and Sonora was sure for a minute that she'd hit him.

The bar door opened and closed. Sam. His look of bewilderment hardened as he turned from her to the men.

They were already scrambling into the truck. Sonora saw no blood, no sign anybody was hurt. Her luck had held, she was still a terrible shot.

The pickup's engine caught on the second crank. Tires screeched as the truck pulled away.

'We'll be back, bitch.'

'Yeah, and this time there'll be two of us,' Sam yelled.

Sonora looked for the girl, saw she was gone. Ten points for brains, if not manners.

Sam opened the passenger door of the Taurus. Gave Sonora a look. 'Accidental discharge tomorrow morning while you're getting ready for work. Get *in*.'

She got in. He started the car, slammed the gears into reverse, pulled out of the parking lot.

'When the hell did you decide you were Clint-fucking-Eastwood?'

Sonora looked at her feet. 'Why don't you calm down and hear my side of it?'

He wasn't listening. 'Those are probably the only three rednecks in Kentucky without a gun in their truck, you're lucky one of them didn't come up shooting. What would you have done then?'

Sonora shrugged.

'What *is* it with you these days, girl?'

'What is it with *me*? What is it with them? I got no patience for this stuff anymore, Sam.'

'No patience for what, Sonora, real life?'

'Hey, it was a rape in progress. Didn't you see the kid? They were trying to force her into the pickup.'

'Oh, well, then just blow their heads off, you got cause.'

'I think so, and you would've too, if you'd been there.'

'Maybe. And maybe we're feeling a little bit pissy these days, how about that?'

'Sam, you know me— '

'Your point?'

'I've seen you do worse.'

'You have not.'

'Fine, just shut up about it.'

'*Sonora*— '

'*Drop* it, okay?'

'What you going to do if I don't? Shoot me? What's so funny, girl, nothing here funny.'

Sonora closed her eyes and folded her arms. 'Interesting, isn't it, Sam? Women live with the implied threat of violence from men, and that's all right. Turn the tables and you don't like it much.'

'That's got nothing to do with this, Sonora. Don't put me in that pig category just because I'm male. You're a police officer and you're on duty, and you've got procedures.'

'It felt good, Sam. For a minute or so, it felt really good.'

'Let me know when you get fantasies about handcuffing men and setting them on fire.'

'If you think you're funny, you're not.'

Chapter Fourteen

It was three-thirty AM when Sonora and Sam parted company in the parking lot on Broadway. The downtown street lights cast a blurred yellow glow on the rain slick pavement. Some of the office buildings were lit, all of them empty.

Sonora got into her car and rolled the window down.

Sam leaned an elbow on the open sill. 'Going home, Sonora? Not strapping on a six shooter and ridding the city of vermin?'

'Home to *bake*, how's that for innocent?'

'I'm going to grab a few hours sleep, then go in early. You don't make it in on time, I'll give out the informant story.'

'Thanks, Sam.'

It was usually the other way around. His daughter's illness did not always coordinate with the murder rate. Sonora worked double time and lied liberally to cover for him when Annie was having a bad spell.

Sonora grabbed Sam's sleeve before he could get away.

He looked at her. 'What?'

'I didn't tell you this 'cause I was mad. I had a weird message on my answering machine. The office machine.'

'I get weird messages all the time, Sonora. Usually it's my wife.'

'This was a woman— '

'So's my wife.'

'Quit playing and pay attention. She didn't say much, but she did say "you'uns."'

That caught him. He leaned into the window. 'You think it was her?'

'Yeah.'

'What'd she say?'

'Just hello, you don't know who this is, but I'll call back.'

He thought for a minute. 'I wonder why she's calling you.'

Sonora shrugged.

'If it is her, Sonora, then she likes the chase. She may be one of those nutcases looking for a police playmate.'

'It's not like we thought she was normal.'

'Good point. Watch your back, kiddo.'

Sonora watched him get into the car, turn and wave. She glanced up to the fifth floor of the dingy brick building, looking at the lit offices of homicide. Fluorescent light poured through bent, yellowed venetian blinds. In spite of the chill, someone had opened a window.

She was glad to be going home.

Her car made the usual straining noises as it ascended the hill. Her engine would not last much longer on the streets of Cincinnati.

The rain had stopped, but the garbage piled up and down the sidewalk was sodden, raindrops glistening on dark plastic under the glare of headlights. A woman leaned out of a two-story window, tattered yellow curtains thrust to one side. In the light from the apartment, Sonora could see that the woman had coarse blonde hair and a hard look. She smoked a cigarette, gazing listlessly at the wet, garbage-filled streets.

Cincinnati was depressing after dark. Sonora rolled up the windows and settled in for the drive to the suburbs. She felt out of sync, equally pulled by the squad room and the home fires. Fires, she thought.

Home fires. Car fires. Mark Daniels up in flame. Keaton Daniels . . .

A horn honked and she jerked herself upright. She was in the wrong lane. She swerved to the right, hands trembling on the wheel. Sonora rolled the car window down, breathed chilled air, and leaned forward in her seat, driving slowly.

God, it was so easy. One minute you were driving, the next you were asleep. Was that what it had been like for Zack? Had he woken up before the collision? Felt pain?

There had been no alcohol or drugs in her husband's bloodstream. Sonora hadn't needed the coroner's confirmation. Zack had fallen asleep behind the wheel because he was exhausted. It tired a man out, juggling a wife, two kids, a full-time job and the blonde of the week.

Sonora turned down her street and pulled to the side of the driveway, careful not to block the black Trail Blazer parked in front of the garage. Clampett met her at the door, eyes bleary, tail wagging. The children, Heather most likely, had brushed out his fur and tied a ribbon around his collar.

Sonora gave Clampett a gentle nudge with her knee to make him move away from his ever ecstatic perusal of the garage. The house had the hushed peacefulness it acquired when the children were finally, deeply asleep. Sonora heard the hazy burr of static coming from the television in the living room. She went through the kitchen, set her purse in a chair, saw that there were dishes in the kitchen sink. Popcorn kernels littered the floor. Smears of chocolate syrup and rings of melted ice cream glazed the table and cabinets. Sonora wondered if they'd eaten the ice cream or spread it around with a brush.

She grabbed a blank pad of stick-up notes and scrounged for a pencil in the small tin of odds and ends on the microwave.

I AM NOT THE MAID, she wrote in large block letters. NO TV OR VIDEOGAMES TOMORROW TO HELP

YOUR MEMORY. NEXT TIME CLEAN UP YOUR MESS. LOVE, MOM.

She stuck the note on the refrigerator.

Sonora walked into the living room where her brother was asleep on the couch. The sports section of the newspaper was fully open and draped over his head and shoulders. His cowboy boots were on the floor. *He* did not have holes in his socks.

Sonora turned the television off. Her brother sat up, shoulders hunched forward, and rubbed a hand across his face. He reached for the round-lensed glasses that sat on the arm of the couch, slid them on his nose and blinked. He looked very much like Heather, except that his hair was blond.

Sonora sat in the rocking chair and closed her eyes.

'How many drinks of water do you give Heather when she goes to bed?' His lisp was very faint – only noticeable when you listened for it.

'One. How many did you give her?'

'Sixteen.'

Sonora shook her head. 'Idiot.'

He yawned and stretched. 'About dinner.'

'Yeah?'

'The deal was a home cooked meal for baby-sitting. Hungry-Man TV dinners— '

'You didn't read the fine print. I *owe* you a homecooked meal.'

'That's six in the hole.'

'You hear about that guy burned up in the car?'

He pushed his glasses back on his nose. 'That *yours*?'

Sonora nodded, closed her eyes. 'Man I'm tired, and I still have to bake cupcakes.'

'You don't want to go in the kitchen.'

'Too late. You look exhausted, too. Did you play with the kids all night?'

'Horsey rides and piggyback for Heather. Monopoly with

both of them. It's very energetic, the way they play. I can never figure out why you have to run around the table *twice* when you land on a railroad.'

'You could stick them in front of the TV.'

'Always the devoted mother. What time is it?'

'Four AM. Like in the middle of the night.'

He shook his head at her. 'Why are you making cupcakes? Bakeries, dork. You've heard of them?'

'These have to be Mommy-baked.'

'Lie.'

'Heather would know. Mine are always misshapen. They plump out.'

'Remember the night I was here and you grilled chicken?'

'Thank God you carry a fire extinguisher in your car.'

'Come on, get moving, I want to see how you charcoal broil your cupcakes. Can I use your phone?' He picked up the cordless mounted on the kitchen wall, punched in his code, and listened for messages. 'By the way, Sonora, you had a pretty strange call right around dinnertime.'

'Leave a message?' Sonora got a mixing bowl from the cabinet and studied the box of cake mix. Duncan Hines. Eggs, water.

'No. It was a woman. I go "hello" and she starts singing.'

Sonora looked up from the back of the box of cake mix, trying to keep the oven temperature in her head. Bake 375. 'She what?'

'*Sang*. An old Elvis song. *Love Me Tender*.'

'That's not an Elvis song.'

'He sang it, he made it his.'

Sonora scratched her cheek. 'Wait a minute, I don't get this. She sang *Love Me Tender* to you over the phone?'

'Yeah.'

'Sing good?'

'So so.' He hung up. Grimaced.

'What?' Sonora asked.

'Big crowd at the saloon tonight. A lot of people there for line dancing lessons.'

'That's good.'

'Yeah, but the girl who teaches went home sick and it looks like the flu, which leaves me with problems tomorrow. I can't cover for the kids, unless you want them at the club.'

'Not on a school night.'

'Oh, and Chas called. Wanted to know where you were, didn't believe me when I said you were working, and wants you to call no matter how late you get in.'

'Damn. Fine.'

'So don't call him.'

Sonora picked up the phone, punched in a number, rolled her eyes. Stuart looked at her.

'Not home. At,' she looked at her watch, 'four-sixteen AM. He did this on purpose.'

'Had you call and then doesn't answer?'

'If he's there.'

'Not all guys are like Zack,' Stuart said. Sonora looked at him and he grinned. 'Some are worse.'

'Boggles the mind, don't it?' Sonora got a large spoon out of the silverware drawer, and pretended not to notice that her brother was peeling her stick-up note off the refrigerator. He rinsed ice cream out of the bowls and loaded them in the dishwasher. Sonora could not remember ever seeing him do one dish the entire time they were growing up. She started to say something, then closed her mouth. In all the years they had fought over the bathroom, insulted each other, and been rude to one another's friends, she had never pictured her brother baby-sitting her children and cleaning her kitchen.

'Oh my God,' Stuart said.

'What?'

'Chocolate syrup on my polo shirt.'

'I'm going to an autopsy first thing tomorrow. Guess what kind of stuff I get on my shirt?'

Stuart cringed. 'Aren't you going to use a mixer?'

'I can't find it.'

'It's in Tim's room.'

'I'll just use a spoon. The lumps will probably bake out.'

'Do you think you should fill the little cups things so full? That's probably why they stick out like that. Sonora, didn't Mom teach you any of this stuff?'

'Yeah, I'm Donna-fucking-Reed.'

The phone rang as she was finally getting to bed. She picked it up on the third ring.

'What's so important you have to talk now, Chas, or don't you know it's the middle of the night?'

Silence. A giggle. Sonora frowned.

'You'uns sound like a girl in a snit. Don't tell me you got man trouble in the middle of everything else.'

You'uns. Sonora caught her breath. 'Who is this?'

'Don't play games with me, Detective, that kind of crapola is for men friends, not girl friends.'

Sonora sat up in bed, hand sweaty on the receiver. 'Girl friends, huh? So how about we get together and have a good talk?'

'Shop till we drop and go get some fancy desert?' The voice had a wistful twinge. 'You and I both know we'd wind up in one of your little interrogation rooms.'

'We like to call them interview rooms. Be nice to have someone to talk to, don't you think? I bet you have a lot to say.'

'If you're tracing this call, Detective, won't do you no good. I'm at a pay phone, and it ain't my usual place.'

Sonora listened for bar noises. Nothing.

'He's cute, isn't he?'

Sonora frowned. 'Who?'

'Keaton, don't pretend, I can tell you like him.'

'You going to kill him?'

Dead silence. 'You take the direct approach, don't you? Acting like a three here.'

Sonora frowned. A three?

'How about this? I stay off him, if you'uns do the same. You won't believe me, I know, but I don't want to kill this one. He reminds me of somebody.'

'Who?'

'Just . . . a guy I used to know.'

Keep her talking, Sonora thought. 'Look alike?'

'It's more than that, Detective. It's a certain kind of thing, an energy, a feel about him. Like he really sees me. It's the way he makes me feel. He puts me in the place I want to be.'

'You know him, then?'

'I know him. He don't know me.'

Sonora cocked her head. 'What do you want from him? Why do you want to hurt him?'

'I don't want to *hurt* him. I want to be important. In his life.'

You got that, Sonora thought. 'You telling me you kill men to be important?'

Laughter. 'You got to admit, it's a sure fire way to get their attention.

'Sure fire? Cute.'

'And they deserve what they get. You be honest, Ms. Detective girl, you'uns would see my point. You must have these thoughts. These men deserve it. This can't be a whole new idea, or you always been good?'

'Always,' Sonora said, thinking of the men in the pickup.

'If that's true, you cain't be happy.'

Sonora frowned. 'What does happy have to do with it?'

'Nothing, for good girls who do what they're told. Don't you see how that sets you up? Be miserable for the sake of everybody else. Never get what you want, 'cause that's bad. Build your life around some man, or you're nothing.'

Sonora took a breath, wondered if she was out of her mind. 'What makes you think I'm so good? I shot at three men in a pickup tonight.'

Silence. Keeping her off balance a little, Sonora thought. Hoped.

'You did not. Not a good girl like you.'

Sonora frowned. Was that a train in the background? 'Believe it or not, suit yourself.'

Silence. Then, 'Why would you do that? Police work?'

'I had my reasons, like you have yours. You do have reasons, right?'

'Nice try. It's funny, I didn't expect to like you.'

A click, and the connection went. Sonora grabbed a pencil and wrote on the back of a box of Kleenex, trying to get the conversation down verbatim, wondering in the back of her mind if she'd stirred the pot a little too hard.

Chapter Fifteen

The blade would hit the skin at nine AM. Sonora made it to the coffee pot in the lounge by eight-forty. She poured herself a cup, and wandered down the brightly lit hallway in search of the pathologist.

A sign taped to the green tile wall said BODIES *MUST* BE TAGGED AND BAGGED. At the bottom was a handwritten scrawl that said '*Please don't tie the pull tags on the bag together!*'

'Sonora.'

She turned. 'Eversley, yo. I was looking for you.'

'You wandered right past like a zombie. These early morning chop sessions must be hell on a girl with a social life.'

'I don't have a social life, I have children.'

'You must have had one some time or other.' Eversley sat on the edge of the desk, smiling smugly. His eyes were grey, his face round and ravaged by old acne scars. His hair was dark and wiry, and if he carried a bit more weight than would be advised by the American Heart Association, it made him look cuddly in a sweater. Something in his attitude suggested perpetual exasperation.

He glanced at a clipboard on the desk. 'You would be here for the crispy critter?'

'I would.'

'At least it's recognizably human. We got one in last week that would fit in your microwave.'

'Homicide?'

'Down girl. Somebody smoking in bed in their mobile home – otherwise known as an invitation to infernoland.'

'Who's up this morning?'

'Dr. Bellair.'

'Ah, well,' Sonora said. It meant everything by the book – goggles, apron, shoe covers and gloves.

'This one did not go gently into that good night. Talk about your date from hell.'

Sonora leaned against the edge of the desk, close enough to Eversley to smell his shaving lotion. She wished he wouldn't wear scent in the autopsy room, where one more smell, in the cacophony of other odors, was nothing short of an assault on the senses.

She yawned. 'This guy wasn't a date, he was a victim.'

'I heard about this one, Sonora. He was handcuffed, right? S & M.'

'It's not a sex thing, Eversley. If it was a sex thing, it's going to be like this, don't you think?' Sonora raised her arms in the air, holding them out to the sides. 'Or this.' She moved her hands over her head. 'He'd be cuffed to the head rest, or the door handles.'

'He'd have to have a hell of a wing span to catch both door handles.'

Sonora pulled her hands forward, wrists together, waist level. 'Instead, he's cuffed to the steering wheel, like this. You could call it the prisoner position.'

'You could, but I wouldn't.'

The soft tread of rubber-soled shoes caught their attention.

Even in dark blue scrubs, Stella Bellair had an air of dignity and elegance that managed to be distancing. Her posture was erect, her air of professionalism and courtesy rarely breached. She wore her hair in a chignon, tiny coral earrings adorned her ears, and her ebony skin, perfectly made up, glowed with health and well being.

Sonora wondered how she managed. Bellair's schedule

was as demanding as her own, and she was the mother of three. Why did Sonora know the woman's home was immaculate? Why didn't she wonder such things about men?

Eversley bowed. 'Good morning, Stella.'

'Morning all. Is the DB out of Xray?'

Eversley nodded. 'I saw Marty wheeling him out about fifteen minutes ago.'

'Coffee,' Bellair said, heading back down the hall to the lounge.

Eversley slid forward on the desk. 'Okay, picture this. Guy meets Girl. Guy gives Girl a ride. Guy gets the wrong idea. Girl— '

Sonora felt the vibration of the pager that hung from an empty belt loop at her waist. 'Hang on, Eversley.' She pulled the beige phone across the desk. 'Dial nine to get out?'

'What a good guesser. Nine is exactly the number you want. How'd you hit on it, are you some kind of psychic genius?'

'Can't deal with the living, so they handle the dead.'

'That is *so* offensive.'

Sonora chewed her bottom lip as she dialed. 'Tell me this. *Why* is it always nine? And why is it nine one one for emergency? What is this nine thing? Why . . . yeah, hello, Blair here.'

Sam's voice was thick with exhaustion. 'The brother called.'

'Keaton Daniels called in?'

'Yeah, that's what I said, he called in.'

'So what's up?'

'Thing is, Sonora, he wouldn't tell *me*. Said he wants to see you right away, and it's got to be you.'

Dr. Bellair walked by, heading for the autopsy room. Sonora realized that Eversley was gone. They'd be starting any minute.

'Will he keep?'

'I told him you'd be a couple hours. He said he was at his apartment. Number is— '

'The Mt. Adams address? I got that.'

'Wait. Your son's algebra teacher called too.'

'Who?'

'A Miss Cole. She said you should call her. Want the number?'

Sonora swiped a coupon for a BUY ONE GET ONE FREE chicken dinner off the desk and flipped it over. The price of a two piece dinner had gone up again. 'Yeah, Sam. Oh two six. Okay. Jesus. Anything else?'

'You hear back from your new buddy? Sonora?'

'Yeah, I did, and it's not so funny, Sam.'

'What'd she say?'

'We'll talk later, gotta go.' She hung up, listening to sputters.

Sonora headed down the hallway, nodding once to a surgical resident working off his bout of indentured servitude.

She went past the viewing window, where families could look through meshed glass to identify their loved ones, provided features were intact. She passed a sign warning of Biohazard, wondered what was up in algebra, and paused outside the green swing doors by a metal cart that held, among other odds and ends, goggles, shoe covers, and plastic aprons. She skipped the apron, but took time for shoe covers and goggles. The gloves, coated with something powdery to make them go on smoothly, were way too big, leaving an inch of latex hanging loose from her fingers. She double checked her camera awkwardly through the gloves, made sure it did, indeed, have film and working batteries, then went through the double swing doors.

There were several autopsies in progress, the sound of running water, large grey trash cans overflowing with waste. The smell of blood was strong, but overpowered by the cloying scent of Calgon Vestal Lotion Soap.

Dr. Bellair, hands on her hips, was studying a set of Xrays illuminated on the wall. Eversley was looking over her shoulder. Bellair pointed.

'Right there.'

Eversley nodded.

'What you got?' Sonora asked.

'Bullet frag.'

Sonora scratched the back of her head. 'You mean he was shot too?'

'Talk about your overkill.'

The gurney carrying Mark Daniels' body was moving, as if by magic, toward the table. Sonora craned her neck, saw that Marty was at the other end, blocked by the rise of Mark Daniels' head. She took a cautious step backward to avoid being run over. Marty always swore he could see where he was going, and no one liked to argue and lay themselves open to a charge of political incorrectness toward dwarves, but a month ago he'd given one of the pathologists a solid thump, and last week he'd knocked over one of the technicians. With Marty, of course, it might have been intentional.

He eased the gurney beside the examining table – stainless steel, raised edges, water hoses, and drains.

'Nothing about it in the hospital report,' Eversley said.

Bellair turned away. 'They had other things to deal with. Let's get him on board.'

Marty shoved his stool up under the head of the table and climbed to his perch. Like most dwarves, he was solidly built and broad featured. Sonora noticed that his gloves fit snugly, but his hands were larger than hers. His hair was brown, coarse and curly; his thick handlebar mustache going grey.

Two women, both senior medical students, took their places beside the table. The brunette, Annette something or other, Sonora recognized, the redhead she did not. Annette, as usual, was unfathomably hostile, her dippity-do hair flipping up neatly all the way around. She had disliked

Sonora on first sight, and Sonora saw no reason not to return the favor.

The bag was unzipped, and everyone except Sonora took a hand in lifting Mark Daniels from the gurney. They rolled him face down on the table. Sonora rubbed the bridge of her nose, thinking how uncomfortable he looked. The backs of his thighs and his buttocks had not been burned. Blood had pooled there after death, giving the skin a dark, bruised-looking lividity. A small trickle of blood ran from Mark Daniels' nose and trailed to the table.

'No clothes, right?' Sonora said.

Eversley sounded exasperated. 'Hospital says they're at the morgue, morgue says the hospital has them, EMT won't be available— '

Bellair was shaking her head. 'From the look of these burns, Detective, there aren't going to be any clothes to speak of. The ER doctor could tell you for sure, but with burns like these, the clothes would have been embedded in the skin, unless it was a belt buckle or something.'

'The arson guys didn't find a thing. I'm just double checking. Actually, we think the killer took them, so if you find a fragment or something, let me know.'

They all nodded thoughtfully. Everyone in the room liked being in on the whodunit stuff.

The body was turned, supports positioned. The neck sagged, the eyes wide. Nobody home.

Eversley picked up a hose and began to rinse the body. Marty worked his fingers along the back of the white, sluglike head.

The redhead was touching Mark Daniel's belly. 'Is this a knife wound?'

Sonora grimaced. 'Come on. Not a gun and a knife.'

Eversley touched the split in the skin. 'I'd guess it's a fissure from the burns. Let me grab a magnifying glass.'

Bellair pushed the recording pedal with the slip-covered toe of her shoe, and began her external examination of the body. The others, Sonora included, stood poised at the edges of the table, waiting to take the puzzle apart.

'Subject is white male, age twenty-two, sustaining several— '

It was long and tedious, the burned skin carefully examined with a five-power magnifying glass. Sonora yawned and stood on one foot, and wondered if Tim had been turning in his algebra homework.

She studied Mark Daniels' concave belly, the flattened buttocks, the hairless blistered scalp, and tried to connect what was left to the snapshots she'd seen. He would not get the chance to follow in his big brother's footsteps.

Eversley held up his camera. 'Another Kodak moment.'

They took turns shooting the blistered scalp, the charred stump of ear, the second and third degree burns, the blackened stubs of the hands. Bellair probed the bullet wound, and Sonora made notations in her notebook. The gloves were hot, and her fingers and palms were sweating inside the latex. Bellair wrestled the ventilator tube from Daniels' open mouth. The plastic popped and buckled.

Eversley put his camera back in the cabinet. He arched his back and stretched. 'Get your scoopers people. Time to make a canoe.'

Sonora heard the whir of the small circular saw, the blade cleaving a Y-shape at the top of Daniels' chest. The thick layer of skin pulled away like a heavy apron, exposing a butcher shop panoply of meat and fat, and fouling the air with the dark, human smell of an open body cavity. As always, the yellow globs of fat made Sonora promise herself that she would begin regular exercise. Tomorrow. First thing.

'I don't feel so good,' Sonora said mildly.

Eversley and Bellair looked up sharply, always in expectation that anyone outside the closed circle of death specialists would give way and hit the floor. It was considered bad form to go from the morgue to the emergency room – even worse to make the complete circle and come back dead from the ER with a fractured skull.

'Just kidding,' she said.

Bellair's expression was tolerant. Eversley stuck out his tongue. He took a large pair of lopping shears and cut through Mark Daniels' rib cage, and the orchestrated mayhem began. The intestines were scooped out, the internal organs removed, weighed, then set on a cutting board where a med student took slices and chunks and put them in specimen bottles.

Bellair took a cup of blood from the chest cavity and the redhead used a syringe to extract urine from the bladder.

'No gallstones,' said the brunette. She wrestled a knife across the tough yellow-opaque membrane of the gall bladder. Bellair slit the stomach, and Sonora suddenly smelled the loud odor of bourbon.

'Bourbon. Undigested popcorn. Some other stuff here, eaten a few hours earlier. Eversley can figure it out in the lab.'

Sonora made a note. Mark Daniels' last meal. Bourbon and popcorn – Cujos?

Sonora looked up in time to see Marty peeling the scalp over the top of the head. It pulled away like skin from a chicken, looking like a thick Halloween mask, and exposing the blood-reddened skull beneath the skin. Marty took a circular saw and cut through the back of the skull, a fine grind of bone clouding the air like chalk dust.

He took the carefully cut pieces of skull away, and Sonora thought of removing the shell from a horseshoe crab. Marty was precise and orderly, and instead of crab meat, his reward was Mark Daniels' brain.

'Epidural hemorrhage,' Marty said.

Sonora looked up. 'A blow to the head?'

Bellair raised a hand. 'Maybe.' She examined the tough membrane covering the skull, and cut the back section. 'I'd say this is from the heat.'

Sonora picked her camera up, and took a picture of the skull and membrane Bellair had exposed, then stepped back out of the way.

The sounds that came from the med students cutting boards made Sonora think of boning chicken. It was all much too much like what one found in the meat department at Winn Dixie, which, Sonora thought, at least provided a small insight into cannibalism. She hadn't eaten meat for several weeks after her first autopsy.

Bellair was frowning. 'Soot in the air passages. Pulmonary edema.'

Sonora made notes on the details of Mark Daniels' agonizing death.

And it was over at last, Bellair pulling off her gloves, intestines and various odds and ends belonging to Mark Daniels packed into a plastic bag, tied off, and left to rest between his legs.

Even dead people had stuff to keep up with.

Eversley wadded his soiled gloves into a ball, tossed them underhand into an overflowing trash can. 'You know the accelerant?'

'Gasoline.'

'I'll get back to you on the carbon monoxide levels, and the levels of hydrogen cyanide or sulfide nitrous oxide.'

'What's the cyanide from?' Sonora asked.

'Died in a car, right? All that stuff is petroleum-based plastic. Which means it burns like hell and gives off toxic gas. Likely he's dead from a combination of carbon monoxide and cyanide.'

'Not the burns?'

'They didn't help. But if it was just burns, he would have hung on for about three days, probably even lived. We'll see what the carboxyhemoglobin levels are, but cyanide disappears from the blood and tissue at a rate that in no way relates to the concentration.'

'Tell me what you're saying, Eversley.'

'He likely died of a combination of carbon monoxide and hydrogen cyanide poisoning. The cyanide levels will be hard to pinpoint, especially if the EMT was smart and gave him thiosulfate.' He looked at Bellair. 'They do that?'

'Wouldn't cyanide have killed him in a matter of minutes?' Sonora asked.

'Nope. Even with a hefty dose. Don't opt for the cyanide capsules if you ever hit death row.'

'Thank you, Eversley. I'll write that down.'

'It isn't a fun way to die. DA could make something of it in court.'

'Eversley, he was handcuffed, doused with gasoline, shot in the leg, and set on fire. DA should be home free.'

'Plus you got pictures. Because the defense attorney— '

'Eversley, you got to quit watching so much TV.'

Chapter Sixteen

Sonora had always liked the Mt. Adams area – the townhouses crowded cheek by jowl, teetering over the hillside, overlooking the river and the city proper. The gears of her car made whirring sounds as the street rose at a twenty-five degree angle.

A man stopped on the sidewalk and paused to look at the window display in the kind of jewelry store where they didn't bother to show prices. Something about the man, the set of his shoulders, the very shape of him, made Sonora hit the brakes and look back over her shoulder.

He did not notice, did not even look up, and it took no more than a quick second glance for Sonora to know that this was not Zack, didn't even look all that much like him.

She pulled the car back into traffic, feeling the sag in her shoulders, an ache in her back. She hadn't done this in ages, and she hated herself for it, that quick moment of recognition – yes, there he is – paths of logic in her mind setting off warning bells – no, Sonora, this can't be right.

For months after Zack's death she had unconsciously looked for his face in every crowd – mall, movie, grocery store – expecting, God knew why, to run across him at the Dairy Mart buying Shredded Wheat. Some part of her held those everyday mundane images, some part of her refused to believe that she would not walk into the bathroom and see him shaving.

The nightmare really was over.

She realized that the man reminded her of Zack because he looked angry – angry because she worked long hours, or because the kids were noisy, or because he was unhappy and any unhappiness was her fault, and life was unjust, and no one ever treated him right. Angry just because.

Sonora inched the car up the steep hillside, moving into the residential part of Mt. Adams.

Years ago the area had been favored by university students, but the Volkswagens and Kharmen Ghias had given way to four- wheel drive Jeeps, Audis and Saabs. Every other townhome had been gentrified, and everything, from the facade of a bar called Longworth's, to the Buckeye Security signs in a sprinkling of front yards, and the trimmed and beribboned sheepdog prancing down the sidewalk, said YUPPIE loud and clear.

For Sale signs were common.

Sonora passed Rookwood Pottery, all wooden beams and English Tudor attitude, maneuvered around a blue truck that said H. Johnson Moving and Storage, and smiled to herself when she spotted a townhome that was in bad need of paint, with a yard gone to weeds, and an old church pew on the front porch. Rebel heart.

The church pew proved to be too much of a distraction, and she barely missed a brown metal dumpster that said Rumpke on the side.

If she did not have children, Sonora thought, she would live here. Provided a bag of money fell on her head.

His was one of the better ones – a renovated, slender, three-story building of reddish pink brick trimmed in the shade of dark blue that the paint stores called Early American. The tiny patch of lawn was neatly landscaped and lovingly groomed.

Keaton Daniels had the front door open by the time she was parked and halfway down the walk. He was unshaven and did not look well, beard stubble against chalk white skin. He wore khakis again, a white tee shirt, thick cotton socks.

In Sonora's mind came the image of the brother, violated on the metal gurney, Marty massaging the scalp before peeling the face away, and baring the skull beneath. Sonora pushed hair out of her eyes, trying to shed the image, focusing on Keaton. I do not want to see this man on an autopsy table, she thought.

'Mr. Daniels?'

He nodded and opened the door, mouthing polite things that ran together and sounded absent and empty.

He bypassed the living room and headed into the kitchen. Light streamed into the breakfast nook. Daniels led her to a round oak table covered with white terrycloth, a half-filled coffee cup at one place, along with a brittle looking piece of buttered whole wheat toast, one large bite off a corner.

A red dishcloth was thrown across the middle of the table. A rolled-up newspaper was thrust to one side, the red rubber band peeled off, the paper uncurling. A stack of mail sat next to the plate, two or three envelopes ripped open. Sonora saw a water bill. Visa.

She took out her notepad and sat down across from the interrupted breakfast and waited, chin in hand, elbows on the tablecloth.

Daniels did not sit. He rested a knee in his chair, and shoved a thick finger toward a cheap white envelope with an Elvis stamp, canceled.

'I didn't go out yesterday, I didn't even get my mail. But this morning, I tried to at least get back in some kind of routine, so I made breakfast, got the paper and stuff.'

Sonora checked the tape recorder, saw it was working, then resumed eye contact. Daniels leaned his weight on the knee.

'All that time, this was sitting in the mailbox.'

He picked up the red dishcloth and uncovered a Polaroid snapshot. The picture was upside down, from Sonora's point of view. She moved Keaton Daniels gently to one side.

Mark Daniels looked through the open window of the

car, shirtless, hair wildly mussed. His hands were cuffed, stretched to the limits of their rings as he tried to pull them free. Sonora could see something wrapped through the steering wheel and looped around his waist. His hair looked wet, like he was sweating. No, she realized. Gasoline. He'd been doused with gasoline.

Just before ignition, Sonora thought. The look on his face was one she hoped never to see on someone she loved.

Sonora had gone through some nasty little caches before, but she had never known a killer to send one of the pictures to the victim's family. She sat down slowly in the hardbacked Windsor chair.

Her first impulse was to throw the dishtowel back over the picture, but the cop took over and she let it be. Keaton Daniels was beside her, pointedly looking away.

She took his arm. 'Come on.'

She had liked the look of the living room when she'd come in, the honey beige love seat nestled between two worn bookcases filled with paperbacks, a few hardcovers, children's books and games. An old walnut desk sat perpendicular to the couch, making a corner of comfort amidst the black leather and chrome furniture tastefully grouped on the other side of the room.

Sonora looked from one side to the other.

'The good stuff belongs to the guy who owns this place,' Keaton told her. 'His company sent him to Germany for nine months. The junky stuff is mine.'

'By all means, the junky stuff.' Sonora sat on the love seat and Keaton sat on the edge of the cushion beside her.

'There's more,' he told her. 'I called my mother after the picture came. I was afraid *she'd* gotten something.'

'And?' Sonora had her notebook out again, the recorder going.

'No. But she had an odd visitor. She's . . . she's in a sort of convalescent home. She's young but . . . it's complicated.'

'What kind of visitor?'

'A young lady. My mother's words. Who wanted to talk about Mark, and about me.'

'About you? Did your mother describe this young lady?'

'Small and blonde. Kind of fragile.'

Sonora ran a hand through her hair. 'Name?'

'Wouldn't give one.'

'What did your mother think of her?'

'She was puzzled. She didn't like the woman's questions, she was too *familiar*, that's how she put it. She means— '

'I know what she means. So what happened then?'

Keaton clutched the arm of the couch. 'That's pretty much all I could get out of her. I told her I'd come and see her, I'd see that it was all right. That made her happy. She likes her sons to come running.'

The bitterness came and went quickly, but Sonora wondered if the role of big brother and elder son wore thin.

'I'll go with you,' Sonora said.

He inclined his head toward the kitchen. 'What about that?'

'We'll have a technician look at it. See if we can pick something up.'

'Fingerprints?'

'Prints, saliva on the seal of the envelope, hair. Whatever.'

'That would be something,' he said woodenly.

It would also be unlikely, Sonora thought. This killer was too intelligent to lick the envelope.

The papers were calling Mark Daniels' killer the Flashpoint killer, a term culled from a quote by an arson investigator who had been discussing the flashpoint of the fire. Around the department they were calling her Flash.

Sonora wondered if there would be more pictures. It could get a whole lot worse. She studied Keaton Daniels, wondering how he'd hold up.

He caught her eye, held her gaze. Something changed,

and she realized she was breathing a little too hard. She felt high-strung, suddenly, and nervous.

'Did you change your locks?' she asked abruptly.

'Yeah.'

'No, you didn't.'

'What?'

'I'm a cop, remember? I know when people lie to me.'

'Must be hell on your kids.'

'It is, and don't change the subject. If your problem is the expense, I know somebody who will do a good job for a cut rate. Look, I'm not trying to be a pest about this. But this killer may have your house keys. She's called you, sent you a picture, maybe even gone to see your mother. I'm worried about you.'

It was true, but she hadn't meant it to sound so personal.

He moved away from her on the couch. Shrugged. 'I had some idea that if she came here, I could take her on.'

'Pictures change your mind?'

He nodded.

'Good.' Sonora glanced back at the front door. Glass panels lined both sides, which meant locks would not keep the killer out. 'You might want to think about an alarm system.'

'I'm subletting. I can't do something like that without permission.'

Sonora leaned against the desk, faced him. 'I've got something I want you to take a look at.' She dug into the briefcase, maroon vinyl, a gift of loving bad taste from her children who had spent some time saving up for it. She took the sketch and sat it on the couch beside Daniels, then stood in front of the desk.

The artist had worked with Ronnie Knapp for two solid hours, and Ronnie had been happy with the results. Sonora had made a point of asking him, later, in private. People often said the sketch was good when the artist was in the room – afraid of hurting his feelings.

The woman in the profile was blonde and unsmiling, though she did not look ethereal to Sonora. That kind of quality would be hard to catch.

Keaton Daniels frowned, but his eyes held the light of recognition.

'I don't know,' he said.

'Keep looking. She says she knows you, but you don't know her.'

'She *says*?'

'She calls me too.'

He looked ill. Went back to the picture, chewed his lip. 'I can't be sure, but she's familiar. Like I've seen her around, or something, but I can't place her.'

'Anything comes to mind on it, let me know. Look, I need to make a call, can I use your phone?'

'Sure. One right there, and one in the kitchen.'

'Let me take care of things in the kitchen. You get ready, and we'll go pay a call on your mom.'

'Do you think she's in danger?'

'I wouldn't think so, but I'd like to hear what she has to say.'

Sonora went into the kitchen, took the red cordless phone off the wall mount, looked at the picture of Mark Daniels while she dialed. Eversley's words from the morning autopsy echoed in her ears.

Another Kodak moment.

Chapter Seventeen

Keaton Daniels' mother lived in a convalescent home in Lawrencetown, located between Cincinnati and Lexington, on the Kentucky side. The 'home' was several miles down a two lane rural road. Sonora followed Keaton's rental, a navy blue Chrysler LeBaron. He turned left into a dirt and gravel drive – more dirt than gravel – and stopped beside a wood and brick ranch house that had been built sometime in the sixties or seventies.

Keaton led Sonora to the side of the house and up three steps to a concrete patio. A rusty grill, red paint flaking off, sat next to a wet mop. The grill was full of water. Lumps of white, burned charcoal floated in soot-streaked sludge. Old lawn furniture, black wrought iron, floral print vinyl, was stacked in the corner. The cushions were torn, the chairs missing legs.

Daniels knocked at a screen door that opened into a dark cluttered kitchen.

'They expecting us?' Sonora asked.

'I like to drop in unexpectedly.'

Sonora glanced over her shoulder. The house was surrounded by tobacco fields, stubbled with the withered brown stalks of stripped burley. The lawn was patchy and full of clover.

'Well, Keaton, oh my word.' The voice was loud and hard edged, and a woman opened the screen door in obvious invitation. 'Keaton, honey, I'd thought you'd come sooner. Come in, come in, bring your little girl in.'

Keaton stepped up into the kitchen and was gathered into

an awkward hug that neither he nor the woman seemed to find palatable.

'This is Police Specialist Blair,' Keaton said.

'Police?'

'She's a homicide detective, Kaylene. About Mark.'

The woman's mouth opened wide, exposing stubbles of yellowed teeth, one going black, several missing. She was a hefty woman, solidly built, and encased in a loose tent-like print dress, gaping armholes exposing a grimy beige slip. The woman was braless and her breasts sagged onto the expansive soft belly. Her hair was grey, sparse, pinned into a bun. Her eyes were pale blue, the whites yellowed, like wax build-up on a kitchen floor. She had a faint but noticeable mustache on her upper lip.

Sonora wondered if Keaton Daniels hated his mother.

'Honey, this whole thing is jest awful, jest awful.' She led them through the dark kitchen to a dining room and den that had obviously been added on. The family pictures on the walls perpetuated every nasty rural stereotype Sonora had ever heard.

'All my people were upset about your brother, Keaton. We're all family here. And honey, your mama. Your mama like to die. I wished you could of come up just that night.'

Keaton looked stricken.

'I'm afraid Mr. Daniels was with the police all night,' Sonora said.

Kaylene opened her mouth, then closed it. 'Oh well. Well then.'

The den wasn't dirty exactly. In fact, Sonora decided, it was clean. But the furniture was old, the flowered orange and yellow couch worn through on the armrests. An avocado green easy chair with a footstool had newspapers in the seat and a soiled lace doily on the headrest. A space heater glowed orange in the corner of the room. The fireplace was boarded up, and a black wood burning stove sat in front of the hearth. There were baby pictures of toothless infants with unusually large heads, and a bronze pair of baby shoes sat atop a stack of *Reader's Digests* on the mantle.

Keaton glanced around the room, and over his shoulder. 'Is my mother in her room, Kaylene?'

'That's where she is, hon. You go on, go on, I know she's wanting to see you.'

Keaton looked uncertainly at Sonora.

'Take a few minutes alone,' she said.

He nodded and moved down a corridor to the left. Sonora wondered if that was where Kaylene's 'people' were. If so, they were a quiet bunch.

'Come on and sit down, honey. I guess I should say Detective.' Kaylene settled onto the green easy chair and patted the footstool in front.

Sonora wondered if she was expected to sit at the woman's knees. She settled on the edge of the couch and hoped Keaton would get a move on. She'd felt safer working undercover narcotics.

Sonora put a tape in the recorder. 'How long have you run this home, Mrs.— '

'Oh, you can call me Kaylene. But if you need it for your records, my married name is Barton, and my maiden name is Wheatly.'

'Kaylene Wheatly Barton.'

The woman gave her a royal nod. 'Honey, you want some ice tea, or a pop?'

'No thanks.'

Kaylene picked up a Popsicle-stick fan that had a romantic picture of Jesus on the front – brown curly hair, soulful eyes, white skin. Angelic sheep and storybook children clustered around his knees.

'I don't know about you, but I'm burning up. I got to keep it warm for my people, because they get cold. Blood thins, I guess, when you get old. Mr. Barton says the blood will thin.'

Sonora began to feel fascinated by this woman with bad teeth who called her husband *Mister* Barton.

'How long has Keaton's mother been here?'

'Long about four years.'

'What's wrong with her?'

'I guess, you know, it's her laigs.'

Must mean legs, Sonora decided. She heard the deep male mumble of Keaton Daniels' voice.

'I understand she had a visitor.'

'You must mean that little girl come by yesterday.'

'What was her name again?'

'Well, Lordy, Detective, you know she never did say. Just told me she was a friend come to call. Mr. Barton told me this morning I ought not to have let her in, but I didn't know. She didn't hurt nobody. But, oh, Miz Daniels, she was awful upset after. Awful.'

'What did she say when she came to the door?'

'She come to the front door. Most of my people's family come to the side door there by the kitchen, we hardly use the front. And she says she's here to see Miz Daniels. Well, she's a pretty little thing. Tiny, you know, and that blonde blonde hair, not quite down to her shoulders, and wavy like. Brown eyes, and pale skin, but her cheeks was bright red. Scarlet, like she'd got a fever. I thought she might be sick even, and she seemed kind of shy. So I let her in, and took her to see Miz Daniels. I was expecting to see family and such, with Mark kilt like that.'

Sonora nodded.

'She's in there, and I was in the kitchen, making up some corn pudding for supper. My people love that corn pudding. It's sweet and they like that. I got the recipe from my cousin. She wrote a cookbook once, self publish by my brother-in-law.'

Sonora nodded again. Patient, always.

'And then I hear crying. I might not have heard much in the kitchen, but I was going through the den to check on Mr. Remus, 'cause he needed his Hayley's Flavored MO.

My people have schedules, you know, and they don't want to miss. It upsets them.'

Sonora was unclear on exactly what was scheduled, and had no intention of asking.

'So I pass by Miz Daniels' room on the way to give the Hayley's Flavored MO to Mr. Remus, and I see her door's closed. Now that's odd, I'm thinking, because I like my people to keep the doors open, so I can just check on them and such. But it's closed, and I think I hear something, kind of a bird noise almost, then voices. So I go on and get Mr. Remus his Hayley's, and I'm there awhile, 'cause he don't like that mint flavor, he likes the regular, and he can't make up his mind to take it. So finally, finally, I just say, well, now, Mr. Remus, I'll just leave it here while you make up your own mind.'

Something about the way she said make up your own mind made Sonora think of Sam, and she smiled, and Kaylene smiled back and kept on talking, and everything felt friendly in the room.

'So I just leave the little plastic cup on the dresser. I put it in little plastic cups just like they do at the hospital, because I don't cut corners, you know, like they do at some places. I do things right, though what they charge for them little cups is just nasty.' She nodded her head and blinked.

'Everything's gone up.' Sonora leaned back on the couch and uncurled her fist. Patience. Patience.

'Now when I go on out of Mr. Remus's room, I see Miz Daniels' door is open, and Miz Daniels is up on her walker, though you can see her laigs is bad and hurting her something nasty. And that little girl is leaving, but they don't hug or nothing. Now you would think, if she was a niece or something, she might give Miz Daniels a hug, and might check with me to see if Miz Daniels needed anything. But I tell you I saw right off something funny was up. Because Miz Daniels looks mad as can be, and her eyes are red like, and the tears is just a running down her cheeks.' Kaylene pressed her fingertips to her own cheeks, then cocked her head to one side and frowned.

Sonora waited expectantly.

'Sorry, I just thought I heard one of my people.'

'Was the girl upset?'

'No, she seemed kind of excited like. Really, she seemed sort of like my dog when he's got that cat down the road in a corner.'

'Smiling?'

'No, don't think so, but smug, that's what I'd call it. That shyness was kind of gone, and she seemed pretty pleased. And I didn't get a nice feeling, looking at this girl. The feeling I got was nasty.'

Sonora made notes. She dug in the vinyl case and took out the sketch of Mark Daniels' killer. 'Is this anything like her?'

Kaylene took the picture with eager hands.

'Well I just don't know, it could be. My reading glasses are in the kitchen. Let me get those, so to get a better look.'

Sonora followed Keaton Daniels down the thinly carpeted corridor to an add-on that had obviously been built to accommodate Kaylene's 'people.' The ceiling was low, and Keaton dwarfed the hallway. His footsteps were quiet, the whole house was oddly hushed, and Sonora realized that Daniels had different tennis shoes on – Nikes this time.

Kaylene Wheatly Barton had not been sure that the woman in the sketch was the same girl who had visited, but her description – tiny, shy, unsmiling – dovetailed with the impression Sonora had from the bar owner of Cujos. Sonora did not like the feeling she got from this killer, as if Mark Daniels' death was just the starting point for what she had in mind.

Keaton stopped suddenly and Sonora bumped into him.

'Sorry.' He put a hand on her arm and Sonora was aware of the weight of it. He leaned down and spoke softly. 'She's being difficult. I told her she has to talk to you, but I don't know.' He scratched the back of his head. 'She used to be very normal, your All-American mom.'

Sonora touched his shoulder. 'It'll be all right.' She moved around him and went into the tiny cubicle. 'Mrs. Daniels?'

Aretha Daniels was on the tall side, and had likely been slender most of her life. Her waistline had thickened, and her shoulders slumped forward, back rising in a hump that meant advanced osteoporosis. Her hair was dyed jet black, and she wore black-rimmed cat glasses with an old lady chain.

She sat on the edge of a single bed that was made up with a worn green bedspread of cheap ridged cotton. There was a chair near the bed, plastic with a walnut veneer, Harvest yellow padding, a waiting room kind of chair. The walls were paneled with fake walnut, there was no window. A small table sat beside the bed, the surface overwhelmed by a stack of magazines – *Good Housekeeping, Ladies Home Journal, Mature Health*. A box of Puffs blue tissues was half full, and a glass of water with lipstick stains on the rim sat on top of a magazine that featured the fresh, intelligent features of Hillary Rodham Clinton.

Three grey cartridges had been tucked into the tissue box for safe keeping. Gameboy cartridges. A book of crossword puzzles lay open on the bed, a dull-pointed pencil wedged in the gutter between the pages. Sonora smelled perfume – White Shoulders – and mentholyptus.

Aretha Daniels was hunched over a Gameboy, feet propped on the bottom rail of the bed. She sucked enthusiastically on a cough drop; Sonora saw it glisten on the edge of her tongue. Aretha Daniels' thumbs moved quickly.

'Fireball,' she muttered, her face mirroring the dull intensity that Sonora thought of as the videogame look.

Sonora recognized the recurrent bar of music that rolled forth from the hand held console. Super Mario.

'Mrs. Daniels, I'm Police Specialist Sonora Blair. I

work homicide for the Cincinnati Police Department. I'm handling Mark's case.'

The woman glanced up. 'Sonora? That's unusual.' She went back to the game.

Keaton sat on the bed beside his mother. Tension was apparent in the controlled way he put an arm around her shoulders. Very close to ignition, Sonora thought.

'Mother. Put the game on pause and talk to Detective Blair.'

Sonora winked at him, turned the chair backwards and straddled it, resting her chin on top. Aretha Daniels watched her out of the corner of one eye, and Sonora got the feeling she was annoyed by imagined disrespect. Good.

'Keaton tells me you're a schoolteacher.'

The woman rose slightly on the edge of the bed. 'I *was* a school teacher. I haven't taught since my husband's death. My legs gave out on me.' She patted her knees and winced.

'Are you in pain? Should I ask Kaylene to get you something?'

'Young lady, I am in pain every minute of my life. I wish there *was* something you could get me.'

Keaton Daniels winced, but Sonora ignored him. As did his mother, who put the Gameboy down on the bed, and gave Sonora a sideways suspicious look.

'All right, young lady, you want to discuss Mark. Very well. When are you going to catch his killer?'

'If I don't track her down this week, then we're talking months, years, or never.'

Mrs. Daniels' hand hovered over the Gameboy. She pulled it away and pursed her lips. '*Never* is not acceptable.'

'I don't like it either, so help me out. Because I think you talked to your son's murderer yesterday, and I want to know everything she said.'

Aretha Daniels made a choking noise. 'That horrible little girl that came yesterday. It was her?'

The irritable Mom-voice was gone. Aretha Daniels sounded cowed and old. Sonora turned her chair sideways and leaned toward her. Keaton moved close to her on the bed and she put her hand over his.

Sonora's voice was gentle. 'Tell me everything you remember.'

Aretha Daniels rubbed the top of Keaton's hand, and took a breath. 'She was Keaton's friend. That's what she said.'

Keaton's look was intense, guarded.'

'She talked about Mark. No, that's not exactly right. She wanted to know how I felt about Mark's death. She actually asked me that. At the time I thought she was simply . . . awkward. Socially. But she kept at it, kept questioning me.'

'What kind of questions?'

'Well, like, wasn't it awful, how he died? Did I think he was in a lot of pain?' Aretha Daniels swallowed and clutched Keaton's arm. 'Did I think about it, imagine it? Did I think he . . . think he . . .' The tears came suddenly, and Aretha Daniels sobbed.

Keaton pulled his mother close and slipped a wad of Puff tissues out from under the Gameboy cartridges.

She blew her nose. 'She wanted to know if I thought he had cried. If I thought he had *called* for me.'

Sonora felt the heat rise in her cheeks, felt the ulcer acknowledge the call to arms, her jaw clench as the anger flooded her senses with an intensity that seemed dangerous, at the very least to her stomach.

'And the whole time she was watching me. It's hard to explain. It was like she was hungry for what I had to say, but her eyes were . . . odd, somehow, the expression. And she never smiled. Not even at first when I said hello.'

Sonora knew that Aretha Daniels' had been afraid, and that the fear had shaken her, and hurt her, and that she would never admit it.

'Then what happened?'

'I told her to leave.'

Keaton's jaw was clenched. 'I want you to come and stay with me a while, Mom.'

'Keaton, no, I won't. I will never be a burden on you.'

'You aren't a burden and I want you to come.'

But he didn't, and all three of them knew it.

'Did she say anything else?'

Aretha Daniels shrugged, lifted a hand, let it fall.

'Did she ask you about Keaton?'

'At first, Keaton was all she talked about. I thought maybe she . . .' She turned to her son. 'I thought she was some kind of a girlfriend. That maybe she was the reason you and Ashley— '

'No, Mother.' Repressively.

Aretha Daniels looked across the room at Sonora, her gaze an accusation of a sort. 'You have children.'

'Two,' Sonora said.

'Ages?'

'Six, my daughter. A son thirteen.'

'Thirteen? No wonder you look tired. Up late worrying, I suppose. Keep him in hand, it will pass.'

Sonora smiled, but felt oddly comforted. 'I hope so. There seems to be a problem with algebra.'

'At that age, it will be a lack of organization and study. Likely as not he hasn't been turning in homework. Be firm with him, Detective.'

'Yes ma'am.'

Aretha Daniels looked at her sharply, as if sniffing for sarcasm. She patted Keaton's cheek, then pushed him away gently.

'You should go, it's a long drive home for you.'

'Mom, come on. Come home with me a while.'

Aretha Daniels picked up the Gameboy and stared at the tiny screen. She patted Keaton's knee. 'Be careful, son.'

Chapter Eighteen

Sonora went from the porch steps into the muddy yard, and took a deep breath. Keaton Daniels walked beside her, steps quick, hands deep in his pockets.

'Is there any place to eat around here?' Sonora asked.

'Probably something in town. Dairy Queen at the next exit.'

'I've got to feed my ulcer. Meet me at the Dairy Queen, we need to talk.'

He nodded, started to say something. Sonora waved him on. She wanted out and away. She did not like leaving Aretha Daniels behind in this farm-hell. She got her engine started first, gravel sputtering beneath the wheels of the Taurus. Keaton wasn't behind her when she turned onto the narrow two-lane road, and she looked back over her shoulder. Daniels was hunched forward over the steering wheel of his car, head bowed.

Sonora grimaced and hit the accelerator, heading down the winding road toward the blessed interstate. She kept an eye on the rearview mirror until Keaton's blue LeBaron showed up behind.

By the time Sonora pulled into the crumbling asphalt parking lot of the Dairy Queen, she was queasy and tired of the car smell. She parked next to the inevitable pickup, and Keaton pulled up beside her. She dug her cellular phone out of her purse.

Yes, the kids were home. Yes, the kids were safe. Yes, their grandmother, Baba, was coming to pick them up. Heather asked when she was coming home, sounding wistful. Tim asked if she had her gun and if it was loaded, and told her to be careful.

Sonora tucked the phone into her purse next to the gun and went into the Dairy Queen. Keaton was inside, studying the menu. He moved close to the cash register. Ordered fries, a barbecue, a Sprite.

'For here,' Sonora told the girl behind the counter. 'Chili dog, onion rings, and a Coke. Yeah, I want chili on it. That's usually implied, with a chili dog, right?'

Keaton looked at her. 'Be nice, Detective, this is a small town.'

The food came on red plastic trays. It was late afternoon, well past the lunchtime crush, and they had their pick of sticky tables.

'Over here.' Keaton took a wad of napkins and wiped a frosting of salt from a corner table.

A fern in a basket over Sonora's head dropped a leaf on the seat beside her.

Keaton Daniels stabbed a french fry into a white paper cup full of catsup. 'Nice place to leave your mother, isn't it?'

'Why is she there?'

'Her choice. Kaylene is supposedly a cousin of some cousin two hundred times removed. And my mother . . . my mother is nuts.'

'I take it you weren't consulted?'

'My mother made the decision so she wouldn't be a burden. Pays her own way, except Kaylene calls me on the sly every month or so needing money for what she calls "Mama's extras".'

'Do you pay?'

Keaton looked at her.

'I'm a cop, I'm nosy.'

'Sometimes.' He took a large bite of barbecue. 'My mother didn't used to be like this. The woman who limited my television when I was a kid now has carpal tunnel from playing videogames.'

Sonora looked at the chili dog, wondered how the ulcer would handle it, toyed with an onion ring.

'What was your mother like? When you were a kid?'

Keaton stacked three french fries and ate them in a wedge, sans catsup. 'She was a teacher. Where I lived, most of the mothers were stay-at-homes. Not like now.'

'What grade did she teach?'

'Elementary school mostly. Middle school for a while, then she was a principal.'

'Not surprised.'

'She was good at it. Good with the kids, but no nonsense. She would come home everyday, pick me up at my grandmother's, or whoever I was staying with, and she'd be all full of energy and the things that happened during the day. Always had funny stories to tell me and Mark. She always seemed more interesting than the other moms. I work with teachers, older women, and they remind me of what she was like back then. The ideal mom time. I miss her. It's almost like—'

Sonora had the feeling he was going to say 'like she's dead.' He stacked up three more french fries, then leaned back, chewing.

'So. You married?'

Sonora laughed. 'No. My husband's dead.'

Keaton tilted his head to one side. 'You're the first woman I've ever met who laughed when she said her husband was dead.'

'Cop humor.'

'Whatever. You're easy to talk to. Is that because you're a woman? Do you think women cops are easier to talk to?'

Sonora shrugged, ventured one bite of chili dog.

'I'm not being sexist. I know from my own work, men and women are different, have different strengths. Is it better for a cop to be male, do men get more respect?'

Sonora thought about it. 'Once in a while when I worked patrol, I'd answer a call, say a prowler call, and people would ask why they sent a little thing like me.'

'Is it weird being the only woman in male territory?'

'There are other women. I'm one of the boys at work. After work, no, I get left out a lot. But I see these guys all day, I have two kids, it doesn't break my heart. I don't like it when people think I get a promotion just because I'm female.'

'I know exactly what you mean.'

'Yeah? How's that?'

'Hey, I got hired *because* I'm a man. I get picked for committees *because* I'm a guy. See, if I advance, it's because men always get preferential treatment. They all think I have the advantage because I'm a white male.'

'Do you?'

'Maybe I'm just a damn good teacher.'

'How many men are there, teaching elementary school?'

'I used to be the only guy at my school, my old school.'

'You were the only man there?'

'Only. Custodian, principal – all female.'

'Is that good or bad?' Sonora started getting serious on the chili dog.

'Both. I liked being different, being the unusual one.'

'And bad?'

'You know how women, when they work together, their periods synchronize? How'd you like to go to work in a building with forty-five women all having their period?'

Sonora coughed violently. Keaton leaned over and patted her on the back.

They were eating ice cream. Sonora had gotten to that point where the food had been on her stomach long enough to make the pain of the ulcer go away. She felt pretty good. No ulcer pain and a hot fudge sundae.

She shook her head at Keaton. 'My situation *is* tougher.

Look, even the little things. One assignment I had, women had to hike three floors to get to the bathroom. Men never have to put up with that stuff.'

He poked the bottom of a frozen lime push-up. 'At my school there *was* no men's room.'

'They plant a tree in your name?'

'No, they just declared the bathroom unisex.'

'So?'

'So? I go in, there's a tampon dispenser on the wall. Three women combing their hair and pulling up their pantyhose. You think I feel welcome? Like I'm comfortable in there with a magazine?'

Sonora was eating french fries now, Keaton working on an order of onion rings. He pulled the streamers of onion out of the thick crunchy batter and ate them separately.

'Any time they need a piano moved – ask Mr. Keaton. One of the teachers wants help carrying in boxes – ask Mr. Keaton. I'm the school brute.'

Sonora stuck a straw in the milkshake. 'The men are way overprotective. Sam's been my partner, more than five years. Even now, I know there are times he just wants me to stay in the car.'

Keaton peeled a piece of chocolate topping off his ice cream cone. 'Try this. The first teaching job I got offered I lost, because I wouldn't coach the basketball team. I guarantee you the women don't have to coach.'

Sonora nodded. 'The minute I get promoted, I get jokes about my love life. And guys that don't have half my smarts, honestly they don't, they get these great assignments.'

'How'd you get homicide?'

'A lot of reasons, one of which is I write a good report. The clincher was because of a creep named McCready.'

'Why, he your superior officer?'

'No. You really want to hear this?'

'Yeah, I do.'

'Okay, let me back up to the beginning. I'm in uniform, and I get a call. A woman comes home and somebody has robbed the house. I'm first on the scene.

'So I'm looking around. And this woman, she's upset, you know, trying not to cry, because she's got her little boy, he's maybe two. And the house is a mess. Whoever has been in has ransacked the place, turned it upside down, pulled all the woman's underwear out of the drawer. And the whole time I'm in there, I get this weird feeling, something's not right. Just a feeling, my intuition, okay?'

Keaton nodded, leaning forward.

Sonora stared at a smudge of mustard, but she saw the house again, the woman, pale, biting her lips, holding her little boy, sleepy-eyed and slack in her arms. They had come home from the grocery store, and the trunk of their car was still open, still full of bags, when Sonora arrived alone in her patrol car. It was past the baby's nap time. Sonora remembered that he kept rubbing his eyes, laying his flushed pink cheek against his mother's shoulder. The mother had been young, blonde hair tied in a ponytail, nose and cheeks pink with sunburn.

It had struck Sonora that nothing was actually missing. The TV was there. Radio. Loose cash on the dresser.

She had done it by the book. Asked the woman to wait outside, called for backup, gone through the house room by room. Endured the tolerant kindly look from the husky black patrol officer who had come at her call.

Getting the details down for the report, it had dawned on her that her best friend in elementary school had a house just like this one, and that there was an obscure, little used attic entrance in the closet ceiling of one of the bedrooms.

She'd gone to check. Sure enough, an attic entrance, but no smudgy hand prints on the cover, which was wedged neatly in place. A child's stool lay on its side next to the open closet.

Sonora had stood on the stool, still barely able to reach, and had had to ask the cop, Reilly, to give her a boost. He had been good-natured but skeptical, offering to go up in her place. She knew from the glimmer of amusement in his eyes that this was going to be a 'story' tomorrow at roll call.

She dislodged the attic cover, sweat staining the back of her uniform, though it was cool in the house, air conditioning going full blast. The attic was dark, tiny slivers of light coming in from a ventilation grill up under the eaves.

The attic was hot, smelled of mildew. The air was thick and close and her cheeks were flushed. She hesitated. If someone was there, she would be exposed. But Reilly was looking impatient. Any minute now he'd take over and send her off to the kitchen to finish taking the report.

Sweat rolled down her temples as she stuck her head up into the attic, eyes adjusting slowly.

No floor, just a bare bones skeleton of wood supports, and thick pads of pink fiberglass insulation. Something large in the corner, huddled to one side.

Sonora took her gun from the holster, thumbed the safety off. With her left hand, she took the flashlight off her belt and flipped it on.

The spread of light revealed a man with a gun aimed at her head. Their guns went off simultaneously. His misfired. Her bullet tore through the man's windpipe; he was dead before the ambulance arrived. His blood had soaked the ceiling of the hallway outside the bedrooms.

It was the only time she had fired her gun in the line of duty. She had killed one Aaron McCready, out on parole, a PFO with a history of rape, drug trafficking, and public disorderliness.

At the time, she had felt lucky. Passed over. Then two weeks later Zack had his accident and was dead.

'What's that?'

Sonora looked up.

'What's PFO,' Keaton asked.

'Persistent felony offender.'

He leaned back. 'What if you hadn't looked? Think what if you had left him in the house with that woman and her little boy.'

She shook her head. 'I don't think about it. I dream about it. But I don't think about it.'

'It's hard to explain. The guys will be all together like a football huddle, and they'll have this kind of laugh. Then they'll look at me funny, like they forgot I was there.'

Keaton ate a spoonful of chili. 'Listen, I know about those conversations that stop. Only mine are in the teachers' lounge. Usually, it's about M-E-N. Or childbirth. That's all they talk about, the agony of labor. I mean, God, how bad can it be?'

'You don't want to know.'

'Why do you assume that?'

'What?'

'That I don't want to know? They look at me and launch into this big discussion of basketball. Like, I'm a guy, so all I can talk about is sports?'

'Let's just say they don't ask me to the poker games.'

'Count your blessings. I'm the only man in America who has to go to baby showers. And they always think my gifts are funny, no matter what I buy.'

'*Parties*? Do you know how many men want to see my handcuffs?'

'At least you're not some kind of male madonna. Tell a woman at a party that you teach first grade and she gets all starry-eyed. Like you're the Mother Theresa of elementary school. Puts a real damper on any kind of intelligent conversation.'

Sonora picked up a chicken finger, then laid it back on the paper box.

Keaton Daniels picked up a pork fritter and chewed halfheartedly. The glass doors of the Dairy Queen began to open and close, and people were lining up at the counters. Sonora glanced over her shoulder. Keaton looked at his watch.

Sonora thought, with a certain urgency, about the women's bathroom. And what it would be like if there were three men in there, checking their flys, jock strap dispensers on the wall.

'What's so funny?'

'Nothing. I think I have a junkfood hangover.'

Keaton started stacking trash. 'You know, at home and stuff, I eat salads. Fruit and cottage cheese.'

'I hear denial.'

Outside, the temperature had dropped. The sun was going down, the sky grey. They walked silently to their cars, pausing by Keaton's blue LeBaron.

He put a hand on the door handle. 'Day after tomorrow I bury my brother. Maybe I should buy a suit.'

'You don't have one?'

'Just my khakis. Teacher clothes. Most of the children I teach – suits mean divorce lawyers. Makes 'em big-eyed and quiet.' He cocked his head to one side. 'You'll be there?'

'Unobtrusive.' Sonora was aware of the roar of traffic on the interstate, the papery patter of brittle leaves blowing across the broken asphalt.

Keaton closed the car door, rolled down the window. 'Too bad we're not in one car. We could drive home together.'

She raised a hand and went to her car, smiling but uneasy. She had been thinking exactly the same.

Chapter Nineteen

Sonora took the elevator up to the fifth floor, where homicide looked out over downtown Cincinnati. She leaned against the wall, tried not to think about the embarrassment of riches she had consumed at the Dairy Queen.

The front booth was empty now, after hours, though an extraordinary number of detectives were working late tonight – most of them on her case. She heard sobbing as she walked down the hall.

Sam steered an elderly woman toward the exit – she was tall, big boned, and her hair was set in an old-fashioned finger wave. She held a lace-trimmed handkerchief to her eyes.

'Hi, Mrs. Graham.'

'Detective Blair, how are you, dear?'

'Surviving. You?'

'Better, now that I've gotten everything off my chest.' She patted Sam on the cheek. 'Are you sure I'm not under arrest?'

'No ma'am, Mrs. Graham. I need you, I know where you're at.' He took a bill out of his wallet. 'Now you take that, and don't be waiting at the bus stop after dark. Get you some dinner and a cab, you hear me?'

The woman patted his arm and folded the bill carefully. 'Do you think I should set it aside for the legal fees?'

'No, ma'am, we have legal aid for that.'

Sonora smiled sweetly and watched Mrs. Graham into the elevator. 'What was she confessing to this time?'

'Daniels, third one today. Must be a full moon tonight.'

Sonora stopped by her desk, saw the message light on the answering machine said two. She pushed the button. The volume was up, and Heather's sweet voice filled the squad room.

'Mama, guess what, I learned to belch the alphabet today.'

Several detectives looked up from their desks.

'Help me out here, Sam, I forget how to turn this off.'

'No way, I want to hear.'

At Z the squad room erupted in applause. Sonora grimaced, waited for the second message. A detective in the Atlanta police department. She scooted forward in her chair and dialed the number he'd left.

'Detective Bonheur.' The voice was male, black, pleasant.

'This is Police Specialist Blair, Cincinnati. I have a message you called?'

'Yeah. About that NCIC report you put out on the arson murder. You file VICAP with the FBI?'

'Not yet.'

'Just curious if you'd talked to them. Said your victim was a white male, age twenty-two, handcuffed to the steering wheel of his car and set on fire?'

Sonora was guarded. 'Yeah, you got something similar?'

'Pretty distinctive, don't you think?' He made a groaning noise, and she pictured him settling back in his chair. She wondered if it was sunny in Atlanta. She should move south. Cincinnati was ever overcast, ever grey.

'Had one a lot like it about seven years ago, almost to the day. That's what made me wonder. But mine didn't use handcuffs.'

'It was a she?'

'No question. Victim survived.'

Sonora sat forward in her chair. 'Tell me about it.'

'Man name of James Selby. White male, he'd be about twenty-six or seven the time it happened. He'd been in a bar drinking. Not a bad place, yuppie hangout. When he left, a woman approached him in the parking lot. Said she had car trouble. He told me at the time that he thought she looked familiar. I think he'd seen her in the bar, nodded at her or something. You know how they do.'

Sonora wondered who 'they' were. Yuppies, she guessed.

'He offered to look at the car. She said she'd been having transmission trouble, and she was going to ask AAMCO to come out the next day and take care of it.'

'Pretty smart,' Sonora said. 'Nobody's going to pull out a tool belt and jury rig a transmission.'

'Yeah. So he agrees to take her home.'

'His mama never told him not to pick up strangers?'

'He said it was kind of the other way around. That she seemed shy and scared to ride with him, but afraid to hang around the parking lot. He even offered her cab fare.'

'Nice guy.'

'Too nice. But she said no, just drive her home. She gave him directions, and they wound up way back in a subdivision that was under construction. Some houses finished, most of them frames – a lot of empty lots, earth movers, broken sidewalks.'

'They do that in Atlanta too?'

'Do what in Atlanta?'

'Build the sidewalks, then tear them up putting in houses.'

'Ummm.'

'This victim of yours. How does he describe her?'

'Small. Long blonde hair. Brown eyes, he thinks, maybe green.'

'That might be my girl. Think he'd be willing to take a look at a sketch?'

'Probably if he could, but he can't.'

'I thought you said he survived.'

'Blinded in the fire. Vocal cords damaged. Disfiguring facial scars, nerve damage to his hands. He was in and out of hospitals for three years.'

'See any pictures of this guy before the attack?'

'Nice looking, as I recall. Big, solid build.'

'Dark hair, brown eyes?'

Bonheur seemed surprised. 'Sounds close enough.'

'Did he say if she took pictures, after she tied him up? Use a Polaroid, maybe, or one of those Instamatics?' Sonora heard papers rustling.

'No, not that I recall, and I think I'd remember that kind of detail. On the other hand, you know how it is when people get hurt like that. He had gaps in his memory. He didn't remember getting out of the car, didn't remember the teenage couple who helped him before the ambulance came. He blocked a lot of it, so who knows?'

'Was that it? I mean afterwards, did she bother him anymore? Try to get in touch with his family?'

'Not that I know of.'

'Okay. If I can get my sergeant to approve it, I'd like to come down and talk to you. I'll show you my case file, if you'll show me yours.'

'I'm cool.'

'Any chance of me talking to the victim?'

'I could give him a call.'

She paused. 'How'd he get away?'

'Untied the ropes. She didn't use handcuffs, but I was thinking maybe by now she's perfected her technique. If it's the same one. You ought to talk to a Delores Reese in Charleston, West Virginia. She had something, arson murder, young white male victim. Happened about three years ago.'

Sonora wrote D. Reese and Charleston on a scratch pad. She heard Sam calling her name, the background shuffle as people headed for the conference room.

'Anyways,' Bonheur was saying. 'My girl used a rope – laced it through the steering wheel. I guess with your guy in handcuffs, he didn't have a chance.'

Sonora thought of Mark Daniels under the brilliant lights of the ER. 'No. No chance at all.'

The air was stale, the room thick with the odor of old coffee and tired cops. Sonora tried not to look at the powdered white doughnuts in a grease-spotted Dunkin Donuts box. Sam tossed a file on the table, gave Sonora a second glance.

'Look like you're going to be sick, girl.'

'Dairy Queen, and don't ask details, just get those doughnuts out of my sight.'

Sam moved the doughnuts, sat down, teetered backward in his chair. He pointed to a short, hefty man who drank coffee like it was a chore.

'It's Arson Guy.'

'My friends call me Mickey, my kids call me dad, my wife says you jerk. But here.' He peeled something off his tongue and examined it in the light. 'Here, I'm not a name or a number. Here I'm Arson Guy.'

'Somebody toss that man a cape.'

The door opened and Crick walked in, settled heavily into a chair. 'What you got, Mickey?'

The room went quiet.

Mickey drummed a thick finger on the table, scattering crumbs. 'No wallet, and no keys, except the one that we found on the floor of the car, driver's side.'

'Car key?' Sonora asked.

'No, too small.' Mickey made a space with two fingers. 'Might fit a briefcase, security elevator, or a pair of handcuffs. We're still working on it.'

Sam scratched his chin. 'Why would the key to the handcuffs wind up on the driver's side, where Daniels was?'

'Maybe Flash dropped it,' Gruber said. 'Or maybe Daniels got it away from her.'

'No sign of car or house keys?' Sonora said.

'You asked me that all ready. Nope.'

Crick looked grim. 'So she's got the keys and the wallet, the shirt and the shoes.'

'Trophies,' Sam said. 'Hey, Sonora, you tell the brother to change his locks?'

'More than once.'

A woman laughed in the hallway, and Molliter closed the door. Sonora checked her watch. A cop who sounded happy this late in the day was a cop who was going home. Sonora toyed with her coffee mug, finger smearing the lipstick stain on the rim. The smudge gave her pleasure – the mark of a woman in a room full of men. Plus it kept people from borrowing her mug.

Crick frowned. 'Sanders had court and it ran over, but she pulled the phone records from that bar, Cujos. It's a definite that somebody called Keaton Daniels' Mt. Adams townhouse the night of the killing.'

'Time?' Sonora said.

Crick stretched. 'Nine-thirty, thereabouts.'

'So it was her.' Sonora leaned back in her chair and closed her eyes, seeing Mark Daniels on the autopsy table. She thought of Keaton, and how she had left the tape recorder off at the Dairy Queen while they talked. She opened her eyes and leaned toward Crick. 'We got a problem with the brother. You see the picture Flash sent him?'

Crick looked up. 'Still in the lab, but yeah, I've seen it.'

'Flash has been to see this guy's mother, too.'

'Mark Daniels' mother?'

'Yeah, asking about *Keaton*. No question she's after him, Sergeant. She's called him, sent him pictures. Snags Mark in the bar that Keaton goes to. Kills Mark in Keaton's car.'

'Your instinct again,' Molliter said.

'For Christ's sake, Molliter, look at the behavior here.'

'Hey, don't jump down my throat, Sonora. Think about it. She did the dirty deed, maybe she'll move on.'

'Yeah, and clap three times for Tinkerbell.'

Sam scratched his chin. 'But she's not moving on, Molliter, that's the whole point.' He picked up a file, looked at Sonora. 'What was it she said on the phone? She wanted to be important?'

'It's not just that,' Sonora said. 'She said there was something special about Keaton. She said she didn't want to kill him.'

'You believe her?' Gruber asked.

Crick waved a hand over his head. 'Sanity check, folks, *believe* her? This woman is a manipulative sociopath, she'll say anything to get what she wants.'

'That's the point,' Gruber said. 'What's she want?'

'She wants Keaton,' Sonora said.

Gruber pointed a finger. 'She's calling *you*.'

Crick leaned back in his chair and folded his arms. 'Let's put a little extra surveillance around the townhouse. Get the night man to give Daniels a regular call, check up on things.'

Sonora realized she'd been holding her breath. Exhaled. Knew what the answer would be, but asked anyway.

'How about real surveillance? Somebody outside the apartment at night, and with Daniels during the day at work, or at least to and from the school.'

Crick gave her a small smile, rubbed the back of his neck. 'Sonora— '

'She's after him, Crick, you know she is. Surveille *him* and we'll catch *her*.'

'Sonora— '

'You want another one? Up in flames? You seen the Daniels' autopsy shots?'

'Sonora— '

'I'll put in extra hours.' She waited.

'Oh good. I get to finish a sentence.' He held up a finger.

'One, you're already working extra hours. You going to quit sleeping? Two, something like this, it's open ended. She could hit him now, next week, next month. Could even be next year. We don't have that kind of manpower and you know it.'

Sonora nodded. She knew the load, the budget, the economy. 'This can all be traced back to George Bush.'

Molliter looked up. 'Excuse me?'

Sonora caught Crick's eye. 'You realize she likes games. She's playing catch me if you can. That's why I'm getting the calls.'

Crick gave her a cagey smile. 'Glad you brought that up. Much as the camera loves my face,' he slapped his left cheek, 'Lieutenant Abalone and I have talked it over, and we want you, yes you, Sonora, to do the press conference. Which, by the way, is scheduled this evening in about one hour.'

Sonora swallowed. 'Very funny, sir.'

'Couldn't be more serious. We like the woman-to-woman angle. She does too, obviously. Flash will be watching, and we want her watching you. Maybe she'll call you again. Have a little girl talk.'

Sam grimaced. 'The things you girls talk about.'

'I like it,' Gruber said.

Molliter looked her over. 'She's got a spot on her tie.'

'Look, Sergeant, I don't see what this has to do with giving Keaton protection, and I'm not feeling too good, and I'm really bad at any kind of thing where I have to get up in front of people and— '

Sam shook his head. 'She'll get nervous and throw up. She's scared to death to stand up and talk in front of people. Won't even raise her hand at a PTA meeting.'

Gruber shrugged. 'Just make sure she throws up before they start the cameras.'

Crick raised his voice. 'Just look confident, Sonora. Say you're closing in, that you're going to make an arrest any time now. Be patronizing. Make it clear that you know Flash isn't half as smart as you are.'

'Gonna take some acting to pull that off.' A voice from the back.

'You want her to show the sketch?' Sam asked.

'We sent it over to the television stations this morning when we set this up.'

Sonora looked down at her tie, then over at Sam's. 'Yours is clean. Too bad it's ugly.'

He pulled the knot loose, and tossed the tie across the table.

Sonora looked at Crick. 'Anything else?'

'Withhold the business with the handcuffs. Hold the keys – the small one and the ones that are missing.' He stood up, stretched, looked her up and down absently. 'And comb your hair.'

Chapter Twenty

Sonora took a count of reporters, camera people, pretty faces with microphones. She looked down at Sam's tie. Ugly.

Mokie Barnes, Cincinnati PD's public information officer, gave her a worried look, saw she was watching, and smiled encouragingly. Sonora was not without sympathy. If she were a PR person, she would not consider herself good material either.

Barnes stepped in front of the lights and cameras, said a few words Sonora was too nervous and preoccupied to make sense of, then motioned Sonora to come forward.

The lights from the cameras warmed the room. Sonora had everyone's complete attention. She didn't want it.

She swallowed, throat dry, knees shaky, thinking of the Monday morning quarterbacks at the department who would be watching with critical eyes. She cleared her throat, then remembered Mokie had told her not to. Strike one. She lifted her chin and began to speak.

'Sometime late last Tuesday night, Mark Daniels, age twenty-two, left a local bar with an unknown woman. Mr. Daniels was later rescued from a burning automobile in Mt. Airy Forest, by Patrol Officers Kyle Minner and Gerald Finch. Mr. Daniels sustained severe burns and died early Wednesday morning at University Hospital. Officer Minner was critically injured while freeing Mr. Daniels from his car—'

'Did Daniels live long enough to identify his killer?' Tracy Vandemeer. Right on cue, cooperating, as asked.

Sonora looked sternly into the camera. 'Mr. Daniels was able to give us detailed information on his assailant before he died. We expect to make an arrest very soon.'

'Was the killer the woman he left with from the bar?'

'Do you have her name?'

'Can you describe her?'

'Is the killer a woman?'

Sonora nodded. 'We believe so.'

'How did she kill him?'

Sonora looked grave. 'Mr. Daniels was tied up, doused with accelerant, then set on fire.'

'Was he conscious?'

'Yes.'

'Had he had sexual relations with this killer?'

'We don't believe so.'

'Was this woman a prostitute?'

'How long was he in the car before the officer pulled him out?'

Sonora made a grudging show of reluctance. 'We do not think the killer was a prostitute, but we do not rule that out.'

'Can you describe her?'

'Was she working with a partner?'

'Was Daniels robbed?'

'Did Daniels know his killer?'

'We believe Mr. Daniels met the woman in a bar Tuesday night, a few hours before his death.'

Intense faces. Furious scribbling from the print media.

'Had they known each other long?'

Sonora shook her head. 'We're still working on that.'

'Do you have her name?'

'We can't release that information at this time.'

'Wasn't Daniels from Texas?'

'He was from Kentucky, wasn't he?'

'Mark Daniels was a student at the University of Kentucky, and was working on a bachelor's degree in social work.'

'What do you know about the killer?'

'The woman last seen with Daniels is small-boned and short. She has brown eyes and wavy blonde hair. We have a sketch.' Sonora waited for the cue from the camera man. He nodded and she went on. 'Anybody who has seen this woman, or has any information about this crime, is asked to call the police department immediately, and ask for Specialists Blair or Delarosa.'

'Detective Blair, don't you consider this a rather grisly crime for a woman to commit?'

'I think it's a grisly crime for anyone to commit, and I personally intend to see the perpetrator brought to justice.' God, Sonora thought. I sound like Dragnet. But Crick had said to make it personal.

'What kind of a person does this?'

Sonora thought of her key words. Pathetic. Dysfunctional. 'We're obviously talking about a *pathetic* individual with extremely poor social skills— '

Someone in the back of the room laughed loudly. 'I'll say.'

'A severely dysfunctional individual.' Sonora took a breath. She'd gotten it all in. She looked at them, felt relieved – let them hammer, then wind down. She nodded, did not smile, thanked them for their attention and walked away.

Someone called her name. Tracy Vandemeer smiled maliciously. '*Love* the tie, Sonora.'

Chapter Twenty-One

Mark Daniels' father had been born, raised, and buried in Donner Kentucky. In death, at least, Mark would follow in his footsteps.

Sonora drove and Sam frowned over a map. He smelled faintly of cologne, his cheeks pink and freshly shaven. He had gotten a hair-cut the day before, and he looked younger than ever, different in his best suit.

He refolded the map, pulled down the visor and looked in the mirror, fingering his tie.

'I don't know, Sonora. Yellow? What do you think?'

'I kind of love it, Sam.'

'I hate any tie I don't pick out my own self. That a new lipstick?' he asked.

'Yeah.'

'Too dark.'

Sonora looked in the rear-view mirror.

'Watch *out*.'

She looked up, and slammed on the brakes.

'*Jeez*,' Sam said. 'Your lipstick is fine.'

'You'll be the visible cop,' Sam was saying as they pulled up to the red brick church. White columns gave the structure a feeling of elegance and grace. 'Here, here, park here.'

'I hate to parallel park.'

'Come on, Sonora.'

She pulled to the side of a white Lincoln Continental.

Sam shifted in his seat. 'Molliter and Gruber should be

here already, looking through the crowd. Flash will be tempted as hell to show up.'

'I'm staying close to Keaton. He'll signal if someone looks promising, odd in any way. You watch the girls in the pews, see if they're crying like their hearts will break, or looking smug. Looking hellish at Sandra, or watching Keaton.'

'Yeah.'

'Love that tone, Sam. You don't think he had anything to do with it?'

'No. It was too nice a car to burn up if it was his own.'

Cars were arriving in a steady stream, circling the church parking lot and cruising up and down the main drag, looking for a place to light. Sonora looked over her shoulder, turned the wheel hard to the right.

Sam pretended to wipe sweat from his brow. 'I was sure that Lincoln had bought it, at least as far as the paint job.'

'It's hard to see in this Taurus, Sam.'

'We need teeny tiny cars for teeny tiny cops.' He unbuckled his seat belt and got on the radio. 'I'll bet Molliter's been here a half hour. He's usually early.'

'He's anal retentive.' Sonora laid her head back on the seat. They hadn't stopped for lunch and the ulcer was saying hello. She glanced at Sam, still on the radio, coordinating, and tapped a fingernail on the steering wheel, half expecting Sam to comment on the dark nail polish.

A navy blue Chrysler LeBaron, a rental, pulled up across the street, stopping in a no parking zone. The driver's door opened and Keaton stepped out. He wore the inevitable khakis and a blue striped shirt, dark tie, sportcoat. Reeboks this time, and they looked new.

Sonora laughed softly. 'So he didn't get the suit. Good for you, Keaton.'

He opened the passenger door and helped his mother out onto the curb. She leaned heavily on two canes, her steps slow, short and cautious. Keaton stayed close, looking both ways before they crossed the street, stepping between his mother and oncoming traffic.

They were up onto the sidewalk when he saw Sonora. He smiled and she smiled, and they looked at each other for a long steady moment before he turned back to his mother, gave her his arm, and helped her up the concrete stairs.

Sam clicked the radio off. 'What was all that about?'

'All *what* about?'

Sam looked from Sonora to Keaton, then back to Sonora. 'You know better.'

Sonora flipped hair over her shoulder. Opened her car door. 'Butt out, Sam. There's nothing here for you to worry about.'

'Tell me another one, girl.'

The cemetery was on the outskirts of town and badly in need of mowing. Trees were few and far between, headstones thick across the gentle roll of hills in this community of the dead.

Sonora saw a headstone for a PFC Ronald Daniels who had died at age nineteen. She looked at the month and year of death. Tet Offensive, Vietnam. A tiny American flag speared the ground beside the pinkish marble headstone.

Sonora was aware of intense activity in every direction. Frail elderly men and women being helped into chairs, Keaton Daniels moving from one group to another. His mother, seated up front, wiping her eyes with a neatly folded handkerchief. Molliter, Sam – detectives looking at license plates, faces in the crowd.

The papers had reported that Mark Daniels had lived long enough to describe his killer. Flash would know better than to come.

The temperature dropped as the wind whipped up, sending hats flying. People bowed their heads and shoulders, partly in grief, partly against the wind that tore at their clothes and rippled their hair. Sonora jammed her hands into her jacket pockets, grimacing when the wind carried her tie over her shoulder, and made her skirt billow and bare her legs. The crowd shifted and settled as the graveside ceremony began, and Sonora wondered what was left to be said that hadn't already been covered inside the church.

A car from Channel-WKYC-TV-Live-From-Oxton pulled presumptuously onto the lawn and Sonora groaned, amazed that such a small town had a television station and news team. The *Cincinnati Post* had sent a photographer, who had taken a few quick shots of mourners in front of the church, then gone.

Sonora wondered if some regional opportunist was stringing for a Cincinnati station. At least if they covered the funeral, they'd show the artist's rendering of Flash. Maybe someone knew her.

The reporter was shunned as she videotaped the funeral from a discreet distance, disapproval evident in the stiffly turned backs. Only the children watched openly.

One of the funeral directors, face tensely polite, descended upon the camerawoman, smiling, gesturing, explaining the legal range. The woman went rigid, legs braced, thick, blue-black hair blowing in the wind. She shrugged, moved a few yards away, and lifted the camera.

Odd for her to be working alone, Sonora thought.

The minister called for a prayer. Every head bowed, except Sonora's. She watched Keaton Daniels, sportcoat whipping in the wind. And realized that she was not the only one watching.

The reporter had the vid cam focused almost exclusively on Keaton, and Sonora turned and stared.

The woman leaned forward, arms rigid, and even from a distance, Sonora could see that her complexion was fair, despite the perfectly aligned black hair.

Everything fell into place – a strange woman in a black wig, working a camera alone, focusing on Keaton.

Flash.

Sonora started toward her, pacing herself. Keep it slow and easy; don't spook her. The woman was short, maybe five one, fine-boned and disappointingly average looking. Just as Sonora was wondering what she expected – some physical manifestation of blood lust? – the camera swung reluctantly away from Keaton, capturing his mother and his wife, then moved again, panning the crowd, making a circle and resting at last on Sonora.

Flash let the camera drop, and for a long moment the two of them eyed one another. Sonora paused mid-stride and any doubts she'd had dissolved. The wind blew hard against her chest, and her mouth went dry. The woman tucked the camera under her arm and turned away.

Got you, Sonora thought.

Flash went straight for the car, walking quickly, but not running. Sonora picked up her pace, slowed by high heels that dug into the spongy ground, all the while thinking about the sensible flats in the bottom of her closet beneath the snowboots, also unused.

'Shit,' she said. 'Shit shit.'

Flash was moving faster now, skirting the back of the car. Sonora's purse slid down her arm and she kicked off the high heels and ran, aware that some of the mourners were beginning to turn and stare, aware that if she was wrong she was going to disrupt Mark Daniels funeral and look like an idiot and maybe get a reprimand from her sergeant. The damp grass was a cold shock through the nylon on her feet, and it crossed her mind that if she was going to make a habit of wearing ten dollar pantyhose to work, she would have to start taking bribes.

'Hey, girlfriend, wait up!'

Flash faltered, then slid into the front seat of the car and slammed the door. Sonora thought of her gun, buried amid the rubble in her purse, which she had dropped along with the shoes. She was a homicide cop. Out of the gun habit. DBs didn't shoot back.

Loose gravel bit into Sonora's feet as she hit the pavement. The car engine caught just as she reached the side door. She snatched the handle. Locked.

Sonora made eye contact, saw Flash set her lips in a thin line. Flash jerked the car into reverse in a spurt of acceleration that ripped the metal handle out of Sonora's hand, twisting her wrist with a bruising wrench. Sonora stumbled forward and fell, skidding on her knees. She heard the shift of gears and the growl of the engine being revved, and she tried to scramble to her feet. No time.

Sonora threw herself sideways, vaguely aware that someone – Sam? – was shouting her name. She saw the left bumper of the car veer toward her, saw spots of rust on the metal. She shut her eyes, bracing for the blow.

Sonora felt a rush of air. The tires passed inches from her head. She lay still, feeling the wet ground seep through her jacket and skirt.

Too close, she thought, thinking the unthinkable – Tim and Heather, orphans in the world. She wondered if she had enough life insurance.

It was getting damn personal, this case.

Chapter Twenty-Two

The world was suddenly full of legs and voices, people calling her name. Someone shouted officer down, and Sonora looked up to see Sam crouching beside her. She sat up, aware that her knees were stinging and sore.

'You hit?'

'It was Flash, Sam, get on the— '

'Done, girl, you think you're the only one around here with a brain? Called it soon as I saw you running. You okay?'

Sonora looked at her legs. Balls of nylon hung from a large hole in her pantyhose, and her knees showed tiny pinpricks of blood across abraded flesh. Her kids often came inside with worse, and she'd stick a Band-Aid on them and send them right back out.

She felt mildly disappointed.

A new voice interjected. Gruber. 'What'd you chase her for, Blair? She wouldn't have spooked if you'd just called it in. We could have— '

'Can the Monday morning quarterbacking, will you?' Sam said. 'You going to sit on your butt all day?'

Sonora took his hand, felt hot pain in hers. Gruber went behind her, putting his hands on her ribs, and lifted her to her feet.

They were thick around her, Sam, Gruber, Molliter. She looked over Sam's shoulder, saw Keaton Daniels three feet away, watching. He waved. She waved back with the hand that didn't hurt.

Off in the distance, there were sirens.

Sonora sat sideways on the passenger's side of the Taurus, trying to fill out a report with her left hand. The door was open, and her feet dangled over the side of the seat. She shivered. Her skirt was wet. It was getting cold out.

The radio crackled, the voice of the local dispatcher providing a comforting cop background. Sam sat on the hood of a Kentucky State Police car, talking amiably with a tall man in a Smokey hat.

'It was her, wasn't it?' Keaton Daniels rested an elbow on the car door, a pair of black high heels dangling from his fingers. He handed the shoes to Sonora.

'It was her.' Sonora turned the shoes over, studying the heels.

'Filming it. Filming my brother's funeral.' Keaton spoke through clenched teeth.

'Filming *you* at your brother's funeral. There's a difference, and I don't much like it.'

'I thought you were right-handed,' he said, focusing on the pen in her left hand.

She showed him the wrist that was swelling and taking on a bluish cast.

'I thought she'd hit you. With the car.'

'She gave it her best.'

'But you're okay.'

'Yeah, I'm okay.'

He handed her a slip of yellow notebook paper. 'I'm going back to the house. My great aunt's house. This is the address and phone number.'

'I'm sorry about all this, Keaton. As soon as I hear something, I'll be in touch.'

Her mud-stained blazer was draped over the headrest of the seat. He ran a gentle finger down the torn lapel.

'Be careful, Detective.'

He turned his back and walked away and she watched him

until the sound of heels on pavement caught her attention. Sam came toward the Taurus, gave Daniels a look that was not exactly friendly.

He rocked back and forth on the balls of his feet. 'Word just came in over the radio.'

'They got her?'

'No, she got them. Body of a security guard, over at WKYC-TV in Oxton, multiple gunshot wounds in the back. DB was found near a dumpster that'd been set on fire. And the station car is missing.'

'Flash, then.'

He took a handkerchief out of his pocket, spit on it, wiped mud off her chin.

'Gross, Sam. Oxton people mind if we come take a look?'

'Said to come along. What about your hand? You want to get it looked at?'

'No. You drive, let's hit the road. Know how to get there?'

'Nah.'

'God forbid you should ask directions.'

The road passed through farmland in a succession of hairpin turns. Sonora admired the locals who could regularly drive the posted speed of fifty-five miles per hour and live to tell about it.

Her wrist throbbed and she shifted to a more comfortable position, watched the By-Bee Mobile Home Park go by. The playground out front was abandoned and bedraggled – swings missing from the rusted metal A-frame, a merry-go-round listing dangerously to one side. There was only one board intact on the seesaws, red paint peeling away.

The mobile homes were old, rusting, the parking lot full of pickups, Trans Ams, and Camaros. One of the houses had window boxes, but no flowers. A yellow dog trotted under the swings, nose to the ground.

The speed limit went from 55 to 25 MPH. Oxton was tiny – a feed store, Farmers Food Co-op, Bruwer's Bakery, Super America. A small grocery store advertised MARLBORO LIGHTS and VIDEOS. They passed a CHURCH OF GOD'S DISCIPLES FOR THE LORD. Sunlight glinted on Pabst Blue Ribbon beer cans stacked by a yellow sign warning of hazardous curves. Sam pulled over and studied the map.

'It's a small town, Sam.'

'Yeah?'

'So I see flashing lights, as in emergency vehicles. Over the hill there, see? How many emergencies you think they have in one afternoon?'

'No more than one or two.'

WKYC-TV was housed in a squat concrete cube, the back parking lot fenced off with twelve feet of chainlink topped by barbed wire. Sonora and Sam parked alongside the street in front of an H&R Block and a Yen Yens Quick Chinese.

'I want an eggroll,' Sonora said.

'Let's look at the DB first. If you seriously want to risk Chinese in a town this size.'

Sam got out of the car and headed for the deputy. Sonora hung back to watch, waiting for Sam to work his good ole boy magic.

She put her high heels on, smoothed her skirt, which had wrinkles and mud enough to be attention getting. She straightened her tie and put on more of the dark lipstick Sam didn't like.

Sam wiggled his fingers at her. Go to work, she told herself. Dead body time.

'Deputy Clemson, this is my partner, Specialist Blair.'

Sonora moved stiffly, offered her right hand without thinking. Clemson had a firm grip and she winced, bit her lip, pulled her hand away.

'Sonora came a little too close to whoever it was

stole that car out of the lot, and killed your security guard.'

Clemson looked her up and down and touched the brim of his hat. 'That so? I'd kind of like to get close to that guy myself. Come on around back.' He motioned to the orderly knot of people who stood talking by the curb. 'Y'all move on back, come on now.'

Another deputy appeared and made kindly shooing motions and people backed politely away.

At least things were friendly, Sonora thought. Saw things were not so friendly around back.

The hearse was open, and the DB had already been loaded. A fire engine, OXTON VOLUNTEER FIRE DEPT stenciled on the side, sat next to a burned-out dumpster that dripped water and foam. Sonora peered at the asphalt near the dumpster, noting the thick oily blood stain. She went to the hearse, glancing over her shoulder at Deputy Clemson.

'May I?'

He nodded.

She fished rubber gloves out of her purse and peeled the bloody sheet away.

The man looked like somebody's grandfather, pale blue eyes wide and vacant. Sonora ran her fingers through the thick white hair, noticed that the full mustache was yellow with tobacco stains. She probed the scalp, found an indentation on the left temple. Probably hit his head when he fell.

The body was pliant, only just beginning to cool, but it was heavy, and shifting it was awkward. Sonora was aware that the men watched her. One of them stepped close and helped her turn the body. A deputy. Young.

'Thanks,' she said.

He stayed to watch up close.

The old man wore a brown uniform and a leather jacket that was drenched with stiffening blood. Sonora probed gently, saw two holes on the mid quadrant of the left side of the back. She picked up a limp, heavy hand, noted the gold wedding band, the curly white hairs on the wrist. No wounds on the palms or fingers. No blood. He hadn't fought, or had time to react, which meant the first shot likely killed him.

She pulled the sheet back over the body and looked up to find Sam watching her.

'What you think, Sonora?'

'Hey, he was shot.'

Sam gave her a lazy look.

'Hard to tell with the blood, Sam, but looks like two shots with a twenty-two through the vena cava. He never knew what hit him, didn't put up a fight. Makes sense. She's a small woman, she's not going to want to go hand to hand.'

Clemson opened his mouth, then closed it. 'You said she?'

Sam waved a hand. 'Deputy Clemson here tells me that the guard called in a fire, then went out to investigate. When he did, he left that back gate unlocked.'

Clemson shifted his weight. 'What I can't figure is why he, I mean she, would start that fire up in the first place. Just calling attention to herself.'

Sam stuck his hands in his pockets. 'Car she took was parked over on the other side of the parking lot – which is where the body was found, right? She starts the fire as a diversion while she steals the car, only instead of putting out the fire, the security guard calls the fire department, leaves the fire to burn, and starts looking around the lot. He gets too close and she kills him.'

'Why here?' Clemson said.

Sonora waved a hand. 'Locals in Donner wouldn't know her, wouldn't know she had no business with the car. And excuse me, but this is a small town for a television station. Seems odd to me they even have a car.'

Clemson pushed his hat farther back on his head. 'It

belongs to the owner's son – a little prick who likes driving around with the logo on the side.' He glanced at the body, turned his face away. 'This guy fought in World War Two, got four grandchildren. Wife's been sick the last five years. This is like to kill her.'

'What was his name?' Sonora said.

'Nickname was Shirty. Shirty Sizemore. That's her, right over there. His widow.'

The woman was small, figure wide and lumpy, shoulders sagging. She had a beaten down air about her, a wilt that took years to acquire. Sonora met her eyes, saw intelligence, shock, and, oddly, relief. The same look she'd seen in her mirror the night Zack had died.

Another grieving widow.

Sonora leaned up against the hearse. 'Still got his gun holstered.'

Sam gave her a look. 'What's bothering you, Sonora?'

'I was thinking about Bundy.'

'Ted Bundy? Theodore?'

She nodded. 'Just the pattern. Plans carefully year after year, but then something changes or sets him off, and suddenly he's going on a blitz. Taking big risks. Rampaging through a sorority house in Florida, with the cops on his tail up north.'

'Think she's cutting loose?'

'I'm worried, Sam, I really am. They all do it, sooner or later. If this is her blast off, we're in for it.' Sonora rubbed the back of her neck. 'Any sign of the murder weapon?'

Sam shook his head. 'They'll go through the dumpster when the hot spots cool. Sheriff says the autopsy will be done in Louisville, and he'll get back to me with results. And we've been officially asked to keep our murderers up north where they come from, and unofficially asked to be in on the kill if at all possible.' He yawned. 'You still want an eggroll?'

Chapter Twenty-Three

Sonora went home and took a hot shower before she picked up the kids. She put on a black tee shirt, a pair of jeans and worn boots, then threw on an old flannel shirt to cover the bluish swelling on her wrist. If the kids asked about it, she wouldn't lie, but it was best to tone things down.

Her daughter clung to her when she picked them up, and even Tim gave her a hug. They kissed their grandmother good-bye, then climbed into the back of the car. They reeked of tobacco smoke and seemed subdued.

Sonora waved at her mother-in-law. Baba watched them from the doorway, cigarette dangling from her lips, her three little dogs jumping and scrabbling the screen.

Grandchildren were exciting.

'What's for supper?' Heather asked.

'Whatever we pass on the way home.'

They rented a movie, and Heather and Tim curled up on the den floor while Sonora built a fire in the fireplace. Once the blaze was small, but steady, Sonora settled on the couch with two Advil, a Corona, and a heating pad for her wrist. Clampett put his head in her lap and licked the bottom of the beer bottle. Sonora pushed his nose away.

'You guys sure you don't want to watch *Witness* first? It's a classic.'

Tim rolled his eyes. 'Mom, we've seen that movie so many times, we know all the dialog.'

'Can we make popcorn?' Heather asked.

Sonora fed Clampett a mushroom. 'Have to do it yourself, I'm not getting up.'

The doorbell rang, three times quickly.

Tim laughed. 'Yeah, right. Want me to go?'

'Not after dark.'

'Probably just some lady with a gasoline can.'

Sonora pushed the dog off her lap and gave her son a look. She turned the porch light on and squinted through the peephole in the arched wood door.

Chas stood on the front steps, bouncing up and down on the balls of his feet. He wore new jeans, a shirt that had likely just been removed from an LL Bean box, and an Outback hat with a feather in the brim.

Sonora considered not opening the door.

Chas set a shopping bag on the porch, folded his arms and shifted his weight to one foot, mouth small and tight. Really, it was amazing how much he was reminding her of Zack.

'*Mama!*' Heather's voice was shrill. 'Clampett's eating your pizza!'

Sonora sighed. Opened the door. 'Hello, Chas.'

He took off his hat, pushed back the straight black hair, silver at the temples. He had broad cheekbones, a dark complexion, blue eyes. 'Hey, babe. You didn't need to dress up, just for me.'

Sonora maintained silence.

'May I come in?' He said it with such meek politeness, Sonora felt guilty.

He was good at that, she thought. Giving guilt. She pushed the screen door open, and he stepped through just as Clampett came running, Heather right behind.

'Chas!' Heather wrapped her arms around his waist. Clampett pawed his leg, tail wagging, thumping the wall.

Chas stepped backward, patted Heather awkwardly on the top of her head, then nudged her away. He looked at Sonora. 'We need to talk. Privately.'

Heather backed away, chin sinking to her chest. She pushed her glasses up on her tiny button nose and Clampett licked her elbow.

Sonora squatted down next to her daughter, winked, and gave her a hug. 'Go watch your movie, Heather. Take Clampett with you.'

'Will you come too?'

Out of the corner of her eye, Sonora saw Chas grimace. So handsome, she thought. Such a prick.

'Later, sweetie, you go ahead.'

Sonora watched her daughter trudge toward the den, head bowed, dog at her heels. Any doubts she might have had were gone. Chas bent close to kiss her hello, but she turned her back and led him up the stairs into the living room.

'Sit down, if you want.'

He paused by the back of the couch. Heather and Tim had been playing with Tim's miniatures, and the floor was covered with plaster cast mountains, fake trees, painted archers and dragons. One of the pillows had bite marks, and Clampett had clearly had an accident beside the coffee table.

Sonora sat on the edge of the couch, stiff backed and regal – queen of her domain, God help her. 'You want to sit down?'

Chas curled his lip. 'You need to do something about your dog.'

Sonora felt her cheeks turn red. 'He's just old.'

'Maybe it's time to put him out of his misery.' Chas sat close to her on the couch and gave her a confident smile. It dawned on her that he had a habit of sitting too close, standing too close, grabbing hold of her arm. 'You've been dodging me, Sonora.'

Time for a dramatic pause, Sonora thought, waiting it out.

Chas frowned, leaned back against the couch, closed his

eyes. 'I've had a long day, baby. Hell, I've had a long week. I'm dead tired and mega-stressed.'

'Aw, gee.'

He opened his eyes, folded his arms. 'Okay, so you're mad. I've talked to Sam and your dad. Even your mother-in-law.'

'You talked to my dad?'

'I know you don't get along, Sonora, but I wanted to let him know my intentions.'

'Which are?'

He rummaged in his bag, pulled out a Dove bar, and smiled.

No, Sonora decided, a smirk, not a smile.

'Chocolate. And better than chocolate. Diamonds.' Chas held a black velvet box up in the air, just out of reach. 'Make me happy, Sonora.'

'I'm supposed to jump for it?'

His lips tightened and he leaned close. 'Stop playing games, Sonora, and tell me what's on your mind.'

She took a breath. 'I don't like you, I don't love you, and I don't respect you.'

His mouth opened, then closed, and he swallowed. The smirk came back. He had decided to be amused. 'Is that all?'

'You remind me of my dead husband. That is not a compliment.'

'Maybe he's better off dead.'

'Maybe I'm better off.'

He shook his head slowly. 'I thought you'd be happy to get married, I *know* you would. There's something going on you're not telling me.'

'Maybe I don't like the feather in your hat. Or that you whistle *Carmen* all the time. Maybe I don't like it that you play competition Frisbee.'

'What's wrong with Frisbee?'

'Nothing, unless you call it *ultimate* Frisbee and get intense.'

'Talk to me, baby. It's that incident with the car, am I right?'

Sonora cocked her head to one side. 'It's reason enough, don't you think?'

'I promise, I *promise* you. Nothing like that will ever happen again.'

'No, it won't, you're right about that.'

'It wasn't that big a deal, Sonora.'

She leaned forward, into his face. 'It *was* a big deal. You went off. For no reason, out of the blue, you go nuts behind the wheel. You hit that Volvo on *purpose* and had the unmitigated gall to get out and tell the driver it was *my* fault for making you mad. You used the car like a weapon— '

'Oh, I can't believe I'm hearing this. So now you're abused?'

'Get out, Chas. You make me tired.'

He stood up, walked three steps, then turned around, smoothing the thick black hair, his pride and joy. 'You've got someone else, don't you?'

'This discussion is over.'

He tossed the velvet box on the floor by her feet. 'Don't you even want to look at it?'

'No.'

'I have champagne in the bag. You want to keep it to celebrate your aloneness tonight?'

'Take it and go away.'

He grabbed the bag and the box, but did not notice the Dove bar wedged between the center couch cushions. Sonora followed him to the door.

He looked back at her over his shoulder. 'We could be a dynamite couple.'

She inclined her head in the direction of the den and the kids. 'I'm past the couple stage, Chas. I'm a family.'

'Be picky if you want, Sonora. But it's not going to be

easy to find someone willing to put up with a pissy dog and two kids.'

'What's difficult is finding somebody worthy of the privilege.'

She closed the door in his face. Heard applause. Tim stood on the staircase next to Heather, who ran and put her arms around Sonora's waist.

Tim shook his head. 'Good going, Mom. You'll never get married at this rate.'

Sonora was aware of thunder, and a tiny tap on her shoulder. Lightning cracked and lit the room. Heather stood beside the couch, eyes wide, thumb in her mouth. She was neatly belted into a white bathrobe with pink rosebuds, and wearing her favorite kitty slippers – two sizes too small. She had likely been roaming the house for a while, trailing her favorite blanket.

The room went dark again, dimly lit by the glow of the television and the tiny green lights on the VCR. Harrison Ford was on screen, fixing a broken birdhouse.

Sonora moved Clampett off her feet, shoved the half-eaten Dove bar out of her lap, and raised the end of the quilt to let her daughter under.

'Scared of the storm?'

Heather nodded, crawled onto the couch, and laid her head on Sonora's shoulder.

'Mommy?'

Sonora yawned, closed her eyes. 'Hmmm?'

'Will you be home when I wake up in the morning?'

The phone rang, and Clampett opened his red-rimmed brown eyes. Sonora pulled her arm out of the cocoon she'd made with the heating pad, and reached for the cordless, realized her hands were shaking. Flash calling? Who else, this time of night. Phone taps were in place. She swallowed.

'Sonora Blair.'

'Sonora. I'm sorry, I know it's late, I've been on the road all night.'

She recognized his voice immediately, as well as the cadences of panic. 'Keaton? What's wrong?' She glanced at her watch, squinting. One-thirty AM.

'I just got home, to the townhouse. And there's another one of those envelopes. Like the other one, you know?'

'I know, Keaton.' Use his name. Keep him calm. She pulled Heather close.

'It feels like there's two pictures in there this time.'

'You haven't opened it?'

'No.'

'Don't open it, okay? Keaton?'

'Okay.'

'Look, I'm coming over, just sit tight. I'll be there as soon as I can.' She rang off.

Heather sucked her thumb, blue eyes stoic. 'You got to go again, Mommy?'

'Yeah. But I'll get Uncle Stuart to come keep you safe in the storm.'

'Mom?'

Sonora looked up. Saw Tim in the stairwell, still in bluejeans. She looked at her watch. 'Why aren't you in bed?'

Clampett padded up the stairs, licked the boy's bare toes. Tim scratched the dog's ears.

'You got to go to work, Mom?'

'Afraid so.'

'Don't forget your gun.'

'I won't. I'll get Stuart to come.'

'I can take care of things.'

'I know. But he's still coming.'

Tim nodded. Seemed glad. He was young, Sonora thought. And it was the middle of the night. And Flash was out there, somewhere.

Chapter Twenty-Four

The townhouse was dark, though a light glowed from the back. Sonora parked at the curb and shut the car door softly. The street was still, the houses dark and silent. In the background came the roar of the highway.

Sonora's boot heels were noisy on the sidewalk. The front door was open, the storm door shut. She rang the bell, and waited – tried the handle, found it unlatched, and went inside.

Keaton Daniels had left a trail. A canvas briefcase had been dropped in the foyer, a tie unknotted and hung over the bannister that curved into the living room. The kitchen light was on. Sonora could see a stack of mail on the table, a curling newspaper.

A bottle of gin was open, next to a half-filled glass.

The mail was scattered. *Men's Health*, *Gentlemen's Quarterly*, *Highlights For Children*. A Master Charge bill, good news from Ed MacMahon, pizza coupons, something official from the legal firm of James D. Lyon. A cheap white envelope next to the one from the legal firm, torn across the top.

He hadn't been able to wait. Sonora glanced at her watch and saw that it was two-forty. She had left him alone too long.

The pictures were Polaroids, one sitting crooked. Sonora resisted the urge to straighten it up. She focused on the pictures, shivered, sat down slowly, and put her head in her hands. Then looked again.

In the picture on the left, Mark Daniels struggled with the handcuffs. Sonora could see the sweat rolling down his temples. She looked closely. Something odd, something in his fingers.

The second picture was the bad one, taken just as the fire licked the top of the car window, and Mark Daniels faced death. His mouth was closed. He was not screaming.

Sonora went to the back door and looked out at the tiny, sloped yard that was enclosed by an eight-foot privacy fence. She flipped the porch light on. Keaton Daniels had his back to her, hands jammed in his pockets. He was looking over the fence, to the city lights below.

The rain had not come, but there was thunder crowding close. Sonora walked across the yard, grass curling around her boots.

'Keaton?' she said softly.

He didn't seem to hear. She touched his shoulder and he laid a hand on top of hers and squeezed.

'Don't say anything.' His voice was thick, as if he'd been crying.

Sonora kept his hand, and moved in front of him.

He had changed in some subtle way that troubled her, as if once he was *there*, and now he was *here*. The funeral, just that afternoon, seemed miles and years away. She squeezed his hand, took a step toward him, her shirt just a hair's breadth from his. He did not back away. She took his face between her hands, and stood on her tiptoes to kiss him.

He hesitated, and her stomach tensed and fluttered. Then he bent close. He grabbed her hard, his tongue in her mouth, and she felt the sandpaper bristles of his unshaven cheeks, the soft chill wetness of his tears.

When she pulled back he caught her hand. She laced her fingers in his and squeezed. Tonight he was vulnerable. Tonight would be taking advantage.

'You shouldn't be alone, Keaton, can I drop you somewhere?'

'No,' he said.
'You're sure?'
'Sure.'
'I'm going back in the kitchen for a minute. Stay here.'

She went through the house to her car, got a paper grocery bag from the kit of stuff in the trunk, put the pictures and envelope in. She stacked his mail, glanced out in the yard. He had his back to her. She was halfway to him when he turned.

'You're leaving?'

She nodded. She could think of no words of comfort, no words to take the pain away. 'I'll call you.'

'Sure.'

She paused at the gate, hand on the latch, and turned to see he was watching. 'I'll get her,' she told him.

Chapter Twenty-Five

Sonora carried the paper bag up to the fifth floor of the Board of Elections building to homicide. She saw a shaft of light beneath Crick's door, waved at Sanders, who'd pulled the eight PM to four AM shift. Her favorite.

'Something up?' Sanders asked.

'More pictures.'

Sanders scooted back in her chair, pushed hair out of her eyes with a hand that shook. 'From Flash?'

Sonora nodded.

'Bad?' Sanders said.

'Bad. Anybody in the lab?'

Sanders shook her head.

Sonora headed for the swing door that joined homicide and CSU. 'Better here than in the trunk of my car. Let Crick know, will you?'

She left the Polaroids on Terry's desk with a note. Was leaving just as Crick and Sanders came in.

'Sonora?' Crick said.

'Over there, Sergeant.' She pushed past him. She wasn't up for another look at Mark Daniels, brave, agonized. She checked her watch. After three. AM at that. Her message light was blinking.

One from Delores whatshername, returning her call. Another from a cop in Memphis, unsolved arson/homicide. Sonora made a note of his name and number.

'Sonora?'

She jumped, though the tone of voice was gentle. Crick

looked angry, as usual. Sonora did not have the urge to tell him to loosen his tie, because he'd already taken it off. She rested her elbow on the desk, propping her chin.

'You still here?' he said.

'Such a detective. You see the pictures?'

He answered with a grimace. 'Wonder how many more like that she's got.'

Sonora shrugged. 'Not sure Daniels can take too many more.'

Crick rocked back and forth on the balls of his feet. 'Not sure I can. Maybe Terry will get a print this time. And Blair, go home, you look like hell.'

'Sir, I got a message here from a homicide cop in Memphis. Three years ago they had a murder pretty similar to the Mark Daniels' killing.'

'Think it's Flash again, huh?'

'Even better than Atlanta, except the victim didn't survive. Killer was a woman, and she used handcuffs.'

'So now you want to go to Memphis.'

'I'm also playing telephone tag with a Delores something or other in West Virginia.'

'*Another* one?'

'Yes sir.'

He rested a hand on the back of her chair, making it creak. 'You file VICAP with the FBI?'

'Not yet. You think we could get some kind of voice analysis?'

'To tell us what? She's a homicidal maniac? That she's dangerous? That she's going off big time?'

Sonora bit her lip. 'Point taken.'

'Sorry, didn't mean to blow off on you, Sonora. Hang on.' He went to his office, left the door gaping. She heard a file drawer open, a curse, the file sliding closed. Didn't quite catch, from the sound of it. Which bugged her. She got up and went to the doorway.

Crick waved a thick booklet of papers. 'Here we go.'

'The drawer didn't catch.'

'What?'

'File drawer.' Sonora crossed the room, pushed the drawer, second from the bottom, with the toe of her shoe. Heard the click. Felt better.

'You happy now?' Crick said.

She pointed to the booklet. 'You know and I know the FBI won't come in on this till we have a name, address, and signed murder warrant. Why are you giving me this at three o'clock in the morning?'

'So you'll go home and leave me alone. It's negative reinforcement. Plus it covers our ass, proves we tried everything.'

'Here's everything for you, sir. She has a rural background, and probably grew up in a small town – somewhere in Kentucky where they say you'uns. My guess is she's been snagged on some kind of shoplifting charge, some time in her life. She's been setting fires for sexual gratification since she was a teenager, maybe younger. She tortured animals for fun when she was little, and she likes to watch the families of her victims suffer. I'd bet my last penny she's stalking Keaton Daniels, and I will tell you again we should stick to this guy like glue.'

'How about an address for her, Blair. You got that?'

'Will I get an address by filling out this form?'

'Never know till you try.'

'Make you a deal. I fill out the form, and you clear me for Memphis and Atlanta.'

'You fill out that form, and I'll get back to you.'

She stayed put. Looking at him. Willing him to agree.

He growled. 'Anything else, Specialist Blair?'

'No sir.'

'Go away.'

Chapter Twenty-Six

The parking lot was well lit and empty. Sonora slammed the car door and checked the locks. She had a weird, unsettled feeling, and she turned and scanned the back seat. Empty. Should have looked before she got in.

She started the engine, glanced up at the foggy windshield, and saw that someone had traced a three over the driver's side.

Flash?

The cellular phone rang, as if on cue. Sonora picked it up, listened.

'Hey, girlfriend, how you doing? Keaton get my package okay?'

Sonora flicked on the headlights, checked the rear-view mirror. No one, no one close. Flash was likely around somewhere. Watching.

'Yeah, we got it.' Sonora pulled the car out of the lot. She turned left, heading toward the river, trying to remember where all the pay phones were.

'We?' A pause. 'Funny, isn't it, that you knew it was me right off in that graveyard today. See, I think we're connected, you and me. I think— '

'How'd you get this number?'

'Forget how I got it. Maybe you gave it to me. Maybe I am you, maybe I'm your dark half. Maybe you did the killings and don't remember. Maybe you're six and I'm three.'

'What's that supposed to mean? Make some sense, why don't you?' Sonora scanned the streets. Empty.

Silence on the other end. Then, 'Okay, girl, let's talk about you.'

New tone of voice, Sonora thought. Change of tactics? New buttons to push?

'It wasn't no stroke now, was it? What killed your mama?'

Sonora hit the brakes, pulled the car to the curb. 'What are you talking about?'

'You know, my mama died, too, when I was real little. At least you were all grown up.'

'What happened to your mother?'

'We're talking about yours, Detective. Your mama. The doctors never was too sure what happened, isn't that right? Too many pills, or what. You could of said the word, but no, no autopsy for *your* mama. You think she took them pills herself, or you think your daddy give 'um to her? Or maybe he just held a pillow on her face, when she's all doped up. Think she knew? When it was happening? You should see people's faces when they know they're going to die. They get the funniest looks.'

Chapter Twenty-Seven

It was cold in the conference room, early morning chill. The smell of new coffee was comforting. Sonora took a small bite from a plain cake doughnut, barely aware of the buzz of voices. She had not slept. She had laid in bed and closed her eyes and seen Mark Daniels, cuffed to the steering wheel, flames licking the side of the car. Saw her mother, looking grumpy and sad in the coffin.

Sonora pulled her bottom lip and watched Sam trace a thick forefinger across the map.

'Right along the Big South Fork here. And around this part of southern Kentucky, particularly near the Tennessee border. I mean, it's a joke to a lot of people, but in some of these rural areas they say you'uns like we say y'all.'

There was a ripple of snickers.

'We?' Gruber was grinning.

'We'uns from farther south. And by the way, fuck all y'all, which is another thing we say in the south.'

Sanders looked up. She was the rookie in the group, thin and young, hair cut short and swingy. 'Do you think maybe—'

The door opened. Sergeant Crick walked into the room, black lace-ups polished and shiny, a burly grey sweater stretched over his shoulders and chest. Terry followed, looking distracted. She wore a soiled blue smock and a strand of hair had come loose from her ponytail.

Crick settled at the head of the table and waved a hand. 'Terry?'

She pushed her glasses back on her nose. 'We lifted a print from one of the pictures.'

Sonora looked up. 'You mean Flash didn't wear gloves?'

Terry tucked the strand of hair behind her ear. 'I'm pretty sure she did. Thin ones. But she has very pronounced friction ridges, and she touched the surface of one of the Polaroids, which is very porous. Plus, it's been humid with all the rain we've had, and warm for this time of year. Which helps. We got lucky.'

'Is it a good print?' Sam asked.

Terry smiled, catlike.

Sonora leaned forward in her chair. 'Where did she leave the print? Where on the picture?'

'On Mark Daniels' face.'

Crick looked at Gruber. 'Your turn.'

Gruber gave them a lazy smile. 'We went back to the neighborhood canvas. Had some houses we missed the day of the killing, nobody home. Sanders here found a lady who noticed a bronze Pontiac off to the side of the road, near the park. She thinks it was there that whole day before Daniels was killed. It's a little picnic area there, on Shepherd Creek.

'Anyway, this woman notices the car because she lives across the street, and you notice strange cars in your neighborhood. So we figure, okay, if Flash leaves her car so she can make her getaway that night, where does she go when she drops it off? And a ways down the road we got a Dairy Mart and a BP Oil, both with pay phones. We pull the phone records, and find somebody called a cab from BP Oil the afternoon Daniels was killed. We talk to the guys that work there, and one of them remembers seeing a blonde making a call. The hair's a little different from the sketch. He said she had real short bangs, said they looked funny. Ragged and uneven. So we got the cab driver who picked her up. Took her to a place downtown. Shelby's Antiques.'

'How far was it from the car to where Daniels was killed?' Sam asked.

Gruber opened his mouth, but Molliter held up a hand. His voice was flat.

'Maybe I should answer, since I'm the one that walked it off.' He pointed a freckled finger at the map. 'It takes eight minutes, walking briskly, to get from the kill spot, to the area where the car was parked.'

'Longer in high heels, and after dark,' Gruber said.

Sonora frowned. 'Provided she went by the road.'

Molliter gave her a patient look. 'She's not going to go crashing through the underbrush down that hill in a pair of high heels.'

Terry took off her glasses and rubbed the two red spots on the bridge of her nose. 'She changed her shoes.'

Sonora nodded.

'Come on, girls. She's got track shoes in a tiny little purse?'

'Big purse,' Sonora said. 'She's got a lot of stuff to carry. Plus her feet aren't as big as yours, Molliter.'

Gruber was nodding. 'Remember, she's got to have her rope and camera, so why not tennies?'

Sam waved a hand. 'And she gets the gasoline out of Mark Daniels' car. You found that melted plastic next to the gas tank, right Arson Guy?'

Mickey looked up. 'Absolutely. Makes more sense to siphon it than to carry it around.'

'Anything on the type of rope?' Crick asked.

'Garden variety clothesline. Find it in every hardware store in town.'

Sam rubbed his nose. 'So how did she get to this Cujos if her car's in the park? Taxi there too? Catch a bus?'

Gruber's eyes widened. 'Good point.'

'Check it out,' Crick said.

A knock at the door gave him pause. Crick raised an eyebrow, and Molliter went to the door, muttered something, walked around behind Sonora's chair, and dropped a package on the table.

Sonora looked up from her notes. She shook the package, then peeled the tape back, which ripped the paper and brought all eyes to her side of the table. Mickey paused, then continued.

'Is it ticking?' Sam whispered over her shoulder.

Sonora peered inside. A note, and something small, square, covered in foil. She took the foil pack and put it in her lap, tried to open it quietly, peeling the edges slowly back.

Toast – two pieces. Whole wheat, lightly browned, delicately buttered with the crusts cut off. Sonora scratched her chin and reached into the mailer for the note – a piece of lined second grade paper, thin and grey.

The handwriting was strong, made with a thick black felt tip pen, slanted steeply to one side. Sonora squinted and held it close to her face.

I WOULD HAVE MADE YOU BREAKFAST. K.

Sam looked over her shoulder. 'What is it, girl? Your face is turning red.'

Sonora snatched the note from his probing fingers and jammed it deep into her jacket pocket.

'Nothing.' The room was suddenly silent. She looked up to find Crick looking at her. 'Sorry, I miss something?'

'Arson Guy said the key they found goes to handcuffs, but not the cuffs used to bolt Mark Daniels to the steering wheel of his car.'

Sonora settled the package in her lap. Thought a minute. 'This makes no sense. You absolutely sure?'

Mickey scratched his chin. 'The key we found would never fit the cuffs on Daniels. Whole different manufacturer.'

'One of those pictures Keaton got, it looks like Mark is holding something. You can't quite see it, but his fingers are pinched together.' Sonora held her hand up, thumb and forefinger touching. 'And that patrol officer, Finch, he said Mark was screaming about a key, that he kept saying it over and over. Maybe he *wasn't* calling for his brother. Maybe he was talking about the key to the cuffs.'

Sam cocked his head to one side. 'So he's got a key to the cuffs, but it's the wrong one?'

'Doesn't make sense.' Molliter tipped his chair backward. 'None of this works for me.'

Sonora thought of that last picture of Mark, fire following the wick of rope wrapped around his naked, vulnerable body, the awful look of knowledge on his face.

Gruber made a noise and Sonora looked at him, knowing the thought hit him the same time it hit her.

She cleared her throat. 'Try this. Flash gives Daniels a key to the handcuffs and he thinks he's going to be able to get away, right up till the last minute, when he gets the key in the lock, and finds out it doesn't fit.'

'Let me get this straight. She cuffs them to the wheel— '

'Why does Daniels let her do that?' Gruber crumbled a chunk of iced caramel doughnut.'

'Could be a sex thing,' Sam said. 'Let me cuff you and love you.'

'What kind of guy would go along with that?' Molliter's face was red, and a film of perspiration lined his upper lip.

'Nine out of ten,' Gruber said.

Sonora snorted. 'What do you mean what *kind* of guy, Molliter? Are you saying if he spreads his knees for some girl he just met, he got what he deserves? That what you're saying?'

'Enough of that,' Crick said.

'He's made remarks like that about women victims. What do you think with the shoe on the other foot, Molliter? Is it different now?'

'Listen, Blair— '

'I said *enough*.' Crick's voice was impressively authoritative. Sonora decided she would imitate it the next time she was mad at her son. A Crick voice. Something to cultivate.

Sanders bit her lip. 'Aren't we forgetting that Daniels was shot? That was in the autopsy report, wasn't it?'

Sonora nodded. 'Okay, she threatened him with the gun, he gave her trouble, and she shot him in the leg. Snap on those handcuffs, boy, or I'll shoot you again.'

Molliter's face was bright red. 'But what's the point? The key doesn't fit. Why give it to him?'

Sam waved a hand. 'Somehow or other she gets this guy's wallet and his clothes and gets him handcuffed to the steering wheel. Now, face it, men aren't threatened by a little thing like Flash. They're not going to take her seriously. She probably has to shoot them just to get their attention. She's smart. She gets a gun on them and she's got the power before they even know they got a problem.'

'So it's not a sex thing.' Molliter sounded relieved.

'Not for the men,' Sonora said.

Sanders raised her hand, chin level. 'Going back to that geographic thing— '

'I think we were on the *porno*-graphic thing,' Gruber said. 'And I don't know about the rest of you guys, but this sure takes the fun out of picking up women.'

Sanders smiled. Cleared her throat. 'I wonder— '

'We get anywhere on park witnesses?' Gruber asked.

Sanders' cheeks went dark red, and she raised her voice. 'Sam? Aren't there several community colleges in that area of Kentucky you were talking about? The places you pointed out on the map?'

Sam gave her an encouraging nod.

'Then I was wondering. Maybe she went to school there.

We might check with some of the community colleges and see if they have any history of arson, or— '

Gruber waved a hand. 'She could have gone to school anywhere, Sanders, if she went at all.'

Sam was shaking his head. 'No, if she did go, Sanders could have something. The rural kids stick close to home those first two years. It's cheaper, for one. And they go to a school with their own, instead of heading off to a large university where people look down their nose at 'em. Then they're either happy with a two-year degree, they drop out, or transfer to a university that disallows most of their credits.'

Sanders looked at Sonora. 'You were talking about going back to her early years. If she went to college, there might have been some unexplained fires. We could talk to the campus police.'

Crick started stacking papers. 'Good idea, Sanders. Get on it today.'

'Out of the mouths of babes,' Gruber said.

Sonora looked at Sanders, saw the woman's red face, waited. Sanders picked up her papers, eyes downcast.

'Okay,' Crick said. 'Gruber. Stay with the taxi and the transport. See if you can pick Flash up after the antique store. Sonora, you and Sam take the store itself. Molliter— '

Molliter checked his watch. 'I have a possible suspect due in. Late, already.'

'This early and he's late?' Sam asked.

Gruber grinned. 'She. Hooker, on her way home from work.'

Molliter blushed. 'She may pan out, as an informant. It's always possible our killer is a prostitute.'

'Go to it.' Crick rubbed the back of his neck. 'Any more phone calls, Sonora? Hang ups, anything?'

Sonora glanced at the floor. Did she really want to tell Crick and everyone else what Flash had said about her mother? She wondered how Flash had gotten the number to her phone, how she'd found out the things she had no business knowing.

'No sir.'

It was the first lie, a gentle lie, to protect a part of herself that needed to stay private.

Chapter Twenty-Eight

Sonora listened to her daughter sob on the other end of the phone.

'It's my tea set that Santa Claus brought me. The one I use for the ponies.'

Sam walked by, mouthed 'antique store,' and pointed at his watch. Sonora nodded at him. Okay already. The side of her neck was aching. Too much time on the phone.

'When's the last time you had it, Heather? Maybe it's just in the closet, in all the mess.' If it was, Sonora thought, it might never be seen again.

'I had it out on the back porch. Somebody's tooken it.'

Taken it, Sonora thought. 'That's what happens when you leave your stuff outside, Heather.' She glanced up to see Sam shaking his head at her. Mean mommy. Sonora closed her eyes and swallowed nausea. Too early for the ulcer, but here it was anyway. Lack of sleep. Unless it was something else, like . . . no, no. It couldn't be that. Sonora glanced at the calendar on her desk and realized her period was late.

'Mommy?'

'Look, Heather, I'm sorry you feel bad. Mommy's at work right now, but we can talk about this some more when I come home. Look under your bed and in your closet. Maybe you didn't leave it outside.'

Tim's voice echoed in the background. 'I bet it's under your bed. Come on, you dork, I'll help you look.'

Sam settled on the corner of Sonora's desk as she hung up. 'Now can we go?'

'I'm ready if . . . excuse me, Sam. There's Sanders by the coffee maker. Time out for baby-training.'

'Baby-training?'

'Be right back.'

Sonora leaned against the bathroom wall and folded her arms. Sanders gave her a nervous look, then turned to the mirror, digging in her purse for a brush, lipstick. It gave Sonora a pang to realize that she made the other woman nervous. She thought of Flash, and girl conversations over the phone. Sonora grimaced. *Not the same*. Sanders looked at her and she folded her arms.

'I'd say sit down, but for obvious reasons, I don't think either of us would be comfortable that way.'

Sanders laughed, and bit her bottom lip.

'I know this sounds offensive, Sanders, but you don't have a penis do you?'

'*What?*'

'Now, you could buy yourself a penis in the back of one of those magazines they pore over down in vice, but it wouldn't be the same would it? So save yourself some confusion and hurt feelings. You're not going to be one of the boys. This isn't woman-to-woman stuff, I'm telling you the same thing my sergeant told me eight years ago, okay? Don't let guys like Gruber interrupt you every two seconds. They're not going to take you seriously, you put up with that.'

'I don't want to be rude.'

'*They're* being rude.'

'So you're saying I should file a complaint?'

'You want to file a complaint because you got interrupted?'

Sanders folded her arms. 'Then what do I do?'

'You handle it, and you better do it now, because it's going to get worse if you don't. Draw a line and don't let anybody step over it, and don't hold a grudge. Oh and Sanders, when you do take a stand out there, try not to smile.'

'Smile?'

'My observation is that women always smile no matter what. I bet Bundy's victims smiled before he killed them. You're a cop. Don't smile when people are giving you grief.'

'You've given me a lot to think about.'

'Good. It's one reason I like working with women. They think.'

Chapter Twenty-Nine

A wooden carousel horse sat in the display window of Shelby's Antiques. The white enamel was chipped and worn, the red and blue roses painted round its neck drab and faded. For the first time in her life, Sonora had the urge to buy an antique.

A cluster of bells at the top of the front door jangled as she and Sam walked in. Sonora went directly to the horse and checked the price tag that hung around its neck. Her urge to buy an antique went away.

It was a large store, crammed full of furniture and shelves that held displays of dolls and bins of odds and ends – flea market stuff, which Sonora always thought of as junk. She found the thick odor of old things unpleasant. There were tin trays that said Coca-Cola, Betty Boop postcards, tiny, colored-glass bottles, playing cards from New York City. Coke bottles, moldering books, World War Two medals, china dolls, plastic dolls, a teeny little tea set. Much of the small stuff hailed from the forties and fifties, with an old-fashioned aura of tackiness Sonora found depressing.

She passed a rack of white gauze dresses that swayed when she walked too close. She fingered the smallest, touching the delicate cotton, the yellowed satin ribbon, the row of tiny pearl buttons.

'Blue Willow plates!' Sam moved to a table by a pile of books. 'Shelly's got one her grandmother gave her. You've seen it, it's on the wall in the kitchen. Shelly would love this place. She would eat this up with a spoon.'

Sonora walked deeper into the store, warped tile beneath her feet. She passed a Victrola and a stack of LPs in worn jackets. The one on top was Carmen.

A woman stood behind the counter, manning a polished brass cash register. Her hair was very dark, parted in the middle, flipped under. Her figure would have been considered wholesome and fine in the fifties. She wore dark lipstick and had heavy brown eyebrows. A pair of glasses hung from a chain around her neck. She was studying a stack of papers, making notations in ink. Sonora would have guessed her to be a PhD, teaching anthropology or medieval literature at an ivy league university.

The woman looked up and smiled, and Sonora reached for her ID.

'Morning. I'm Specialist Blair, Cincinnati Police Department, and the man over there admiring the Blue Willow plates, is Specialist Delarosa. I'd like to ask you a few questions.'

The woman put her glasses on, took her time studying Sonora's ID, cocked her head sideways to get a good look at Sam.

Sonora fumbled with her recorder, peeling cellophane from a fresh tape. 'I'm a homicide detective, I'm investigating a murder.'

'A murder?'

Sonora nodded. 'I'm sorry, I didn't catch your name?'

'Shelby Hargreaves. I'm part owner.'

'H-A-R-G-R-E-A-V-E-S?'

'Yes.'

'Were you here last Tuesday? I was wondering if you waited on a woman that afternoon – I have a sketch. It would have been around . . .' Sonora glanced at her notes. 'Sometime after lunch. Two, maybe three. You were here then?'

'I was here all day. I was in early, around seven, and didn't leave till after nine.'

'This lady is blonde, between twenty-five and thirty-five. Small boned. I've got the sketch here, but it's not one hundred percent accurate, you understand?'

'You could be describing yourself, Detective.'

Sonora grimaced.

Shelby Hargreaves frowned over the drawing, then tapped her cheek with a short fingernail that shone with clear polish. 'I think so. Yes, if this is the one I'm thinking of, I helped her myself. She came in a taxi.'

Sonora kept her face noncommittal. 'You noticed that?'

'It's unusual, don't you think? Most people drive their own car, or walk, or maybe take a bus. They don't take a taxi to go shopping.'

'How about when she left?'

'I don't think I noticed. She didn't ask to use the phone, so she could call a ride. She just went out. Headed toward town, I'm pretty sure.'

'Toward town,' Sonora echoed. They could check bus schedules and cab companies. 'How long was she here?'

'An hour and a half, maybe two hours. She was a browser. I think she'd been in before, because she had certain areas she went to – like she knew where we kept the things she liked.'

Shelby Hargreaves slipped the glasses off her nose and rubbed her eyes. 'She was very much in her own little world, that one. Came walking in all business, then wandered slowly down the aisles, like an enchanted princess. Antique magic.'

Sam walked toward them down the aisleway, turning his head now and then as something caught his eye. 'You watch all your customers that close?' he asked.

Hargreaves shook her head. 'Not usually. But she had an acquisitive look. She wanted things, touched them, like a spoiled little girl at a candy counter. I call it greedy fingers.'

Sam grinned and Hargreaves gave him a particular smile.

'What kind of things did she look at?' Sam said.

Hargreaves leaned both elbows on the counter. 'Dolls were the main fascination, and what I call the miniatures. Doll house furniture. She liked that little tea set over there, did you see that?'

Hargreaves moved from behind the counter and led them to a small child's tea set.

Sonora frowned. Something here that bothered her.

'This set is too small really, for the size doll she wanted, but she wouldn't look at anything bigger.' Hargreaves led them down the aisle. 'She looked at these for a long time.'

They were displayed on a mahogany sideboard – china dolls, exquisitely dressed, blue marble eyes fringed by thick dark lashes, lids that opened and shut. Some of the dolls wore earrings, and one had a parasol, trimmed in lace, and delicate bisque rouged cheeks.

'My daughter would love these,' Sonora said.

Hargreaves nodded and grimaced. 'It's only adults, collectors, who have these kinds of dolls nowadays. It's hard to remember sometimes that they were made for children.' She pointed to a boy doll dressed in brown velveteen pants and jacket, ivory lace at the sleeves and throat. 'She looked at this one quite a while. Too expensive, I guess. He's a German bisque boy. A character doll, see the painted eyes? It's a Simon & Halbig. But she didn't go for it. She didn't like the hair. It's blonde, you see, and she wanted dark hair. I wound up getting her one I had downstairs. It wasn't in mint condition – it was missing an arm, and the cheek was scuffed. And it's not marked, so I can't be one hundred percent sure who made it, which decreases the value.' She leaned close to Sam. 'Most people, they don't like the missing limbs, and they use that as a major arguing point to bring the price down. Unless they work on dolls themselves, they won't buy. But this girl hardly seemed to notice.'

'I wish I could see it,' Sonora said.

'I've got another like it, a girl. Come with me, I'll show

you that.' She led them into the next room, which was filled with larger pieces – furniture, spinning wheels, cabinets. A wide staircase led from the center of the floor to the basement. Sam motioned Sonora ahead, and followed close at her heels.

It was musty smelling downstairs, and cold. The merchandise wasn't as choice. There were a lot of books – old, blue-jacketed Nancy Drew books, Hardy Boys adventures, military paraphernalia. Hargreaves moved purposefully past a dusty, vintage sewing machine, her heels noisy on the yellowed tile. She stopped in front of an open cupboard that was teeming with dolls – many of them missing limbs, some of them nude or headless, all of them battered and worn. The misfits.

'It's a very unusual doll, the one she selected.' Hargreaves reached for a girl doll, about seventeen inches tall. It wore a blue plaid dress; a satin ribbon had somehow been attached to the painted-on hair. 'This one is actually marked. It was made in Brooklyn by Modern Toy Company, sometime between 1914 and 1926. My guess is it's an early one, so I'd say 1915 or 16.' She handed the doll to Sonora.

There was a brown stain on the front bib of the dress, but the white knee socks were surprisingly clean, the yellow shoes unmarked. The arms of the doll were oddly muscular, like drumsticks, and the striated hair and porky little face were painted on. The doll had an oily look that Sonora did not like.

Sam took the doll and waved its little arm. 'Sawdust.'

'Right. The body and head are shaped with cork, but the limbs are stuffed with sawdust. They're jointed.' Shelby Hargreaves pulled up the doll's dress. 'See here? Discs at the shoulders and hips.'

'How did she pay?' Sonora asked.

'Cash,' Hargreaves said.

'Did she buy anything else?'

'Odds and ends for dollmaking. I have a box of stuff out

in the back.' She inclined her head toward two heavy swing doors. 'I let her poke through that, and she picked up a few things. Come on, I'll show you.'

Sonora took the doll away from Sam, smoothed its dress back over its knees.

The back room had a rough cement floor, and was dark and drafty. Slits of sunlight shone through cracks in an accordion-style delivery door, which was shut tight and padlocked. A naked bulb hung from the ceiling, providing a cone of dim light and an abundance of dark and shadow.

Sonora looked at the exposed wires, the dust, the dry brittle furniture. Fire hazard, she thought.

Most of what was back in the storeroom looked broken and abandoned. An old metal baby crib, bars lethally wide at the top and narrow at the bottom, was stacked next to an iron bedstead, a wooden Indian, and a Coca-Cola sign. Shelby Hargreaves squatted next to a battered, avocado green storage trunk, opened the latch, and lifted the lid. Sonora looked over her shoulder.

A macabre collection, this motley conglomeration of doll eyes, sawdust stuffed limbs, tiny, unattached hands, and doll heads. A threadbare baby bonnet lay next to a torn parasol and a pair of teensy eyeglasses. There were shoes and felt kits, a few paintbrushes, what looked like molds for heads. Sam reached in and picked up an odd tool, shaped something like a Tootsie Roll Pop.

'What's this for?'

Shelby Hargreaves touched the grey metal. 'An eye beveller. Made by a company in Connecticut. It's used to make an eye socket. There's a better one in here.' She rummaged through the trunk. 'I *know* there's another one. Unless Cecilia sold it or moved it. It surely didn't get up and walk off by itself.'

Sonora exchanged glances with Sam.

'Now that bothers me,' Hargreaves said. 'I'll have to check with Cecilia. I suppose she must have sold it.'

'Did this girl buy anything from the assortment here?' Sam said.

'She bought some eyes. Brown eyes. Blue ones are more popular, but she wanted the brown. I tried to sell her something to replace that arm.' She held up a sagging sawdust limb. 'This might have been made to work, but she didn't want it.'

There came the faint but unmistakable jangle of the bells over the front door.

'Excuse me, I'd better get back upstairs.'

Sam gave her a hand up, which made her cheeks turn pink. She dusted off her skirt.

'Look around all you like, detectives. If you'll close the trunk when you're done, I'd appreciate it.'

Sonora waited till she heard the clatter of heels on the stairs, then squatted next to the trunk, picking things up, putting them down.

'No eye beveller,' she said.

'Reckon Flash took it?' Sam asked.

'No doubt in my mind.'

Chapter Thirty

Sam's radio went off as they walked out of Shelby's Antiques. Sonora propped her feet up on the curb and leaned against the Taurus. She looked through the window at the carousel horse.

Sam put the radio back on his belt.

'What's up?' Sonora asked.

'Sheriff called from Oxton, about the security guard? Louisville ME did the autopsy this morning. Definitely a twenty-two, three bullets. And they found the car she took.'

'Where?'

'Parked way out of the way, some rural road or other called Kane's Mill. They figure she stashed her car, crossed a railroad bridge on foot, and hiked about six miles into town to the TV station. Maybe changed clothes in a McDonald's or something – should be they'll find witnesses. She'd have to be hauling a good sized pack for the video camera. Afterwards, they figure she lost her tail on the backroads, doubled back to where she had her own car stashed, and switched. They found strands of synthetic black hair caught in the car door, and the driver's seat was set as far up as it would go – just right for shrimps like you and Flash.'

'Thanks, Sam. Mind slipping your wrists into these handcuffs?'

He grinned. 'The car was wiped, but they got one or two prints, not good ones. Plus they found an X-Acto knife that nobody from the television station claims. The kind of thing a hobbyist might use.'

'I think we know what her hobby is. Did you tell Crick that our girl likes to play with dolls?'

'He thought it was pretty interesting that she made a point of getting a new one hours before she killed Daniels. A boy doll at that. And that it was important enough for her to pay cab fare, like it was part of some little scenario she had cooked up.'

Sam's radio went off again. He raised one eyebrow; Sonora shrugged. She had a worried feeling, as if something important had slid by.

She rewound the interview tape, put the recorder next to her ear. Hargreaves' voice was distinct and pleasant – she'd be good on radio.

'*. . . and what I call the miniatures. Doll house furniture. She liked that little tea set over there, did you—* '

Sonora felt a hand on her shoulder and jumped.

'Girl, you okay?'

'Yeah, sure. What's up now?'

Sam frowned. 'Dumpster fire, at the school where— '

'Keaton?'

He nodded. 'Evidently Flash went after one of the teachers.'

Sonora headed for one side of the car, and Sam for the other. She buckled her seat belt. 'So what happened?'

'That's all I know. Daniels called it in himself. Blue Ash PD didn't want us pulled in.'

'How long ago?'

'Couple hours. She's long gone, and Crick is pissed.'

'So am I. Thank you, Blue Ash.'

'Cut 'em some slack, Sonora, for them it's a routine dumpster fire.'

'There are no routine fires where Keaton Daniels is concerned.'

'Why's she going to show up at his school, Sonora? Helluva chance she's taking.'

'You understand the word obsession? Why do ex-husbands shoot their ex-wives at the office? I wish to God Crick would keep somebody with him.'

'Live in the real world, Sonora.'

Chapter Thirty-One

The burned-out dumpster was at the far end of the Pioneer Elementary School playground. Sonora stood on the hood of a Blue Ash patrol car and peeped inside. The fire had gobbled the top layer of trash. She wished Arson Guy was around. If the fire had burned deeply in one spot, it likely had smoldered, which might mean a cigarette tossed in. If, on the other hand, there was an accelerant— '

She heard a recognizable click and turned her head.

'Just leave your hands where they are.' The voice was female and shaking with excitement. Sonora got a quick look out of the corner of her eye.

The Blue Ash patrol officer was black, fine boned and slender, looking more like a teacher than a cop. She wore the uniform with spit and polish.

Sonora made sure her hands stayed put. 'Excuse me, officer. Sorry, can't read your name tag from here. Bradley?'

'Brady.'

'Officer Brady. What the hell do you think you're doing, pulling your gun there? If this is your car, I promise, I haven't scratched the paint.'

'Identify yourself, please.'

It dawned on Sonora that the Blue Ash police would be looking for a short blonde. This was getting irritating.

'The woman you're looking for is thinner than I am,

much as I hate to admit it. And her hair is shorter and lighter blonde.'

The uniform was looking around for help. No one was close. She pulled the radio off her belt.

Sonora laughed. 'Come on, Brady, please, don't embarrass me like this. I'm a detective, I work homicide for the city. That's my partner there in front of the school, talking to the good old boys. You know him? Sam Delarosa?'

'Got some ID?'

'Right here on my belt.'

'Keep your hands up.'

'If I fall on my butt, it's on your head, so to speak.'

Brady did not smile and she kept her gun steady. Sonora turned sideways, hands in the air. She hoped Sam wouldn't notice, she'd never hear the end of this. Brady inched closer, squinting at the ID.

'If you're satisfied with the little plastic picture, I'd appreciate it if you'd holster your gun, Officer Brady.'

'Sorry.'

'Nah, you never can tell.' Sonora sat on the hood of the car and swung her legs over the side.

Brady nodded glumly. Her hair was trimmed close to her head, and her face showed the uncertainty of extreme youth.

'You been here long?' Sonora asked.

'Since the call came in.'

'So what's the story?'

Brady leaned against the car and began to talk. Good old girls, Sonora thought, as she listened.

The call had come in a little after two. Brady checked her notes. Two-twelve, to be precise, which Sonora could see she was. It had been Physical Activity time and there were two primary classes on the playground. Sonora looked around the lot. It was a nice school, and judging from the facilities, was run by a fat cat PTA. A map of all fifty states was painted on the asphalt – educational hopscotch. There was a slide and a swing set and monkey bars, freshly painted in vibrant shades of all the primary colors, with cypress mulch cushioning the dirt beneath.

There had been two groups outside. One of them should have been the Daniels' class, but they had traded time with Vancouver's primary so they could schedule in a performance by a traveling puppet show. Instead of being outside, Daniels and his kids were indoors, watching *Rumpeltstiltskin*.

Vancouver had noticed a woman hanging around the edge of the playground, and was on her way over to check her out, when one of the children fell off the monkey bars. When she got that settled, she saw the woman talking to one of the children. She challenged her. The woman came at her, scratched her face, shoved her to the ground, and ran away.

Sonora frowned. The playground was vulnerable, placed on the other side of the school parking lot, away from the main buildings. The school was surrounded by houses on two sides. A limited access highway ran along the back, with a small hill and a thin strip of trees and bushes between. The back of the school was fenced with four feet of chain link, but there was no fence on the left side. Easy access, Sonora thought. Wouldn't even have to climb the fence.

'Any idea what this woman said to the child?'

'She wanted to know who his teacher was. He said Miss Vancouver, and this woman said wasn't he in Mr. Daniels' class? Then that's when the teacher came over.'

'She hurt much?' Sonora didn't see an ambulance, but it would have come and gone by now.

'No, not really, just shook up.'

Sonora looked for Sam. His shoulders were stiff and he was waving his arms. The side door of the school swung open and Keaton Daniels walked out with a man whose rumpled suit and air of authority said police. Trailing behind was a short man who wore his pants hitched below his belly, and slicked back his thinning black hair with something sticky. The principal, Sonora guessed. Whoever he was, he did not look happy.

Neither did Keaton. His jaw was set and he had that wary and guarded air she was beginning to know. Sonora slid off the hood of the car.

The cop in the suit eyed the ID hanging from Sonora's belt and gave her a hard look. She didn't know him. She got along with Blue Ash homicide people, but she didn't sense any rapport with this one.

The cop cleared his throat. 'Excuse me, Miss— '

'Specialist Blair.' Sonora held up both hands and pointed at Sam. 'I'm just one of the troops, sir. The man you need to argue with is over there. Mr. Daniels, may I have a word?'

The cop gave Keaton a hard look. 'We'll be in touch.'

The principal's smile was tense. 'Think about what I said, Mr. Daniels. We'll talk again in the morning.'

Keaton jerked his head in an unfriendly nod. Sonora fell into step beside him and they left the others behind.

'They want me to leave, you know that?' He looked at her sideways and kept walking. 'Like I would. Like I can't protect my kids. If I'd been out here I would have *had* her. God, it would have been so easy.'

Not as easy as you think, Sonora thought. Now probably wasn't the time to bring it up.

They went across the playground, past the monkey bars and basketball goals. Keaton looked first left, then right.

'What are you looking for?' Sonora asked.

Keaton scratched his head. 'One of the kids in my class said she saw a woman out here two days ago, watching us at PA. She said the woman was standing by the water. I'm trying to figure out what the hell she . . . surely it couldn't . . .' He moved off toward the line of trees that ran between the back of the school and the interstate, stopping in front of a deep puddle of mud, two feet by three, shadowed by a clutch of adolescent oak trees. Keaton looked down at the muddy water. 'You think this is what she meant?'

Sonora shrugged. Looked for footprints. 'Anything is possible, Keaton.'

He glared at her. 'She's not running me off, not me, babe. I'm not leaving my kids, or quitting my job, or changing my life.'

'Can they make you? Quit?'

Keaton stared off toward the school. 'They'd have to go through channels. Offer me something administrative downtown, and even then, I don't think they could force it. If the principal wants to get nasty, he can start shading my evaluations, but that takes time.' He lifted his chin. 'Why, you think I'm wrong? You think I'm risking my kids? I can take care of them, Sonora. If she comes back here, fine with me.'

Sonora nodded at him. 'School got smoke alarms?'

'Of course.'

'How about your apartment?'

He put his hands in his pockets. 'Four as of last night.'

'I'm up to five now, at my house.'

He gave her a second look. 'Your house?'

'Just paranoid. I've got two kids, remember. You change your locks yet, Mr. Daniels?'

'*Mr.* Daniels? What happened to Keaton?'

'What happened to the locks?'

'Using the mom-voice on me, Detective?'

'You think she's not dangerous because she's female, Keaton?'

'I think I can handle her.'

'Your brother couldn't.'

Chapter Thirty-Two

Sonora drank from a can of Coke as she headed toward her desk. The message light on her phone was blinking. Chas, no doubt. Constant, predictable and annoying. Twice she'd returned his calls, but he never seemed to be home.

She remembered calling Zack, nights he worked late, returning calls to find he wasn't there. Guess where I am, Sonora? Let me throw it in your face. Only this time, the nasty tricks didn't work, because this time, she didn't care.

Her stomach went from nausea to pain. Ulcer or not? She'd picked up a test at the drug store yesterday. Sooner or later she would work up the nerve to use it.

Sonora leaned against her desk, pushed the button. Not Chas, amazingly, but her brother, sounding perturbed.

'... something funny with your phone. You got call forwarding to my place now or something? Because that woman who sings is calling over here at the saloon. Normally I wouldn't mind, but she doesn't sing all that well, okay, and *Love Me Tender* isn't one of my favorites.'

Sonora chewed a fingernail. Could this weird caller be Flash? Why would she call and sing? Flash was getting to her, big time, maybe she was just seeing her everywhere. On the other hand, how many strange women were out there making calls to Sonora, and why now? There were no coincidences in a murder investigation. Just paranoid homicide cops.

Sam wandered in from the direction of the men's room, adjusting his belt. 'Molliter's got his hooker, you want to go listen up?'

Sonora looked at him, frowned. 'I don't have call forwarding.'

'No kidding? Can we focus here, Sonora? Gruber and Molliter have her in the interrogation room right now.'

'You mean interview room.'

'I mean hot witness. Gruber says she may know the killer.'

'Thank god for the witness fairy.'

'Girl, you are so cynical. Your problem is you just don't like Molliter. Come on, let's peek.'

The witness was small and rail thin, and she sat in the chair sideways, her feet curled under her. She smoked with hard, jerky motions, fingers trembling around the cigarette. Her jeans were shredded from stem to stern, and she wore red lycra bicycle shorts beneath. Her dirty cowboy boots were brown suede with tassels, the heels showing a pyramid-shaped pattern of wear. She wore a red and black plaid shirt, eye makeup, and her spiked yellow hair was greasy.

Molliter sat near the tape recorder, a dark green monster that took up the right-hand corner of the table. Gruber said something about coffee and headed out. Sam intercepted him in the hallway.

'So what's she say?'

Gruber poured coffee in a Styrofoam cup. 'She says black, and six packs of sugar.'

Sonora nodded. 'That ought to hit her good, she's already shaking. She needs something, but it's not sugar.'

Gruber shrugged. 'She works the trade, Sonora, and she's white, so that's like a given, you know? Course if she's no better at it than you were when we worked vice— '

'What's she say about the killer?'

'Hooker friend of hers, named Shonelle, who likes to work

with cuffs. She's telling Molliter all about it right now. I better get back in there before he embarrasses himself.'

'Physical description fit our girl?'

'Not even close. Taller, different complexion, and hails from "Nawth Carolina".'

'So how's this Shonelle wind up hooking in Cincinnati?' Sam asked.

Sonora pushed hair out of her eyes. 'Maybe she's a Bengals fan.'

Gruber folded his arms and gave her a lopsided smile. 'Something to do with an *arson* thing. No conviction – no surprise, you know their hit ratio. Supposedly this Shonelle was getting hassled and brought in every time a fire broke out, so she decided she needed a change of pace. Came to Cincinnati.'

Sam looked at Sonora, then back to Gruber. 'How'd you get on to this? She just waltz in the door?'

'I told you, Molliter knows her, from vice. She says she and Shonelle used to be buddies. But I don't hear friendship when she talks, you hearing me?'

Sonora nodded.

'Says when Shonelle talks about the johns, she says she's going to set their pants on fire.'

Sonora grimaced. 'Oh sure. Tailor-made. Lock 'em up, and I'm out of here.'

Gruber waved a hand. 'Don't sneer at me, that's what she says. Says she's been suspicious because Shonelle stole one of her regular customers, and this guy, who used to come around every couple of weeks, hasn't been back. And when Sheree – her name is Sheree La Fontaine— '

'Of course it is,' Sonora said.

'It's on her driver's license. Anyway, when Sheree asks Shonelle about this john, Shonelle just gets a funny look, and kind of laughs, and says she took care of him for good. Roasted him.'

'She actually used those words? Roasted him?'

Gruber nodded.

'She give you a description of this Shonelle?'

'To the wire, babe, right on down to the fuchsia orchid tattooed on her left shoulderblade.'

'What's she like?'

'Black, redheaded, tall and curvy. Big bazooms – Sheree swears they're fake. Oh, and a trick knee.'

'Say that again,' Sam said.

'That's how *she* put it. They both work the other side of the river. Shonelle used to dance in a club called Sapphire, but can't anymore 'cause of the knee.'

'No disability on that, huh?' Sam said.

'So did she give you a name on the john who got roasted?' Sonora asked

'Said he called himself Superdude.'

'*Superdude*?'

'Yeah, well. More imaginative than John Smith.'

Sonora cocked her head sideways. 'Smells worse than the morgue. She given you a description of Superdude?'

'Not yet, but hang around, and I'll ask.'

He headed for the interview room, and Sam filled two coffee cups. Sonora didn't want it, but took it anyway so she would not have to field queries about the ulcer. The doughnuts were wearing off, and the pain was going from background irritant to foreground agony.

They headed for the two-way.

Molliter was still hunched over the recorder, and Gruber had pulled a chair close and was leaning forward, face friendly. Sheree glanced at the two-way now and then. Once she waved.

'They think we don't know that they know,' Sam said.

Sonora grinned. Anybody who watched TV knew, little children knew. But the two-ways were useful because you could babysit a suspect a lot easier if you could peep in from the hallway – just to check on the little things, like whether they were climbing the walls or punching holes in the ceiling. They'd had one guy try to get out that way. Sonora always figured he'd have had a better chance with the front door. Or just by waiting it out. You couldn't keep a suspect forever without the DA nailing you to the wall. Not in real life.

Sheree took tiny sips of the coffee. Gruber was smiling and patient, and Molliter, as usual, looked sour.

'You sure you don't know any name other than Superdude?' Gruber said.

'He didn't use American Express, okay, he left home without it.' Sheree pulled a cigarette from a new package of Camels that Gruber had given her along with the coffee.

Gruber lit a match. 'How about what he looked like? He was a regular, so— '

'So yeah, I saw more than his face. No more than five inches. I'd say average.'

Molliter coughed and Gruber nodded seriously. 'That's good, but we need something to tell him apart from all those other average guys. How about the rest of him? Like his face, build. Hair and eyes.'

Sheree gave him a playful smile. 'Pubic hair?'

'You want to tell me about it, I'll listen.'

'Lot of things I could tell you about.'

Sonora wondered how old Sheree was. Impossible to tell, with hookers, the streets aged them quickly. This one looked forty and acted fourteen.

The girl seemed bored suddenly, glanced again at Molliter, then took a deep drag of her cigarette. 'He was kind of on the tall side, nothing major. Five eleven maybe, six feet. Sort of skinny, you know, stringy kind of build. Hair was reddish brown, and I think his eyes were green.'

'Anything else you notice about this guy?' Gruber said.
She shrugged.

'You told us all kinds of stuff on Shonelle. Do the same for me on the guy.'

'I told you. Tall and skinny.'

'So what kind of nose he have? Big nose?'

'Just a . . . just a regular nose.'

'Tattoos? Dark eyelashes?'

'Sure. No. I guess his eyelashes were light.' Sonora blew air between her teeth.

'What?' Sam said.

'She's describing Molliter. There is no Superdude.'

'Looks like Molliter's eating it up.'

'Molliter would. They should see if she'll take a lie detector. Right now. See if she will.'

'We can't do one today, anyway.'

'I know that, but she doesn't. I'll be right back.' Sonora went into the bullpen and veered left, sticking her head into officers' quarters. Crick was in front of the terminal, his sausage-thick fingers working the keyboard over with swift, heavy jabs.

'Sergeant?'

'Yeah, what is it, Blair?'

'Gruber and Molliter tell you anything about this witness they got?'

'So, what about it?'

'I been watching, Sergeant, and I'm telling you she's pulling their chain.'

'What makes you psychic?'

'Come on. She says this missing guy is named Superdude, and when they asked her for a description she gives them Molliter. Let's just say I got a feeling. Looks to me like she's got it in for this Shonelle she's trying to pin.'

'Oh, well, Blair, if you got a feeling say no more.' Crick leaned back in his chair. 'She give much detail on the description?'

'Precious little. Broad and vague, and when Gruber led she was happy to follow. The only thing that does strike me is the girl herself. She kind of fits the general description. Short and blonde. Bent.'

Crick pulled at his bottom lip. 'How about we offer the lady a lie detector?'

'My thoughts exactly.'

'Okay.' He went back to the keyboard. Sonora stayed in the doorway. 'What now?'

'That dumpster fire makes it pretty clear. Flash is sticking close to Daniels.'

'No, Blair.'

Sonora leaned against the doorjamb. 'What about that trip to Atlanta? That cop, Bonheur, has no problem with me going down there, looking at the case file, talking to the victim.'

'How you going to do that? They using mediums, or making do with Ouija boards?'

'I told you, sir, the victim survived on this one. Untied his ropes and got away.'

'No handcuffs?'

'No, but a lot of other similar elements.'

'I'll think about it.'

'Are you inclined to say yes?'

'Maybe. Are you inclined to go away? Listen, Blair, you talked to Sanders?'

'No, why?'

'She's onto something. Run along now, and bother her.'

Chapter Thirty-Three

Sonora stood with her back to the bathroom door, bolt digging into her rib cage, thinking she might need to be sick again. The back of the toilet was littered with wadded cellophane packets, an empty box, a wrinkled instruction sheet.

She held the white wand limply, tears rolling down her cheeks. Both windows pink. Why pink, she wondered, why not black? This could not be happening, not to her, not now. Men like Chas should not be spreading genetic material.

Sonora picked up the instruction sheet, hand shaking. She studied the succession of little pictures in the directions, vision blurred by tears. The outside door opened and she heard footsteps.

'Sonora? Sonora, you in here?' Sanders. Sounding chirpy and excited. 'Sonora?'

'Yeah, yeah, I'm here.'

Sonora reread the instructions. Took a breath. Both windows were supposed to start out pink. For negative results, wait five minutes and pray the window on the left turns white.

There was still hope. She looked at her watch, wondering how long it had been.

Sanders' voice was melodious. 'Crick said to talk to you and let you know, because I think I may have found her.'

'Who?' Sonora leaned against the wall. Breathed in and out. Listened to the beat of her heart. Time to look, time to check that little window, or wait another minute?

'Who? Oh, you're kidding. I was checking community colleges in those parts of Kentucky that Detective Delarosa— '

'*Sam.*'

'Sam was talking about.'

Sonora's grip tightened on the wand.

'And I've got a possible that looks really good – fires *and* a suspicious death, and there's a picture, a yearbook picture. They faxed it, and it came through pretty good. Could you come out and look at it, please?'

Now. It was time. Sonora swallowed, felt her stomach flipflop, and raised the wand in a shaking hand.

Left window white.

Sonora closed her eyes and leaned into the metal door. 'Thank God, it's an ulcer.'

'What?'

'Just one second, Sanders.' Sonora took a deep breath. Nah. She was done being sick. She pushed hair out of her eyes, came out of the stall.

Sanders held up a thin white slip of fax paper. 'You think this might be her?'

'Give me one minute.' Sonora bent over the white porcelain sink, grimaced at the familiar rust stain that circled the drain. Her knees were weak. She cupped her hands under the faucet and rinsed her mouth.

A small idea came to mind. She could make those calls and visits from Chas disappear with one message left on his machine – just tell him her period was late. Sonora looked at her reflection. Was she that much of a bitch? She thought maybe she was.

Sanders tapped a toe in a soft, annoying staccato. Sonora looked in the mirror.

'Okay, Sanders, what's her name? This girl in the picture?'

'Selma Yorke.'

Sonora decided that Sanders was holding her breath. She wiped her hands on a brown paper towel.

'Give it here.'

Chapter Thirty-Four

Sonora had that feeling she got when the case was finally breaking. They had a name. They had Selma Yorke.

It was definitely her picture in the yearbook. Sans wig, but Sonora knew the face, the *look* of her.

She had been featured twice. Once in the traditional rows of students, unsmiling and shy, hair waving in pale blonde rivulets, bangs longish and combed to one side. The other picture was a group shot of young girls in long white dresses, posing on a wide sweeping staircase. Perfumed and made up, eyes shiny with excitement, each and every one with a bouquet of tiny pink roses. Selma was the standout, the one who ignored the camera, looking off in the distance with a sour expression. She held her bouquet tightly in one hand, letting it trail to the side, as if she couldn't care less about the flowers, but had no intention of letting them go. Her bangs were ragged and short, angled awkwardly as if they'd been snipped by an angry child. Sonora remembered when Heather had cut her bangs with little plastic safety scissors. They had looked much the same.

Selma Yorke.

Sanders hunched over over the phone book, limbs loose, eyes downcast. 'She's not in here.'

Sam looked at Crick. 'We going to pick her up or circle?'

'Pick her up, if we can find her.' Crick squinted at the computer terminal. 'Never been arrested in Cincinnati. No

Ohio driver's license. We can run it and see if she's got a Kentucky or Tennessee license.'

Sonora crooked a finger. 'Come with me, Sanders. Sam and I will show you how it's done.' She glanced at her watch. 'You guys just give me half a minute to make one quick call.'

'Didn't you just talk to your kids?' Sam asked.

'I have to leave one short message for Chas. Only take a sec.'

Sonora put a video tape of *The Crying Game* up on the counter. It was a slow afternoon, so there wasn't a line.

Sanders stood beside her, looking nervously over one shoulder. Sam was in front of the popcorn machine. He bought a large bag, crammed a handful of kernels into his mouth. Sonora opened her purse and dug in her wallet.

'Do you have an account here?' The clerk was male, in his late teens.

Sonora nodded. 'I forgot my card.'

'Name?'

'Selma Yorke.'

He tapped the keyboard. 'Is your account at this location?'

'No, it's at the other one.'

'That's Selma Yorke at 815 Camp Washington?'

Sonora nodded, smiled, paid three fifty and signed for the movie. Sanders was bouncing again. They headed for the parking lot and Sam wandered out with them.

'Popcorn?'

Sonora took a handful.

'How can you *eat*?' Sanders looked at them over her shoulder as she headed into the road. Sam grabbed her elbow and held her back, pointing a salty finger at an oncoming brown truck.

'UPS stops for no man, or woman.'

Sonora licked salt off the palm of her hand. 'No one, Sam. Sounds better if you just say no *one*.'

The truck moved by in a cloud of exhaust and Sanders danced ahead. 'What now?'

'We could watch the movie,' Sonora said.

Sanders laughed and Sam looked at Sonora. 'We were young once.'

The sign said WELCOME TO CAMP WASHINGTON. The tiny group of houses lay just under the interstate, one street over from the slaughter yards. Railroad tracks were in spitting range, and old brick warehouses were a couple of blocks away. Sonora rolled the car window down and listened to the backdrop roar of traffic. It was still light out, drizzly. Humidity made the air thick and sticky, in spite of the chill. Sonora heard the metallic squeal of brakes on rail bed. She closed her eyes. This was what Selma Yorke heard at night when she lay in her bed. These were the noises and smells that framed her life.

Sanders leaned over the back of the seat. 'We could knock on the door and see if she's home.'

Sam raised an eyebrow at Sonora. 'What you think?'

Sonora gave Sanders a look. 'Remember. She's not under arrest. We don't have a warrant. We just want to talk.'

'Got your gun, Sanders?' Sam said.

Sonora opened her car door. 'Leave her alone, Sam.'

The house was old, two stories, nearly hidden behind a large leafy oak tree, and caged by a tall ragged hedge that almost concealed a rusting chain link fence. The lawn was scrubby, weed-infested bare dirt. The windows of the house were crusted with grime, the interior secreted behind gauzy curtains that looked filthy, even from a distance. A tire swing sagged from a tree in the front yard, suspended by a rotting rope.

An empty bird nest sat in the crook of a rusting gutter pipe under the eaves of the house. Sonora heard the coo of a dove. She walked across the spongy grass, boot heels sticking.

She's not here, Sonora thought. But her heart was pounding and her palms were coated with sweat.

She stood away from the window and the door, letting Sam knock. A significant number of police officers were killed on front porches, even on minor calls.

No one answered.

Chapter Thirty-Five

Sonora was alone when the call came through. The paperwork was done, and she was listening for the umpteenth time to Gruber's interview with the woman who'd spotted Flash's car. She came out of her daze on the second ring, looked around and realized that the guy on night shift was at dinner.

'Homicide, Blair.'

'Girlfriend, we need to talk. Phone booth half a block down by the parking lot. Get over there now.'

Selma. Sonora caught herself before she called Flash by name. 'Let's talk here.'

The line went dead. Sonora ran her hands through her hair, grabbed her blazer, and headed for the elevators.

The streetlights blazed over deserted sidewalks, office buildings lit and empty. Sonora was glad to have the Baretta in her purse. A car cruised slowly, muffler loud. Sonora made eye contact with the driver – lone male – who speeded his car and disappeared.

The ring of a phone sounded as the throb of the car's engine trailed away. Sonora ran the last few steps. Picked up the receiver.

'You'uns didn't have much of a childhood, did you?' The words were flippant, the tone was not. Selma Yorke's voice was thick and draggy.

Sonora shivered. 'My childhood was fine, what's it to

you? It's you that had a bad childhood, you're getting us mixed up.'

'I did it for you, you know. I felt sorry for you, after talking to him. I mean, it was all threes for you, wasn't it, girlfriend?'

'What do you mean, threes?'

'People have personalities and bad luck, just like numbers. You never notice that before? Three is bad news. And that brother of yours a one.'

'A one?'

'You know, a *one*. Shy and outcast, nobody liked him. That bothered you a lot, didn't it? Kids are mean, he was all the time getting beat on, and then your daddy getting mad at him for not sticking up for hisself, adding fuel to the fire.'

Sonora's purse strap slid down her arm. 'Tell me about your daddy.'

She might never have spoken.

'Then you go and marry a man just like him, just like they say in the shrink books. Make you happy, he's dead now?'

'Does it make you happy, the men you've killed? Is that why you do it?'

'You'uns think I'm a total mess, don't you, you think only good girls have nice feelings. I tell you this. I knew a boy once, just a boy, like Keaton. Made me feel like I was . . . like I was important, like I was a part of him. The thing is, I always have been all by myself. And I liked it that way, except sometimes I'd get to feeling funny. Like I was going so far inside myself I wanted to scream? You ever feel like that?'

'No,' Sonora said.

Silence again, then a choked laugh. 'That's why I like you, you always say just what you think. Maybe you don't know how it feels. But it's noises, inside of me. Like mama in the fire.'

Maybe it's your conscience, Sonora thought.

'You ever hear whale songs, Detective? That's what it sounds like, inside of me. Look, I know I'm different. I've always known that, always been on the outside, looking in. This boy, Danny, he was like Keaton. He made the bad feelings go away. Being with him was like . . . like being high. It felt good. I didn't think I'd ever feel that again. I see men, and they look like him, like Danny, but they don't work, they don't give me that feeling.'

'Does Keaton give you that feeling?' Sonora said.

'Good to know you're catching on.'

'What was that business on the playground?'

'I was missing him. I had to see him.'

'Don't give me that,' Sonora said. 'What you're doing is hunting him.'

'Don't you see?' Selma said. 'That's where you come in. I helped you. Now you help me.'

Chapter Thirty-Six

By the time Sonora made it back to the squad room, the phone was ringing again.

'Homicide, Blair.'

'Ms. Sonora Blair?'

'Speaking.'

'Ma'am, I'm calling from University Hospital, concerning a Charles F. Bennet. Are you a relative?'

Ex-significant other, Sonora thought. 'I'm his, um, his friend.'

'Ma'am, Mr. Bennet has been in an accident and—'

'A fire?'

'No ma'am. A car accident.'

'Oh. How bad is he?'

'He's in emergency now, but—'

'I'm on my way.'

It was raining again, just like the night Mark Daniels was killed. Sonora felt like she was dreaming as she went through the automatic doors into the waiting room.

Quiet night. Two people watching television, one uniformed police officer on the phone.

'Sonora Blair, here about Charles Bennet.'

The clerk was middle-aged and tired, eyes blue and bloodshot. 'Yes ma'am, if you'll take a seat, someone will be right with you.'

The police officer looked over his shoulder. 'Excuse me, ma'am, did you know Mr. Bennet?'

Did? Sonora nodded.

'I wonder if I might ask you a few questions.'

Sonora brought her ID up out of her purse. 'All you want, but I'd appreciate knowing what happened.'

'You're homicide?'

'Yeah. He's dead, isn't he?'

The uniform hesitated. He was an older man, close to retirement, and his eyes were sad. 'I'm sorry, he was DOA.'

Sonora nodded, feeling stiff and numb.

The uniform put a hand on her shoulder. 'Hit and run, he never saw it coming.'

'Any leads on the car?'

The officer shook his head. 'No witnesses. Got shards of broken headlights in his shirt pocket, and tire marks on . . .'

'It's okay.' Sonora straightened her shoulders. 'I think I better have a look.'

The pretty face was gone. There were tire marks on the crushed chest, windpipe and larynx. For the first time in a long time, Sonora looked at death and felt ill.

She turned away, saw the clothes piled on the counter. The shoes were in good shape, pants in tatters, shirt all gore. The familiar jacket was stiff with blood. Sonora fingered the sleeve, then gave it a second look.

There had been four leather buttons – one had been torn away, leaving three. She checked the other sleeve. Three buttons again, one missing.

I've helped you, now you help me. Three and three. Proof of what she already knew.

Selma Yorke.

Chapter Thirty-Seven

Sam handed Sonora a beer, and sat on the end of the couch. He scratched Clampett behind the ears. 'You doing okay over there, Sonora?'

'I don't know. Tell you the truth, I don't feel so good.'

'Tell you the truth, you don't look so good. Have a big drink of that beer.'

'Hang on a second, I think I hear Heather.'

'She's fine, the kids are asleep, I checked them both just a minute ago.'

Sonora took a sip of beer, leaned back and closed her eyes. 'This is so unbelievable. It's hard to . . . I'm not happy about this, Sam.'

'I didn't figure you would be.'

Sonora opened her eyes. 'I mean, I may have been pissed and all, but I'm not glad he's dead. He was . . . it made me sick to look at him.'

'What's the matter with you, hon, nobody's going to think you're happy over this.'

'Selma does.'

Sam sat forward. 'You talked to her?'

Sonora swallowed. 'A couple of times.'

'You mean stuff we don't have recorded?'

'Once on a pay phone. Once on my car phone.'

'And you didn't *say* anything? What the hell's going on with you?'

'I . . . she . . . she knew things, Sam, really private stuff.'

'Private? What are you playing at girl, there's nothing private between the two of you.'

Sonora blew air between her teeth. 'Wrong, Sam. She knows things, *personal* things, stuff she's got no business knowing.'

Sam put a hand on her shoulder. 'Okay, Sonora, let's take this slow and think it through. Tell me what she knows.'

'Things like . . . like my parents. You remember that business when my mom died?'

Sam set his beer on the end table and gave Sonora a sideways look. 'You saying she knew that you think your dad—'

'Yeah. She knew that. *All* about that.'

Sam got his thoughtful look. 'What else? Anything?'

'About my brother, growing up. And about Zack.'

'You talk about this kind of stuff to just *anybody*, Sonora?'

'Jesus, Sam, of course not. You. Just you. And you didn't tell her, did you?'

'You have to ask?'

'I haven't told anybody else. Well, my brother. But he wouldn't talk to her.'

'What about the obvious here, Sonora, boyfriends? You were over the moon about Chas for a while there, you give him all the intimate details?'

Sonora picked her beer up, put it back down. 'Oh.'

'Oh, she says. I take that as a yes.'

'But why would he, I mean how could she . . . you think she's been, like, dating him?'

'I admit it's a stretch, but who else could it be? Any signs he's been seeing somebody?'

'Yeah, right, I should know them by now.'

'Would Chas tell all like that to somebody he barely knew?'

'I think maybe so, especially since he was so mad at me. Jesus, this is so weird.'

'You ought to pick your fellas a little more carefully, girl.'

'So she did do it. She killed him. If you could have heard her on the phone, going on about threes.'

'I wouldn't know about that, would I, since you been holding out? But, Sonora, jacket buttons don't prove murder. Can't build a case book on something like that. We need to get a look at her car, get the physical evidence. We'll run this by Crick in the morning, play up the sympathy bit over Chas so maybe he won't kill you.'

Sonora put her head in her hands.

'You okay?'

'I feel lost, Sam. Like I'm falling. I don't know how to put it, I just know it feels really bad. It makes me wonder.'

'Wonder what?'

'If this is like the way she feels.'

Chapter Thirty-Eight

Records from Selma Yorke's alma mater showed that she had gone to high school in Madison, Kentucky – a small town, barely on the map, resting in a valley at the foot of a mountain raped by strip mining. Sonora looked at the raw wound of land, thinking that Selma had grown up with it.

There was one restaurant on the outskirts of town. A Pizza Hut.

The two-lane road twisted and turned, leading them downward toward the river. Woods pressed on both sides, relieved now and then by a sprawl of mobile homes and box-like whitewashed houses. Men sat outside on front porches and smoked.

Sonora stared out the window. 'What are these guys doing? It's a working day.'

'Maybe they work night shift. Maybe there is no work.'

'And maybe they're just watching the marijuana grow.'

'Watch your stereotypes, girl.'

'Lookit, Sam, there are dogs under that porch.'

'Don't point, Sonora, it's not polite.'

Sonora pushed her nose against the glass. 'You know, I think I've seen that house already.'

'They just look alike.'

'This is the second time that woman in lavender pedal pushers has waved at me, Sam.'

'There's a little grocery about a mile down the road. We'll get directions there.'

'How do you know?'

''Cause we passed it a couple times already.'

The sign over the screen door said Judy-Ray Food Mart. It was warm inside, poorly lit. Almost everything was old – the linoleum, the shelves, the dairy case. Only the stock was new – bright colored wrappers on old metal shelves. There was a large selection of cigarettes and chewing tobacco. Sam helped himself to both, along with a packet of peanuts, a Moonpie, and a bottle of Ale-8 One.

'Hidee,' he said to the girl behind the counter.

She wore acid washed jeans and a woven belt that said DONNIE'S GIRL on the back. Sonora stepped aside and let Sam do his stuff.

She was hungry. She eyed the counters and settled for tiny white powdered doughnuts, a packet of cashews and a Coke. Sam opened his packet of peanuts and poured them into the bottle of Ale-8 One.

He grinned at the girl behind the counter. 'Wonder if you could help me out some.'

Sonora wandered to the back of the store, opened her pack of doughnuts. Checked out the movie rentals.

All the latest films. Rural wasn't rural anymore.

'Sonora?'

She swallowed a mouthful of doughnut. 'Yeah?'

'Come on, girl. We took a wrong turn, but I know where I'm headed. It's out of town, no more than fifteen minutes away.'

Sonora settled back in the car, wondering what Sam meant by town. The grocery store? The mobile homes?

He sat beside her, drinking Ale-8 One and crunching peanuts. He seemed happy.

'I'll be damned, they *said* a chicken on the mailbox. This has got to be it.'

A faded plastic chicken sat on top of a dented mailbox. Some joker had shot a bullet through the chicken's head.

Sam turned into the drive, and gravel crunched beneath the tires of the car.

The house was small, two stories, painted blue with white shutters. Children's toys, bright colored plastic, littered the sagging porch and the sandy, dirt-packed yard. Clumps of grass and weed had turned brown. Sonora could see a tire swing and a burned out barn behind the house.

'This looks a lot like where she's living now,' Sam said.

'Yeah, and see that, Sam?'

'The barn? Fire follows this girl, doesn't it?'

There was no screen in the storm door, just a warped metal frame. Sam knocked on the sun-bleached wood.

They waited. Sam knocked again and the door was opened by a woman in a blue cotton dress. The thick hams of her calves were encased in heavy stockings and showed like stumps beneath the hem of her dress. Her navy blue leather shoes, Papagallos, looked brand new.

She opened the door wide. 'You'uns must be the police. Come in, won't you?'

You'uns. Sonora exchanged looks with Sam. They were in the right place.

'I'm Marta Adams, Selma's aunt. Ray Ben, the police are here.'

The living room was small, the wood furniture polished and slick. A braided rug gave a cozy Early American look. The furniture was maple, and there was a profusion of end tables, coffee tables, side tables – all covered with ceramic animals, seashells, ashtrays, and coasters. There were doilies on the arms of the floral chintz couch. Heavy green curtains kept the sun out.

Ray Ben Adams sat at the edge of his recliner. In spite of being skinny everywhere else, his belly bulged over his belt buckle. He wore black leather work shoes, the lace-up version, and a blue, oil-stained work shirt that had his name printed on the pocket. He had sideburns, an angular, sunburnished face, and his hair was grey streaked and greasy. His brown eyes were bloodshot. Oil and dirt had permanently stained the cuticles around his fingers.

He took a deep drag of his cigarette, smoking it down to the filter, and stubbed it out in an ash tray that said Myrtle Beach, South Carolina. He stood up to shake hands.

Marta Adams fanned her blue dress out behind her, and sat on the edge of the couch. Beside her, on an end table, was a large, worn black Bible, reading glasses folded neatly to one side. Marta Adams crossed her legs and the nylon sang.

'You'uns want to talk about Selma, that right?'

Sonora nodded, thinking that Marta Adams was the kind of woman you could imagine waiting tables, calling people honey, and snapping gum. Her favorite brand would be Dentyne.

'What's she done?' Ray Ben asked.

Sonora set the recorder on the coffee table and slid in a new tape. She was on the verge of saying 'nothing', then decided that would be an insult. She and Sam hadn't come all the way out here for nothing.

'We're homicide detectives, Mrs. Adams. We think Selma may be involved in a case we're investigating.'

'Homicide? You mean murder?'

Sam nodded. 'Yes, ma'am, we mean murder.'

Ray Ben pulled a package of Winstons from his shirt pocket. 'You think she done it?' He offered the package to Sam, who looked wistfully at Sonora, then declined. Ray Ben struck a match and inhaled tobacco. Sonora's head began to hurt.

'That's what we're trying to figure out.'

'What'd she do?'

Sonora looked at him steadily. 'Handcuffed a man to the steering wheel of his car, doused him with gasoline, and set him on fire. Sir.'

Ray Ben sagged in his chair. Marta Adams tightened her lips and settled back against the couch. Large tears rolled down her cheeks. She took a crumpled wad of tissue from the bosom of her blue dress.

'When's the last time you talked to Selma?' Sam's voice was gentle.

Ray Ben cleared his throat. 'Mama, maybe we better not talk to these folks. We don't have to say a word, if we don't want to.'

Marta Adams patted her husband's knee. 'We'll do what the Lord would want us to, Ray Ben. She's beyond us, we known that a long time.'

He swallowed hard and took a deep drag of his cigarette. Sonora was tired and the tobacco smoke irritated her eyes. She thought of her children. Stuart would look after them. They were okay.

'What you want to know?' Marta Adams asked.

'Just tell us about her,' Sam said. 'Anything you can think of.'

Marta Adams fiddled with the top button of her dress. She blew her nose delicately and with apology, and began to talk.

Selma had come to them at age five with nothing more than a doe-eyed baby doll that played Brahms Lullaby, and the soot-stained nightie she had been wearing when a fireman carried her out of her burning bedroom to safety. Both parents, Marta's sister, Chrissy, and her husband, Bernard, had died of smoke inhalation.

It had been a fire of suspicious origin, starting in the living room. There had been speculation that little Selma was playing with matches, but the final conclusion was that a cigarette had ignited the couch. Bernard had smoked.

The baby doll had reeked of smoke, but Selma pitched a fit when they tried to wash it or get her a new one. They let her keep it. It was all she had.

She did not smile or talk the first year she was with them. Shock, they were told. She was an intelligent child. Her parents – Bernard in particular – had been 'yuppies' (this confided in an embarrassed whisper) and had started her in Montessori schools by age three.

After she was with them a year, she resumed talking. They did not make a big deal of it, they were warned not to. The smiles never came.

She had been an uncomfortable child.

Selfish. They hated to say it, but it was true. She didn't like to share, but Marta and Ray Ben had five of their own, and sharing was par for the course. Her nickname had been Magpie. She liked pretties, not necessarily valuable. There was no predicting what would catch her eye, but whatever did had a way of migrating to her secret stash. Sometimes she buried things, then forgot where, and would dig the yard up trying to find them. Made little holes everywhere.

She was mesmerized by mirrors and water, puddles and lakes. She'd sit and look into the river for ages, not moving a muscle. But she hated the ocean.

'The waves scared her. We went to Myrtle Beach once, and she wouldn't go in the water. Said it was too big and too noisy.' Marta Adams looked at Ray Ben and he nodded.

No, she did not get along with other children. She was uninterested in the other kids, preferred her own company, and played alone for hours, taking inventory of all of her treasures.

Dolls? Oh, yes, she loved dolls. She would scream till her face got red if you touched one of her dolls. Ray Ben had tried to fix one once, they were always losing the arms and legs, and Selma had not liked it one bit. She hadn't cared about the missing limbs, not like Marta's little girls, who would die a thousand deaths over a Barbie who'd lost a leg.

Sometimes, Ray Ben spoke up suddenly, she secretly mutilated the other girls' dolls, so they would pass them on to her.

'You don't know that,' Marta told him.

'I seen her do it once.'

No, no, the barn had burned a couple years after Selma had gotten there, but she'd only been seven at the time. Seven years was too young to blame. It had been a terrible fire. They had lost an old milk cow and a goat, and their entire crop of tobacco.

The kids had cried for weeks about the animals. Except Selma. She didn't cry unless she was mad.

They tried to give her religion. The minister of their Baptist church went the extra mile with Selma, but she was never grateful. They had church on Wednesday night, Sunday morning, and Sunday evening. They said grace at every meal, and had a Bible reading after supper most nights.

None of it rubbed off on little Miss Selma Magpie.

Sonora looked at Sam. There was spite in the way Marta Adams said 'Miss Selma Magpie.'

'That was her nickname?' Sam's voice was honey.

Marta Adams laughed, but her eyes were cold. 'I guess we did call her that, a few months after she come. Most of the kids had nicknames.'

'What was she like as a teenager?' Sonora asked.

Ray Ben stubbed out a cigarette. 'She was trouble, that's what she was.'

'Now, Ray—'

'You said tell them the truth, Marta. Tell them the truth.'

Marta looked at the wall. 'Those were difficult years.'

'I'll say they were. She drank and she smoked, refused to go to church with us on Sunday, and did things with boys by the time she was thirteen.'

Marta Adam's face turned dark red. 'Ray Ben.'

'It's true. We caught her, didn't we?'

'Not *boys*. That one boy.' Marta Adams bowed her head. 'It's a wonder that child never got pregnant. The truth is, no matter how much I punished that girl, she done as she pleased, even when she was little bitty.'

'When did Selma leave home?'

Marta sniffed. 'Two months after she turned fifteen, she walked out this house and down that road, and we never seen her again.'

Ray Ben shook his head. 'She never called, she never wrote, never so much as sent us a card. We ain't heard one word out of that girl since she left.'

'Did you adopt her?' Sonora asked.

'We always meant to, but just never got around to it. She always went by Adams, though, like the rest of our kids.'

Sonora frowned. 'That was how long ago?'

'When she up and left? Been, oh gosh, eleven years. November, I think, 'cause she went with no coat and it was cold. Just took that old worn-out jean jacket and her doll.'

'And the roll of money I had on my dresser, *your* best earrings, and Jester's little pistol.' Ray Ben did not seem to have fond memories.

'A twenty-two?' Sam asked.

'Sure was. Cute little thing.'

Sonora looked at the thick curtains, wishing she could see outside. She pictured Selma aged fifteen, going down that gravel drive for good, all alone in the world. Three years later she had enrolled in Ryker Community College under the name of Selma Yorke. Where had she gotten tuition money? ID? High School transcripts?

'Did she graduate from high school?' Sam asked.

Ray Ben shook his head. 'She was smart, but she didn't do nothing with it.'

Sonora would have given a lot to know what had happened in the three years from fifteen to eighteen. Selma had taken college courses in business and accounting for close to two years, leaving in the middle of her last semester, after a dorm caught fire just before Easter vacation. A boy had died in the fire – a dark-haired, brown-eyed boy. Sonora had seen his picture in the year book. He had been studying business administration, was on the intermural football team. He'd been on the swim team, and was accounted a champion at table tennis. Dead now, eight years, in a fire of suspicious origin.

'Your sister's last name was Yorke?' Sam asked.

'Yes. She married Bernard Yorke. He worked for Ashland Oil. Had a real good job, made good money.'

'More than we ever did,' Ray Ben said. 'For all the good it did him. We still wound up raising his daughter.'

And what a fine job you did of it too, Sonora thought.

Sam leaned toward Marta Adams. 'What was it that made her leave all of a sudden?'

'We didn't say all of a sudden,' Ray Ben said.

Sam smiled gently. 'Middle of the school year. It's cold out, she's fifteen years old. Must have been something.'

Ray Ben shrugged.

Marta Adams looked at the floor. 'That was just Selma. She did stuff like that.'

Chapter Thirty-Nine

The principal's office of Jack's Creek High School was a square box, the walls concrete block, the floor over-waxed linoleum. The yellow pinewood desk was cluttered, and one of the filing cabinets hung open. The chair behind the desk was undoubtedly the most comfortable in the room, but it was empty.

Sonora sat in a straight back wood chair next to Sam, waiting for the next teacher.

'Get the feeling she wasn't much liked?' Sam was saying.

Sonora nodded. The principal had been new and young, and did not know Selma Yorke, but he had lent them his office and instigated a parade of teachers who did.

Someone knocked at the door.

Sam looked at his watch. 'Last one.'

The woman was past retirement age, tall and broad shouldered, with well rounded hips but no extra weight. She wore a blue print dress that hung loosely to mid calf, thick cotton socks and scuffed deck shoes. Reading glasses hung from a chain around her neck. Her hair, grey and white, was thickly plaited and hung down her back.

'I'm Ms. Armstead, the art teacher.'

Sam stood up and shook her hand. 'Specialist Delarosa, and this is Specialist Blair.'

Armstead nodded at Sonora and sat down. She inclined her head toward Sonora's recorder. 'Are you taping this?'

Sam smiled at her. 'We record all our interviews, standard procedure.'

Sonora leaned forward. 'Ms. Armstead, the principal talked to you already, didn't he, about a student named Selma Yorke?'

'I don't remember all of my students, Detective, and this *was* over eleven years ago. But the fact is, I do remember Selma, very well.'

Sonora and Sam exchanged looks.

'Why very well?' Sam asked.

'I'm an art teacher, and Selma was very talented. Talented and . . . tortured.'

Sonora settled back in her chair. 'Why do you say that – tortured.'

'I'm speaking internally. Let me give you a for instance. We always do a unit on portraiture – one student models and the others sketch. Selma couldn't do it, she could not draw another human being. Sometimes she would sketch a number, instead of a face. It was weird, it made the other children uncomfortable. She was not well liked. She tried, I'll give her that. I saw the child sit there, time after time, pencil in hand. She would break the lead, tear the paper. One particularly bad day she went to the rest room and . . . and cut off her bangs.' Armstead's voice went breathless. 'I went to her. I took her aside, but she was a difficult child to get close to. I will tell you honestly that I did not like her. But I did respect her talent. I haven't had another student like Selma.'

Good, Sonora thought. But Armstead looked bereft.

'Had she done anything like that before? Gotten mad and cut her bangs?' Sam asked.

'When I gave them the self-portrait assignment, Selma couldn't even begin. She got very angry, then came in the next day, bangs chopped right off, the same thing. She was very apathetic. Said she'd take a failing grade for the project, moped around the room while the others were working. Then she came to me and asked if she could draw Danny instead.'

Sonora looked at Sam. 'She mentioned a Danny. A couple of times.'

'Tell us about him,' Sam said.

'Daniel Markum. He was older than she was, twenty-two, twenty-three. His brother went to school with Selma, and he worked the family farm and ran a repair shop from the house. Some of the teachers thought he shouldn't have been fooling with a girl as young as Selma, but she was crazy about him.'

Sonora leaned forward in her chair. 'Did she do it? Draw him?'

Armstead nodded. 'A very credible job, she *was* talented. She did him, but never anyone else.'

'Have you seen her since she left? Heard from her?'

Armstead shook her head. 'I did what I could when she was my student, but we were not close. I kept things, some of her work, locked away in my private cabinet. Would you like to see?'

A bell rang just as they left the principal's office, and the hallways flooded with kids in blue jeans. Armstead led them past a thinly populated trophy case, through double doors into 101-A – the art room.

The walls were covered with vibrant masks of papier mâché, bright greens, yellows, blues. Armstead went past a paint-streaked sink and opened a locked cabinet. Her head disappeared and Sonora heard rustling noises.

A girl peered in the doorway and looked at Sam. She grinned and left.

'Here we are.' Armstead brought out a fabric case and unzipped it over her desk, took out a canvas and held it up.

It was thickly painted with throbbing, dark color.

'Selma loved to paint. Disturbing things, hot hard colors as you see here, very abstract. The other students, the other teachers, thought it was just splatters on canvas. Ignorance.' Her voice sounded clipped and irritable. She rummaged in the satchel and pulled out a square of canvas paper. 'This is the sketch she did. Danny Markum. The likeness is good.'

Sonora held the sketch by the edges. It had been done in charcoal, by a hurried, almost frantic hand, and something about it disturbed her. The likeness to Keaton Daniels was superficial, but marked. She passed it on to Sam.

He looked up and caught Armstead's eye. 'What happened with her and Danny?'

Armstead winced. 'She did this just before the . . . that business at the river.'

'What business at the river?' Sonora asked.

'You don't know?'

Sam shook his head.

Armstead settled slowly into the chair behind the small square desk. 'Nobody really knows for sure what happened that night, and there were a lot of versions flying at the time, let me tell you.' She looked out the window, seeming far away. 'I told you Danny had a brother, Roger, and he was in Selma's class. Selma was jealous of Roger. She was jealous of anybody that went near Daniel, but Roger in particular.

'The two of them, the brothers, had a habit of going night fishing once a week. It was a sore point with Selma. She had a thing about the river. Anyway, Selma was always agitating to tag along, but Roger usually talked Daniel out of letting her go. This one night, Roger said Selma came anyway, fought with Danny, then stormed off. The story goes that after Selma left, Roger went back to the car for more beer. And when he came back, Danny was gone. Nothing there but his fishing pole and bait, and a half empty beer can.'

'They doing a lot of drinking?' Sam asked.

'Probably. More than they should, no doubt. They dragged the river and found Daniel's body. The official ruling was that he waded out over his head and drowned. He couldn't swim. Most of the kids around here can't.'

'Then the rumors started,' Sonora said.

Armstead propped her chin on her elbow. 'More than just rumors. Roger made a big fuss. He said Selma came back and pushed Danny in. But the sheriff let it go. He said that Selma loved Danny and, after all, she was a little thing, and Danny was a solid six foot. But they . . . they found one of Selma's earrings in the mud. Selma said she lost it the first time, when they had words.'

Sam looked at Armstead. 'The *first* time? She said that?'

Armstead nodded. 'I heard her say it, here in class.'

'You tell the sheriff?'

'I . . . yes.' Armstead traced a finger across the desk. 'Roger wouldn't let it be.'

'Is that when she left?' Sonora asked.

'Not exactly. Not long after that, Roger had an accident. He was working late in the family tobacco barn, and a fire started. He didn't make it out.'

Sam spoke gently. 'Any ruling on how the fire started?'

Armstead spoke through clenched teeth. 'Someone emptied a gas can that was there for the tractor, and then dropped a match. Roger never had a chance.' She looked up at Sam. 'Everyone said Selma did it. And *that* was when she left.'

Sonora and Sam exchanged looks.

Armstead took the canvas paper from Sam. 'It's a very focused sketch, don't you think?'

Sonora thought obsessed would be a better word. 'Ms. Armstead, do you think Selma killed Roger? Do you think she killed Danny?'

Armstead raised a hand in a gesture that looked hopeless and tired. 'I wouldn't – I couldn't know. I will tell you that after Danny died . . . she tried to draw him, but she couldn't.'

Chapter Forty

Sonora looked up at the fifth floor of the Board of Elections building, saw that all windows were lit. She looked at Sam.

'Go home, babe, see your kiddo. How's she doing?'

'They're still running tests, Sonora. Always running tests.' He chewed his lip. 'Naw, I better— '

'Go *home*, Sam.'

'Go home, okay. Call if you get something.' He leaned across the seat and kissed her cheek. 'You're looking tired, Sonora.'

'I am tired, Sam.'

He watched her walk from the car to the side door – cop watching cop in at cop headquarters. Sonora glanced up at the video camera in the doorway.

The elevator was slow. She rested her head against the wall, thinking she would like it if Sam kissed her more often.

Her phone was ringing as she walked in. She almost passed it by, then thought it might be Stuart or the kids.

'Homicide, Specialist Blair.'

'Hello.' The voice was high and fluting, vaguely familiar against a noisy background. 'This is Chita Childers. You know, from Cujos?'

Sonora's heart beat kicked in hard and heavy. Tell me she's there, she thought. Tell me she's there.

'He's here.'

Sonora leaned against her desk. 'He?'

'Yeah, um, that guy, you know? The one in the picture?'

Sonora felt a chill, then her heart settled. Keaton, of course. 'Solid build, dark curly hair?'

'Yeah.' Chita was chewing gum, which over the phone sounded like a wad of plastic in her mouth. Sonora wanted to tell her to spit it out.

'Thank you, Ms. Childers. I appreciate the call.'

'Should I try to keep him here or something?'

'No. He's not a suspect.'

'Just a law abiding citizen having a drink, huh?'

Sonora pictured Chita Childers behind the bar, hands on her slim hips.

'You might want to know that he's asking after her. That blonde in the jean skirt. He's not a cop is he?'

'Did he say he was?' Sonora asked.

'No.'

'He's not.'

'So I shouldn't have called, huh?'

'Certainly you should have. I appreciate it.' Women always needed to be reassured, Sonora thought. 'If you see the other one—'

'The girl?'

'The girl. Don't approach her, and call me right away.'

'Will do.'

Sonora called home. 'Stuart? Don't wait up, I'm going to be late. Can you stay?'

'Bartender went home with the flu twenty minutes ago. I was going to wait till the kids went to bed, then take off. You think they'll be all right, or you want me to stay?'

'They should be all right, just make sure they're all locked up and the alarms are on.'

'No problem. Case breaking?'

'Side issue. Trying to keep John Q Public out of trouble.'

'Maybe John Q wants trouble.'

'He's going to get it, he doesn't watch out.'

Chapter Forty-One

Sonora ran a pick through her hair and reapplied her makeup, smearing Sulky Beige heavily across her lips. She looked in the rear-view mirror. Nothing she could do about the hard exhaustion in her face, and the newly acquired slump to her shoulders. She straightened her tie when she parked the car, then changed her mind and stuffed the tie in the glove compartment.

Cujos was winding down – it was late, a week night. Sonora wondered if Selma was around, watching him, watching her. She paused in the doorway, and people stared. Something about her always said cop.

Keaton sat by himself a few feet from the bar where he could see the front door, the rest rooms, and the television. He was close to the end of his beer. His khakis were wrinkled, but his shirt was freshly pressed and he had shaved after five. He looked tired and pale and wonderful.

Sonora rested a hand on the chair across from him. 'Hello, Keaton Daniels.'

'Sit down. I saw you on the news tonight, and I was wondering about all those developments you mentioned.'

Sonora sat and smiled sadly.

'It's all hype, isn't it?'

'It's not breaking yet, I won't lie to you. But it's moving and picking up speed. And I *will* catch her.' She tilted her head sideways. 'Provided you don't beat me to it.'

He smiled, and she liked it that he didn't try to deny it. 'Am I in trouble?'

'You got a gun, Keaton?'

'Yeah, you mind?'

'Got a permit? Know how to use it?'

He nodded.

'Then no, I don't mind. Just don't take it to school with you.' She leaned back in her chair. 'Been here a long time?'

'Since eight.'

'Long night.'

Chita Childers leaned across the bar, trying to get their attention. 'Last call! Either of you want anything?'

'I was thinking about toast,' Sonora said. It was out of her mouth before she had time to think. Bad girl. No can do. Brother of victim. Be smart.

Keaton stood up and took the jacket from the back of his chair.

God he looked good, she thought.

Chita Childers stared at them. 'Going to call it a night, huh?'

Keaton smiled at Sonora.

'I'll follow you home,' she said.

The streets of Mt. Adams were lined with parked cars, giving the neighborhood a tight, squeezed feeling. Keaton took Sonora's hand and led her up the walk to the front porch. He fumbled with the house key and Sonora wondered if he was nervous. She was.

'You ever get those locks changed,' Sonora asked. She looked over her shoulder. Scanned the dark streets.

Nobody, no movement, no car out of place. Selma couldn't be everywhere at once, one person couldn't do twenty-four hour surveillance. Maybe she wasn't out there.

And maybe she was.

'Yeah, I got the locks changed. We're safe.'

The house was dark, just a light over the sink in the

kitchen. Keaton headed for the lamp, but Sonora put a hand on his arm, and he left it dark. The blinds were open, and the streetlights gave the room a shimmer of illumination. Keaton closed the front door and locked it.

He took Sonora's hand and led her to the edge of the couch. 'Stand close to me, like you did the other night.'

Sonora let her purse slide off her shoulder and drop to the floor. She draped her blazer over the arm of the couch, then moved toward him, not quite touching. Was she really going to do this? She studied his face, shadowed by darkness. Yes. She was.

Keaton put his arms around her, and she stood on her tiptoes and dipped her tongue into the hollow of his throat, a butterfly flick. He kissed her, swiftly and hard, and after awhile she broke free.

They stood still for a moment, breathing deeply. Keaton put his hands on her hips and pulled her tight against his body. She closed her eyes, feeling his warmth, his hardness, the beat of his heart against her chest.

He traced the line of her neck and shoulder with the thick pad of his thumb. She placed a finger against his lips, parting them slowly, touching his tongue, lightly grazing the bottom edge of his teeth.

With her other hand she unbuttoned the top buttons of her shirt, and unlatched the front hook of her bra. She arched her back, felt her hair slide across her shoulders, bit her bottom lip when he bent forward and put his mouth on her breast.

They shed their clothes quickly, awkwardly. Light spilled in from the street and turned their flesh milky white.

Sonora sat on the couch and pulled him close in front of her, took him into her mouth. He wrapped a hand in her hair and said her name so softly she thought she imagined his voice.

His breath came in short gasps, and the hand tangled in her hair tightened into a fist.

'*God.*'

Sonora laughed.

'Come upstairs,' he said.

The stairs were bare wood, and caught the light. Sonora's hand slid against the bannister on the way up, and Keaton guided her through the open hallway toward his bedroom.

Outside, a car door slammed.

'You okay?' Keaton asked. He stroked the small of her back.

'Just jumpy.'

It was dark in the bedroom, blinds drawn tight. Sonora saw the white glow of a digital clock. Keaton put both hands on her shoulders and pressed her back against the edge of the bed. He pushed her legs back till her knees were high, then traced the inside of her thigh with his tongue.

She grabbed the headboard and shut her eyes. His touch made her jerk, and he paused for a moment before he resumed, relentless and slow. He moved on top of her, his mouth over hers. She grabbed his shoulders.

'Keaton.'

She shut her eyes and tried to hold him back. Now was probably a bad time to tell him she wasn't on the pill. She relaxed and let him resume, just once or twice more, and then she thought of pregnancy and babies and how easily she got caught.

'Keaton, I can't— '

He kissed her neck. 'Yes, you can. Yes, you can.'

'Keaton, I get pregnant at the drop of a hat.' The words came out in a strangled rush. He stopped moving inside of her and raised up on his arms. 'So to speak,' she said.

'Sorry. Should have asked.'

The bed creaked when he got up. She heard a drawer open and close, the crinkle of a foil packet. He climbed back into bed and stretched out beside her, kissing her again. She swung her legs over his hips and sat on top of him. He put a hand on her belly, and then he was inside again, and now it was safe, and she rocked on top of him, slow and sure.

And then she was overwhelmed, suddenly, and closed her eyes, lost just before his soft groan.

Sonora sank slowly to Keaton's chest. He put his arms around her, scratching her back lightly, making her shiver and smile.

'You hungry?' He sounded sleepy and peaceful. Kind.

'Starved, how'd you know?'

'Your stomach's growling.' He turned a lamp on beside the bed. The room was all dark wood and masculinity. He opened a dresser drawer and pulled out a large white sweatshirt. 'Put this on if you're cold.'

She slid the shirt over her head. The cuffs hung past her wrists.

'Be right back.' He went into the bathroom. Shut the door.

Sonora went to the dresser, checked her hair in the mirror, noticed a newspaper clipping with her picture. Next to the clipping was a hardbound notebook that had *Journal of Investigation* printed in bold black letters on the front.

Private, of course. She turned the cover.

My brother is dead now, the police are tracking the killer. The detective in charge is a woman. She strikes me as tough and capable. She has a smart mouth, but underneath I think she is kind.

Sonora grimaced, then smiled. Interesting to get those first impressions.

I will be dogging her every footstep. I want Mark's killer caught. But I am getting ahead of myself. I think this all started with phone calls, right around Easter, when Ashley and I began falling apart.

Sonora heard the toilet flush. She closed the journal and moved away.

Keaton came out of the bathroom wearing a dark blue bathrobe. He took her hand, leading her down the stairs through the dark silent house, and they laughed for no particular reason. Sonora felt like a child who was getting away with something.

He turned on the lights. Darkness was thick against the windows and Sonora blinked at the harsh, cheery brightness of his kitchen.

'I was hoping you would come, so just in case.' He opened the refrigerator and waved an arm.

Chocolate-covered strawberries, frozen yogurt, egg rolls. Classic Coke in bright red cans.

Keaton Daniels smiled proudly. 'Girl food.'

Chapter Forty-Two

Sonora left Keaton's townhouse well before dawn, with a full stomach, a sleepy ulcer, and a long hard kiss.

'You really go to work this early?' he asked, as she hunted through the living room for her clothes.

'Umm. Where is my . . . oh, there it is. Here's your towel back, and thanks for the use of the shower.'

'Can I talk you into some breakfast? You said last night you wanted toast.'

'I lied.'

The phone rang. Keaton frowned, looked at her. 'Think it's for you, some cop thing? Nobody calls me this early.'

Sonora shook her head. 'I didn't give your number out. Nobody knows I'm – answer it, why don't you?'

He took the extension in the living room. Said hello. Listened. She knew who it was by the sudden set of his shoulders, the hand by his side closing into a fist.

He hung up.

'It was her,' Sonora said.

'Yeah.' His voice was tight, so different from the way he'd sounded minutes before.

Sonora yanked her boot over her foot. 'What, Keaton? What'd she say?'

'She said she'd pay me back. She'd pay both of us back good.'

Sonora drove through the dark streets – it was garbage day again, and plastic bags clogged the curbs. She had called home, of course. All was well. She cruised out of the Mt. Adams area, and wound down to Broadway onto the bridge, just as the sky got lighter. She glanced over her right shoulder, saw the mountains were fogged in. A train whistled. Three large road locomotives strained at the upgrade, pulling a fully loaded unit train – Kentucky coal, headed north.

She wondered how adults – herself in particular – expected teenagers to be sensible about sex, when they were dumb themselves. Do as I say, not as I do.

It started to rain, and Sonora turned on her windshield wipers, squinting through the grey haze and drizzle. The river was greenish at the edge, grey and brown toward the middle. The local access bridge was brightly lit and Sonora passed through the stone crossing. Lights from the parking lots in Riverfront Stadium made reflections that looked like torches coming up from the water. The roar of trucks on the interstate sounded lonesome.

Sonora glanced at her brother's saloon, snug in its berth on the waterfront. She had no regrets about investing Zack's death benefits in Stuart's business, but had lately been wondering what she was going to do about sending the kids to college. Surely by the time Tim was out of high school, she and Stuart would have enough return on investment to send Tim to Harvard. Provided he passed algebra.

Sonora took the exit to Covington. The steep hilly streets were quiet. She drove past tall narrow houses, packed close together, painted in an astonishing range of colors – stately red brick to lime green. All of them looked dingy in the gloom. There were high rise hotels, the big clock tower, Super America, Big Boy Burgers, Mainstrasse Village and the sign for the Visitors Center. Cincinnati kept its sin on this side of the river, and Covington was a small town, big city-satellite mix of stately churches, dingy houses, motels, and bars that featured Girls, Girls, Girls and XXX movies.

Sonora passed Smith Muffler shop (*Free Installation*), Kentucky Fried Chicken (*Finger-Lickin' Good*), and Kwik Drive-in (*Kools, Camels & Savanna Lights*). She breezed past Senior Citizens of Northern Kentucky, and turned into the empty parking lot that served the legal offices of McGowan, Spanner & Karpfinger – uncomfortably located across from Red & Orange Liquor Shoppe and Angel's Bar, featuring GIRLS DAY & NITE.

Sonora saw a hunched figure in a black leather jacket through the glass of a brightly lit booth. The lawyers were not pulling all nighters, but if they had been, their BMWs would be safe. Ruby was on shift.

Sonora walked across the freshly patched asphalt, finding nothing much and everything in particular of interest. Cop attitude. Ruby, as always, had her head bent over a book.

A tiny CD player spewed jazz with a state of the art quality that had cost thousands in speakers and amps just ten years ago. A pink and white box of Dunkin Donuts was open and empty, and Ruby was sipping Evian water, and scoring notes on blank sheets. Ruby acknowledged Sonora with a nod and put out her cigarette.

Sonora opened the door of the booth and leaned her shoulder against the edge. 'Hey, girl. Have I come at a bad time?'

Ruby gave her a sideways sloppy smile. 'The great composer at work. I'd offer you a doughnut, but I ate them already.'

Sonora had never been able to pinpoint Ruby's age – somewhere between twenty-eight and forty-eight. She was big boned and fleshy, skin a deep blue black, and her hair was thick, abundant, and rigid with tight curls some women paid big bucks to achieve. She was deft with makeup, and wore purple lipstick and a nightstick on her belt as if the two always went together.

'Ruby, you ought to be studying.'

'I know. What you smiling about, you just get laid or something?'

'I've been over there at girls girls girls, dancing on tables all night.'

'I have to say it agrees with you.'

'Speaking of dancing. You know a working girl named Shonelle?'

'Shonelle, hmmm. She danced at the Sapphire, didn't she? The one jacked up her knee?'

'Jacked up?'

'*Messed* up. Sonora, you are so *white*.'

'Yeah, yeah, be a bigot. How about Sheree La Fontaine, you know her?'

Ruby shut her eyes. 'Skinny little girl with fake blonde hair that she doesn't wash good more 'n once a week?'

'That's the one.'

'What's going on? I've seen that evangelist cop hanging around, what's his name, Molliter?'

'Molliter.'

'I hear he has an AK-47 stashed in his basement in the burbs. Cincinnati's finest. Who protects us from you guys?'

'You need protecting, Ruby?'

Ruby patted her nightstick and the huge revolver on her hip.

Sonora flipped open the lid of the Dunkin Donuts box and scooped up a crumb of chocolate frosting.

'This have anything to do with that dude got roasted in his car?'

Sonora licked her finger and nodded. 'Tell me about this Sheree La Fontaine and Shonelle.'

'No love lost, that's for sure. Always fighting over . . . get ready. Clothes.'

'Clothes?'

'See, they both work the streets, right? And some of the girls, I'm talking about Sheree here, stash clothes in out of the way places around their hangouts. Might need a switch during the night, sometimes they change if the cops run them in, you know the drill. And Sheree says Shonelle keeps taking her stuff, and buddy they got into it big time last month. I'm talking a hair pulling, cussing, spitting cat fight.'

'What's the dope on this Sheree, anyway?'

'From down south somewhere, the Carolinas I think. I hope she's not par for the course, because if she is and the south does rise again, we all be in for some shit.'

'Could you get a little more specific?'

'Weird, Sonora, even for an addict. Sits in the bars and lights matches. Shonelle is twice her size, but went after her, digging with those fingernails like a maniac. Course, hooker addicts aren't exactly your average bear, you get me?'

'You see her around the night the Daniels kid got killed?'

'Let me think. That was . . . Tuesday week, that right?'

Sonora nodded.

'You know, come to think, I did see her. Around midnight, getting in a car with some john. I didn't get much look at the guy, so I don't know if it was your boy.'

'My guy was up in Mt. Adams at midnight. On his way to die.'

Ruby looked grim. 'Yeah, well.'

Sonora yawned. 'I got to go home and kiss my kids before they go to school.'

'How they doing?'

'Good, except my son's flunking algebra. How's yours?'

'She's fine. Potty trained, finally, thank you Jesus.' Ruby glanced down at the page of notes, then looked back up at Sonora. 'Me and my ex, you know, we just don't go good together. But he's helping me with tuition, and he keeps the baby sometime. Now, most girls I know, their ex just walks off and leaves them with the babies, never even looks back. Lot of anger out there, Sonora. Lot of girls I talk to just nod and say maybe this guy got burned up, maybe he brought it all on his own head.'

'He didn't, Ruby.'

'Hell of a way to go.'

Sonora nodded. 'Listen, there's no food in my house. There an all-night grocery store anywhere close?'

'Nothing but that Kwik Stop, and they charge an arm and a leg.'

'I look rich to you?'

Chapter Forty-Three

Sonora was thinking that she had bought everything except milk, when she turned the corner toward home. In a split second of clarity she saw the flashing blue lights, the police cars, the open front door. Remembered Selma's words – *I'll pay you back good.*

Sonora slammed on the brakes, opened the car door, and was on the pavement as the parking gear caught and the Nissan rocked backward. Out of the corner of one eye, she could see the wary stance of the patrolman in the second car, see his hand cover the gun on his hip as she ran toward his partner.

'What the hell's going on here?'

The uniform on the radio was young, dark hair cropped short. He clicked his radio off, blinked. 'Everything's all right, ma'am.'

'This is my house, okay? I've got kids inside.'

The screen door slammed. Stuart headed her way, taking the porch steps two at a time. His shirttail hung over his jeans, and his shoelaces were untied.

'Where are the kids?'

'They're all right, Sonora. Everybody's okay.' He ran a hand through his hair, making it stick up on the side.

Sonora folded her arms, closed her eyes a short moment, took a deep breath.

'Ma'am, did you say you live here?'

It was the one who had touched his gun. Light brown hair, thick neck.

'Detective Blair, I work homicide. And yeah, I live here.'

The dark-haired one, the steady one, was nodding at her. 'We got a call, 911, possible intruder— '

Sonora heard the door open. Heather ran toward her, arms out, face tear-stained and pale. Something bad.

Sonora looked at Stuart. 'Where's Tim?'

'Right here.' Tim shut the front door and followed his sister down the steps.

Sonora put her arms around Heather, gave Tim a hug. He did not pull away. She lifted Heather up in her arms, groaned as the weight of her growing child hit her in the small of the back.

'So, what's up kid-lets?'

'Let me tell it,' Tim said. 'We heard somebody outside the house, and— '

'She pulled on the knob, Mommy! On the back door, we saw her.'

'Her?' Sonora swallowed hard.

Tim folded his arms across his chest. 'I thought it was you. I almost opened the door. But Clampett was barking, and he yelped and I looked out the curtain, and it *wasn't* you.'

'So then what?'

'She knocked on the glass real hard!' Heather burst into tears and buried her face in Sonora's shoulder.

Tim looked tense and young. 'I called Uncle Stuart, and he called 911. That was right, wasn't it?'

Sonora put a hand lightly on her son's shoulder. 'It was perfect.'

He nodded, cheeks flushed, lips tight. 'We can't find Clampett.'

Stuart bent down to tie a shoe. 'We'll find him, Tim.'

Sonora set her daughter down. 'Did you get a good look at this woman, Tim?'

'Short hair, like to here.' He touched his collar bone. 'Blonde. She was little, like you, Mom. She looked funny.'

'Funny?'

He shrugged. 'Weird.'

The patrol officer grinned and tousled her son's hair. 'I bet I could put my feet up and let him write the report.'

Sonora looked at her brother. 'You get a look at her?'

'Long gone by the time I got here.' He bent down, picked up Heather, balanced her on his hip. She wore nothing but a nightgown, and her long thin legs had chill bumps.

'Cold, baby?' Sonora put her blazer around her daughter's shoulders. She looked at the uniforms. 'You guys had a chance to take a look around?'

'Just a quick one.' Thick neck.

Sonora nodded. 'Stuart, why don't you take the kids inside and— ' Sonora heard a whimper and looked over her shoulder. The three-legged dog bounded toward her, something yellow streaming from the side of his mouth. Clampett barked, doggie breath frosting white in the chill air.

Sonora braced herself as the heavy muddy paws landed against her shoulders. Clampett's tail swished back and forth, thumping Heather's bare legs.

'Want to dance, pup?' Sonora put her hands on the dog's soft muzzle, pried open the black-rimmed jaws, wrestled a large round lump off the back of the thick ham tongue. Clampett barked and jumped, and Sonora twisted sideways, playing keep away.

The dark-haired cop looked pale. 'What is that?'

Sonora held up the soggy blonde head so he could see. 'Barbie. Or parts thereof.' She studied the wet, plastic doll head, wondering about prints.

It was muddy out in the yard. Stuart took the kids inside to make hot chocolate while Sonora walked the perimeter of her property, circling closer and closer to the house, the dark-haired uniform at her heels. The volley ball net sagged across the middle of the backyard, and the lawn was overgrown and brown, thick grass limp with dew.

She wondered what Flash had thought of the plastic kiddie pool filled with trolls and algae-coated water, the basketball wedged under the rusted-out slide, the plastic playhouse so full of old toys the door bulged open.

There were footprints outside Sonora's bedroom window, and another set by Heather's.

The thick-necked cop rounded the corner of the yard and jogged over, hand holding the radio snug to his belt. 'CSU van is on the way. I asked your brother to stay inside with the kids for the time being.'

Sonora nodded and sat down on the bottom porch step. The uniforms moved discreetly away and talked together in low voices, pretending not to notice while Sonora put her head on her knees.

Chapter Forty-Four

Sonora slopped coffee into her lipstick-stained mug. She was late, the task force had already assembled. Her phone rang before she could get away from her desk. Sonora sighed and picked it up.

'Hey, girlfriend, how's the kids?'

Sonora sat back down. Gritted her teeth. 'You listen to me— '

'No, you. I'll make you'uns a deal. Leave Keaton alone, I'll leave them alone. Think about it.'

The line went dead. Sonora's palms were slippery on the receiver, and the phone smacked hard on the desk when she lost her grip. She took a breath, hung the phone up gently. Closed her eyes, opened them. Took a notepad off her desk and headed for her meeting.

They were watching a videotape of the latest press conference. Sonora squinted at the screen, wondering if it was her imagination, or if she was showing just a hint of double chin.

Gruber looked up. 'That's a nice tie, Sonora, but what happened to the one with the catsup on it?'

Crick shushed him. 'Watch for the next part, it's good.'

Onscreen, Sonora cocked her head to one side and told the reporters that the investigation was moving forward swiftly, and it was only a matter of time. Yes, she was the case detective, and would make the arrest herself. The DA's office was waiting for lab results, merely a formality. They had been lucky with witnesses, and, quite frankly, the killer had made a number of careless mistakes.

If the killer wanted to talk, Sonora was certainly available, and she gave her number. It would be in the perpetrator's best interests to turn herself in. She would be handled sympathetically, the police department would see that she got the proper help, and a lawyer would be provided free of charge.

Yes, the perp was a woman, a sad case, very disturbed, pathetic really, not particularly bright.

The room got quiet. Normally, this last would bring a howl of laughter, and the theory that Sonora would be the next victim. Sonora rubbed her eyes and wished she was as close to arrest and wrap up as the confident woman on screen.

'Good job, Sonora,' Crick said.

Gruber crossed a heavy foot over one knee. 'Yeah, too good. I don't like what happened at Sonora's house this morning, kids and all. I think you're throwing her out there, sir, and look what we get.'

'Action, reaction,' Crick said.

Sonora felt her face get warm and pink.

'Yeah, with Sonora's neck on the line.' This last from Molliter.

Sonora was surprised. Then wary. Was this camaraderie, or overprotection? Did it matter, with her children caught in the middle? What would they say if they knew where she'd spent the night?

Crick looked at Sonora. 'CSU get anything?'

'Not a lot. Partial right thumb on my daughter's window. Toe smear in the mud. Terry also told me Sheree La Fontaine's prints don't match the one they took off the Polaroid that Flash sent to Keaton Daniels.' Sonora did not look at Molliter.

Sanders tapped her chin. 'Sir, I was wondering if we could utilize the feds on this.'

Gruber hooted with laughter. 'Utilize the feds? That's sweet, honey. Then maybe we can teach the Aryan brothers to sing *We Shall Overcome*.'

Sonora rubbed her eyes, kept her voice low key. 'We've asked for help in that quarter, Sanders, but it's just a formality. Leave no stone unturned, you know? FBI doesn't come in unless there's a signed warrant with the suspect's name.'

'Yeah, they're happy to take the collar, long's they don't have to put out.'

Molliter folded his arms. He looked unhappy. 'Look, Sonora, maybe you're overdoing it on this Daniels guy.'

'What's that supposed to mean?'

'She may just move on to the next victim.'

'It's pretty clear she's fixated,' Sam said.

Sonora kept her mouth shut. Dangerous ground.

Gruber waved a hand. 'Okay, but why has she got this thing with Sonora? It's almost like they're rivals or girlfriends or something. I mean, Sonora's a cop— '

'I told you, it's catch me if you can,' Sonora said. 'It happens.'

Crick folded his arms. 'It happens when the perp is flipping out. Which makes her that much more dangerous.' He pointed at Sonora. 'You still want to go to Atlanta?'

'Sir?'

'Been talking to your buddy down there, Bonheur. Selma Yorke's name showed up in the file of possibles they put together after the attack on James Selby.'

Sam put a hand on Sonora's shoulder. '*Here* we go, darlin'. Here we go.'

'Blair,' Crick said. 'About what I said earlier – action, reaction. What do *you* think set her off?'

Sonora swallowed. 'TV interview, obviously sir.' Bad policewoman, she thought. Her chest was tight. Was that what guilt felt like? Had Zack felt this way when he cheated?

Crick was nodding. 'What would you say to one of those radio call-in things? Think she could resist talking to you?'

Sam shook his head. 'I don't like this.'

'We'll have somebody with her kids,' Crick said.

Sonora cleared her throat. 'It's just— '

'Just what? If she reacts that much to a taped interview, I think she'll go nuts to talk to you live.'

'Talking on the radio would make me nervous, sir.'

'Get over it, Blair.'

Chapter Forty-Five

The city of Atlanta throbbed with sunshine and noisy traffic. Sonora squinted and put on a dark pair of sunglasses. An unmarked police car pulled into the circle drive in front of the hotel and parked illegally. A black man in a lightweight tan suit got out of the car, leaving the driver's door hanging open.

'Detective Sonora Blair?' He pointed large fingers at her like a gun.

'You must be Bonheur.'

They shook hands. He wore a diamond encrusted wedding ring and his grip was firm. He was built like a football player, hair close-cropped and balding at the top. He opened the passenger door of a pale blue Taurus and motioned Sonora in. She would have thought it was funny he drove the same make of official car she did, if her head hadn't been pounding so hard.

'Thought there was going to be two of you.'

'My partner had to stay behind. Little girl is in the hospital.'

'Too bad. Got your suitcase and everything. You all checked out?'

She nodded, slung the suitcase in the back, and settled in the front seat.

'What time you get in?'

'Three AM. Fly back out tonight around six.'

'Running you ragged, aren't they? First name's Ray.'

'Sonora.'

'You like Atlanta, Sonora?'

Sonora took her sunglasses off and looked at him. 'Ray, I *love* Atlanta. It is vastly superior to Cincinnati, which when I left it was gloomy and grey.'

'That's the north for you.'

A horn honked, and Ray switched lanes quickly. He drove the car in short jerky spurts and Sonora put a hand on her stomach.

'You know, talking on the phone and all, I kind of got the impression you were white.'

'Excuse me, Ray?'

'White, you know, not green, like you are now. You feeling bad or something?'

'Having a Maalox moment.'

'Ulcer, huh? You know, my wife has a cure for that.'

'Maybe I should give her a call.'

Bonheur changed lanes again, cutting off a Subaru. The driver flipped a rod and Bonheur shook his head. 'You don't want to. My wife's cures are usually worse than the disease.' He gave her a sideways glance. 'How about we go downtown and let you get a good look at the case file. Then we can go out and see the crime scene. Maybe grab an early lunch. We have an appointment with James Selby around twelve-thirty, quarter to one.'

'He okay about talking to me?'

'Yeah, but it's been a long time since it happened. He blocked a lot of it, right after.'

'You have him hypnotized?'

'DA nixed it. Said too much chance of planting suggestions that would seem like memories. Didn't want to muddy his credibility as a witness, not that it ever came to court – we didn't get close. But I've talked to this guy since, and he's been filling in the gaps. Hard to know, though, if it's real or not. You can read the transcripts of what he said right after it happened, and decide for yourself.'

'She ever get in touch with you?'

'She? The killer?'

'Yeah.'

He looked at her. 'You mean like some woman on the edge of the investigation, trying to help or be involved?'

'Yeah, sort of.'

He shook his head. 'We watch for that, with the weird stuff, but I don't think it ever came up. Why, you got somebody?'

'She calls me.'

'The killer does? You sure it's her?'

'I'm sure.'

'What's she say?'

Sonora talked. He listened. Frowning. Then rubbed his chin.

'Sounds like it's got to be her. Sounds like she's losing it, too. Happens sooner or later. Takes more risk, more fantasy, to keep 'em happy.'

'You think she wants to get caught?'

'Hard to tell. That business with her coming to the house, that's creepy. Your kids safe right now?'

'Oh yeah.'

'She wants to get caught, she can always turn herself in. I think she likes the game.'

'I think she may be . . . trying to connect. She's angry.'

'They all are.'

'Serial killers?'

He grinned at her. 'Women.'

James Selby lived in a brick cape cod on the opposite side of town from the crime scene – which in Atlanta during afternoon traffic meant a two-hour drive. Waxy-looking ivy hugged both sides of the house. There was a square plaque in the front yard, announcing the name of the security firm that watched the premises. Sonora had noticed similar plaques in a lot of the yards. Atlanta had a crime rate that thrived with the magnolia blossoms.

Selby's front door was wood plank and horseshoe-shaped, with black metal hasps at the top and bottom that made Sonora think of Lutheran churches. The door had been painted dark red sometime in the last month, and a new, freshly polished brass kickplate ran along the bottom. Sonora heard windchimes.

Bonheur galloped up three red brick steps to the tiny front porch and rang the doorbell. Sonora followed slowly, hand on the wrought iron railing. Off in the distance came the burr of a lawn mower.

Bonheur touched her shoulder. 'Brace yourself. He's been through a lot of operations. Spent the better part of three years in the hospital, and if you think he looks bad now, you should have seen him then.'

The door opened and swung inward, and a man appeared in the shadowed hallway.

'James. My man.'

'Ray. Good to see you, come on in.' The voice was the low rasp of severely damaged vocal cords.

Sonora followed Bonheur up the front stoop into the dim, tiled hallway.

Even in the thin light, James Selby was startling. Sonora felt her stomach sink as she took in the elongated, scarred features, one sightless eye lower than the other. His hair grew in a patch on the back of his scalp, blending with a bad toupee. His face looked like it had melted, smeared, then frozen. The neck was thickly scarred, one hand misshapen, the forearm curled forward.

Bonheur touched Selby on the shoulder. 'Standing beside me here is Detective Blair. I told you about her.'

Selby's thin, slash lips stretched into a smile. 'Good to meet you, Detective. Forgive me, do you use Ponds Moisturizing Cream?'

'Yes.'

'I like the way it smells. Very fresh, better than perfume. My sense of smell is fantastic since I lost my sight.'

'Please don't tell me what I ate for lunch.'

Selby laughed, a raspy bark. 'Come in, we'll sit for a while.'

He led them into a dark living room, and switched on a lamp. Late afternoon sun slanted in from French doors that opened onto a brick patio. A golden retriever lay like a sphinx next to a shabby green easy chair. The dog wore a thick leather harness on her back and watched James Selby's every move, tail thumping the floor.

'That's Daffney, by the way. She'll play cute and show you her tummy, but I'll have to ask you not to pet her. She's a working dog and she's on duty.'

Daffney immediately rolled to her back, front paws paddling the air. Sonora thought of Clampett and hoped the kid next door was being diligent about letting him out.

'I think that bulb's burned out, on your lamp there,' Bonheur said.

Selby looked up. 'Is it? Let me get another one.'

'Don't bother, James. We got enough light from the window.'

'If you're sure.' He held up a plastic board. 'Look at this, Ray, this is something new.' He turned his head toward Sonora. 'It's a Braille Writer – works so that you can write and read left to right, instead of backwards. I'm testing it. They have this great questionnaire for feedback. Not in Braille, though.' He laughed again, hoarsely.

Sonora glanced around the room. There were no knickknacks and precious little furniture. A grand piano sat in one corner, black, highly polished. Sonora and Bonheur sat at either end of a floral patterned couch that had the look of a valuable antique. There were food stains on the upholstery.

The fireplace was choked with charred lumps of wood and thick grey ashes. A green rag rug in front of the hearth was thickly coated in dog hair. Sonora pictured the man and the dog, sitting in this room on chilly nights, the only light from the glow of the fire.

Shelving along the wall held stacks of CDs, and one picture in a wood frame. Sonora crossed the room for a closer look.

Selby cocked his head to one side, and the dog watched, eyes alert. 'You're interested in the picture, Detective Blair? I'm afraid that's my vanity showing, leaving it out. I like people to know what the man inside looks like.'

Sonora picked up the frame. The print was eight by ten, black and white. The focus was slightly off.

'That was taken a few months before it happened.'

They all knew what 'it' was.

The photograph showed James Selby sitting at the piano. A girl sat beside him, her arms wrapped tightly around his waist, her heart-shaped face porcelain pretty. A fire flickered in the fireplace, and the photographer had caught the reflection of the flames in the surface of the polished piano.

Sonora felt a twinge of dread. This could be Keaton, she thought, looking back at James Selby. They had been so very like – brown eyes, dark curly hair, that solid presence.

Sonora stared through the French doors to the algae-scummed birdbath, the snarled cluster of rosebushes, the weeping willow tree – James Selby's backyard that she could see and he could not. She took a breath, and sat back down on the couch.

He looked different to her now. He was the man in the picture.

'Tell me your story,' she said.

Selby waved a hand self-consciously, as if she had not come cross country to hear him. 'Ray's heard all this before.'

Sonora wondered what his voice had been like. Low and sexy? Had he sung in the shower? She opened her purse, and set out the recorder.

'Forget Bonheur, he can always take a nap. Take your

time, Mr. Selby. Tell me everything you remember, and I'll bring you her head on a stick.'

Selby looked up sharply. 'Ray, I like this woman.'

'No doubt she earns her ulcer.'

Selby tucked a small cushion under the curled arm, then draped his good right arm on the side of the chair.

'In the beginning, Detective Blair, there were phone calls.'

He had practiced this, Sonora thought. He had everything thought out and worked through.

'The calls began after Easter, lots of them, calling and hanging up. Sometimes she would talk. She'd say, hello there, James. Nothing else.'

Sonora put a fist under her chin.

He had met her at a bar, his usual place. He'd had the vague feeling he'd seen her before.

He had moved away fairly quickly. He was pretty good looking and it wasn't unusual for a woman to strike up a conversation. But that night he was there with the guys, and he wanted nothing more than the traditional beers after Wednesday night softball.

Sonora heard pain in his voice. And pride. She wondered about the girl in the picture.

He left the bar around ten. It was a weeknight and he had to be at work by eight.

Where did he work?

A bank. He was a teller, on his way up. He'd liked the job a lot.

She'd approached him in the parking lot, hands nervously twisting the strap of a large leather bag slung over her shoulder. It was an old mail bag, scuffed and worn, and he'd asked her about it. She said she'd gotten it at a flea market.

'Flea markets and antiques,' Sonora muttered.

Selby shifted the crippled arm.

She had car trouble. She'd had her transmission replaced

and now the engine wouldn't start. He'd offered to take a look – a skiffy transmission shouldn't keep the engine from catching – but she'd said no. It was under warranty. She'd have somebody come out and take a look at it in the morning, could he just give her a quick ride home?

She had looked over her shoulder when she asked him, and had seemed small and scared. Selby laughed here, saying he'd thought she was nervous of him. He was a big guy, six feet and solid, and he'd offered to lend her cab fare.

That had seemed to reassure her. She'd nodded shyly, not smiling, and opted for the ride. That was why he was so sure she was nervous of him, because she never smiled. He thought she was afraid.

'James, did you see her car, at the bar?' Sonora asked.

'Uh . . . I didn't check under the hood or anything. She said it was a transmission thing. I didn't get the feeling she wanted me to take a look or anything. She seemed resigned, you know?'

'So you never actually saw the car?'

Selby was quiet. 'Guess not. I don't really remember.'

Bonheur shifted sideways in his chair. 'We followed up on the car angle. Checked the lot at the bar the next morning. Went to repair shops. Never got anywhere.'

'Her car was in the subdivision, dropped off ahead of time,' Sonora said. 'Don't you think?'

Bonheur scratched his chin. 'Could of had two.'

'Maybe. We place her using cabs, maybe buses.'

'You saying she stood outside that bar crying car trouble but no car?'

Ballsy, Sonora thought. 'Takes your breath away, doesn't it?' She looked at Selby. 'So she's got you feeling protective, and you offer to take her home. Then what?'

Selby settled deeper into his chair. 'She gives me the address, but I couldn't place it. She told me the subdivision was new, no way I'd know it. Actually, she said you'uns. No way you'uns would know it.' He swallowed. 'The way she said it. Made her seem ... smalltown, kind of. Vulnerable.'

Sonora nodded here. This was Flash.

They wound up on the outskirts of the city, in a remote area where they were just starting to build houses. Only a smattering of new homes in the front of the subdivision were occupied. He had protested, thinking they'd gone the wrong way. He began to wonder if this woman was some kind of mental case, or if he was being set up for a robbery. He was getting worried, and very sorry he'd picked her up.

Pull up here, she'd told him. And suddenly she had a gun, a twenty-two derringer, small even in her delicate little hand. This is a robbery, she'd explained, unsmiling, voice soft. She wanted his wallet, that was all. He'd handed it over without a word, annoyed with himself for picking her up, thinking this would be too embarrassing to report to the police. Wait till he told the guys at the next softball game.

She kept reassuring him over and over that she wasn't going to hurt him – that she was afraid of him, and needed get away time. She tossed him a looped clothesline and told him to wrap it around his wrists, legs, and belly, and thread it through the steering wheel. She took the keys out of the ignition and the car registration out of the glove compartment. Then she'd looked up at him and said, by the way, before you get fancy with the rope there, hand over your clothes.

That was where he'd turned balky. No way was he taking off his clothes, too weird. She'd explained in a firm, matter-of-fact voice that she would put his clothes and car keys together about a hundred feet from the car. That would slow him down, and give her plenty of time.

But she had gone strange on him in a way he could not explain. Her eyes were empty, her speech mechanical, as if she wasn't seeing him, as if he wasn't there. Somehow, they weren't connecting.

He stood his ground. She shot him in the leg. Selby's

voice still echoed surprise after all these years. He never believed she would shoot him, not without working herself up to it. But she hadn't hesitated.

Sonora nodded slowly. So this was how little Flash had gotten the man tied up.

At first, Selby was saying, he had been so shocked he hardly felt the pain. Flash demanded his shirt and he handed it over. He remembered he fumbled one of the buttons and she had leaned over and ripped it off, and kept it, clutched in her left fist, right hand steady with the gun. He'd grabbed at her when she got close, and she'd shot him again, the bullet hitting his shoulder.

He was bleeding and hurting, so she'd helped him loop the clothes-line around his hands and waist, passing it through the steering wheel. She had tied the knots herself – not very well. He'd done a half-assed job looping the rope around his hands, but she hadn't protested.

She rolled down her window, grabbed her bag, and got out of the car. He watched her from the rear-view mirror, though he was getting dizzy and had to concentrate not to pass out. She went to the gas tank, tried to open it, but it was the locking kind. She found the key on his ring – very cool about the whole thing – then pulled plastic tubing and an empty Coke can out of the bag. She put the tube in the gas tank, sucked the end of it, and inserted it through the key hole opening of the Coke can, filling it with siphoned gas from the tank of his car.

The whole time she worked she hummed. A small part of his mind kept trying to place the song.

She took the dripping Coke can and splashed gasoline in his eyes.

He remembered crying out, rubbing his face on the bare skin of his shoulder, while she splashed gas into his lap, the front seat of the car, and all along the loose end of the clothesline that she pulled out of the window to the pavement below.

He heard her fumble in the bag, saw a flash, and opened his eyes long enough to see that she had a camera and had taken his picture.

He was sick now, the gasoline fumes making him nauseous and dizzy, and his thoughts weren't connecting too well. He smelled the burnt head of a match. He opened his eyes to the nightmare vision of a ribbon of flame eating its way up the clothesline, and (he hesitated here) the woman pulling up her skirt and wedging a hand between her legs.

Seconds, was the thought in his mind. He only had seconds. And suddenly the gun didn't seem to matter a hell of a lot.

He got untangled from the rope fairly quickly, but it took some fumbling to unlock and open the car door. That was where he'd made his second bad mistake. If he'd gone through the window he might have made it out in time – at least not been burned quite so badly. But the gasoline fumes exploded just as the car door opened, and he was engulfed in fire.

Here the memories got sketchy. He thought he'd dropped to the ground and rolled, and he'd swear she'd stayed to take pictures.

After this point, everything in his mind was dark and vague, but he had the impression that someone had driven by, honking their horn. He'd always wondered about that. Had it been somebody trying to summon help . . . or had it been her?

Her, Sonora thought, but said nothing. The dog snored, the clock ticked. Dusk was grey in the room.

Ray got up, put a hand on Selby's shoulder. 'You all right there, James? Can I get you a beer, or a glass of water?'

James Selby covered the scarred hand with the good one. 'Funny how it comes back so clearly. I even remember what she was humming.'

Sonora nudged the dog with her foot.

Selby turned his unseeing eyes in her direction. 'It was that one Elvis used to sing. *Love Me Tender*.'

Sonora sat forward on the couch. 'You *sure*?'

Ray was watching her, the wary cop look. 'What?'

'Someone's been calling my house, that's all. Singing that song.'

'A woman?' Ray asked.

'Yeah, a woman.'

Selby leaned toward her, face folding into the semblance of a frown. 'Be careful, Detective.'

Chapter Forty-Six

Sonora was restless on the flight back from Atlanta. She had asked Selby if there had been anything after the attack. More phone calls. Notes, maybe. Pictures. The question took him by surprise, and earned her a sharp look from Bonheur.

Nothing else, he had assured her.

She hit the bathroom before they landed, running a pick through her hair, leaving it draped over her shoulders rather than tied back. She took a moment for a coat of bronze lipstick. There wasn't much she could do about the greenish pallor, air travel never agreed. She'd feel better once her feet were on the ground.

The flight landed on time. Sonora ignored the baggage pickup snarl with the superior air of one with only carry-on luggage. She paused in front of a bank of phones. Selby had looked too much like Keaton, before the fire had eaten his face.

She called the Mt. Adams apartment and a voice answered after the third ring – a voice she knew well.

'Sergeant Crick?'

'Speaking.'

'This is Blair, what the hell's going on?'

Crick's tone was grim. 'She's been here.' Sonora's knees went weak.

'Daniels got home from school around four-thirty this afternoon—'

Flash had been waiting for him, Sonora thought.

'—and found the door part way open, the side window smashed.'

Why? she thought. Why did he go in? Idiot. Keaton.

'So he went to a neighbor's house and called. Sonora? You still there?'

Sonora leaned against the wall, the tile cool on her cheek. 'Listen, Sergeant Crick, this connection's bad, I can hardly hear you. Is Daniels okay?'

'He's shook, but he's all right.'

'I'm coming out.'

A crime scene van and a swarm of official cars were stacked along the streets near Keaton Daniels' townhouse. Sonora was stopped by a uniform on the sidewalk out front. The officer eyed her bluejeans, dusty boots, leather jacket.

'Can I help you, ma'am?' His voice was stern – one of the uniformed types who used courtesy like a blunt instrument.

Sonora flashed her ID.

The officer apologized, but stood his ground. Sonora gave him a second glance, and he moved reluctantly off the sidewalk, into the grass and out of her way. She went up the front step slowly, boot heels loud on the concrete, and walked into the living room.

Keaton Daniels was on the couch, looking stunned and being ignored by the bevy of crime scene officers. Sonora heard Molliter's voice, saw Sam headed down the stairs, two at a time. He gave her a warning look.

'Blair.' Crick's voice was a bark, and he didn't seem happy.

Sonora raised an eyebrow. 'I told you he needed protection. Keaton?' She touched his shoulder and took his hand – ice cold. She sat on the edge of the coffee table and leaned close. 'You okay?'

He nodded, looked relieved to see her.

'Keaton, are you cold? You want a sweater or jacket?'

'I'm okay, Detective.' His voice sounded dull, a monotone.

Sonora looked over her shoulder. 'Anybody found this man a cup of coffee?'

Crick was watching them, eyes narrowed. He singled out a patrolman. 'Find the man a cup of coffee.' He motioned Sonora up the stairs. 'Crime scene guys are still working things over, but let me give you the tour. The bathroom is the worst.'

Sonora pretended to be confused about which way to turn.

'She took a shower, used the toilet.'

'How'd you figure that out?' My fingerprints will be all over this place, Sonora thought, peering in through the doorway.

'How do you think, Blair? Hey, be careful, don't touch.'

The guest bathroom, so tidy before with fresh towels and expensive peach soaps, was now a mess. Sonora stayed in the doorway, thinking that she was likely the last person to use the bathroom before Flash. She felt queasy suddenly, and her head hurt.

The bath mat, thick, white, and fluffy, had been rolled up and jammed in the corner behind the commode. One of the drawers under the sink was open part way. The toilet lid was up and Sonora took a quick look. Yeah, okay, Flash had used the toilet and left a wealth of clues as to her current dietary habits.

The shower curtain had been yanked sideways and one corner had torn loose from the rings and sagged into the tub. A sopping wet washrag had been thrown on top of the bath mat, and the soap was in the bottom of the still wet tub, melting and stuck to the porcelain.

Wadded into the corner of the stall was a thick blue towel. Sonora wondered if Keaton had changed the towels. Please God, he had changed them.

'*Blair?*'

'Sir?'

'I said we got pubic hair out of the drain and . . . you with me here?'

'Yes sir. Excuse me, I've been to Atlanta and back in the last twenty-four hours.'

'You should have slept on the plane. Anyway, we may get something off the towel. God knows, this place is lousy with physical evidence, which will do us no good whatsoever, unless we catch this bitch.' Crick grimaced. 'Terry says she's a natural blonde.'

Sonora opened her purse and dug out a bottle of Advil. She poured three tablets into the palm of her hand and swallowed them dry.

'Take a look over here in the bedroom. Something you better see.'

Terry was stripping the sheets from the bed as they went in. Sonora felt her knees go funny as she looked around the room. Dark bronze lipstick had been smeared across a pillow case, the shade close to Sonora's own.

Sam was pointing a flashlight onto the dark floor of the closet. 'She took his *shoelaces*. And tore buttons off some of the shirts.' He squatted down on his haunches, touching nothing. 'Looks like a tennis shoe outlet in here.'

Crick touched Sonora's arm and pointed her to the clothes dresser. The newspaper photo of Police Specialist Sonora Blair had been wadded, then ripped into three pieces. Keaton's *Journal of Investigation* was gone.

'That all?' she asked.

Crick put his hands behind his back and cocked his head to one side. '*That all*, she says. I would think it would get under your skin a little, Blair. Because this is a dangerous woman, and I get the *serious* feeling she doesn't consider you good people.'

'This surprises you, sir? After coaching me through the press conferences? I would have thought you'd be happy.'

'You just be careful, Blair.'

'What else did she do?'

'Went in the kitchen and took a fistful out of a macaroni and cheese casserole. Ate some of it, we think, and smeared the rest on a dish towel.'

'She'll be in trouble looking for leftovers at my place, I got a thirteen-year-old.'

'Funny girl.'

He crooked a finger and ushered her into Keaton's tiny private bath. Sonora frowned, followed.

The counter top was crowded – Braun electric razor, worn black toothbrush, deodorant. No peach soaps shaped like roses. Crick shut the bathroom door. He closed the lid on the oak toilet seat and waved a hand.

'Go ahead, Blair, make yourself comfortable.'

Sonora perched on the edge of the tub, folded her hands in her lap. 'Yes, Sergeant?'

Crick scratched the side of his neck. He was a big man and he took up a lot of room. His knees were too close and Sonora pulled away.

'Look, Blair, I ought to call you in my office and come up on this in a more delicate way, but we've worked together a long time. I want you to consider this an *unofficial* question. And be honest, Blair, for your sake and mine.'

She was cold suddenly. She swallowed.

'Is there something going on between you and this Keaton Daniels?'

Sonora cocked her head to one side. 'Something going on? He's Mark Daniels' brother, Sergeant, and I think he was the intended victim all along. Sam and I have questioned him silly, and spent some time trying to gain his trust. We're trying to keep him alive. I consider that part of the job.'

Crick rubbed the top of his forehead. Sonora noticed that his eyes were bloodshot, lids swollen.

'Look, Blair, I've been in touch with Renee Fischer. You heard of her?'

'Forensic psychiatrist. Used her on the Parks thing, didn't they?'

Crick nodded.

'I hear she's good,' Sonora said.

'She is. She's just getting started on Flash, but she called me early this morning. Said she'd been up all night, going through what I gave her.'

'And?'

'She says there's obviously something about Daniels, something different from the usual victims.'

'We knew that.'

'Yeah. And she's looking at you as a cross between a confidante and a rival.'

'I'm the cop trying to bring her in, makes perfect sense.'

Crick looked at her.

'Your point? Sir?'

'Okay, you're the one after her hide. Fine, Blair, if that's as far as it goes. But that's your picture there, on top of the dresser in this man's bedroom, and Flash didn't cart it up here, I asked.'

'What did Keaton say?'

'He said he clipped all the articles about the investigation.'

'There you go.'

'I didn't see any other articles.'

'I guess he hasn't had time to put together a scrapbook, Sergeant. Why don't you get specific, sir, and tell me just what the problem is. Or is there a regulation against my picture on this man's dresser?'

'No, Blair, and there's no regulation against fucking him either, but you damn well better *not* be.'

Sonora spoke through clenched teeth. 'You don't have these little talks, these kinds of suspicions and speculations, when it's male cops and female witnesses.'

'Don't give me that sexual harassment crap, unless you want to make it official. I want you to listen to me, Blair, and for once in your life don't interrupt. If there *is* something going on between you and Daniels, we got problems. The woman is dangerous, and I want her before she goes off again.' His voice lowered and went gentle. 'I've known you a long time, Sonora. I've never seen you dump a case, I've never seen you cross the line. If something's going on, I want you to tell me, and tell me *now*.'

Sonora stared at him, stony faced.

Crick threw up his hands. 'You fucking Daniels or not?'

Sonora folded her arms. '*Not*.'

Chapter Forty-Seven

'Sam, I'm in *trouble*.'
'Sonora—'
'*Shit*, Sam.'
'Don't panic, girl. Get yourself together, before somebody hears us. We'll talk later.'

Sam lit a cigarette, and Sonora didn't complain. They sat in the parking lot of the Sundown Saloon, looking at the still sludge of the river. Sam flicked ash out the open window.

'You should have told him the truth.'
'You said that already.'
'Yeah, but Sonora, he's right, it does affect the investigation. You were the last one in the bathroom before Flash, suppose those are your hair samples?'
'You think that hasn't got me worried?' Sonora took a deep breath and looked out the window. 'What are you going to say if Crick asks you about it?'
'You mean if I know you slept with the guy? You want me to lie for you?'
'Yeah.'
Sam flicked the cigarette butt out the window. 'Remember back when we thought we were the good guys?'
'Thanks, Sam, you always know how to make it all better.'
'You okay now? I'd like to go home.'
'I'm going to get the kids and go back to the house.'

'You're going to get them up? It's two AM. Let them sleep at your brother's.'

'I promised I'd get them tonight. Besides, I want them home in their own beds so I can get them off to school okay.'

'Come on, then. You herd Tim and I'll carry Heather.'

They closed the car doors softly – habits acquired on stakeouts. Sonora felt bad suddenly, the ulcer again, and she leaned against the side of the car.

Sam turned to look at her. 'You coming?'

'In my own good time. Sam?'

'What?'

'Something I was wondering. This guy in Atlanta, this Selby. He said the calls started up after Easter. And it just dawned on me that Keaton said the same thing.'

'I don't remember him saying that. And I've gone over all the transcripts at least four times.'

Sonora remembered that she had read it in Keaton's *Journal of Investigation*. 'He said it, Sam, okay?'

'Pillow talk?'

'It's interesting, don't you think? I mean, what's the big deal about Easter?'

'Eggs, bunnies, religion. Could be a lot of things. Sonora?'

'Yeah?'

'Let me know, will you? When you find out?'

'Find out what?'

Sam grinned. 'Whether or not Keaton changed the towels.'

Chapter Forty-Eight

The kids slept in the car on the way home. Sonora carried Heather to her bed, and guided Tim into his. Clampett had made three messes, in spite of being let out regularly by the boy next door, who had dutifully deposited the mail and newspapers on the kitchen table as instructed.

Sonora left her carry-on bag in the hall. She flipped through the mail in the kitchen, finding monthly greetings from Master Card and her utility company, and a reminder that it was time for the children to visit their dentist.

She paused in the dark hallway, feeling the ulcer, too tired to move but too wired to sleep. A long soak in a hot bubble bath would be good, right about now.

She had just belted into a bathrobe when the phone rang. Please be Keaton, she thought.

'Sonora?'

It was him.

Sonora kept her voice formal. 'Thank you for checking in, Mr. Daniels. Are you at your wife's house?'

'No. Red Roof Inn, exit seven off seventy-one north.'

'I'll be in touch as soon as I know something.'

'Sonora— '

'I'll be in touch, Mr. Daniels.'

'Oh. Thank you, then.'

'Good night.' Sonora hung up, switched the phone to the children's line. Called information, Red Roof Inn. He answered on the first ring.

Sonora caught her breath. 'Sorry, Keaton. My line is monitored right now, I'm calling on the kids' phone. You okay?'

'No.'

'We need to talk.'

'How about dinner tomorrow night?'

'Not possible. Keaton, I'm in trouble here, about you and me.'

'I was getting that impression tonight. You acted funny.'

'I lied to my sergeant. About us. I told him it was strictly business.'

'Is it?' He sounded cold suddenly, wary.

'I don't usually sleep with witnesses. Look, I have to ask you about the towels.'

'The towels?'

'In the bathroom. When we . . . got together. After I took a shower, did you change the towels?' She held the phone clamped tightly in her fist.

'Oh. Sorry, no I didn't. Is it a problem?'

'There's physical evidence, Keaton. Hell, they found pubic hair in the bathtub drain. It could be mine or hers. They think it's hers, but we know better. It could be either of us.'

'What did your sergeant say?'

'I didn't bring it up, Keaton. I'd prefer not to get fired, considering my kids and the state of my bank account. Mortgage and all, you know?'

'Sorry, I must be dense, this really is trouble.'

'It really is. Another thing I need to know. I saw on your dresser before I left for Atlanta, your *Journal of Investigation*.'

'That was private.'

'I didn't read it.' Just the first page, she thought. 'Was it there when Flash got into your apartment?'

'Flash? Is that what you people call her? Is this some kind of a cop joke?'

Sonora winced. 'It's slang, and it's not a joke, it's real life in the world of a police officer. I'm sorry if you're offended. Was the journal out when Flash came through your apartment? Did she take it, or did our lab people get hold of it?'

'She took it.'

'I see. What was in there?'

'Personal things I'd just as soon no one else read. It started out as a log of investigation, but there's also things about my brother. And about you.'

'About me?'

'Yeah.'

'Damn. That journal is going to piss her off big time. You take care of yourself, Keaton, and watch your back. Call me at the first sign of trouble.'

'Do I understand you to mean that's the only time I call you?'

Sonora closed her eyes. 'Afraid so.'

'For how long? That we can't see each other?'

'Till I catch her, Keaton. And bring her to trial. And convict her ass.'

'Yeah. I see.' He hung up.

Sonora set the phone down gently. Maybe not the bubble bath routine. Maybe just a very hot shower.

She checked the kids – both sound asleep. Clampett was stretched in the hallway between their rooms. He lifted his head when Sonora walked by. Whimpered.

'Want to go out?'

He wagged his tail and got up with a painful, jerky movement that made Sonora notice the white fur rimming his black lips, the sagging muzzle, rheumy eyes. She crouched low and hugged the dog, thinking from the smell of him it was high time for a doggie bath.

'Go out, Clampett?' She headed down the hallway, turned off the alarm. A cold shock of air wafted through the door, and Clampett slowed. Sonora nudged his hind end with her knee, and the dog kept going. Slowly.

'Good boy.'

She flipped on the back porch light. Waited. Clampett disappeared into what was left of the garden. Sonora reset the alarm and went to take her shower.

The bathroom was still neat – the kids had not had a chance to shed clothes, pull down towels, toss washrags, and leave lumps of toothpaste in the sink. Sonora turned the shower on hard and hot, closed her eyes as water streamed across her shoulders.

She was rinsing shampoo out of her hair when the burglar alarm went off.

Sonora left the water running, grabbed a towel and stepped over the side of the tub, wiping suds out of her eyes. Her robe hung from a hook on the back of the door. She grabbed it just as the doorknob turned, then caught on the snap lock.

Sonora froze, jammed wet arms into the sleeves of the nubby terrycloth robe, belted it quickly, and opened the door.

The hallway was empty.

She checked the children – mother first, cop second. Tim was asleep in spite of the alarm. Heather sat bolt upright in bed, clutching a stuffed penguin.

'Stay put,' Sonora said.

Clampett barked, the hysterical bark, guard dog aroused. His toenails raked the back door.

Sonora smelled smoke just as the detector went off. The earsplitting buzz made the hair stand up on the back of her neck.

She ran down the hallway. The front door stood open, broken panes of glass in the foyer. She heard footsteps – someone running across the sidewalk. She was torn, but she'd seen enough fire scenes to know how quickly a house could go up.

A car door slammed as she headed into the kitchen.

The fire was on top of a pizza pan, pictures curling into

flames. Sonora grabbed a dishtowel and smothered the tiny blaze. She heard footsteps, saw her son.

'Fire's almost out. Go see to your sister.'

The dishtowel was blackened and smoking and she tossed it into one side of the sink and turned on the water. Outside, Clampett sounded suddenly far away.

Sonora looked down at the instamatic Polaroids. Saw her son's face, this time sound asleep. She frowned. Recognized the bed she'd just hauled him out of. Stuart's place. Her hand trembled as she flipped the second picture.

Heather, clutching the penguin, cheeks round and soft in sleep. Same nightgown she wore right this minute. The pictures had been taken hours ago at Stuart's.

Sonora took another dishtowel and waved the air beneath the smoke detector. The alarm stopped. Silence, except for the shower running. She took a deep breath. Went to the phone, hit the automatic dial button for her brother. The squeal of a disconnected line was loud in her ear.

'I'm sorry, the number you have called is not in working order. Please— '

Tim and Heather stood in the doorway, close together. They asked no questions, which told Sonora how shook they were. She clutched the edge of the kitchen counter.

'Somebody broke in, and I'm worried about Uncle Stuart. I'm going to call for help, then all of us are going to get in the car and go check on him. We're staying together, got that?'

They nodded.

'Can Clampett come?' Heather asked.

'You bringing your gun?' Tim said.

Sonora bit her bottom lip. 'Yes to both questions.'

Both children looked satisfied.

Chapter Forty-Nine

The windshield fogged as the car spiraled downhill. Sonora opened the window, smelling the river, listening for sirens. Her hands were unsteady on the steering wheel, and Clampett's doggie breath was moist on her shoulder as he leaned over the back of her seat.

'Heather. Get the dog.'

'Mommy, are you okay?'

'Drive faster,' Tim said.

'Everybody's seat belt fastened?'

The riverboat rose out of the water, a smoking black skeleton. Blue lights from police cars strobed across red pulses from the ambulance and fire trucks.

'*Mommy*.'

Sonora caught her breath. 'Maybe he wasn't home. Stay in the car, I'll go check. Hang onto the dog.'

The first person she recognized was Molliter. She was about to call to him when a uniform stepped into her path.

'I'm sorry, Miss— '

'I'm a cop,' she said.

He looked dubiously at her wet hair, still sticky with shampoo, the sweatshirt, bluejeans, Reeboks, no socks.

'This is my brother's place.'

His look went from tough to pitying. 'Could you step over here please, ma'am?'

It was Molliter who came to the rescue. Molliter who waved the uniform away, and sent someone to sit with the kids. Molliter who took her to a smoke-grimed fireman who offered her a blanket and a sweaty handshake.

'Did you bring anybody out?' she asked.

He hesitated. He had blue eyes, big shoulders. He looked past her to Molliter who said, 'Best tell her what's going on,' in a flat tone of voice.

Cop tones, she knew them.

'You say your brother was inside?'

'Maybe. He lives on the third floor. There's a storeroom up there, next to his apartment.'

'Right about where would that be, ma'am?'

Sonora pointed.

The fireman gave her a look of sympathy. 'I'm sorry. We weren't able to get him out in time.'

He glanced over her shoulder at the waiting ambulance. Sonora followed his gaze, aware, for the first time, that the paramedics were standing around. Waiting.

'He's in the ambulance?' Sonora said.

'Uh, no. Actually, our man went in and— ' The fireman cleared his throat. 'Clearly, the victim was dead, and it was . . . it was obviously a matter for the police.'

'Obviously a matter for the police,' Sonora echoed. She wondered what the fireman had seen that made the upstairs apartment so clearly a matter for the police. 'When can we go in?'

'Still pretty hot up there, ma'am.'

Molliter touched her elbow. 'Let's find you a place to sit, shall we?'

Sonora agreed that would be nice.

Her hair was dry by the time Sam and Crick arrived.

'Long time no see,' she said.

'You don't have to be tough tonight, Sonora.' She didn't know Gruber was there till he touched her shoulder.

'She can't help it.' Sam crouched down on one knee. 'Shelly's here.'

Sonora let a breath escape. 'Good. Where?'

'In the car with your kids.'

'What about Annie?'

'At the hospital.'

'Of course, Sam. Sorry. Can't believe I forgot.'

'That's okay, honey.' He squeezed her shoulder and she put her hand over his. She thought for a minute she might like to cry, but the urge quickly passed.

Crick edged close. 'Sonora, I can't believe this is happening. Did I hear right? Flash was at your place tonight?'

Sonora nodded.

'Thank God your kids are all right.' He shifted his weight. She realized he was talking to her in a tone of voice she'd never heard. Maybe it was the voice he used with the babies in the church nursery. 'Sonora, we're going in now. I want you to— '

'Please. Sergeant Crick. Let me come in.'

He got that look of infinite patience. 'Not a good idea.'

'Your brother, you'd go in.'

'I'll leave it up to you, Sonora. My advice is stay away.'

She nodded. Dropped the blanket that had been around her shoulders. She picked it up off the ground, shook it out, folded it, then frowned, not sure what to do. Crick waited as if he had all the time in the world. Gruber took the blanket from her matter-of-factly.

'Let's go,' Crick said.

He had a flashlight. Sonora followed, Sam on one side, Gruber on the other, Molliter bringing up the rear.

It was hot inside, acrid with smoke. Sweat filmed the back of Sonora's neck, dripped down her spine. She felt hot and cold, a tense flutter in her chest. She was breathing hard. Tasting salty sweat on her upper lip.

She went up the side of the stairs, thinking how much her brother had loved this place. The smoke-singed tables and charred wet carpet seemed vaguely familiar. She glanced over her shoulder at the bar. Thought of Stuart developing his palette during his restaurant days, sampling leftover drinks from the night before while cleaning the bar the next morning. Thought of him looking after the kids, feeding them TV dinners, playing Monopoly, giving horsey rides.

Thought of him in the bad old days, walking home alone every afternoon.

Crick faltered at the top of the stairs, and Sonora took the lead, first one in the tiny, well-equipped kitchen. The pictures that Heather had colored and taped to the refrigerator were torn and shredded. The round glass table was over on its side, and the drawer that held kitchen knives gaped open.

'The oven's still on,' Sonora said.

Sam looked thoughtful. 'They were baking cookies tonight, weren't they? Stuart and the kids?'

Sonora nodded. Opened the oven door. Cookie sheet, no cookies. 'My guess is he was in here baking when she surprised him. Looks like they fought.'

'Mess could have been made by the firemen,' Gruber said.

'They're not going to rip the pictures off the refrigerator.' Sonora pointed. 'Bedroom's that way.'

Gruber and Molliter headed down the dark hallway. Sam patted Sonora's shoulder.

'Let me go in first a minute, okay?'

She nodded, reluctant now.

'You all right?' Crick said. He wiped a handkerchief across the back of his neck.

Sonora said yes, heard the snap of rubber gloves from the bedroom, the drip of water down the wall, the roar of traffic on the bridge across the river.

She looked at her feet. 'I think I'm going in now.'

'If you're sure.' Resignation and fatigue in Crick's voice.

She started in just as the others came out.

It was Sam's face that changed her mind. He put an arm around her, and turned her away. 'Don't be going in there, honey. It was pretty quick. He didn't suffer long.'

Sonora hid her face in Sam's shoulder and squeezed her eyes shut, thinking how kind he was to lie.

Chapter Fifty

The children did not know what to make of her. She had laughed when she broke the news of Stuart's death, then apologized and laughed again. Tim had looked at Heather and said, 'You know, we may have to commit her.' Then all three of them had burst into tears.

Sonora still had her funeral dress on, but the kids had changed into bluejeans.

Tim looked at the clock in the airport restaurant. 'Baba's going to make us miss the flight.'

Sonora grimaced. 'She'll come rolling in at the last minute. No one in your father's family is punctual. It's genetic.'

Heather waved her new Barbie doll. 'Thank you for all the presents, Mommy, and my new jeans.'

'You sure we can afford this?' Tim asked.

Sonora gave him a look. 'You like the Walkman?' They were young, she thought. Young enough to be distracted by pretties.

'I wish you could come with us, Mommy.'

Tim ate a large bite of hamburger. 'How come you can't? You're off the case, aren't you?'

Sonora put her finger in a wet mark on the table. 'Yeah, I'm off.'

'That's mean, Mommy, when you work so hard.'

'No, hon. I can't work it anymore. Them's the rules, and they're good ones.'

'It would be upsetting, dork.' Tim looked at Sonora,

grimaced, and exchanged looks with Heather. 'She's doing it again. *Mom*. Why are you looking like that?'

'What's wrong, Mommy? And don't say nothing.'

Tim put his french fry down. 'Is it because of Stuart, or because we're going? We can stay with you, Mom. I'm not afraid.'

Sonora rubbed her eyes. 'It's Stuart. I'm going to be upset about this awhile, okay? Aren't you guys upset?'

Heather stuck her thumb in her mouth.

Tim shrugged. 'I loved him, okay? But I never miss people. When they're gone, they're just gone. I still have my life.'

Sonora chewed the knuckle of her left fist. Hard words from a thirteen-year-old. Which worried her more than tears. 'Eat up, kids.'

Heather put her hands demurely in her lap. 'It's very good, but I'm not hungry. Mommy, are you going to be lonely?'

'Clampett will keep me company, and I've got some stuff to do that's going to keep me busy.'

'What stuff?' Tim said.

Sonora wiped her clean hands on the thin and unsatisfactory paper napkin. She poured salt in her palm and ate it. She hadn't done that since she was Tim's age.

'But where are we going?' Heather said.

'Atlanta,' Tim told her.

'But after Atlanta.'

Sonora squeezed her daughter's hand. 'Won't know till you get to Atlanta. Baba's going to pick. Why don't you talk her into taking you to a beach?'

'The ocean?' Heather said.

'That's where beaches are.'

Sonora scowled at her son. 'Be nice. I'm counting on you. I'm counting on both of you. Look after each other and be good. And do your schoolwork.'

'How long are we going to be gone?' Tim asked.

Sonora frowned. 'I don't know, I haven't thought that far. Probably till Visa cancels my card.'

Chapter Fifty-One

The first picture came in the mail late that afternoon. Two more arrived the next day.

Chapter Fifty-Two

Sonora sat on the couch in the living room, thinking about walls. The phone rang. She did not count the rings, or notice when they stopped.

Walls were not the sort of thing one normally noticed. She knew that, in the back of her mind – knew that so much time staring at walls was not a good thing. But there was something about a wall that was steady and undemanding, muting somehow. Walls dulled the senses, which in turn dulled the pain.

She was glad the kids were gone. It was good to know they were safely tucked away at the seaside with a grandmother who might smoke too much, and make Heather sneeze, but who would nurture them. Nurture was hard right now. Sonora was relieved not to have to do nurture.

And dealing with the kids would definitely take away from wall time.

She heard a bark. Got up to open the back door, felt the wind across her face, sniffed it like a bouquet.

So much for her quota of daily activity.

Clampett nudged her knee, licked her fingers. Sonora scratched his neck under the worn leather collar. The angels might turn their backs, but not her trusty dog.

Chapter Fifty-Three

Sonora was asleep on the couch when the doorbell rang. She opened her eyes. Rubbed a hand over her face, licked dry lips. She looked at her watch, saw it was two o'clock. AM or PM?

The doorbell rang again. PM, she decided. Felt like afternoon.

She opened the door, blinked at the man who stood on the front porch. Felt Clampett's presence by her side.

The man was somewhere between twenty-eight and thirty-eight, which was a nice age bracket for a girl who was interested, which she wasn't. He wore jeans and a white cotton shirt, had high, broad cheekbones, a baby face, wavy brown hair.

Nice shoulders, Sonora thought.

The man picked up a rose petal from the soft stems and pieces that littered the front porch.

'Somebody been sending you flowers, pretty girl?'

Sonora wondered if she should tell him that the rose petals had spilled from funeral flowers. She looked down at her worn jeans, thin white tee shirt, thick white socks. She decided that she was not a pretty girl and that this man annoyed her.

'I don't want any,' Sonora said.

'Now hang on and give me a chance. See, your dog there hasn't barked or growled once. Dog knows I'm good people.'

Sonora put a hand on Clampett's collar. 'This is the

world's best dog. In honor of this dog, I'm going to give you thirty more seconds.'

He grinned. 'I'm from across the river, honey, I'm not sure I can talk that fast.'

'Give it a shot.'

He rocked back on his heels. 'You're Blair, aren't you? Homicide cop working the case where the guy was cuffed in his car and burned up?'

Sonora straightened her back. 'Let's see some ID.'

He reached into his back pocket and she tensed. 'No room in there for a weapon, honey, not in this pair of jeans.' He handed her a badge, and she looked it over, squinting.

'Deputy Sheriff Jonathan Smallwood. Calib County, Kentucky?'

He propped an elbow on the wood rail of her front porch. 'Sorry about what happened to your brother.'

She nodded. Word like that spread quickly, cop to cop.

'That's the main reason I drove up here. After I heard about your brother. I got a story to tell you.'

Sonora opened the screen door. 'Maybe you better come in.'

Smallwood paused at the edge of her living room, gave her a look over one shoulder and shook his head.

'You been eating anything at all?'

Sonora curled up on the couch, cross-legged, pretending not to notice when Clampett jumped up on the next cushion and laid his head in her lap. House rules for dogs had gone to hell.

Smallwood opened the curtains, stirring the dust, letting a latticework of sunshine in so bright Sonora blinked. He gathered up glasses, wadded tissues, pizza boxes, and disappeared into the kitchen. He stacked newspapers and set them on a chair.

'Feel better?' Sonora said.

'No, but you will.' He settled into her rocking chair. Crossed one ankle over his knee. 'Once upon a time.'

Sonora leaned close.

It had been five years since he'd come across the car burning hotly on an out of the way county road where the savvy parkers knew to go. It had been hot out, early September, and he shuddered when he described the blackened figure fused to the steering wheel – eyeless sockets, arms pulled forward, pugilistically locked.

The car had belonged to one Donnie Hillborn, and dental records had confirmed that the blackened body was indeed Donnie, the older brother of Vaughn Hillborn, hotshot football player, currently being courted by the University of Tennessee, the University of Kentucky, Duke and Michigan State.

Donnie had been a local embarrassment. Donnie had been gay and proud of it.

There had been numerous oddities at the scene. A key in a charred fist. The smell of gasoline inside the car. A Coke can in the weeds nearby that had held gasoline and not Coke. No shoes, belt buckle, or signs thereof, anywhere on or around the body.

'Could of burned up, I guess.' Smallwood glanced at Sonora.

'Not if the body didn't.'

He looked thoughtful. 'Officially listed as a traffic fatality, despite the lack of tire marks or collision damage.'

'Autopsy?' Sonora asked.

'Wasn't one.'

'Why does this smell so bad? Why cover it?'

Smallwood rubbed the back of his neck. 'It's the sports thing.'

'You've lost me.'

'The family didn't want it investigated. They figured it was some kind of hate thing. Because Donnie was gay.'

'You've *got* to be kidding.'

'This is a very out of the way county in Kentucky. A man can go to LA and walk around with false eyelashes and a cosmetics bag and people don't look twice. But where I come from . . . don't tell me Cincinnati's an oasis of tolerance. You people just concentrate your vice on the other side of the river in Covington.'

'We let Maplethorpe stay.'

'Been lynched in Calib County.'

'I take your point, Deputy. How'd the family manage to swing it? Money?'

'You birth a football player, it puts you in the catbird seat.'

'Come on, I don't get this.' Sonora tickled Clampett just under his left ear. 'Nobody's going to cover up a murder because somebody's kid plays good high school ball.'

'And you looked so intelligent, too.'

'Explain it better,' Sonora said.

Smallwood rocked back in his chair. 'I'm not saying who the family talked to, or where the pressure connected. Could have been local, could have been the sheriff. Could have been somebody at the university, some alumni. All I know is, the death of Donnie Hillborn becomes a tragic traffic fatality, and Vaughn gets pretty serious about going with UK.'

'And did he? Might give you a clue as to who put pressure on who.'

'We'll never know. Six weeks later, he was dead too.'

Sonora lifted her head. 'Of what?'

'Accident, out on the farm. Hillborns had a little place, way out from town. Barn caught on fire. Vaughn was inside, trying to get his horse out. Ironic, isn't it?'

'It's crap, and you know it.'

Smallwood looked at her. 'They found a cigarette butt.'

'Kid played football, he didn't smoke.'

'It's Kentucky, everybody smokes.'

'So what did you do, Smallwood, you leave it alone?'

Clampett jumped off the couch and put his nose on the deputy's knee. Smallwood rubbed the dog on the side of the neck.

'Believe me, I tried, and I caught hell for it.' Even now, five years later, Sonora could hear the frustration in his voice. 'The thing is, these people never went anywhere, except to Lexington now and then to shop at the malls. Hillborn was a good kid, studied hard, worked the family farm. I've looked at every face in town, more than once, and I can't make sense of it. I thought at first it was some kind of nutcase passing through, but Vaughn died too, so that don't hold up.'

'What did Donnie Hillborn look like?'

'Big guy, solid. Six-two.'

'Dark curly hair and brown eyes?'

Smallwood looked at her. 'Yeah.'

'Sounds like my girl's involved.'

'I thought so, that's why I'm here. What do you know about her?'

'Selma Yorke. Small, wavy blonde hair. Never smiles.'

'That's it?'

'Watching men burn up in their cars brings her to sexual highs. She takes pictures.'

'Where would she run across Hillborn and his brother?'

'She likes brothers.' Sonora's throat closed. She swallowed.

Smallwood's look was full of pity. 'I've never seen anybody like that in Calib County, and I'd know.'

'You said Vaughn went into Lexington. Maybe he caught her eye there.'

'I checked. He'd been doing recruiting trips for months, training, studying, and working on the farm. He hadn't been to Lexington since Easter, and the only place he went was Sears, to get some Craftsman tools and his taxes done at the H&R Block.'

'Why didn't you call me three weeks ago?'

'You're not listening, are you? The case is closed and I'm not here, and the investigation does not go on. But I have copies of the investigation reports in the trunk of my car, and if you want them they're yours.'

'I'm not working the case. Why don't ... Hold up a minute. You said he went to Lexington around Easter?'

'Yeah.'

'To get his taxes done?'

'Yeah, at H&R Block. At the Sears.'

'Sears. Hell, yes, next to the Allstate Booth. Ashley Daniels works for Allstate, in a mall. It's *taxes*. April fifteenth. It's not Easter at all, it's the tax thing. It's H&R Block.' Sonora put a fist under her chin. 'Be interesting to find out how many of Selma's victims got their taxes done there.'

'Don't mind my look of confusion, honey, but have I helped you out?'

'Yeah, you've helped me. Thank you very much, Deputy Smallwood. I didn't see you, I didn't talk to you, and you can clean up my living room any time you want.'

He shook her hand warmly. 'You're rocking chair is real comfortable, and I'm nuts about this dog.'

Chapter Fifty-Four

The office was familiar and strange – her desk unnaturally clean no messages on the answering machine. Sonora smelled old coffee and felt like she'd left yesterday and a hundred years ago.

She ducked into Crick's office before anyone saw her.

He was frowning at a computer printout, but when he saw her he smiled.

'Home from the wars,' he muttered, and motioned to a chair. 'How are your children?'

She sat down. 'Taking it so well it scares me.'

'Kids are tough. How are you progressing on the nervous breakdown?'

She laughed. Realized she hadn't in a while. 'Very well, thank you, sir.'

'I see you're wearing a clean shirt and tie. This mean you want to ease back into some work time?'

Sonora nodded.

'Good. You know you can't do active work on the Daniels case, but we can use you to consult. Or you can wash your hands of the whole thing, and nobody'd blame you a bit.'

'You know better. Get prints, anything off the pictures?'

Crick shook his head. 'We've been watching Selma's house, but there's no sign anybody goes there. We're trying to get a court order to search the premises. So far judge says no go.'

'I've had to get my kids out of town, my brother got torched, and the judge says no go?'

Crick's face was expressionless.

'What happened to Molliter's big witness?'

'Got a body turned up at the morgue, looks like it may be her. Molliter had court today. He'll ID it tomorrow.'

'I could go. I saw her in interrogation.'

'That would help.'

They looked at each other.

'Would a cup of coffee help you work your nerve up, Sonora?'

'Sir?'

'So you can say whatever it is you've got on your mind.'

Sonora tilted her head sideways. Took a deep breath. 'You remember that conversation we had in Keaton Daniels' bathroom?'

Crick's eyelids drooped slightly, but he stayed quiet.

Sonora sat on the edge of her chair and looked at the floor. 'I slept with Keaton Daniels, and used his shower. The physical evidence you got out of the bathroom – it could be her or it could be me.'

'I see.'

'Selma was out there. Watching. She knew I spent the night. She called and said she'd pay us back, both of us.'

Crick looked at her.

'That's why she showed up at my house. And his.'

He placed his fingers together, carefully. 'No wonder you were worried.'

'Still am.'

'Sonora. It's a wonder she didn't take your babies out with your brother.'

She gritted her teeth. 'Not a minute goes by, I don't think about it. Maybe she's getting a conscience.'

Crick pointed a finger at her. 'Pay attention. They never, *ever*, get a conscience. She didn't kill your kids because it didn't suit her at the time. Maybe it didn't fit in with her fantasy. Because that's what these killings are, they're her fantasy. That's why she does what she does, she's acting it out. And she's got no limits on what she'll do to make it happen. Make no mistake. If she'd felt the slightest urge to kill them, she would have, without a second thought.'

Sonora nodded, sat back in her chair. 'There's more.'

'I don't want details, Sonora.'

'I had a visitor. A deputy from a remote part of Kentucky who had a story to tell me.'

'He slept with Keaton too?'

'Selma hit there. Two brothers, both dead in fires, one burned up in his car. A few months before it happened, one of them had his taxes done at H&R Block.'

'So?'

'So. H&R Block in a booth at Sears. These booths are usually located next to the Allstate counter, or they used to be. You following me?'

Crick frowned. 'Not really.'

'Daniels' wife, Ashley, is an Allstate agent. Her booth is right next to the H&R Block office every year, I checked. These killings happen in the fall, but it's usually after a few months of phone calls and stalking. Keaton said his calls started in April. And Selby, that guy in Georgia, that's when his started. April. Think April fifteenth. Taxes. H&R Block. You get it?'

'You saying she's some kind of tax accountant? Works for the IRS?'

'For H&R Block. Not hard to get on there, it's seasonal, they train people. Perfect for her psychological profile – intermittent, undemanding employment. When tax season is over, she's got time and a long list of possible victims. Name, address, income. Deductions.'

'Yeah.' Crick rubbed his chin. 'Ties in with that weird thing she has with numbers. What is it, threes and nines?'

'Threes are evil, ones are shy.'

'Obviously not your average bear, this girl.'

Sonora looked at him. Waited. 'Crick, drop the shoe, will you? Yell at me now, please, and get it over with.'

He leaned back in his chair, gave her a sad smile. 'Normally I'd transfer your ass, the very least. I'm cutting you a lot of slack. I think you've had enough grief, Sonora.'

She stared at the floor. 'You don't seem surprised. I take that to mean I'm a lousy liar.'

'Not at all. It's her that convinced me. Something set her off enough to stalk you, and kill your brother. Could be the cop angle, could be more than that. I thought there might be more. Your kids came damn close to the edge there. If it gives me nightmares, God knows what it's doing to you.'

Sonora chewed her knuckles.

'Look, Sonora, it's good your kids are out of town, but they can't stay away forever. We need to keep Flash stirred up and angry. We need to keep her off balance.'

'You want me to sleep with Keaton again?' The look he gave her made her sorry she'd said it.

'Radio call-in show, remember? We decided to let Sam take your place, but you know it'll work a hell of a lot better with you. Problem is, this business with your brother. It'll draw a lot of attention.'

'That's what you want, isn't it?'

'Might not be what you want.'

'What I want,' Sonora said. She let her hands rest between her knees. 'What I want, is to catch her.'

Chapter Fifty-Five

Sonora walked carefully on the freshly mopped tile floors, watchful of wet spots. The morgue was quiet, the lights off in most of the offices. From somewhere came a voice that sounded like Eversley.

'Yeah, sure, another mysterious disappearance. First my chicken coupon, now this. You telling me the DBs are taking this stuff?'

Sonora passed the refrigeration unit. The thermometer showed a temperature of 55 degrees. Inside the viewing window, she saw the forlorn body of Sheree La Fontaine, lying like a ramrod on a gurney, a towel balled around her feet.

Marty stood patiently beside her. 'Hate to say it, Detective, but we've had DBs in here that looked healthier than you do.'

'I'm in the right place then, aren't I?'

He inclined his head toward the body. 'That her?'

'That's her. Sheree La Fontaine. Working girl from the other side of the river, hails from North or South Carolina.'

'Wasn't she a suspect in that Daniels thing?'

'Not anymore. I take it cause of death would be the stab wounds to the throat?'

'We'll make a pathologist out of you yet.' Marty made a notation on a chart. 'Sign.'

Sonora scrawled her signature.

'I thought Molliter was coming in.'

'His day off and he had to be in court, so they're already paying him time and a half, plus I was in the neighborhood. On my way to do a radio thing, call-in show. I'm a celebrity expert. Cop and victim.'

Sonora sat back in the chair, loosened the high heels on her feet, decided that when she got home she would throw them away. She looked out the window. It was dark. She had talked to the kids right before she left. They were fighting with each other and enjoying the beach.

She took a sip of water and wondered if there was time to go to the bathroom.

A man in blue jeans and an olive green pullover sweater sat behind a board of controls. He smiled at her. He knew she was nervous, and he'd been working hard to do the impossible and make her feel at ease.

He stroked the thick black mustache over his lip. 'Don't forget the ten little words we can't say on the air.'

'You'd just lose your license, I'd lose my job.'

He looked reassured. 'Here we go, then. If you have an uncontrollable urge to cough or throw up or something, just hold up one finger and I'll cover. Ready, two, three . . . and this is Ritchie Seevers on the air tonight with Specialist Sonora Blair of the Cincinnati Police Department's homicide unit. Specialist Blair is . . . I'm right, aren't I? The lead detective on the Mark Daniels' murder investigation?'

'I was the lead detective, yes. Not anymore.'

Seevers touched his forehead. 'Of course. For those of you who've been living in a vacuum, Specialist Blair's brother was the latest victim of the Flashpoint Killer. Detective Blair is here to talk to us about the ongoing investigation of the truly heinous murder of Mark Daniels, who, as you likely remember, was burned alive in his car. She's also going to give us guys some safety tips.' He laughed here, at the notion of men needing safety tips. 'And if any of *you* out *there* have questions for Specialist Blair, be sure and give us a call.'

Seevers paused, and Sonora wondered if she was supposed to make a comment. She could not think of anything particular to say.

Seevers smiled and went on. 'Detective Blair, do you . . . let me interrupt myself, I think we have someone on the line.'

'Hello?'

The voice was female. Sonora felt her heartbeat pick up.

'Yes, hello, you're on the air with Ritchie Seevers and Specialist Blair of the Cincinnati Police Department's homicide unit.'

'Oh. Hi, Ritchie. I listen to you all the time? And I wanted to ask a question.'

'We're all ears here, but first would you tell us your name.'

'Rhonda Henderson.'

'How you doing, Rhonda, and thanks for calling in. What's your question?'

'My question? I just wanted to ask. Umm. So you're a girl and you're a police officer. Do you carry a gun like the men?'

Sonora crossed her legs and leaned back in the chair. 'All police officers are required to carry a gun.'

'Do you like, know how to use it?'

Sonora sighed, realized the big exhale was not such a great idea on live radio. Seevers went through a round of patter. Answered another caller, this one male. Sonora shifted her weight, trying to ease a knot of tight muscles in the small of her back.

'Ma'am, are you the police officer whose brother got killed in the saloon fire?'

'Yes, I am.'

'You must feel awful.'

Seevers shot her a sympathetic look. 'Thank you for calling, sir. We appreciate your sympathy.'

'You going to kill her when you run her down?'

Sonora crossed her legs. 'It's my job to uphold the law, sir, not break it.'

'But if it was my brother and I was you, I'd break her neck.'

'I'm mainly interested in seeing she gets off the streets.'

'How long's that going to take? I guess since she's killed one of your own, so to speak, I guess now maybe you folks will do something about bringing her in.'

'No one understands your frustration better than I do, sir, but we've had a team of very fine officers tracking this woman from day one. All of them have worked around the clock, and will continue working long hours till she's caught.'

'Yeah, but . . .'

Sonora felt heat rising in her cheeks. She tried to focus, thinking this was too soon after Stuart, that she was going to lose it and screw everything up. Seevers was waving at her. Another caller.

'I just want to know, where is your sympathy for this poor girl?' The voice was older, female with an angry edge. But not Flash.

Sonora sat back in the chair, mouth open. Where was her sympathy?

'I mean, get real, why don't you? You know and I know that only *men* kill for no reason. I assure you this poor girl's the victim here.'

Sonora leaned close to the mike. 'Ma'am, I sat in emergency with a twenty-two-year-old college student right after he was pulled out of a burning car. I guarantee you *he* was the victim.'

'You just say that because he's your brother.'

'He was not— '

The woman's voice jumped an octave. 'You don't know what these guys did to this poor girl. Maybe they *forced* themselves on her.'

Sonora made an effort to sound calm and steady. 'Ma'am, I'm going to have to stop you, and make it clear that the Flashpoint Killer stalked her victims, that she— '

'You know, you're not exactly an objective party though, are you, Detective?' The voice was low now, tight.

Sonora bit the inside of her cheek. Selma had twitted some dark pool of feminine rage. There'd be no dealing with this one. Sonora wondered how many more like this there were out there.

'And I mean, no matter what *you* say, which we really can't trust 'cause of your brother and all, but no matter, you know very *well*, miss, that this girl probably got the shaft all her life. She could of been raped, you just don't know what kind of horrors might— '

Who are we talking about here, Sonora thought. You or her? She set her jaw.

'I do know, ma'am, that whatever her background, she's got no right to tie innocent men up and set them on fire. And that objectivity has nothing to do with tracking this woman down like the *dog* she is, which the Cincinnati police department *will do*.'

Seever's voice came through with just the right touch of mellow, belied by the sweat on his brow. 'And we thank *you* ma'am, for sharing your viewpoint.'

Sonora leaned back in the chair. She had made it through Stuart's funeral without shedding a tear, enduring the looks and whispers of everyone who watched and waited for her to crack. Seevers handed her a wad of tissues.

'We have time for just one more— ' Seevers was looking a question, and Sonora swallowed and nodded her head. 'Ritchie Seevers, with— '

'Hey, girlfriend, it's me.'

Sonora's throat went dry. She looked at Seevers. His eyes were large, and a sheen of sweat popped across his forehead. He had exactly what he wanted, Sonora thought, and wasn't sure what he was going to do with it.

'I just called to tell you bye,' Selma said.

Sonora frowned. 'Why good-bye? You going somewhere?'

Selma laughed. 'You'uns don't ever miss a chance, do you?'

'Why are you leaving?'

'You know why. It's gone bad. I got to go looking.'

A victim, Sonora thought. She'd be stalking again.

'What is it you want, Selma? What you looking for?'

Long silence, and when the words came, they came slowly. 'A place that makes me happy.'

'Happiness comes from within,' Seevers blurted, pop radio psychology bubbling forth.

There was a pause. 'Not in me,' Selma said. Like she was sleepy.

Chapter Fifty-Six

Crick rubbed the back of his neck. Gave Sonora a look. 'Track her down like a dog?'

Gruber cleared his throat. 'I believe the actual words were 'like the dog she is.' I got to say, sounded good to me.'

Crick turned sideways. 'Lieutenant Abalone did *not* agree.'

'Hey, she's human,' Molliter said.

'I am not.'

Sam looked at her. 'You're not human?'

Sonora frowned. Realized she was tired and not making sense. She had that awful feeling – tight chest, panicky flutters, hot and cold chills. 'She sounded so weird, don't you guys think?'

'You're the expert,' Sam said, 'she talks to you.'

'She was weird. Like . . . sad. Toned down. Almost pathetic.' Sonora looked at Crick. 'You talked to Dr. Fischer about this?'

'Yeah, but I don't have to. You're not feeling sorry for her, are you?'

'No. Course not.'

'Good. That poor little me voice is just a nice piece of work that'll come in handy if we ever jerk her butt in front of a jury.'

'That sounds like Crick talk, not shrink stuff.'

'Yeah, well, Fischer talked a lot about degrees of stimulation, depressed states of— '

'What's that got to—'

'Let me finish. In a nutshell. Flash is fading. She needs a jolt to pick her up.'

'Maybe she'll go home,' Molliter said.

Sam shook his head. 'She's depressed, not stupid.'

Crick shrugged. 'Been watching the place from the get go. She knows we're there, she won't come back.'

'Let's go in then,' Sonora said. 'Take Fischer's opinion to the judge.'

Crick shook his head, opened his mouth. 'They won't—'

There was a knock on the door, and Sanders poked her head in. 'Sir?'

Crick ran a hand under his shirt collar. 'Why the hell are we all crammed in here? No, don't back away, come in, Sanders.'

'She can sit in my lap,' Gruber said.

Sanders put a hand on her hip. 'If you didn't eat so many doughnuts, you might have a lap.'

Sonora saw Gruber's look of shock, closed her eyes, smiled a little.

'Ashley Daniels just called,' Sanders said. 'A woman who identified herself as Police Specialist Sonora Blair stopped by her office, her Allstate booth, just a little while ago.'

Sonora scooted her chair sideways. 'What's this?'

'I got her to describe the woman. She was small and blonde, and Mrs. Daniels thought she looked familiar.'

Crick cracked his knuckles. 'You ever meet Ashley Daniels face to face, Sonora?'

'Briefly.'

'It's Flash,' Sam said.

Sanders nodded. 'The woman wanted Ashley Daniels to go with her. For questioning. But when Mrs. Daniels asked to see ID—'

'Good girl,' Gruber muttered.

'The woman said she'd left it in her jacket in the car. She tried to get Mrs. Daniels to go with her down to the parking lot, but she wouldn't go. So the woman said she was going to go get it, and she'd be right back. But she didn't come back.'

'Okay,' Crick said. 'She went for the wife. She's going to blow.'

'We got to put somebody on Keaton, sir.'

'Yeah, we'll have to. We stirred her up. I don't want his death on my head.'

Everyone was moving, on their feet.

'But why's this woman seem familiar?' Molliter said. 'Ashley Daniels thought she looked familiar, right?'

Gruber waved a hand. 'Probably because they worked within thirty feet of each other for several months. We confirmed. Selma Yorke worked at H&R Block in the Sears at Tri-County Mall. All her co-workers say she had black hair.'

'Wig. Probably same one she wore to Mark Daniels' funeral,' Sam said.

Gruber looked at Sonora. 'We also got her connected up to an H&R Block in Atlanta. Lennox Square, mile away from the bank where James Selby was a teller. It's a definite he got his taxes done there.'

'She used the same name?' Sonora asked.

'Workers get bonuses if they continue one year to the next.'

'All right, surveillance on Daniels.' Crick looked at his watch. 'Judge Markham leaves for Hilton Head and a week of golf in one hour, after which Judge Hillary Oldham will be on call. Oldham used to practice law with Lieutenant Abalone's brother Samuel, and she likes cops. I'm going to get a court order out of this. I want a look inside that house.'

'Can I ride along?' Sonora asked.

'Sonora— '

'Please. In appreciation of doing the radio thing.'

'I'm supposed to thank you for that?'

Chapter Fifty-Seven

They took exit 1846–passed a chili place, Isadores Pizzaria, warehouses, old stockyards. The Camp Washington Community Center had bars on the windows. A sign on the door designated it as a child safe place. A worn poster on a telephone pole touted THE ULTIMATE CHALLENGE – THE MEANEST MAN CONTEST.

Overhead came the roar of cars on the interstate. It was grey out, a fine mist of rain in the air. Sonora rolled down her window, heard the squeal of brakes on railroad tracks.

She glanced at Sanders, who sat on the edge of her seat in the back of the Taurus. 'Sam, we need to make a stop on the way back. Sanders wants to get Gruber a dozen doughnuts.'

Sanders giggled and Sonora grinned. Good old girls. Sonora glanced out the window at a billboard that said *Ever Toast A Friend?* and showed a car in flames. The warning on the bottom said *Friends Don't Let Friends Drive Drunk*.

Her smile faded.

The house was grey and bleary, here at the end of the day, tucked behind a cluster of trees that were leafless and forlorn. Sam eased the Taurus into a tight spot behind a rusting, mustard-yellow Camaro. A large woman in maroon polyester pants and a black sweatshirt watched them from her front porch. There was a plastic Santa Claus hanging under the woman's porch light. Sonora wondered if it was left over from last year, or if the woman was early with her decorating.

Sam got out of the car, stiff legged. 'Crick made sure to let the guys watching the house know we were coming, Sonora. Didn't want 'em getting excited and taking you into custody.'

'Thank you so much.'

This time she knocked at the front door. No answer. Sam used the key he'd gotten from the landlord. The door swung open with a creak and sagged sideways – warped, ancient, and unloved. Sam motioned Sanders around to the back of the house, then stepped forward, gun ready. Sonora followed at his back.

The living room was tiny, and coated in filth, and it looked like the world's biggest flea market, garage sale, basement from hell. Sonora took a breath of stale, sour air, thinking that Selma Yorke could be three feet away and they'd never know it. Cardboard boxes, sagging and old, were stacked in every available space, most of them filled with old magazines and dusty, yellowing newspapers. Plastic laundry baskets brimmed with old clothes, jewelry, worn shoes, hats, purses, books – everything that was ever in the bottom of a closet or stuffed back in a drawer.

Sonora poked through a laundry basket with torn webbing, finding old baby clothes, a high button shoe, a strand of bright orange beads – the kind children would stash in a dress-up box. Everything was coated with a fine layer of grime.

Things were acquired and abandoned. Owning was enough.

The kitchen was neat and clean. The appliances were old, the white enamel chipped in places, rusting around the chips. The linoleum was cracked and had holes and creaked loudly beneath their feet. The countertops were crowded. Sonora counted five bread boxes – most of them old, battered and ugly. A chipped plate, mug, and fork sat in the white, rust-stained sink. The dishes looked clean. Sonora touched them. Dry. She ran a finger along the bottom of the sink. Dry again. She went to the refrigerator – a short, old fashioned box shape with a wide metal handle.

Not much inside. A large can of Hawaiian Fruit Punch, the triangular openings on the metal top orange with rust. Juice had dried and formed a pink crust in the edges.

The shelves were stocked with white Styrofoam take-home boxes, wrinkled McDonald's bags, a red and white box from Kentucky Fried Chicken. A white bag was full of stiff, cold hamburgers in blue and white cardboard boxes – White Castle.

The crisper was empty. No fruit. No vegetables. Sonora checked the freezer. Popsicles and freezer pops. Fudgsicles. Dixie cups with ice cream – vanilla with swirls of fudge, vanilla with swirls of strawberry. Jell-o pops. Pudding pops. Ice cream sandwiches from Sealtest. No Breyers, no Hagen Daas, no Chunky Monkey from Ben & Jerrys.

The laundry room was a revelation – empty Coke cans lined neatly on the shelves, three fresh new bundles of clothesline, looped and held together by a sticky paper wrapper.

'It really is her,' Sam said. He went to the back door and waved at Sanders.

Sonora headed up the bare wood stairs. They were warped, impossible to climb quietly. She paused in the narrow, dark hallway, smelled dust, heard the tick of a clock. Heard Sam, coming up the stairs behind her.

'Bathroom,' Sam said, pointing.

The room was tiny and smelled of mildew. The woodwork had been stripped from the wall, showing a dark grungy gap between the warped end of the brown-stained linoleum and the water-spotted plaster wall. The medicine cabinet hung open, empty shelves orange with rust and dirt.

Selma Yorke had left a handful of cosmetics. A fat pink tube of Maybelline mascara, black-smudged, lay sideways by the sink. Sonora spotted the stubby end of an eyeliner pencil, no cap, and a tube of brownish red lipstick. Talcum powder spotted the dry sink, caked in the lumps of aqua toothpaste that dotted the basin. Sonora looked in the trash can.

'What you got?' Sam stood in the doorway, one eyebrow raised.

Sonora looked at him over her shoulder. 'I hate it when you do that.'

'Sneak up on you?'

'Raise one eyebrow.'

'That's 'cause you can't do it.'

Sonora tilted the trash can forward. Wads of pink bubble gum. A Fudgsicle wrapper, streaked with dried chocolate. And a sprinkling of baby-fine blonde hair.

'She cut her hair. Looks like she just snipped the bangs. Old patterns, Sam.'

'Old patterns and new trouble.'

A soiled towel showed smears of brown, orange and blue. Sonora sniffed and smelled turpentine. Black mildew spotted the caulking along the sides of the tub.

Sam flicked a finger. 'Reckon there's pubic hair down there in the drain?'

'Yeah, yeah, have your fun.'

They split up. Sonora walked into the bedroom on the left, finding an unmade, wrought iron single that brought jail-house bunks to mind. The sheets had pulled from the foot of the bed, exposing a yellow-stained grey-striped mattress. The pillow was flat, trailing feathers from an open seam. There were no blankets.

The walls were plaster, dirt over old avocado green paint. The carpet was thin, green, sculptured.

The dresser was cheap, the top drawer empty. The other three drawers were stuffed with wadded clothing, so full they did not close. Bits and pieces swelled over the edges – jeans, underwear, nylon shorts. Sonora went to the closet.

The double metal doors were shut tight.

Sonora put a hand on a loose plastic knob and yanked. The door stuck, squeaked, then gave way to a rumbling avalanche that tumbled to her feet.

Dolls. Old, new, modern, antique. Barbie, Chatty Cathy, Thumbelina. China, plastic and bisque faces. Stray arms, legs, heads, little dresses, little shoes, marble and painted eyes, wide open, unseeing.

Sonora heard footsteps, Sam calling her name. She stirred the mass. Nothing real. Just dolls and doll parts.

'Sonora?' Sam stood in the doorway, gun at the ready. 'You okay? I heard you squeal.'

'Did not.'

'Looks like Annie's room in here.' He jerked his thumb toward the other bedroom. 'You better come see.'

It was the better of the two bedrooms, and ran along the entire back of the house. It had originally been two rooms, but the separation wall had been knocked out. There were two windows along the back, ragged curtains thrust to one side to let light in through grimy panes.

On the left hand side was a workshop – hammer, nails, scraps of wood in one corner, a portable Black & Decker table saw. A sturdy easel had pride of place in the center of the room, and a wood shelf held paints, brushes, turpentine. Stacks of canvases were propped against the wall and stuffed in the closet.

Sonora studied the work, unfinished, but long dry, on the easel.

The colors were angry. Dirty reds, orange and brown. The paint was thick and full of chunks – plastic buttons, shoe laces, little bits of clothes glued on. A patch of cold ice blue was incongruous on the left hand side, oddly unrelated to the rest of the picture.

'Look at this, Sam. Look at this stuff.'

He turned the stacks of canvases facing the wall. 'Jesus H. Christ, Sonora, this is weird-looking shit.'

'Now we know why she takes the clothes.'

'Take a look over here.'

Wood boxes were stacked four high and three across, most of them two feet by two square, joined together in a huge and bizarre dollhouse.

Each box was a still life and all the dolls were male, dressed in clothes that had been rudely cut and stitched from men's blue jeans, cotton shirts, khakis. Some of the dolls sat at desks, some played baseball. The first one stood behind a roughly constructed counter in a crude facsimile of the lobby of a bank.

James Selby, Sonora thought.

She stretched out a hand, but did not touch the brown-eyed doll that stared blankly from behind the counter.

There was a gap in the dollhouse. The next to last wood box was missing – had that been Mark Daniels? The last box was empty, the wood raw and newly sawn. Sonora wondered who had been slated to go inside. Stuart? Keaton? A shoebox sat in the windowsill over the empty wood box. Sonora peeped inside.

The tea set was tiny and made of porcelain, perfect for the fingers of a very little girl. It was too fragile for a young child; it would not be a practical gift. But it was sweetly painted with blue forget-me-nots, and had a tiny tea pot with a lid, six round plates, and four cups and saucers. When Heather found it beneath the Christmas tree last year, she had left her other gifts in a pile of colored paper and ribbon, lined up all her tiny horses, and become lost in a child's fantasy where ponies drank out of teacups, wore ribbons in their tails, and conversed with little girls in nightgowns.

Sonora clutched the edge of the windowsill, and sat down on the floor. In her mind's eye she saw Selma Yorke drifting through the lawn around her house, where Tim and Heather slept and played and took their baths. She saw Selma's greedy fingers on Heather's little tea set, and wondered if one of the Barbies in the closet full of dolls had been abandoned outside by her forgetful daughter, then snatched up by a woman who handcuffed innocent men to steering wheels and burned them alive in their cars.

'Sonora? You just get tired all of a sudden?' Sam crouched beside her, looking unhappy.

'It's not like I didn't already know she was hanging around the house, right? I just need to sit down for a minute.'

'Honey, you are sitting down.'

Chapter Fifty-Eight

Sam and Sonora sat in the parking lot of a Taco Bell, engine idling.

Sam patted her shoulder. 'You cold, Sonora? Want my jacket?'

She did, but shook her head no. Sonora watched raindrops trickle down the car window. 'It's more comfortable to think people like Selma don't have feelings. But they do.'

'I know. But Sonora.' He touched her knee. 'Lots of kids are abused. Only a rare few turn into killers. If you could be there when she does what she does, if you could see her face when she kills. You wouldn't have sympathy for her at all.'

'I know.' She squeezed his hand. Sam winked and eased the car toward the drive-in window.

'Come on, girl. Eat something, you'll feel better.'

'Get me some rice.' Sonora dug the cellular phone out of her purse.

'What you doing?'

'Checking messages.'

'Why don't you take it easy for ten seconds while we get something to eat?'

Sonora sat with the phone in her hand. Punched in numbers and listened. Sam took a plastic bag of food from the window.

Sonora looked at Sam. 'Shelby Hargreaves.'

He parked the car next to a handicapped spot. 'Woman at the antique store?'

Sonora nodded. 'Wants me to call. Give me your pen, let me write this number down.'

'Here.' Sam handed her a Coke.

She unwrapped a straw and stuffed it through the slot. Liquid bubbled up over the plastic lid and spilled on her pants. She took a drink, then propped the cup against the back of the seat.

'You're going to spill that,' Sam said.

Sonora put the phone to her ear. 'Ms. Hargreaves, this is Specialist Blair, Cincinnati P.D.'

'Detective Blair. Good.'

Sonora watched Sam bite into a bean burrito. He ate them bland, no salsa.

'Look, it's that doll I told you about – the German bisque boy that this woman looked at, but didn't buy? It's missing. It's got to have been stolen.'

Sonora rubbed her forehead. 'You're sure?'

'It was here last night, but when I came in this afternoon, it was gone. I've looked all over for it, and nobody remembers selling it. And it's not in the inventory receipts.'

Sonora felt nervous flutters in her chest, the panicky hot and cold feeling. 'It was good of you to call, Ms. Hargreaves.'

'I just— '

'No, I appreciate it. You've been a big help.' Sonora hung up, saw Sam was looking at her. There were bean smears on the edge of his mouth. She handed him a napkin. 'Selma went to the antique store and took the other doll. It's now, Sam, she's gearing up for another hit. She's going after him.'

'She took the other doll?'

'*Somebody* did, and we both know who.'

'Okay, stay calm, girl, we got Daniels covered. Just need to get hold of Blue Ash and let them know.'

'I'm calling the school.' Sonora made the call, went through the rigamarole of identifying herself, asking for Keaton.

'I'm sorry, Mr. Daniels is in class. I can take a message.'

'This is an emergency. Call him to the phone, please.'

'Just a moment, then.'

Sonora rubbed a fist on her left knee. Took a sip of Coke. Sam ate another bite of burrito, chewing slowly.

The voice came back to the phone, sounding breathless. 'I'm sorry, he doesn't answer his intercom. The Chapter One reading teacher is in the room and says he'll be right back. I'll have him call you then.'

'I'll wait.'

'But . . . I think he's in the little boys' room!'

'For God's sake,' Sonora muttered.

'Pardon?'

'No, pardon me. I need you to give him a message just as soon as he comes out. No, wait, let me talk to your principal.'

'He's at Central Office.'

'Okay. You're aware of Mr. Daniels' situation?'

'We all are.'

'Good. You can understand, then, that it is important for him to get this message. Tell him not to leave the school under any circumstances. Not until he hears from me, by phone or in person. My name is Blair. Detective Sonora Blair.'

'Detective Blair. Got it. I'll deliver the message myself.'

'Do me a favor, will you? Go stand outside the men's room, and see he gets it as soon as he comes out.'

The woman promised she would in a very small high-pitched voice. Sonora hung up and chewed her lip. 'I got a bad feeling, Sam.'

'He's okay, don't panic here. We got him surveilled.'

'I want to go to the school.'

'Crick wants you out of the way, you know that.'

'Sam, Blue Ash? This is their territory and they're doing the surveillance at the school, right? Our people don't pick him up till he's on the way home. I want to go over there. I want to see him, I want to warn him. I got—'

'A bad feeling, I know.' Sam wadded the burrito wrapper and tossed it into the back seat. 'Okay, we're going. Eat your rice on the way.'

Chapter Fifty-Nine

The parking lot of the Blue Ash Pioneer Elementary School was a gridlock of buses and parents picking children up in the rain. Two Blue Ash patrol cars blocked the circle drive, blue lights flashing.

'For God's sake, girl, quit chewing the strap of your purse.'

'*Something's happened*, Sam.'

'Wait till I stop the car, Sonora!'

She left the door hanging open. The concrete walk was wet. Small children with backpacks and lunch boxes huddled beneath the overhang. Sonora forced herself to slow down.

A uniformed officer stood in the front entrance, hand on her hip. Officer Brady. She recognized Sonora and waved her on.

'They're in the office.'

Sonora nodded, didn't break stride. She turned the corner and went through the doorway.

'It's *her*.'

Sonora heard the gun being drawn, and put up her hands. 'Hey, I'm a *cop*.' She had their attention, anyway, a knot of uniforms, two men in plain clothes, several women in suits.

Sam ran in behind her, waved his ID. '*Damn* good way to get yourself shot, Sonora.'

'Leave me alone.'

'Or hit by a car. What you doing jumping out like that?. You— '

Sonora felt someone tap her shoulder. The man was short and round, had a thin wedge of white hair and a red face that probably meant high blood pressure.

'Excuse me for interrupting your argument. I'm Detective Burton, Blue Ash.' He looked at Sam. 'You guys partners, married, or what?'

'Same difference,' Sam said. 'Is Daniels okay?'

Burton touched the top button of his shirt and loosened his tie. 'Daniels is gone.'

Sonora sagged against Sam. 'I knew it. I told you I had—'

'A bad feeling. I know.'

Burton motioned to a black plastic couch. 'Why don't the two of you sit down, and let's see if we can't get to the bottom of this.' He turned to a woman sitting in a chair that had been pulled away from a desk. He was gentle and he talked slow. 'Ms. Sowder, there's no need to feel bad. Nobody's blaming you.'

The teacher was white faced and grim. She nodded.

'Now he told you he was just going to be gone a little while, and that he'd be back shortly, that right?'

'That's right.' Sonora stood up. 'Excuse me, Mrs. Sowder, I'm Specialist Blair. Did you get the impression—'

Burton waved a hand. 'Detective, I'd—'

'Burton, look, this is your jurisdiction, okay. I know I'm jumping right in the middle here, but it's my investigation, and while you and I squabble, this killer is going to off Keaton Daniels. Just let me talk to her a minute, *please*.'

The please stuck in her throat, but turned the trick. Burton waved her on.

'He didn't check out with the front office, Mrs. Sowder, that right? Did you get the impression he was sneaking away?'

The teacher rubbed her eyes. 'It wouldn't surprise me. He seemed really upset. And he also . . . he asked to use my car.'

'Your car?'

'He said his was stalling out, and could he take mine. He said he'd be back in about twenty minutes.'

'But he didn't say where he was going?'

'No, but he was . . . compelling. He was frantic.'

Sonora frowned. 'And he knew that if he didn't come back in twenty minutes you wouldn't walk off and leave the kids.'

'Of course not.'

'So he knew they were safe.'

'Yes. I've been teaching in his class all year. We have a good working relationship. We're friends.'

'And he did take your car?'

'Yes.'

'But didn't say where he was going or why?'

'I think it had something to do with his wife,'

'His wife? Why?'

'He had a message from her, so he called her from the office. That's when he came back and said he had to go out just for a short, time, and would I watch the kids.'

Sonora peered into Keaton Daniels' rental. Rain drenched her head and shoulders and dripped off the end of Sam's nose.

'Three things we know,' Sam said. 'One, he didn't want to take his car, or check out officially, which means he wanted to sneak away. Two, he left in the middle of the school day and didn't tell anybody he was going except that Mrs. Sowder. Three. What was three?'

'His wife.'

'Yeah, his wife called. A woman who said she was his wife, anyway.'

'It was her. Secretary recognized her voice.'

'Come on, girl, let's get out of the rain.'

Sonora leaned back against Keaton's car and bit the back of her hand. 'Just let me *think*, Sam.'

'That's the problem, Sonora, you can't think, you're too upset.'

'*This* helps?'

They stared at each other. Sam's tie was plastered to his shirt. Sonora's hair hung in wet wavy strands along her shoulders.

'God, Sam, Flash is going to kill him. He may already be dead.'

Rain splattered the pavement and a steady stream of cars flowed through the circle drive. The crush of children gradually began to dissipate.

'Let's try the Allstate Booth,' Sam said.

Burton surrendered the phone like a gentleman. Sonora reached into her jacket pocket, found the business card Ashley Daniels had given her that first day. She twisted the phone cord, counted three rings.

'Allstate, Beatrice Jurgins.'

Sonora identified herself, asked for Ashley Daniels.

'I'm sorry, she's out of the office. Can I take a message or can I help you?'

'Look, this is an emergency. I have reason to believe Mrs. Daniels is in some danger, and I need to speak with her at once.'

The voice on the other end went up an octave. 'She's not here.'

'Where is she, do you know?'

'She had an appointment. Somebody called, and she asked me to cover for her in the booth. A hot lead, she said. I figured it must be life insurance.'

'When was this?'

'She got the call this morning. She said she had to meet a prospect on their lunch hour.'

'She give you a name?'

'No, but . . . hang on a sec. Maybe she put it down in her book.'

Sonora waited. Looked at Sam. His hair was wet

and sticking up on one side. She smoothed it back in place.

'Hello? You there?'

'Right here,' Sonora said.

'Okay, I looked on her desk. She's got her book with her— '

Sonora's stomach got tight and painful.

'*But*,' the tone was triumphant, 'she wrote Ecton Park on a scratch pad, and I'll bet that's where she went.'

'Ecton Park? Seems strange for her to be meeting a client in Ecton Park, don't you think?'

'Not if you can sell some life. And she did say she was catching them at lunch.'

'Them or her?'

'It must have been a her, because she put on the fake glasses. She does that when she writes a woman, because Ashley's a dish and she likes to tone it down.'

'She make a habit of meeting clients in out-of-the-way places?'

'Ashley's careful. If she doesn't know somebody, she tries to meet them in the office. But we have the fall life contest going right now, and Ashley's really close. Could mean a trip to Hawaii.'

Sonora sighed. 'When is she due back?'

There was a long silence. 'She's already late.'

'Not careful enough, then. Thank you, Ms. Jurgins.'

Sam wiped his face with a handkerchief. 'You say Ecton Park? That's in Mt. Adams, right where Keaton lives.'

'Yeah, and it's outdoors and wooded. Just exactly what appeals to Flash. I think Selma's got herself a hostage, and Keaton's gone to rescue his wife.'

Sam was nodding. 'I'll call Crick.'

'Do it from the car. Let's hit the road.'

'*I'm* driving.'

Chapter Sixty

'It's a big park,' Sam said.
'She'll be by the water.'
'Fine, Sonora. That could be one of about five different places.'

'What kind of car did that teacher drive?'
'Sowder? Toyota Corolla.'
'Find the car, find Keaton.'

Sam drove past the conservatory and a rusted-out water tower. Sonora saw a pool of shallow greenish water next to an empty gazebo. Raindrops spattered the surface.

'What's that?' Sonora asked. 'A skating rink?'
'No, fountain. Turned off for the winter.'

The Taurus glided close. Made a shark pass by a lone car parked by the fountain – a shiny black Datsun Z.

Sam looked at Sonora. 'You know the make of car Ashley Daniels drives?'

'Black Datsun Z.'
'Anybody inside?'

Sonora squinted through the rain-streaked window. 'Hard to tell, the windows are fogged. I'm getting out.'

Her leg brushed the wet back bumper of the Datsun and her jacket plastered to her back like a second skin. She shivered, looked in the window, knocked on the glass. Tried the handle of the back door and found it unlocked.

Sonora wrenched the door open and crouched close to the ground, gun at the ready.

Nothing but the sound of rain. Insurance manuals and

a briefcase were scattered across the back cushions. A red leather purse lay on the front seat, passenger's side. A console in the middle held a large paper cup from Rallys, and a mounted car phone. A dark stain ran down the side of the upholstery.

Sonora opened the driver's door.

There were dark brown smudges on the rim of the steering wheel, and blood pooled over the accelerator and gas pedal. A black slingback pump, left foot, sat on the car dash.

Sonora heard footsteps and looked up into Sam's face. Rivulets of rain ran down his cheeks. She took a breath.

'This does not look good.'

Sam grimaced. 'Just talked to Crick. Park patrol did an extra round a few minutes ago, spotted the secretary's car up the road, near the main park entrance at an overlook.'

'Anybody inside?' Sonora closed the door of the Datsun and headed for the Taurus.

'Guy wasn't sure, he didn't think so. Crick told him to glide in and out, business as usual.'

Sam backed the Taurus out of the circle drive, and made quick work up the hill. Crick was there ahead of them, looking into the empty Toyota Corolla.

Sonora put a hand on the door handle.

'*Wait* till I stop, Sonora.'

Crick turned when he heard their footsteps.

'Nothing,' he said.

'Look in the trunk?' Sonora asked.

Crick shook his head. 'Not yet. Crowbar's in the back of my car.'

'I'll get it,' Sam said.

Sonora paced the parking lot, went to the edge to look out toward the river. It was hard to see in the drizzle, and she held the palm of her hand up, shading her eyes from the rain. Concrete stairs led from the overlook to another parking lot below, where there were cars, a swing set, another fountain that had been turned off. An overlook at the end of the lot gave a less lofty view of the river, which was grey now, churning with rain.

The steps were steep, leading down the side of the cliff. A man and a woman slipped into view, then disappeared.

'That's them,' Sonora said.

Sam and Crick were at her elbow. 'Where?'

She wasn't sure who had asked the question, maybe both. 'On the stairs.'

'I looked when I got here, I didn't see anybody,' Crick said.

'They passed into view just a second ago.'

'You sure?'

'Hell yes, I'm sure.'

Sam started for the stairs, but Crick held his arm.

'You go charging off after them, she'll shoot him, and you.'

'I'll shoot her first.'

'Let's try to keep Daniels alive. We'll drive down, then go on foot.'

Sonora looked down the cliffside, squinting. Something there, a path of some sort. Which made a certain sense. People never stuck to the stairs.

She pointed. 'I'm going that way.'

'Sonora— '

'Just to keep them in view. Everybody gets in the car, they could go anywhere. They're close to the bottom already. I won't approach, Crick, I'll just keep them sighted.'

'Okay, go.'

'I'm with her.'

Sonora headed for the path, Sam at her heels. The closer they got, the steeper it looked.

'Shit, Sonora, we're never gonna make this.'

Sonora grabbed the trunk of a tree, knees aching at the incline of the hillside. The dirt had turned gluey in the rain, slippery on the top. Her shoes sank in the brownish black sludge.

Six feet down the slope her feet stuck, then slid. She landed on her knees in the mud. Sam grabbed her arm and pointed. Spoke in a whisper in spite of the distance and the rain.

'Look, see? There they are.'

Two drenched figures headed toward the river overlook.

'Run, Sonora.'

Once they got their momentum going there was no way to stop. Rainwater pooled at the base of the cliff, and Sam and Sonora splashed through. Sam looked toward the parking lot.

'You see Crick?'

'No, and I don't see Keaton either.'

'Must have gone over the guardrail.'

'Okay, Sam, you circle left, I'm going behind them that way.'

Sam looked one more time for Crick. Nodded. 'Go, girl.'

Sonora straddled the railing, climbed over the hill to the brush. On her left was the Kentucky River. She could see Barleycorn's Floating Restaurant, and knew that if she went the other way she'd find the remains of the Sundown Saloon.

There was grass underfoot, waist high weeds. Her shoes were heavy with mud. The rain picked up, her clothes streamed water. She half-ran half-walked, moving down the path. Rounded a bend. And there they were, no more than three yards ahead. Just out of reach.

Sonora stood still for a moment, catching her breath. Her spine felt tingly, palms suddenly wet. It was almost absurd, the tiny blonde next to the large, broad-shouldered male.

In her mind's eye she saw the bloodstained shoe in Ashley Daniels' car, the fan of blood-soaked upholstery.

She raised her gun, aimed with the utmost care. Keaton was still too close, but he was pulling ahead. She waited till he was clear. Held her breath and fired.

Selma Yorke flinched and turned around, blonde hair dark with rain. No hit.

'Police,' Sonora said. 'Selma Yorke, you are under arrest. Stand aside, Mr. Daniels. Move it, move now, drop that gun— '

'Sonora, she's got Ashley stashed out here in the woods. She's hurt, but she's still alive.' Keaton held up a jacket, sun-yellow around splotches of blood.

Selma looked at Sonora. 'You found me.'

That first time Sonora had seen her, there in the cemetery, it had been a letdown, how drearily normal Selma looked. Today, even with the short blonde hair plastered with rainwater, she was oddly pretty – cheeks pink and flushed, an edgy air of energy and purpose. She met Sonora's eyes just for a moment, then looked away, gaze shifting like a lightning flash. Sonora had seen it twice before, this inability to focus and meet a gaze. Both times from someone on the verge of major breakdown.

'Put the gun down, Selma.'

Selma cocked her head to one side. 'You'uns could have shot me right in the back. How come you didn't?'

'I tried, I'm a bad shot, that's all.'

Selma laughed, but Sonora registered the flicker of pain that came and went.

'Come on, Selma. Put it down, and we can go somewhere dry and warm and talk.'

Selma shook her head. 'This isn't about us, Detective. This is about me. Me and him.' She put her gun to Keaton's head.

The nightmare, coming true. Sonora gritted her teeth. 'Let it go, Selma. You don't have to do this.'

'I do have to.'

'No, you don't.'

'I want to.'

Sonora steadied her aim. 'Out of the way, Keaton.'

'Don't move,' Selma told him.

Keaton looked at Sonora. 'Look, if there's any chance—'

'Ashley's dead, Keaton. Her car's full of blood.'

'You *know* she's dead?'

'I saw her body, now *move*. Go!'

'Girlfriend, you'uns are fibbing and you know it.'

Keaton looked at Sonora and she knew, from the expression on his face, who he believed.

'Keaton, she's playing with you.'

He shook his head. 'I've got to see her. I want to see Ashley.'

Selma looked at Sonora. 'Want to?'

Golly gee, Mom, look what I did. Sonora knew better than to refuse.

'Come on, Detective. You first, then him and me. And you lose your gun now, or I'll shoot him right here.' She put the muzzle of the gun at the hollow of Keaton's throat, and Sonora remembered kissing him there, and the way his arms felt when he pulled her close.

She blinked, set the gun on the side of the path. Wondered where the hell Sam was.

Selma motioned with her head. 'That way. Toward the river.'

Sonora turned her back and walked.

She waited for the gun to go off, another little game, but the sound of footsteps and heavy breathing let her know they were no more than a few feet behind. Up until now, all her energy had been focused on the chase, bringing Selma in. She would be grateful, now, if she could bring Keaton out alive.

She picked up the blood trail as they moved down hill, a rusty smear on a sapling. She imagined Ashley Daniels stumbling down the path, thought of the blood-soaked shoe in the car, the forced march through the rain. She wondered if there was the smallest possibility Keaton's wife was alive.

The mud caked on the hem of her jeans slowed her down.

Sonora smelled the river, the rain, realized that if she lived, she'd never be able to look at the muddy waters of the Kentucky without remembering.

She saw the footprint out of the corner of one eye, a long smear where someone had fallen. Saw Ashley Daniels' black slingback pump lying on one side, caked with mud. Sonora turned and faced Selma.

'Where is she?'

Selma pushed hair out of her eyes. 'Keep on going and I'll show you.'

'I don't think so.' Sonora pointed to the shoe. She heard Keaton's intake of breath, saw him surge toward the edge of the path.

'*No.*' Selma had the gun up.

He'd never survive a shot that close, Sonora thought.

'She goes,' Selma said.

Sonora moved to the edge of the path. Looked over her shoulder. Keaton was white, rain running down his cheeks. She was afraid to turn her back, afraid he'd be dead if she moved too far away.

Selma moved the gun. 'Right down there.'

There would have been more blood, Sonora decided, if not for the steady drum of rain. The ground sloped steeply, and she braced herself by hanging onto the thicket of trees. She could see Selma and Keaton, when she turned her head, knew they were watching.

A patch of yellow caught her eye, sunny yellow showing behind a fallen tree. Sonora slid down the slope to look.

It was the feet that bothered her the most, the ripped stockings and torn flesh. She imagined Ashley Daniels, bleeding and afraid, stumbling through the woods to her death.

Her manicure was intact, she had not fought. Her white silk shirt was sodden, showing the outline of the lace demicup bra, pink flesh beneath. Her shirt was liberally stained, as if she'd had a lap full of blood.

She'd been shot once, in the stomach. Sonora looked at the black gaping wound, surprised that Ashley had lived as long and walked as far as she had. There were drag marks through the leaves. Ashley had likely collapsed on the path, losing the shoe, and Selma had dragged her a few feet into the woods – not far – hiding her behind the rotting tree.

And now Selma was marching them right past the body; to where? The river, no doubt.

Sonora went through the motions, touching the cold wet hand, the side of the neck, avoiding the wide open violet eyes, the oddly grumpy look on Ashley Daniels' face, as if she had merely been inconvenienced, rather than in exquisite pain and fear.

Sonora looked back up to Keaton and Selma. She could make a break and run. She knew it and so did Selma. Might even catch Selma – should be cops everywhere by now. But she'd never get Keaton out alive.

Sonora headed up the slope, saw Keaton watching her, a hungry look. She avoided his eyes, grimaced at Selma.

'Now what?'

'The river,' Selma said. She pointed with the gun. 'Let's go.'

Sam would be close, Sonora thought. Crick, and uniforms, and reinforcements. Time was on her side.

'Okay, the river.'

'Wait a minute.'

Sonora and Selma looked at Keaton as if they'd forgotten he was there.

'Did you . . . what did— '

Sonora touched his arm. Selma flinched and moved in closer. Sonora kept her voice low and calm.

'It wasn't her, Keaton. She's down by the river, probably, like Selma says.'

'She's over there,' Selma said. Flatly. A dangerous tone in her voice.

Sonora swallowed, mouth so dry she wanted to stick her

tongue out and catch a drop of rain. Keaton shook his head, eyes taking on a flat glaze that made Sonora reach for him. He twisted sideways, a fast graceful pivot, and grabbed Selma by the throat.

Sonora surged toward them, saw the frown on Selma's face screw into a mask of rage, knew she would be too late. The shot was deafening, and so close Sonora almost felt the impact.

There was a moment of quiet as they stood together, like a trio of close friends, Keaton and Sonora shoulder to shoulder, Selma small and clutching the gun, the ragged fringe of short wet bangs like spikes across her forehead.

Keaton did not fall or groan or even seem to be aware of the crimson blossom spreading across his chest. He kept his grip on Selma's throat.

Sonora felt rather than saw the gun come back up. She shoved Keaton sideways, and he let go of Selma and fell. Sonora landed hard on his chest, waiting for the bullet that she knew would come.

But it didn't. She felt Keaton's blood warm his shirt and hers, felt the swift hard beat of his heart.

'Get *away* from him.'

Sonora turned her head sideways. Selma was still on her feet, legs apart, bottom lip caught beneath little white teeth.

'Out of the way, girlfriend. Bullet go right through you into him, no difference to me.'

'I thought he was different, Selma.'

'You'uns thought wrong, we both did. I need to keep looking, that's all. Now you got about thirty seconds to move.'

Sonora hung tight to Keaton, warm, solid, and wet under her chest. 'No.'

'You'uns don't believe I'll shoot.'

'Yeah, I believe it.'

Selma looked at her. 'So now what?'

'You're under arrest. You have the right to remain silent— '

They said Selma never smiled, and it came and went so quickly Sonora wasn't sure it was ever there. And just like that Selma was gone, running toward the river in the rain.

Sonora moved off Keaton, put a palm flat against the hole in his chest. The bleeding had stopped, the pressure of her chest against his cutting the flow. His face was white, lips purple.

He opened his eyes. 'Why'd you stop me? I could . . . I could have had her.'

'Keaton— '

'Don't touch me.' He jerked suddenly, eyes fierce. 'Did she suffer? My wife?'

'No,' Sonora said.

'You always tell me lies, Sonora.'

She left him, chest trickling blood in the mud and the rain. Later, when the nightmares came, she would dream of him there, chest rising slowly with each painful breath, yards away from Ashley's body.

Sonora ran down the path toward the river, wondering why Selma hadn't shot her when she'd had the chance.

Rain pelted her head and the drenched jacket slapped her thighs. Her breath came hard. She ripped the jacket off as she ran, threw it down on the pathway, ran harder.

Sonora heard the gun go off just as she caught sight of the river, water swirling around Sam and Selma's knees as they struggled for control. Sam fell backward, taking Selma with him, brown droplets spattering Sonora as she ran full tilt into the river.

Selma came up first, small blonde head like a seal. She looked like a very little girl, wet, angry and afraid. Sonora felt the shock of water, warmer than she'd expected, and she wrapped her arms around Selma's shoulders, thinking with surprise how small-boned and fragile she felt.

'Sam!'

He surfaced just as Sonora called his name, still alive, strong, in one piece.

'Thank God,' Sonora muttered.

Selma screamed and Sonora tightened her grip, but Selma bucked sideways and slipped away. Sonora pitched forward after her, missing and going under. She was back up in a second, coughing, rubbing her eyes.

'I got her,' Sam said, and he pulled Selma up out of the river, one hand on her neck, the other a tight fist in her hair.

Chapter Sixty-One

The basketball goal had not been in the budget, but had proven to be a good investment. Sonora threw shot after shot. She was getting good. She played every time she saw Selma in her head. She played a lot.

Sometimes, late at night when she could not sleep, she wondered what would happen if she and Selma were merged into one – wondered which side would dominate, the good or the bad. Did she have enough good in her to balance Selma's bad? Was there a good part of Selma – or could there be? What would a good Selma be like?

Sonora thought of her brother, the hot charred remains of his little apartment in the saloon.

Nothing good in Selma Yorke.

So why hadn't Selma killed her that day in the rain? Killed her and gotten away?

The front door opened and Tim and Heather came out onto the porch. They looked at each other, whispered something, and stood at the edge of the driveway, bundled up in their jackets and gloves.

Sonora wished she could make her mind go blank. She had not slept more than an hour or two a night since she'd brought Selma in. She lay in bed, wide eyed, hour after hour. The only time she felt sleepy was when she was driving. Which was bad timing, any way you looked at it.

'Mommy?' Heather looked at Sonora, eyes serious behind the tiny gold-rimmed glasses. 'Come in now, Mommy. It's cold.'

'I'm playing.' Sonora bounced the ball hard on the concrete.

Tim and Heather looked at each other, exchanged more whispers.

'Mom, want to watch *Witness*?'

'No, thanks.'

'Want some chocolate?'

'You kids go ahead.'

Tim frowned. 'Can we play basketball with you, Mom?'

'Don't you have homework? Algebra, Tim?'

'We did our homework, made up our beds, and cleaned our rooms.'

Sonora stopped and looked at them. Really looked. Doing their homework, making their beds, cleaning their rooms – that caught her attention. Offering her chocolate, her favorite movie. And something like a catch in their voices.

She had been looking at them and not seeing them for too many days in a row. There were times when it had to be like that – real life moms with real life jobs, and intervals where your attention and focus slipped away, and you told the kids to hang in there, let me catch this killer, then we'll get your school clothes, your new shoes, spend one day in the malls, and one at the movies or something fun.

But there were limits. And she realized, looking at them standing side by side, breath fogging the air, what babies they were. And how much she expected of them. Too much, maybe.

High time she got back to looking after them, instead of the other way around.

She should tell them she loved them, should tell them how proud she was of them both, but before the words came, Tim had snatched the ball.

'Mom, you're looking pitiful out here. If you want to shoot, do it like this.'

The ball slid through the net and Heather snatched it up and tossed it into the air. It went wild and rolled in the street. Sonora heard a car engine. Ran to the edge of the driveway.

The car came to a halt, and the driver motioned Sonora ahead. She hurried across the street and the driver waited, motioned her back. Patient of him, she thought, and took a second look.

Keaton. He parked in front of the house and got out of the car.

The children watched from the driveway. They looked annoyed. One moment they'd had her attention, and now it was gone again.

Keep this short, Sonora thought. She bounced the ball on the sidewalk. 'Good to see you up and around.'

'You didn't come and visit me at the hospital,' Keaton said.

He had lost weight, too much weight. His eyes held a hunted look that gave Sonora the panicky feeling that maybe time did not heal all wounds, that scars could run too deep. She wanted to touch him, brush the back of her hand on his freshly shaven cheeks.

Don't touch me, he had said. *You always tell me lies*.

Sonora kept the ball bouncing in a slow steady rhythm. She had called the hospital every day until he was out of danger, but saw no reason to bring it up.

'Let's walk a little,' he said finally.

Sonora handed the basketball to her son. 'Play with Heather, I'll be back in a minute.'

Heather had her solemn look, chin down, and Sonora hesitated, then ran back and hugged her, whispering promises of the dinner they would cook, the fire they would build in the fireplace. It took a promise of Victoria's Secret bubble bath to bring the chin up and the smile out.

Sonora stood up, brushed Heather's hair out of her eyes, saw Keaton still and patient. She noticed a startling touch of grey in the hair at his temples.

He waited till she was beside him before he started walking. 'I missed Ashley's funeral. Did you go?'

'Yes,' Sonora said, trying not to remember.

'I'm glad. So, what's going to happen with her?'

They both knew who he meant.

'She'll plead insanity, and I think it'll fly. Then she'll be put in an institution for the criminally insane and she'll never leave, hopefully. But she won't be executed.'

He put a hand on her arm. 'I wanted to thank you for saving my life, that day. And to tell you that you're a very good cop.'

He bent down and kissed the top of her head. They walked back to the driveway and the children, who were staring wide-eyed and watchful.

Keaton snatched the ball from Tim and dribbled it up to Heather. She shook her head.

'I never have got a basket. I'm too little.'

He lifted her high in the air beneath the net. 'You just need a little extra height.'

Heather threw the ball and it touched the rim, rolling around the edge. Sonora held her breath. The ball fell through the hoop.

'Swisher!' Heather said, waving a hand in the air.

Chapter Sixty-Two

Sam put a cup of coffee on Sonora's desk. She said thanks, but didn't look up, intent on getting her lipstick straight.

'Why don't you call it quits, girl?'

Sonora glanced at Sam. He was glaring at her, rubbing the back of his neck.

'I mean it, Sonora. We got her up one side and down the other. We're putting files to bed every which of way, the case book is a beauty. We got more physical evidence . . . quit looking in the mirror and talk to me.'

'Sam, we've had this conversation.'

'You don't have to be the one talks to her, Sonora.'

'She wants me.'

'Who cares? You still feel like you owe her?'

'I do owe her.'

'Sonora.' He took hold of the mirror, but steadied it instead of snatching it away. 'Look, girl. Look at your eyes. Look at the shadows *underneath* your eyes. Now I talked to Crick, and he said all you got to do is say the word.'

Sonora looked into the mirror, remembering her first week working homicide.

She'd been invited to a drunken pub crawl in honor of one Burton Cortina, who was moving to Fraud & Forgery. He had been kind to her, taking the time to make her feel welcome when she was brand new and shy.

They'd talked amiably and loosely, strangers who'd had too much to drink and the comfortable knowledge that their paths were unlikely to cross in the near future. They had both confessed homicide their highest ambition, and had a beer on it. Sonora had been unable to look at him without pity.

'You think I'm crazy, giving it up, don't you, Slugger?'

Sonora shrugged.

'I know how you feel, probably better than you do yourself.' He had glanced in the mirror behind the bar, then faced her with a dead look in his eyes that she'd seen on other cops, older cops. 'All I can tell you, Slugger, is that one day it gets to be enough.'

That was all he'd said, but the words had stuck, hanging over her head like a threat.

'I'm okay, Sam.'

'Yeah? And how's your ulcer?'

'Gone.'

'Gone? No kidding?'

'No kidding.' Sonora blew on the mirror, fogging her reflection. It was true. Since that day by the river, the anger she'd felt for who knew how long had drained away, giving her a centered, steady feeling. She didn't hate them anymore – not her dead husband, not Chas, not her father. Not Selma. The ulcer hadn't twinged since.

Sonora checked her watch. Almost time. She called home to check on the kids – in the middle of these long sessions with Selma Yorke, she needed to hear the voices of her children.

They were fighting over the last blueberry bagel. Sonora told them to split it – radical thought – and hung up. Checked her watch again. Grabbed her notes.

Gruber gave her a thumbs up when she passed him in the hallway. She peered into the interview room. Selma was already there, sitting complaisantly beside her lawyer, Van Hoose. Van Hoose always managed to keep a poker face, but was often pale and shaky by the end of each session. Sonora saw major counseling in his future before the year was out.

She studied Selma, as she always did, wondering if Dr. Fischer was right, if she'd been reaching out, going through some weird metamorphosis. Wondered about the anguished Selma in the phone calls. Wondered why a woman who could douse someone with gasoline and set them on fire, wouldn't shoot her when she had the chance.

Sonora pushed through the door, startling the lawyer but not Selma, who sat quietly, hands on the table. She had cut her bangs again, which meant things were not going well. Her brown eyes were bloodshot, hands steady. She wore prison denims. She looked small.

'Hello, Selma.' Sonora nodded at the lawyer, who said hello. She put a fresh tape in the machine, sat across from Selma. Tapped a pen on the edge of the table. 'Selma, you want a Coke or something?'

'No.'

Sonora made a note in her interrogation log. It was her habit to keep track of everything – time-in, time-out, every offer of refreshment, cigarettes, bathroom breaks. No rubber hose in Cincinnati.

'Let's talk about your brother today,' Selma said.

Sonora pushed away from the table. 'Let's not. Let's talk about the fire again, where your parents got killed.'

Selma frowned. 'We already talked about that.'

'Did you do it, Selma? Did you set that fire?'

There was a tap on the door. Sonora got up, frowning. Gruber.

'Sorry. Phone call for the counselor, supposed to be urgent.'

Sonora looked over her shoulder at Van Hoose.

'I'll take it. Only be a minute.' He left the room like he was glad to go.

Sonora closed the door behind him. Turned off the tape recorder, looked at Selma. Bad seed? Anything good, anything salvageable? She was having long talks with Molliter about this, and neither one of them was happy.

Sonora sat down and leaned across the table. 'Just you and me, Selma. Did you set that fire?'

'I got something for you.' Selma reached into her pocket, and Sonora felt her heart skip. Selma slid a cassette across the table.

Sonora picked it up, read the label. Whale songs.

Sonora swallowed. 'This what your parents sounded like, the night they died?'

Selma looked at the floor. 'All of 'em sound like that. Stuart did.'

Sonora felt the wash of tight, panicky breathlessness that came whenever she thought of her brother.

'Why didn't you kill me that day in the park?'

Selma looked up. This time there was no question, no mistake. Selma Yorke smiled, lips curving gently in a way that was eerie and sensuous.

And Sonora wondered who had who.

EYESHOT

For my buddy, Jim Lyon
Couldn't ask for a better friend

Acknowledgements

My thanks to Robert Youdelman, P.C., Attorney At Law, who graciously took time out of his demanding schedule to keep me out of trouble.

To Detective Maria Neal, Criminal Investigation Section, who was available for questions and to talk plot, and who counted up body parts and told me what I was missing.

I count myself lucky to work closely with three talented and brilliant people – my agent, Matt Bialer, my HarperCollins editor, Carolyn Marino, and my Hodder & Stoughton editor, George Lucas. It is a rare privilege to tap the instincts of three people whose opinions and creativity I trust.

To artist Steve Sawyer, and entrepreneur Cindy Sawyer, who made themselves available on a moment's notice, to discuss plot and artistic vision.

To the Tennessee State Trooper who kindly did not arrest me while I was parked beside I-75 scouting locations for body parts.

To the students and staff at the University of Cincinnati, who were kind enough to provide maps, directions, and insights.

To Doug Collins, who was good enough to act as my videographer when I did walk-throughs of the murder.

To Sharon Hilborn and Tamra Gormley of the Commonwealth Attorney's office, for questions answered.

To the usual gang of helpers and readers, my kids, Alan, Laurel, and Rachel, who screen to the best of their ability during deadline days up to and including facing down law enforcement, to Bill Swinford, one of my favorite attorneys, for being a friend.

And my thanks to Lindsey Hunter and all my buddies at Silverstone Farm who help me work and train and play with my horses. See you in the next book.

eye-shot: the distance that a person can see; range of vision

World Book Dictionary

Peter Peter, Pumpkin Eater
Had a wife and couldn't keep her
Put her in a pumpkin shell
And there he kept her very well

Children's nursery rhyme

Chapter One

It was one of those moments when Sonora hated police work.

Butch Winchell sat across from her in the interview room, laying the family snapshots out on the table. There was brown-eyed Terry, three years old, Power Rangers sweatshirt barely covering a pouchy tummy. And baby sister Chrissie, struggling sideways in her lap, fine hair a wisp at the top of her head, sister's hand clutched in a tight and tiny grip.

Their mommy was missing.

Sonora liked it that the Winchell kids had normal names. None of the soap-opera specials – Jasmine, Ridge, Taylor or Noelle. She ran a finger along the edge of the table. Outside it was ninety degrees and sunny, but it was cold in the interview room. Everywhere in the city people were going boating, swimming, out to movies.

Homicide detectives never had any fun.

Sonora looked across the table at her partner, Sam Delarosa. If the baby pictures were bothering her, he'd be worse off. Softer hearted.

He smiled at her, gave her his 'come hither' look. He was a big guy, big shoulders, dark-brown hair side-parted and falling in his eyes. He looked young for his age, boyish – though Sonora, who knew him well, noted the careworn signs of worry around his mouth, and at the corners of his eyes. He had the kind of small-town, country-boy, Southern charm that made women want to confide in him, and men automatically include him as one of the boys. There was no doubt that he was the kind of guy who opened doors for women, watched football, and didn't like to shop. His normality was one of the things that attracted Sonora. They'd worked homicide together for five years.

And it was the second 'come hither' look Sonora had gotten out of him this week. She was sure they had put all that stuff way behind them. He must be messing with her mind.

She smiled back, heavy on the eye contact, and he gave her a second glance before his eyes went back to Winchell.

'Her name is Julia, Detective Blair.' Winchell laid one more photo beside the rest. He looked up at Sonora.

Just like her kids, Sonora thought. Quick to pick up on a moment of inattention. She pushed hair out of her eyes. Too long, too curly. She wondered if cutting it would tame it down or pouf it up.

She picked the picture up off the desk.

It was a quickie photograph, Kodak Instamatic, with the sticky glaze of constant handling. She gave it a long look, passed it across the table to Sam.

There was something breathtaking about Julia Winchell.

The hair was magnificent – red-lit brunette, thick and curly, rising from a widow's peak, pulled back from a heart-shaped face. She had a high forehead, a touch of severity about the mouth. The lips were lush, heavy at the bottom, the eyes almond-shaped, deep brown, with well-defined eyebrows. She had narrow shoulders, long slim fingers, delicate porcelain wrists.

She was the kind of woman you would expect to find vacationing in Paris, or exploring the countryside of southern Italy. She would order clothes from J. Peterman, shop at Abercrombie & Fitch.

Hard to believe the woman in the picture could be the wife of this ordinary man who looked petulant, uncertain, and afraid.

Married young, Sonora thought.

Winchell picked up the Styrofoam cup of coffee Sam had brought him and raised it to his lips, but didn't drink.

Bad coffee? Sonora wondered. Nerves?

'Mr. Winchell, would you like a soda or something?' she asked.

He shook his head. He'd be a medium to small, if attractiveness was measured like teeshirts, black hair wet with gel, heavy black rims on the glasses, a round sort of face. Sloping shoulders, paunchy stomach. The kind of extra weight nobody noticed on a man. The kind of extra weight that sent women screaming to the salad bar.

Somebody's brother, somebody's cousin, somebody's killer.

Sonora figured on a high probability that the man sitting across from her had killed his wife, provided she turned up dead. She might just have run away from home. Back when Sonora had been a wife, she'd wanted to run away from home.

But not enough to leave two little children behind, both babies still.

Winchell hunched forward in his chair, shoulders tense. He had hollows of darkness beneath his eyes. 'You can't see it in the picture, but she's also got a tattoo on her ankle.' He pushed the glasses back on his nose. 'It's not cheap looking, okay? She did it graduation night when she was a senior in high school, and her mama wanted to kill her. It was just kids cutting up. She and her friends had been out to a Chinese restaurant to eat, and decided that they should get their birth year symbol tattooed on them somewhere. Hers is the year of the dragon – she was born in sixty-four. None of the others went through with it – can't blame them, if they were born in the year of the rat or the monkey or the pig or something. It's really kind of neat looking, blue and green with red eyes and a long red tongue.'

Sonora leaned forward, memory stirring, cop instinct on edge. 'Did you say left ankle?'

He hadn't said. Sam looked at her.

'I think . . . yeah, it was her left ankle, definitely.'

Both men looked at her expectantly.

Sonora didn't care to elaborate, not with Butch Winchell and those baby pictures staring her in the face. It wasn't the kind of theory you shared early – not if it involved a severed leg found alongside the interstate highway. It was a long shot anyway. The leg had turned up a whole state away. Julia Winchell had disappeared in Cincinnati, Ohio, not where-some-ever, Kentucky. What gave Sonora pause was the way the leg had been taken off.

It was sweaty work, cutting up bodies. Most killers took the hard road, sawing the leg straight off at the thigh, with the usual combination of brute force and ignorance. Working from the joint was a lot easier, same as boning chicken. In the instance Sonora was thinking about, the top of the leg had been severed at the ever so practical hip, but the foot had been taken off over the ankle, well above the joint. Inconsistent, she'd thought, when she'd heard the story. It had bothered her at the time.

A dragon tattooed over the ankle bone might explain it. A killer intelligent and cool-headed enough to consider the practicalities of dismemberment was not likely to leave a tattoo for easy identification.

Sonora sat back in her chair. 'I'm confused, Mr. Winchell. Do you and your wife live in Cincinnati?' From his accent, they'd have to be Southern transplants. Unhappy in Ohio, like other Southern transplants. It would be interesting if they were from Kentucky, home of bourbon, race horses, her partner, Sam, and various and sundry body parts.

'We run a diner in Clinton.'

'Clinton is where?' Sonora asked.

Sam scratched his head. 'Tennessee, isn't it?' His area of the country.

'Yes, sir, right outside of Knoxville. That's where I grew up, Knoxville. I . . . we bought the diner four years ago – it's just a little place in downtown Clinton. But it's a beginning, and for us . . . for me, anyway, it's a dream come true.'

Sonora noticed that Winchell was clenching his fists. She figured the diner was a point of contention in the marriage. Dream fading in the day-to-day grind of reality.

'Julie up and decided a while back she wanted to go to this conference here. In Cincinnati.'

Sonora knew where here was.

'A restaurant conference?' Sam asked.

Winchell looked at his feet. 'Nope. This was one on running a small business – tax advice and everything geared for people whose business is small-scale.' He shrugged. 'Pretty much a waste of time if you ask me.'

'Did she?' Sonora said.

'Did she what?'

'Ask you.'

He grimaced. 'Julie is an independent female, which I admire, usually.' Lip service, Sonora thought. 'I didn't really think we could afford it. Especially not the air fare. Julie said she'd drive and keep expenses down and we could take this off on our income tax.'

Sonora nodded. 'So it was already a sore subject when she left.'

He opened his hands wide. 'It was settled. But then the transmission went out on the Mazda. My opinion was, she ought to call it off. Car repair bill coming in . . .' He took a breath. 'Her point was we'd already made the deposit to the people running the conference and we weren't going to get that back. The air fare on short notice was ridiculous. So she did a car rental – got a weekly deal. That way she wouldn't leave me without a car, and she'd have wheels while she was up there. Here, I mean.'

'Pretty determined to get away,' Sam said mildly.

Winchell's hands hung heavily between his knees. 'She said she needed some time to herself.'

'How far is it?' Sonora asked. 'You say the conference was here, in town. How far from Clinton?'

'It's about a four-hour drive, give or take.'

'Okay,' Sonora said. 'So then what happened?'

'She, um, she didn't come home.'

Sonora nodded, kept her voice gentle. 'That much we figured. It would help if you could go into a little more detail. When was the last time you talked to her?'

'Well see, what happened was kind of odd. I was supposed to pick her up at the car rental place. She was going to be driving down late that Sunday afternoon, after the conference. But she didn't show up and she didn't call. I couldn't get her at the hotel. We'd sort of fixed the time around six – that I would pick her up at the car rental place around six o'clock. And since I didn't hear from her, I just went on out there, see if she'd show up. And she didn't.'

'How long did you wait?' Sam asked.

'About forty-five minutes. I had both the kids with me. All excited because Mommy was coming home. But Mommy didn't come home.' His voice broke and he rubbed his chin hard. He was getting a five o'clock shadow and the stubble of beard rasped against his fingers. 'Nobody at the rental place had heard anything from her. If it had been just me, I'd have waited longer, but the baby was getting tired and Terry was fussy. So I went on home.' He took a breath. 'The minute I get the car in the garage I hear the phone ringing. So I run for it, leave the kids strapped in their car seats. But whoever it is hangs up. Fifteen minutes, and it rings again and it's her. Julie.'

Sam nodded. Winchell bit his lip.

'She was upset, I tell you that from the get go. I could tell she'd been crying.' He closed his eyes and ran his hands through his hair.

Sonora wondered if the gel made his fingers sticky. It had dried, so maybe not.

Winchell opened his eyes. 'She told me that something

had happened. She said she couldn't come home for a while – she had to take care of it.'

'What was *it*?' Sonora asked.

Sam gave her a look. He thought she interrupted too much.

'I don't know,' Winchell said.

Sonora frowned. 'How come you don't know?'

Winchell leaned forward, close to Sonora. 'See, used to be, her first question would have been the kids. Are they okay, you know, the whole worried Mommy bit.' He shook his head. 'She didn't even ask. Not at first.'

'Did you *ask* what the problem was?' Sonora said.

Sam rolled his eyes.

Winchell looked at his hands. 'I don't . . . we didn't get to that.'

'You mean you had a fight,' Sonora said.

'It wasn't a fight.'

'What was it then?'

'I just . . . here she is going on about how she can't come home, and not one word about how I'm making out with the kids, who I've had on my own all this time, with precious little help.'

Sonora exchanged looks with Sam. Shocking – married people having a fight. Next on *Oprah*. She wondered how often Julia Winchell had handled the kids on her own with precious little help. Knew better than to ask.

'She got mad and hung up.'

'And you haven't heard from her since? Nothing at all?' Sam asked.

Winchell shook his head. 'No, and it's not like Julie. She's no grudge-holder. She'd of called me if she could. Now if it was her sister, that'd be something else. But Julie, she gets mad fast, then it blows over. And even if she was mad at me, she'd call just to see about the kids and talk to them. Only thing that's kept me going is I know she's got to be alive. I just don't know where or what's going on.'

Sonora cocked her head to one side. 'How do you know that?'

Butch Winchell smiled at Sonora – a social smile from a man who looked like he needed last rites of the heart. Sonora had seen other men look that way – killers, some of them. She studied his sad eyes, the large white hands (*the better to strangle you with, my dear*). The fingers were artistic and delicate compared with the chunky heaviness of the rest of him.

He scratched his cheek. '*Somebody's* using our credit cards. The limits are all run up.'

Chapter Two

Winchell was not a stupid man. He should not have missed the endless possibilities – none good – of his credit cards maxing out. He just wasn't ready.

Sonora stacked the snapshots, smiled at Winchell in a noncommittal way. Pity would scare him, right about now. It would be better all around if he was thinking straight.

'Just a few more questions, Mr. Winchell. Details to clear. You said Julie had – has – a sister. If you could give us a number, I'd like to give her a call. Also, what about her hotel? Did she check out? Have you been over there?'

Winchell's lips went tight. 'She's staying at that Orchard Suites place down by the river. According to them she hasn't checked out, but she won't answer any calls and the guy as much as told me nobody'd seen her. But he wouldn't let me into her room. She's using a credit card that's just got her name on it, or they might of let me in. They don't seem to care that I'll be footing that bill.'

'Speaking of which, we'll need your credit card numbers, the last statements.' Sonora cleared her throat. 'Also, was your wife hospitalized any time recently? Her latest medical records might help us out.'

Winchell pushed his glasses up on his nose. 'With the babies, she was. I can get that for you.'

Sonora smiled again. 'Sooner the better.' She checked her watch, waved a hand at Sam. 'Detective Delarosa can get this going for you. Maybe get some of the basics faxed. Sam?'

He nodded, gave her a watchful look, turned a gentle smile on Winchell. 'There's a phone we can use out here.'

Not going back to his desk, which butted right up to hers. Good Sam, Sonora thought. He, at least, had picked up on the significance of the hospital records. He always hated asking that question, because sometimes people cried.

Sonora took the picture of Julia Winchell and her two babies and headed for her desk.

She settled into her chair, checked her watch. Two o'clock. Two hours till shift change. The peculiar Friday feel of restless energy and ennui was thick. Sunlight streamed through the windows like a beacon.

Sonora dialed a number she was beginning to know by heart. She listened to it ring. Conversations with Smallwood were getting more and more frequent.

She'd met him months ago, on his day off, when he'd left Caleb County, Kentucky, to tell her about a local murder that dovetailed with one of her own. She'd been going through a bad time, then, and his voice on the other end of the line had gotten more and more welcome.

He fed her the interesting pieces of the bad and the ugly he came across in day-to-day work and gossip – a sort of cop to cop come-on.

'That you, Smallwood?' Sonora pictured him in his deputy's uniform, one foot on the desk.

'*Girl.*' The voice was country Southern, and deep.

'Answer me a question.'

'Yes, I do accept your kind invitation to dinner. Or is that supper, in Cincinnati-speak?'

'Pay attention, Smallwood. You remember that severed leg you were telling me about?'

'Always business with you, isn't it? Yeah, I remember.'

'Where exactly was that found?'

'Down I-75 south, between London and Corbin.' His voice got sharper, more focused. 'You got something?'

'I don't know. Hope not, actually.' She spread the pictures

of Julia Winchell's little girls across the desk. 'You ever hear any details on the victim?'

'Nope, but it's not like I would. I know somebody down there, though – she's going with my cousin.'

'Nice to know you fit the typical Southern stereotypes.'

'Let me put you on hold real quick, and I can find something out.'

'Is this a Cincinnati quick, or a long Southern minute?'

'Knit something, why don't you?'

The line clicked, and Sonora balanced the phone on her shoulder, turned in her chair, saw Gruber doing the same.

'We've got to stop meeting like this,' Gruber said.

On hold and stirring up trouble, Sonora thought. He was from New Jersey, dark and swarthy – sad brown eyes. And an air of challenge women found interesting. He'd picked up weight, all of a sudden, but he still looked good.

'Is this the secretary? Can I speak to a real cop?' Smallwood, back in her ear. 'You there, Sonora?'

'Where else would I be?'

'I could think of a couple of places. Anyhow. Results aren't back from the state lab, but unofficially the victim is female, between the ages of twenty-five and thirty-eight, leg severed over the ankle, but taken off at the hip joint.'

'Blood type?'

'A positive.'

'Any scars, tattoos?'

'Not that I know of.'

Sonora made a note.

'You going to tell me what you got?' Smallwood asked.

'Missing person, woman from Clinton, Tennessee, disappeared up here at some kind of seminar.'

'I must be missing something. Why would her leg be showing up in Kentucky? This be because she's from Clinton? Think maybe this leg just kind of migrated on home?'

'Pay attention, Smallwood, and listen to how a real cop

thinks. This woman has a tattoo, a dragon, right over the left ankle bone. I just thought it was funny. Killer took off the leg at the hip joint, which makes perfect sense, though none of them ever do it, do they? Then he goes and sweats the foot off over the ankle, which makes no sense at all unless there's a tattoo he's trying to hide.'

'You say this vic is from Clinton?'

'Yeah.'

''Cause London's on the way there.'

'Is it?' Her next stop was going to be a map.

'South down I-75. Maybe not such a long shot after all. You getting cop twitches on this, Sonora?'

'We call it instinct, Smallwood.'

'Maybe you want to come on down then.'

'Maybe.' Sonora looked up, saw Sam and Winchell headed her way. 'I'll get back to you, Smallwood, and thanks for the help.' Sonora hung up, smiled at Winchell, who trailed Sam like a baby duck following his mama. Cop imprinting.

She picked up a high-school transfer paper she needed to fill out for her son, and waved it in the air. 'Just for the record, Mr. Winchell, can you tell me your wife's blood type?'

His eyes went flat. 'A positive.'

Sonora turned the pictures on her desk face down, so she didn't have to look at Julia Winchell's babies.

Chapter Three

The Orchard Suites Hotel was on the Ohio River in Covington, right across the bridge from Cincinnati. Sam eased the Taurus up and down the parking lot.

'No sign of the rental on this end,' he said.

'What color was it again?'

Sam looked at her. 'You mean you've been looking up and down your side and you don't—'

'Nineteen ninety-five Ford Escort, red. Just double checking.'

'Tell me about that leg again. You say it had a tattoo?'

'No, Sam, I said the foot was cut off well above the ankle—'

'That would be the shin.'

'Thank you, *doctor*. Think about it, Sam. Hip taken off at the joint, which makes the most sense.'

'Except nobody ever does it that way.'

'But this guy *did*. So why's he take the foot off *over* the ankle joint?'

'Cut there first, saw how much trouble it was, got smarter on the next cut and did it at the joint.'

Sonora frowned. Sometimes she didn't like it when Sam made perfect sense. 'Maybe. Or maybe he was cutting it off over a tattoo. This victim was a female between the ages of twenty-five and thirty-eight and the blood type matches Julia Winchell's.'

'Face it, Sonora, most victims of that kind of crime are young females. And half of America has A-positive blood.'

Sam pulled the car into the circle drive in front of the lobby. 'I wonder what Julia Winchell was upset about.'

'Probably going home.'

'She was pretty damn set on getting up here. You think she was fooling around on him?'

'You saw the picture.'

'You got to feel for this guy, Winchell,' Sam said.

Sonora slammed the car door. 'Not if he did it, I don't.'

It was cool in the hotel – not quite chilly, but a relief from the heat and humidity rising in gasoline-tainted waves from the asphalt parking lot. The lobby was wide and noisy, full of fountains and people in sports shirts and sandals. A tired-looking woman in lime-green shorts herded a knot of pre-teen girls out the front door. Two of the girls turned and looked at Sam. There were giggles.

'I think I'm the butt of a joke,' Sam said.

'A familiar sensation I'm sure.'

'You always get bitchy in the heat.'

The desk clerk was tall and had bushy eyebrows, and a nervous habit of clearing his throat. He handed Sam a card key.

'There was a man here, earlier, asking about her. He said he was her husband.'

'Black hair, glasses, name of Butch?' Sam asked. The clerk nodded. 'That's the husband.'

'We have to be very careful about who we—'

Sonora waved a hand. 'No problem, I'm glad you brought it up. You definitely didn't let him in?'

'Definitely.'

A good thing, Sonora thought. Winchell was never officially in the room. If they got forensic proof he was, that would nail him. 'She got any messages?' Sonora asked.

'I could look,' the man said.

Sonora looked at the man's name tag. Van Hoose. 'So look already.'

He ducked to the other side of the counter, and Sam gave Sonora his rudeness-disapproval frown.

'Seven.' Van Hoose handed Sonora a computer printout. 'This is a list of the calls she made. And here are the messages, never picked up.'

Sonora looked it over, followed Sam as he said thanks and moved away from the desk. One of the numbers seemed familiar.

Sonora looked up at Sam. 'We got your public library. A bunch from Winchell. Return a call to what looks to be another room in the hotel.' Sonora went back to the desk clerk. 'That what this is? One of the other rooms?'

He nodded.

'Look that up, why don't you, and let me know who was staying in that room at the time the call was made.'

Van Hoose hesitated. But they were the police after all. He went to his computer.

Sam drummed his fingers on the counter. Sonora laid her hand over his to make him stop.

'The call came from a Mr. Jeffrey Barber in room three twenty-seven.'

'Checked out when?'

'July sixteenth, on a Sunday.' He handed Sonora a slip of paper. 'This is the name, address, phone number and plate number he filled out for registration.'

Sonora smiled. 'We may have to hire you, Van Hoose.'

'What's your procedure when a guest disappears?' Sam asked.

Van Hoose shifted his weight to his left foot. A bone popped in his hip. 'We check the credit, and if the card's good, we keep the room a while.'

'How long?' Sonora asked.

'Honestly? It's a management call. Depends on the guest's credit and how bad we need the room.'

'Okay.' Sam patted the desk. 'Thanks.'

Sonora followed him through the lobby to the elevators. Punched four.

'They got free breakfast with the room here,' Sam said.

'Very important,' Sonora agreed, closing her eyes. She leaned against the back wall of the elevator, which stopped at the second floor to let in two couples, freshly bathed, perfumed, panty hose and heels.

Sonora wondered what Smallwood was doing tonight. Probably not working.

The elevator stopped. Sonora got the rat-in-a-maze feeling she got in hotel corridors.

She gave Sam a look out of the corner of one eye. 'You seem to know your way around this place.'

'This is where I bring my women. They like that river view and I like the breakfast.'

Julia Winchell's room had that hotel air of maid service around clutter. It opened onto a sitting room: TV, desk, table, and chairs. Hunter-green couch. There was a bar with a coffee pot and small refrigerator. The room was freshly dusted and vacuumed, pillows plumped. Stacks of paper, books, and a small, open briefcase crowded the top of the desk.

Sonora gave the couch a second, wistful look. Her dog Clampett had chewed up the cushion on the one in her living room, and it left a trail of stuffing every time someone sat down.

She peeped into the bedroom. The bed was made, and a teddy had been neatly folded on the ridge of pillows that stretched across the king-size mattress.

Sonora picked it up, smelled the wave of sweet flowery scent, fingered the soft black silk, admired the spaghetti straps that criss-crossed along the back.

She heard Sam whistle as he opened and closed the tiny refrigerator behind the bar.

'Old pizza,' he shouted.

'Save me a piece.'

'What?'

'Look in the bathroom, Sam. Count the toothbrushes.'

His steps were heavy in the hallway. Sonora knew he could walk lightly if he wanted to. She'd heard him do it once or twice.

He put his head in the bedroom doorway. 'Two. Both dry as a bone.'

Sonora waved the nightgown. 'I guess she wasn't just here for the river front view.'

'Poor son of a bitch.'

'I assume you mean the husband. Who now has a very good motive.'

'Keeps us in business.'

Sonora headed for the dresser drawers, wondering if Julia Winchell was the kind of hotel guest who unpacked.

She was.

Sonora found a silk nightie, slate blue, Victoria's Secret price tag hanging from the side seam. She had one like it at home in her closet, hooked over her lingerie bag. Julia had paid full price for hers; Sonora had waited for a sale.

Which might mean a special occasion, as far as Julia Winchell was concerned.

She had a tendency toward white or black, tailored shirts and khaki pants, longish skirts, straight-cut, size eight. She shopped at The Limited, spent a lot of money on shoes that were well worn, and size seven and a half.

A full assortment of makeup cluttered the bathroom counter – neat but not obsessive. Julia Winchell had brought her own makeup mirror. Bubble bath from home.

Sonora took a quick mental tally. Mascara, eyeliner, blush, two shades of lipstick. All partially used, nothing new except one of the lipsticks. Sonora opened the older tube, rolled it out. Rum Raisin Bronzer.

There were theories that you could read a woman's character by the shape of her favorite lipstick. Sonora had seen an article on it once in the *Inquirer*.

She looked back into the bedroom at the black silk teddy, the crisply ironed white shirt, hanging on the back of the bathroom door. There was a quietness in the room, already a layer of dust on the worn floral suitcase. Julia Winchell wasn't coming back.

'Sonora?'

It was the way Sam said her name that got her attention – a particular tone of voice. Sonora felt a familiar tingly feeling in the base of her spine, the same feeling she'd gotten when Winchell mentioned Julia's tattoo.

She put the tube of lipstick back on the bathroom counter. 'What, Sam?'

He had his back to her, a sheaf of paper in his left hand.

The phone rang.

Sonora raised an eyebrow at Sam. He nodded, and she picked up the desk extension. There were several phone numbers jotted down on an Embassy Suite scratch pad, one with a 606 area code. Julia Winchell was from Tennessee, which was 423 – as Sonora knew from calling Smallwood. She was pretty sure that 606 was Kentucky. The leg had shown up in Kentucky.

'Hello?' Sonora pitched her voice low. At a guess, she'd say Julia Winchell was an alto.

Silence.

'Hello?' Sonora said again. She heard a click, looked at Sam. 'Hung up.'

'Sit down, Sonora. You should look at this.'

'What is it?'

'I think I know why Julia Winchell decided not to go home, and it isn't what you think.'

'What is it?'

Sam had Julia Winchell's open briefcase on the couch. He moved it to the floor, picked up a sheaf of papers that looked like handwritten notes and a newspaper clipping with ragged edges.

She settled on the couch. Sam handed her a folded newspaper clipping. 'Let's start with this. Recognize the picture?' He sat on the arm of the couch, knee touching hers. He tapped the newspaper. 'Look at the date.'

Sonora got her mind off the knee and looked at the paper. It was a Saturday edition of the *Cincinnati Post*, folded to the Metro section, dated July fifteenth, the day before Julia Winchell had been supposed to drive home to Clinton. She raised an eyebrow as she read the caption.

District Attorney Gage Caplan put closing arguments before the jury today in the trial of ex-Bengal football pro Jim Drury, accused of running down Xavier University co-ed Vicky Mardigan. Drury, a popular hometown boy made good and local celebrity, attended Moelier Catholic High School, a school well known for nurturing football players. He has done spot coverage for local television stations during the football season for the last nine years. Mr. Drury played for the Bengals from 1979 to 1986.

Sonora looked up at Sam. 'Caplan's going for vehicular homicide.'

Sam grimaced. Vicky Mardigan had been dragged thirty-eight feet down Montgomery Avenue, and left to die in front of the White Castle in Norwood. She was breathing when the 911 team got to her, but hadn't survived the night.

'You think Caplan has a prayer of nailing him?' Sonora asked.

Sam shrugged. 'Drury says she walked out in front of him. How's Caplan going to prove otherwise? His word against a dead girl's.'

'Sam, he dragged her half a mile down the road.'

'He says his foot slipped when he tried to hit the brake. And there were no alcohol or drugs in the guy's blood – that'll work against Caplan.'

'You've heard the rumors.'

Sam nodded. Every cop had. Drury was a known maniac on the road. Short-fused, he took his anger out behind the wheel. He'd been pulled over time and again by uniforms, but he was Drury, for heaven's sake. He usually signed an autograph and went on his way.

'Yeah, Sonora, but you can't take rumors to court. I've worked with Caplan a couple of times – no question he's good. Most of 'em, you hand them the case file, they look it over fifteen minutes before they go into the courtroom, if you're lucky. Caplan does his advance work, and he charms the shit out of the jury.'

'Gee, Sam, thanks for the visual.' Sonora's foot itched. She rubbed her shoe against the carpet, wondering if she should take it off and go for total ecstasy.

Sam turned sideways, so he could look at her. 'Julia Winchell left a lot of little notes behind in that briefcase, Sonora. She saw a murder. Or thinks she did.'

Sonora gave Sam a lopsided smile. 'By chance she mention the killer's name?'

Sam grimaced and Sonora thought he looked sad. He tapped the news clipping in Sonora's hand. The one with Gage Caplan, ace District Attorney. 'As a matter of fact, she did.'

Sonora tilted her head to one side. 'Somebody he's putting away?'

'No, Sonora. Him.'

Chapter Four

Sonora looked at Sam. Looked back at the picture in the clipping. 'Did I understand you? You're telling me Julia Winchell saw a murder—'

'I'm saying she thinks she did.'

'And the killer was Gage Caplan? *This* Gage Caplan?' Sonora waved the clipping. 'Champion of the underdog, defender of law and order, friend to cops, kids, yada yada yada?'

'How many times do I have to say yes?'

'Until I get you to say no. *Who*'s he supposed to have killed?'

'His wife.'

'His wife? That establishes a motive, I guess.'

'Seriously, Sonora—'

'Seriously, Sam, his wife is alive and well. They had a picture in last week. Caplan the family man. Wife and little kiddy.'

'*First* wife, Sonora. This all happened eight years ago.'

'So why didn't she bring it up eight years ago?'

'She did. Nobody believed her. And she only saw the guy – she didn't know his name. Till she picked up the newspaper two weeks ago, and there he is.'

'Give me details, Sam.'

'I don't have details.' He stood up, pointed to the sheaf of papers on the desk. 'This is all I got. Notes. Stuff she jotted down.'

'It's thin. Except . . .'

'Except what?'

'This list of calls she made. I thought one of those numbers was familiar. She was calling the DA's office.'

'Look, Sonora, I'm not saying it's true. Calling the DA's office proves not a thing, except she may have had a screw loose.'

'Her husband doesn't describe her that way.'

'He maybe is the one who killed her.'

'If she's dead.'

'There is that.'

Sonora smoothed the clipping out on her knee. Frowned at the headline. CAPLAN CLOSES IN. The picture had been taken in the courtroom, side-angle view, Caplan talking to the jury. He was a big man in a nice suit – not too nice, you'd never picture this guy wearing a pinkie ring. He was attractive – carrying a lot of extra weight, the way ex-athletes often do, but it sat well on him. His hair was thick and full, razor cut.

A District Attorney with definite jury appeal. And popular in the ranks.

Sonora skimmed the article.

The defense attorney was Judith Kelso, another hometown girl, which was a smart move on Drury's part. She was a short, squat blonde, and she was moving hard and heavy. Much had been made of Drury's squeaky-clean blood test, his all-American hard-jawed good looks, his community service with the Shriners, his struggle to be a good father to his kids, despite the divorce. This was a golden boy, who deserved the benefit of the doubt.

Vicky Mardigan, a nineteen-year-old from Union, was not pretty. In her pictures she looked chunky and small and she had a bad complexion. The photos from the accident scene were hard to take. The jury had needed a recess.

Women's rights groups had picked up the case, for reasons that were not clear to anyone. They were holding vigils downtown, trying to take back the night. Sonora wasn't sure they'd ever had it.

In the bullpen, Drury was getting three-to-one odds in a new twist on the usual football betting pool. Caplan was the only reason Drury's odds weren't better.

Business as usual.

Sonora laid the newspaper clipping gently on the coffee table. 'Make a prediction, Sam. Is Caplan going to convict?'

'If anybody could, he'd be it.'

'See, that's the problem, Sam. I agree with you. Almost every cop in the city agrees with you, including, I might add, our chief of police.'

'We could let it go,' Sam said.

'We got records of phone calls back and forth between the DA's office and this hotel room. Phone calls both ways.'

'And she's missing.'

'Maybe she'll come back,' Sonora said flatly. She looked up, caught both her own and Sam's reflection in a mirror that hung over the desk.

Two unhappy cops.

'She ain't coming back,' Sam said.

Chapter Five

The shift had changed over and everyone else had gone off duty except Molliter, who was on nights. Molliter was a tall, rangy redhead with a sour look. Known to be religious. He was at his desk, eating pineapple rings from a square Tupperware container.

Sonora shuddered. Settled at her desk. 'My phone light's not blinking.'

'No messages? Where are your kids?' Sam asked.

'Heather's at some skating thing. Tim's at the mall hanging out and annoying the security guards.'

'How'd they get to these places?'

'A combination of their grandmother, one parent with a van, and a friend's big brother who drives. Wait till your Annie gets older.' Sonora watched him out of the corner of her eye. Last year, it would not have been a safe comment. 'How's she doing?'

'Two Bs, the rest Cs on the last report card. She's behind but she's catching up.'

Sonora opened her bottle of tea. It was nice to ask after Annie and get something other than a medical report. This time last year she'd been in the hospital, enduring blood work and testing in an ongoing battle against leukemia.

Sonora peeled the yellow-and-white tissue paper from her sub sandwich. 'Okay, Sam, you take this Barber guy and I'll take Julia's sister.'

'I'll take the sister.'

'No, I will.' Sonora saw no telltale smear of tomato sauce

on the paper. She opened the bread of her sandwich. 'Gross, what is this?'

'Crab and seafood salad. You got mine.'

They switched sandwiches.

'You got a nice phone voice, Sonora – Barber will talk to you.'

'You just want the sister because you hope she looks like Julia.'

'What is this?' Sam asked.

'It's Snapple, Sam. Mango Madness. I thought you'd like it.'

'Real cops don't drink Snapple.'

'Give it here then.'

He pulled the bottle out of her reach.

Sonora dialed the number Butch Winchell had given her, got a busy signal, and put the phone on redial. She chewed meatball and jalapeno pepper and was halfway into the sub when the phone rang once, and was answered immediately.

Sonora swallowed hard. 'My name is Blair, Detective Blair, and I'm trying to reach a Liza Harden?' She grabbed a pen with greasy fingers, heard Sam snicker.

The voice was wary. 'I'm Liza Harden. I'm sorry, who did you say you were?'

'Detective Blair, with the Cincinnati Police Department. A Mr. Butch Winchell has reported his wife, Julia, missing, and he gave us your number and said—'

'Oh, yeah, I'm her sister.'

Sonora flipped open a notepad. 'Do you have a few moments to talk with me, Ms. Harden?'

'*Of course.*'

'Have you seen or talked to your sister any time recently?'

'I talked to her . . . um, a few days ago. Sunday morning, the seventeenth.

'Sixteenth,' Sonora said.

'Whatever, I talked to her that Saturday night too.'

'When she was in Cincinnati?'

'Yeah. Really, I talked to her every night she was there.'

Phone lines humming, sister-to-sister. 'Do the two of you usually talk every day?'

'Um, no, only when . . .'

'Yes?'

Harden cleared her throat. 'Just when there's stuff going on. When we have things to talk about.'

'What was going on?' Sonora asked. Harden did not answer. 'Ms. Harden, have you heard from your sister at all since Sunday morning of the seventeenth?'

Harden's voice softened. 'No. I haven't.'

'Don't you think that's odd?'

'Yes. I didn't know what was going on. Butch called me and he said he was headed your way. He didn't find her?'

'No ma'am, he didn't. And you're sure she hasn't been in touch?'

'Absolutely.'

The woman sounded definite. Truthful.

'Ms. Harden, I know you don't want to betray any confidences here, but we're concerned about the whereabouts of your sister. Do you think it's possible she might have left her family, um, willingly?'

Harden's voice went flat. 'No, I don't.'

'No doubt?'

'You know about the affair, don't you?'

Sonora thought about it. 'Can you confirm that there was an affair, and give me the man's name?'

'Yes, there was an affair, and no, I don't know his name. But she didn't run off with him, Detective. The affair was not going well and he was the last thing on her mind.'

'What was on her mind, do you know?'

Harden took a breath. 'It sounds . . . dramatic. But my sister saw a picture in the paper. A picture of a man she thinks killed somebody eight years ago. She was upset about it, and she was going to the police.'

'I can double check, but we have no record of her filing—'

'I talked her out of it. Of going to the police. I thought she would just make an ass out of herself. She decided she'd look into things herself, don't ask me how. I was hoping she'd give up on it and come home. It seemed . . . pointless.'

'She didn't give you any idea what she intended to do to check things out?'

'No, but we got interrupted.' Harden's voice took on a rough edge. 'That whoever it was she was seeing was at her door, upset about something, God knows what. He was very high maintenance, that's one thing she did tell me, and driving her up the wall. She said she'd call me later, but she never did.'

'You must have been worried.'

'Very. But I wasn't quite sure who to tell.'

'What do you know about this murder she thinks she saw?'

'No "thinks" about it, Detective, Julia isn't a nut. She told me about it, but it's been years.' Harden paused. 'I know it happened when she was on campus. She went to the University of Cincinnati, did you know that?'

'No,' Sonora said.

'Look, I've got a date and he should be here any time, and I've got ten minutes to put on makeup and get these electric rollers out of my hair. Can I think about this and call you back?'

Sonora gave her the number and hung up. Ten minutes was going to be a hell of a rush. She looked over at Sam. 'How'd you do with Barber?'

'He's a photographer. He's not home. It's Friday night and nobody's available.'

'Let's get out of here.'

Chapter Six

Sonora was dawdling in the parking lot, not sure she was ready to leave Sam, not sure she was ready to launch into the Mom thing. She got into the Blazer, put the key in the ignition so she could roll the window down and talk.

'I want this Chevy,' Sam said.

'Tim wants me to keep the Nissan so he can drive it when he gets his license. You don't want to buy that one, do you? I'll give you a deal.'

'I know it too well.' He slapped the top of the Blazer. 'You ever want to sell this, you let me know.'

They looked at each other. The sun had gone down but it was still hot. Sam had sweat on his upper lip.

'What you going to do tonight?' he asked.

'Go home. Clean house. Pay bills.' For some reason, she had been going to say call her brother. Maybe because it was his car she was driving. He had left her everything in his will.

'What?' Sam said.

'Don't ask me why, but I was going to say call Stuart.'

Sam squeezed her shoulder. 'I wish I could tell you these things go away, Sonora. I think you just learn to live with it.'

She was. Learning to live with it. One brother, murdered in hot flame and agony, because he was related to a homicide cop after a serial killer.

Someone honked a horn, and Sam looked over his shoulder and waved. A regulation-blue Taurus unmarked cop car pulled close alongside the Chevy, loose gravel crunching beneath the tires.

Gruber and Sanders. Sonora gave Sam a look. If there was ever a mismatched pair of cops . . .

Gruber was a hard-ass guy from New Jersey, with an attitude to match his experience. Sanders was the little girl next door who wanted to grow up to be a mommy and a schoolteacher.

'You guys forget the way home?' Sonora asked.

Gruber rubbed a hand across his face. 'Home? Where's that?'

Sanders stuck her head out the window. She had straight brown hair that hung to her shoulders. 'Another clown down today.'

Sam nodded. 'We heard. Lion's Club Fair, same thing?'

Gruber shifted the car into park. 'Yeah. Bobo's in the dunking booth throwing out insults to the crowd, waiting for somebody to bean him with a ball. Instead, some guy cuts him in half with a thirty-ought-six, bolt-action rifle.'

Sonora rested an arm on the open window of her Chevy. 'Doesn't anybody see this guy coming?'

Gruber snorted. 'Hell, yeah, lots of people. You going to argue with a guy with a deer rifle and an attitude?'

Sanders shook her head. 'Those poor clowns, sitting on that perch in the booth. There's no place they can go.'

'Except under,' Gruber said. 'They got Bobo clowns quitting in droves.' He held up a bag of doughnuts, stuck them through the window over Sanders' head. 'Help yourselves, guys, courtesy of my partner here.' He saluted Sanders, who grimaced at the doughnuts.

'We're trying to set up a stakeout,' she said. 'Catch this guy coming.' Sonora was looking into the bag, deciding between caramel iced and chocolate sprinkles. Sam took cinnamon cake. 'I'm going to wear a clown suit and sit in the booth and Gruber's going to collar this sucker, you see if we don't.'

Gruber turned and looked at Sanders. White powdered sugar flaked the beard stubble on his strong handsome chin. 'Who says *you*'re doing the decoy? You got dimples. Cops with dimples can't be decoys.'

'It's a regulation, I think.' Sam licked cinnamon off his fingers.

Sanders folded her arms. 'I already talked to Crick. He said whosoever shall fit into the clown suit with vest underneath shall therefore be the clown decoy.' Sanders smiled at Gruber. 'We already got the suit; I've tried it on, and you'll never fit.'

'Wha— is that the reason behind all the sub sandwiches and pizzas and candy bars you been bringing me?' Sanders smiled gently, and nodded. 'I thought you *liked* me. I bet I've put on fifteen pounds in the last three weeks.'

'Maybe more,' Sanders said.

Gruber stuck a finger in his waistband. 'God bless. Now what am I going to do?'

Sonora took the bag of doughnuts off his hands. 'Do what women do.'

'Which is?'

'Induce vomiting.'

Chapter Seven

Sonora drove with the windows down. Stuart had loved country music all his life, and for some reason, lately, she found herself listening to his tapes. She stopped at a red light, turned the volume down.

She had been a die-hard rock fan all her life and did not want to be caught listening to country.

It was a long drive home, all the way into Blue Ash. She got to the house after dark, which at least meant she did not have to notice how much the lawn needed mowing.

She headed up the stairs from the garage, saw, with no surprise, that her kids were on the floor in front of the television set. Clampett leaped off the couch, trailing clumps of yellow foam stuffing, tail wagging and thumping the wall. He stepped on Sonora's foot and jumped for the bag of doughnuts.

'Hi, kids.'

Tim looked up. He was on his back, one leg bent, head pillowed by the only couch cushion free of dog bites. His hair was black, close cropped, which gave him a tough look he cultivated. His jeans were oversized and bagging. Sonora always wanted to tell him to pull them up.

'What's in the bag, Mom?'

Heather got up. 'Doughnuts, stupid.' She pushed her glasses back on her nose. Her hair, dark and fine, streamed loose from a braid. 'Can we have some?'

'If you can get to them before Clampett does.'

'Mom,' Tim said. 'Can you wait a while before you go

into the kitchen? Me and Heather are going to clean that up later on.'

Sonora overslept the next morning. She drove fast, dropped Tim off at a friend's, and Heather at her grandmother's. Homicide had no respect for weekends.

She headed for the city, wondering how she could justify being so late. She decided to stop and talk to Caplan on the way in, go through the motions, meet Sam and regroup. No one would know how long she had talked to him, or waited around until he could talk. She could go to the office like a worker bee, instead of slinking in, hanging her head.

It was a plan.

She didn't know where Caplan lived, but it would be a good bet to try his office. There was a chance he'd be working. Even if he'd given his final arguments, he had to prepare for the sentencing segment, in case he won. The Drury thing was probably muscling in on his weekends.

There were cars in the parking lot, which Sonora found encouraging.

She went through a door into a hallway, heard laughter, a young male shouting, 'Yeah, right,' then a female voice, also young, that said, 'You sure you don't want me to stay?'

Sonora got the feeling, as she rounded the corner, that the woman would have liked to stay. A male voice, rich with the medium depth of a good baritone, said, 'Hell no, you kids get home and enjoy what's left of your weekend. I'll see you first thing Monday morning. Early, the both of you.'

The kids, Sonora saw, were a man and woman anywhere from twenty-two to twenty-five, wearing jeans and khakis, Saturday casuals. They had the sheen of up-and-coming youngsters who had sufficient pocket money and fun on what weekends they took from the office, and the pale complexion of kids who worked long hours.

Sonora immediately recognized the man at the door who

was waving them off. He wore his shirtsleeves rolled up and his strong forearms were criss-crossed with glints of gold-brown hair. His body type might have been called fat in a man more unattractive, but not this one. His clothes fit him well, and he wore them with the air of comfort a man gets when he is happy with who he is and where he is going. His hair was dark tobacco-brown, the waves well cut and under control, and he had the big shoulders and muscular build of a man who is good at physical things.

He smiled at Sonora, a one-sided smile, and she noticed that his eyes were very blue. He folded his arms, cocked his head to one side.

'You have the world-weary air of a cop.'

The 'kids' in the hallway gave Sonora a long look.

'You're Caplan?' she said. Just making sure.

'We haven't met.'

His handshake was firm, and he covered her one hand with both of his and gave her a speculative look, the kind a man gives a woman. Sonora had not expected him to be quite so taking in person. Like all the best DAs he had a certain presence that would be a plus in the courtroom, or anywhere else, and she liked the steady way he returned her look, and the intelligence she read in his eyes.

She was glad she had worn the silky white shirt. 'Specialist Sonora Blair. Homicide.'

He grinned. '*Really*. Surprised we haven't run across each other till now. You brought down that nutcase last year, Yorke, wasn't it? Serial killer? Liked to play with matches?'

'Selma Yorke,' Sonora said. 'Liked to play with matches' was one way to describe a woman who handcuffed men to the steering wheels of their cars, doused them with gasoline, and set them ablaze.

He looked over Sonora's shoulder at the two in the hallway, made shooing motions. 'Get along and get rested up. I'll be working your butts on Monday.'

They obeyed immediately, footsteps echoing.

Caplan waved an arm, cop-friendly. 'Come on in, and excuse the mess. Trying to nail myself a vehicular homicide, so we're working late nights and weekends.'

'I appreciate your time. Your name is legend you know.' Sonora caught the smile, boyish and on the edge of shy, as she followed him through the doorway.

It was a busy room, too many desks in too small a space, and it had the familiar tired smell of old coffee and cold pizza that Sonora recognized from long nights in the bullpen. The trash cans were full, some of them overflowing. One desk still had a light on and a typewriter uncovered and was snugged in an alcove right outside of the open office Caplan led her into.

His desk was as close to immaculate as a desk could be after weeks of intense work. A brass lamp cast a pool of light over the flat black surface, set in heavy, well-polished mahogany. An open briefcase housed an Apple PowerBook, taking up the slick and dusted right corner. His computer was set to the left on an arm of mahogany, and the screen was up – color monitor.

Not government issue, Sonora thought, looking at the bookshelves, the credenza, the flowered love seat and oriental carpet. Looked like something you would find in a well-heeled law office, where they handled things like bankruptcies and corporate taxes.

Brought a few goodies from home.

A double-frame holder sat on a book shelf, off the desk, non-traditional. Caplan couldn't see it but everyone else could. On one side was the picture of a little girl, six or seven, maybe a bit younger than Heather. The child was Amer-Asian, hair jet-black and shoulder-length, eyes slanted and cornflower-blue. Her skin had a fragile porcelain look, and she wore a red velvet dress with a sash so big that either end of the bow peeked out from both sides of her tiny waist.

Her smile was wide but unconvincing, and she looked tense. Her eyes were sad.

The companion picture was a contrast of informality. The woman wore wide khaki shorts that stopped at her knees, chunky waist cinched with a drawstring belt. Her sleeveless blue denim shirt looked worn but comfortable. She had chin-length, thin, dark-blonde hair, an odd sort of clown nose, and a figure that an unkind person might dismiss as dumpy.

She looked shy, as if she knew that she was unphotogenic, and that the camera would not be kind.

'My family,' Caplan said.

Sonora nodded, muttered 'lovely' under her breath. The woman could not be the biological mother of the little girl, but those big blue eyes looked like Caplan issue.

Sonora took the newspaper clipping from her briefcase, and handed it across the desk. 'Good picture.'

Caplan did a double take when he recognized himself, then leaned back in his chair. 'My wife went out and bought a dozen newspapers when this came out. Sent them to all her relatives. She grew up on a farm, so I guess she figures that when the barn cats don't scare the mice, these will.'

Sonora gave him a sideways smile. 'Don't add that one to your collection, it may be evidence.'

Caplan scooted his chair in close to the desk, smile fading. 'What do you mean, evidence?'

The relaxed feel of the room went away. Caplan had a wary look that put Sonora on guard.

'I've got a woman who's come up missing. Julia Winchell. She had this clipping in her hotel room.'

He shook his head, a look of polite perplexity wrinkling the brow. Sonora was watching and he knew it. It made them both nervous.

'Julia Winchell? Sorry, I don't know her.'

Sonora nodded. He said the name as if it meant nothing. She studied him, thinking that probably it did.

Caplan rocked from side to side in his chair. 'It's odd, though. I mean, whoever she is, she clearly cut this out with a purpose. You think she has some connection to the case?'

Sonora waved a hand. 'Anything's possible. We're just in the initial stages. She's not from around here.' Caplan leaned back and waited. He wasn't going to ask. 'She's from Tennessee,' Sonora said. 'In town for some sort of small business convention.'

'Married?' Caplan asked, voice dry.

'Married. Two little kids.'

He was nodding. 'You know, it's possible . . .'

Sonora waited. Let him say it.

He waved a hand. 'Sometimes the family thing is overwhelming. Wife gets away from the diapers and the house a couple days, gets swept off her feet. She'll probably call in a week or two when the novelty wears off.' Caplan scratched his chin. 'I know I sound a little hard. It's not something I'd say, except to someone like you, who knows the business.'

'We think it's possible she witnessed a murder.' Sonora smiled. Bland.

'No kidding? She file a police report?'

Sonora shook her head. 'It was something that happened a long time ago.'

Caplan pulled his ear. 'That's kind of weird. You think maybe she called our office or something?'

'No stone unturned. That's why I'm here.'

'Which makes you good at what you do.' His voice stayed friendly, but he had an air of preoccupation. He tugged the middle desk drawer. It stuck, and he yanked it hard. 'Messages,' he muttered, dislodging a fistful of pink telephone slips with jagged edges. A pencil fell to the floor and Sonora could see the edges of an unruly stack of papers and old envelopes. Caplan shoved the drawer shut and flipped through the messages, humming.

'Revolution' – the Beatles.

He looked up and caught Sonora's eye, brows raised. 'Nobody here by that name, but my secretary may have screened it, or someone else could have taken the call. It's been a mess around here lately.'

Sonora looked at the immaculate desk.

'Bea should be gone by now. We're in pretty good shape, so I told everybody to leave at noon. I've got to get home myself. My wife's expecting her first child, and she's been feeling bad the last couple of days. Probably the heat. Anyway, I'll ask Bea on Monday if she took a call like that, have her check with the staff. I'll get back to you on it.'

Sonora nodded. 'Appreciate your trouble.'

He shook his head. 'Not at all. Two little kids, huh? What ages?'

'Three and fourteen months.'

'Um.' He looked truly regretful. He was a family man. He had kids of his own. 'Anything at all I can do to find their mama, don't hesitate to ask.'

Sonora shook his hand again. 'Thank you.'

He stood up. 'Is that blouse silk?'

It wasn't, but Sonora wasn't about to say rayon. She wasn't about to say anything. He was hitting on her. Damn.

'Stay in touch, Detective. We could do the lunch thing, when my schedule clears.'

'Let me know what your secretary says.'

'About my schedule?'

'About those phone calls. And thanks for your time.'

Sonora turned away, wondered why the secretary had left her lamp on and her typewriter uncovered, if she had gone home. She looked over her shoulder at Caplan, caught him watching her butt. She inclined her head. 'This your secretary's desk?'

Caplan moved across the room behind her, looked out. 'Yep.'

Sonora waved a hand toward the lamp, the typewriter. 'Maybe she's still here.'

Caplan put both hands on Sonora's shoulders and scooted her gently out of the way. He turned the lamp off. 'I don't—'

Something landed hard very close by, and a woman's soft voice could be heard, muttering.

Caplan pursed his lips. 'Maybe she *is* here. I sent her home a little while ago, but Bea's a real hard worker.' He headed toward an open door behind the desk. Sonora saw metal file cabinets, a copy machine, stacks of paper, forms, envelopes. 'Bea? You in there?'

Sonora trailed him through the door.

Caplan opened his arms wide and grinned. 'I thought you went home an hour ago.'

'First I heard of it.' She was black, thin, close to retirement age or beyond, and though there were lines of fatigue from her nose to her lips, and bags of exhaustion under her eyes, her smile was sweet, and she greeted Sonora with genuine warmth.

'Bea, this is Detective Blair. She's a homicide investigator from downtown.' He waved a hand. 'Bea Wallace. Runs the office and everybody in it.'

'So long as I've got you fooled.' She leaned against the open file cabinet, then rocked back on her feet, looking from Caplan to Sonora. 'How can I help you out?'

The accent wasn't local, but from farther south. Maybe Kentucky, but, to Sonora's ear, she'd guess Tennessee.

'I'm trying to track a woman who went missing a couple weeks ago. Julia Winchell. According to our phone records, she called your office here, several times.'

Bea Wallace folded her arms, closing the file cabinet with her back and resting up against the dull gray metal. 'Say that name again?'

Sonora turned sideways, facing her. 'Julia Winchell. She probably asked for Mr. Caplan. She clipped his picture out of the newspaper.'

'Julia Winchell. The name doesn't ring any bells. But

we've been getting all kinds of calls since we started the Drury prosecution.'

'I bet you have,' Sonora said.

Bea Wallace tapped her cheek. 'We did get one strange one though, come to think of it. Little girl wanted to know what the statute of limitations was on a homicide.'

'There isn't one,' Caplan said.

'What I told her. And she wanted to know if I could give her any details about . . .' She glanced at Caplan. 'About a particular homicide.'

'Which particular homicide?' Sonora glanced at Caplan, saw that his stance was solid and tense.

'She'd caught that article about you in the paper, Gage. The one that gave that background stuff on your first wife. Sorry. She wanted to know if they'd ever caught the killer. How long Mr. Caplan's been a district attorney. That kind of thing.'

Caplan nodded, thin-lipped and grim.

Sonora gave Caplan a sideways look. No doubt, then, that the call was from Julia Winchell. She had the usual cop's aversion to coincidence.

'What'd you tell her?' Caplan asked.

Bea Wallace shrugged. 'She didn't sound like the typical nutcase, but how can you tell? We've had a lot of calls since the Drury thing started. This kind of case brings out the bad ones.'

'In droves,' Caplan said, and grimaced.

'I don't like it when they get personal about Mr. Caplan. So I didn't tell her anything.'

'She call back?' Sonora said.

Bea looked down. 'Just once.'

'What about?' Sonora asked.

'Wanted to know what Mr. Caplan's wife's full name was. His first wife.'

'And she was killed?' Sonora said.

'Murdered,' Caplan said. 'Brutally.'

'She wanted to know if they'd ever caught the killer.'

Caplan shifted his weight, stared at a spot on the wall, somewhere between Sonora and Bea Wallace.

Sonora pushed hair out of her eyes. These people did not give ground easily. 'And you said?'

Bea Wallace stood still, both feet planted side by side. She would not meet Sonora's eyes. 'I said no. They did not catch the killer.'

Chapter Eight

The parking situation tipped Sonora off – after hours, no special events, and yet all the slots in front of the Board of Elections building were filled, both sides. These were not cop cars. Cops tended to drive two types of car. The older guys, the guys with families, favored the beige Taurus or Camry, cars that didn't stand out to the highway patrol, cars that were the interstate equivalent of Stealth bombers. One could tote the kids in comfort, and indulge in an excess of speed without the embarrassment of glad-handing a brother officer into forgiveness. The younger cops drove Chevy Malibus and Camaros, with souped-up 454 engines for speed, and modified turbo 400 transmissions that gave torque and muscle.

The underpaid press tended toward Chevettes, Vegas and Escorts.

Sonora looked at the mix – a Lincoln, an LTD, a van, Chevy Blazer, one small blue Mazda. Looked like John Q. Public.

She headed into the building, took the elevator to the fifth floor. She heard the buzz of voices as soon as the doors opened. The noise reminded her of high-school hallways between classes. She passed the empty glass booth of reception and went through the swing door into homicide.

She veered sideways immediately, reflexes excellent, to get out of the way of a woman who walked past with the air of the person in charge. Sonora did not recognize her.

She was tall and big-boned, wings of gray in the swept-back coarse brown hair. Her dress was that deep shade of purple that seemed to appeal to British royalty and women past menopause. The dress was belted in the middle, setting off a well-toned, nicely proportioned figure, though the shoulders were large, and the hands and facial features oddly mannish.

The woman caught Sonora's look, lifted her chin, and breezed past, finding herself face to face with the swing door. She turned and frowned, and Sonora leaned up against the wall, arms folded, thinking that this was a woman people were probably at pains not to cross.

'Where *is* this mythical coffeemaker, or can I persuade someone to actually get me a cup?' She looked at Sonora expectantly, and held a mug out, as if in supplication.

Sonora noticed that the mug was her turquoise Joseph-Beth Booksellers cup. 'You don't want *that* one.'

The woman braced her legs. 'What?'

'That mug. You don't want to drink out of that one – it's got lipstick stains on the side.'

The woman turned the mug on one side and squinted, then pursed her lips. 'You're right.' She curled her lip, handed the mug to Sonora. 'Thanks.'

'Anytime.'

Sonora continued down the hallway, stopping at the coffeemaker that steamed on the table by the left hand side of the wall. She wondered how the woman in purple had missed it. She put coffee and cream into the mug, rocked it gently to disperse the white powder, smiled when the mix turned the right shade of mocha brown, and headed for her desk, noting, as she went by, that both interview rooms were full.

'Sonora?' Sam leaned out of Interview One, right behind her.

He loped down the hallway, brown hair sliding into his eyes. His tie was loose, shirt ballooning from the waistband of his pants. He looked boyish and tired, as if he hadn't slept.

'How'd you get all these people here so early?' Sonora said.

'I guess they get out of bed before you. You up all night cleaning and paying bills and doing the Mom-thing?'

Actually, she had let it all go to hell and curled up with a book. She gave Sam a noble look, tinged with sadness. 'I chose to be a single mother. I'm not complaining.' She yawned and covered her mouth. 'Stopped at Caplan's office on my way in.'

'Yeah? How'd it go?'

Sonora frowned. 'A little weird.'

'Weird how?'

'Just a feeling I got. Everything he *said* was right, anything I can do to help, all that. But he told me his secretary had gone home, and she hadn't.'

'Arrest that man.'

'I got the feeling he didn't want me talking to her.'

'Maybe he wanted you to go away so he could get his work done and go home.'

'Maybe. But she did call. Julia Winchell. The secretary talked to her.'

'What did she want?'

'She wanted to know about Caplan's first wife. And how she got killed.'

'Nancy Drew at work.'

'Which is what I need to be. It's wall-to-wall cars outside. How many people you got up here?'

'Five or six,' Sam said. 'Hundred. Locals. Called and invited to drop by.'

Sonora hid a smile. 'Who's the sweetheart in purple?'

'Valerie Gibson, the conference coordinator.'

'Scary.'

'I'll take her,' Sam said. 'You cover the couple in Interview Two. Molliter's working the lady in One.'

'I thought he was on nights.'

'He wants the overtime and we need the help.'

Sonora gave Sam a hard look. 'What's wrong with the couple in Two?'

Sam smiled sweetly, and scooted down the hallway, fast enough to let her know she'd been stuck. She stopped for a minute outside the hallway to peep in at them, saw the woman, sixtyish, rummaging in an expensive-looking tapestry purse, waving one hand in the air. The man sitting next to her was frowning and watching intently, as if his life depended upon what might or might not come out of the purse.

Sonora took a sip of coffee and ducked inside. The woman was unwrapping sticks of Wrigley's Doublemint gum. She gave one stick to her husband and unwrapped another, looked up and caught sight of Sonora.

'Are you the secretary, miss?'

The woman would be short when she stood up, Sonora thought. Five two at the most. Still taller than Sonora herself, but a good deal heavier. She wore a lavender blouse that looked more like real silk than rayon, and looped in a big bow across the collar that had been buttoned tightly around her neck. The ends of the bow fluttered across what she would undoubtedly call her bosom, and dipped below the high waistband of the navy skirt that flared and folded, the hem line mid-calf. Her shoes, under the table, looked sensible and new, the toes squared, the heels chunky. The oval lenses of her glasses magnified her eyes.

'I'm Police Specialist Blair. I'm a detective.'

'Gum?' the man said, chewing discreetly.

Detectives merited gum, Sonora noted. 'No thanks.' She shook both of their hands and sat down. The woman set her purse on her lap.

Sonora gave them a smile that was likely more preoccupied than friendly, threaded a reel of tape into the old war-horse of a tape recorder, and asked them both to state their names.

'Barbara Henderson Miller,' the woman said, eyes big and alert behind the thick lenses of her glasses. 'And this is my husband—'

'Alford C. Miller,' he said, leaning toward the recorder.

'What's the C stand for?' Sonora asked, thinking maybe 'crabby.'

'Carl,' he said. And blinked.

Sonora rubbed the back of her neck. 'As I understand, one of you, both of you—'

'Both,' Mrs. Miller said. Alford nodded.

Sonora was not surprised that they had not needed to hear the question. These people would know their answer before you knew your question.

'Both of you attended this small business conference at the Orchard Suites?'

Mrs. Miller's purse slid sideways and a checkbook, flowered glasses case, and roll of butterscotch Lifesavers spilled out. The Lifesavers hit the floor and rolled under Alford's chair. Mrs. Miller caught the checkbook and glasses case, pressing them into the folds of her thick polyester skirt.

'You didn't close it, Barbie.' Alford leaned sideways to pick up the butterscotch Lifesavers.

'I *did* close it, I heart it snap. Didn't you hear the snap?' She looked at Sonora.

'I wasn't paying attention. Are the two of you local? You live in Cincinnati?'

'We live in Union,' Alford said.

'So you didn't stay at the hotel?'

Mrs. Miller took a tight grip on her purse. 'Oh yes we did. We like staying in hotels. You get breakfast.'

'It comes with the room,' Alford explained.

Sonora took a breath, let it out slowly. 'Mr. and Mrs. Miller. Did either of you see or talk to Julia Winchell during this conference?'

'Well, how could we not? It wasn't that big a conference,' Mrs. Miller said.

Alford thumbed his ear. 'You mean that black-headed girl Detective Sam showed us? In the picture?'

'Yes.'

'He play football in school?'

'He was on the badminton team,' Sonora said. She did not want to get into Sam's glorious football history.

Alford was still working the thumb. 'That can't be right. UC doesn't have a badminton team. Do they?'

'He went to school in Kentucky,' Sonora said.

'We certainly *did* notice *Mrs.* Winchell,' Mrs. Miller said.

'Pretty little girl,' Alford said absently. 'She seemed very nice at first.' He gave his wife a dark look and both of them nodded.

'At first?' Sonora said. With these two it might be best just to let them talk, provided she could keep them on the subject.

Mrs. Miller leaned forward, facial features going tight. 'She seemed nice at first, maybe a little offish, keeping herself to herself some.'

'Shy,' Alford said.

'Reserved. With some people, not with everyone. For instance, Mr. Jeff Barber certainly seemed to be a particular friend.'

Sonora made a note. Alford leaned forward and cut his eyes sideways. Sonora was tempted to print GO TO HELL on the notepad, but she couldn't pay attention and write upside down at the same time.

'I take it Mr. Barber was enrolled in these courses too?'

Alford shook his head. 'Not courses. It was a one-week conference. Lectures, panel discussions, workshops. Really, it should have been a *two*-week thing. That would have been more effective.'

'But double the tuition,' Mrs. Miller said.

'Maybe, maybe not. With economies of scale—'

She was losing them, Sonora thought. 'Can I get either of you a soda, cup of coffee?'

Their heads swiveled as one, their eyes bright, as they allowed that a soda would be a welcome thing.

'Let's clear up this Barber thing before I run out to the machine.' Sonora had kids. She knew how to do this. 'When you said they were good friends. Did either of you get the feeling they knew each other before?'

'They *said* not,' Alford said.

'You asked?' Sonora looked at him.

He nodded.

'They certainly got *very* chummy *very* fast.' Mrs. Miller gave Sonora a significant look.

'For instance?'

'Oh, but I don't like to say.'

'Mrs. Miller, I'll remind you that Julia Winchell has been missing for over fifteen days, and she has two young children waiting at home. You need to answer all of my questions to the very best of your ability.'

Alford made the kind of clucking noise you would make to a horse. 'That just makes it that much worse, when an irresponsible young mother can't behave.'

Mrs. Miller leaned forward. 'Does her husband know anything about all this?'

Sonora closed her eyes, shutting the two of them out for three precious seconds. 'About all what?'

'About the way she was carrying on!' Mrs. Miller let go of the purse and it hit the floor, spilling contents, which Sonora was now able to inventory with her eyes closed. Mrs. Miller looked at Alford, heading him off. 'I *did* snap it shut – the catch is broken. And I've only had this purse a few months. I think the store should take it back. Don't you think?' She looked at Sonora.

Alford was on his hands and knees, picking up the butterscotch Lifesavers. 'Did you keep the receipt?'

No, she hadn't kept the receipt.

Sonora leaned back in her chair, placed both hands flat on the table. 'You said that Julia Winchell and Jeff Barber were' – she looked at her notepad – 'in your words, "carrying on." Tell me exactly what you mean.'

'They weren't the only ones.' Alford. Off on a tangent.

His wife nodded. 'You must mean that MacMillan woman. *Sylvie.*'

Alford leaned forward. 'First of all, they *sat* together. Every single class.'

'Saved each other seats,' Mrs. Miller said.

The two of them slid their chairs in closer to the table.

'Anything else?' Sonora asked.

'They laughed. A lot. She had this little way of turning her head sideways when he talked.'

'Very cute,' Alford said.

'*Coquettish.* And one day, at a workshop, she came in late and *he* wouldn't let us start till she got there.'

Sonora wondered how to spell 'coquettish.' She wrote down 'flirty.'

'Don't forget that Friday,' Alford said.

Mrs. Miller patted the table. 'That's right. We went to Montgomery Inn. We can't have the ribs. We have to order the chicken for our digestive systems, but we like eating down on the river. So we gave ourselves a little treat and went there for dinner.'

'Which *he* called supper, I heard him!'

Mrs. Miller nodded. 'And they were already there. *Just* the two of them, in one of those half-circle little booths, sitting very close together.'

'And?' Sonora asked.

'They seemed very happy,' Mrs. Miller said.

Alford nodded. 'They were having the ribs.'

Chapter Nine

Sonora left the Millers pining over ribs. She peered into the two-way of Interview One, saw Valerie Gibson waving an arm in the air, and Sam cringing. She went in quietly.

Gibson was holding forth. 'One of the best conferences we've ever had. A very congenial group, with a palpable *esprit de corps.*'

Sonora decided that any woman who used 'palpable' and '*esprit de corps*' in one sentence deserved to be interrupted.

'Sam, can I see you just for one minute?'

Gibson swiveled sideways and raised one eyebrow. '*That* is the secretary who took my coffee cup.'

'I'm just a temp,' Sonora said.

Sam made soothing noises at Gibson and followed Sonora out. He shut the door and leaned against the wall, giving Sonora a look.

'Get anything out of her?'

'I think what you mean is did I get anything useful? Which is no. Anything out of your couple?'

'Unmitigated joy.' She leaned her back against the wall, lowered her voice. 'It does looks like our girl was ...' She paused, picturing Julia Winchell's haunted face in the photograph, her two children. Remembered how unhappily she herself had been married way back when. She had been about to say 'doing the nasty,' but changed it to 'stepping out.'

Sam cracked a smile. 'As in *stepping* out or stepping *out*?'

'Shut up, Sam. She was getting close to this Jeff Barber guy at the conference, just like we figured.'

'Close, Sonora? That Victoria's Secret Special looked very close.'

'Yeah, have it your way, Sam. She was fucking Jeff Barber. Any luck yet tracking him down?'

'None yet. Want me to give him a call?'

'Now would be good.' She followed him into the bullpen. Waved at Sanders, who was at her desk, on the phone.

Sanders had a high-wattage glow that made Sonora decide the call was definitely personal.

Young love.

She thought of Keaton, and pushed his image out of her head. When a relationship went bad it was always better to sever the connection, and not do the back-and-forth agony dance. Better, but hard. He would always hold her peculiarly responsible for the death of his estranged wife, even though she'd saved his neck. It was not fair, but it was real life.

Sometimes it seemed the whole world was paired off except her. She was getting tired of lying to people about what she did Friday nights.

'Sonora?' Sam tucked a wad of tobacco into one cheek.

'What you got, Sam?'

'Jeff Barber runs a photography studio in a strip mall out on College. We talked to his wife—'

Sonora raised an eyebrow. 'So there is a wife.'

'Yeah, *I'm* shocked. Wife said he'll be working in the darkroom all day. Probably be home late tonight, maybe around ten.'

'So he didn't run away. I bet he'd rather talk at the studio.'

Sam moved his shirt cuff off his wrist, looked at his watch. 'Let's wrap this thing up here, and go out together.'

Sonora smiled. She was not going back into that room with that couple. 'Why don't you hold the fort here, Sam?

I think I better jump on this Barber thing while I can. See you later.'

She put her coffee mug down, then picked it back up. Better take it along to be safe.

Chapter Ten

The strip mall, out exit seven in Montgomery, was dying the slow tortured death of buckled asphalt, grass sprouting through the cracks, broken concrete headstones for parking spaces. A blue mail-drop box showed four pick-up times, the latest at six PM.

Most of the storefronts were dark. Barber's studio was next door to a pet store, Animal House, front door propped open with a brick. A condenser dripped rusty water onto the worn concrete sidewalk. Sonora heard the squawk of a parrot and the shrill sweet chatter of parakeets. According to a hand-lettered sign in the front glass partition, they were running a special on 'Animal Science Diet.' Sonora thought of Clampett, content to eat whatever was on special. He was getting on in years. Would he live longer if she put him on an animal science diet? She wondered what an Animal Science Diet was.

The humidity was making her hair curly. Frizzy, actually. The F word. She straightened her tie, and pushed the door open to Barber Studio Internationale, thinking he could call it 'Internationale' till the cows came home, but tomorrow this would still be Cincinnati.

There were yellowed wedding pictures in the window – a bride gazing happily into a bouquet of white roses that were too beautiful to be real. Another shot showed a pregnant woman in a white flowing robe holding a pink rose to one cheek in a soft camera focus that said Madonna, Madonna, Madonna. A heavy silver cross hung around her neck.

Sonora gave the picture a second look, thinking that it would be more realistic to have the woman bending over a toilet tossing her cookies. She wondered how that would look in soft focus.

Little brass bells tinged as she entered the studio, but the man inside was singing along with Roy Orbison in a duet of 'Crying,' and didn't hear her come in.

Sonora put her hands in her pockets and rocked back and forth on her heels. She had on new Reeboks, white high-topped Freestyle, with 'Reebok' stitched in shimmery silver on the sides. Sonora liked her tennies new and unscuffed. She admired them for a moment, then looked around the studio.

A lot of vinyl in that state-park shade of brown used for signs and picnic tables. The carpet was indoor-outdoor, thin and reddish, and there was a green couch next to an old silver ashtray – the old, freestanding kind that opened in the middle to make a chasm for cigarette butts and ashes. It was the kind Sonora had liked to play with when she was a child. The kind her mother had told her to leave alone.

The vocals swelled, harmonizing with Roy's, '*cry-ee-ee-ee-ing.*' A man pushed his way through a saloon-style swing door, caught sight of Sonora, and stopped dead.

'You're among friends,' Sonora said. 'I'm an Orbison fan.'

He watched her, like a startled mule deer making its mind up whether to spook and run.

Where would he go? she wondered.

He was exactly what she had expected. Handlebar mustache, thick, black and long enough to chew. Eyes deep-set and brown, shadowed by half-moons of fatigue. His lips were thick beneath the mustache and he needed a shave. His hair was longish, like he was overdue for a haircut, collar-length in the back, shorter on the sides, and parted to one side.

His shoulders were stooped, like an old man's, though he looked to be no more than thirty-five or -six.

'I sing "Blue Bayou" in the shower, myself,' Sonora said. She wanted him off guard and friendly. For starters.

He gave her a sad smile. In the dog world he would be a basset hound and would howl on the night of the full moon, and at ambulance sirens. He went over to the boom box and shut the CD off, looked over his shoulder at Sonora. 'My guess is you're getting married, am I right? Second time around, and this time it's going to work?'

She held out her ID. 'You guess wrong. Police Specialist Blair, Cincinnati PD.'

His eyes took on a glaze of shock. He licked his lips. 'What exactly is a police specialist?' His voice had gone down an octave.

'A detective. In my case, homicide.'

'Homicide,' he repeated.

'Forgive me, Mr. Barber, but you look like a man expecting bad news.'

'Would you . . . would you like to sit down?'

Sonora looked at the couch. She'd sat on worse. In her own living room. 'Thanks.'

Chapter Eleven

Of course he smoked. Generic brand, white packaging, cigarettes that smelled as bad as they looked. The air-conditioner was laboring, and it gave off a sour musty smell.

A small picture of Barber, a woman, and two children was displayed in a frame on the coffee table. If Barber had taken the shot, it would go a long way toward explaining the lack of Saturday afternoon clientele.

'Nice family,' Sonora said, picking up the picture. The help-meet had curly brown hair, chin-length, a full face and glasses. The children were school age, first and second grade, from the looks of them. One boy, one girl, standard issue, bowl haircuts.

'They were.'

Sonora checked his left hand. Saw the thick gold band. 'Were?'

'Died, all three of them. Ran up under a tractor trailer truck on I-75. My wife and daughter went instantly. My son hung on a couple of days. Happened five years ago.'

Sonora looked into his face, saw that he was smiling the bland sheepish smile people plaster over a welter of grief. His demeanor was apologetic. He had not meant to bring tragedy into the room – it was just there ahead of them.

She told him how beautiful his children were, and that she was sorry.

'What were their names, your kids?' Sonora asked.

'Christy and Wesley. Christy for my sister. Wesley for Kathy's dad. Kathy was my wife.'

The names came awkwardly on his tongue, and Sonora looked at his eyes and decided that he mentioned them almost never, but thought of them every day.

'You've remarried?' Sonora said.

He looked puzzled. 'No.'

'We called your house. Talked to a Mrs. Barber—'

'Ms. My sister. She goes over and leaves me dinner every day.'

'That's nice.'

'It would be if she could cook.'

Sonora gave him a half smile in acknowledgment of the hit, but wondered why he didn't let his sister off the hook, if he didn't want the meals. She slid back on the couch. 'Mr. Barber, how long have you known Julia Winchell?' She watched his face. 'You do know her, don't you?'

'I, uh, I met Julia at a conference on running a small business.'

He liked saying her name, she could tell. Red flag number one.

'When was the last time you saw her?' Sonora took out her mini recorder. Checked the tape, turned it on. 'Excuse me, let me ask that again. Mr. Barber, when was the last time you saw Julia Winchell?'

He moved sideways, shoulders low even when he sat. 'At that last workshop, I guess. The one on dealing with the IRS.'

'And that was the last time you saw her?'

He nodded.

'Say yes,' Sonora said, tapping the recorder.

'Sorry. Yes.'

'When was that, exactly?'

'Saturday, late in the afternoon. The fifteenth of July.'

'You call her? Afterwards?'

Pause. 'No.'

'Has she called you? Written you? Gotten in touch with you in any way?'

'Why would she? You haven't ... has something happened?'

'Mr. Barber, have you called Julia Winchell since that last workshop on the IRS? Her hotel, her home, whatever?'

'No ma'am.' Very softly lying.

Sonora sighed, rubbed her forehead, held up a finger. 'Number one, you're making this hard.' Another finger. 'And number two, you're not helping me. I see your point of view, believe me, but I got to tell you you're not helping yourself at all here.'

She was playing with him. Julia Winchell had gone somewhere, if only to a shallow grave by the side of the road. And if suspect number one was the husband, the lover was candidate number two.

'Work with me on this,' Sonora said.

'I'm not sure what you—'

'Describe your relationship with Mrs. Winchell.'

His color drained, left hand making a fist. 'Is she ... You said you were a homicide detective. Is Julia ... did something happen to her?'

'Were you expecting something to happen to her, Jeff?'

He bit his lip. 'No. But—'

'But what?'

'*Please*, just tell me.'

'She's missing, Jeff. She hasn't been seen or heard from for two weeks. She hasn't called about her children for fifteen days. You may be the last person—'

'To see her alive?' he asked.

'Jeff, you keep harping on that. Why do you think something happened to her? You do, don't you?'

'I don't know.'

'You know.'

'I don't.' He gave her the puppy-dog look.

It probably worked, with kinder females than she'd ever be. She wondered how long he'd been trading on his tragedy.

Glanced at the picture of his family. 'If your children were missing their mother—'

'Please don't do that. Don't use my children.'

Sonora nodded, pursed her lips. 'Mr. Barber, it might be a good idea for you to answer my questions downtown, as they say, and you with the attorney of your choice.'

'But *why*? If she's missing—'

'See, you're not working with me on this, Jeff. And I don't understand why you won't help me. I'm not an unreasonable person.' She opened her arms wide. 'But, if you won't work with me, it makes me think you've got something to hide.'

'I *will* work with you.'

'You're going to have to do better than you have been.'

He nodded at her.

'Jeff, let's start at the beginning.' She pitched her voice low now, quiet honey. 'What was your relationship with Julia Winchell?'

He put both palms on his lap and wet his lips. 'We were friends.'

'More than friends,' Sonora said. A statement.

'She was married,' he said flatly, and looked at Sonora. She stayed quiet and he shifted sideways in his chair. 'We hit it off, we were friends. Men and women can be friends.'

Sonora waited. She had conversations like this with her son. Waiting for the truth to come. Barber looked around the room the way Tim did when he didn't want to tell her something. Were they looking for a way out? Of a conversation?

Sonora kept her voice soft and matter-of-fact. 'I'll make it easy on you, and tell you what I know. You and Julia Winchell were having an affair. It's not like a new concept, okay, Jeff? I'm sorry to intrude into your privacy, but if you care for Julia you'll help me out.'

'I cared for her. I loved her.'

'Tell me this, Jeff.'

He waited, expectant.

'Why are you using the past tense?'

Chapter Twelve

Jeff Barber was not happy to be downtown at the Board of Elections building talking to Sam. Barber was having a break and a ham sandwich with catsup.

Sergeant Crick stood in the hallway, arms folded. He glared at Sonora. 'Catsup? On a ham sandwich? And you let him?'

Sonora yawned, covered it with her hand. 'I'm not his mother.'

'If you were, I'd tell you to get him a haircut.'

Crick was clearly in his usual good humor, Sonora decided. He wore a shirt that hung loosely across swollen biceps, the collar buttoned tight across the short thick neck. His air of disapproval was a constant and he was broad and massive and intimidating, until you got to know him and were legitimately afraid.

'How long they been boinking?' Crick asked.

'He won't admit to the boinking. He says they just met at the conference.'

'He's full of shit,' Crick said.

Sonora inclined her head. 'True.'

Crick shifted his weight from his left leg to his right. One of his bones popped. He had brown eyes, intelligent and wise, and he stood too close.

'So, Sonora, why *don't* you believe him? Just because he looks like a lying shit?'

'For one, the sister says there was somebody. For another, Julia Winchell brought lingerie with her. One black teddy, and one blue nightie.'

'Maybe she always wears them. Call up her husband and ask him.'

'I was just thinking there might be a kinder way.'

'Like *please* does your wife wear black teddies? Since when were you kind?'

'See,' Sonora said. 'You caught me. I'm not being kind. I don't know if Butch Winchell knows his wife was fooling around. If he does, we got motive. I'd kind of like to have my stuff straight and hit him with it when I can watch his face.'

Crick scratched his nose. 'Let's say they been screwing a while, long enough for this little girl to get her lingerie together. Theorize on that. How you going to prove it? The sister ever meet him?'

'No.'

'Know him by name?'

'No.'

'So then?'

Sonora leaned back against the wall. 'See if he's ever been to Clinton, Tennessee. See if they went to school together, way back when. Phone records. Maybe he's been calling her house. He called her hotel room, we got that cold.'

Crick shook his head back and forth, clearly unimpressed. 'He'd brush that off in no time. Say it was conference stuff. What's this guy do for a living?'

'Photographer.'

Crick frowned at her. 'Hell, there you go.'

'Pictures?'

'If they just got together, maybe no, maybe yes. But if the sister and the nightie hunch prove right, they've known each other a while. What photographer could resist taking pictures of his lady love?'

'Think so?'

'I was in love once. I think so.'

* * *

Sonora waited outside the door of Interview One while Jeff Barber ate the second half of his sandwich. Sam sat across from him, watching him chew and swallow. Sonora considered inviting Sam out for a conference, decided no. He could follow her lead. Anything else would look too contrived.

She heard footsteps behind her, heavy and light.

'*Sonora.*' Gruber. Sounding pissed.

She turned sideways, saw that Sanders was with him, thin-lipped, cheeks flushed. She'd never seen Sanders angry, but this might be it.

'This is my personal life and nobody's business but mine. We are not going to have this conversation,' Sanders said.

'Oh yeah we are.' Gruber had his jaw set hard.

Sonora looked at him. 'If Sanders says we're not having this conversation, we're not. I got work to do, and kids at home eating pizza and watching MTV and *Mayberry* reruns instead of doing their chores. I'd like to get back to the house to make sure they're not conducting satanic rituals at the end of the driveway. You know kids today.'

'See? She's too busy, anyway.' Sanders folded her arms and puffed air between her lips. Sanders petulant and angry in the space of a minute.

Sonora looked at her, then back through the two-way. Barber was still chewing. He ate a Frito.

One more bite of sandwich, and she was going in.

'Here's what we want to know,' Gruber said. 'Is how can you tell if the guy you—' He looked at Sanders and lowered his voice. 'The guy you're crazy about, is married.'

Sanders leaned close. 'The symptoms are these—'

Sonora held up a hand. 'Why are you asking me?'

'We figured you'd know,' Gruber said.

Sonora gave him a look. 'I don't even want to think about why you said that.' She looked back through the two-way. Barber was on his last bite. There was catsup and a large white breadcrumb on the left corner of his mouth.

'Look, Sonora, if we're bothering you.' Gruber waved a hand.

'You *are* bothering me, but I'll give you what I got. One. When's he call you, Sanders? Between eight and five? That means he can't call you from home.' She glanced at Sanders, saw her go still and watchful. 'Two. Did he fall in love and decide you were soulmates in the first forty-eight hours? Married guys are usually in a hurry. Three. Does he watch the clock when you guys are together? Because if he's married, he's usually supposed to be somewhere else. And four . . .' Sonora glanced back through the two-way. No more ham sandwich. She was definitely going in. She looked back over her shoulder, and saw Sanders heading down the hall toward the ladies' room.

'She left after three,' Gruber said. 'What's four?'

'You're a guy, you were married, you probably already know.' Sonora headed through the door into Interview One.

Barber was not glad to see her. She handed him a napkin. 'Catsup on your mouth.'

He took the napkin and wiped his lips, crumbled it into a ball.

Sonora sat on the edge of the table, swinging her right leg. Barber still had the breadcrumb hanging from his mouth. She knew it was going to drive her crazy. 'Okay. Let's speak hypothetically here.' She looked at Sam, who poured a handful of Fritos into his hand and shoveled them into his mouth.

Barber crossed his legs, thighs pressed tightly together. He flipped a wave of dark hair out of his eyes and the breadcrumb fell off the corner of his mouth. Sonora breathed a sigh of relief.

'Now, Jeff, let's say, just for the heck of it, and hypothetically you understand, that while you been here talking to Sam and eating your sandwich, that I got a court order and went to your photography studio there. And let's say I found pictures of Julia Winchell. Pictures taken *before* this conference. I'd have to decide you've been lying to me here, and I'd want to know why. I might suspect you of something awful. I might have to talk to your friends and neighbors and also, not incidentally, to my sergeant and a judge about my suspicions of you.' She stopped talking for a minute, watchful. Heard Sam crunch more Fritos. Sonora leaned in close. 'We got witnesses, Jeff. People who know the two of you were together, people who will testify that you and Julia Winchell were having an affair.

'Now, Jeff, Julia's been gone fifteen days – as far as we know, in touch with nobody. Her husband's worried about her. *I'm* worried about her. What I don't understand is why *you're* not worried about her. It makes me think you already know what happened to her.'

Barber leaned forward, elbows on his knees, and covered his eyes with his hands. He looked like he was going to be sick.

Could have been the sandwich, Sonora thought.

She noticed that his palms were large and square. She pictured them around Julia Winchell's neck. Cop imagination.

Sonora gentled her voice. 'We need to find her, Jeff. We need you to talk to us, tell us everything you know. I think – I get the feeling that you know something that could help me find her. You need to talk to me, Jeff. Talk to me for Julia's sake. You care too much about her not to help us. Don't you, Jeff?' Sonora took a breath. 'Jeff? You with me here?'

He raised his eyes, hands still covering his mouth. 'Of course I care.' The words were muffled behind the thick fingers.

'If you care you'll talk to me.'

He looked from Sonora to Sam. 'I think ... I think something did happen to her.'

Sam quit crunching Fritos.

Sonora nodded at Barber. 'Been worried about her, haven't you?'

He nodded.

'It's got to have been hard for you. Nobody you can ask, nobody you can talk to. How long you been worrying, Jeff?'

'Since she didn't call.' He swallowed so hard it made Sonora's throat hurt. 'She was supposed to call. We were going to . . . to meet together. But she didn't, and so I knew something had to be wrong.'

The male ego, Sonora thought, glancing back at Sam. Something had to have happened to her, or she would have called.

'How long have you two been . . . together? Jeff?'

Barber let his hands drop between his knees. 'I was down in Knoxville picking up a lens a buddy of mine was selling. He was retiring, getting rid of a lot of his equipment, and I went down to buy stuff off him. They're doing a lot of construction on I-75 down near Knoxville, so this guy tells me my best bet getting home is to take Maybryhood Road and go through Clinton. That way I bypass all the mess and the traffic tie-up. Said there was a good place to have lunch there – the Blue Moon Diner. Near some place where some twins used to have a restaurant, I don't know. But that's where I met Julia.'

He said her name with a gentle hunger.

'So you met her in the diner,' Sonora said.

Barber brought up a bright red flush. 'A woman like that, running a diner in Clinton, Tennessee? Have you seen pictures of Julia? She had beautiful cheekbones, a kind of round, Slavic bone structure. I asked if I could take her picture. I did, and went home. Could *not* forget her. So we – we talked on the phone, a lot of that. I told her about this conference, the small-business thing.'

'Whose idea was it for her to come up?'

'Mine. But she wanted to come. I think she did.' He

frowned. 'She wasn't happy at home. I mean, she wasn't *un*happy, but she wasn't happy either. To be honest, she was fine either way without me. But *I* wasn't fine without *her*. It's like . . .' He looked at the wall. 'It's like she woke me up. I've been on autopilot since . . . for a while now. First it had to be that way, then it just got to be the way it was. I mean stupid stuff. Like I didn't notice how ratty and dusty my office was, till I got Julia in my life. I don't know what I'll do without her.'

You could clean your office, Sonora thought.

Sam leaned sideways. 'When was the last time you saw her?'

'We had dinner at the Montgomery Inn, the one on the river.' His voice had gone low and gravelly. 'We were supposed to go out again the next night. But there wasn't a next night.'

Maybe she had indigestion, Sonora thought. 'What happened?'

'I went back to my room late. We were supposed to meet for breakfast – they have a breakfast buffet. It comes with the room.'

Sam nodded, man-to-man. The importance of a breakfast buffet was not lost.

'She called my room early that morning. Said for me to go on without her. She seemed distracted and, I don't know, kind of angry. I thought she might be mad at me, so I tried to talk to her, but she said she'd call me later.'

'Did she?'

'I didn't wait. I thought something was wrong. Like between us. So I went to her room.'

Might be true love, Sonora thought. Passing up that breakfast buffet.

'What was up?' Sam said.

'She had a newspaper. One of those ones they leave outside the door. I wish they hadn't.'

'Why's that?' Sam said.

'She had it folded back to a picture of that prosecutor who's going after that Bengals player. Drury.'

Sonora nodded. 'Keep talking.'

'She said she saw this guy Caplan kill somebody eight years ago.'

Sonora looked at Sam, then back to Barber. 'Tell me exactly what she said.'

He swallowed. 'It happened while she was in school.'

'She say what school?' Sam asked.

'University of Cincinnati. I mean, people get killed around there every year. I thought she must of meant some kind of thing in the streets. But she said this happened inside. And she saw it.'

'Did she report it?' Sonora asked.

'She told the security guard, but when she took him back inside there wasn't anybody there – no body, no murderer. Guard thought she was a crank. But she was really sure about it. She got a good look at this guy, and she's sure it was Caplan.'

'Who got killed? Did she know the victim?' Sam asked.

'It was a girl, that's all she told me. And she was pregnant.'

'Anything else?'

'That's all. She was trying to decide what to do about it. She felt funny about going to the police, since it had been so long ago. Eight years. She was going to look into it, that's what she said.'

'Look into it how?' Sam asked.

Barber shrugged. 'I know she went to the library, because she asked me for directions on the best way to get there. Said things had changed so much in the last eight years she couldn't find her way around. I wanted to go along with her, but she said no. That's the last time we talked.'

'Did you call her again?'

'Yeah. But it was like I was on the back burner all of a

sudden. She got real busy, and I could never catch her in her room. Since then, no calls, no letters.'

Sonora tilted her head to one side. 'You wrote letters?'

He nodded.

'Where'd you send them? Not to the house, is my guess.'

Barber shifted in his chair. 'She had a post office box,' he said. Matter-of-factly.

'Let me get that address off you,' Sonora said. Matter-of-factly.

Chapter Thirteen

Sonora was working from home, which was not always a good idea, because it meant she could watch the kids while working, a possible oxymoron. But it did allow her to wear sweatpants and not comb her hair.

From the kitchen came the clink of Heather's spoon against a cereal bowl. The rustle of cellophane. Clampett, asleep on the couch behind Sonora, was suddenly awake.

'Let her eat,' Sonora said to the dog.

Clampett yawned. Stretched and stepped down from the couch on top of the map she had opened out on the floor. He was a big dog, in excess of a hundred pounds, thick coat, blond, three-legged. He'd shown up on their back porch years ago, hair thick with mats, burrs and ticks spread liberally about his body, stomach running on empty. The kids liked to make up stories about his shady past.

The current fiction involved Cuba and political asylum, mainly because of Clampett's interest in a fake plastic cigar the kids had stashed in the dress-up box in the laundry room.

Clampett licked Sonora's wrist, and tasted her pen. A stream of saliva dripped from the dog's mouth and landed somewhere in southeast Ohio. Sonora shoved him sideways, and he padded into the kitchen.

Sonora squinted at the map, looking for where she'd traced I-75 with the pen. Red, she decided, was not the color to have used. The map was already full of red lines, and hers was lost in the shuffle. She frowned and wondered what color she should use. The map was a rainbow, no color noticeably missing.

'Clampett, *no*.' Heather's voice, from the kitchen.

She found the line she'd traced just under a hole from one of Clampett's toenails, followed it to where the map left off in northern Kentucky.

'Dammit.'

She snatched up the map, turned it over. Ohio, Indiana, northern Kentucky. Everything but Tennessee, which was what she needed. She folded the map, wondering if she had a map of Tennessee in the glove compartment of her car. The map did not want to go back into the original accordion folds. Sonora unfurled it and tried again.

'Clampett, *stop*.'

A bowl clattered against the kitchen floor. The map bunched when it should have folded and Sonora wadded it into a large ball, and threw it across the room.

The doorbell rang.

Sonora looked at her watch. Eleven AM. Sunday morning. Seventh Day Adventists?

She got to her feet slowly, the small of her back stiff and achy. Boy, were these guys in for it! She ran down the stairs, opened the front door. The heat and humidity hit her like a glove in the face. She could almost feel the air-conditioning being sucked away, and it wasn't even noon yet.

Sam stood on the front porch, glancing over his shoulder at a pickup truck pulling a maroon fishing boat.

'That hurts,' he said, grimacing, turned to Sonora and screamed.

'Oh shut up. I don't look that bad.'

'If you say so.'

Sonora noticed that *he* looked good. Freshly showered. Khaki pants and a denim shirt.

'You're going to burn up in that shirt,' she told him.

'I'll roll up the sleeves and show my biceps.' Sam followed

her in through the door. 'You got anything I can eat while you get a shower?'

'We going somewhere?'

'To work, girl. Talked to the Clinton, Tennessee sheriff's department.' He checked his watch. 'Something like an hour ago. Julia Winchell's turned up.'

Sonora paused on the steps. Sheriff's department. So Julia Winchell was dead. She hadn't realized she'd been hoping. 'Where'd they find her?'

'Some of her. Head, hands, and feet, bound up in a plastic trash bag. Snagged on somebody's trotline in the Clinch River. Guy went out and checked it early this morning.'

'Positive ID?'

'Not confirmed, but the sheriff there seemed pretty sure. Garfish had gotten into the bag, but there was the long hair and the widow's peak.'

'She had a widow's peak?'

'Yeah. Didn't you notice, in the pictures?'

'I guess.'

'Anyway, we've been invited to go down for a look, and I said we'd be on our way.'

'Why didn't you call me?'

'Line's busy.'

'Use the business one.'

'That one's busy too.'

Sonora headed into the kitchen. 'You dialed it wrong, Sam. Nobody's been on the phone all day. Heather just got up, and the boy never stirs till late afternoon.' She glanced at the kitchen extension, saw two blinking red lights. 'Well hell.'

'Hi, Heather,' Sam said.

Sonora glanced at her daughter, absently pulled the long dark hair off her shoulders and out of the cereal bowl. 'Heather, give Sam some Lucky Charms, while I go kill your brother.'

Tim was still in his bed. The room was thick with dust

and an electric guitar was parked on the floor next to a practice amp. Sonora stepped over a pile of clothes that emitted an odor that would do a locker room proud.

'Mom, do you mind not just barging into my room?'

Tim's hair, black, was short and spiky and stuck up from where he'd been sleeping on it. His face had broken out along the chin. The sheets of his bed were wadded along the side and he had clearly been sleeping on bare mattress.

'Off the phone,' Sonora said.

'But, Mom—'

'And then you explain why you're on my business line.'

His eyes widened. 'I thought it would be okay, because it's Sunday.'

'It's never okay. I'm a cop, Tim. People get murdered on the weekends too. Consider yourself a prime candidate.'

He glared. Mothers rarely amused fourteen-year-olds. 'You don't have to yell.'

'This, I promise you, is not yelling. Why are you talking to two people at once?'

'I'm doing a conference call.'

Sonora looked at her son and wondered if teenagers went through phases so you wouldn't miss them when they moved out.

'You have one minute to get off. Sam's here. I have to go to work. They found—'

'Something horrible. I don't want to hear it. Mom, everybody's going to Kenneth's to swim. Can you drop me on your way?'

'What about Heather?'

'I have to *babysit*?'

Sonora backed out of the bedroom. She shut the door hard.

Sam wandered into the hallway, cramming a handful of dry cereal into his mouth. 'What's with the phone?'

'He's fourteen years old and he's having a conference call.'

'If that boy's got a girl on each line, I'm going in there to shake his hand.'

'What was it,' Sonora said, 'that led me to procreate in the first place?'

'Probably too much to drink.' Sam picked up the map, tossing it up and catching it. 'Have a moment with maps, did you, Sonora?'

Chapter Fourteen

The sheriff's office was in a cinderblock building next to the Farmer's Co-op. Sonora opened the door of the Blazer and let Heather and Clampett out. It was too hot to leave them in the car.

She looked at Sam. 'You know, if you die and go to hell, you could wind up here.'

'Speak up, Sonora. Make sure we get off on the right foot with the locals.' He opened the door.

'Hang on to Clampett's leash,' Sonora said, glancing at her daughter. She could use some cleaning up. Her pale-blue shorts were loose around her thin, tan legs, and her white tank top was smeared with grape from a cup of Hawaiian shaved ice they'd stopped for on the way down. She wore plastic sandals with silk daisies on the front. Her toenails needed trimming. Her shoulders were pink with sunburn, arms broken out in goose bumps from the chill inside the police station.

Clampett's toenails clicked against the worn yellow linoleum, and he zigged and zagged through the small lobby, sniffing. Heather held tight to the leash, along for the ride.

'That dog taking you for a walk?' The woman behind the desk was tiny and thin, hair cut short, dyed white blonde. Her eyes were thickly circled with eyeliner, expertly applied. She had a deep tan that gave her young skin the patina of alligator hide, cigarette husk in her voice.

Sonora put her ID on the woman's desk. 'Detectives

Blair and Delarosa, Cincinnati Homicide. I think Sheriff Sizemore is expecting us.'

The girl looked at Sonora curiously, then glanced at Sam. The nameplate on her desk said Sylvia Lovely.

Good name for a porn star, Sonora thought.

'It's that Julia Winchell thing,' Sam said. 'You didn't happen to know her?'

The girl shook her head. Her neck was long and pretty. Her earrings dropped all the way to her shoulders. She glanced at Sam's left hand, noticing the wedding ring.

'No, I didn't know her.' She leaned over her desk, picked up the phone, punched a button. 'Monte? You got those folks from Cincinnati here waiting.' She looked up. 'Said to tell you he's real sorry for the wait, and he'll be off the phone in just a minute.' She nodded her head toward the couch. 'Y'all can take a seat if you like, shouldn't be but a minute. Can I get anybody a pop? We got coffee made up, too.'

Old coffee, Sonora thought, judging from the smell.

Clampett was licking the bottom of a blue can of Cherry Coke when a door opened and Sheriff Monte Sizemore walked into the room.

He was taller than Sonora, which wasn't saying much. His hair was brown, cut short in the way of state troopers and marines, gray-flecked at the temples and across the top. His uniform was well pressed and had likely been spotless when he'd put it on that morning. The bottoms of his shoes were mud-crusted, and the cuffs of his pants had been drenched, then dried into mud-stained wrinkles. There was a large round stain over his left knee and his shoes squeaked.

He shook hands with Sam and Sonora, bent down to say hello to Heather and Clampett.

'How long you been on the case?' he asked Heather.

She smiled and dipped her head, pushed her glasses back up on her nose and leaned against Clampett, who drooled down her leg.

'I think your puppy wants his own Coke,' Sizemore said.

Heather tilted her chin. 'I already gave him a drink of mine.'

Sonora grimaced, wondering if Clampett had gotten his drink before or after she'd gotten hers.

Sizemore patted Heather's shoulder. 'I got a granddaughter about your size. She loves to draw horses. How about if Sylvia gives you a pad of paper and a pen and you draw me horse while I talk to your mama?'

Heather frowned. 'I don't know how to draw horses.'

'Then draw something else,' Sonora said.

Chapter Fifteen

Sizemore led them to the break room, shut the door. He limped, just barely. The door creaked as he closed it.

'Need to oil that,' he muttered, heading across the floor.

Sonora stood close to Sam, spoke under her breath. 'Tell me he's not heading for that old refrigerator.'

'Probably next to his lunch.'

The refrigerator was Harvest Yellow, one of the double-wide models, and it hummed. An erratic trail of water snaked out the left side, staining the shiny linoleum. Grilled shelves were stacked against the wall. Sonora remembered when Harvest Yellow had been all the rage for kitchen appliances. Now everything was black and white. The new black and white. The old black and white wouldn't cut it.

Sizemore took a fork off the top of the refrigerator, wedged it into the latch, and opened the door.

Sonora, standing close, felt a cold breath of air, smelled the dark ominous odor. She took a step closer.

Bottles of Seven-Up and Orange Crush lined the inside door, held in place by a bowed and scratched band of aluminum that was working loose near the door hinge. Sonora looked over her shoulder and caught Sizemore's eye.

'I needed someplace quick, Detective. We got your little girl's drink out of the machine.'

She nodded.

The shelves had been removed to make room for a Coleman cooler that sat on the bottom over the crisper bins. The cooler was faded red, scratched across the front, as if someone had gotten malicious with a key.

Sizemore bent to pick up the cooler, and Sam stepped forward and took one end, guiding the cooler to the floor.

The smell gathered strength.

Sizemore straightened up, groaned and touched the small of his back. He wiped sweat from his forehead with a neatly folded handkerchief.

'Y'all want a look, I guess.'

Sonora leaned down and opened the lid, tilting it back on its hinges.

She was immediately engulfed in a whangy miasma that hit with the force of a ripe garbage dump – a fetid mix of fish, rotting meat, and blood.

The bag was a Hefty cinch top, drawn tight and double secured at the neck with a wormlike strand of fishing line. It was shiny black and damp, sweating beads of condensed water.

'Is this the original bag?' Sonora said. It looked to be in too good a shape.

Sizemore spoke through his handkerchief. 'No, that bag was ripped open, and fish had been into it. The original's in there, though. What's left of it. I double bagged it just to keep . . . anything from falling out.'

Like when you buy canned goods at the grocery, Sonora thought. She reached for her purse, and a pair of latex gloves.

Sam fished a tiny pocket knife out of his blazer and cut the fishing line.

'Let me put some newspapers down,' Sizemore said, moving quickly. He slid a thick wide padding of newspapers onto the floor, and Sonora removed the bag from the cooler.

A thick splat of water stained the front page of the *Clinton Register* right over the article about trouble at the Main Street McDonald's. Sonora held her breath, taking air in nasty shallow snorts. Water streamed down one side of the bag as she rolled the top away.

Plastic garbage bags had long been a boon to criminals and home-owners alike, storage being a problem in many lines of work.

A small foot bulged through a ragged tear heel first, meat sagging, bone exposed along the top of the foot. Long black hair was twisted through the toes. The interior bag was battered brown plastic, stained and smeared with things uncomfortable to imagine. It was open at the top, revealing more black hair. Sonora pushed the shredded plastic to one side, and began to unpack.

The tally included one severed head, face hidden by heavy black strands of hair. In her mind's eye, Sonora saw the picture of Julia Winchell with her two little girls gathered into her lap. She held the image, trying to match it to the head that dripped onto the pad of plastic and newsprint.

She reached back into the bag, removed two hands and two feet, the right one taken off at the ankle, the left severed well over the joint. Sonora gently peeled and unwound the long black hair that stuck to the face like cellophane against an iced cupcake.

The face was swollen pale and unrecognizable. The mouth was open and Sonora took the flashlight Sam handed her and pointed it inside. The meat of the tongue was gone, eaten back to the nub. The woman had small white teeth and no cavities, a tiny delicate mouth, turning black with rot.

The right eye was a gnawed, empty socket, thick with unhatched fly larvae.

'She's been outside some,' Sonora said.

Sizemore was nodding. 'Old boy who found her left her out in his minnow bucket while he decided what to do. Brought all this up on his trotline, first thing this morning.'

'His minnow bucket,' Sonora said softly, with a sigh. The left eye was still intact, small blood vessels swollen and burst. She looked up at Sam.

'Strangled?' he asked.

'Looks like. Petechial hemorrhaging, so strangled or hung.'

Sam grunted as he stretched the latex gloves over his thick hands. One size fit all – which meant they hung over the edges of Sonora's fingers, and went with difficulty over Sam's.

'Go slow,' Sonora said. 'These have been in the water awhile.'

'Slippage?' Sam asked.

'Looks like.'

He picked the right hand up carefully. Bits of flesh had been nipped away, and what was left was pale white around the midnight-blue mottling of rot. The flesh was swollen, giving it a thick, glovelike look, and it had been in the water long enough for the pelt of skin to start coming loose from the structure of bone.

She had small hands, even swollen with gas and bloated with water, and they looked tiny and fragile in Sam's thick long fingers. The index finger was gone on the right hand, just above the knuckle joint, and Sonora thought of torture and hungry fish, and wondered which it was.

'Any defense wounds?' she asked.

Sam turned the hand palm up and shoved it in her direction. 'I don't see anything. What do you think about the chop?' He turned the edge up, for better viewing.

Sonora turned her head to one side, squinted.

Clean severing, leaving the fine-tooth grain of a serrated cutting edge.

'Some kind of saw,' Sonora said.

'Chain saw?' Sizemore asked.

Sonora shook her head. 'Too fine for that.'

'Hacksaw,' Sam said, glancing over his shoulder at Sizemore. 'Don't you think?'

The sheriff swallowed but stepped forward, took a hard look.

Sonora knew he wanted to leave them to it, and wished

that he would, but he was too polite to go, and she was too polite to ask.

'I've used a hacksaw a time or two,' the sheriff said, voice deep and tight. 'I'd say could well have been, though tell you the truth, I don't have my reading glasses on, and I'm not much used to this end of the job.' He looked at the stub of index finger. 'I'd say a gar got hold of that right there.'

'Excuse me,' Sonora said. 'What the hell is a gar?'

Sizemore looked at her kindly. 'Kind of a cross between a fish and an alligator. Little legs and sharp teeth.'

'Ick!' Sonora said, and shuddered. She tilted her head to one side. 'What you think, Sheriff Sizemore? Is this Julia Winchell?'

He looked away from the floor, and studied the outer wall, as if there were a window there. 'I can't say for sure, but with that hair and all, and her up and missing, I'd say so.'

Sonora reached for the left foot, turning it to one side to expose the ankle. The skin was coated with moss and snagged leaves. She pushed them away, revealing a mask of blackened decomposition. She wondered if there was a dragon tattooed underneath.

Chapter Sixteen

Julia Winchell's killer had run into bad luck when the plastic bag containing her severed head, hands, and feet had snagged on a trotline draped across the bottom of the Clinch River.

Sonora looked across the water to a small park. She wished Heather was on one of the swing sets, instead of crammed in the back of the sheriff's car with Clampett, air-conditioner straining in the hot humid air. The sun was formidable, and beer consumption was high amongst the spectators of the softball game across the river. Sonora smelled charcoal and hotdogs, saw the large black grill, the thin drift of smoke. The softball players seemed out for blood, in spite of the afternoon heat. Likely a grudge match, Sonora decided.

Sheriff Sizemore looked over at Sam. 'Not to interfere, but your brakes were squealing on that Blazer. They feel mushy when you drive?'

Sam smiled good-naturedly. 'Felt fine to me.'

Sizemore shrugged, pointed through the trees. 'The ol' boy who dredged up that garbage bag lives back there. Got a mobile home just behind those trees. Not far.'

Sonora looked over her shoulder at the trim fields, green and fragrant against the water. 'All this land his?'

Sizemore shook his head. 'Belongs to Cleaton Simms, been in his family for years. No, this ol' boy used to do some handiwork for Cleaton's daddy – he still helps keep the tractors up and the machinery going. Name's George Cheatham. Hell of a mechanic, but he's old now, and slowing down, and his wife is in bed most the time with the diabetes. He looks after her.' Sizemore glanced up and down the river. 'It's a good spot, out here. George does a lot of fishing.'

The mobile home was vintage fifties, aluminum-painted sky-blue so long ago the color was mostly memories and paint flakes. It was hidden behind the trees, all the windows cranked open with old-fashioned levers and sticks. The front door was propped open, screen door shut. The outside metal looked like it would be hot to the touch.

There was no breeze. Sonora could not imagine the mobile home being anything but unbearably hot inside.

A stack of old tractor tires was a presence on the left. One had been set down and filled with sand. A plastic sand pail and broken-off shovel, both a faded yellow, sat to one side of the tire, and a child's Tonka dump truck sat on top. An orange cat sat in the middle of the sandbox, blinked, turned his back and began digging.

Sizemore noticed Sonora's look. 'Their grandkids come sometimes. Cleat fills it up with sand for them every year.'

The screen door creaked and the sheriff raised a hand. He looked at Sam and Sonora. 'This is George Cheatham. This is the old boy that found her.'

Cheatham wore khaki work pants, mud-stained around the bottoms, heavy work shoes, unlaced, tongues flopping, and a worn white teeshirt that hung loose on his thin neck and arms. His skin had the rough and red bronze veneer of years of work in the sun, and his hair was short and fine and steely gray. He walked slowly, like his back hurt, and dragged his feet. The toes of his shoes were scuffed and scarred, so dragging his feet along was more habit than reluctance to make their acquaintance.

'George, these are the detectives from Cincinnati I told you about.'

George nodded. His hand shook when he offered it to Sonora and he looked a little white around the lips. Sonora glanced over his shoulder. She saw a curtain move in a window of the mobile home. It was too bright out to see inside. Probably the wife, wondering if they were coming in.

'I'm Specialist Blair, this is Specialist Delarosa.'

Cheatham shifted his weight like his feet hurt. 'Y'all like to come on in and sit down? Get out of the sun?'

'I appreciate the offer, Mr Cheatham. But what would really help us is if you could just tell us what happened and show us where you found the . . . the bag. Let us take a couple of pictures.' Sam held up a camera.

Sonora put a fresh tape in her recorder. Sweat trickled down the small of her back. The heat was making her queasy.

Cheatham nodded. His mouth worked in nervous little chewing motions. 'My boat's down this way. Y'all want to see?'

Sonora glanced over her shoulder – the sheriff's car was out of sight behind the trees. She nodded at Sam. 'Head on down. I want to check on Heather, then I'll catch up.'

'Want to bring her down?'

Sonora glanced at Cheatham. He wouldn't talk freely about dismembered body parts with a seven-year-old around. Neither would she.

'Nope.' Sonora headed back through the trees.

A man stood next to the sheriff's patrol car, his back to her, arms resting on the open window. She could see the top of Heather's head, and Clampett sitting in the driver's side. The front dash was fogged with dog drool and snout marks.

The man wore a faded pair of Wranglers, a white cotton teeshirt. Cute butt, which didn't stop Sonora from wondering what he was doing chatting up her seven-year-old, and why Clampett didn't bark.

Her feet hit gravel and the man turned.

'Girl, you look like you're going to tear my head off. Don't you recognize me?'

She didn't right at first. His hair was longer than the last time she'd seen him, thick and brown, and his face was tan. He looked fresh-scrubbed and cool, sunglasses hanging from the neck of the teeshirt. His cheeks were pink from a fresh shave, arms more muscular than she remembered, coated with coarse tan hair.

'Smallwood.'

He gave her a sideways look, fluttered his lashes provocatively. 'You can call me Deputy, if you want.'

'I'm still trying to figure out why my dog doesn't bark at you.'

'I have a way with animals. Usually sheep.'

She was going to shake his hand, but he gave her a hug instead. She caught the faintest whiff of scent. He smelled good. She liked it when men smelled good. She wished she wasn't so hot and sweaty.

He nodded at Heather. 'These rookies get younger every year.'

'It's take-your-daughter-to-work day.'

'Mom's going to take me to the morgue when I'd older,' Heather said.

'*Much* older,' Sonora muttered.

'*And* teach me to shoot.' Heather gave him a cheerful grin. 'Mommy, I'm hot. Can Clampett and me get out of the car?' A film of sweat coated her forehead, and her cheeks were flushed.

'Yeah, hop on out.'

'What's going on?' Smallwood asked.

Heather was fumbling with the door handle, and he opened the door, gave her a hand out.

Sonora stepped away from the car, voice low. 'Got a find here that may match up to what you got in London.'

'Head, hands, and feet,' Heather said. She looked at Sonora. 'That lady in the office told me.'

'Good of her to bring you up to date. What brings you out here, Smallwood?'

He smiled. 'This is Southern law enforcement. We all know what goes on in each other's backyards. Plus, we did kind of find the leg on our watch, if it turns out to be a match.'

'Did you know Julia Winchell?'

He shook his head.

'You want to walk down with me, talk to the guy who found her, take a look around?'

Smallwood glanced at Heather. 'What you going to do with little bit here?'

'Take her along, I guess. It's too hot to sit in the car.'

Smallwood glanced across the water to the little park full of swing sets, softball players, lush green grass and noisy children.

'Why don't I take her over there till you get done with your business?'

Sonora hesitated.

Smallwood smiled patiently while she turned the pros and cons over in her mind.

'You sure you don't need to go down there with me?' she asked.

'I've seen a trotline before.'

'Not like this one I bet. And how you getting over there to the park?' She glanced at the sheriff's patrol car.

'I've got my Jeep just over there. You didn't think I walked down from London, did you, Sonora? Brought my dog, too. We'll take yours along, and they can keep each other company.'

Sonora frowned. 'Clampett's kind of big. He can be a little aggressive.'

Smallwood grinned. 'I figure Tubby can handle the shock.'

'Don't let Clampett hurt him.'

Smallwood laughed and Sonora gave him an uneasy look.

'Heather, you want to go to the park with Deputy Smallwood, and swing on the swings?'

'Clampett's coming with me?'

'Yeah,' Sonora said. 'You make him behave, and you be good too.'

Smallwood put his sunglasses on. 'Everything's under control, Mama. You go ahead and do the nasty down there, and I'll take the dogs and the kid to the park.'

Sonora hugged Heather, told her again to be good, and headed back the way she had come. She turned back once, as she hit the tree line, and looked over her shoulder. Heather was skipping along beside Smallwood, asking him about Tubby, Clampett at her heels, tail wagging.

Sonora frowned. She was very cautious about allowing men into her children's lives. She barely knew this man and she'd broken relationship rules already. Not that she was planning to have a relationship.

She brushed hair out of her eyes and headed back through the trees to the water that had hidden Julia Winchell for the last couple of weeks.

Chapter Seventeen

When Sonora came through the trees to the muddy edge of the river she heard the hum of insects, and the low, easy laugh of men just beginning to feel comfortable with one another. Sizemore and Cheatham had known each other for years, and Sam could always be counted on to work that good-ol'-boy magic that is the special province of Southern men.

They were sitting on an old yellow rowboat that had been turned over to expose flaking paint and a hull that had been scraped raw.

Sam was eyeing a white plastic bucket with a John Deere symbol on the side, flies thick at the edges. 'How long'd you keep it in there?' He got up and peered inside, grimaced.

'Keep what in there?' Sonora asked.

George Cheatham looked up. 'The, um—'

'The plastic bag,' Sheriff Sizemore said, at the same time Sam said, 'Make a guess, girl.'

Sonora looked inside the bucket, which held about three inches of dirty brown river water, two tiny silver fish with meaty white bellies, and something dead that seemed to have the teeth and tail of a fish, and the hands and feet of a 'gator. Dead flies skimmed the top of the water.

'What *is* that?' Sonora asked, pointing to the 'gator thing.

'Water dog,' George said.

'Gar,' Sizemore told her.

Sam looked at Sonora. 'You really never saw one before? They bark when they're on shore.'

'They do not,' Sonora said, frowning at him, but Sizemore

was nodding his head. 'Was it – that gar thing – was it in the bag with the . . . was it in the bag?'

Cheatham nodded. 'Smell of blood attracted it, then it tore on in there. I kilt it with a baseball bat I keep in the bottom of the boat.'

Sonora looked at the boat, mud banked against the edges where it had dripped water. She looked back in the bucket. A sliver of brown plastic floated next to the gar, whose damaged head swelled and bloated in the heat. More flies arrived, circling the top of the bucket. Sonora felt the sun on her head, the sweat running down her back. Her shoes were caked with mud.

They would have to take that gar back, and analyze the stomach contents.

Sam clicked his recorder on. 'Mr. Cheatham was just getting started on his story.'

Sonora settled next to Sam on the overturned boat. Cheatham turned another five-gallon bucket – this one said Papa Jeff's Mild Golden Pepperoncini on the side – and sat on the edge. He scratched his chin.

'I run the trotline out last night around dusk.'

Sonora looked at Sam and he whispered in her ear. 'Fishing line. Baited all the way across, goes across the river, sits on the bottom, maybe, and snags fish.' He looked up at Cheatham. 'What'd you bait it with, Mr. Cheatham?'

'Cookie dough and night crawlers.'

Sam looked interested. Nodded his head.

'Went down real early this morning, 'bout six-thirty when the sun come up, and brought up the line. Found this bag hanging off the middle. So I pull it up and dump it on the bottom of the boat there.' He rubbed rough palms together, making raspy noises, like cricket legs at dusk. His left shoulder twitched at regular intervals.

'Never seen nuthin' like it before and never hope to again. That water dog up and crawls across my foot and I bash it good with my bat there.' He nodded toward the stained aluminum bat. 'And I head on home, shaking like nobody's business, I don't mind telling you.'

'Did you check the rest of the line?' Sonora asked.

Cheatham nodded. The shoulder twitched.

'Anything on any of the other hooks?'

Cheatham shook his head. 'Nuthin' of a unusual nature. Turtles. Got a good-sized wide-mouth bass. Good eating for tonight, anyhow.'

Sonora watched for the shoulder twitch. 'Then what happened?'

'I come close to heaving the whole mess on back in the water, then I start to wondering where's the rest of her? So I poke around a little where the line was, but didn't find much. I didn't look too hard – it was giving me a funny feeling, sitting out on that boat with . . . you know, in the bottom.'

Sonora glanced out across the river. 'Right about where were you, Mr. Cheatham?'

He rubbed the back of his neck. Pointed to the right, away from the ballpark. 'Right down there just a piece – see where that tree's laying sideways like? Had one end of the trot line tied around it, but I hid it on the other side. Didn't want nobody messing with it.'

Sam nodded.

Sonora looked out over the water, picturing the old yellow boat bobbing in the ripples, the park quiet, sun just up, accordions of reflected light skimming the water's surface. Fish jumping, making ripples. Cheatham emptied his last cigarette out of a crumpled pack of Camel Lights, struck a wooden match on his black-rimmed thumbnail. The acrid smell of burning tobacco drifted around their heads. Cheatham inhaled deeply, dragging a good way into his last cigarette like a man starved.

Sam took pictures. Jack Cheatham sat on the upturned bucket, cigarette loose on the left side of his mouth, a hesitant smile on his face, like a man who's been trained to smile for the camera, no matter what.

Chapter Eighteen

Sonora watched them from a distance – Heather going up and down in the big swing, Smallwood pushing her higher and higher.

There was no parking this far back in the park, so Sam edged the Blazer off the road into the grass. He put the car in park, tapped the steering wheel, looked at Sonora, and grinned.

'So that's the famous Smallwood. He still calling you every couple of weeks?'

Sonora nodded. She watched Clampett, on his feet, circling the swing set, growling at any child or adult who came within fifteen feet of Heather.

He seemed to tolerate a smaller dog, who sat and watched Smallwood and panted in the heat. The dog was packed tight as a sausage casing, with short blue-gray fur and black ears. He watched the playground with a look of intelligence that was unnerving.

'Where'd the little dog come from?' Sam asked.

'Smallwood's. Weird-looking mix.'

Sam shook his head at her. 'That's a Blue Heeler. Cattle dog. I haven't seen one since I was a kid.'

'I'm glad Clampett didn't hurt it.'

Sam laughed. 'You been worrying about the wrong dog, Sonora.'

She shrugged and got out of the car. Heather was smiling, swinging higher and higher, hair blowing, and Sonora felt sad.

It was the Daddy thing. Zack was an absentee father when he was alive, and Sonora knew that, if he had lived, their marriage would have ended around the time she had buried him. But Heather and Tim were missing out on the strong male influence.

On the bright side, there had been insurance money.

Chapter Nineteen

Sonora let out a sigh when she saw the McDonald's across the street from the Winchells' small blue house.

'What?' Sam said.

'McDonald's,' Sonora told him.

'You hungry?'

She looked pointedly at her daughter. Sam nodded, and pulled into the parking lot. Sonora turned around and looked at Heather.

'Can Clampett have a cheeseburger?' she asked.

They left Heather locked in the Blazer with the windows down, Clampett gulping a cheeseburger, Heather working on a chocolate sundae. The first chocolate smear was already drying on the passenger's side headrest, and the windshield was fogging with Clampett's warm breath. Sonora had left the radio playing, and shown Heather the house, catty-cornered to the McDonald's and across the street that Heather was under no circumstances to cross.

Sam and Sonora headed down the sloping asphalt parking lot toward Main Street, which was torn up and clogged with trucks, men in hard hats, a steam roller, and a huge lighted arrow mounted on a trailer that kept traffic herded into one slow-moving lane.

Mounds of dirt were piled on the side of the road. Broken concrete and asphalt were liberally mixed in the reddish brown soil like raisins in a muffin.

Sonora glanced down at her Reeboks. These were her

oldest pair. Probably be easier to throw them away than clean them up. It was six PM, but the sun was still high. It felt like the middle of the afternoon.

The Winchells' house was fifty, sixty years old, red brick that had been whitewashed, the paint peeling. Mounds of dirt were humped at the end of a gravel drive. The yard was sparse, weedy, but trimmed. There were flower boxes in the front window, thick with pink and white begonias.

A rusty red wagon sat by the edge of the driveway. It had been packed with stuffed animals. A tiny bicycle, no more than two feet tall, lay across the front porch.

Sam picked the bicycle up, set it gently on the sidewalk beside the front steps. He looked at Sonora.

'I should have stayed with football.'

Sonora knew what he meant. Times like this she wished she was a secretary. 'Football gave *you* up, remember?'

'If I forget I have you to remind me.'

Sonora took a breath, and tried to relax. Her back felt rigid and achy. She rang the doorbell, heard thumps – small feet on hardwood – and an angry screech. The door stuck, then opened. Winchell held a baby in the crook of his left arm. His sleeves were rolled up and the front of his shirt and top of his pants were wet. Sonora recognized the child from the pictures that still sat on her desk in Cincinnati.

Butch Winchell pushed his glasses back on his nose. 'Hi.'

The baby was wrapped in a yellow terrycloth towel that was draped and hooded over the top of her damp, drippy head. She grinned at Sam and Sonora, showing a spread of tiny milk teeth.

'*Move*,' she said.

Winchell glanced down at the little girl. 'This is Chrissie. Her first word was "move," the second was "mine." Must come from being the second child.'

Possible future in police work, Sonora thought.

'Mr. Winchell,' Sam said.

Winchell held up a hand. 'Come in, and we'll talk.'

He was oddly relaxed and matter-of-fact. He led them into a living room with polished hardwood floors. A cheap but colorful oriental rug, rose and black, warmed the room. There were wood shutters on the window, and the walls had recently been painted a soft yellow. The furniture was old, Salvation Army era, but there were mahogany bookshelves built into the walls, a stone fireplace, and a television tucked into an antique oak pie safe.

With the ease of experienced parents, Sonora and Sam negotiated the color books, crayons, and Leggos that littered the floor. Sonora settled on the edge of an old green couch. She avoided the armrest, which had a mysterious yellow stain. Sam took a recliner, maroon vinyl, that looked as if it had survived – barely – the kittenhood of a series of bad cats. Foam spilled from a tear in the cushion. Sam tucked it back in absently, realized what he was doing, and quit.

'Let me put Chrissie in her sleeper,' Winchell said. 'Be right back.'

Sonora waited till she heard his footsteps on the staircase. 'You called him, right?'

Sam looked at her. 'You were standing right there when I did it.'

'I mean, you told him why we were coming out here, right?'

Sam nodded. 'Told him it would be a good idea to have someone with him. Maybe to look after the kids.'

Something was pressing into her back. Sonora fished behind her and pulled out a worn blue book with a cracked spine and tooth marks on the corner.

Dr. Seuss. *Green Eggs And Ham*. She handed it to Sam, looked at her watch. They had a four-hour drive back.

Sonora drummed her fingers on the armrest, away from the yellow stain. She noticed a little girl, the three-year-old, staring at them from the hallway. She stood in the shadows and her features were hard to make out. She was small, tummy swelling over her shorts and pouching out from under a chocolate-smeared teeshirt that was getting too small.

'Come on in,' Sam said.

She took three steps forward. She wore pink flip-flops and held a half-eaten cookie high up over her head. She had tucked a purple weed into her hair, snug behind her ear.

'Why you got that cookie over top your head?' Sam said.

'Got it at the Mortons' next door. Didn't want Bernie to get it.'

'Bernie that hungry?' Sam asked.

'Bernie's always hungry. He's a dog.'

She took a bite of cookie. 'My name is Terry. Are you here about Mama? Daddy says we're having a bad year.'

Footsteps again, on the staircase. Slow. Winchell came down the stairs with the baby in one arm, and a folded playpen in the other. Sam was on his feet in an instant, reaching for the playpen.

'My little girl had one just like this,' Sam said, unfolding the yellow-meshed square and setting it in the center of the room.

The baby screamed, leaned toward Terry and the cookie. Terry shoved the cookie toward her sister.

The baby's mouth popped open, soft lips pursed. She nipped off the end of the cookie, chewing hugely, exposing pink gums. Chocolate-tinged drool spilled down her chin into the folds of her neck, and soaked the collar of the rose-pink sleeper.

'Terry, I just got her cleaned up.'

The little girl put the cookie behind her back. 'I'm sorry, Daddy. Want me to get a wash rag?'

'Please.'

Terry looked at Sam. 'Will you help me turn on the water?'

Another conquest, Sonora thought. He even got to the young ones.

'You bet I will. Go on and pop that little one into the pen, Mr. Winchell. I'll keep an eye on your babies.' Sam looked at Sonora and she nodded.

'Mr. Winchell, while Sam's doing that, let's go into the kitchen for a minute and talk?' Sonora smiled at him and pushed through floor-length wood saloon doors.

It was a small kitchen, dark, imitation-redbrick linoleum peeling away from the edges of the wall. A metal highchair, butter yellow, was scooted up to the edge of the table. The metal food tray was clumped with baby oatmeal which, Sonora knew from experience, would now have the consistency of concrete. A baby spoon, the end shaped like Mickey Mouse, was on the floor under the table. Two laundry baskets sat next to the back door.

There were dishes on the counter, an open loaf of bread near the sink. The table was old brown Formica, stainless-steel legs, and cluttered with a two-day supply of milk-filled bowls clotted with dead soggy cereal. An open box of Sugar Frosted Flakes sat next to a box of Fruit Loops. A plastic mug shaped like a parrot had slipped on its side, a trail of dried orange juice snaking to the edge of the table. A bottle of Flintstones vitamins, three left, one purple Fred and two green Dinos, was open next to a sticky-looking salt-shaker. There was no pepper in sight.

Pictures ripped from color books were taped to an almost new double-wide refrigerator. You could get ice cubes and ice water out of the door. Sonora wanted one like that.

She thought of Julia Winchell, facing this dark cramped kitchen every morning. Working long hours only to come home to laundry, bills, kids.

Much like her own life.

The room at the Orchard Suites would have been an oasis – a two-room suite with maid service and a complimentary breakfast buffet right off the lobby. Black silk teddy on the pillow at the head of the bed.

Was Julia Winchell having an affair because there

was trouble in her marriage, or because she needed a vacation?

'Excuse all this mess,' Winchell said. He pressed his back to the counter in front of the sink, and licked his lips.

Sonora nodded. 'Mr. Winchell, Detective Delarosa talked to you on the phone about why we're here.'

'I got Kool-Aid in the refrigerator. Or I could make you some ice tea.'

'No thanks.'

'It's grape.' There was sweat on his forehead.

'No thanks.'

'Want to sit down?' Winchell pulled two chairs away from the cluttered table, chair legs scraping the linoleum, making black scuff marks that barely showed against the red.

Sonora noticed that Winchell's pants hung loose, his eyes dark-shadowed. Not sleeping or eating. His cheeks were pink and smooth. Probably shaved for the first time in a long time right after Sam's call.

'Mr. Winchell, is there anyone you want to have with you tonight? Maybe help you out with the kids?' she asked.

Winchell was smiling at her, shaking his head. He picked a spoon up off the table, fingering the bowl. Sonora saw that his hand was perfectly steady.

'Mr. Winchell, I think it's possible we may have found your wife.'

He kept smiling. Sonora watched him, wondering if she was getting through.

'If we have found her, Mr. Winchell, the news isn't good. It's bad.'

'I know what you're saying.' The smile had gone shy, but it was still there, and the look in his eyes was sober, the voice deeper and more gravelly.

She was getting through.

'We've found ... remains ... that we think are Julia's remains. You can go to the sheriff's office and make a formal identification, but we thought it might be easier, at first, if you took a look at a couple of pictures.'

Sheer torture for him now. Sonora took the pictures from her blazer pocket quickly and handed them over. He made no move to take them. Sonora brushed crumbs and clutter to one side of the table, and laid the pictures out, avoiding milk rings and sticky spots.

They'd done what they could in the sheriff's office, laying the head back against the steel table as if Julia Winchell was resting, pulling a white sheet up to her chin to cover the raw, fish-eaten wound of the severed neck, unwrapping the hair from the face. The sheriff had cut a piece of black construction paper and placed it over the empty eye socket.

Still, by no means pretty.

The skin had that pearly gray-white translucence of death, black-tinged with putrescence. And the hands, laid on the table, severed wrists hidden by the sheet, were still missing fingers, one gnawed to the bone.

'*God.*' Winchell shuddered and looked away, closing his eyes. 'It's not her.'

Sonora frowned. 'Mr. Winchell, I'm sorry, would you take another look so we can make sure?'

He looked again, eyes narrow, head tilted sideways as if he couldn't face the pictures head on. He shook his head. 'No. I'm sure, I'm definite. This isn't Julie.'

Sonora took the pictures and put them away. 'Mr. Winchell—'

'It's *not* her. How about some Kool-Aid? Be glad to pour you a glass.'

He was bringing out the heavy Southern artillery. Blunt courtesy to the right palate for TKO.

'All right, Mr. Winchell. I don't have any more information for you right now, but I'll stay in close touch.'

'Of course. Thank you. I'll do the same.'

'There's one other thing.'

He waited, hands still in his lap.

'Detective Delarosa mentioned this to you on the phone, I think. We need blood samples from your children, so we can run a match with this victim, check the DNA. That way we can make a positive ID – in this situation, or in anything else that might crop up.'

He licked his lips. 'Could you maybe get the DNA stuff from Julie's sister?'

'We've been in touch. She'll be meeting us at the clinic in about an hour, give or take, but we still need samples from the children. The Sevier Boulevard Clinic is staying open. We've made arrangements already. Unless you prefer your own doctor?'

'Is there any charge for this?' he asked in a soft voice.

'No sir, no charge.'

He nodded. 'I need . . . a little time. Clean Chrissie and Terry up, and do some stuff here in the kitchen. Can I meet you there, say half an hour?'

She would never get home. She thought of Heather, waiting, waiting. 'That would be fine.'

Sonora turned away, taking a breath as she escaped the kitchen. Sam was in the living room, reading *Green Eggs And Ham* to the girls, who were both cuddled in his lap.

'Sam?'

He held up a hand. 'Almost done.'

Terry glanced up at Sonora, but her absorbed gaze was immediately drawn away when Sam turned the page and showed a new picture. Chrissie bent forward, mouthing the corner of the book.

'Be right out front,' Sonora said.

She had to get out of the house. She headed out the door, screen whanging shut behind her.

She was across the street, no more than a couple of feet from the Blazer, when she heard Winchell call her name. He was standing in the side yard, waving his arms. Sonora figured he'd come out that back kitchen door, bypassing Sam and his little girls. He was pitched forward, body tense.

Sonora looked back at the Blazer. Clampett's head was thrust out the window. She could hear him bark and snarl because someone had dared open the passenger's side door of the car parked next to theirs. Laid back and easy at home, he was a hellacious watchdog on the road. Heather was pulling on his neck, trying to get him to hush.

Sonora headed back across the road. A pickup truck, loaded with gravel, went by slinging small rocks at her feet. She waited for traffic to slow, then break, but cars kept coming in an endless stream, giving her an occasional glimpse of Winchell, pitched forward on his toes, wiping sweat from the back of his neck.

There was a dump truck coming, right behind a white Lexis, ponderously gathering speed. Sonora dashed through the gap, climbed over the gravel and dirt piles, headed down the weedy unpaved driveway back up to the Winchell house.

Butch Winchell had deflated somehow, face sagging, hair sticking up on one side where he'd run his hands through. He did not meet Sonora's eyes. He took his glasses off, cleaned them on his shirt.

'Mr. Winchell?' Sonora said gently.

He was out of breath, as if he'd been the one darting through traffic. They both were breathing hard.

'Yes, ma'am. I think . . .' He rubbed his forehead with the heel of his hand, put the glasses back on. 'I changed my mind, Detective Blair. It's Julie.'

'I know.'

Chapter Twenty

The waiting room was cold enough to make Sonora shiver – a good thirty-degree drop from the heat and humidity outside. Sam paced in front of Sonora, Heather up on his shoulders, sleepy but game.

A woman in pink sweats and a white polyester jacket leaned out into the waiting area from one of those equipment-laden rooms where medical people always made you wait.

'We're ready now, Detective.'

Sam looked at Sonora 'I'll go. I'm more used to it.'

Something in his tone of voice gave Sonora a twinge of guilt. He'd logged more than his fair share of hospital time with Annie. Sam put Heather gently on the floor and walked into the examining room, with Butch Winchell and his two little girls.

Heather sat cross-legged on the floor in front of Sonora. Her teeshirt and shorts had seen a lot of action for one day. She needed a bath.

'Where's Sam going?'

'They have to take blood samples from Mr. Winchell and his little girls.'

'How come Sam has to watch?'

'Maintain continuity in the chain of evidence.'

A wail came through the closed door. Heather put her head against Sonora's leg, and Sonora reached down and lifted her off the floor, settling her sideways into her lap.

They sat quietly, listening to the babies cry. Sonora heard

a car door slam, saw headlights, noted quick light footsteps. The glass door opened, bringing in a wave of humid heat and the sound of crickets, and a woman who, at a distance, resembled Julia Winchell.

She had the same kind of hair, brown-black and sleek, with the lush richness Sonora had only seen in Vidal Sassoon commercials. She wore blue jeans, lace-up hiking boots, an orange teeshirt that said JAZZERCIZE. She was tallish, five six or seven, with high cheekbones. Her hair was cut chin-length, straight and swingy. Her brows were dark, eyes almond-brown. She walked very precisely, careful where she put her feet.

Sonora wondered how like she was to her sister. Families, in her experience, shared mannerisms and quirks of speech even more than physical similarities. Tribal trademarks, she thought. Had Julia Winchell kept her nails so long and meticulously polished? Did she turn her head sideways like that, chew her hair when deep in thought?

Sonora had the familiar urge to know the victim. She had an image, fueled by one Kodak snapshot, and the remains that had been snagged and dragged by the trotline.

Sonora shifted Heather off her lap, stood up. She flipped the ID, knew Heather was watching. For some reason the kids always liked to see her show the badge.

'Detective Blair, Cincinnati Police Department. You're Liza, aren't you? Julia's sister?'

The woman swung her head sideways and tilted it up. 'Liza Harden. Yes, I'm Julia's sister.' They shook hands. 'I've talked to you on the phone a couple of times, haven't I?'

There was no Southern in this woman's voice. Sonora wondered where she was from, and how she'd wound up in Knoxville.

'Thanks for coming,' Sonora said.

Liza Harden looked away. 'Did Butch . . .' She took a breath. 'Did Butch think it was her?'

'If you don't mind, Ms. Harden, it would be best

if you took a look yourself, and formed your own opinion.'

'Sure.'

She was going all stony-faced. Sonora decided they'd better get the blood samples first.

Chapter Twenty-One

Sam and Sonora packed the blood samples carefully into the back of the Blazer. It would have been nice to rent a room for the night, but they decided it would be best to get the physical specimens back to Cincinnati and into the hands of the CSU guys. Neither of them wanted to sit in front of a jury and explain how the blood had sat overnight in the parking lot of the local Budget-Tel.

Sonora sat in a booth at the Shoney's Inn Restaurant, non-smoking, next to the salad bar, and ordered a Coke.

Liza Harden went for coffee, in spite of the heat.

'Where's your little one?' Harden asked. Her eyes were red-rimmed and glazed. She seemed to want to talk.

Grief took people that way, sometimes, stunned them into an honest purge of thought and emotion. Sometimes they said things they were sorry for later. Sonora had always thought it was a good time to talk to people, if you had the stomach for it.

Harden put three packs of Equal into her coffee cup, caught Sonora's look. 'If you think this is bad, you should have seen Jules. She put – no kidding – eleven of these in every cup of coffee. Fifteen in her iced tea.' Harden smiled, eyes misty. 'Last Christmas I went to Sams and bought one of those *huge*, econo-boxes of Equal – must have been ten thousand packs in that thing. I wrapped it in red foil and put it under her Christmas tree as a joke. That thing weighed a ton. She kept picking it up and fooling with it. She thought I got her, like, hand weights or something.'

Sonora took a long sip of Coke, savored the jolt of sugar and caffeine. 'Your sister have a good sense of humor?'

'Oh *God*, she was funny. We always did the joke thing at Christmas. One year she gave me these horrible disco earring balls – I mean, purple sequins, the height of tacky. And I was thanking her, you know, and thinking, what in the *hell*! She got to laughing and told me my real present was in the trunk of her car. That's what started it, it was her. So the next year I got her a goldfish – Jules hated fish, she could not stand to be around aquariums, said they were tedious beyond belief. She got me an M&M dispenser. I'm not going to be able to stand it this year. Christmas and no Jules.'

She covered her face with her hands. Sonora waited.

Harden wiped her eyes with a napkin, blew her nose. '*Sorry*.' She looked up, eyes bright. 'Where's your little girl?'

'She and Detective Delarosa went to Wal-Mart to pick up . . . a cooler.'

Harden did not seem to find any particular significance in the need for a cooler. Sonora did not explain.

'You have any other kids, Detective?'

'My son is fourteen. Heather is seven.'

'Where is he?' Harden asked.

It was a sore point. 'I don't know. No one answers where he swore up and down he would be.' Sonora brought out her recorder. A tape was inside, ready to go.

Harden gave her a wary look.

'I take it that you and your sister were close?' In this instance, a rhetorical question, but Sonora always made a point of starting with the easy stuff. She could listen to Liza Harden talk about Julia for thirty seconds, and know they were close.

She wondered what it was like to have a sister.

Liza Harden nodded.

'How was her marriage?'

'I *knew* you were going to ask me that. It was fine, I guess.'

'How fine could it be? We both know she was having an affair. You never met this guy?'

Liza Harden's eyes went narrow for a moment. She leaned back against the turquoise pad of the booth. 'No, I didn't want to. I like Butch, and I felt funny about it. I told her if this guy lasted more than six months, I'd meet him then.'

'How'd Julia take that?'

'Told me to go fuck myself.'

'Had she done anything like this before?'

Harden looked at Sonora, reached for her coffee cup, and put it back down. 'No.'

Sonora raised one eyebrow. 'You sure?'

'Yeah, I know, I hesitated. Far as I know this was Julia's first walk on the wild side. She didn't know how these things work. But I do. I've done it before.'

'Okay. Julia know about that?'

'Some of them. I didn't tell her at first – I thought she'd, you know, be all shocked and disapproving. But I fell in love and got upset and called her once.'

'What'd she do?'

Harden shook her head. 'It was the first one I told her about, and she *laughed*. Then I was the one who was shocked. She said she had no idea I'd been having all the fun, wanted to know all about it. That's what got me wondering if her marriage was all it was cracked up to be. She even asked me . . . never mind *what* she asked me, but let's just say it was pointed.'

Harden refilled her coffee from the brown plastic pot, ripped open a blue packet of Equal. 'Believe me, we weren't raised like this.'

'How long did your sister have a private post office box?'

Harden frowned. 'You know about that? She got it about two, three months ago. Right after she met this guy.'

'She open it just for him?'

Harden shrugged. 'Yes and no. Let's say he was the catalyst. But I'm the one who talked her into it. Went with her, paid the first six months' rent on the thing. See, I didn't know if her marriage was in trouble. My experience is: people say, no, we're fine, fine – oops, guess what, we're getting divorced. That's the way it was for me, some of my friends. The reasons may take years but the actual divorce seems to hit all of a sudden. A post office box is a good thing to have.'

Sonora nodded. Harden continued. 'She had a safe deposit box at a bank, too, and a checking account in her name only, different bank from the one she and Butch used. One hundred dollars in the bank account, three hundred in the box. We put it in together. For emergencies. I've been divorced before. I know how this stuff works.' She dipped her spoon in and out of the coffee cup, scattering brown drops of liquid on the imitation-woodgrain table.

'Sounds like serious trouble,' Sonora said.

Harden's look was intent, as if she had tales to tell. 'It's a good idea to be prepared. Remember, I've been there, seen friends go through it. Seen how the person you said forever with, had children with, turns into a weird nasty stranger. I can't decide whether divorce just turns people mean, or if you're just seeing them the way they really are for the first time.'

'What was going on with them? Julia and Butch? From a sister's-eye view.'

Harden set the spoon down. 'I think, in all honesty, her marriage was no better or worse than any other. They've been running the diner for four years – putting in unbelievable hours. And they started their family about the same time. Two little girls – beautiful as they are – and the diner. They've actually been doing pretty well with it the last couple of years, but it's an impossible load.'

'Butch do his fair share?'

Harden shook her head. 'What man does? And anyway, the diner is his big dream. Jules was fine with it, but she was getting restless. She felt like she'd spent four years busting her ass, getting the diner off the ground, making babies like a hill woman, and she was wanting just a little time to herself. To get centered, is how she put it. Butch didn't get that, and the more she tried to pull away, the harder he kicked. If he'd have let her breathe a little, they probably would have been okay. That's why that affair of hers was going nowhere.'

Sonora raised an eyebrow, waiting.

Harden laid her palms down on top of the table. 'Because the guy needed a keeper. His wife and kids died in a car accident a few years ago, and he grabbed my sister like a lifeline. He was . . . demanding, and difficult. She used to joke that now she had four kids on her hands, the girls, Butch, and . . . this guy. The last time we talked, she said she thought she'd made a mistake. That she was feeling . . . I don't know . . . claustrophobic and out of breath when she was near him. I think she was trying to figure out how to get rid of him without hurting his feelings.' Liza Harden rolled her eyes. 'Ain't no way, of course. And then this big exciting plan to meet in Cincinnati gets made, and she goes up on wings of love, and finds after a few days this guy is driving her nuts.

'*Then* she sees that guy's picture in the paper, and she's off on that like you would not believe. It's been a lot of years since it happened. I was surprised by how upset she was over it.'

'She say who this alleged killer was?'

'Some DA – got his picture in the paper, trying some old jock for running down a girl from Xavier.'

'She give you a name?'

She frowned, pursed her lips. 'She mentioned it. I'd know it if I heard it.'

'Helphenstine? Reynolds? Caplan?'

'Yeah, that was it.'

'Which?' Sonora glanced at the tape to make sure it was running.

'Caplan.'

Sonora kept her expression matter-of-fact. 'How sure was she?'

Harden waved a hand. 'We talked about that, you know? 'Cause it's been eight years. And she only saw him maybe a few seconds. It's been eight years, and people change. Plus he was crying when she saw him.'

'Crying?'

Harden nodded. 'Isn't that weird? I can't remember exactly what she said, but I think he was holding some poor girl under water, she's gagging and thrashing around. And the whole time he's holding her under, tears are running down his face.'

'Sweat,' Sonora said.

'Jules said crying. It weirded her out.' Harden folded her arms and leaned back into the booth. 'Julia told me she was going to go to this guy's office and meet him. Maybe on some pretense. She didn't think he would remember what she looked like. I told her not to confront him. If it is him, she tips her hand. If it's not, she looks like three kinds of idiot, right?'

'Why didn't she go to the police?'

'Well, you know, Detective, the whole thing is pretty thin. She sees a picture in the paper of a guy she thinks committed a murder nobody believed happened eight years ago. She wanted to check things out a little. Look at it on her own. And forgive me for being blunt. I don't know what it's like with you guys, as in police officers. But your average citizen's usual contact with prosecutors isn't likely to be pleasant. Ever been a witness to a crime? Better to be a criminal. Jules witnessed to a car accident once, and foolishly tried to be a good citizen. Never a good idea.'

'I wish I could say I didn't agree with you.' Sonora glanced at the recorder. What the hell, Harden was right. 'About this murder your sister thinks she saw. What was your gut feel on it?'

'I don't know. I admit, when Jules called me, I thought it might be some kind of an escape thing. Play detective. Beats going home to a man who's driving you nutso, or dumping a lover who's doing the same. But now, after what happened to her, it kind of makes you wonder.'

'You have a key to the post office box?' Sonora asked.

Harden nodded.

'Where is it?'

'On my key ring.'

'I meant the box.'

'In Knoxville. Couldn't have one here and the whole town not know about it.'

'How far a drive?'

'About thirty-five, forty minutes.'

'Is your name on the paperwork?'

'Had to be. Otherwise they'd send the bill and stuff to her house, and Butch would have found out.'

'Good. My partner should be here—'

'Hell, no, I'll take you right now. I want to see what's in the box.'

Chapter Twenty-Two

The post office branch where Julia Winchell had her secret post office box was in a small strip mall on Kingston Parkway, Knoxville's main thoroughfare. They passed through an endless string of offices, malls, movie theaters, restaurants, BlockBuster Videos, liquor stores.

Liza Harden braked for the parking lot speed bump a split second before she hit it. She drove a dingy white Toyota Carolla with navy interior. The air-conditioner worked, barely, flooding the cab with an odor similar to that of a dirty gym sock. The car squeaked, shocks on overload, and Sonora decided that if her son drove this badly when he turned sixteen he would not get his license.

'Forgive the smell,' Harden was saying. 'I don't know *why* it does that. It's either the smell or no air-conditioning.' She glanced sideways at Sonora. 'You got a preference?'

Southerners, Sonora thought. So gracious.

There were plenty of parking spaces. Liza Harden stopped the car just before it hit the curb. Her front tires grazed concrete. She turned off the engine, pulled the emergency brake into place, and looked at Sonora.

'The afternoon Jules and I came here was her first real day off – no kids, no restaurant – in months. If that tells you anything.'

Welcome to real life, Sonora thought, wondering what Harden did for a living. She got out of the car.

Harden walked ahead into the post office – small glass doors partitioned the outer lobby from the service counters that were locked up tight. She bypassed the first inlet of boxes, leading Sonora into the middle alcove.

'Thirteen seventy-five,' Harden muttered. She considered and rejected the various keys on her ring. 'Ah. Here's this. It looks good.'

She inserted the key into the lock while Sonora said a small prayer.

It was one of the smaller boxes, letter-size and long. The key turned and the door swung open with a squeak. Sonora moved sideways, edging Harden aside as politely as possible.

Inside she saw a brown envelope, rolled to fit, along with three standard-size letters and a box of Cocoa Puffs, advertisement-size. Harden held a hand out expectantly.

Sonora handed her the cereal.

'What about the mail?'

'I've got it.' Wariness dropped like a blanket between them. 'I have a form and a receipt you need to sign, when we get to Clinton. Paperwork's in my car.' Sonora glanced at Harden. No clue to what she was thinking. 'It will be better if these get opened up in the lab, with the crime-scene guys. Get what evidence we can from them.'

Harden folded her arms. 'Feel free to make me that speech about how you're going to catch my sister's killer. That was always my favorite scene on *Crime Story*.'

Chapter Twenty-Three

Sonora tucked her daughter into the back seat of the Blazer, folding her jacket into a pillow, using a worn but clean beach towel that had been left in the car from the last lake trip to use as a makeshift blanket. She used the middle seat belt because it was adjustable, and Heather could lie down. She snugged it up till it looked comfortable, wondering how safe it would be.

'When's Sam coming?' Heather asked. Her eyes were closed.

'Just in a minute.' Sonora heard the door of the sheriff's office scrape the concrete stoop. The men's voices and footsteps had the quick measured pace that meant they were carrying something either awkward or heavy or both.

The back hatch of the Blazer opened. The air outside was cooler now, but not by much. They'd turn the air-conditioner up high when they hit the road, and Heather would need the beach towel to keep the chill off while she slept.

Sonora hoped she would sleep.

'Move it back this way.' The sheriff's voice, instructing Sam, who slid an oversized metal cooler into the back of the car.

Heather's eyes opened to slits.

Sonora patted her head. 'Go on to sleep, kidlet. We got a long drive ahead.'

Heather nodded slightly, and turned on her side. Sonora listened for heavy, regular breathing. Little seven-year-old girls did not need to know that the cooler in the back section of the Blazer held a severed head, two hands, and two feet.

She shut the car door gently, and went to the back of the Blazer. Sam latched the back hatch gently. The cooler, heavily packed with ice, did not move.

Sonora shook Sheriff Sizemore's hand, signed his clipboard of papers.

'I'm sure you people are the ones ought to have this stuff. You got the facilities. And, like you say, you got reason to believe she was killed up in Cincinnati, which makes it your baby.'

Sonora was not sure who he was reassuring.

Sam shook Sizemore's hand and clapped his shoulder. Their reasons for thinking the crime originated in Cincinnati were thin. But Sizemore wasn't arguing.

'You've been a whole lot of help, Sheriff. Run a good outfit, for a country boy.'

Sonora thought she would never have gotten away with it, but Sizemore grinned.

'You folks just find the fella did this, and put a tag in his ear for me. I don't want to see this one ground under the heel of that Aldridge boy over at the state police. Ain't money or pussy in it, he ain't interested.' He looked at Sonora, and turned pink around the ears. 'Excuse me.'

She really hated it when they remembered she wasn't one of the boys. 'Money doesn't offend me,' she said, deadpan. 'And you can't fault a guy who likes cats.'

'We won't trouble the state boys any,' Sam promised. 'And you got my number. Give us a call, if you hear anything.'

'You bet.'

Sonora looked back over her shoulder in time to see the sheriff actually tip his hat. She waved and headed toward the driver's seat, bumped into Sam.

'It's after dark, girl, I'll drive.'

'I'll drive.'

'You remember last time when I asked if you wanted to

pull over and let me drive for a while, and you said you would if you could find the side of the road?'

Sonora glanced at Heather in the back seat. 'Okay, you drive.' She got into the passenger's side and put on her seat belt.

Sam adjusted the rearview mirror and looked at her. 'Can't fault a man for liking *cats*?'

Gravel spun under the car tires as Sam backed the Blazer out of the lot. He glanced up in the rearview mirror, slammed on the brakes.

'What now?' he muttered.

Sonora heard knuckles against her window, and rolled it down. The sheriff again, red-faced and out of breath.

Please God he doesn't want those body parts back, Sonora thought. They'd signed for them, completed all the paperwork. Invested in a cooler.

'That back right tire looks low,' Sizemore said.

'We'll get it checked when we fill up on gas,' Sam said.

Sonora smiled and waved. The sheriff nodded and headed off.

'You notice the tire looking low, Sam?'

'No.'

'I guess we can check it like you said. When we get gas.'

'Hell no, the tires are fine.'

'You didn't even look. What if it is low?'

'I ain't checking it.'

Chapter Twenty-Four

They hit fog going over the mountains that bordered the Tennessee state line. Sam squinted, following the taillights of the truck ahead.

'So then what happened? Anything in the post office box?'

'Two letters and a brown envelope.'

He glanced at her, then looked back at the road. Swirls of clammy white drifted across the lights. The road was almost invisible.

'Don't slow down too much – we'll get rear-ended,' Sonora said.

'Open that mail.'

'It'll make me car sick.'

'Then you drive and I'll read it.'

Sonora glanced back at Heather, breathing deeply and evenly, eyes shut tight. Her hand rested on her cheek, vibrating with the movement of the car.

At the next bathroom break, she would call home, and this time Tim would be there. She did not like driving home late at night, in the fog, wondering if he was okay. She glanced back toward the cooler, bent down to the maroon vinyl case by her feet.

The zipper seemed loud in the cab of the car, road noises muffled by the fog and darkness. She looked at the white envelopes.

'Turn the fog lights on, Sam. Switch on the left. Next to that other one.'

'What other . . . oh, here.' He clicked a switch. The beams of light changed, penetrating the mist instead of reflecting back. 'Girl, you could've brought this up a while ago.'

Sonora opened one of the envelopes. 'Bill from Victoria's Secret. Julia Winchell ordered a black silk teddy and a wonder bra.'

'Big?'

'Medium.'

'I meant the—'

'I know what you meant. She owes forty-two dollars and sixty-eight cents. Guess what the interest rate is on this thing, Sam? It's God-awful. Guess.'

'Wages of sin.'

'Sam, it's not sin, it's lingerie.'

'What else you got?'

Sonora opened the other white envelope. 'Stuff from the conference, looks like. Information on panels and stuff. "The Small Business-Person Interfacing With The Local Chamber Of Commerce." My God, no wonder she had an affair. Anything would be better than listening to this crap.'

'Typical. Get the information out after everyone's left town.' He gave her a sideways look. 'What's the balance on your Vicky's Secret account?'

'About the size of the national debt.'

'What kind of stuff do you buy?'

'Every flannel nightgown they sell.' She held up the big brown envelope.

'Open that,' Sam said.

Sonora looked it over. 'Cincinnati postmark. Dated . . . let me count on my fingers here. Twenty days ago? Yeah. About the time she was calling home saying she wasn't coming back.'

Sonora was getting queasy. She took a breath, closed her eyes, and ripped open the envelope. Inside was a cassette tape. 'Property Of Julia Winchell' had been written on a label in black felt pen. On the other side, 'PERSONAL,' in capital letters.

'Whoa,' Sonora said.

'What?'

'It's a cassette tape.' She held it up.

'Give it here, let's play it.'

'No, don't put it in my player, it eats tapes. I've lost two Bonnie Raits, one Rod Stewart and a Beatles in the last six weeks.'

'Doesn't anything you own ever work?'

Sonora shrugged.

'I don't blame it for spitting out Rod Stewart.'

'Are you trying to start a fight?'

Chapter Twenty-Five

Sonora bent the bobby pin, pushed it into the lock on her son's bedroom door. The door jammed, but she shoved harder, and slid through the narrow opening.

Tim was sound asleep in his bed. Dirty clothes, dropped in the doorway, made a pretty good barrier.

They had called at a rest stop somewhere near Berea, Kentucky. Tim had been home, cooking a frozen pizza, no clue as to where anyone was, no clue Sonora was looking for him. He had seemed genuinely shocked that his mother might be expecting him to make it home somewhere in a two-hour range of when he'd said he'd be in.

Sonora ventured another three feet into the room to retrieve the cordless phone, placed with precision in the boot of a shiny black roller-blade skate. She took another look at her son, grimaced at the glass that held what looked like old, furry orange juice, and scooted back through the door.

A relief to see him home safe, asleep in the bed. Tomorrow she would ground him.

'Two days, or three?' she asked Sam, who was heading down the hallway, Heather over one shoulder.

Clampett knocked Sam sideways, leaped at Heather, then turned his attention to Sonora, pinning her to the wall with his front feet.

'Get down,' Sonora said.

The dog dropped to three legs immediately, and took the sleeve of Sonora's shirt in his mouth.

'Drop,' Sonora said.

Clampett wiggled and wagged.

'*Drop!*'

'Two or three what?' Sam asked.

Sonora twisted sideways, opened Heather's door with her free hand. She followed Sam into the bedroom, walking sideways, dog still attached to her sleeve.

'How long I should ground Tim.'

'My mama would have blistered me and grounded me for a month.'

Sonora straightened Heather's unmade bed.

'You going to worry about toothbrush and jammies?'

Sonora shook her head. Heather was barefoot. Her little sandals stuck out of Sam's pants pockets. 'She hasn't stirred since we dropped the cooler off.'

Sam took the sandals and set them on Heather's dresser next to a stuffed penguin. Sonora settled Heather in the bed and covered her up. They left the room, pulling the door almost shut. Clampett tried to nose his way back in. Sonora took his collar.

'Time for you to go out.'

Sam shook his head. 'Too late. Better check the hall by the kitchen.'

'He's just glad to be home.'

'The wee of joy. You got a boom box for cassettes?'

'Yeah, if it works.'

'If it does, I'll give you five dollars.'

Chapter Twenty-Six

Sonora sat back on the couch and took the first sip of a Corona. The bottle of beer was icy cold and a small wedge of lime floated at the top. She tasted lime pulp on her tongue, leaned back into the couch, and pulled a quilt over her legs.

Sam looked up from the tape recorder. He sat awkwardly on the floor, too big to be cross-legged comfortably, like Sonora.

'You could turn the air-conditioning down.'

Sonora closed her eyes – her new response to suggestions she didn't like. Passive resistance. She was learning it from her youngest, the resident expert.

Sam picked up the recorder and tilted it sideways. 'When's the last time you cleaned the heads on this?'

'Never.'

Clampett padded in, tail wagging. He nudged Sam, bulking him with sheer size. The boom box slipped out of Sam's hand and he dropped Julia Winchell's cassette.

Clampett had it in his mouth before Sam or Sonora could move.

'*No.*' Sonora set the beer on the floor, grabbed the dog by the mouth. '*Drop.*'

Clampett looked at her, brown eyes apologetic. But his jaw muscles were tight, and he clamped down harder.

Sonora smacked his nose.

The dog stared at her, wagged his tail.

She tried to pry his jaws apart. Clampett ducked his head, held on harder.

'*Drop*, dammit.'

Sam took the dog by the collar. Tried his jaws. 'At the rate you're going, that dog's going to think his name is dammit.'

'Get him a cookie – sometimes he'll trade. Get the chocolate chip ones in the top of the pantry.'

Sam went into the kitchen. Sonora tried the dog's jaws. No luck. Clampett gave her a sad look. He was a retriever. He was retrieving. His expression begged for understanding.

'*Drop*,' Sonora said. 'Sam?'

'No cookies.'

'I just—'

He peered around the corner, held up an empty, crumpled Chips Ahoy bag. 'This it?'

'I just bought those yesterday. Okay, there are sausage biscuits in the freezer. Get me one of those.'

'Frozen?'

'Clampett won't care – he eats firewood.'

Sonora heard the freezer door open and close.

'Gone,' Sam said.

'Couldn't be. Not already.'

'Empty box in the freezer. Want me to throw it away?'

Sonora heard him tapping cardboard against the counter. 'No, I want it as a keepsake. Look in the fridge for leftover meatballs. Drop, Clampett.'

Drool slid down the side of the dog's muzzle and hung in a line of saliva.

'Sam? Meatballs?'

'Nope.'

'What *is* in there?'

'Pickles.'

'The one thing he won't eat. Okay. Oh, shit, he's chewing. *Stop* it, Clampett.' Sonora held his head.

'Don't you have any dog biscuits or treats, or did the kids eat those too?'

'Go back in my bedroom, and look in the shoe box on the back left-hand side of the closet.'

'Don't give him a shoe. Smack him.'

'I already did.'

'Let me get a rolled up newspaper after him.'

'No, that just makes him playful. He thinks it's the hit-the-dog-with-the-newspaper game. Go get that shoe box.'

Sonora listened for Sam's footsteps in the hallway, heard the squeak of her closet door opening.

'Jeez, Imelda—'

'Get the shoe box, and keep the mouth.'

She heard rustling noises. The bedroom door shut.

'I'm not going to even ask, Sonora, why you keep Oreo cookies in a shoe box in your closet.'

'For emergencies, obviously. If it isn't nailed down or healthy, the kids inhale it. Clampett's lucky he can run fast.'

Sam looked at the three-legged dog. 'Looks like they've been snacking on him.'

'Cookie please. No, hold it up.'

Clampett looked at the Oreo cookie, strained forward. Sonora kept a tight hold on his collar.

'Drop for a treat,' she said.

Clampett opened his mouth and the cassette hit the floor. He jumped for the cookie and snapped it out of Sam's hand. Sonora grabbed the tape and wiped it on her shirt. Clampett looked from her to Sam, black cookie crumbs on his muzzle.

'Give him another one,' Sam said.

'Chocolate is bad for puppies.'

'And firewood isn't?'

Sonora put the cookies back in the shoe box and stuck them in the refrigerator. Clampett curled up like a tiny puppy on three quarters of the couch. She rescued her beer.

Sam pushed her sideways into the dog and took the end of the couch.

'This is cozy,' Sonora said.

Sam held up the tape. 'Specialist Blair, please explain to the jury why there are tooth marks on Exhibit A?'

'Shut up and play the tape.'

Chapter Twenty-Seven

The first noise out of the boom box was a squeak, followed by a hiss and a string of noises you don't want to hear when you value the tape inside. Sonora looked at Sam, when, like magic, a woman's voice came through amid the crackle of cheap cassette and dirty heads.

Sam grinned.

Sonora wondered how often she and Sam had wished out loud that a murder victim could talk. This one was going to.

'*This is Julia Janet Harden Winchell, recorded in the Orchard Suites Hotel in Cincinnati, Ohio.*'

Her accent was hard to describe – a unique blend of midwest Chicago and Southern Tennessee. It hit the lush lower registers. She spoke slowly but without hesitation.

Sonora closed her eyes, picturing the long dark hair, the widow's peak, full cheeks, dark slanted brows. Even dressed in the jeans and torn sweatshirt she'd been wearing in one of Butch Winchell's pictures, she had a Victorian look about her, an air of fragile quality.

No wonder Jeff Barber had pursued her across state lines. Sonora wondered what it was about him that had attracted Julia – fill a room with men and she could have had her pick.

Why did she go for Barber, a needy, difficult male? Was she acting out some doomed karma, forever selecting men who would be dependent and smothering, always going for the wrong guy, like every other woman alive?

Good question. No answer. Sonora sat back, closed her eyes, and shut everything out, except Julia Winchell's voice.

'An odd and upsetting thing has happened, and I am setting down my thoughts and my memories on tape. I am a believer in fate. I think this had to have happened for a reason.'

Sonora noted the clear enunciation, the self-confident tone of voice. She wished that she, too, believed in fate. It might make her job a little easier.

'Today I opened the newspaper and saw the face of my killer.'

Sonora exchanged looks with Sam. *My killer*. Presumably she meant the guy she'd seen all those years ago. But she was dead now, and she'd said *my* killer. The tape played on.

'When I opened that newspaper I saw a face I saw eight years ago. His name is Gage Caplan, and he is the Cincinnati District Attorney who is prosecuting that ex-football-player who ran down the Xavier University co-ed. It is so strange, to have a name to go with a face I can't get out of my head. And to find him in the DA's office.

'Eight years ago I was in school at UC, the University of Cincinnati, living in the dorm. I was having a bad day – one of my sinus headaches, plus I'd lost my purse. So I took a Contac and went to bed early.

'Just when I was about to fall asleep, I remembered one place I might have left my purse that I hadn't looked. I had met a girlfriend for lunch, and we'd connected up in the media room in the Braunstein Building. I thought maybe I left it in there. I'd looked everywhere else.

'It was dark out, by now, and raining hard. Not a good idea to be wandering around campus by myself. But I had fifty dollars in my purse, and my driver's license, and my Sears credit card, plus my address book that I've had since my second year of high school. Plus all my keys and a new pair of pearl earrings Liza got me for my birthday.

'I decided that muggers and rapists didn't like the rain any

more than anybody else, and that the purse might not still be there the next morning, if it was there at all. So I went.

'*It was cold out and I was wearing those dumb sandals everybody wore then. I stepped in a puddle first thing, and got my feet wet. I was wearing a jean skirt and no tights because of the sandals, and because my legs were still tan from the summer. And I got cold.*

'*So when I finally got in the building it was warm, and I had seen a security guard up at the top of the building, smoking, so I felt safe. That was the funny part. Feeling safe.*

'*I went up to the media room – it was on the fourth floor, which is important. The media room was open, but there was nobody in there. But there was my purse, right on the table where I left it. First I checked the wallet – my money and everything was there, even the earrings. And my head started feeling better, so some of it must have been stress.*

'*I remember walking down the corridor, feeling sleepy from the pill – it was just a Contac – and thinking if I could make it back safe across campus to my dorm room, I could curl up in bed with a book and a Snickers bar that was also in the purse, and I remember thinking how great that would be.*

'*I know I heard a door close somewhere, but I didn't see any people. All the lights were on. I know I was making squeaky noises, and little wet footprints on the linoleum. My feet were slipping and I had to go slow. I turned left to go down the corridor – I was kind of turned around, trying to go out the other exit that would be closer to central campus.*

'*I remember seeing a little black door that said three. Which I thought meant I was on the third floor. Which I wasn't. More on that later.*

'*I'm walking along and I hear noises. Funny noises, but kind of awful. I heard, like, a sort of cry, then a groan and gurgle. And a man sort of growling at someone. Then somebody crying.*

'*I looked around. One of the office doors was open. There was a pink sweater hanging on the back of a chair – I don't know why I remember that, but I do.*

'There was nobody in the office. Whoever it was, it looked like they just went away for a minute – you know, leaving the door open like that. And I heard some weird stuff, thumps and cries and water splashing or something, coming from across the hall from the ladies' room.

'I went in there slow. I was kind of holding my purse across my chest – don't ask me why. I was kind of embarrassed, but there was nobody around. I was scared. It was all kind of weird and out of place.

'The bathrooms in that building are laid out kind of funny. You go inside in kind of a little hall. Then you turn a corner, you turn right and it opens up into the usual thing – mirrors and sinks and stalls.

'I heard water, and someone gasping, like they were coming up for air, and a woman – her voice was young and soft and she was like, crying. In a panic.

'I remember she said "please" and "the baby."

'So I didn't think at that point: I just ran in.'

The voice stopped and the tape ran in silence for a while.

'This part I remember really well.' The voice had gone flat. *'He was . . . he had her down on the floor, bent over the toilet, like she was being sick. But he was holding her head in the . . . in the toilet bowl. I saw it in the mirror first, the top of his head. She came up again. She was fighting him, gasping, and he got down on his knees, and pushed all his weight, one hand on the back of her head and one on the back of her neck.*

'She was a little thing. I couldn't figure how she lasted like she did, because he was a big guy, and he looked strong. She was oriental. She had black hair. At first I thought she was fat, but then I saw she was very pregnant.

'And then he . . . I could see he was crying. So weird. I mean he really was crying. And he pushed down on her so hard, she just didn't have a chance. She hit her mouth on the rim of the toilet. The seat was . . . the seat was up, I guess. And I saw blood spurt from her lip and go down the side of

the toilet bowl. And he . . . he slid her head – her mouth – off the rim, and shoved her head down in the water. And I think she must have swallowed a lot of water all of a sudden or passed out because you could see her just go limp.

'*And I yelled or screamed at him to stop. And he saw me. And he looked so . . . stunned, I guess. Tears running down his cheeks. And he kind of strained toward me. I think he was going to come after me, and she moved. At least I think she did. It happened fast – it was hard to tell. But he decided to keep her under, instead of coming after me. He kept her down, her head in that toilet.*

'*But he watched me. I was going to go and try to make him let her up, but she wasn't moving and I was pretty sure she was dead. And he was such a big guy. So I ran for help. I wanted somebody to try and save the baby, if nothing else.*

'*Just before I could move, or run, or whatever, he said . . . he said, "Hang on just a minute, will you?"*

'*I . . . it was such a shock, because he sounded so normal. Hang on, be right with you, I can explain. It was funny, because he had a really nice voice, kind of gentle and calm. And I just stood for a second and we stared at each other. And then I started crying, I think, and I ran away.*

'*I ran down the hall and there was a room with the door open and full of people. I couldn't understand why they didn't come when I screamed, but when I went inside it wasn't people, it was mannequins. That was . . . horrible. And I ran out back in the hallway, wondering if the person with the pink sweater had come back, but then I thought whoever it was wears teeny pink sweaters won't be much help either way. If it had been a big old gray sweatshirt I might have risked it.*

'*I remember seeing an exit sign and thinking—*'

The sound of a telephone ringing came through loud and startling.

'*Oh, shit.*'

There was a sound like bed springs before the click of the machine shutting off.

Sonora looked at Sam. They listened, for a while, to the hiss of empty cassette tape. Julia Winchell didn't come back.

Chapter Twenty-Eight

Sam wandered into the kitchen, opened the refrigerator, and came back in the living room with the Oreo cookies, drawing Clampett's and Sonora's immediate attention.

'I am eating these only because I need a sugar hit to get the energy to drive home. Why are you frowning at me? I'll share.'

'Julia Winchell said the woman drowning in the toilet was oriental.'

'Yeah, so?'

'Caplan's got pictures in his office. His little girl is blue-eyed, Amer-Asian. Which means her mother—'

'Could have been the woman in the bathroom. Hm.' He crunched a cookie, dribbling black crumbs down his shirt front. 'What were they doing on campus?'

'How the hell would I know?'

'You are tired and cranky. We'll figure this out tomorrow.' He reached down, rubbed the back of her neck.

She closed her eyes. 'You're tired too. Spend the night, why don't you?'

'Remember what happened the last time I did that?'

They both smiled.

Sonora shrugged. 'Kids are here, this time.'

'They're sound asleep,' Sam said.

'The bedroom or the couch?'

'I couldn't resist you. And it would be a shitty thing to do to Shel.'

She was not going to listen to the wife lecture. Anyway, she liked Shelly, and she wasn't sure, but she thought she might feel guilty. Sonora rolled sideways on the couch, pulled the quilt off of Clampett and over her head.

'You going to roll up like a worm in a cocoon or walk me to the door?' Sam asked.

'I'm not moving.'

'If you walk me to the door I can accidentally kiss you good night.'

'Lock up on your way out.'

Chapter Twenty-Nine

The air-conditioning in the bullpen was emitting a sour smell that reminded Sonora of Liza Harden's little Toyota. She had come in early, around six, in spite of the late night, but Sergeant Crick was still in ahead of her.

He sat at Gruber's desk, rolling his chair from side to side. He looked like he had slept.

'Hold up your foot, Sonora.'

'What?' Her eyelids ached, and her head was hurting. She also thought she might want to throw up, some time or other. No sleep gave her a queasy feeling in the morning.

'Your foot. Hold it up.'

Sonora lifted her left foot, aware that her white hightop Reeboks were getting dingy and worn. Maybe new shoelaces would perk them up. She was not supposed to wear them to work, and she hoped Crick was annoyed. If she had to put up with queasy, he could put up with annoyed.

'Damn, girl, look at those.'

Sam, over her shoulder. Sonora looked from Sam to Crick.

'I *like* these socks,' she said.

'Hot pink,' Crick said. 'Reeboks and pink socks? You looked at the dress code lately, or you pushing for a transfer to vice?'

'It's just so we know she's a *girl* cop,' Sam said.

Sonora nodded at them. 'Soon as Gall's starts selling pink handcuffs, I'm first in line.'

'At least we know what to get her for Christmas.'

Sonora put her arms on the rests on her chair. 'While you're admiring my socks, sir, I was wondering what you could tell me about Gage Caplan.'

Crick's look was wary. 'The DA Caplan?' He folded his arms. 'Who wants to know?'

'*I* want to know. His name's come up in the Julia Winchell investigation.'

Sam settled at the edge of her desk, winked. 'Sleep well?'

'Better than you.'

'Come up how?' Crick said.

Sonora glanced over her shoulder, and saw Molliter, working at his desk, finishing up the night shift. Pretending not to notice their conversation. Caplan was a popular district attorney. He liked cops. He respected them. He put perps in jail. He had a lot of friends in the police department. One of them was Molliter.

Sonora looked at Crick. 'Let's go in your office.'

'This chair does not fit my butt.' Crick got up.

The coffeemaker was on in Crick's office, baking old coffee into toffee-like sludge at the bottom of the glass pot. Crick flipped the switch, waited for Sonora and Sam to settle. He sat behind his desk and smiled. Sonora did not like that smile.

She was a little bit afraid of Crick – most of them were a lot afraid. He had smarts, he had integrity, and he backed his people up. She'd misstepped badly in the Selma Yorke case last year, and here she was, still working.

But being a cop was like being in the army. Crick was a superior officer, not in the rank and file, and, in Sonora's experience, as soon as a fellow officer left the rank and file they had motivations and agendas that were not obvious and to be avoided.

'Don't trust me?' Crick asked, showing his teeth.

Sam was looking at her like she'd lost her mind.

'I'm organizing my thoughts.'

Crick smiled again, a real one this time. In appreciation of a good sidestep, Sonora suspected.

'Julia Winchell witnessed a murder eight years ago.' Sonora expected questions, but Crick did not interrupt – just stayed quiet and coiled like a cat well versed in the art of looking sleepy and bored before the pounce. 'She got a clear and long look at the killer. When she went for help and came back, the killer was gone.'

'Big surprise,' Sam muttered.

'The body was gone too. In short, nobody believed her and she had to let it go.'

Crick leaned sideways. Still no comment.

'So anyway, Julia Winchell comes to town for a conference. Opens the newspaper. Sees a spread on Caplan, over that ex-football-player and the hit-and-run.' She looked at Crick. 'She recognized him, sir.'

He looked at her and sighed. 'Say the name, Sonora. I want to be real clear on this.'

'She identified District Attorney Gage Caplan as the man she saw murder a woman in the bathroom on the UC campus.' Sam was leaning back in his chair with his feet stuck out, but his chin was up.

Crick looked at Sam, soft but watchful. 'This bring back memories, Delarosa?'

Sonora looked from Sam to Crick. Decided, for once, to keep her mouth shut. Sam had run into trouble, of the higher-up political kind, just before they'd become partners. Which was why he'd gotten the rookie-female-partner award. Which was why promotion was not in his line of vision.

'You want off?' Crick asked.

Sam shook his head, slow and deliberate. 'I wouldn't mind seeing Sonora off it, sir. She's got kids.'

'We've all got kids,' Sonora said.

'Not Sanders. Not Gruber'.

'Gruber? He's probably got some somewhere,' Crick said.

'He and Sanders are busy on the Bobo thing. You sure you want to tangle with the DA's office, Sonora?' Crick was clear-eyed, almost sincere.

She actually hesitated. She'd had enough of being the cop you stared at last year when she'd tracked Selma Yorke. Lost her brother and a large chunk of her reputation in the fallout. Neither she nor the kids needed any more fallout.

'We caught it, sir.'

Crick nodded. 'Let's look at what we've got here. A prominent district attorney has been accused of murder by a nutcase who has subsequently disappeared, then been found in pieces on the side of the road.'

Sonora gritted her teeth. Julia Winchell was *her* baby. She'd decide if the lady was a nutcase. 'You saying *she*'s a nutcase because she had the bad taste to get herself dismembered?'

Crick sighed. Looked at Sonora. 'You look like the dachshund in the yard next door when my collie goes over the fence. I'm calling her a nutcase because she sees murders where the bodies disappear and the perps are sort of local celebrities.'

'She was pretty clear about what she saw,' Sam said.

Crick was still looking at Sonora. 'Exactly what did she see?'

'A man drowning a woman in the ladies' restroom in the Braunstein Building on the UC campus. The victim was oriental, and very pregnant.'

'Very convincing,' Crick said. 'I just don't remember a body turning up on the UC campus, and I think I would remember a pregnant oriental female drowned in a toilet.'

'Winchell went for help and when she came back the body was gone.'

Crick ran a hand over his face, rubbed vigorously. The growth of beard sounded scratchy against the rough-callused palm. 'Yeah, you mentioned that before. I was just thinking – didn't I just see this plot on a movie of the week a couple months ago? Brian Dennehy? Suzanne Sommars? I bet she had repressed memory, or something.'

'Not repressed memory, sir. The body was gone.'

'Swam away, no doubt.'

Sam got up, left the room. Sonora heard file cabinets open and close. She placed her fingertips together, tapped the back of her nails together.

Crick grimaced. 'Don't do that.'

'What, sir?'

'That thing, there, with your hands.'

Sonora held her hands up like they used to in old M&M commercials. 'Julia Winchell was strangled and cut up in pieces and strewn like so much garbage from here to Clinton, Tennessee.'

'Yeah, I get you, dragging a woman to Tennessee is heinous.'

'It doesn't make *her* a nutcase.'

'It doesn't make her sane. She had a lover, right?'

Sonora hesitated.

Crick put a hand out, cupping his ear. 'What's this I hear?'

A file drawer slammed shut. Another one opened.

'Yes sir, she had a lover.'

'That Jeff Barber guy. The photographer, if I remember correctly. Do I remember correctly?'

'Yes sir.'

'Fooling around on her husband. And you bypass the jealous husband and the lover and go for this convoluted non-obvious bullshit?'

'Okay, sir. We agree it's usually the husband. But—'

Sam came back in, pushing the hair that slid into his eyes back with an impatient gesture that was as familiar to Sonora as the wistful feeling that came with it. He stood next to her chair. Solidarity. And he had a triumphant air that seemed to put Crick on his guard.

'We've all heard yada yada yada that Caplan became a

DA after his wife was murdered and the killer never found,' Sam said.

Crick leaned back until his chair creaked. He folded his arms.

'This is the file, and a picture of the first Mrs. Gage Caplan.' Sam put an open folder and a spread of pictures on Crick's desk. Sonora saw them upside down.

Black hair. She would have been pretty once – but not in the shot that captured her curled in fetal position around the mound of belly, hair stuck to her delicate neck.

Sonora picked up one of the pictures. The woman's eyes were wide. She was Asian. Small and petite.

'Where's the autopsy report?' Crick was rummaging. Sam passed it across the desk, and sat back down in his chair.

'Sir?' Sonora said.

Crick held up a hand. Achieved silence. Sonora wondered why Crick's holding up a hand brought immediate obedience. When *she* held up a hand people tended to comment on her nail polish.

She considered the way he held the hand. Nothing special. Maybe it was the size of the hand.

'Delivered of a perfect baby girl, death by asphyxiation, minutes after the mother.' Sam winced. 'Micah Caplan. Cause of death, drowning. Found her body by Sonier Creek. Signs of struggle . . .' Crick frowned, kept reading, then looked up at Sam and Sonora. 'Either of you looked at this?'

Sonora shook her head.

'No,' Sam said.

Crick got up and shut the door. His walk was slow and deliberate. Sonora knew from the tense and in-check way he moved that somebody was in trouble.

He sat back in his chair, voice oddly subdued. 'Two things.' He held up thick fingers. 'Fragments under her fingernails match skin samples taken from her husband.

His answer – she had a habit of scratching his back during lovemaking, and they'd had relations that afternoon.'

Sonora looked at Sam.

Crick held up another finger. 'Second. Cause of death was by drowning. ME made a note here, flagged it. Lungs contained traces of surfactants, phosphorous, hypochlorite bleach – samples were consistent with any number of household cleaners. He wasn't happy. The creek had its share of pollution, and while said elements can certainly be found in trace quantities . . . basically, what he saying here is that wasn't creek water in her lungs.'

'If she drowned in the toilet, that's where she'd get all that crap in her lungs,' said Sonora. 'The surfactants, the bleach. That's all cleaning fluid.'

'I want his car,' Sam said. 'He scattered her down the side of the road – his car's got to be a gold mine.'

Crick's tone of voice was dampening. 'If he used his car. This is not some juvenile we're dealing with. He's a DA, he works the system. We move too soon, and take the car, even if he doesn't get us blocked, we could blow the whole case. What's the story on the vic's car? It was a rental, wasn't it?'

'Haven't found it yet,' Sam said.

'That's not what I want to hear.'

Sonora pulled her hair back and tucked it under the collar of her shirt. 'He did it, didn't he?'

Chapter Thirty

Sonora had a great deal of curiosity about Gage Caplan's wife, so when the white Nissan Pathfinder pulled up in front of the Caplan household, and she saw a woman behind the wheel with a dark-haired child in the passenger's seat, she forgot her irritation with Caplan for keeping her waiting in front of his house.

His power play was childish and interesting. A gauntlet thrown down – why? Because he was guilty? Too important to be bothered?

She watched his family, wondering why they did not go into the garage. The Pathfinder was stark white and pretty new-looking. It had the air of a car kept snugly in the garage.

The little girl hopped out quickly, jumping off the side of the Nissan and closing the door. It did not catch. She looked to be ten or eleven – hard to tell because she was petite and likely small for her age. Her hair, blue-black and shiny, hung chin-length. She wore tiny jean shorts fringed à la Dogpatch with white lace on the pockets and hem. Sonora caught a flash of a loose red teeshirt and beige lace-up hiking boots – all the rage – before the little girl disappeared around the front of the Pathfinder.

Colleen Caplan was quite pregnant. The little girl gave her a hand out and Colleen said something that made them both laugh.

She was graceless in her pregnancy, backside broad and spreading. She wore shorts that hung long and loose just above her knees. Her legs were pale – no sun. She wore thick cotton socks, and high-top white Reeboks just like the ones Sonora had on. A red maternity teeshirt hung like a lampshade over the shorts.

Sonora got out of the car, shut the door softly, and headed up the driveway toward Gage Caplan's wife.

It was a face only a mother could love, yet oddly endearing, like a boxer puppy: ugly and cute. She had a thick round nose, a round face, marzipan-blonde hair that was chin-length and straight, parted to one side, and a thin feathered fringe of bangs.

Her complexion was rough, face flushed, and she seemed to move in a fog of preoccupation. She looked worried. Her brow was wrinkled in the kind of deep grooves few people earned till their sixties or seventies.

Colleen had not noticed Sonora, but the little girl had. The woman hopped sideways in an awkward movement that was as playful as it was gauche. The little girl said something and tilted her head and Colleen Caplan turned and saw Sonora.

Her mouth made an O, and her shoulders sagged, and the worried look settled back on her face. Sonora felt like the black cloud that came with every silver lining.

'Hello,' Colleen Caplan said with a dutiful but wary politeness. 'Can I help you please?'

Sonora smiled, reached for her ID. 'Specialist Blair, Cincinnati PD. Are you Mrs. Caplan?'

But she had lost the woman's attention.

'That's so amazing!'

Sonora frowned at her. Surely not the woman cop thing. Please not the do-you-pack-heat-like-the-big-boys? question.

'Your purse! You just found your ID like that right in the top of your purse! How do you do that?'

'I dug it out before I got out of the car,' Sonora said.

'No, don't tell me that, you'll ruin it!' Colleen Caplan

gave her a real smile, big and broad and spreading across her face, making her cheeks puff up and her eyes go small. 'Pockets!' She patted voluminous side bulges in her shorts. 'I don't carry a purse. I can't find anything in it, so everything is in pockets.'

'You can't find stuff in your pockets, either,' the little girl said.

'This is Mia.' Colleen patted the top of the little girl's head. 'She is my pride and my joy and the light of my life.'

It was said lightly, with a fond smile, and Sonora got the feeling that Colleen Caplan often introduced Mia that way, and always meant it.

'We lost the garage door opener again.' Mia bent over and picked at one of the laces on her hiking boots.

'But I do have my keys!' Colleen Caplan patted her pockets again and frowned. 'At least I think I do.' She seemed out of breath in the heat. Her neck looked sweaty. She peered into the Pathfinder. '*There*.' She opened the door. A huge set of keys hung from a cobalt-blue fuzzy ball that Colleen Caplan held up and waved at Sonora.

Sonora moved around to the other side of the car, opened and closed the passenger door that had not caught earlier.

'Mrs. Caplan, I was supposed to meet your husband here, and—'

'*Come in* then. We have air-conditioning!'

There was no doubt, Sonora thought, looking at the house, that the Caplans had air-conditioning as well as every other household convenience, but Colleen Caplan's words throbbed with such unbridled enthusiasm that Sonora had to smile. And it was very hot.

'Thank you, I will.'

Chapter Thirty-One

They went through a side door into the kitchen, which looked clean enough beneath the kind of clutter that accumulates very quickly with a kid in the house. Sonora, looking at Colleen Caplan, almost said two kids in the house.

There were open cans of Chef Boy Ar-Dee Ravioli on the cabinets, a wad of damp paper towels at the foot of a huge white double-door refrigerator. Sonora looked at the fridge. It had an ice-maker and ice water in the door, just like the one in the Winchells' kitchen, except newer. Maybe she would put one on her Sears charge account, and pay it off in six-dollar monthly increments for the rest of her natural life.

The house looked brand-new. There was a breakfast nook in the kitchen with an oak table. Everything was white white white. Spotlights showed that there were no cobwebs over the gold-knobbed cabinets.

'Mrs. Caplan—' Sonora said.

'Call me Collie.' She opened the refrigerator, which was full of bright red cans of Coke and shiny green cans of Mello Yellow. She smiled over her shoulder at Sonora. 'Soda? We also have coffee and wine.' The last was added awkwardly. A sentence she threw in for sophisticates who liked such things.

'A Coke would be great,' Sonora said.

'Let me find the cookies and we'll sit down.'

Where to sit proved to be a problem, with Mia peeping into a white-carpeted living room with the air of one in front of a museum exhibit. She looked over her shoulder at Collie. 'She's company. We can sit in here if it's company.'

Collie Caplan pursed her lips, stopped mid-stride.

'Oh no we can't,' Mia corrected herself, sounding regretful. 'The no-food rule.'

'You know, honey, it's my house too.' Collie smiled but it was a small, tight thing, and it did not light her eyes. She looked worried. She looked tired.

Sonora looked at the white brocade couch. 'Please don't ask me to go in there and eat a cookie.'

Something like shame passed over Collie Caplan's face. She straightened her shoulders, winked at the little girl who watched her, hands clasped behind her back.

'Don't be silly, Mia. Spills can be cleaned up, I had the couch scotch-guarded.'

Something uncompromising in her voice. Sonora and Mia followed her into the living room.

'Sit down,' Collie invited.

Sonora looked around the room, chose a wingback chair in hunter-green leather, set her legs between the edge of the chair and a footstool. Even if she'd been inclined to put her feet up, which she wasn't, there was no doubt in her mind that footstools in this house weren't for feet.

Collie sat on the edge of the couch. Mia settled beside her, thighs touching.

Something about the two of them together, side by side, muscles tense, poised for flight, made Sonora sad.

She told herself to be careful of jumping to conclusions about Gage Caplan, knew when she did that it was a wasted effort. The conclusions were coming fast and furious.

'Collie, want your back pillow?' Mia asked.

'No thanks.' Collie's voice had gone quiet. Sonora saw dark circles under the woman's eyes. A lot of sleepless nights. Which might be due to the pregnancy, or might not. Collie patted Mia's leg. 'But thanks for asking. Why don't you take the cookies down to our den and watch a video?'

'Can I watch *Pulp Fiction*?'

'No.'

Mia grinned suddenly, the smile of a kid who was testing the waters. 'It's time for Ricki Lake.'

'That will broaden your mind,' Collie said darkly, but Mia was already gone. Sonora waited but did not hear the sound of a television.

'Did my husband say he was going to meet you here?' Collie asked.

Sonora nodded.

'He probably just got held up. I'm surprised he agreed to leave the office. You know the jury's out?'

'He told me they were waiting on a verdict, but he thought it would be awhile.'

Collie licked her lips. 'Maybe the jury came in.'

They looked at each other.

'I hope he nails this guy,' Sonora said.

'If anybody can do it, it's Gage,' Collie said, serious now.

'I hear a lot of good things about him,' Sonora said, but Collie seemed to pick up on something in her voice, and her eyes went narrow and watchful. 'How long have you and Mr. Caplan been married?'

'Five years.' She twisted her khaki shorts in one thick finger.

Sonora smelled vanilla, noticed the dry chips of potpourri in a crystal bowl by her shoulder. Next to the potpourri was a candy dish, with a clump of hard candy, red-striped pillow shapes, that had stuck together. It was the kind of candy no one ate, no telling how long it had been there. Added a touch of color, at any rate.

'Did you know his first wife?'

Collie shook her head, twisted her finger first one way, then the other. 'She was the prettiest thing, just like Mia. Mia's not mine, you know, but she *is* mine, if you know what I mean.'

Sonora knew what she meant. Collie and Mia were what she and Heather were, on a good day – what she and Tim had been, before aliens took him away and left her with a teenager.

She knew a good mother when she saw one.

'Mia was only two when Micah died.' Collie got up, opened the seat of the piano stool in front of a gleaming black grand piano, rummaged, looked over her shoulder at Sonora. 'She played. Gage bought this piano for her on her birthday the year before she died. He keeps all her music and her pictures in here. Sometimes Mia likes to look at them.'

The photo album was dingy white vinyl, bought in less affluent days. There were sticky fingerprints on the front cover. Likely Mia thumbed them quite a bit. Collie handed the album to Sonora, opened in the middle.

'This is our favorite. Mia's and mine.'

Micah had been small and slight in the way of many Asian women. Her eyes were blue like Mia's, face very round.

'Micah was Korean, Japanese, and American mixed. She got adopted by her dad when he was in the Korean War. They – her parents – they live in Kentucky.'

Sonora looked up from the picture. 'Where in Kentucky?'

'London.'

London, Kentucky was the last place Julia Winchell had bought gas, according to the records from her BP Oil account.

'What's their name?'

'Ainsley. Grey and Dorrie Ainsley. They're Mia's grandparents, so I see them a lot. They've really been good to me.' Collie was moving back to the couch, hand tucked into the small of her back. 'Dorrie and me – and *I*, I should say – we have a lot in common.' She grinned at Sonora. 'Both of us have Amer-Asian daughters. And neither of us could have kids of our own.' She settled back on the couch so carefully, Sonora could almost feel the backache. She patted her belly.

'This is some miracle baby. I really tried everything before I met Gage. Spent a fortune, time, money, and effort. My first husband and I did. I explained all that to Gage before we got married. But he had Mia and was absolutely positive he didn't want any more.'

She stared at the wall over Sonora's left shoulder. 'Got one anyway!' She scratched the end of her nose. '*I* was thrilled. For me, it was a dream come true. If somebody would of told me all those years ago I would finally have one of my own . . . I guess it would have saved me a lot of wear and tear and medical bills.'

'What happened to your first husband?' Probably shouldn't have asked, Sonora thought. But she was curious.

Collie looked at the floor, then back up at Sonora. 'Left me. One of those office affair things. They're married. Got kids.' She bit her bottom lip. 'Both real happy. She seems like a real nice girl.'

Sonora cocked her head to one side. 'Has everyone gotten so civilized that the ex-wife has to speak well of the woman her husband was fooling around with?'

Collie's mouth opened, then she laughed. 'No, really. I feel sorry for her because she's married to him. Believe me, he's fooling around on her too. I thank God for Gage every day.'

Sonora forced a smile. She did not think that Gage Caplan was a husband any sane woman should be thankful for.

She looked down at the picture of Micah. She was wearing one of those fuzzy pink mohair sweaters with white pearl buttons. She held Mia up to the camera, eyes squinting in the sun. Mia was maybe three months old, and her mouth was curled in a toothless baby smile, gums pink and bare, hair a soft black wisp on her head.

'It was terrible how she died,' Sonora said mildly, watching Collie.

Collie nodded, and Sonora saw she had the worried look

that was beginning to be familiar. 'They never caught him,' she said softly.

'They suspected Mr. Caplan, didn't they? For a while?'

Collie sat forward, arms wrapped around herself like she was cold, though her face was flushed, and a line of sweat filmed her upper lip. She nodded.

'Did you know him then?' Sonora asked.

'No. I wish I had. It was a terrible time for him. I could have been a comfort to him. You know, Gage has a very sad side to him he just doesn't let most people see.'

'I'm sure he has a lot of sides to him,' Sonora said.

Collie's look was intelligent. 'I can't decide if you like him or not. Most women do, you know.'

'Do they?' Sonora asked.

Collie nodded. 'Oh yes. And they think, why did he marry *her*? Big nose and overweight.' She glanced at her belly. 'I look like this even when I'm not pregnant.'

'Since we're being blunt . . .' Sonora said. Collie looked at her. 'Have you ever had any suspicions that Gage had something to do with Micah's death? I mean, did it never cross your mind?'

'That's blunt all right.'

Sonora nodded, kept smiling. In her experience, you could say very outrageous things if you smiled.

'No, of course not. It's never crossed my mind. I know Gage. Do you know exactly how she died?'

'Yes,' Sonora said, but Collie kept talking, like she'd never heard.

'Somebody drowned her in a creek. They took her purse. It was weird, because no one could understand what she was doing there. Gage thinks maybe somebody hid in the backseat of her car, or forced her off the road. And of course what he never tells anyone is about the overnight case they found in the trunk of the car. An overnight case with a sexy negligée.'

'He told you.'

'I'm not just anyone. I think it's very . . . very good of him not to bring that up. Not to try and hurt her reputation. When everyone suspected him.'

'If another car forced her off the road, there might well be scratches on the paint of her car. There weren't.'

Collie scooted back on the couch. 'You know the case pretty well.'

'I've studied it.'

'Then you know she was pregnant.'

'Kind of blows the nightie theory.'

Collie rubbed the back of her neck. 'Not necessarily.'

'It's thin, Collie.'

'Seven and a half months pregnant. A perfect baby – a little sister for Mia. I used to think about that all the time. It had to be some kind of a monster, to kill her like that when she was pregnant.'

It had been Sonora's experience that pregnancy did not give a woman any protection from violence. Sometimes she wondered if it made her a target. She did not share these thoughts.

'Do you think it happens very often?' Sonora asked kindly.

'What do you mean?' Collie was twisting her shorts again.

'That a stranger kills a pregnant woman for no particular reason? Yeah, her purse was missing. But she still had her engagement ring on. Big diamond, it's in the report. She wasn't molested.'

Collie's lips turned down in a deep frown that would have been comical on her clown face, if her eyes had not been so sad.

'I just don't get this. I don't get what you're trying to tell me.'

'I'm sorry,' Sonora said. 'I'm not trying to tell you

anything. I do know the case pretty well. Is there anything you want to ask me?'

'No,' Collie said. Quickly. With force.

Denial was an amazing thing, Sonora thought. But she was on shaky ground.

The phone rang, and Collie jumped. 'Sorry. Excuse me.' She got up, headed into the kitchen. 'Hello? What? No, I do not want a maintenance agreement on a freezer. Well for one thing, we haven't bought one. No. Thanks. No problem.'

The phone clicked into place. Collie came back, moving slowly, an anxious look in her eyes. 'Are you reopening the case? Micah's death? Do you have new evidence, or something?'

'No, we're not reopening that case, not right now. I'm looking into something else – a missing person. Would you know if your husband has had any calls from a Julia Winchell, anytime in the last few weeks?'

Worry swept across Collie's face like a storm warning. 'I . . . we had quite a few hang-ups a couple weeks ago. But no, as far as I know, nobody by that name called here. Our number's unlisted, for obvious reasons. We don't give it out much.'

The phone rang again. Collie laughed, but the smile did not reach her eyes. 'Right on cue.'

She headed back to the kitchen, hand pressed into the small of her back. Sonora heard her pick up the phone, pitch her voice low. Sonora could not make out the words. She wished Sam was along. He was the best eavesdropper. She'd been to one too many rock concerts.

She heard Collie calling softly to Mia. 'Get fixed up, honey. That was Daddy on the phone. The verdict's in.'

Sonora heard Mia's gasp. 'Did Daddy win?'

'Yes, sweetie, Daddy won.'

Sonora bit her lip. At least she knew why she'd been stood

up. The good news was Gage Caplan got a conviction. The bad news was Gage Caplan got a conviction.

She was going to bring down the DA who nailed Jim Drury?

Joy.

Chapter Thirty-Two

Caplan had sent Sonora a message through his wife, which Sonora found high-handed. A request for a favor – he was clearly in the mood to ask.

Would she drive Collie and Mia into town so they could join him and his staff in an impromptu and informal celebration? In return, he would take some time to let Sonora ask those questions she needed to ask.

If he had thought to annoy her, he had guessed wrong. He would be full of himself, in his element. Guard down. She looked forward to watching him.

She would have said she was almost enjoying the chase, but a look at Collie Caplan, strapped uncomfortably into the passenger's seat, and Mia, sitting stiffly in the back in a clean denim jumper and black patent leather shoes, quelled any little thrill of the hunt.

If she got Caplan they were out a dad and a husband. If she didn't, they got to keep a killer.

Sonora glanced at Collie – pregnant, like Micah. What had made Gage Caplan kill a wife who was seven months pregnant with his child? Why could he not wait until the child was born?

Unless the child was the point.

Not his? Could he be that sure?

Collie had made it clear, whether she realized it or not, that Caplan was not happy over her pregnancy.

Plenty of pregnancies began with reluctance, Sonora thought.

She needed to know why the first wife had to go.

Chapter Thirty-Three

The office was a mess. Boxes of files, loose rolls of faxes, and a coating of multicolored strings of confetti.

They were drinking champagne out of little plastic champagne glasses. Mia edged close to Collie, who edged close to Sonora. Collie took Mia's hand, and Sonora noticed that the second Mrs. Gage Caplan was trembling.

It could have been a scene from a movie. A young woman, blazer off, in a tight black skirt and tuxedo-style white shirt, perched on the edge of a desk, legs swinging, medium-high heels slipping off one slender ankle. She wore a gold ankle bracelet. Sonora noticed Collie studying it.

Collie's ankles were very likely thick and swollen in this heat and at this stage of her pregnancy.

Gage had his sleeves rolled up precisely two turns, exactly right for the sexy man about town. He looked good. He felt good. Physically large, dominating the room with presence and personality, a come-and-get-me-and-I'll-eat-you smile on his face. He had a nice tan.

Sonora wondered how he managed the tan with all the hours he had to have been putting in.

Collie had changed out of the shorts, making the unfortunate choice of a maternity ensemble that was just cause to have the designer shot or sentenced to a pregnancy of his or her own. It was a two-piece affair, in palest pink – tiny puff sleeves and an overblouse draping a pleated skirt with a stretch panel in front.

Sonora had seen better-looking lampshades.

The overblouse tied in the back, empire style, with a big bow that would have been appropriate for Mia. It had large pockets, and baby blocks sporting the ABCs had been stitched on each side.

Sonora had always wondered why you could never find maternity clothes in shiny black leather.

'Here they are!' Caplan's voice was a boom of pleasure. Collie blushed. 'Come on in – we don't pay rent on the hallway.'

A smatter of laughter, cool amusement from the girl in the ankle bracelet.

'Come on, Mia. Give Daddy a hug and tell him you're proud, then I'll get you your first glass of champagne.' Caplan poured a tablespoon of liquid into a glass, handed it to his little girl. He squeezed her chin, and she smiled up at him.

'I knew you'd win, Daddy.'

There was a wave of approval and Caplan picked Mia up and set her on the desk next to the girl with the ankle bracelet.

The room went tense. Sonora looked up, watchful. For a moment everyone seemed to hold their breath, looking from Collie to Ankle Bracelet. Sonora knew, then, that Caplan and Ankle Bracelet were deep in an affair, one of those office things that everyone knows about except the wife.

And, while Collie did not know, she sensed something. She looked like a deer in a spotlight, awkward and large in her pink puffed sleeves amidst the leather-briefcase set. Her lower lip trembled.

Caplan turned, smiled at her with such tenderness that Sonora doubted what she had just seen. 'My beautiful wife.'

Too precious by half, Sonora thought. Rude to ask for a barf bag?

A lesser man could not have carried it off, but Caplan

managed. Sonora looked around, decided she was the only one there feeling nauseous.

Formidable, she thought.

'Detective.' Caplan handed Sonora a glass. He turned to Collie. 'I know, I know, you're pregnant. We have to be careful of the *bay-bee*. Help me celebrate with *just* a taste.' He pushed a glass into her hand. She pulled her hand away but he reached for it and made sure she had the glass secure in her fingers before he let her go. She smiled at him.

Quit smiling, Sonora thought.

Collie did not drink.

'It's a major victory, you know.' He spoke softly. If Sonora had not been standing so close she'd never have heard him. Someone was telling a joke. 'Celebrate with me, Collie girl. It's our big day.'

'*Mr*. Caplan.' Bea Wallace swooped over to Collie and relieved her of the glass. She smiled at Collie. 'Men.' Looked over at Caplan. 'Sometimes I think you have the brains of a gerbil.'

It took him aback. Sonora hoped, for Bea Wallace's sake, that she was a state employee and impossible to fire.

Caplan gave them a smile. '*Don't* drink then. This wife of mine has a mind of her own.' He looked at Sonora. 'Between the two of them, they'll keep me from getting a swelled head.'

'Too late.' Sonora said it softly enough that she did not think anyone heard. But Bea Wallace cracked a reluctant smile, and Caplan gave her a look.

'Pardon?'

'I said it's late. Maybe we should talk some other time. After your celebration.'

'No, no. Come on in my office a minute.' He raised his glass at the room. 'Party on without me.' No one paid any attention except Mia, watching Daddy-The-Hero. 'The detective and I have business. I'll be—'

'Hell, Gage, don't you ever get a break?' someone asked.

He stiffened. He did not like anyone saying hell in front of his little girl, Sonora guessed. He waved a hand, turned to Collie. 'Starting tomorrow, I'm taking some time off.' He grinned at Mia. 'How'd you like to go down to London and see Gramma?' He looked at Collie. 'You and me can take the canoe out. We haven't done that in ages.'

Sonora saw Collie's hesitation, the shadow in her eyes.

'It'll be hot,' Collie said.

Gage tucked his chin to his chest. 'Sorry, hon. I was just wanting a break.'

'Oh no, we can go. I can wear shorts, we can swim. It'll be fun.'

'You sure?'

'Sure.'

He squeezed Collie's shoulder. 'There *is* more to life than eating and sleeping, I promise.' He waved Sonora into his office.

She noted Collie's crestfallen droop and Bea Wallace's frown. She studied the fold of flesh that lapped over the starched-back collar of his shirt.

I *will* get you, she thought.

Chapter Thirty-Four

Sonora was disappointed when Caplan closed the door, and she had a chance to look around his office. She had expected to dislike him for keeping it neat and orderly, in spite of the pressures and long hours he'd been working to put Drury away.

But the computer was still up and humming. One file cabinet was open.

Caplan moved a stack of files and video tapes off a chair. 'Why don't you take the one behind my desk? You might be more comfortable, everything else is in such a mess. Just let me do one thing . . .'

Caplan scooted behind his desk – box of files under one meaty arm – and touched the keyboard of his computer.

The sounds of a crowd going wild filled the room, with the loud announcement that '*Elvis has left the building.*'

Caplan grinned. 'Better than a beep.'

'This chair's fine,' Sonora said, taking the one he'd cleared. She rested one foot on the edge of a box of papers. Waited for him to get comfortable in his chair. His intercom buzzed. Bea Wallace sounded harassed.

'WSTR, on line three. You want to take it?'

'Tell Sly I'll be issuing a statement at four-thirty, as planned.' Caplan paused. 'But tell him I'll beep him and try to talk to him personally first, if I get a chance. Oh, and if the *Inquirer* calls, put 'em through.'

Caplan looked up at Sonora, leaned back in his chair. 'I'm all yours.'

'Congratulations on the verdict. I honestly didn't think you had a prayer.'

'Me neither.'

'And you still prosecuted? You're either honest, ethical, and not too bright. Or a big-time gambler.'

He smiled at her, twisting gently from side to side in the well-padded leather chair. His eyes were very blue.

'Enjoying yourself?' Sonora asked.

'A prime moment,' Caplan said.

Mistress and wife toasting his success in the next room, television and newspapers at four-thirty to announce the big victory in court. A man riding so high might well believe he could get away with murder twice.

'So. Detective Blair. No blacks or Indians in homicide these days?'

Sonora tilted her head to one side. 'Both, I think. So?'

'So what did you do? Who'd you piss off? Must have been that thing last year when you brought in that serial killer – what did you guys call her? Flash?' He stuck his tongue in his right cheek, making it puff out. 'Heard you slept with a witness, or some such thing. I guess somebody in this man's army is out to get you, Detective.'

'I don't follow you.'

'Smart girl like you? Come on. Here you are on my doorstep again. Questions, concerns, problems.' He waved a hand. 'You suspect me of some kind of involvement in this Julia Winchell thing, God knows what or why. Cards on the table, Madam Detective? I'm a popular guy, I got your clout, I got your pull. I'm the hot potato, so I'm just curious how I managed to land in your lap. You got my sympathy, though, you surely do.'

'That's kind of you,' Sonora said mildly. 'Maybe we're in the same boat. You went up against the football alumni, and I'm going up against a popular district attorney. But hey. Worked for you, didn't it? You're my hero, I guess.'

'What is it you want, Detective?'

'Your alibi, Counselor.'

'My alibi for what?'

'Tuesday, July eighteenth, from, say, eleven-thirty AM till eleven PM.'

'Pretty broad time spread you got there, podna.'

Sonora opened her notebook, and looked up innocently. 'You have a problem answering the question?'

Caplan shook his head, cheeks drawn, bottom lip pursed. 'No. Let me think a minute.' He closed his eyes. 'Working, I think. Pretty much all I have been doing, these last few weeks. But no, I remember that Tuesday because Collie and Mia went up to Cleveland to go fishing with Ralph. Ralph is her dad.' He said the name like it was funny.

'They catch anything?'

'Collie? Doubt it. Dad probably did. I think Mia said she got something. Pretty excited about it, as I recall.'

'So you went home about what time?'

'Two-thirty. I'd left my laptop at the house, and I had a file I wanted on it. And I hadn't had lunch. I knew Collie and Mia were in Cleveland with old Ralph, so the house would be quiet. I went home, put on some sweat pants, made myself a sandwich and worked till late.'

'How late?'

'Some time after eleven. I stopped and watched the news, drank a brewski. Claire Pritchard was on with the stock market report, so it was already part way over. Must have been between eleven and eleven-thirty.'

'Anybody come to the door?'

He shook his head. 'If they did, I didn't know it. Never heard the doorbell, but sometimes I don't hear it when I'm working at home.'

'Anything else?'

He paused. 'A confession.'

Sonora raised an eyebrow, wary of his tone.

'I made myself *two* sandwiches. And ate a box of glazed Krispy Creame Doughnuts.' He slapped his gut. 'As you can see, I'll eat anything. Oh, look, she's trying not to laugh. Don't hold it in, Detective, could be harmful to your health.' He was smiling, but his eyes looked sad. 'This brings back memories, Detective.'

'Of what? Micah's murder?'

'I was under suspicion then, too.'

'And now?'

He shrugged. 'I survived that: I can survive anything.'

That Sonora might believe. 'Anybody call while you were there, at home?'

'Several people. I didn't pick up. Bea knew where I was, but nobody else did. I was hiding out, trying to get some work done. You don't believe me.'

'I think what we've got here pretty much counts as no alibi.'

'Pretty much.' He picked a pencil up off his desk, balanced it in the groove between his nose and upper lip. 'Tell me, you think I ought to grow a mustache?'

'That's of absolutely no interest to me.'

'What is of interest, then?'

'What did Julia Winchell look like?'

'Never saw her.'

'Want to see a picture?'

'No.'

'You kill her?'

'No.'

'You cut her up?'

'God, no. Can't even carve meat.'

'If you did cut her up, what tool would you use?'

He looked at her. Perturbed, finally.

'You own a hacksaw, Mr. Caplan?'

He hesitated.

'Let me help you on this one. Your wife says you own a hacksaw.' She hadn't, but Caplan didn't know that.

'I guess I might have one out in the garage somewhere. So?'

Sonora leaned back in her chair, stretched out her legs. 'Most of the men I know have a pretty accurate mental inventory of what tools they have, in the garage or anywhere else.'

Caplan grinned. 'I'm not most men. I'm pretty secure about my tools, so I don't spend a lot of time taking inventory. You impressed?'

'Believe me when I tell you that I'm not. Are you willing to submit blood and hair samples, Mr. Caplan?'

'For what possible reason?'

'How about a look in your garage? Turn over that hacksaw?'

'Play by the rules, Detective. I have faith in our system of justice. Get a court order and I'll cooperate.'

Sonora stood up. 'Enjoy your victory, Mr. Caplan. We'll talk again soon.'

'I'm sure we will.'

Sonora headed for the door.

'Detective. I was wondering.'

She paused, hand on the doorhandle.

'What *does* it take to impress you?'

She studied him a minute, caught sight of the file drawer that was hanging open. She indulged herself and crossed the room, snapped it shut. As she headed back to the door, she looked at him over her shoulder.

'I guess if you got away with murder twice, that would impress me.'

Chapter Thirty-Five

Sonora walked into the women's bathroom in homicide and headed for the sink. She was hot and sweaty and wanted to wash her face. She should not have made that last comment to Caplan. Never issue a challenge to a stone-cold killer – she had learned that the hard way.

A stall door was just swinging shut, then it opened. Sanders came out.

'They've been here again,' she said.

Sonora went and looked into the stall. The toilet seat was up. 'You know, they're each and every one of them detectives. You'd think they'd know better than to leave clues.'

'Are they never going to get the men's room fixed?'

'Last I heard they're still trying to trace the smell. Some kind of backup in the drain somewhere.'

Sanders grimaced. 'They can smell it all the way back in Crime Stoppers, and I don't want to be mean, but I am sick of these guys coming in here. They're messy. They're *gross*. I found—'

'Please don't tell me.'

'But what can we do about it?'

Sonora pushed hair out of her eyes and looked in the mirror. Short hair would not suit her face, and if she got it cut she couldn't pull it back. She looked over her shoulder at Sanders. Still there. 'You prepared to fight dirty, Sanders?'

'Like how dirty?'

Sonora took off her shoe, smashed the tampon dispenser.

'Never use your gun for this sort of thing, Young Sanders. I knew a guy used his gun to hammer in a nail and shot his thumb almost all the way off.'

'You're *breaking into* a tampon dispenser?'

'Un petit larceny. Here.' She tossed a cardboard box to Sanders, who actually caught it. 'Men are funny creatures, Sanders. Vulgar, crude. But squeamish about the oddest things. Spread these around. It will definitely get rid of the single guys. May work on the married ones too, some of them anyway.'

She glanced at Sanders' feet, looked back again to make sure. High heels again. Sheer black stockings, instead of the usual thick leotards. 'Lunch with the married guy?'

Sanders blushed, deep, dark, satisfying red.

Sonora looked away. 'Sorry. None of my business.'

'I suppose *you*'ve never done anything like that in your life.'

'Sure I have.'

Sanders leaned against the stall door. 'How'd it turn out?' She teetered back and forth on the balls of her feet, anxious, hopeful. Ready to call 1-900-Psychic to see if all would be well in the name of true love.

Sonora sighed, leaned up against the wall. 'I know what you want me to tell you. You want me to say he left his wife and kids, and married me, because we were soulmates and it was meant to be. Don't let me forget the part where we lived happily ever after.'

Sanders' voice was very small. 'These things do work out sometimes, you know.'

Sonora looked at her kindly. 'Yes, they do. I've even known people where it worked out.'

'It did?'

'Yes.'

'But not for you?'

'For me it was like a virus. I got it once, got over it, and am immune to catching it ever again.'

'I wish I knew for sure if he was married.'

'Okay, here's a quick check. How long did you know him before he said he loved you?' Sanders opened her mouth, but Sonora held up a hand. 'You don't have to tell me. Just remember, single guys are impossible to pin down, and married guys tell you they're committed in forty-eight hours – they're in a hurry and they got no freedom to lose.'

Sanders sat down on a toilet seat and put her head in her hands.

Sonora sighed. 'How long?'

'The first night.' Sanders' voice had dragged down at least two octaves.

'Look, this isn't like some kind of exact science, Sanders. For all I know, this love of yours is a straight-up soulmate. I've never met him, I can't judge. Come on girl, get up. Decorate.'

Sanders dragged little blue boxes out of the dispenser. 'It's the married thing that's driving me crazy. I have to *know*. Would you . . . Gruber wants to tail him. See where he goes at night.'

'You know, there is a simpler way. You could just ask him, point blank.'

'I did.'

'*And?*'

'He said he didn't know.'

Sonora burst out laughing.

'I don't think it's so very funny,' Sanders said.

'I know, Sanders. I wasn't laughing when it happened to me.'

'What should I do?'

'Ask him this. Ask him, when he turns over in bed at night, is there a woman there with him? If there is, tell him he might be married.'

Sonora took a good long look at Sanders and made up her mind. Hopeless romance wasn't worth a second look. Keaton was hopeless. She decided to have dinner with Smallwood.

Chapter Thirty-Six

Sam was at his desk when Sonora went into the bullpen. He looked up as she settled into her chair.

'I already listened to your messages for you.'

'Gee thanks, Sam. How come?'

'I didn't have any. And also, because somebody else was listening to them.'

Sonora stopped and looked at him. 'Somebody was listening to my messages?'

Sam nodded.

'Who?' Her voice was quiet but hard.

Sam gave her a wary look. 'Molliter.'

'He say why?'

'Said it was an accident.'

'How could that be an accident?'

Sam shrugged. 'And by the way, Visa says your payment is overdue.'

'Tell me something I don't know.' Sonora flipped through the large stack of bills. She'd brought them to the office thinking she'd get to them sooner. Another fantasy gone to hell. Why was Molliter listening to her messages?

'Oh, and your son called. He wants to know if you could take off work early and drop him at some kind of all-age show in what I warn you is a sleazy part of town. And you'd need to pick up three of his buddies.'

'Hey, Blair. Your little girl still belching the alphabet?' Gruber. He looked tired and depressed, tie hanging to one side.

'She's got refinement now, Gruber. She's quit with the alphabet and moved on to *Figaro*.'

Sam looked up. 'Really? The whole score?'

'No, just the first few measures.'

'That's still pretty damn amazing.' Gruber settled into his chair and sighed. 'This dieting shit is not for me. You ever heard of this fat-burning diet?'

Sonora shuddered. 'There are about a million of them. How's the clown thing going?'

'Guy uses deer slugs. So even if we get a weapon, which so far no luck, not like he leaves it behind, but even if we get the weapon, they won't have rifling to ID it with. He could wrap the damn thing and send it Fed-Ex with roses, we couldn't nail him with it.'

'The guys getting hit have any connection?'

'Well, gee, Sonora, you mean besides being clowns in dunking booths who insult one guy too many?'

Sonora looked at the sludge in her coffee cup, and thought of going to the bathroom to rinse it out. Sanders was probably still in there, crying or decorating. 'So what are you saying, Gruber? These guys are getting killed because they're obnoxious?'

'You got any better ideas?'

'They *are* obnoxious,' Sam said.

'Best lead we got is stuff from the guy's shoe. Just don't ask me yet where it's gotten us.'

'What shoe?'

'You didn't hear? Cinderella dropped a tennie. Wal-Mart's own version of a Nike. We been thinking about going door to door with every deer hunter we know and inviting them to try on the golden slipper. We're just awaiting authorization to go out and buy us a velvet cushion to carry it on.'

Sonora dumped the sludge into Molliter's coffee mug and filled her cup. Put in a double portion of cream to turn things light brown, instead of tobacco brown. Time to branch out. No sense getting into a rut.

'So what was it?' Sam said.

Gruber scratched his chin. 'What?'

Sonora looked up. 'The stuff on the bottom of his shoe. Bubble gum? Name, rank, and serial number?'

'Creosote,' Gruber said.

Sonora leaned against Sam. 'Creosote. Where do you find creosote?'

'Places,' Gruber said.

Sam stuck his tongue in his cheek, thinking. 'Telephone poles. Maybe this guy's a pole climber for the phone company.'

'Ought to be easy to find if he uses a deer rifle to reach out and touch someone,' Sonora said.

Sam nodded. 'Poor son of a bitch is probably just trying to find his own true voice.'

Gruber looked at them. 'You guys through? I mean, I don't want to interrupt if you got more of this shit to get out of your system. And don't think just because I already heard all these bad jokes at least twice is any reason not to carry on there.'

Sam grabbed Sonora's coffee cup out of her hand, took a sip. 'I don't think our humor is appreciated.' He leaned close to Sonora. 'Before I forget, you had one more message on your machine. Somebody from Money-Wise Rent-a-Car wants you to call them back.'

Sonora looked at him. 'That's Julia Winchell's rental company, Sam. You're just sitting on this?'

'They said personal.'

'I told them to ask for me personally.' Sonora frowned. Now Molliter knew they'd found Julia Winchell's car. She didn't feel good about that.

'It's got to be somewhere,' she said. 'We could call the psychic hotline, or we can call the guys from Money-Wise. What would you do, Sam?'

'I'd get more sleep so I wouldn't be such a . . .' He looked at her. 'Irritable person.'

Chapter Thirty-Seven

It drizzled on the way to the airport. Sam drove, air-conditioner on high, window steaming as cold air mixed with hot humidity and tiny slips of rainwater. The roads were slick in spots, drizzle mixed with baked grime and oil spills.

'Turn the wipers up a notch,' Sonora said.

'Who's driving, girl, you or me?'

The windshield wipers were on the low, occasional setting. In between swipes the drizzle piled up into what Sonora considered to be intolerable levels.

'I thought Money-Wise didn't have an office at the airport, Sonora?'

'I'm not telling you a thing till you turn the wipers up.'

'Why do you have to see? I'm the one driving.' He turned the wipers up a notch.

Sonora glanced in the rearview mirror. It was just on five and traffic was getting slow and thick.

'No, Money-Wise doesn't have offices at airports, ever. But for some reason, this car's in the B lot with all the other rentals.'

'How'd they find it?'

'Their guys cruise the airport lots on a regular basis. Most people don't realize Money-Wise doesn't have offices at airports – cars get left there all the time.'

'So how come it took two weeks to find it?'

'That's what I asked. Guy I talked to said there were two possibilities. One, it just got there. Two, it's the busy season. Nobody's had time to cruise for cars. Sam, the rain's stopped and that squeak is driving me nuts.'

'You want the wipers off now?'

The representative from Money-Wise Rent-a-Car was young, hair trimmed short, neatly dressed in a suit in spite of the heat. He stood with an air of possessiveness next to a red Ford Escort. The first thing Sonora noticed about the car was the windshield, which was cracked.

'John Curtis.'

The kid smiled at Sonora, shook her hand gravely, and called her ma'am. She wondered what the possibility was that her son would turn out this way. She wondered if she wanted him to.

The asphalt parking lot was spotted with damp, from the rain. The air had gone steamy, and Sonora's hair was curling on her shoulders. She lifted it off her neck, thought about cutting it very short.

Sonora gave Curtis a second look. His skin was white and sweaty, eyes red-rimmed. Out late drinking, she knew the signs.

Typical All-American boy.

Sonora heard Sam muttering into a radio. 'Got a key?' she asked the boy.

'Yes, ma'am. But I'm not supposed to—'

'We're impounding the vehicle, which is now evidence in a murder investigation. You know how long it's been parked here?'

'Not exactly, no ma'am. We found it after lunch, a couple of hours ago. It was on our hot list, so I called Mr. Douglas as soon as we found it.'

'And this is normal procedure? Cruising airport lots for your rentals?'

'Oh, yeah. People leave them here all the time. Most rental places have airport offices and they assume we do too. But we don't have one-way rental. You can't, like, rent a car in Cleveland and leave it in Cincinnati.'

'Have to take it back where you picked it up?'

He nodded. 'Which means we have to be careful when we do cruise the lots. Sometimes people leave them in the airport lot and want it there when they get back. They're not too happy if it isn't there waiting for them.'

Sonora nodded. Curtis had the air of someone who faced the firing squad when a customer got unhappy.

Sonora touched Curtis's arm. 'Look, it's hot out, and you'll excuse me for being blunt, but you look like you're going to vomit in my crime scene, so—'

'We were out late, entertaining clients. Is this a crime scene?'

'Yeah, and you look like you entertained real well last night. Why don't you go on inside where it's air-conditioned, find yourself a men's room, and throw up? We'll talk some more when you're done.'

He gave her a grateful look, headed for the terminal, moving fast.

'Did I hear you tell that kid to go throw up?' Sam. At her elbow, cheek full of tobacco. He was wearing some kind of shaving lotion that made her want to get closer. She didn't.

'Yeah, so?'

Sam got closer to the car. Sniffed, tentatively. 'No body.'

Sonora dug in her purse for gloves. 'No flies, anyway.' She checked her recorder to make sure it held a fresh tape.

'Kid get in the car?' Sam asked.

'Says not. We'll get his prints just in case.' She pointed to the crack in the windshield. 'What do you think of this?'

Sam circled to the front of the car, squatted in front of the bumper. 'No damage, here. Wasn't caused by a fender-bender. Makes me wonder how it did get cracked.'

Sonora opened the driver's-side door and stuck her head

inside. The car had been shut up, sitting in the hot sun for days. Heat hit, surly and sweaty, and Sonora took a deep breath, sweat trickling down the small of her back. Hot air filled her lungs. If she was a dog, she'd flop down in the shade and go to sleep.

Instead, she leaned awkwardly over the driver's seat and squinted. 'What's this? Sam, we got smears all over the—' She squinted, looked closer. 'Jesus. Is this what I think it is?'

Sam was over her shoulder in an instant.

'Look, Sam. Footprints, right? Heel scuff here. Toes here and here, smeared like a kick, then dragged across the glass.' Sonora pointed, not touching, not quite.

Sam pointed at a spot to the right of the steering wheel. 'Point of impact. Must have been a hell of a kick.'

'Big struggle, and she kicks the windshield.' Sonora got out of the car, walked around to the passenger's side, opened the door. 'Dent, right here in the armrest. Ah. Okay. Let's say her head's here, butted up against the door.'

'If her head put that dent in the headrest, it was some kind of struggle.'

'No blood anywhere I can see, so he didn't cut her up in here.'

Sam looked at Sonora. 'He *killed* her here though. Look at that windshield.'

'ME says her hyoid bone was broken, and she had patriarchal hemorrhaging in that left eye.'

'Conclusion, strangulation.'

Sonora felt queasy. The heat was getting to her. 'So let's say he's driving. She's sitting here.' Sonora pointed. 'He stops the car, turns sideways, leans over her, puts his hands around her neck.'

Sam nodded. 'Her head slips down to the armrest, she kicks like a son of a bitch and cracks the glass in the windshield.'

'But he's a big guy and she's dead. Why didn't he clean up?'

'Time? No paper towels?'

'He had time to play butcher and button button with the body parts.'

'Interrupted?' Sam said.

'Maybe. This is her car. He kills her in the car, then moves the body someplace where he can take his time. Meanwhile his car is clean.'

'Yeah, but then why does he drop her car off at the airport and not clean it up?'

'He's not going to want to be seen with her car. And now he's got a body on his hands, he's got to get it to a safe place. Remember that guy we found with his wife in the trunk?'

Sam grinned. 'Wasn't his lucky day.'

'It's a pretty safe bet the car rental guys are going to clean up the car. If this had been Avis or Hertz, the car would have been processed and cleaned that day or the next. Maybe he doesn't realize Money-Wise doesn't do airports. You didn't.'

Sam spit tobacco and nodded.

'There you go, then.' Sonora stuck her head back in the car and sniffed. Hot vinyl. Baked armorol. 'I think she died here, Sam. I think he strangled her right here in the front seat.'

'Makes it our jurisdiction then, for sure. She may have been dumped all the way up and down I-75, but she got killed in Cincinnati.'

Chapter Thirty-Eight

It was close to seven when Sonora got home. The sun was still high and hot and it hadn't rained at her house. She pulled her car into the tiny garage space her car occupied between boxes full of she did not know what, garbage bags, and kids' bicycles. She could not understand how she wound up with two kids and five bicycles, but she knew there had to be a good reason, because Tim had explained it to her once.

Heather was sitting on the front stoop wearing last year's swimsuit. Her chin was propped on her hand and she looked thoughtful.

Sonora got out of the car, skirting a hockey stick, and an open bag of unused grass seed from a yard project, unfinished, as usual. She could not look at the garage without getting depressed. She did not look.

She left the garage door open, and went up the front steps.

'What you doing, kidlet?'

'Hi, Mommy.' Glum.

'What's wrong?'

'I was going to swim, but Clampett won't get out of the pool. Can you take me swimming, Mommy?'

Sonora considered it. Public pools. Band-Aids floating in the water. Children screaming. The humidity and the heat and trying to fit into last year's swimsuit. Attractive.

'Did you forget? It's Grandmommy night. And I have a date.'

Heather lifted her head. 'Is it that guy who took me to the park?'

'Yes.'

'Will he bring his dog?'

'Heather, I never try to predict what a man will do on the first date.'

Sonora went in the front door, thinking clothes, hair, makeup. Someone had left a squeeze-bottle of Aunt Jemima's genuine imitation maple syrup in the foyer, and the find had been discovered by an orderly line of fat black ants, their bodies sleek and shiny like patent leather.

She was going to have to readjust her thinking. House, then clothes, hair, and makeup. Should have arranged to meet him somewhere else.

Chapter Thirty-Nine

Sonora realized, as they walked in the front door, that she had given Smallwood the wrong signal when she'd told him the kids were at their grandmother's and the coast was clear.

Calm, that was the word she remembered using.

She could not very well explain that she did not always feel like dealing with the capricious manners of children who had never liked a man on a first date, and had even gone so far as to get rid of one in particular by asking him if he was their new daddy.

Single men had a habit of not believing you when you said you were not looking for a father for your children. And it was insulting to explain that you did not wish your children to become attached to someone who might very likely be a temporary presence.

Nope. Smallwood had assumed she wanted sex.

Clampett was as friendly as ever, which meant that Sonora had to drag him by the collar into the backyard so that Smallwood could regain his balance.

'How do you take your coffee?' Sonora asked.

'In a beer can.'

Subtle, she thought, opening the refrigerator. 'You're not getting any of that Bud Lite around here, Smallwood.'

'What you got?'

'Corona.'

'In a pinch.'

She shoved a bottle in his general direction. 'You want to bite the cap off, or do I look for the opener?'

He smiled the smile of a man who was almost ready to make his move.

What to do? she thought. She ran the list of body parts and possibilities, deciding in advance what would and would not be allowed. She thought of Keaton. She did not want to think of Keaton. She went back over the mental seduction list, checked off a few more boxes.

That should keep her mind off things.

They sat side by side on the couch with the lamp on low. Outside, heat lightning arced against a black sky, and the wind began to blow.

'Mind if I get rid of the light?' Smallwood asked.

You could make fun of men for their lack of subtlety, but really, what *were* they supposed to do? She couldn't say she hadn't been warned.

It had been different with Keaton. She had been sure with him.

Sonora turned the lamp off.

Smallwood scooted closer, put his arm around the back of the couch, touched her temple with his fingertip.

'Thanks for having dinner with me,' he said.

'Thanks for the dinner.'

He ran the finger up and down her temple with a firm pressure that felt good. Then he leaned close and kissed her.

He tasted like beer and he kissed like a man who would not be hurried. He kissed well. But he didn't kiss like Keaton.

Sonora leaned close and Smallwood slid a hand into the back of her blouse.

Too fast, she decided, but did not do anything about it. She closed her eyes, still feeling the wine buzz, liking the way his hands felt on her back.

His fingers were firm on her skin. Pressing. Slipping beneath the thin strip of bra line. She wasn't quite sure when it unfastened, because he pulled her close, into his lap, so that she was facing him.

His right hand went round her neck, fingers stroking her behind the ear. 'Such a pretty neck,' he said, softly, in her ear.

And when he said it like that, so softly, she believed that maybe she did have a pretty neck.

She was an equal-opportunity lover. She began unbuttoning his shirt, which he seemed to take as encouragement. Fool.

But then he moved his hands to the front of her blouse and lifted it over her head, pulling her into his now bare chest.

Sonora put her head on his shoulder. Definitely not on the list. He kissed the side of her neck, grazing the skin ever so lightly with his teeth. He dipped his head low and took her into his mouth, hands moving up under her skirt, tracing the insides of her thighs.

More things, not on the list.

He had the top of her pantyhose in his fingers, and he was pulling them down, slowly, over her legs.

The next moments were awkward, but familiar, the kind of moments that made women snort when men spoke of betrayals in terms like 'our clothes just sort of came off.' Twisted pantyhose, and socks and shoes, and shock that, yes, a condom was more a necessity than an option. Men were such innocents, Sonora thought. They seemed not to have the faintest idea about babies and AIDS.

And somehow she wound up bare, in his lap, which any man might take as a yes. But when she looked at his face she saw Keaton's face. She closed her eyes and pretended. Smallwood sat up and she wrapped her legs around his waist. He pulled her in close until he was touching her, and he would have been bewildered and appalled if he had known she was still making up her mind whether or not to do it.

She rubbed herself on him, gently up and down, and

he made a noise that let her know she had his undivided attention.

He felt good. God, he felt good.

She lowered herself ever so slowly until he took her shoulders and pushed.

They both sighed.

He wrapped his arms tightly around her back, pulling her in close and hard, and something about the position made him hit her in just the exact right place.

She thought she might not get rid of this couch after all.

He kissed her while he made love to her and she liked that very much. She came quickly and hard, Smallwood right behind her, gentlemanly, as always.

Chapter Forty

Sonora woke up suddenly, feeling like she couldn't breathe. Her left foot and arm were numb. She was still on the couch, and Smallwood had her encircled in a tight grip. She knew she was breathing, but did not feel she was getting enough oxygen. She felt hot.

It was a feeling she remembered from years ago, sliding down that long icy slope toward divorce – but Zach had died before they'd gotten to the courtroom.

Panic attack. Smallwood. Not a good sign. What on earth had possessed her to wind up on the couch like this?

Sex, she guessed. That old thing.

It was heavy dark out, probably around two or three. She had taken her watch off, so she wasn't sure.

She missed Keaton. She missed how familiar he was, and comfortable, and right.

She wanted a long hot bubble bath and her very own bed, all to herself. Mainly she wanted to be able to breathe. The first thing she needed to do was get out of this death grip.

She moved Smallwood's arm slowly, and when that didn't work, shoved and got up. He stirred. She went into the bathroom, decided it was best not to turn on the light and look. She brushed her teeth, splashed water on her face. It helped a little but not a lot.

She looked into the mirror, saw the outline of her face in the dark. That's what you get when you bring a man home and move too fast. Trapped.

Now what?

She headed back toward the kitchen, saw Smallwood standing in the hallway. He smiled sleepily and pulled her into a hug. She hugged back politely, but she wanted him to leave. He muttered something, headed into the bathroom, and she went into the kitchen thinking sex was one level and intimacy was another, and maybe things worked better when you were ready for both at the same time.

The light over the sink had gone out. She opened the refrigerator, reached for one of the emergency cans of Coke she had hidden in the vegetable crisper. She put one on the counter for Smallwood. Rubbed her forehead. Wondered how long he planned to stay. Wondered why it was up to him.

Maybe Sam's Southernness was wearing off on her and she was getting too polite.

She did not particularly want to think about Sam right now. He violated the three rules of successful singlehood – don't sleep with married men, your co-workers, or your friends. She wondered who she *was* supposed to sleep with.

If Smallwood said anything to anyone about what had happened between them, she would deny the hell out of it. Then she would kill him.

She noticed a shadow in the doorway and looked up.

He had not bothered to put on any clothes.

She held up the Coke. 'This or beer?'

She handed him the Coke before he answered. No more beer – she wanted him to drive. He took the Coke, but didn't open it.

'I'm not an insecure man, so there's no way I'm asking how it was.'

Sonora wished he would not make her laugh. It made her like him too much. 'Oh baby, oh baby, I want you. Feel better now?'

'It'll do.' He scratched his stomach absently.

She wondered if she knew him well enough for him to

be scratching his stomach in her kitchen. Ridiculous. She'd just slept with the man.

'You have a nice comfortable bed somewhere, or are we stuck on the couch?'

She wondered why he expected to stay all night. And why she was finding it difficult to object. Somewhere, someone must have written rules about this, and she wished she had a copy: *First encounters entitle both parties to fifteen minutes in the host's bathroom, and twenty minutes of post-coital small talk is considered polite; anything else is pushing it.*

She knew she was being a pig. In the movies, they always woke up together in the morning, unless the men snuck out and left the woman a note. It had always seemed calloused on the man's part, but she began to see the point.

If he was expecting omelets and fresh-squeezed orange juice, he was going to be disappointed. There was nothing in the house but Lucky Charms.

She would never have had this problem if this had been Sam. She pictured him suddenly, reading *Green Eggs and Ham* to Julia Winchell's babies.

Focus, she told herself. Think fast.

Sonora frowned at Smallwood. 'Sorry if the phone woke you up.'

'The phone?'

'Yeah, that's what got *me* up, but I was hoping you'd sleep through it.'

'Something up?'

Sonora sighed. 'Heather, again.'

'Your little girl? She okay?'

'Oh, she's fine, she's just missing Mommy. She does this. Says she wants to spend the night, then I get these' – she glanced at the clock on the stove – 'these three AM phone calls and she's homesick for Mommy.' She made a silent apology to Heather, who generally tramped off to overnights without a backward glance for anyone except Clampett.

'You need to go pick her up?'

Sonora ran her hands through her hair. 'I don't know. Usually I just go over and get her, but maybe it's time she outgrew this kind of thing.'

Smallwood put the Coke back on the counter. 'Don't do it on my account. Maybe you better go on and get her.'

'But what are you going to do? Did you get a hotel room?'

'Nah, I was just going to drive on back.'

The hell you were, she thought. She had felt guilty about throwing him out. Now she felt better.

She followed him into the living room, watched him put on his clothes. He smiled at her while he pulled his pants up, gave her a quick kiss and fastened up his jeans. Now that he was leaving she was a little bit sorry to see him go. He was very cute.

'It's a long drive,' Sonora said. Not that she gave a shit.

'Hell, I do it all the time. I've had a good sleep, I'm fine.'

'Well,' she said. 'If you're sure.'

Sonora took a long hot bubble bath (pineapple and mango), then curled up into a tiny ball beneath her favorite blue quilt. It felt so good to have the bed to herself, that she let Clampett up to share it.

But she could not sleep. When she closed her eyes, she saw Keaton, and wondered if she would ever feel that way about anyone again.

Clampett scratched frantically. He looked at Sonora and gave a mournful whimper.

Flea bath, she thought, visions of flea bombs and daily vacuuming dancing in her head. Bad idea, letting him up on the bed.

She patted his head, rubbed a silky ear. 'Let me bring Caplan down, okay Clampett? Then I'll take care of you.'

She spent the rest of the night curled up with autopsy reports. Cop glamor.

Chapter Forty-One

Sonora arranged to meet Sam early, at Baba's. Heather had forgotten her stuffed penguin and Sonora had promised to drop it by. And they could catch the sixty-four exit about five minutes from her mother-in-law's street.

No one was awake at Baba's, so Sonora left the penguin on the kitchen table, locked the front door on her way out. Sam was waiting for her in the circle driveway, leaning up against their official Taurus, arms folded. He looked like he'd just stepped out of the shower, fresh-shaved, cheeks still pink. It was already getting hot out. His sleeves were rolled up. White cotton shirt, khaki pants.

'No tie?' Sonora asked.

'It's in the car. You tied yours wrong.'

'Please. No criticism before coffee.'

'*Ooou*, it's cranky this morning. When did you get to bed last night?'

Sonora gave him a second look. She had not mentioned dinner with Smallwood. 'I was up all night with autopsy reports. Julia and Micah. Tell me why the district attorney didn't indict when Micah died.'

'They don't usually go after the grieving husband unless they've got a pretty sure thing. And his family has money, I think.'

'I've gotten death-penalty convictions on less stuff than they had him on. I mean, Sam, she had skin frags under her nails. And he said she scratched his back during sex? Her body is found by the creek, and she's supposed to have drowned there, but there's no creek water in her lungs? That makes sense?'

'It may not make sense, but it doesn't convict Caplan.'

'He's got no alibi during the time of the killing. He had scratches, which he said were from hiking. I saw the shots they took of his arms and those scratches looked fresh.'

'Sonora. His wife was seven months pregnant with his child. She was held under water in a creek on a rainy night. You going to convince a jury a man's going to pull something that vicious, you better have it sewed up tight. He's not just killing the wife, he's killing the baby. And don't forget that little overnight case she had in the backseat of the car.'

'Yeah, Collie, his other wife, she brought that up. Like at seven months pregnant, Micah is having a thing.'

Sam put on his turn indicator, pulled into the parking lot of a McDonald's, and went for the drive-up window. 'You hungry?'

Sam ordered an Egg McMuffin and coffee. He looked at Sonora. 'What'll it be?'

'Three hash browns, and a large coffee with cream.'

Sam made her wait till they were on the interstate and down one hash brown before he swallowed a large bit of Egg McMuffin and cleared his throat to talk.

'The overnight case made it look bad, Sonora.'

'She was seven months pregnant. At the end of the day with her feet swollen double you think she's off to meet a lover? You think Caplan didn't pack the damn thing himself and stick it in the backseat?'

'Yeah, actually, I do. And I also think we're going to catch six kinds of hell going after him. And I think he'll be hard as hell to convict. You haven't been into the office this morning, but I have.'

'What do you mean?'

'On your desk, and mine. A thousand and one little messages. Inquiries from everybody who is living and breathing in the DA's office. Some of them I thought quit years ago.'

'What do they want? Are they threats?'

'Threats? Get real. Of course not. Just requests for information, cooperation, copies of this that and the other. Pain-in-the-ass make-work on every case you and I ever touched, and some that we didn't.'

'That's good, Sam. We're getting to him.'

He didn't answer.

'Sam? You want to back off?'

'Hell, no. Let's fuck up our careers and go after the bastard.'

Chapter Forty-Two

It was a little after eleven AM when they took the second London exit and headed left down a two-lane country road that led them past a tiny, white washed Baptist church. The highway had been a wagon train of cars from Ohio, towing boats. They'd passed two exit signs for Laurel Lake, Holly Bay Marina.

'Drop the other shoe,' Sam said to Sonora.

'No, no, that last rest stop should hold me for a while.'

'Maybe twenty minutes. I mean the sign. I'm waiting for your nasty remark.'

'The Dog Patch Trading Center? I figured they had one in every Kentucky town.'

Sam put his right turn indicator on, moved the Taurus out of the intersection. It was a narrow road, a lot of twists and turns, nobody doing less than fifty. Sam was in his element. He had a smile on his face. The closest he ever got to looking angelic.

A car towing a houseboat passed slowly, crowding them close to the edge of the road.

'Why is it all these people with boats come down from Ohio,' Sonora said. 'We got lakes in Ohio. We got rivers in Ohio.'

'We got laws in Ohio.'

They passed farmland. A tractor parked at the crest of a hill.

'I don't get that,' Sonora said.

'Boating laws in Kentucky are about as common as

unicorns and what they have they don't enforce. You can come down here, drink till you can't stand up, and drive like a maniac through the water.'

'You kidding?'

'Absolutely not. Hell of a lot of fun.'

'What about the tractor?'

He looked at her. 'What tractor?'

'The one we passed. Why did they leave it at the top of the hill? Seems like one push, and—'

'We're here, Sonora.' Sam pulled the car up, parallel to the yard. There was no curb between the lawn and the street. Sonora opened her door and got out.

The house was a freshly whitewashed wood-frame nestled on a large corner lot. A white picket fence surrounded the backyard, and on every tenth picket rested a wooden bluebird, sporting a lush red beak.

Sonora wondered how they had nailed the bluebirds up there. As she got closer, she saw that each bird wore a little tiny coat that she thought might be called a weskit, and each had a different facial expression, more human than birdlike.

There were flowers everywhere, herded neatly into beds that were bordered by landscape timbers. There was a birdbath in the front yard and a bird feeder by the driveway.

The metal storm door had dents in the middle and wasn't hanging true, but the front door looked like it had been painted a deep crimson just last week. A heart-shaped door knocker, made of wood, said WELCOME.

The man who came to the door had a big smile and a large hearing aid, clipped behind his right ear. His brow was wrinkled, in spite of the smile, and Sonora decided he was worried.

People tended to look worried when the police came to their door.

'I'm Detective Blair. This is my partner, Detective

Delarosa.' Sonora showed her ID. 'I talked to Mrs. Ainsley a few days ago about coming down.'

The man nodded and opened the door, offered his hand. 'I'm Grey Ainsley. Come on inside.'

The house was cool, windows thickly covered, but all the lights were on and it was cheery. The carpet was thick and new, covered with a multitude of bright area rugs. Grey Ainsley led them to a couch and invited them to sit.

'I'll go and get Dorrie – it's supposed to be Dorothy, but nobody gets away with calling her Dorothy or Dot.'

'I *hear* you Grey, I'm coming in. This isn't Buckingham Palace – I don't have to be announced.'

Grey exchanged looks with Sam, who grinned, and Sonora saw a quick kindling of the mysterious thing called male rapport. Too bad she could not send them out to play.

Dorrie Ainsley had a small-girl candy voice, mid-register and soft. She was short, and she walked slowly, leaning on a cane and taking Grey's elbow gratefully.

'Let me put you in your chair,' Grey said, settling her into a white brocade chaise longue.

Sonora looked around the room for pictures. A large shot of Collie hung on the wall next to one of Mia and Micah sitting on a pink ruffled bed with a huge stuffed alligator. Sonora made a count. Four of the granddaughter, two with Micah, and one of Collie. None of the son-in-law. Interesting.

'Excuse me for stretching out like this.' Dorrie winced as she settled back on the chaise. 'I have terrible knees – degenerative arthritis.'

'She can barely walk. She needs to get those joints replaced.'

'I think I'd like to give them a little more time for research. I want them to get it right.'

'They do a wonderful job with hips,' Grey said.

'Hips aren't knees.'

Sonora noticed lines of pain on the woman's face. Likely she'd given the matter plenty of thought.

Sam was looking around the room.

'Enough knick-knacks in here to start a store,' Grey said. 'Dorrie makes them. She paints.'

'Did you do the bluebirds on the fence?' Sonora asked.

It was the right thing to say.

Dorrie's smile got big and Grey leaned forward. 'Did you notice their faces at all?'

'Oh, honey, she couldn't see something like that from the street.'

'But I did,' Sonora said. 'They had people faces.'

Grey laughed and slapped his knee. 'Painted one for everybody in the family. Kids, grandkids.'

'Do you have one for Mia?' Sam asked.

Grey was nodding. 'Mia, Micah, and Collie. We've just about adopted that Collie.'

It was a conversation stopper. Grey fiddled with his hearing aid. Dorrie leaned forward.

'Let me get you something. A cup of coffee or some lemonade?'

'No thanks,' Sonora said. Sam shook his head. 'We're investigating the homicide of a woman named Julia Winchell,' Sonora said.

The Ainsleys were politely attentive, guarded.

'According to phone records from her hotel room up in Cincinnati, she called your house a day or two before she disappeared. We're pretty sure she was down here.'

Sonora did not explain about the credit-card receipts. Either Julia Winchell was here, or someone used her card.

Grey was shaking his head. 'Name's just not familiar. I don't think we know her.'

Sonora took a picture out of the maroon vinyl briefcase that her children had saved up for and bought for her birthday two years ago. She passed the picture across the coffee table, around the potpourri.

'It's Micah's friend.' Dorrie had a stricken look. Her voice, soft at the best of times, went so quiet that Sonora barely heard her.

'She was here?' Sam asked.

Dorrie nodded. Grey's hand went to hers, and she squeezed it. He moved his chair closer to hers.

'You say she's dead?'

Sonora kept her voice as kind as possible. 'What did she say when she called? Why was she here?'

'She called and said she went to school with Micah. To college.'

'UC?' Sam asked.

'No, Micah went to Duke.' Grey's voice was gruff, but his chin went up. Proud daddy.

Sonora exchanged looks with Sam. Julia Winchell was not an old college buddy of Micah's. Julia Winchell went to UC.

'She did teach at UC,' Dorrie said. 'On a research grant. Micah was—'

'She was smart as a whip,' Grey said. 'One of those Asian whiz-kids. I found Micah in an orphanage when I was in Korea. She was one-third Japanese, one-third Korean, and one-third American. The kind of ancestry that pisses everybody off. Three years old and about this high.' His voice cracked. He held his hand low to the ground.

'I can't have children of my own. I think that's why Collie and I bonded so well right off.'

Grey squeezed Dorrie's knee. 'Except now Collie's expecting this miracle baby.'

Dorrie nodded, smiling gently, and Sonora wondered why women like Collie and Dorrie had trouble carrying children when they were both clearly top-of-the-line mom material.

'I'm sorry. You're here to talk about this other little girl, not Micah.' Dorrie handed the picture back and Sonora leaned forward to get it.

'I think there's a connection, Mrs. Ainsley. Talking about one is going to lead to the other. What did she say when she called?'

Dorrie thought for a minute. 'She asked if she could stop by and see me. She said she and Micah were best friends in school. I didn't . . . I didn't want to be unfriendly. But when Micah died, there was a lot of notoriety and we got bad phone calls.'

'Whole world's going bad,' Grey said.

Sonora thought of the bluebirds on the fence.

'I told her she could come, but then when she got here I just felt funny. It didn't seem to me like she knew my daughter. And I got worried, and I guess I panicked. What I did, I called Mia's father, I called Gage, and asked if he knew her, or if Micah had ever mentioned her. She said her name was Jenny Williams.'

Sonora looked at Sam. Jenny Williams sounded plenty made up.

'Did he know her?' Sam asked.

Dorrie nodded. 'Well, he did. I mean, not right at first. But we talked about it and he remembered her after a minute or two. I gave him her number at the hotel in case he wanted to check her out. He said it was safe to have her in. That Micah had mentioned her, now that he'd come to think about it. Grey was here and he took her out to see the bluebirds – you know, on the fence. That's when I called Gage. And when I described her and . . . you know, she was really very striking. The kind of girl you remember. And she had that tattoo. The little dragon over her ankle. It was so odd because she seemed like the last kind of girl to get a tattoo. But as soon as I reminded Gage about the tattoo, he remembered her.'

Sonora exchanged looks with Sam.

'So he was definite about that? That he knew her?'

'Oh yes. He said that she and Micah were real close, and for me to roll out the red carpet. And I did. She ended up staying to lunch.'

Sam leaned back on the couch, stretched his arm out across the back. 'What do you think, Mrs. Ainsley? She really know your daughter?'

'Nothing she said about Micah rang true. She talked about how hard Micah worked and how she loved to study – and, to tell the truth, Micah never did follow that Asian stereotype. She had American habits, didn't she, Grey? Liked to be out having fun, doing stuff with her friends. She was just so smart, she hardly had to crack a book.'

Even at Duke, Sonora thought. Very smart.

'And she said she and Micah used to go out for pizza all the time. Only, Detective, my daughter was allergic to tomatoes and she stayed away from pizza, because the sauce made her break out all around her mouth.'

Grey put a hand on the back of the chaise longue. 'We didn't know who she was, but she didn't really know our girl.'

'She did ask a lot of questions, though,' Dorrie said. Grey's mouth went hard and he set his jaw.

'What kind of questions?' Sonora asked.

Grey leaned forward. 'See, she said she hadn't known about it when Micah died. So she was wanting to know what happened, and if they ever caught the guy that did it.'

'How well do you get along with your son-in-law?' Sonora asked.

Dorrie looked at Grey. Then they looked away from each other.

'We get along fine,' Grey said. Woodenly.

Sonora looked at both of them – neither would meet their eyes. 'He controls the grandchild, that it?'

Sam rolled his eyes and Dorrie made a noise of protest. But Grey looked her right in the eye.

'You got the size of it. And believe you me, he works it, every chance he gets.'

'Oh, Grey, don't.' Dorrie put a hand in the crook of his elbow.

He patted the hand absently, but did not take his eyes off Sonora. She recognized a man sorely in need of venting.

So did Sam. 'Mr. Ainsley, would you take me around back to get a look at those bluebirds?' He grinned, friendly, at Dorrie, who tried to smile back. 'I didn't get much of a look when we came in. If you don't mind, I'd like a chance to see them up close.'

'Glad to. Let me show you around.' Grey stood up, headed toward what was logically the kitchen. Sonora heard the hum of a refrigerator shifting gears.

She studied Dorrie Ainsley. The back door banged shut – official exit of the men – and Dorrie took a deep breath.

Sonora tried to think of an easy way into son-in-law territory. 'Mrs. Ainsley, what kind of impression does Gage make on your friends?' She waved a hand. 'Family?'

Dorrie's eyes lowered, then her head came up. She lifted her chin. 'People always like Gage. He's full of . . . full of fun, when he's in the mood to charm.'

Sonora was nodding, friendly, sympathetic. She dug her nails into her palm. You could not just open a valve to people's minds and let the information trickle out. Sam was right when he preached patience, patience, patience. She would never tell him that, though.

'What about when he wasn't in the mood to be charming?' Sonora asked.

She looked up, caught Dorrie Ainsley's eye. Whatever she had said, it had been the right or the wrong thing. The woman was swallowing hard again and her eyes were filling with tears. She dug her fingernails into the tender palms of her hands.

It was painful, watching her try not to cry.

Sonora let her voice take on the strong but soothing cadence that worked so well. A combination cop/mom voice. She wished, sometimes, that someone would talk to her like that.

Dorrie Ainsley looked down at the recorder. 'He's not

. . . he's never been anything but nice to all of us. He was a wonderful—' Her voice cracked and she took a breath. A shudder went like a wave through her small stooped shoulders.

Sonora waited, but Dorrie Ainsley could not finish the sentence.

Sonora hoped she could count on Sam to give her plenty of time. She turned off the recorder. There were things she needed to know.

'It's the grandchild thing, isn't it? Mia? Your daughter's dead and he's in control now. It's up to him when and if you get to see her. And he holds that over you.'

Dorrie Ainsley looked at her steadily. 'I have to keep her safe.'

'His own daughter? You have to keep her safe?' Sonora did not know why she was surprised, not if Caplan was the man she thought he was. It was meeting him, she guessed. He was funny. He made her laugh.

People did not lose their sense of humor when they killed.

Dorrie Ainsley had a hard look in her eyes and the tears were gone.

The woman could barely walk and she had a soft side that led her to paint human faces on bluebirds. Sonora had no doubt that she had crocheted the Afghan that was draped over the back of the couch. But she had Caplan's number, and she was dealing with him.

'He's not the man you think he is,' Dorrie Ainsley said.

Sonora thought perhaps he was.

Chapter Forty-Three

'He killed my little girl.'

Sonora glanced at the recorder, decided it was too risky. 'Tell me about it.'

'You've read Micah's file, or whatever it is you people keep?'

Sonora did not like being called *you people*, but she let it pass, like she always did.

'His skin was under her fingernails. He had scratches – whatever he said they came from, liar. He lies – he's pathological. He lies like he breathes the air. I've seen him do it a hundred times. And Micah was *not* having an affair.'

Dorrie Ainsley shook her head like a woman who has heard all the arguments before and does not want to hear them again. 'Being born and raised in a small town doesn't make you stupid. People are people everywhere you go. I thought Micah *should* have had an affair – in her shoes I would. I would have gotten a divorce. But she was afraid of him. You think what happened there by that creek was the first time he tried it? No, ma'am. That was just when he finally got her.'

'I need details,' Sonora said. She flipped on the recorder.

Dorrie Ainsley either didn't notice or didn't care. 'He bought her a horse. A horse they could *not* afford, believe me. I don't know where he got the money.'

Sonora waited.

'You have to understand the timing on this. Micah was

eight weeks pregnant with Mia, and she'd already had two miscarriages. This – the miscarriages – were before she married Gage. Now you and me know that losing two is hard, but it doesn't mean you can't have any. But Micah was convinced she couldn't carry one to term. She even told him not to marry her if he wanted kids.

'Then he goes and gets her a horse when she's two months along? It's not like *he* knew a thing about horses, and Micah was *afraid* of them.' Dorrie picked at a seam on the chaise. 'She was afraid of a lot of things. Micah was timid. I don't know if Grey and I overprotected her – but I just think that was the way the Lord made her. And Gage was always making her do things that scared her, and she was always trying to please him.

'He was so different when they first met. He was always athletic and energetic and liked to do things, but he treated Micah like she was a little china doll. And Grey and I – we welcomed him. We liked it that he took such care with her. At first we did. And then it was too late. She was in love with him, and dependent on him, and they got married and there was nothing I could do.'

'What happened with the horse?'

'Nothing. The lady at the stable watched Micah ride and gave her some lessons, then told them to get a quieter horse. Gage lost interest, and they were in a money crunch, as usual, so they sold him. And you can't tell me he didn't fool around on her the whole time they were married, but it took her forever to figure it out.'

'You told her?'

Dorrie Ainsley shook her head. 'Not my place. She never asked me, so I never said so.'

'How'd you know?'

'At my age, Detective, you know.'

This, Sonora decided, she would accept for the time being.

She tapped a finger on the armrest of the couch. 'Did he do anything besides buy her a horse?'

'It sounds silly, doesn't it?' Dorrie's voice had gone flat. 'It's hard to make people understand about him.'

'I understand,' Sonora said. 'But I need it all. The more you give me . . . the more I'll be able to do my job.'

'And what do you consider your job?'

'To find Julia Winchell's killer. And if I solve an older homicide that's still on the books, that's my job too. And it may take the one to convict on the other, so talk to me, and don't worry about how it sounds.'

She could play devil's advocate later, with Sam. And Crick would be quick to deflate anything flimsy. 'Give me something I can use in court.'

'I would if I could. All I know is, Gage always was making her do things that scared her. Little stuff, mean things. Petty. It sounds stupid, but there's this section of road between here and Cincinnati. It's steep and curvy, and not too bad. It's I-75 – you probably came down it. But Micah always hated that part. And I guarantee you, every time they came home he'd get sleepy around Berea and they'd stop and change over so she would have to drive that part. And she told me, she'd say, ask him, you know, to let her drive the first hour or two out of Cincinnati. She didn't mind the way they drive up there, which is what scares me. It was the mountains that made her afraid. You want to know what I think?'

Sonora did, and she nodded, but there was no need. Dorrie Ainsley did not normally get to talk frankly about her son-in-law to someone who understood, and she was on a roll.

'I think that drive was a punishment for coming home.' Her voice broke and the tears came. 'He was punishing her for coming home, to see her mama. And *sometimes* he didn't ask her to drive, but that was when it was his idea to come.'

Sonora felt her face getting warm and her stomach knotted

and she waited for the pain, but it didn't come. The ulcer really was gone.

But she knew what kind of man Gage Caplan was. She'd been married to one once.

Dorrie knuckled the tears with an impatient gesture that was almost harsh. 'Much as you might think he dotes on that little girl, he was in a rage when Micah told him she was pregnant.'

'You know that for a fact?'

'I *do* know it for a fact. If you could have heard her voice on the phone . . . she was so . . . so crushed. She cooked him this romantic dinner, with candles in the pewter sticks her Aunt Gracie gave her when they got married, and she was so excited. But he . . . but he . . .' Her voice dropped to a whisper. 'She never told me all the things he said. She was too embarrassed. All I knew was what I heard in her voice. And it was bad.

'And then him coming down here and saying, "I'm going to be a *daddy*!" And picking Micah up and twirling her around. Like he couldn't be happier. He *cried*. He took me aside and told me in private he was scared that something would happen to Micah or the baby, and I guess he had no idea Micah had called me when he acted so bad. And to look at him now you'd think he was just crazy about that child. But here's what I know. He's a good daddy and a loving husband when people are *looking*. Not that I'm saying he knocks them around, or any of that normal abuse.'

What a world it was, Sonora thought, when knocking your wife and child around could be called normal abuse. But she knew what Dorrie Ainsley meant.

'But when people aren't watching, he's something else. I don't know what, but it's bad.'

'You said you needed to keep your granddaughter safe.'

'I've been keeping her safe since before she was born. I honestly think – and even Grey thinks I'm crazy – but I honestly think that if I didn't have Micah stay with me those last couple months, Mia would never have been born.'

'Why did she stay with you?'

'We told Gage that the doctor said Micah had to be flat on her back those last weeks, but it was a lie. But that was what we told him, to get her down here, where I could take care of her.'

'Was Micah afraid?'

'Oh yes. I'm her mother, I could tell. But it's not like she'd say so: everything was under the surface and unspoken. It was a wonderful time, those two months. I'd say, Micah, if you feel well enough, you best get up and not lay in bed all day. We rented tons of movies. Watched TV. Read a million books. And she and Grey would take long walks, and go down to the lake, and I'd have their supper waiting. I fixed all their favorite stuff and we were a family again.' Dorrie placed her hands in her lap. 'I think of those two months as a gift.'

'How did Gage take it? The two months she was here?'

'He . . . I expected him to be difficult and he wasn't. It was almost like he was relieved. I couldn't believe he was just going to let her come down here, but he was nice as you please. He was so nice it gave me bad dreams.' She stared at the floor. 'Doesn't make sense, does it?'

It made sense to Sonora.

'But I know he found out we lied to him after Mia was born, because the doctor talked to Micah later, when it was just her and me, and he made a point to tell her that she could have more kids if she wanted. And that if she got pregnant again, she didn't need to stay in bed all that time unless something unforeseen came up. So he *had* to have talked to Gage about it. Gage must have told him what we said and the doctor set him straight. But Gage never said one word to us about it.'

'Odd,' Sonora said.

'Everything with Gage is under the surface.'

Sonora thought of Caplan's desk the first time she'd seen his office. Clean, pristine desk and bookshelves, drawers stuffed with such a jumble they barely closed.

'Did the police talk to you when Micah died?'

'I called *them*. I knew he did it, and so did that Detective Byer. But the DA's office never took it on. Gage was a lawyer himself, and he knew people. I mean, they investigated him. It's just, Gage is . . . he's a charmer. People like him. And then he goes to work for those people! I talked to a lawyer about getting custody of Mia, but I didn't have a chance. All I would do is cause a big mess.

'Then Gage called me, after things died down. We'd had a lot of words, I have to tell you. And he said that he knew that the trouble between us – that's how he put it – was just my grief taking over. And he hoped I would *settle down*. That's what he said, settle down. Because he said Mia loved me and was asking for me and it would be better for her if we got along.' She swallowed hard. 'You don't know how hard it was for me to back down. But I did. Because it was the best thing for Mia. So I apologized and I ate crow. *Then* he tells me he thinks there should be a cooling-off period.' She took a breath. 'He didn't let me see my granddaughter for a year. She was only three years old, then, same age as Micah when Grey brought her home to me. And if you don't think that was a happy day . . . If I could go back to that day, I'd take my little girl and just hide.'

Dorrie Ainsley looked Sonora straight in the eye and, if she'd expected to see sorrow and grief, she was mistaken. Sonora knew stone-cold hatred when she saw it. This was a woman who had homicidal fantasies about the death of Gage Caplan.

'If it wasn't for Collie I don't know what would have happened. But thanks to her I see a lot of Mia and I love Collie like she was mine. She's a sweet thing. I can't imagine why a highrolling son of a bitch like Gage married her. She's too good for him. But it was a godsend for Mia, and for me and Grey.'

But Sonora knew exactly why Gage had married her. Vulnerable, unattractive – but intelligent, playful, fun. Strength of purpose just when you expected her to fold. A quality woman with a clown face.

This was one he could break, and control, and play with for a while.

Chapter Forty-Four

In the best of all possible worlds, which this was not, the men would not have come back in until Sonora was ready to be interrupted. They did not head back into the living room, for which she was grateful, but settled in the kitchen. Sonora heard the refrigerator door open and close. The clink of ice in a glass.

'Can I get you something?' Dorrie Ainsley slid forward on the chaise longue, but Sonora shook her head. 'This little Jenny girl that came to see me. You say her name is Julia? Who was she, then? Was she one of Gage's girlfriends?'

'No ma'am. She wasn't one of Gage's girlfriends.'

The refrigerator door slammed again, and Grey came in, followed by Sam, holding two glasses of lemonade.

'How about that?' Grey handed a glass to Sonora, and one to Dorrie. 'You girls doing an awful lot of talking. Probably need something to—' He looked at Sonora, face darkening to a dusky red. 'Not supposed to call you girls, am I?'

Sonora smiled. Ten points toward being politically incorrect.

He gave her a second look, then turned to Sonora. 'She's been crying, so I guess you're all filled in on the Gage-and-Micah situation.' He sat down on the edge of Dorrie's chaise longue. 'We got no choice but to get along with the boy. No matter what we think happened. It isn't an easy thing.'

'No,' Sam said.

'But it's been a whole lot better since he married Collie.'

Not for Collie, Sonora thought.

Grey was nodding. 'Over a hundred and ten percent. She makes it easy on us. She was scared to death to meet us, bless her heart. She and Gage come down to use the cabin, and no telling what he told her, but—'

'What cabin?' Sonora asked.

'We have a cabin down on Laurel Lake. It's got a little dock, and we have a boat we take down there, to fish and swim. It's real pretty. It was one of Micah's favorite places. I think Gage and Collie get down there more than he and Micah did – Collie likes to take Mia out there. I pretty much give them free rein of the place. Dorrie and I just don't get out there, and I get to see my granddaughter when Gage and Collie bring her down.'

'They're supposed to come in the next couple of days,' Dorrie said. 'They're going to leave Mia with us and take the boat out, though dragging Collie out in this heat with her so pregnant seems the height of stupidity. But maybe that's just me. I don't like it when it's this hot.'

Sonora considered the cabin, thinking that if Caplan killed Julia Winchell in the rental car, like she thought, he'd have to have somewhere private to butcher the body.

'What time did Julia Winchell leave? That day she came down?'

Dorrie looked at Grey. 'A little before one, wasn't it?'

'Yeah. She had a drive back, and she was anxious to hit the road.'

'And how far is it from here to Clinton?' Sam asked.

'No more than an hour, hour and a half.'

'You stay on I-75 to get there?' Sonora asked.

'Up until you get to the exit,' Dorrie said.

Sonora exchanged looks with Sam. He stood up.

'You folks mind if we take a look at that cabin?'

'Hell, no,' Grey said. 'Take you out in the boat, too, if you want to go.'

Chapter Forty-Five

The cabin was a good sixty feet from the lake, one of those vacation home packages, with a roof that slanted in a V and a wood deck wrapped all the way around. Sonora heard the waspy buzz of a boat engine, somewhere close on the water. There were other houses, close by and in sight, scattered at random in the trees, all with boat docks and trails to the lake.

Would Caplan have brought Julia Winchell here? Lots of people around, in the summer, lots of people to see.

But at night, with the body wrapped in plastic, he could have lugged her in under the trees. People were camping, fishing – who was to say he wasn't lugging a sleeping bag or something for the boat?

Grey led them up onto the porch, engine running on the blue Chrysler LeBaron in an attempt to keep the interior cool for Dorrie, who had insisted on coming along. He seemed shy suddenly, shoulders stiff, wiping his feet on the deck for no particular reason.

He unlocked the front door and pushed it open, but did not go inside. 'I best let you do your job. I'll go keep Dorrie company in the car. Holler if you need something.'

Sonora smiled at him, relieved. It was inhibiting to search a house under the homeowner's worried eye, and she was grateful Ainsley had the grace to go back to the car.

Sam nodded thanks and Sonora led the way.

It took a minute for their eyes to adjust, even with the lights switched on. All the windows had blinds and they were down and shut tight, like eyes that would not see. Sonora sniffed. Some odor here, familiar, but she could not place it.

'What's that smell?'

'I don't notice anything,' Sam said.

Sonora headed to the kitchen, sniffing again. Just a trace. She could not place it. A sort of clean chemical odor, and she knew it was common as eggs. What was it?

The cabin was immaculate. Living-room carpet newly vacuumed, tread marks showing. None of the furniture was new; everything had the second-hand air of things that were pre-owned and serviceable. There were prints on the wall of farms in winter – the kind of thing that provided color for under twenty dollars.

Sonora checked the kitchen sink. Dry as a bone and gleaming. She opened the cabinet underneath. It was the usual lair, dark and scummy. A green cleaning bucket, an open canister of Comet – yellow top, so it had a lemon scent. Sonora sniffed it, frowned. Not the smell she'd noticed – it was too lemony. A sprinkle of the blue-yellow powder had spilled onto the bottom of the cabinet. Sonora opened the door wide. The cleaning supplies had been crammed in so tightly that a plastic squirt bottle of Windex had fallen sideways on top of the Endust and the Four Paws Pet Stain Remover. The can of Raid (Kills Bugs Dead) was lying sideways across a black box of ant traps.

But on the right-hand side was an empty spot, a blue dusting of Comet trailing across the circle of empty space. Sonora picked a yellow tab of cardboard off a pile of blue dust.

It had come from a box of garbage bags, Dairy Co-op House Brand, the large lawn-and-leaf size.

Julia Winchell's head, hands and feet had been tied in brown plastic bags, lawn-and-leaf size. Sonora wondered if they could match the roll.

'Find anything?' Sam said, sticking his head in the door.

Sonora rocked backward on her heels and lost her balance.

'Sorry, girl, didn't mean to scare you.'

'I meant to do that. No, really, my knees were tired.' She looked up. 'Got your little penlight?'

'Yeah.'

'Shine it in here.'

'Sonora, if it's something horrible will you just tell me first?'

'You never did get over the time they sent you into that dark room when you were a uniform and you screamed.'

'Damn right I screamed. Place was dark as an oven, and when I turn on the light there's a body hanging from the ceiling fan? What would you do?'

'No body parts, Sam. Come on, shine it in.'

He squatted down beside her, groaned when his knees cracked.

'Getting too old for this, Sam.'

'All ex-football-players have bad knees. Even the young ones.'

'So you must've had yours for years.'

The light made bright circles in the dark recesses of the cabinet.

'Did you know that when you say "must've" it sounds like mustard?'

'You know, Sam, you are the only person who tells me things like that. Thanks for being a friend.'

He studied the light a minute. 'Is this doing anything for you? Because it's not doing anything for me.'

'Okay, see that?'

'See what?'

He was close enough to kiss and he had that little smile that Sonora didn't see very often, and the tone of voice he'd used to say 'see what?' was without a doubt flirty.

Her voice, worldly wise and jaded, came back to haunt her, and she had a mental image of herself, preaching to young Sanders, about how she had taken the cure and was henceforth no longer interested in married men.

She wondered if there was some universal force that got set in motion to make people eat crow when they made noble pronouncements.

'There, Sam. In the scrum, by the Comet.'

'I . . . Sonora, I think it's a clue.'

'Pull me the hell up off of this floor and I'll explain it to you.' She held up her hands.

Sam stood up, bent over her. He still had that smile. 'What will you give me, if I do?'

'Anything you want.'

'Yeah, I heard that about you.'

She shoved him out of her way, wondered if he knew he'd just missed being kissed by an expert. 'Okay, here's the deal. See, under the sink, the clear spot? Something's missing.'

'There are no sponges, either.'

'What?'

'No sponges, no cleaning rags. See, look in that bucket. Plastic gloves and a toilet brush. No sponges. Where are they? Because somebody's gone over this place, and they had to use something.'

'Used the sponges to clean up something nasty, like blood and guts and bits of bone?'

'Eye of newt.' Sam lowered his voice. 'So that's the big clue, Sonora? Empty spot under the sink?'

'The big clue is a tab from a box of garbage bags that were bought in Cincinnati.'

'Lawn-and-leaf size? Brown? Like we found her in?'

Sonora nodded.

'Millions of them out there.'

'We need to find the box. Match the one we found to the roll.'

'Yeah, plus we need to find a murder weapon and walk on water. All in a day's work.'

'Remind me to stick a gold star on your forehead.'

Sam looked at the carpet. 'Okay, you think Caplan was up to no good, right here in the in-laws' cabin. Let's run with it. Where's the vacuum cleaner? Might be interesting to burrow into the bag.'

'Being a cop means never having to say you're normal. Let's try the closet.'

'First one finds it buys lunch.'

Sonora headed toward the stairs that led to a loft. There was a closet, in the pocket of space beneath. She put her hand on the knob, then looked at Sam over her shoulder.

'Wait a minute. *First* one finds it buys lunch?'

He grinned.

She opened the door and looked inside. 'Extra blankets, a humungous jar of banana peppers.'

'Banana peppers? You liar.' He was there, looking over her shoulder. 'Banana peppers. One of those things you buy at Sam's Club when you start getting carried away.'

'But no vacuum cleaner.'

They checked upstairs, and found a loft bedroom that had a pine dresser with color books and crayons, and a little girl's swimsuit hanging in a genuine cedar closet. A comfy red quilt was spread across a double bed, but there was no vacuum cleaner.

Sonora peered out through the bedroom window. The river looked green and clean, shocks of sunlight bouncing off sedate ripples. It was a good deal cleaner than the Clinch River, where they'd found Julia Winchell's remains.

Sonora wondered where the rest of her was. Were there more arms and legs, discarded by the side of the road, awaiting discovery? Had they been carried away by animals?

Where was the torso?

'What you looking at?' Sam said.

'Boat house, or tool shed. Some kind of thing.'

He looked over her shoulder through the blinds.

The tool shed was up the slope from the muddy edge of the water, about a hundred yards from a wood picnic table that bordered the tree line on the left side of the property. It was the kind of inexpensive storage shed you could buy at Sears and put together in an afternoon, the kind where you stored your lawnmower and grill.

Sam squinted. 'Can't tell from here, but looks like a combination lock on that door. I'm sure Grey will let us take a look. Think there might be a vacuum cleaner in there?'

'God knows. Make sure Grey doesn't follow us down there.'

'I wasn't planning to. Don't backseat cop, Sonora.'

Chapter Forty-Six

A fly buzzed Sonora's head as she picked her way down the muddy path that led to the storage shed. She listened for the telltale hum of thick black swarms, but heard nothing out of the ordinary. A breeze blew in off the river.

No body parts, she decided, trying not to feel disappointed.

Sam was muttering. 'Eight, twenty-six, four. Eight, twenty-six, four. Eight—'

'Why don't you write it on the palm of your hand.'

'Hush.'

The door on the shed was bowed in so that Sonora could see the particle board flooring. It was beige with an overlay of grime, and red rust flaked the doorhinges. Sam worked the combination lock, fingers thick and graceless. The lock clicked open. He glanced at Sonora over his shoulder.

'Drum roll right about now.'

'Ta da, Sam.'

The door stuck when he shoved it, but he put his shoulder into it and it slid out of the way, a metallic squeal heralding progress.

It was dark inside. Sonora smelled oil, dust, with lake water and mud overtones. No odor of putridity, no swarm of flies or maggots, tattletales of gore. Sam had the large black Maglite, cop-issue, and he held it high over his shoulder, as they'd been taught to do years ago.

There was a sawhorse on the right, dirty and faded beach towels hanging over one end, an old six-power boat engine mounted on the other side with a vise clamp. The engine looked dry and rusty, crud fouling the propeller. A dark spot on the floor beneath had dried raisin black years ago.

'Oil,' Sam said, catching her look.

She nodded.

A bottle of Clorox sat to one side of the sawhorse, snug to the right-hand side by the wall. A stack of inner tubes was piled in the left-hand corner, some of them still partially inflated. Cecil the Sea Horse, a pair of pink water wings, an orange ring, a purple life vest that had seen better days, and a Mae West that looked like it had been run over with a truck. A red tube-shaped bicycle pump was hung on the left wall, along with a rack of tools. Back in the left corner, behind the vests and water toys, was a red upright Eureka vacuum cleaner.

Sonora pointed.

Sam grinned at her. 'If he did bring her here, that bag will be a gold mine. All it takes is some hair. Carpet fiber from the car. Blood traces.'

Sonora went in careful, watchful for spiders. 'You can't vacuum up blood stains, Sam.'

She pulled rubber gloves on, studied the Eureka. POWERLINE was written down one side in black. 9.5 AMPS.

'Canisters work better than uprights,' Sam said. 'When it comes to dust mites—'

'When it comes to dust mites, I'll call you.'

'They're all around you, Sonora.'

'Vacuum cleaners?'

'Dust mites.'

It was hot and close in the shed. Sweat ran down Sonora's back. She smelled hot metal. She was tired and annoyed. She was never at her best in the heat.

She popped the hard-shell front of the Eureka. '*Yes.*'

Sam squatted next to her. 'I don't know about you, girl, but I never thought I'd be this happy over the contents of a vacuum cleaner bag.'

'Face facts, Sam, it's a glamorous job.'

Sam shone the light along the floor. 'Look what else.'

'Toolbox!' It was black plastic, from Sears. Sonora bent down and flipped the latch. 'What you want to bet there's a hacksaw in there?'

'Too good to be true, but if there is, I'll start believing in the Fairy Godmother Of Evidence.'

Sonora used a gloved finger to poke through socket wrenches, pliers, a hammer. She lifted the top tray and looked into the bottom of the box. She turned her head to where she could see Sam.

'Bring the light over, and get ready to clap for Tinkerbell.'

'Why?'

'Hacksaw. Right here, in the bottom of the box.'

Chapter Forty-Seven

They took the toolbox outside to the picnic table to get a better look. Sonora squinted, tripping on the path. The sun was high and bright and it took a long minute for her eyes to adjust after the darkness of the storage shed. The picnic table was well shaded. It felt good to stand in the shade and feel the breeze coming up off the water.

Sam laid the top tray to one side. He picked up the hacksaw with a gloved right hand. His left was bare.

'Why are you wearing one glove?' Sonora asked.

'Don't need but one. These suckers are hot.'

Can't argue with that, Sonora thought, feeling her own hands sweating inside latex.

A boat went by on the lake – the boat looked as if it had been painted with blue glitter and it looked new. The man driving wore a red life vest and white swim trunks. He waved at Sonora. Even as far away as she was from the water's edge, Sonora could see he was very tanned.

Her girlfriends were always complaining that they did not know where the men were. Maybe they were all at the lake.

Sam held up the hacksaw. 'Damn. This thing looks new, it's so clean.'

'Not hardly. Paint's cracked all along the handle. And look at all the other tools.'

'They're a damn sorry mess. Look at the claw end of the hammer.'

Sonora looked. Dried mud and a tangle of grass were

caught between the two metal prongs. She thought about what Caplan might have cleaned the hacksaw with, remembered the Clorox bottle in the tool shed, the smell in the cabin kitchen.

'Okay, Sonora, you got that shit-or-go-blind look, so what's in your head?'

'Clorox.'

'Say again?'

'There was a bottle of Clorox under the hobbyhorse in the shed.'

'Hobbyhorse? What hobbyhorse?'

'On the left-hand side.'

Sam walked back to the shed, looked inside, made a snorting noise. '*Saw*horse, Sonora.'

'Did you see the Clorox?'

'Yeah. Think he used it to clean the saw?'

'Could be. That's the smell I noticed when we first went inside the cabin. I smelled it in the living room and in the kitchen. And that place under the sink that's cleared out? I bet that's where it used to be.'

'Bleach. To clean up.'

'Look at the rest of his stuff.' Sonora pointed to the toolbox. 'Everything an oily, dirty mess.'

'Just one notable exception.'

'If that vacuum cleaner bag pans out, Sam, we could make half a casebook on that alone.' Sonora sat on the edge of the table and looked out at the lake. The water was blue-green and lazy. 'He strangles her in the car, and brings her here, where he gets his private time, undisturbed.'

'Think we can nail the guy with stuff from a box of garbage bags, a clean hacksaw, and one vacuum cleaner bag?'

Sonora gave Sam a lopsided smile. 'Caplan could probably pull it off.'

Chapter Forty-Eight

There was a kid sitting on the hood of Grey and Dorrie Ainsley's blue Chrysler. He looked to be about seventeen, but he had the wide-eyed stare of a child. He was eating mandarin oranges out of a can with his fingers. A yellow striped sweat bee darted in and around the lip of the open can.

It landed on his index finger and he did not notice it till he brought it close to his mouth. He screamed, threw down the can, and scooted off the car, bare legs squeaking across the metal.

He began to cry.

'*Bees.*' He rubbed the back of his legs, which were red from where they'd been sweat-stuck to the hood of the car.

Grey put a hand on the boy's shoulder 'Bee's gone, Vernon. It's okay now.'

Sam had set the toolbox down, ready to go to the rescue. He picked it back up again. They had put the hacksaw back inside, and latched it securely.

Grey lowered his voice. 'This is Vernon Masterson. His family has that mobile home we saw on the way up, the double wide. Vernon, these are the police officers I was telling you about.'

'Hello, Vernon.' Sam extended a hand.

'Go on and shake,' Grey told the boy.

Vernon stuck out his left hand.

'Other one. 'Member how I told you.'

'Other one.' Vernon put the left hand behind his back and extended the right. 'Shake?'

He and Sam shook hands. Vernon looked at Sonora. 'Shake?'

'Absolutely.'

His hand was sticky with mandarin orange juice. Tears had left tracks in the sweat-reddened cheeks. His white Hanes teeshirt was oversized and his cut-off shorts went to his knees; he wore red flip-flops and there was a dirty Band-aid on his left big toe.

'You catch bad guys. Grey told me.'

Grey picked up the mandarin orange can. Vernon held his hand out.

'No, Vernon, I better throw this away. It's dirty.'

'Mama says I can have as many of the mandarin oranges as I want because of no fat.' He kept his hand out.

'Yeah, but these have been on the ground, Vernon, so they're dirty.'

'Dirty.'

'That's right. You wouldn't want them.'

'No, I wouldn't want them.'

Sonora thought of her own two children, healthy and bright.

Vernon's hair was cropped close in a butch cut, and the stubble was blond. He had a heavy case of acne. His eyes were brown and soft looking, like a deer's. He smiled at Sonora. That was what was charming about him, she thought. A teenager who smiled.

'You catch criminals, too?' he asked.

'Only the ones that don't run too fast.'

He grinned and thumped his nose. 'I run really fast. Celly says so.' One of his front teeth was crooked. 'And Mr. Gage puts criminals in jail.'

Grey secured the lid on a metal garbage can, fitting it snugly over the lip. 'Gage and Vernon are big buddies.'

Vernon held his hands wide. 'Big buddies. We go fish and do trains. He's not putting me in no jail because I'm good.

If I'm not good, he would have to turn me in because of the job. *Even* friends.'

'You like to fish?' Sam asked.

Vernon grinned hugely. 'I like to get them and then throw them back. I like to see the splash.'

'Well, there you are, Vernon, pestering people again.' A girl came out of the trees, barefooted, smiling.

'Hey, Celly,' Vernon said.

'Hey yourself.'

He went to her like a dog to its master, and gave her a great big hug, which she returned with absentminded enthusiasm. What could be seen of her legs was brown and slim, and an ankle bracelet glinted over her left foot. Sonora wondered if Julia Winchell had worn an ankle bracelet to set off the tattoo.

This girl wore a sleeveless jean jumper that hung calf-length and looked lightweight and comfortable. Sonora had seen them for sale at The Limited. Her arms were tan and muscular, and she had a scoop-necked baby tee, in a soft powder pink, underneath the jumper. A gold, heart-shaped locket hung around her neck.

Her hair looked freshly washed and shiny – a professionally highlighted light brown. Her toenails were painted a shell shimmery pink that coordinated with the baby tee. When she got close, Sonora could smell that unisex perfume that they gave out in samples in all the major department stores.

She looked at them all, smiling in an absent, friendly way, then she looked behind them and frowned.

'Gage around?' she asked.

The voice was high and girlish and Sonora revised her estimation of the age. Fifteen or sixteen. She could pass for twenty. She and the boy were no more than a year apart.

Brother and sister, Sonora decided, studying the kids' faces.

Sweat was beginning to work its way through the girl's makeup. She looked hopefully at the cabin.

Sonora, watching Celly, realized she had this sort of thing to look forward to in a few years with Heather.

'Gage isn't here,' Grey said.

'Oh. Well. I mainly came over to make sure Vernon wasn't pestering nobody.' Celly turned to leave, but Sam stopped her by putting out a hand to shake.

'Detective Delarosa. Cincinnati Police Department.'

Her eyes got large and interested, and, as she shook Sam's hand, her air of disappointment dimmed.

'Celly Masterson.'

Sam clapped a hand on Vernon's shoulder.

'This is your brother?'

'Yes, sir.'

Sonora caught Sam's look at being relegated with one well-placed 'sir' to the legion of the old and she grinned and tried to catch his eye.

He ignored her. 'You know Mr. Caplan?'

Celly nodded, unable to contain the enthusiasm, and the warm look that immediately gave her away.

'When's the last time you saw him?'

She moved closer to Vernon, arms tight by her side. 'Is something wrong?'

Sam smiled at her. 'Why would you think that?'

'I don't know.'

Grey was watching her. Dorrie rolled the car window down, turned off the engine.

Everyone seemed to sigh. Sonora realized how annoying the engine noises had been, now that they were gone. A large bird flew overhead.

'Osprey!' Vernon jumped up and down, pointing.

Everyone looked except Sonora. The tension that had suddenly sprung up began to ease. Dorrie waved at the girl.

'How's your mama, Celly?'

'She's fine. Working herself to death.'

'Heard from your dad?'

'Nope.'

Only in the South, Sonora thought, would it seem perfectly natural to interrupt a police investigation with neighborly chitchat.

But Dorrie was setting the girl at ease and establishing adult control, so she kept her mouth shut and waited.

Grey folded his arms and leaned back against the car. 'You were up, weren't you, last time Gage and Collie brought Mia down to swim?'

'The cookout? Yeah. When Gage put that barbecue sauce he made up on all the burgers.'

'They was good,' Vernon said. Then he frowned. 'Mama said for me not to bother you folks.'

'You're a buddy, not a bother,' Grey said.

Sonora looked at Celly. 'You see him since? I think he was down one night, a couple of weeks ago.' She watched the girl, thinking she might lie.

'If he was here, I didn't see him.' Frowning. Puzzled.

But the girl had acquired a wary look, with none of the smugness of a teenager pulling one over, or the wide-eyed innocence of one putting on.

'You see him, Vernon?' Sam asked, looking at the boy.

Vernon shook his head. '*No* sir. But if he come up after dark, I wouldn't of, 'cause I go to bed every night at nine o'clock. Nine o'clock is later in the winter. In the summer it's a kid bedtime, 'cause outside it's still light. But I need to go on to bed because of my medicine routine.' He looked at Sam with apology. 'I may be seventeen, but I am still a kid.'

Sam clicked off his recorder.

Celly sighed and tugged Vernon's teeshirt. 'We better get on home. Nice seeing you all.' She glanced at Dorrie. 'How is Mrs. Caplan doing? She had that baby yet?'

'Baby hasn't dropped yet, Celly, so I say we got another six to eight weeks.'

'Tell her I said hi.'

Celly turned away but not before Sonora saw the wistful look that passed across her face. She knew exactly what the girl was thinking – that to be Mrs. Gage Caplan, and pregnant with his child, would be close to heaven on earth.

Not an analogy that came readily to Sonora's mind.

The boy and girl headed off, Vernon plucking at Celly's dress and talking nonstop, she not paying any attention. Sonora wondered if her feet hurt, going barefoot like that.

Grey waited till they were out of earshot, then inclined his head toward the toolbox. 'Find something?'

Sam grimaced. 'Hate to leave you without your toolbox, but—'

'That's not mine, it's Gage's. I don't give a hoot in hell what you do with it.'

'It's Gage's toolbox? You identify it for certain as belonging to him?' Sonora had the recorder going, but they'd used it enough with the Ainsleys that it had become nothing more than background.

'Hell, you think I keep my own tools crapped up like that?'

Dorrie leaned out the window. 'Grey, simmer down.' She glanced at Sam. 'He keeps his tools neat and put away. His mother always told me he never even broke his crayons when he was little. He's as picky as they come.' She leaned out the window, pushed his hip playfully. 'Probably do you good to break a crayon once in a while.'

'I don't think it's *picky* for a man to keep his tools in order.' His shoulders were stiff. 'A man who can't keep his tools in order is a sorry kind of a fella, if you don't mind me saying.'

Another strike against the son-in-law from hell, Sonora thought.

'His initials are right here.' Grey headed toward the picnic table, pointing. 'Spent a fortune on the box, and next to nothing on what's inside. And everything inside a tangled-up dirty mess. I hate lending him anything, because he never cleans anything up.'

Except for the hacksaw, bleached clean, likely with that bottle of Clorox, Sonora thought. She'd take that along too.

Sonora had been aware of the crunch of gravel beneath tires, and she was just turning to take a look when she heard Grey's intake of breath, saw Dorrie go white and clutch his arm.

Sam said 'son of a bitch' under his breath.

On some subconscious level, she must have known what to expect, because, when she turned and saw the red Cherokee Jeep Laredo with Gage Caplan behind the wheel, she did not feel surprised.

Chapter Forty-Nine

Caplan nosed the Jeep right behind Grey and Dorrie's Chrysler, blocking them in. He shut the engine off, got out of the car.

He had a big grin, dark sunglasses.

His suit coat had been draped over the headrest on the passenger's seat up front. His tie was loose, the cuffs on the navy pinstriped shirt rolled back.

'Hello, Mama. Grey.' He walked to the Chrysler, a man in no hurry, leaned down and brushed Dorrie Ainsley's left cheek with his lips.

Grey stumbled forward to shake his hand.

The Ainsleys looked older, all of a sudden. Beside them, Caplan seemed to reek of strength and robust health.

'Detective Blair . . . and you must be Delarosa. I don't believe we've had the pleasure.'

Sonora looked at Sam. He had a faint smile on his face.

'Yeah, I'm Delarosa. You're Caplan, that right?'

They shook hands, like boxers anticipating a grudge match, neither one of them in a hurry.

'Detective Blair, I have to say I'm surprised to find you here.'

'Why do I doubt that, Mr. Caplan?'

'I don't know, Detective, why *do* you doubt it?'

She wondered how he'd known they were there. The Ainsleys could have called, but one look at Dorrie's white face put that one to rest.

Molliter? Was he Caplan's conduit into the investigation?

Somebody was.

Caplan had a smug smile. 'I just came by to see my in-laws.'

'Just happened to be in the area, a four-hour drive from home?'

Caplan shook his head. 'If you'd swallow that one, you wouldn't be much of a cop, now would you, Blair? I'm here to make plans with Dorrie and Grey for a surprise baby shower for my wife. I'm bringing her down in a couple days, and I thought it would be fun to surprise her.' He smiled at Dorrie. 'Isn't that right, Mama?'

Dorrie swallowed. Looked at Sonora, then back to Caplan. 'That's fine with me.'

'Don't whisper, Mama. People can't hear you when you whisper. Grey will have to turn up his hearing aid.'

Grey clenched his hands into fists. 'I can hear her fine. If you can't, Gage, that's your problem.'

Caplan gave him a lazy look, no more than a flick of the eyes. 'Detective Blair, I see you've collected yourself a few goodies. If I'm not mistaken, that's my toolbox your partner is holding.'

Sonora saw Sam's hand move, saw that he'd clicked the tape recorder on.

'Sam, set the toolbox back down on the picnic table there. Let's let Mr. Caplan make absolutely sure that these are his tools.' Sonora smiled at Caplan and waved a hand toward the picnic table.

Caplan returned the smile. Patient, waiting. Sonora watched him. Was he making mistakes? Was she making mistakes?

He knew the hacksaw was clean. And he knew Grey and Dorrie would have already identified the toolbox. He had nothing to lose here.

Why was he there? she wondered. It told them immediately that he had an 'in' to their investigation. Why show his hand? What did it buy him?

Caplan went to the picnic table, opened the box of tools. 'Yes, sir, Detective Delarosa, this belongs to me.'

Sam pointed to the hacksaw. 'This yours too?'

'Yes sir, it is.' Caplan smiled slowly. 'What were you planning to do with my tools, if I may ask? And ... is that a vacuum cleaner bag?' He looked over his shoulder at Dorrie. 'Late on the spring cleaning this year?'

Sonora cocked her head to one side. 'Now don't tell me, Caplan, the vacuum cleaner bag belongs to you too?'

Caplan looked at his in-laws. 'Folks, both of these detectives are out of their jurisdiction here. Did they show you any kind of a search warrant? Any paperwork at all?'

Grey was still.

'Folks?' Caplan's voice had acquired an edge.

Dorrie Ainsley said no, very softly.

Caplan shook his head at Sonora. 'Detective, you must know better than this. You're miles out of jurisdiction, two whole states away. You're collecting evidence from a private residence without a proper search warrant. Even a man's trash has protection under the law, thanks to our friends in Washington, DC. You can't come in and carry these off without taking a big risk everything you've got here will get thrown right out of court.' He looked over his shoulder at Dorrie and Grey. 'This is the kind of sloppy police work that makes my job so difficult.'

'We've got permission,' Sonora said. She looked at Dorrie. Back me up, she thought.

Caplan shook his head slowly. 'I don't think so. Not for a minute.'

Sonora watched Dorrie Ainsley. Saw the struggle.

'They already have my permission, Gage.'

Grey sighed softly, looked at his son-in-law eye to eye. 'We felt sure you would want us to cooperate with the police. You're kind of on the same side, aren't you, Gage?'

Caplan gave him a gentle smile. 'I'm sure the both of you are doing what you feel you have to do, and whatever happens, happens.' He put his hands in his pockets. 'In a way, you know, I admire you, both of you. I always have.'

Caplan's shoulders sagged, just a little. But Sonora looked into his eyes, and knew that inside, Caplan was smiling.

Chapter Fifty

Sonora did not know what had woken her up. In her mind she could hear Dorrie Ainsley, telling her that Collie and Gage would be taking the boat out. She wondered if Collie was a good swimmer. If she wore a life vest out on the lake.

How well did a woman swim when she was seven months pregnant?

Sonora turned onto her side, decided she could not think until she went to the bathroom, so she did that, then got back into bed, stopping to get her blue quilt out of the closet.

She propped up her pillows, made the bed up, except for the spread, and curled up in the quilt to keep off the chill of the air-conditioner.

It often happened this way, a moment of complete mental clarity just as she was waking up, when she was able to look at things practically, unemotionally, objectively. Able to tell if she was denying a problem, or making one out of nothing.

This felt like a problem.

Collie Caplan lived with Gage Caplan every single day. She was alive and well. She had not asked for protection.

And maybe, after what had happened down at the cabin with the Ainsleys, the lake trip would be called off.

There was nothing Sonora could do but close her eyes and go back to sleep, so she could be rested and brilliant enough to catch Caplan before he did it again.

The doorbell rang, and Clampett leaped up with a combination bark and howl that brought the hair up along the back of Sonora's neck. She reached for the pair of sweats she'd left in a wad on the floor by her bed, glanced at the clock. Five-forty AM.

What the hell.

It was still dark out. Clampett stayed by her leg, barking, his ruff standing in a ridge on his back. Sonora looked out the side window by the front door.

A sheriff's car was parked in front of the house, headlights blazing into the darkness. A pudgy blonde with a ponytail and a uniform that likely caused pain when she bent over waited patiently at the door.

Sonora unlocked the dead bolt. She did not like the woman and she did not like her smirk. 'What is this?'

'Are you Sonora Blair?'

'What's going on here?'

'You're Blair?'

Some instinct warned her. 'No, you've got the wrong house.'

'The hell I do.' The woman tossed an envelope on the porch. 'You've been served.'

Clampett growled. Sonora seriously considered letting him out in the yard to play.

Chapter Fifty-One

Sonora met Sam in the parking lot of the Hilton Hotel. He was standing by the Taurus, looking at his watch. 'I see you got my message.'

Sonora locked up the Blazer. 'To meet you here? Good guess, Detective. Where the hell you been all day?'

'In court.'

'*Court?* For what?'

'The Deaver hit.'

'You didn't have anything to do with that case.'

'No kidding? I still got subpoenaed at six AM this morning, said I had to be in court at eight.'

'They came to my place first.'

'I wondered.'

'Bitchy blonde with hips?'

'That's the one.'

'I didn't have to appear until one. Crick got it squashed.'

'*Somebody*'s got prosecutoritis.'

'Let him play, Sam. That much sweeter when we jump his ass.' She followed him across the parking lot. 'So why are we here, baby? You get us a room?'

He smiled in a way that let her know the thought had crossed his mind. 'Thought we might have a talk with Caplan's Aunt Georgie. Get some background on the bastard, I believe were Crick's exact words. Look for a sweet spot.'

'Anything to get out of the heat.'

Sam waved her forward, through the automatic door

into the lobby of the Hilton. A bellboy looked at them, inquiring.

'Where's Suite A, the Alabama Room?' Sam asked.

Sonora shivered. It was ice cold in the lobby.

The bellboy gave a knowing look. 'You're here for the Babylon Models Internationale?' He eyed Sam's suit and haircut. Looked Sonora up and down.

'I don't think so,' Sam said.

'They're the ones who booked the Alabama Room,' the bellboy said.

Sonora shrugged. 'I guess that's who we want then.'

She headed in the direction the bellboy pointed – round a fountain and huge potted plants and a gift shop that sold toothpaste for over three dollars per tiny tube.

Sam was tugging his tie. 'Internationale? Out of Cincinnati? Who the hell they kidding?'

'Not you,' Sonora said, leading the way.

The doors to the Alabama Room were propped open. A blonde in a black power suit stood next to a table, arguing with a man in a brown corduroy jacket. His hair was cut à la *GQ*, and he had the careful beard stubble Don Johnson made popular in the old *Miami Vice* television series.

'I did the last one,' the man said. 'Why won't you take this one?'

The woman shook her head. Her lips were pressed tight. 'Not in my contract.'

'But why? You shy or something?'

She shook her head, glanced at the clipboard.

The man caught sight of Sonora, flashed a smile as reassuring as a shark fin in the water. 'Are you here for the seminar?'

She glanced into the Alabama Room. A coffee urn was set up on a table at one end of the room. Metal folding chairs were placed in front of a dais that was bracketed by a table and chairs on either side. A video was playing on a television at the front of the room – forgettable music with a driving beat and some kind of fashion show where thin girls were gliding down the runway with plastic fruit on their heads to somehow set off summer resort outfits that would be worn by those too rich or too silly to know better.

'We're looking for Georgie Fontaine,' Sam said.

'Go on in and sit down,' the man said. 'She'll be along after the talk.'

'What talk?' Sam said. His voice was rougher than usual.

Probably suspicious of men who wore corduroy in the dead of summer. Sonora peered into the Alabama Room, where an aura of nervous hope and expectation was as thick as the smell of coffee in the corner. Most of the metal chairs were full, girls of all ages with their moms beside them. There were a few lone males, most of them in their teens or early twenties.

Everyone was dressed up. Little girls had their hair piled on their heads, teenage girls had theirs curled and moussed enough for a Vidal Sassoon convention. They all studied each other out of the corners of their eyes, like girls in a Miss America competition.

Sonora looked at Sam, saw he'd have no chance at Miss Congeniality if he kept that scowl on his face.

'What is this, anyway?' she said.

Corduroy Jacket didn't like her question. 'Aren't you here for the seminar?' he asked. 'If you'll fill out this form and—'

Sonora ignored the pencil and clipboard he tried to hand her and flipped her ID. 'Police Specialist Blair, Cincinnati Police. We're here to see Georgie Fontaine, and would appreciate it if you'd track her down.'

Corduroy Jacket had gone very wary, but the blonde was paying attention. She pointed off to the right.

'Headed that way for a smoke.'

'Thanks,' Sonora said.

Sam followed, head swiveling to give the blonde a second

look. A dark hallway veered off to the left. Sonora smelled cigarette smoke, saw a sign that said RESTROOMS. She looked into the dark corridor, saw a woman leaning up against the wall, inhaling from a cigarette as if it was the sustenance of her life.

'Georgie Fontaine?'

'Who wants to know?' The voice held the deep husk of a veteran smoker, the self-confident amusement of a jaded woman of the world, and a hint of curiosity. 'You guys aren't the cops I talked to, are you?'

Sam walked over to the wall the woman had propped a very nice shoe against, and showed her his ID. 'Detective Delarosa' – he waved a hand at Sonora – 'and Detective Blair.'

'Hell, you *are* the cops. Sorry. I had to get away from the youngsters – they've been bitching at each other all day. Should have retired when I had the chance.'

'Could we go somewhere and talk?' Sonora asked.

'Let's get some coffee in that little sports bar by the gift shop.' She glanced at Sonora. 'Duncan should be giving his spiel right about now. He talks slow, they won't need me for a while. Unless he's got the girl doing it.' She peered around the corner, as if reluctant to show herself.

'It's not in her contract,' Sam said.

Georgie Fontaine blew a smoke ring. 'Haven't I been hearing that one all weekend long? Coffee will have to hold me till I get rid of all the kiddos, then I want something long, cold, and alcoholic.' She headed down the hallway, glanced at them over her shoulder.

'Coming?'

She led them the other way around, avoiding the seminar charade in the Alabama Room.

The crowd in the sports bar was thin. The air was filmed with stale cigarette smoke. All of the tables were sticky with beer rings and crumbs, and wadded napkins constituted most of the table decorations. No doubt the night before had been a big success.

A bartender moved slowly on legs like jelly, wiping glasses dry. He did not seem happy to see them.

Georgie Fontaine took the cleanest table in the far left corner of the room, away from a noisy group of men wearing the kelly-green pants and knit shirts that proclaimed golfers. There were four of them, two were smoking. They drank beer and Beefeater Martinis and watched the tournament on television. Sonora felt her head begin to ache.

She took the seat at the table facing the television, because she knew that if Sam could see it he would watch it, no matter what was on. A smattering of applause broke out from the large screen as a man with a pot belly made a difficult shot, and the announcer spoke with the kind of muted enthusiasm used by disc jockeys at classical radio stations.

Sonora put her elbows on the table, felt water soaking through the sleeve of her blouse.

Sam had his recorder out, and Georgie Fontaine was reeling off her name, address, and serial number. She said her age without hesitation. Sixty-two.

'Not possible,' Sam said.

'What isn't possible, sweetie?'

'I couldn't have heard that right. You're *forty*-two.'

'This is what sixty-two looks like in the nineties.' But she smiled at him tolerantly, as she would at a son.

'Just for the record,' Sonora said. 'Gage Caplan is your nephew.'

Fontaine lit up a cigarette, took a quick puff. 'Only one I got. Rest are nieces, and I got three of those. They're easier to buy for at Christmas.'

'Are you and Gage close?' Sonora said.

Fontaine's eyes narrowed.

Could be from the smoke, Sonora thought. But she wondered.

'Never see him.'

'Why is that?' Sam asked.

She waved a hand. 'I work long hours. He works long hours. He's done very well. I'm proud of him.' She did sound proud. Surprised too.

'You see much of your nieces?'

Fontaine rolled her eyes. 'All the time.' It sounded like a complaint but she smiled fondly. 'Babysit their kids when I have some time, which isn't all that often.'

She took another drag on the cigarette, glanced over at the bartender. He avoided looking at their table.

'See much of Mia?' Sam asked.

Fontaine thought about it. 'I saw her once at some Christmas thing. It was right after her mother died, and Gage was kind of at loose ends. Poor baby, I never saw a kid look so tiny and lost. She cried a lot, asking for Grandmama. The other one, Gage's mom, is dead. I remember wondering why he didn't have her down with Micah's folks for Christmas – I think they live in the hills or something. Tennessee or Virginia.'

'Kentucky,' Sonora said.

'Whatever.'

Sam grimaced but did not say a word. Sonora wondered how often Mia had asked for her grandmother, wondered if she'd learned not to ask. Wondered how aware the child was, of the games being played out around her.

'You said Gage's mother is dead?' Sam asked.

Fontaine nodded. 'Very tragic. Gage was just a little guy when it happened, six, I think, if that old. I think he was in school. Kindergarten. Kimmie was maybe seven months pregnant. She'd miscarried once and was trying like crazy to have another child.'

'She was your sister?'

Fontaine shook her head, waved away a cloud of smoke. 'No, my sister has all the girls. My brother married Kimmie when Gage was four or five. Her first husband just ran off and left them and they were living in the projects and really going it hard. Alex was very comfortable, financially, my parents had money and, you know, they gave us a very nice life. Got us started when we left college, then left us alone. We both went into business – me into modeling, then running this modeling school. Alex went into law. Specializing in bankruptcy. Well, consider the last decade or two. He sure hit the right specialty. And loves it. Believe it or not, people need a white knight when they're going bankrupt. Creditors get mean if you don't yank their leash, and if people don't know the law they aren't protected. I know he does a lot of work out of pocket. Which he can do, thanks to good old mom and dad.'

She spoke of her brother with a great deal of fondness, Sonora thought. She spent a lot of time with her nieces. And yet had almost no contact with Gage. Interesting. Was it because he was not really family, the blood issue, or was it something else?

'What happened to your sister-in-law? How did she die?'

Fontaine's face settled into the worn grooves of old familiar grief. Her shoulders sagged and she stubbed her cigarette out in a gold foil ashtray that was full of other butts, some lipstick-stained, at least two shades of red.

When Fontaine spoke, her voice was matter-of-fact. 'She drowned in the bathtub.'

Chapter Fifty-Two

Sam looked over at the bartender, who nodded and headed over. 'How could she die in a bathtub? She epileptic? Pass out?'

Fontaine shook her head. The bartender stood next to Sam, a question in his eyes.

'Coffee,' Sam said, pointing at himself and Sonora. He looked at Fontaine.

She blew a smoke ring. 'Oh, the hell with it, bring me a whisky sour.' She looked at the waiter. 'And wipe the table, if you would, please.' Fontaine moved a dirty glass to one side, and the bartender gave her a mournful look, as if he knew he should never have come over.

'Alex and Kimmie had this big ol' house. Brand-new, out in Indian Hills, land all around. It was a long drive for him to the office, but Kimmie had her heart set on living there. Gage went from the projects to this enormous house. And Kimmie was pregnant when they were married, and they lost the baby. Tore them both all up to hell. I know it was hard on Gage. They had this nursery they put together. Kimmie never had anything, so she outfits her nursery with everything she ever wanted when her first was coming along.'

Sonora nodded. 'How did Gage feel about all of this?'

The bartender came back with a plastic tub. He put all the glasses in the tub, tossed the ashtray in on top, and wiped the table with a drippy rag, leaving a swath of wet beads for everyone to dodge.

'Drinks be right up,' he said.

Sonora reached into her purse for a bottle of Advil.

Fontaine was thinking. 'That's kind of hard to say. He didn't seem to not like Alex, but he didn't seem to like him either. Like Alex was part of the furniture. I know he was kind of clingy with Kimmie; I remember he used to watch her all the time. If she was in the room, Gage was always in touching distance. He was a smart kid. Ahead for his age. Coming out of a bad school, but still sharp.

'I know he kept asking why Kimmie didn't have all that baby stuff when he was born, and she kept trying to explain it was because of Alex. He never did seem to get it. He and Kimmie had this thing where he was the old baby, and this was the new baby. But instead of making him feel better, it seemed to make it worse. He was really . . . bothered. Kimmie and Alex talked about it, but they were so distracted, so in love and excited about the new baby. I know I was worried about Gage getting short shrift there, and I think Mom said something to Alex. But Kim was like a little girl in a fairy tale and I don't think her feet were touching ground. She and Alex were so obsessed with each other it was nauseating. We were all just kind of tolerating them till the "honeymoon" cooled off. And then she lost the baby. And it was like their whole world went dark.

'They locked the nursery door and wouldn't let anyone go in there, and Alex took Kimmie off for a cruise and left Gage with my mother.'

The drinks came. Fontaine sighed softly when she saw the whisky sour. The waiter left plastic cartons of cream and Sam took a drink of steaming black coffee and stacked the creamers into a short and stocky white tower. Sonora opened one, poured it into her coffee.

Fontaine snapped her fingers. 'I almost forgot. I brought pictures.' She rummaged in her purse, a large, shapeless leather one that looked to have endless capacity and was worn down and soft with age.

She took out an envelope with a breath mint stuck to one

side, opened the flap, removed a stack of prints. She laid the pictures out in a row like a hand of solitaire and she snapped them as she laid them down, just like you might with playing cards. Sonora thought of Butch Winchell, lining up pictures of Julia and her two baby girls.

Fontaine pointed a fingernail coated with deep-red polish. 'This one's cute.'

Gage, age three, sat cross-legged in a dingy living room. There was a television on behind him, and the kind of couch people put out by the side of the road (or, Sonora thought, in her living room). Gage's hair was long, curly, and his face was round and full, cheeks chubby like a Gerber baby. Even then he looked like a little linebacker, thick sturdy legs, a solid build. He had a hand crammed deep into a box of Cracker Jacks and there was a piece of caramel corn on the front of his shirt. He was smiling and happy and seemed not to have a care in the world.

The row of pictures told the story. Gage and Kimmie, together against the world. The team. Money very tight. Gage's clothes all with the worn look of hand-me-downs. Christmas trees with a few toys, some giveaway color books, the tiny boxes of crayons they gave away in restaurants. Sonora thought of Kimmie, hoarding those little boxes so her little boy would have more things to unwrap.

There were pictures of the new house – Kimmie twirling in empty rooms, none of Gage here. Where had he been that day?

And pictures of the nursery. Pretty as a wedding cake – white and lacy and coordinated with hardwood cherry baby-furniture canopy crib, bassinet, a little reading nook with a bentwood rocker and a shelf full of brightly colored books.

'You say his mom drowned in the bathtub? Anything funny about it?' Sam asked.

Fontaine shook her head. 'It was tragic, but it was an accident. They had one of those antiquey type tubs – large and deep with feet on it. Alex had it put in special for Kimmie. She'd been having a difficult time with the pregnancy. She had fainting spells. They think she ran the water really hot, and all the blood rushed to the surface of her skin, and she just . . . passed out. And drowned.'

Sonora picked up one of the pictures, held it up. Not a very good shot. Someone had been trying to get the nursery from the hallway. The room was light, sun streaming in, but not centered, and half the shot was of dark hallway. Standing in the shadows, next to the bright sunny nursery, was little Gage Caplan.

A year had made quite a difference. The happy, carefree child was gone, if he'd ever really existed. Gage was looking at the camera and posing with a smile so earnest it was painful to see, knowing that the man or woman wielding the camera had probably not even been aware he was there.

Sonora flipped the picture over. Someone had written NURSERY in block letters on the back. Not NURSERY AND GAGE. Just NURSERY.

Chapter Fifty-Three

Sam pushed the swing door into the bullpen and let Sonora go ahead. 'What about Caplan's current wife?'

'What about her?' Sonora said.

'I don't feel good about her situation. Pregnant. Living with a wife killer.'

'Me either.'

'Maybe we should talk to her. Drop a hint.'

'Oh, yeah. Meanwhile, Caplan will tear our heads off. Besides, I already did.'

Sam stopped at the edge of the desk cluster. 'I've seen ant hives look lazy compared to this.'

Sanders was putting on her jacket.

'Lose another clown?' Sonora asked.

'We've got the killer.'

Sam whistled. '*Way* to go. What happened?'

'Caught the sucker red-handed.' Gruber's voice, as he came in through the swing doors between the crime scene unit and homicide. His tie was loose, and there were circles under his eyes, but his step was light and he had that eager attitude cops get when they circle in for the kill. Sonora envied him. She wanted a warrant for the arrest of Gage Caplan and the same kind of feeling in *her* stomach.

'Thanks, Gruber, I was scared I might have to finish a sentence.' Sanders tilted her head and peeped at him.

He grabbed his chest. 'Direct hit, young Sanders.'

'But what happened?' Sonora asked.

'One-armed Bobo in a dunking booth. We were out

surveiling Indian Hills, and this guy hits. Only Bobo's waiting for him now. Got a handgun in his pocket – don't even take it out. Nails him through the jacket pocket as soon as he catches sight of the deer rifle. Good thing he got him with the first shot. Kick-knocks him off the platform and into the water, and now his gun's with the fishes.'

'Kill him?'

'No such luck. Winged, right arm, but to hear this guy squall you'd think he got repeatedly gutshot with an AK-47.'

'What's he like?' Sam said.

Sanders narrowed her eyes. 'Nebbishy. Skinny guy in cowboy boots and a concave chest.'

Gruber was nodding. 'Oh yeah, I noticed that first thing. Concave chest.'

'Oh, shut up,' Sanders said.

'Uniform is cuffing him, know what he's doing? Crying. Saying don't hurt me don't hurt me, get me a doctor. *Son* of a bitch. What a tough guy.' He looked at Sanders. 'Hospital's going to release him into our custody – we're going over to get him right now, if Sanders here's got her lipstick on straight.'

'I borrowed yours,' she said, eyes shiny.

Gruber glanced back at Sam and Sonora. 'How's your thing coming along? 'Cause if you got time on your hands, you can, like, dust interview one for us.'

Sonora looked at Sam. 'Is it my imagination, or is this man insensitive?'

Sam showed him a middle finger. 'Dust this, babe. We got work. Where's Crick?'

'In his office celebrating, I'm sure.' Gruber followed Sanders out the door.

Crick's door opened just as they got there. He did not look like he was celebrating. His gaze rested on Sonora and her knees went weak. The man did not look happy.

'There you are,' he said. Mildly over the volcano. 'Just the two I want. In my office.'

He didn't have to add 'now.' Sam exchanged looks with Sonora and they went inside. Sonora sat down without being asked because standing up was hard when Crick had that look on his face. Crick did not keep them waiting. He sat on the edge of his desk – too close and too big.

When he spoke, it was in a very steady tone. 'I've had a call from the District Attorney's office, and I want to get a few facts straight.'

Sonora wondered how much trouble Caplan was going to cause. She'd just been to London, Kentucky, to see his in-laws and commandeered his toolbox. For every action there is an equal and opposite reaction – that she had learned in grade school.

'Sonora. How often have you interviewed the counselor alone?' Crick watched her steadily. The cat-at-the-mousehole look.

The question did not sound good. Sonora frowned. 'He was supposed to meet me at his house a few days ago, but didn't show. I talked to his wife—'

'You talked to his wife?'

'Yeah and—'

'Why?'

'Why *what*?'

Clearly, in his eyes, she could see he did not like her tone of voice. But she did not like being interrupted and cross-examined rudely when she was busting her ass on a case.

'Why did you go to his home and talk to his pregnant wife?'

'Why not?'

Crick looked at her. 'Then what?'

'After I talked to his wife? He asked me to drive her to his office, and then he said he'd talk to me there.'

'He asked you to come then? During his big victory celebration?'

Sonora leaned back in her chair. Wary. 'Yeah. He did.'

Crick looked at Sam. 'What about you? Where were you?'

'I was running following-up on this guy Barber, and the people who saw Julia Winchell at the conference.'

'How come you two split up?'

'Just worked out that way,' Sam said. 'Cover more ground in a hurry. We weren't sure she was dead yet. Not then.'

'You're excused, Delarosa.'

He looked at Sonora. He made no move to leave.

Crick did a double take. 'I said you're excused. Detective Blair and I have some private business to discuss.'

Sam kept looking at her. She nodded her head and he got up, squeezed her shoulder with his left hand, glanced back at Crick, and headed out.

'Close the door behind you,' Crick said.

Sam shut the door firmly. Sonora put her hands in her lap.

Crick sighed. Rubbed a hand across his face. 'District Attorney Caplan has had a talk with the lieutenant.'

'I'm sure he has.'

Crick raised an eyebrow. 'Oh you are, are you? And why is that?'

'Because he's a killer. And he's a DA. And I'm going to nail his ass, and he knows it. I'm just surprised it didn't happen sooner.'

Crick leaned back, folded his arms. 'That's not the nature of the complaint.'

'What is the nature of the complaint? Sir?'

'Caplan says you've made unwelcome advances toward him, hounded his wife and family, including his mother- and father-in-law, and shown up in his office at times orchestrated to embarrass him.'

'*What?*'

'Sit down, Blair. Caplan knows about what went on with the Selma Yorke thing last year. About your relationship with a family member of one of the victims. What he said, basically, was that you were at it again.'

Sonora dug her fingernails into the palm of her hand. 'Conceited, arrogant son of a bitch.'

'Is that all you've got to say?'

'You *know* what he's doing. You know Sam and I are getting floods of make-work requests from the DA's office. You know we've been subpoenaed to appear in court on cases we had nothing to do with. And. *How* did Caplan know I was at his in-laws'? We got a leak, sir, otherwise how could he have known?'

Crick laughed so hard it was a howl. 'Got a leak to the prosecutor's office? No shit, I wonder who it could be. I can think of only one in fifty possibilities. And for that matter, how do you know his in-laws didn't call him?'

'I don't believe that, sir.'

'What matters here is what *I* believe.'

'Did you expect Caplan to take this sitting down?' Sonora asked, teeth clenched.

'I know Caplan is riding high since he nailed Drury. I know he gets along with almost every cop who's worked with him in court. I know he's got a lot of friends and a lot of influence.'

'How about the cops that investigated the murder of his first wife? Did they get along with him too?'

Crick didn't answer.

Sonora got up and walked out.

Chapter Fifty-Four

Sonora stopped by her desk long enough to kick the chair over, then headed for the women's bathroom. The door was on a 'slow hinge' and refused to slam. She ran water in the sink and splashed some on her face, aware, suddenly, that something was hanging from the mirror.

A jockstrap.

She had called this one wrong. She wondered what had made her think she could gross out male cops.

She snatched the jockstrap off the mirror, pulled the elastic back like a slingshot, and jettisoned it.

The bathroom door opened and Sam stuck his head in. 'Girl, you in there?'

'Yeah?'

'Correct me if I'm wrong, but that was a male undergarment, wasn't it?'

'So?'

He came in carrying a chair, two Cokes, a package of peanut butter crackers. He jammed the chair up against the door, flipped the latch, and sat down.

'Privacy.' He sighed, handed her a Coke and the package of crackers. 'If your temper tantrum is over, why don't you tell me what's going on?'

'Crick just said that Caplan has put in a complaint about me coming on to him during questioning.'

Sam did not look surprised. The office grapevine was in good working order, no duh. 'You got your tapes, don't you?'

'All he has to say is I turned them off.'

'He ain't got nothing. You're a good cop. Let your record stand.'

Sonora looked at him. 'Idiot. That's the problem.'

'Oh hell. That Keaton Daniels thing.'

He said Keaton's name like it was a disease.

'You never did like that guy,' Sonora said.

'It's not that so much as it was a bad career move on your part.'

'Tell me something I don't know.'

He smiled at her. 'Bitchy under pressure. One of the things I like about you, Sonora. You're not noble. In the South, women make martyrdom an art form.'

'You have that Southerner's way of insulting me politely.'

'Ingrained. But back to my point. It's a man's problem. See, what you want to do is emote and carry on and have long drawn-out discussions on stuff like "how could he?" and "what did I do to bring this on?" If you got a man's problem, use a man's solution.'

Sonora unclenched her jaw. She wanted to say something about the 'emote and carry on' remark, but wouldn't that mean she was emoting and carrying on?

'Just what is a man's solution? Shoot it? Flush it down the john?'

Sam shook his head at her. 'Ignore it.'

'Ignore it?'

'Yep. Then the ball's in their court. Then they got to put up or shut up, and you don't sit there and spin, which is what they want. Don't do that, girl. Just go on with your regular shit.'

Sonora thought for a minute. 'You know, Sam, I'm beginning to understand why men always get the upper hand.'

Chapter Fifty-Five

Crick looked at Sonora, arms folded. He stood outside his office. 'Sudden call of nature?' he asked her.

Sonora felt Sam at her back. 'Yes, sir.'

'That's the only explanation I could come up with. I wouldn't want anybody who works for me thinking they can get up and leave because I say something they don't like.'

'No sir.'

Crick sat back down behind his desk, and started talking before they settled. 'Not a damn thing in that vacuum cleaner bag, boys and girls.'

Sonora sat down slowly, stared at Sam.

'I see by the way your mouths are hanging open, you expected otherwise.' Crick snorted. 'Did you really think he would use a cabin that belongs to his mother- and father-in-law? When he knows damn well they hate him?'

'That would make it all the better, as far as he's concerned,' Sonora said.

'Nice theory, Blair, but it didn't pan out and he made an ass out of both of you. What we got now, boys and girls? We got the counselor, just nailed Jim Drury, and got a lot of good press and pats on the back. His first wife was murdered, heinously, but he's rebuilt his life. New wife, new baby, daughter he adores. He's made himself available to talk to you time and time again. You've been to see his wife, you've been to see his in-laws, you've talked to his step-aunt for Crissakes. You make accusations and took physical evidence from a cabin where you suspect he dismembered a woman he says he never met. And guess what. It's clean. No blood, no hair, no nothing. Now the big vacuum cleaner coup is his trump card, not ours.

'The man's only crime is he owns a hacksaw. Guess how many men do? All you have is a tattooed dead woman who says she saw him kill somebody, and she can't testify, can she?' Crick placed his fingertips together. 'So who in this office is ready to jump up and talk to a grand jury?' Caplan put hand to his ear. 'I'm listening, but I don't hear any volunteers.'

'What about the rental car?' Sam said.

Crick nodded. 'Okay, you're getting warmer, but you're a long way from hot. *Somebody* killed her, but you don't have Caplan's head in the noose. Mr. Caplan has declined to give us hair and blood samples. The rental car could be a major screw-up on his part. He's too smart to screw up so we figure he was short on time and took a calculated risk. Good. He can't have all the breaks, and we'll get something. We got soil samples, for one, which for reasons we cannot figure are similar to the residue on the shoes found at the scene of one of the Bobo killings.'

Sonora sat forward. 'Say what?'

Crick shrugged. 'Don't ask, I can't for the life of me figure out the connection. But we will. Or rather, you will. And Caplan, through channels you understand, has made a very good observation. Which is that he's a long shot compared to Julia Winchell's husband and lover. Man has a point.'

'Sir.' Sonora did not like the pleading note in her voice. She cleared her throat. 'This hacksaw of Caplan's. It had been scoured clean with Clorox, even though all the other tools had accumulations of dirt and oil and rust. Why is it clean? Everything fits in for Caplan.'

'Give me your theory, A to Z.'

Sam shifted in his chair. 'We think he killed her here, in Cincinnati, strangled her in the rental. Then put her in his car and carted her down to the cabin – okay, not the cabin – but somewhere. He cut her up with the hacksaw, put his little packages together, and cleaned up like a DA who prosecutes murders knows to clean up.

'Look at the geography – it fits him. The leg was found right outside of London on I-75 right before you get to Corbin. Another hour or two down the road is the Clinch River, which flows through Clinton, Tennessee. He could have thrown that bag with the head, hands and feet over from the interstate.'

'Why go south? Why go out of his way?'

'Which would you do?' Sonora asked. 'Throw body parts on a trail leading to your house, or on a trail leading to the husband of the woman you've just killed? Assuming you don't want to get caught?'

'Where's the rest of her? Arms, another leg, torso?'

'They may still be out there. Maybe they were carried off by animals,' Sam suggested.

'Maybe he kept some of her,' Sonora said.

'Then he's got a lair,' Crick said. 'But it's not the cabin. Which leaves the rest of the world.'

Sonora chewed a thumbnail.

Crick leaned back in his chair and closed his eyes. He sighed heavily and opened his eyes. 'I made a phone call. Detective Owen Baylor. Know him?'

'His name was in the file. He handled the investigation into Micah's death,' Sonora said.

'Yeah, he's retired now,' said Crick. 'Either of you talk to him?'

Sonora and Sam shook their heads.

'Yeah, I know, and he's miffed a little. He's got a little time on his hands. Plenty enough to talk to you guys about Caplan if you'd come around, that's how he put it. He thinks Caplan did her – Micah. Thought so at the time. It went before a grand jury, but they didn't indict.'

'Why not?' Sonora asked.

'Bad presentation?' Sam said.

'So Baylor says, and he was there. On the other hand, he thinks Caplan did it.' Crick scratched his chin. 'Caplan wasn't in the DA's office then. Baylor thinks that the prosecutor didn't think Caplan did it. Didn't feel like he could prove it anyway, and didn't want to go after the grieving husband unless he could really nail it down. He and Caplan seemed to hit it off. That didn't sit too well with Baylor, I tell you. Still doesn't. Anyway, they got to know each other. Caplan kept harping on catching the killer who murdered his wife, and eventually applied to work as a DA. To put his grief to rest. He gets hired on, and, surprise surprise, he does a helluva job.'

'Experience will out,' Sam said.

Crick narrowed his eyes. 'The two of you. Both in agreement. You think Caplan did Winchell? You think he did his first wife?'

Sam nodded.

'Absolutely,' Sonora said.

'Work from the other end awhile. The one depends on the other. So you get out there to the university, where Julia Winchell saw whatever it was she saw. And you walk it through. And you make it work, or you leave the guy alone and focus on somebody else. We clear?'

'Yes sir.'

Crick stood up and his voice deepened. 'Good. 'Cause I don't like assholes in the prosecutor's office playing games with my people. Rest assured, there will be no more subpoenas. You better be right, and you better bring him in. I'm counting on you two to see I get the last laugh on this.'

Sonora took a deep breath and scrambled out of Crick's office behind Sam. He leaned close and muttered in her ear. 'It's not that I don't trust Crick, but if I see a sheriff's car in front of the house, I'm not going to the door.'

Chapter Fifty-Six

Sam leaned against the wall and Sonora sat in a metal folding chair. The man behind the desk was relaxed, not in any hurry. He had a mustache that was going gray, and wore the blue uniform shirt of campus security.

The office was tiny, desks and cabinets scarred and old, like the ones in the bullpen. Sonora wondered why it was a given that anyone who had anything to do with law enforcement got crappy office furniture.

She'd seen janitors with better accommodations.

The drawers in the filing cabinet had not been closed in years – much too full. Boxes of papers and forms and computer printouts were stacked chest high in every corner, and the files on top of the file cabinet were an exercise in balance.

A round metal trash can had been turned upside down so the security guard, P. Fletcher Hall, could use it as a footstool. Sonora wondered where they threw trash. Although it was possible, looking around the tiny office, that they kept it.

'That clock keep good time?' Sam asked.

'Yeah,' Hall said, attention on the cabinet he was searching.

Sam grinned at Sonora. The clock was missing a second hand.

The guard nodded his head. 'Yep. Here it is. Thought he'd have it; Lieutenant don't throw nothing away.' He read it first, while they waited, which irritated Sonora, then handed it across to Sam, which annoyed her again.

He waited for Sam to read, then grinned. 'The girl was clearly a nutcase, unless it was one of those sorority things. She causing trouble?'

Sonora looked up. 'That what the guy said in the report? Nutcase?'

Sam leaned over and showed her the acorn that had been drawn in the top right-hand corner of the form.

The call had been logged at ten-forty-eight PM. According to the security guard, Marsh, he'd been standing on the top of the concrete bridge that led from the fifth floor of the Braunstein Building, taking advantage from the let-up in rain for a smoke break, when a young woman who was later identified as Julia Harden of Clinton, Tennessee, and a student at UC, had come tearing out of the fourth-floor exit in a condition described as hysterical.

Marsh had watched her, alarmed. She was clearly in a panic, screaming for help. He had been about to call out when she spotted him. It was dark, but the embers of his cigarette were glowing, and there was light spillage from building security lights. She had run in circles for a moment, trying to find the outside staircase that led to the bridge, and was out of breath by the time she made it up.

Sonora knew who not to call in an emergency.

Marsh had clearly been suspicious of drug-induced hysteria. He had spent some time describing her physical appearance, including bloodshot eyes, and respiratory distress, including a cough and a runny nose.

She had been crying and nearly incoherent. She had told him that a pregnant woman was being murdered in the women's bathroom on the third floor.

She had specified the third floor, which, in addition to her appearance, had put him on guard. The third floor was a parking structure.

He led her back into the building and took the elevator to the third floor. When the elevator opened onto the parking structure, she had become hysterical, and in order to placate her, they had searched all of the women's bathrooms, working from the top down.

Nothing out of the ordinary was found.

She had settled on the fourth floor as where the alleged murder occurred, convinced by the presence of the Resource Room/Multi-Media Lab and the mannequins in the fashion design classroom. But there had been nothing to see in the bathroom. No blood. A little water on the floor, but that could easily have been caused by a toilet overflowing.

He had questioned her carefully on drug use, but, other than saying she had taken Contac for a sinus headache, she swore she was clean.

He had suggested taking her to a hospital emergency room, and at that point she had given up, except for insisting on an escort back to her dorm.

Sonora shook her head. No wonder Julia Winchell had never forgotten.

'Marsh still work here?' she asked.

'Dead two years ago, over Thanksgiving. Pancreatic cancer.'

'We take this, or get a copy?' Sam asked.

'I guess I better make you a copy,' Hall said. 'Believe it or not, I let that out of here, Lieutenant will know somehow it's gone.'

Sonora took a last look at the office before she walked out, grateful that there were one or two places left in the bureaucracy that had not been computerized for efficiency. They'd never have found it otherwise.

Chapter Fifty-Seven

Sam's pager went off while they were in the student center, looking for a place to pick up a sandwich. He headed to the bank of phones near the stairwell.

It was quiet inside, dark and cool. The lunch hour was long over and the fast-food outlets were dark, locked behind metal grilles. Midsummer, hot as hell in the late afternoon, very little activity.

Sam was making notes. Sonora sat on a bench and crossed her legs. Her jeans were getting looser. Had the weight-loss fairy finally come?

Sam hung the phone up, and sat down beside her on the bench, flipping open his notebook. 'That was the maintenance supervisor, returning our call. Here's what we got. Braunstein Building stays open and unlocked twenty-four hours a day, people in and out at all hours. Classrooms, offices, and labs for biology, chemistry, fashion design, genetics and biochemistry.'

Sonora tapped the bench. 'Sam, it's all falling into place.'

'Just because the building's unlocked twenty-four hours a day doesn't prove he did it. If you think I'm going back into Crick's office with anything less than solid, you think again.'

'All I'm saying is it shows opportunity. So far, so good.'

'May as well forget lunch, everything's closed down. Let's have at it.' He flipped his notebook shut, stuck it in his pocket. 'They got maps at the information counter.'

The campus could not have been called crowded, though it was far from deserted. The occasional student wore loose shorts, sandals, backpacks hanging off their shoulders. A few suits here and there – administrative types. No one else dressed like that in the heat. A background cacophony of jackhammers and beeping machinery kept a film of grit in the air. Construction workers in yellow hard hats were grimy with heat and sunburn.

Sam studied his map, stopped in front of the ground-floor entrance to the Braunstein Building. A truck pulled up. Sonora saw Sam's mouth move. She waited till the truck, brakes squeaking, lumbered away.

'What'd you say?'

'I said she probably came in right here.'

Sonora pointed. 'Concrete bridge, right up there. Probably where she saw the security guard.' Sonora tried to imagine the place at night, in the rain. 'You really think she saw him in the dark?'

Sam scratched his chin, stepped off the curb, looked around. 'Yeah, probably. There'd be lights on. She might even have noticed him as she went in. I'll buy it. Come on, let's find us some air-conditioning.'

The glass double doors led into a foyer, dark tile, staircase to the left, and a drink machine glowing DIET PEPSI in the right-hand corner. Sam opened the metal doors on the right, like he knew what he was doing.

'I think we should go left,' Sonora said.

'Are you serious? Go right, come on.'

The metal doors slammed behind them, making an echo, like prison. The walls were beige, concrete block. Ugly mustard yellow doors led into the FRESHMAN RESOURCE ROOM & MICROCOMPUTER LAB.

'See that?'

Sonora looked inside. Bookshelves, tables, plastic chairs,

study carrels, and, to the left, a computer lab. The room smelled old.

'It's where she left her purse,' Sonora said. 'I've got the weirdest feeling. Like she's right here beside us.'

'It's the heat, girl. Fried your brain. Do us both a favor and don't mention things like that to Crick.'

A girl in a study carrel looked up. Sonora and Sam ignored her. Police business. They left the lab and moved back into the hallway.

A door squeaked loudly and boomed shut, making what Sonora knew her son would call reverb. Their footsteps were loud. Sonora's Reeboks squeaked. The hall had a yellowed look, linoleum buffed over a heavy wax buildup. Big round clocks stuck out from the wall, like Sonora remembered from elementary school and hospital rooms. The minute hands jerked with the pulse of every second. The lighting, fluorescent and harsh, spilled squares of reflected light on the overwaxed floor.

Sam stopped at the floor directory, studied it for a minute, went left down the corridor. Voices echoed, Sonora could not place where. She imagined Julia Winchell, coming into the building from the dark, rainswept campus. She would be drenched, her feet wet, sandals squeaking like Sonora's tennis shoes. She would pass the glowing drink machine, the metal doors would clang behind her, and she would stand, worried, in front of the resource room.

Her purse would be sitting on a desk, right where she had left it. She would take a minute and look inside – checking for the fifty dollars and the earrings from her sister. And they'd be there. And she'd be relieved, and pleased. She would think that her ordeal was over.

'Here,' Sam said. 'Four-thirty-two. Micah Caplan's office. Her old office.'

It belonged to somebody named Harry, now. There was a cartoon on the door – an alligator, with the caption, 'Trust me, I'm the boss.' The paper was dirty and curling at the edges. Sonora wondered if it had been there eight years ago. She wondered if Micah had put it up.

She took two more steps, then stopped. 'Sam, what floor are we on? I thought we were on the fourth floor.'

'We are.'

'Then how come that little black door has a three on it?'

He walked back toward her. Looked at the opposite wall. 'You mean this?'

'How many other little black doors do you see?'

'It's a dumbwaiter.'

'No kidding. It's still got a three over the top. Why is that?'

'You're worse than my kid. I don't know *everything*.'

'Yeah, but wouldn't you think, if you saw a three over a door, that you were on the third floor? This is where she got confused. This is why Julia Winchell thought she was on the third floor.'

'Don't go overboard, Sonora, it's not going to buy us a warrant.'

'It's indicative, Sam.'

'That I'll give you.'

'Right before Julia heads into the ladies' room and descends into hell, she sees this little black door with a three over it. Which explains why later, when she went for the security guard, she told him she was on the third floor.'

'Which buys Caplan time to make off with the body. Another thing we're going to have to figure out.' He headed back down the hallway. 'Women's restroom, Sonora. The scene of the alleged crime.'

Sonora stood outside the door. She was aware of a metallic background hum, as if they were close to a physical plant. Glass display cases lined the right-hand side of the wall, with printouts and faculty lists mounted under glass.

She wondered how it had sounded, the noises coming from the bathroom that night eight years ago. It was an odd, echoey building. People far away sounded close. You could hear voices and doors closing, and still not see a soul.

What had it been like for Julia Winchell, alone, or nearly alone? Hearing the splash, the choking noises? Having the courage to open the door?

'Sonora?'

'Yeah, go ahead.'

He pointed to the blocky black outline of a stick figure in a skirt, denoting female. 'I think, seeing how this is the ladies' room, maybe you better go in first by yourself, make sure there isn't anybody else there.'

Sonora leaned sideways against the bathroom door and pushed. Behind her, someone came out of a doorway. She caught the dark silhouette out of the corner of her eye, before whoever it was turned a corner and was gone. The bathroom door creaked, and she went in.

'Loud door. Why didn't Caplan hear her?'

'Think what he's doing, Sonora. Micah's making a lot of noise. He's involved. Crying, if Julia Winchell didn't make that up.'

'You think he didn't know a thing till he looked up, then, *voila*! there's Julia? Watching and witnessing?'

'Celebrate the moments of your life.'

The first thing Sonora saw walking into the bathroom was the opposite wall. Julia Winchell must have found that disconcerting. Yellow tile wall, mustard-brown linoleum. Then you veered right, and there was a line of sinks and soap dispensers on the right-hand side, and a row of mirrors, opposite a line of individual stalls.

A towel dispenser and inset trash can were on the far wall. All stall doors were open, all cubicles empty. Sonora opened the door and looked at Sam.

'The coast is clear, come on in and adjust your panty hose.'

'I could probably get arrested for this,' Sam muttered.

'I promise to swear I don't know you.'

They stood side by side, staring into the cubicles, as if there was something to see.

'I wonder which one it was,' Sam said.

'Which what?'

'Stall.'

'That one,' Sonora said, pointing to the one second from the left.

'Why that one?'

She shrugged.

Sam turned and faced the mirrors. 'She saw it there first.'

'The reflection? Probably. Saw something, and turned and looked.'

The bathroom door opened. A girl in plaid shorts and chunky shoes came in, arms bare and sunburned. She stopped suddenly, looked up at Sam.

'Um,' he said.

'It's opposite day, right?'

Sam and Sonora scooted out.

Sam took a deep breath once they were in the hallway. 'What is opposite day, anyway?'

'Pay attention, Sam. We got Julia Winchell running screaming out of the bathroom. She goes . . . this away, maybe?' Sonora headed to the right. The corridor ended in a T. Green swing doors, one propped open, led into a large lab-type classroom. Clustered next to the door were three dress forms and two mannequins.

Sam stopped. 'Look at that.'

'Didn't she say something – what was it? She thought she saw people, but it turned out to be mannequins?'

'Everything's clocking.'

'God, Sam, can you imagine? She sees Caplan in the bathroom, drowning Micah, she runs screaming for help, thinks she sees people, comes full tilt in here and gets . . . this. No people. She must have had nightmares for years.'

'Let's go back to the bad guy,' Sam said. 'What's Caplan do with the body?'

'He knows the cavalry's coming and he's got to move fast.'

'There's a lot of doors, up and down the hallway. He could have gone in any one of them.'

'At night, Sam? Lot of them will be locked.'

'The mannequin room isn't locked.'

'Think he brought her in here?'

Sam wandered in, and Sonora followed. He pointed. 'Right there. Big black trash barrels. Could have put her in one of those, temporarily. Mail cart right there, could have slid her right on in.' He stepped into the hallway. 'Dumbwaiter is right down the hall. Could have loaded her onto that.'

'Suppose someone was at the other end?'

'He's moving fast, now, Sonora, taking risks. How about these lockers?' He stepped out into the hallway. 'Think he could have fit her in one of those?'

The lockers were painted army green. A few had combination locks on them, most didn't. 'Full length. Looks possible.'

Sam opened the locker that was second from the end. 'Get in. She was littler than you are.'

'Hey. She was pregnant.'

'Except for that.'

Sonora ducked and scooted in. 'Easy fit, actually.'

'There must be fifty ways to store this body.'

'So he stashes the body, then waits till Julia and the security guy leave. Maybe waited a couple hours till everything is dead quiet. She was a little bitty thing. He could have rolled her out in the mail cart. I wonder if he planned to leave her here in the building, his original plan, before he got discovered, or if he'd planned that business at the creek all along.'

'We'll never know,' Sam said.

'Unless he tells us.' Sonora chewed a thumbnail. 'If that

guy, Marsh, had made a better search, they'd have found her that night.'

'Sonora, look at it from his point of view. She comes running out and says there's a murder going on in the women's bathroom on the third floor, which just so happens to be a parking lot.'

'People get confused.'

'He looked in every bathroom. There was still nothing there.'

'Let's take a look at that parking garage.'

They headed down the hallway, found the elevator. Sam ushered Sonora in, pushed the button for three. Sonora leaned against the wall, thinking about Julia Winchell, pressed against this very wall, trying to catch her breath, trying to get back in time.

The elevator door opened into a dark cavern of asphalt and noise. The brash sound of a car horn floated in with the smell of oil and gasoline fumes. Sam walked out into the parking lot, looked around, then came back.

'So he doesn't have to haul her body out the front door. He can come down the elevator and put her right into the car. Mighty damn convenient.'

'Hey, Sam.'

'Yeah.'

'There's one other place he could have hid her.'

'What?'

'He could have hung her up, with the rest of the mannequins.'

'You're a sick puppy, Sonora.'

'So is he.'

Chapter Fifty-Eight

Sonora was on the phone with Heather when she heard Sam tell her that Gruber wanted them. She put her hand over the mouthpiece. 'Just one second, okay, Sam?'

'Yes, I promise to read the whole magazine article, but I'm telling you, Heather, it's a come-on. We can't get rich raising chinchillas and the smell is . . .' Sonora paused. 'Heather, listen. You don't worry about the Visa bill. Mom takes care of that. We are not going to raise chinchillas.' Sonora hung up the phone. 'You seen Gruber?'

'Last I saw he was headed into the women's bathroom.'

'Must still be opposite day. Let's see what he knows about those soil samples on the Bobo killer's shoe.'

Sonora and Sam found him washing his hands. He grinned at Sonora as they came through the door.

'You girls ought to clean up once in a while.' Gruber checked his hair in the mirror. 'I got something for you two; don't know if it's of any use. But I know forensics came up with creosote on the carpet in the Winchell rental car. Same as they found in Bobo's tennie.'

Gruber turned the faucet on, slicked down a piece of hair that was lying funny. He reached for the paper towels. Sam handed him one before he got to the dispenser. 'You know, Delarosa, you ever get tired of police work, you have a promising career as a bathroom attendant in your future.'

Sam held out a hand.

Gruber looked at Sonora. 'He expect a tip?'

Sonora nodded. 'I always tip him.'

'Here's your tip, kiddos. Bobo killer is one of those model railroad hobby guys. You know, the ones set up those little tracks in their basement and build little houses and stuff to go around it. He goes train watching on his lunch hour.'

Sam frowned. 'What's that?'

Gruber wadded the paper towel, threw it into the trash. 'It means he watches trains, Einstein. Goes to railroad tracks and switch yards and basically just hangs around like a dork.'

'A train groupie,' Sam said.

'Whatever. But that's where the creosote came from. Railroad tracks.' Gruber headed for the door, looked back over his shoulder at Sonora and Sam. 'Nice bathroom you got here, ladies. Needs reading material.'

Sonora waved him off. 'Everything *you*'d need, Gruber, is scrawled on the walls.'

Sonora's phone was ringing as she and Sam headed out of Crick's office. She tripped over Molliter getting to it.

'I took a message for you while you were out,' Molliter said. 'And I washed your coffee mug for you.' He put the dripping mug on top of her stack of bills.

'You took a message for me? You don't have work? Or were you afraid my answering machine wouldn't get it?'

Molliter took a breath. 'Look, the woman sounded upset.'

'What woman?'

'Don't jump down my throat. Dorothy Ainsley. I told her you'd get back to her.'

Sonora grabbed the phone. 'My seven-year-old lies better than you do, Molliter. Get the hell away from my desk.'

Molliter headed for the file cabinet, hands full of papers. 'I don't know why I try to get along with you, Sonora.'

'Hey, Molliter,' Sam said. 'She was kidding.'

'Homicide, Blair.' Sonora heard noise on the other end,

something like a copy machine in the background, phones ringing. 'Hello?'

'Is this Detective Blair?'

A woman, and she sounded familiar. Sonora frowned, trying to place the voice. 'Yeah, this is Blair. How can I help you?'

'This is Bea Wallace. I'm Gage Caplan's—'

'Chief of staff, yes.'

'I was going to say secretary.'

'What can I do for you, Mrs. Wallace?'

'Mr. Caplan has dictated a chronology of his actions on July the eighteenth. He asked me to fax them to you.'

'I see. And you need the—'

'Yes,' Wallace interrupted. 'I got your message about the fax machine being broken.'

Sonora stayed quiet, thinking. The fax machine was fine. She hadn't left a message. And Caplan knew everything that went on in the bullpen. 'Mrs. Wallace, I really need that chronology right away. I'm sure you understand that in an ongoing murder investigation—'

'Detective, Mr. Caplan has instructed me to . . . I believe the word he used was facilitate. My job is to help you out. Whether or not I want to personally doesn't enter into it.' Her voice was tight, just on the hairy edge of rude.

Smart lady, Sonora thought. She wondered what she had to say, thought a minute, trying to provide a safe venue for her to say it.

'Any chance you could drop by the office and pick it up?' Bea Wallace asked.

Surely not, Sonora thought, with Gage Caplan breathing down their necks. 'Ma'am, my boss has just instructed me not to harass your boss and the last thing I want to do is show up in your office.' Sonora looked over her shoulder, saw Molliter was listening. He'd worked with Caplan several times last year, hadn't he? 'Why don't you meet me out front in the lobby? I should be there in half an hour. That all right? Caplan unchain you from your desk long enough to run downstairs and hand me a piece of paper?'

'Detective, I don't like your tone of voice.'

'Like it or not, Mrs. Wallace, you be there. I'll try not to get held up.'

She hung up, saw Sam staring at her.

'My God, you're in a bad mood.'

'Come on, Sam, we got places to go.' Sonora looked over her shoulder. 'Hey, Molliter. Anything you want to ask me? Like where I'm going? What I'm doing? Will copies of all forensic reports I get make it easier for you?'

He looked at her. 'You're crazy.'

'And you're shit.'

Sam grabbed her arm. 'Come on, girl, you're already in enough trouble for one day.'

Chapter Fifty-Nine

Bea Wallace was standing outside the building when they got there. She held a piece of paper that fluttered in the hot breeze. She looked very solitary, standing close to a fountain, watching the street.

'Park already,' Sonora said.

'Nowhere *to* park,' Sam said. 'You get out and I'll circle around and come back and pick you up.'

Sonora opened the car door part way.

'Wait for the . . . *shit*, Sonora, look before you jump out.'

'Sorry.'

'Go. Now, before the light changes.'

'Thanks, Sam.'

Bea Wallace was looking at her watch as Sonora approached. Her pink striped shirt was coming loose from the waistband of her navy skirt, and it had been buttoned wrong, giving the front a lopsided, unfinished look. Bea Wallace had put on lipstick recently, and was in the process of chewing it off. She stood with her weight shifted to one side.

'Got here as quick as I could,' Sonora said. The wind blew a fine mist of water from the fountain across her face. Felt like heaven.

Bea Wallace gave her a tight smile. 'This is for show, in case the counselor is looking out his office window. I wanted to do this in full view. If he can see me, he won't think twice about this.'

Sonora reached for her recorder, but Wallace shook her head.

'Pull that out and I walk. I value my job. I'm here to do somebody a favor.'

Sonora kept the recorder in the purse. 'Who?'

'Collie. She's a nice little girl, and I don't want anything happening to this one.'

'You said "this one," Mrs. Wallace.'

'I'm well aware what I said.'

'What happened to the last one?'

Wallace looked at her. She had dark-brown eyes, bloodshot, outlined in black eye pencil. She did not look like she had been sleeping well. Which, Sonora thought, could mean she had something on her mind, or that Caplan worked her hard. Possibly both.

'I'm not going to dance with you, Detective. I'm short on time and you look to be short on patience. I don't *know* a thing, but I have worries. The first Mrs. Caplan had one or two near misses before she was murdered. All of them when she was pregnant. And now this thing with Collie and the canoe.'

Sonora moved closer. 'What thing with the canoe?'

'You didn't hear about this? He set it up right under your nose, that day in the office when everybody was celebrating the big victory. Going down to the lake where Micah's mama and dad have a cabin. Mr. Caplan goes there all the time. Collie – she's not much for the water or the heat, and still, they're out canoeing in the middle of the afternoon. And the canoe goes over, and nobody's wearing a vest. I talked to Collie myself this morning. Sometimes that girl tells you things without knowing it. And what she told me I don't like.'

'Canoes go over all the time,' Sonora said. Was this what Dorrie Ainsley had called about? Had she seen the canoe go over?

'This one went over because Gage was conducting a safety "drill."'

Sonora raised an eyebrow. 'With a pregnant woman in the boat?'

'Yeah, and right in the middle of the lake. I don't know how much you know about that area, but that water is miles deep in some places. People dive there. Collie goes under *there*, never see her again.'

'She swim?' Sonora asked.

'Enough that she got to the shore. With no help from our hero. She's really shook up and I don't like the way this sounds. I wonder if you ought to talk to her.'

'Did you?'

Bea Wallace looked at her. 'Tell you the truth, I barely know the woman. But she . . . something about her makes you want to look out for her. She's sure not looking out for herself. She's got a baby to protect. Maybe you can get her to see sense.'

'I don't think she's going to see any kind of sense that doesn't take Mia into account.'

Bea Wallace's lips went tight. 'That's how he keeps her in place. One trick in a bagful.' She handed Sonora the sheet of paper that constituted Gage Caplan's paper-thin alibi. She turned and began walking away.

'Mrs. Wallace?'

'Yes?'

'That fax machine isn't likely to get fixed anytime soon. You need to send me anything else, don't hesitate to call. You can get me at home – I'm in the book.'

Wallace gave her a steady look. 'Tell her to get the hell out, Detective. At least till after the baby is born.'

Chapter Sixty

Collie met them at the door in a frayed pink corduroy bathrobe. It hung loose, buttoned every other one. A long belt hung from the loop on the left and trailed behind her like a tail. She stared at them through the storm door, running a hand through short straight hair, dingy brown streaked into highlights by the sun. Her hair would be almost pretty next time she got around to washing it.

'Afternoon, Mrs. Caplan. May we come in for a minute, and talk?'

At first Sonora thought she was going to turn them away. But Sam was so low-key and appealing, ducking his head shyly and giving her a little smile, as if it would hurt his feelings to turn him away. He always knew when to be nice and when to be tough.

'This really isn't the best time,' Collie said. But she opened the door. She was barefooted. Her toenails had been painted hot pink. Sonora wondered who had painted them. She could not picture Collie bending that far over this late in her pregnancy. Mia, most likely.

Sonora tried to imagine a way for this thing with Caplan to play out so that Mia did not get hurt. She could not think of one.

'Mia's sleeping over with a buddy,' Collie said, as if following Sonora's thoughts. She led them down a staircase off the kitchen into a dark den in the basement.

It looked like the house refuge for messy people. Sonora had the feeling that Collie and Mia spent a lot of time here.

A television was going without sound. One of those shock talk shows, where teenagers were shouting at their parents, whose faces were a despairing mix of hurt, bewilderment, and outrage. Sonora was glad the sound was off.

The downstairs couch was an old beige sectional, forming a cozy horseshoe that was littered with paperback books, Barbie dolls, Bryer horses, and an economy-size pack of M&Ms, plain, not peanut.

'Sit down,' Collie said. 'Can I get you something?' She handed Sam the open bag of M&Ms with an air of distraction.

Clearly the woman had not slept. She stared at Sonora, chewed the end of a fingernail. Sonora wondered if Caplan had passed his sexual harassment complaints on to his wife. She was glad Sam was with her.

Collie put her head in her hands.

Sam leaned forward and touched her lightly on the shoulder. 'Are you all right, Mrs. Caplan? Should we come back at another time?'

'No, I'm okay. Just a headache and an upset stomach. I can't even drive around the block without feeling bad. Pregnancy and this heat, I guess.'

Her eyes had dark hollows beneath, and her lips were dark red.

'I understand fishing is a hobby of yours,' Sam said.

She looked at him dully. 'Um. Yes.'

'Does Mr. Caplan like to fish?'

'No. Not with me, anyway. Gage doesn't really have any hobbies. Except reading biographies.'

'Doesn't build those ships in the bottle, do woodwork, or build model railroads,' Sonora asked.

Collie looked at them. 'Just biographies and ball games on television.'

'You go fishing with your dad a lot?' Sam asked.

Collie sat sideways, looked at him. 'Oh. Yeah, I do. Why are you asking me these questions?'

'When was the last time you got a chance to go up there? Your dad live close?'

'Bowling Green. Mia and me went up in July. Couple weeks ago.'

'That would be the eighteenth? On a Tuesday?'

She waved her hands. 'Could have been, I don't exactly keep the date lodged in my brain. Tuesday sounds right.'

'Catch anything?' Sam asked.

'Mia did pretty good.'

'I'm surprised you got that far away from home, with a baby coming so soon,' Sonora said.

Collie tilted her head to one side. 'My dad called, and he sounded kind of . . . I don't know. Like he really needed me to come up. And I'm glad we went; Mia and me had a great time. My family really made over me. My sister came and we had a . . . it was fun.'

'I spoke with your father, Collie. He said Gage called and asked if you could come up because you were tired and needed to get away. He even canceled his plans for that weekend.'

She clutched one of the buttons at the top of her robe. 'Gage called him?' She sounded out of breath.

'I also heard you had an incident out in the canoe this weekend.' Sonora kept her voice low, matter of fact.

Collie took hold of the loose belt and wrapped it round and round her hand. 'Gage tell you about it?'

'What exactly happened?' Sam said.

'I just . . . it was my fault, I'm so clumsy. Even when I'm not pregnant, I'm a klutz. I just . . . I zigged when I should have zagged, I guess. Fell right out. If it wasn't for Gage, I probably would have gone straight to the bottom.'

'He a good swimmer?' Sonora asked.

Collie nodded.

'Bet he jumped right in after you and pulled you to shore,' Sam said kindly.

Collie was still nodding, but slower, and Sonora saw it

in her eyes. Uncertainty. Hurt. She wondered how much Collie would shield him.

'He jumped in after you?' Sonora said. A question.

'He kind of had no choice – the canoe went right over. It was all my fault,' she said softly.

Sonora wanted to shake her.

'And he towed you to shore,' Sam said.

'It all happened so fast, I just . . . we both made it to the shore, so I guess it turned out fine. Except there he is on one side and me on the other, so I had to wait forever for . . .' She trailed off.

Sonora tilted her head to one side. 'So if he's on one side and you're on the other, he ditched you and left you there on your own in the water.'

Collie looked at her feet, put one bare foot over the other. 'My ankles are swollen.'

'I'm sorry to hear that,' Sonora said. 'He's a good swimmer, your husband. You said so yourself, and other people have told me the same thing. How is it he left you out in the middle of the lake, when you're seven months pregnant, and don't swim all that well? I have a hard time with that, Collie.'

Collie leaned forward as if her stomach hurt. 'Not everybody can be brave when there's a crisis. It's nice if they are, but people are people. You can't make them be heroes. Do you know how embarrassed Gage was for leaving me out there like that? He cried! Don't you dare tell anybody I told you this, but he *cried*.'

Sonora was remembering Julia Winchell's voice, on tape. That the man she saw kill Micah was crying as he held her head down in the toilet. 'When did he start crying?'

'Right before . . . I guess he saw what was coming up and panicked. I know I looked up and he was starting to cry – eyes all red and full of tears – and I remember thinking, well, what in the world? Then the next thing I know, I'm in the water, going under and down. And I was treading, my arms and all, and finally I get my head up. And I'm calling him, and looking for him, and I'm scared to death he's drowned. And the boat is way out of reach, and it's going farther out. And I still don't see him. But then I see that little red Coleman cooler, and thank God. I grabbed a hold of that and kicked with my feet, but I made it. Took me forever, but I made it. Then I crawled up through the rocks and sand. I'd lost my flip-flops. And I sat down, I was so tired. And I look across the water, and there he is, Gage, safe and sound. Just looking at me.'

Sam sat forward on the couch. 'Why weren't you wearing a life vest? If you don't swim well, you should have been wearing one.'

'I know, and I almost always do. But . . . we left them in that tool shed by Dorrie and Grey's cabin, and decided not to go back.'

'Who decided not to go back?'

'I don't remember.'

'Yes, you do,' Sonora said.

Collie licked her lips. 'What are you trying to say?'

'Let me see if the afternoon didn't go more like this. Didn't your husband tip that canoe on purpose? Didn't he make sure you didn't wear a life vest? Didn't he go off and leave you in the water on purpose, hoping you'd drown?'

'Of course not!'

'Really? You were there, Collie.'

'I am seven months pregnant with this man's child!'

'Micah was seven months pregnant when she died,' Sonora said.

Collie stood up. 'This is a miracle baby. We wanted this child forever!'

'We, Collie, or you? How did he react the first time you told him you were pregnant?'

Collie's mouth opened, then closed. 'He . . .' She sank slowly to the couch. 'He yelled at me and screamed at me and broke the picture frame with me and my mom and my dad and my sister. He said any baby of mine would be a . . . an ugly baby. Oh God. I never saw him so mad in all my life.' She put her head in her hand, shut her eyes tightly. 'I know he loves me. He's just difficult sometimes. He's got a high-pressure job, and his childhood. Just not the best. It's not surprising he acts like he does.'

'What he does doesn't surprise me near as much as you, the way you take it, Collie.' Sonora stared at her.

Collie blinked. 'Are you in God's good truth trying to sit there and tell me my husband is trying to kill me? You think I'm just so desperate to be married to Gage, or to anybody, that I'll put up with anything? Is that what you think?'

Sonora kept her mouth shut. It was what she thought.

'Because I'm overweight and have a goofy face and a big nose? I have to take what I can get?'

Sam looked at her. 'I don't believe it.'

'Not that you *have* to put up with it,' Sonora said. 'Just that you think you do. Protect that baby of yours, Collie. Make a formal complaint. Let us open an investigation.'

'I have two babies to protect. Mia's mine too. And unless the laws have changed just recently, the only rights I have toward Mia are the ones Gage lets me have. You going to tell me what to do now?'

Sonora put her business card on the table, jotted her home phone number on the back. 'Call if we can help.'

'Nobody can help me, Detective.'

Sam stood up. 'Take care, Mrs. Caplan. And good luck.'

Chapter Sixty-One

Sonora always thought of mad scientists and old Frankenstein movies whenever she went into the crime scene side of the bullpen. There was always so much going on – vats of liquid, glass cases with who knows what suspended in the middle. The room did not look modern or pristine – in fact, it reminded her of high-school labs, with that same air of aged equipment and people all around mixing chemicals and running experiments that she did not understand.

Terry had a smudge on her cheek. Not unusual for Terry. Her long, straight hair was coming out of the braid, falling across the high broad cheekbones. She was rail thin, wearing white overalls and a lab coat, and she pushed her cat glasses back on her nose and smiled at Sonora.

'You want me to start?'

'Crick wants to do this in his office. He and Sam are there now, waiting for us.'

'Oh.' Terry looked around the lab, as if she were a fish forced to leave her tank. 'I guess.'

She followed Sonora through the swing doors into the bullpen.

'Hey, Molliter,' Sonora said.

He stood at the coffee machine, turned his back.

Crick had a fresh pot of coffee and plenty of extra cups.

Terry helped herself to coffee, and added cream and sugar. She raised both eyebrows and leaned against a file cabinet. 'Let me know when you want me to start.'

Crick waved a hand. 'Start now.'

She nodded her head up and down, up and down. 'You guys have been keeping me busy. Any particular thing you want me to start with?'

'Free hand,' Crick said.

She cleared her throat and went to the end of the room, as if she were preparing to lecture in a hall. Sonora and Sam turned their chairs around so they could face her, and Crick sat down behind his desk.

'Let's start at the beginning, which was eight years ago, with the homicide of Micah Caplan. I've studied the file on that, done a little futzing around, and I can tell you definitively that the water in her lungs did not come from the creek where her body was found. Two months before she was killed there was a sizable agrichemical theft in that area. Very well-organized crime ring going after the dealers – you can get a couple hundred dollars per gallon container – and somebody was ripping them big time. The upshot is that thanks to a well-placed informant, the police were pretty much able to give chase. In an attempt, unsuccessful I might add, to destroy the evidence, one hundred pounds of simazine and twice that of Treflan were dumped into that creek.

'No traces of either chemical were found in Micah Caplan's lungs, but traces were found in her hair and on her clothes.'

'So her killer dunked her in the creek, but she was drowned somewhere else,' Sam said.

Terry chewed her lip and nodded. 'I'd say so. The water in her lungs had traces of surfactants, phosphorous, calcium carbonate, hypochlorite bleach, various detergents. Elements consistent with the kind of chemicals used to clean bathrooms.'

'Toilet water,' Crick said.

'Right.'

'Good. Go on.'

She took a sip of coffee and winced. Hot. 'Cosmetics. There were traces of lipstick and foundation and saliva on the armrest of the rental car. The cosmetics are a match for what you brought me out of the vic's hotel room.'

'Rum Raisin Bronzer,' Sonora muttered.

Terry nodded. 'I studied the soil samples from the rental car – very similar to what we found on the Bobo killer's shoe. I studied the density gradients, mineralogical profiles. Pollens.' She looked at them expectantly.

'Ooooo,' Sonora said.

'Ahhhh,' Sam added.

'Thank you. I came up with oil, pea gravel, creosote present in both samples. But sample one, from Bobo, has pollens indigenous to Cincinnati. Sample two, from the rental, is from farther south. Pollens you'd find in Kentucky and particularly Tennessee, where they have a lot of dogwood and azalea. These pollens are also present inside that plastic bag that held Julia Winchell's head, hands, et cetera. They're in her hair, under fingernails and toenails.'

Sonora looked at Sam.

'It gets better,' Terry said. 'Silica, clay ... let's call it river mud. Consistent with the Clinch River and Laurel Lake area. Found in the soil sample from the rental car, and in that plastic bag of remains.'

'So he used her car. To kill her, then cart her around in later. Dropping off his little packages.'

'The packages were well wrapped then,' Terry said. 'And he didn't do the butcher work in the car. But he may well have used it for delivery.'

Sam waved a hand. 'And there's nothing, not a damn thing, in the vacuum cleaner bag that would make you think Julia Winchell was ever in that cabin?'

Terry shook her head. 'Forget the cabin. You need to start looking for railroad tracks.'

'Railroad tracks?'

'The creosote was in one of the bottom-most layers in

that soil sample. Whoever it is went through the mud, and went across railroad tracks.' She looked at Sonora. 'Wish list. Bring me the box of garbage bags he used. Bring me the box and I'll match the one that had Julia Winchell's remains to the next one on the roll. Then the prosecutor will love you.'

'In this case,' Sonora said. 'Maybe not.'

Terry pushed her glasses back on her nose. 'This guy kills his wives when they're pregnant, that right?' Sam nodded. 'Why doesn't he just get a vasectomy?'

'Be easier,' Sonora said.

Sam looked at Crick. 'Only women could think of a vasectomy as an easy solution.'

Crick folded his arms. 'And for this guy, probably not as much fun.'

Chapter Sixty-Two

Gruber was coming in the door as Sonora and Sam were going out. 'Look, kiddos, your phones were ringing back and forth, one then the other, so I figured it was somebody had both your numbers and going crazy. You know a lady named Dorrie Ainsley?'

Sonora moved faster than Sam, and got to the phone first. The receiver that was off the hook was on Sam's desk. She picked it up.

'Mrs. Ainsley?'

'Is this Detective Blair?' The voice was tight, throbbing.

'Right here, Mrs. Ainsley. I'm sorry, I should have gotten back to you right away, I had—'

'Detective Blair, I just got a call from Mia. She . . . this makes no sense, Detective, but she says she's at a park by the water. Downtown by the river. She says there's a flying pig? And barges?'

'I know where she means,' Sonora said.

'Collie took her down there. She left her at the playground and said she'd be back in about twenty minutes. That was over an hour ago. Mia said Collie hasn't come back. She said that they went to the park in a cab, and that Collie made her pack a bag and that Collie had a bag. Mia tried to call her dad, but she can't track him down. Grey's on his way, but—'

'We'll pick her up.'

'Something else I better tell you. When Collie and Gage were down here, they—'

'Is this about the canoe?'

'Yeah. You know about that?'

'Yes, Mrs. Ainsley. But I appreciate you letting me know.'

'That's what I was calling about earlier. There's something else. Two nights ago I had a phone call from Gage. He . . . he was very upset. Or he acted like he was. He cried.'

Sonora frowned. Bad things happened when this man cried.

'He said that he found out Collie was having an affair. He was afraid she was going to leave him.'

'Do you think this is plausible, Mrs. Ainsley?'

'He said she had one of those online lovers. You know, on the Internet.'

'Is Collie a hacker?'

'I don't know. I know she has a computer she fiddles with. Gage said he got into her e-mail, and that she and this man – this Elvis is what he calls himself – he and Collie have been carrying on for months. He wanted to know if Collie had confided in me about this guy, and what he should do. Whether he should mention it, or hope it played itself out.'

'What did you tell him?'

'I told him he was crazy.'

'What did he say?'

'He said he hoped I was right.'

Sonora pulled the bottom drawer open in Sam's desk. 'You still got that extra pair of cuffs?'

'Yeah, so, come on, girl, we need to pick up that kid.'

'One minute. Where'd Molliter go?'

'You know damn well where he went: I heard you say fuck under your breath when he went over to talk to Terry.'

'Can't hide anything from you, can I, Sam?'

'What are you up to?'
'Trust me – you don't want to know. Where's Crick?'
'Out to lunch.'
'Just as well.'

Chapter Sixty-Three

'What's he want me for?' Molliter asked.
Sonora scratched the back of her head, playing it irritable. 'How the hell would I know? I got stuff to do, and I'm late. He asked me to come get you, I came and got you. Maybe they figured out where the smell was coming from.'

Sonora opened the door to the men's room. The light was off, and the smell was a presence. She had counted on Molliter cringing and being distracted, just long enough.

'Get the light, will you, Molliter?'

'I'm looking for the switch.'

'Somewhere over there, I think.' Sonora guided his hand into the open cuff on the pair that she'd hooked to the drain pipe. The key to good police technique was the advance work.

She had Molliter's cuff snapped while he was still groping for the switch. She took his gun out of the shoulder holster, just to be safe.

'What the hell are you doing, Blair?'

'You been a cop all these years and you don't recognize handcuffs, Molliter?' She flipped on the light. Molliter looked pale and perplexed. And angry. She took a step backward. 'I'll put your gun in your center desk drawer, Molliter. For safe keeping.'

'Man. It *stinks* in here.'

'Yeah. And all you guys are using the women's bathroom, so I don't guess anybody is going to find you.'

'Are you crazy?'

Sonora shrugged. 'I think you're the one, Molliter. Somebody's calling the DA's office and keeping them up to date on this Winchell thing. And now the second Mrs. Gage Caplan is missing, and I don't want Gage getting the play-by-play over the phone. So, to be on the safe side, you're going to spend a while in here.'

'I'll just call for help.'

'I anticipated that.' Sonora took a roll of strapping tape out of her blazer pocket. She covered his mouth quickly: speed was the key here, to keep him off balance. 'I'm sorry, Molliter. You don't look all that comfortable, and with any luck at all, you're going to be here a while. Now, I could be wrong, and if I am I'll owe you a great big apology that you'll never accept, so likely I won't bother.

'I think after a while you'll just get used to the smell.'

He made a noise in the back of his throat. Sonora did not like the look in his eyes. She was glad he was cuffed.

Chapter Sixty-Four

Mia was on the swing set in the third play area they searched. Sonora took a deep breath when she saw her, and Sam squeezed her shoulder.

The little girl had a stoic look, legs pumping, no eye contact or interest in anything going on around her. She swung with precision, up, down, joyless.

It was muggy out and hot. The air was clouded with gnats and the hum of bumblebees. Some of the other children studied Mia. She did not acknowledge their presence.

From the playground, you could not see the river. Sonora wondered where Mia had found a pay phone. She had evidently ranged far and wide.

A small green backpack and a battered blue Samsonite suitcase sat next to the metal frame of the swing set. Mia glanced over periodically, as if to be sure they were still there.

'Mia?' Sonora stood with her back to the sun.

Mia squinted.

'How you doing?' Sam said.

'Fine, thank you.' She stopped the swing by dragging the toes of her hiking boots through the sand.

'Remember me?' Sonora said. 'I'm the police detective that came and talked to Collie.'

Mia nodded.

'This is Sam. He works with me.'

'Did I do something wrong?'

'No, honey,' Sam said. 'We came to make sure you're okay.'

'How did you find me?'

'Your grandmother sent us.'

'You know my grandmother?' Wonder in her eyes. And suspicion.

'Yes. Her name is Dorrie Ainsley, and she lives in London, Kentucky, and she paints bluebirds with faces on them. I've seen them. One of the faces is yours.'

'And one is Mommy, and Daddy, and Collie.' Mia looked at Sonora. 'Did she tell you that Collie didn't come back?'

'That's why we're here. We're going to find her. After we take you home.' Sam crooked a finger and she came running.

Sam carried the blue bag and Mia took the backpack. 'Mia, there's a lot going on we're not sure we understand.'

She nodded. She had been very quiet on the walk to the car, very quiet and watching the crowd. Looking for Collie.

'You sure you have no idea where Collie went?'

'She went to meet the friend.'

Sonora opened the back door of the Taurus, helped the little girl find her seat belt. She was wearing a pair of red cotton shorts today. Shorts and a sleeveless white denim shirt. Her hair was held back with a plastic white hairband. She looked hot.

'Why don't you tell me everything that happened since you got up this morning? Could you do that?' Sonora asked.

Mia nodded. 'First thing, I got up. Then I ate some cereal. Lucky Charms.'

'That's what my little girl likes.'

'You have a little girl?' Mia asked.

'Yeah. Detective Delarosa has one too.'

'They must have been having a sale on little girls that

year,' Sam said. He started the car. Pulled out of the lot where they were illegally parked.

Mia gave them a faint smile. 'Collie was in the shower. She came out and checked the messages. There was one from the car place.'

'What car place? Do you know the name of it?'

'No. But it's the car place where Collie likes to go. I think they must of called while Collie was in the shower and I was still in bed. So Collie called them up and talked a minute, and then she started crying.'

'She . . . why did she cry?' Sonora asked.

Mia shrugged.

'Did the phone ring in between? Did somebody else call?'

'I don't know. I don't think so. I didn't hear it if it did.'

Sonora caught Sam's look. 'Maybe it was a big estimate,' Sam said.

'Yeah, right. Okay, Mia, she cries. Then what?'

'I took her some Kleenexes and a Coke and a cookie.'

Sam looked over his shoulder and smiled at her. 'Want to come and live at my house?'

'Then Collie blew her nose but she wouldn't eat the cookie so I did, because my Lucky Charms were getting soggy.'

Sonora nodded.

'Then she just stopped crying. She said, that's that then. Weird, I guess. Then she hugged me and said she loved me, and that it was time to face the facts. Then she told me we were going to go be with a friend for a while.

'I asked her why. She said it was grown-up business, and that I should do what she told me, and she would try to work everything out. And then she hugged me again and said she would always keep me safe.'

Sonora looked across at Sam. 'We need to go to the house.'

'It's where I'm headed. Mia, did she tell you anything about this friend?'

Mia thought for a minute. 'Just that he was very nice, and very understanding. That he really cared. That he was easygoing and didn't lose his temper, and that he liked little girls.'

Sam looked at Sonora. 'How could she figure all that out on line?'

'Probably told her so himself.'

Chapter Sixty-Five

Sonora half expected Gage Caplan to be in the doorway waiting for them, but the house was empty and unlocked.

Mia ran in ahead of them. Sonora and Sam followed. Mia went straight to the basement calling Collie's name. She was back up in a minute. She did a room-to-room search, looking.

The answering machine was in the bedroom. More white. Bedspreads, white carpet, heavy mahogany furniture, with peach accents on the wall. Expensive and bland.

The closet door was open, a dress on the floor like a blasphemy in the otherwise immaculate room. Sonora pressed the message button on the answering machine.

'Mr. and Mrs. Caplan, this is Wilfred Boggs, calling from Boggs Auto. Please call me at the following number, about your 1996 Nissan Pathfinder, regarding repairs.' Sonora wrote the number down on the scratch pad by the phone, and saw that someone else had written the same number down earlier.

'Should we call them?' Sonora asked.

Sam shrugged. 'No stone unturned. Something made her cry. Want me to do it?'

'Yeah, I'm going to see if I can track down that computer.'

She found Mia sitting cross-legged on the top bunk of her bed. Sonora stood in the doorway.

'May I come in?'

Mia's arms were folded and she was staring into the jumble of sheets, bedspread, and blankets.

'Yes.' Voice barely audible.

'Nice room.'

Mia nodded. Words were too much effort. Sonora looked around the room with a smile, thinking that whoever had put this one together was an opposite to whoever decorated the rest of the house.

The bed was fire-engine-red metal, and there was a desk and dresser, simple, blunt-cut wood: maple. A big bear rug sat in the center of the room and it was evident that the bear head was groomed from time to time. Ribbons adorned the dead fur ears, and someone had colored his teeth with crayons, and stuck the head of a Barbie doll in his mouth. There were posters all over the wall – Patrick Swayze with a horse, a mama cat curled up with her kittens, and a hippopotamus with its mouth open wide.

The book shelf was a jumble of *Fear Street, Sweet Valley Twins*, and some ancient Nancy Drew books. Sonora went to the shelf and picked up a yellow hardback copy of *Mystery of the Striking Clock*. She opened the flap, saw Collie's name written inside in purple cartridge pen.

'Collie gave me those,' Mia said. 'She liked to read my *Sweet Valley Twins* and *Fear Street* books, but made me promise not to tell, so people wouldn't tease her about reading kid books. She'd get Daddy to buy them for me, then we'd sit in the den and eat sandwiches and read. Daddy fusses at us when we do that because he says we don't have enough light. So we try to do it when he isn't home.'

Mia swung her legs over the bed, turned so that her belly was up next to the mattress, and jumped down.

Sonora assumed the ladder was only for the fainthearted.

'Do you think Collie will come back?' Mia asked.

Sonora hedged. 'I don't think Collie will leave you. Remember, she had you pack a bag. She took you along.'

'Just because she has another baby, doesn't mean she

doesn't want me. She already told me that. I'm not going to have sibling stuff. I want a sister.'

'What does Collie want?'

'A baby. A boy or girl will do.'

'Where's her computer, Mia?'

'In the den. But it's got a password. Collie told it to me so I can put on the dinosaur CD and do the kid thing for America On-Line. The password is Mia. She named it after me. The computer is downstairs in the den.'

'Here's what I think. I think you should get something to drink, and eat if you're hungry. Then you should curl up in front of the TV and zone out for a while, try not to worry. And while you do that, I'm going to try and figure out where Collie went.'

'How come Daddy's not at work?'

'Maybe he had an appointment.'

'I have Nintendo in my room. Can I stay in here?'

Sonora nodded, then headed downstairs for the den.

The computer was tucked into a corner, away from the little horseshoe of couch, TV, books, and toys. It sat on a small oak pressboard computer table – streamlined, and no frills – right by a rowing machine and a Nordi-Track that were both heavy with dust.

The computer was not dusty. Sonora sat down in the black, rolling chair, which was much like the one she had at work, without the armrests.

She was not good with computers. She only knew the system she used at work, and the old Apple 2E that she and the kids had had for years. She wished Tim was with her.

She turned on the desk lamp that curved over the work area, and smiled.

A multicolored apple was inset at the bottom of the monitor. Collie had a Macintosh, a Performa 637CD.

Computers for normals. There was hope.

Sonora studied the keyboard. Probably the key in the top right-hand corner with an arrow on it. Nothing else looked likely, and this one would be the logical obvious choice. Sonora pushed the button.

She heard the splay of music that meant she'd hit pay dirt, closed her eyes and smiled.

'Sonora?'

Sam's footsteps on the staircase. He was walking lightly.

'Down here, Sam.'

'Is Mia with you?'

'She's in her room playing Nintendo.'

'Good. I know why Collie bolted.'

Sonora swiveled in her chair, watched him come down the stairs. 'Over here,' she said. She pulled a beanbag chair close to the computer. Sam looked at it, sat and sank almost to the floor.

'Comfy.' He stuck his legs out and tried to get comfortable. 'Had me a little talk with Mr. Boggs. He sounds like a good mechanic, by the way. Anyway, Collie dropped the car off yesterday because it was vibrating like crazy, some kind of problem with the U-joint. Boggs said he'd talked to Gage about it a few weeks ago, but that Caplan said money was tight and he was busy with the Drury prosecution, and was going to wait a while on the repair.

'Evidently Collie got fed up waiting and took the car in herself yesterday. Boggs called to tell her that he couldn't get to the U-joint till he got authorization to fix the exhaust.'

Sonora narrowed her eyes. 'What kind of problem with the exhaust?'

'Well, it seems that Mr. Boggs and his employees had the Nissan running in the garage, and it ran them out. Filled the place with carbon monoxide. They had to air the place out before they could go back to work. When they did, Boggs took a look and found a big hole way up in the exhaust system. He said it struck him as odd. They don't usually break through there, and that you could look the whole system over and not find it unless you were really looking. The upshot is that carbon monoxide has been pouring into the cab of the car, and he thinks it's been going on for a while.'

'I'll be damned.' Sonora twisted from side to side in the chair.

'That's why she bolted. Because if Caplan did make that hole in the exhaust, she passes out behind the wheel, drives the car into a light pole, or head-on across the highway. Remember what she said when we talked to her? She couldn't drive around the block without feeling bad. Put it down to heat and being pregnant?'

Sonora nodded. 'The only thing holding her back was Mia. And if he rigs the Nissan, then Mia likely gets killed or hurt along with Collie and the baby. So now Collie cuts her losses, because now she's got nothing to lose. Why didn't she come to us?'

'Mia, Sonora. She comes to us, she gives up the kid. She's a stepmother – she's got no legal claim. What'd you come up with?'

'I got the computer turned on.'

'Veeeery good.' He leaned forward, came up on his knees, and pushed a square button on the monitor. 'Now you've got a screen too.'

'My hero.' The password barrier came up and Sonora typed in 'M I A.' 'I got the password, too,' Sonora said.

'Your two to my one.'

Sonora pulled the edit screen down and hit finder, then searched for America On-Line. The file came up immediately, again demanding a password. Sonora tried M I A again, and it worked.

'This is too easy,' Sam said.

'It's a Mac, Sam. It's supposed to be easy. Tell the truth. Your Pentium is back in the box because it's such a pain in the ass.'

'The kid uses it.'

'YOU HAVE MAIL!' the computer told them.

Sonora hit the picture of the mailbox. The screen changed

and showed a communication called ELVIS TO COLLIE. She clicked it and pulled it up on screen.

> *Collie, I got your note, and I think you are ABSOLUTELY right. It's not safe for you, or the baby, or Mia. Of course I want you to bring her! We've talked around this before, and if I didn't make myself clear, I will now. I WANT TO PROTECT YOU AND THE BABY AND MIA. I don't want anything to happen to you. Please just do me one favor.*
>
> *When you come to the meeting place, come by yourself, just for a minute.*
>
> *Please understand. I want our first real life meeting to be private. You've never seen me. I am somewhat attractive, but not great. I want you to see me and look at me and not feel pressured. I want you to be able to say, look sorry, I'm calling this off. And I don't want to do that with Mia watching. And remember whatever happens between us, we are friends. There is no pressure on you to be anything but a friend. I will give you safe haven, while you need it.*
>
> *Be careful, and hurry.*

Sonora shook her head. 'Too good to be true. He's telling her exactly what she needs to hear. I never met a man who did that, and it wasn't some kind of con.'

'Look at the screen. Now we've read the mail, it's got a little red check. So evidently Collie didn't get this.'

'She must have. Why else did she leave Mia on the swing set, and tell her she'd be right back?'

Sam pushed a button that said 'KEEP AS NEW.' The check mark disappeared. 'YOU HAVE MAIL!' the computer told him.

'That was easy,' Sam said.

Sonora looked at him. 'But stupid. Why would she do that? So someone could find it?'

'Let's go back into the folder and see if she kept any correspondence.'

'Surely she wouldn't.'

'Why do people do anything, Sonora? Because they're people.'

'This isn't hanging right, Sam. She wouldn't want Gage to find it.'

He ignored her and took over the keyboard.

And hit pay dirt.

A saved file, full of correspondence with her online lover. Elvis.

They had started talking on line three months ago. Just friendly chatting. Two people who needed a friend. Collie was trusting and confiding, and ripe. She opened up to Elvis immediately, commented often on how he always seemed to know when she'd had a bad day, or was upset. Elvis hinted that perhaps he'd found a soulmate.

Soulmate, Sonora decided, was a term that had gotten women in almost as much trouble as 'just this once.' She had seen women, and men, endure years of agony, because they were afraid their sweetie was a soulmate, and irreplaceable. Sonora had not believed in soulmates for years. Her soul was on its own.

'At least we know why she calls him Elvis,' Sam said.

Sonora looked up. 'Why?'

'Didn't you read this one?' Sam scrolled back. 'See? He gives her this sound thing to put on her program that says "Elvis has left the building" instead of beeping. Haven't you ever heard that one? We had it on our computer a while, but it starts to drive you crazy.'

Sonora looked over Sam's shoulder.

Elvis,
   Mia and I got such a kick out of the Elvis thing you gave me for the computer. Believe it or not, Gage hated it. I had to take it right back off because it gave him a

headache. I think he's just tense from this Drury thing. I bet when it's all over he'll think it's funny.

Sonora checked the date, saw the correspondence was early in the relationship.

'Sam, Caplan has that Elvis thing on the PowerBook in his office. How come he tells her to take it off her computer?'

'How come she keeps a file of mail that Caplan can get to with no problem at all?'

'And how come the mail said it hadn't been read, when we know it had?'

'To get the attention of whoever brought the program up.'

'Somebody looking for Collie. Like a homicide detective investigating her death or disappearance. Like a homicide investigator who has already talked to Dorrie Ainsley and been told that Caplan suspected her of having an online affair.'

'What are you saying, Sonora?'

'Try this theory, Sam. Caplan's first wife is murdered. Suspicious enough. The second one gets killed, he's going to be suspect number one. Unless another good possibility comes up. Like some online lover who turns out to be a nutcase.'

'He's the online lover,' Sam said flatly. 'Whole thing has been a set-up from day one.'

'He's in a perfect position. He knows she needs a friend. He knows when she's upset. He knows exactly what makes her tick, so he can be the online lover of her dreams. He knows that when Gage the husband comes home grumpy and difficult, Gage the online lover can leave a little e-mail note to brighten her day.

'Look at the messages. All ego-boosts. You make me laugh. There's no one in the world like you. You're a quick wit, lady. Tell me what you use for bait when you're fishing. But not a lot about old Elvis himself, is there?'

Sam rubbed his chin. 'There's no message about where they met. I looked. Can't find the actual set-up.'

'That's no mistake,' Sonora said.

'So where is she?' Sam asked.

'She may not even be alive,' Sonora said.

'Look for the railroad tracks, that's what Terry said.'

A loud thumping made them both sit up.

'Someone at the door?' Sonora asked.

Sam put a hand on his gun. 'Let's go see.'

Chapter Sixty-Six

The door to Mia's room burst open as they made it to the top of the stairs.

'Collie?' Her face was bright, eyes big, and she ran down the hallway toward the front door.

'Hang on,' Sonora said. Sam moved into the living room. 'Let's have Sam go to the door and you and me wait right here.'

Mia stopped in the hall. Her face was tight and thin, and she cocked her head listening. She took a breath.

'That's Granddaddy.'

'You sure?'

She nodded, straining forward.

'Go,' Sonora said.

As if she could have held her back.

'Where's my little granddaughter?' Grey's voice sounded cheerful, bombastic. Sonora rounded the corner in time to see that the face did not match the voice, until Mia ran into the room. He swooped her up into his arms, and the lines of fatigue and worry eased back. He hugged her tight.

'*Granddaddy*.' She was crying.

'Wassa matter, chicklet? Granddaddy fix it, whatever it is.'

She lifted her head up off his shoulder. 'We can't find Collie. She left and didn't come back, and she's not like that. Something's really wrong, you've got to believe me.'

'Well, heck, yeah, something's wrong. We know Collie

wouldn't go off and leave you, chicklet. Unless she got lost trying to get back.'

Mia looked up. 'You think she's lost?'

'Honey, I've got no earthly idea, and believe me, I'm worried. But it's not like we're going to sit around on our butts, little girl. We've got a plan. We've got two police detectives going to find her – these people are trained professionals and they know just what to do. And you and me are going down to Gramma's to wait. Because when Collie comes looking for you, that's the first place she'll check. Isn't it?'

Mia nodded.

'We got trouble, hon, but we're going to handle it. Now get your bag packed up, while we do some grown-up talk.'

'I already got a bag.' She pointed to the backpack that was still in the hallway.

'*That* little piddly thing? Honey, your gramma's down in London cooking like there's no tomorrow. You going have to stay a while just to eat it all up. Now go get some more clothes and those scary things you like to read. Bring all your favorite stuff. Be a female and don't pack light, 'cause I got that big Chrysler and room is the one thing we do have.' He set her down. 'Go on, baby doll. The sooner you get packed, the sooner we can hit the road.'

Mia seemed lighter, somehow, when she ran down the hall, and Sonora looked at Grey, thinking that she wouldn't mind having him for a grandfather herself.

Grey waited till she was out of earshot, and took a breath. 'What you know?' he said, voice going tight and flat.

Sam gave him a half smile, and rubbed his chin. 'I think the question, Mr. Ainsley, is what do *you* know?'

'What do you mean?'

'I mean that your wife called us forty-five minutes ago, and here you are. It's a three-hour drive at seventy. That Chrysler didn't get you up here in forty-five minutes.'

'You got me there. If you don't mind, I'm going to sit

down on my son-in-law's damn off-limits couch.' He sat, groaned. 'There. Okay, here's what I know.

'Collie called Dorrie a couple days after that canoe thing. She was all worried up. You hear what happened?'

Sonora sat in the leather wing chair, and Sam sat next to her on the footstool. 'We know,' Sonora said.

'Scared her. Scared her a lot. Dorrie and I don't know exactly what Collie is up to, but we trust that girl, and we love her like our own. Here's what she told Dorrie. That if things got really worrisome, and if she got scared enough, she might take Mia someplace where they could be safe. And she said did she have our permission to do that? She said she wouldn't do something like that unless she really had to, but if she did, and we agreed, she promised that she'd keep us in touch so we wouldn't worry. And she said it would be very temporary and very desperate. She said we better not know any details, because we needed to stay neutral. She said Gage might well get Mia back, if only for a while, and he shouldn't suspect we were all in it together. Otherwise he'd keep Mia away from us, like he did that time before.'

Sam tapped his ankle. 'When did Gage call?'

'You mean when he cried on the phone and said Collie was cheating on him with some kind of computer boyfriend?'

'Yeah.'

'Last night. Put me and Dorrie on edge. We talked about it, decided I would come down here, get a hotel room, and just stay close. I'd been on the road an hour when Mia called London. I called Dorrie from a rest stop, and she told me what was up. And I want to say, right here and now, me and Dorrie didn't believe a word Gage said about Collie cheating on him. And what's more, if it is true, then more power to her. I know that boy – he's just trying to turn us against her.'

Sonora looked at Sam. 'I'm afraid it's a lot more serious than that.'

Chapter Sixty-Seven

'Railroad tracks and the river.' Grey looked up. 'You think he's taking her down to London?'

'I don't know.' Sonora looked at Sam. 'Could have been the Clinch River, but he knows the Laurel Lake area. It's not the cabin, but it might be somewhere near there. He knows the area. He's there regularly.'

'Let's call Dorrie and—'

'Think, Mr. Ainsley. You don't want your wife walking into this.'

'We'll call the sheriff.'

'We'll call Smallwood,' Sonora said.

Sam looked at her.

Grey looked in the hallway, saw Mia. 'Come on in, chicklet, I need to ask you a question.' She stood in front of him, hands at her sides. 'Your daddy ever take you train watching anywhere, maybe walking along the railroad tracks?'

She shifted her weight to one foot. 'He likes to go for long walks in the woods, when we go to the lake, but he walks too far, and I don't like to go. He walks for a long time. Collie says it makes him feel better.'

'But you don't know where he goes?'

'Only Vernon knows.'

'Why does Vernon know?' Sam asked.

''Cause Vernon follows him everywhere, even when he's not supposed to. Sometimes Vernon makes Daddy mad.'

Sonora looked up. 'Are there any railroad tracks near your cabin, Mr. Ainsley?'

He frowned. 'There's some tracks and a siding a couple miles out.'

Sam looked at Sonora. 'Terry said to look for railroad tracks and river mud.'

'We got both,' Ainsley said.

Sam nodded. 'Our CSU guys are coming to pick a few things up. Any chance you could stay, and let these guys in?'

'Sure. You two headed to London?'

Sam nodded.

'See you down there if we don't pass you on the road.'

Sam shook his head. 'You'll never catch us.'

Chapter Sixty-Eight

Sam used the blue cop light to get them out of the city. It helped a little. Sonora was on the cell phone, running up the bill.

'I said *Smallwood*. He working or what?'

Sam looked over at her. 'Put your seatbelt on, Sonora. You call Crick?'

'Yeah, he's taking care of it. Drive as fast as you can and not kill anybody – those are his direct orders. Use the light and the state cops will leave us alone.'

'Man, I been waiting for something like this for years.'

Sonora went back to the phone. 'Tell him it's Sonora Blair and it's urgent, with a capital urge.'

Sam glanced at her. 'A capital urge?'

'There's a crisis here, quit picking. Watch that truck, no, dammit.'

'You better sit back and close your eyes. They've got an hour-and-a-half head start. He's not going to keep her around for chitchat.'

'Yeah, but he had downtown traffic around three or so, and you know that's a bitch. Plus he's traveling with a pregnant woman. Unless he's already killed her, they'll be making a pit stop every twenty minutes. Particularly if she's scared.'

'Yeah, but I'm still traveling with you, and you make a pit stop every twenty minutes too.'

'Not this trip. This trip I'll hold it.'

'Hello? Sonora?'

'That you, Smallwood?'

'You sound like you're in a well.'

'Cell phone. I need—'

'Listen, Sonora, I'm sorry I didn't call. I was going to try and get in touch with you tonight. I just got bogged down at work and—'

'Smallwood, this is not about that. Forget that.'

Sam looked at her. 'Forget what?'

'Shut up and drive.' Sonora gritted her teeth. 'Smallwood, we got a problem here, with the Caplan thing, and I'm going to need your help. Number one, we're on our way to London, and it's an emergency situation. We've got the lights flashing, but it wouldn't hurt to let the Tennessee state cops know who we are and that we're okay. We're cleared through Ohio and Kentucky. Crick's working on Tennessee, but if you can help us out any, feel free.'

'Sure, Sonora, but I'm right here. You in that big of a hurry, why not send either me or one of the locals?'

'Funny you should ask. I can't go into details, but Collie Caplan's disappeared and we think she's with Gage Caplan.'

'Doesn't she live with him?'

'Either come up to speed, or just trust me on this, okay? We think they're headed for London, and that he's got some kind of little hidey-hole down around near the cabin that his in-laws have on the lake. Someplace near railroad tracks.'

'What's their last name? The in-laws?'

'Dorrie and Grey Ainsley.' She gave him the address, and glanced at Sam. 'There's a kid that lives near there. His name is Vernon something or other—'

'Vernon Masterson,' Sam said.

'Vernon Masterson. He may know where the place is. He tags along after Gage quite a lot.'

'Sonora, I hate to be negative, but you really think Caplan's going to let a kid find his hidey-hole?'

'Well, gee, Smallwood, this happens to be all I've got. Plus you clearly don't have much to do with children. Kids are sneaky, Smallwood. They find things out whether you like it or not.'

Sam looked at her. 'Forget what?'

Chapter Sixty-Nine

It was nine-fifteen and heavy dusk when Sam and Sonora pulled into the gravel drive that led to the Ainsleys' vacation cabin on the lake. Smallwood's squad car was there, as was a dark green minivan that Sonora didn't recognize.

It was cool, here by the lake. Sonora got out of the Taurus, heard boat engines on the water, and crickets in the grass. Someone had left an orange inner tube on the picnic table. The shed door was open.

The front door swung open as Sam and Sonora made it up on the deck. Dorrie Ainsley stood under the porch light, moths circling.

'There you are. Come on in.'

'Dibs on the bathroom,' Sonora told Sam.

'Don't say hello or nothing,' Smallwood quipped.

'She'll be back, in a minute,' Sam said. 'She just set a record – for her.'

Sonora paused at the bathroom door and looked at him over her shoulder. 'Will you shut up?'

He grinned and waved her on.

She heard the front door open while she was in the bathroom, voices and people moving around. She dried her hands on a towel and hurried out.

Vernon Masterson sat on the couch wearing shorts and a teeshirt. His hair was rumpled and he looked as if he'd been asleep. He blinked at all the people in the room, and sat stiffly beside a woman who patted his leg, and told him everything would be all right.

His mother, Sonora decided.

She looked tired and worried. Her hair was brunette; L'Oreal number eleven, if Sonora guessed correctly. She wore stockings and a skirt and sensible shoes. She looked as if she had not had time to change after work.

'I'm Detective Blair,' Sonora said.

'Katherine Masterson. Vernon's mom.'

Sonora nodded. 'Did they explain that we just want to talk to Vernon?'

The woman nodded. 'I hope you understand. But he'll do better if I'm here.'

Sonora did understand. Mrs. Masterson had no idea who had done what to whom, and she was there to look out for Vernon. In her place, Sonora would have done the same.

'Am I in trouble, Mama?' Vernon asked.

'Just tell the truth,' Mrs. Masterson said.

Sam sat down on the edge of the coffee table across from him. Not too close, but their eyes were on a level. Sonora folded her arms and settled back against the wall. Sam would be good with this.

'Vernon, we're here to look for Mr. and Mrs. Caplan. And we think you know where they might be.'

'No sir, I went to bed at nine o'clock. That's my bedtime every night.'

'I know, Vernon. And that's fine. But you and Gage are pretty good friends, aren't you?'

'Yes sir.'

'And you go on walks together?'

'Oh, no sir.'

'You don't go on walks together?'

'Oh no. I would not follow a friend. Not if he didn't want me to. There might be bees.'

'Didn't you say you played railroad with Mr. Caplan?' Sonora asked.

Sam gave her a look over his shoulder. She decided to shut up.

'Oh no. We were going to. But he never got time. Mr. Caplan works an awful lot. And you don't want to follow him, because there might be bees.'

'Vernon's been afraid of bees since he was a little boy,' Mrs. Masterson said.

'Vernon,' said Sam. 'I'm afraid of bees too. Scare me to death. I hate getting stung more than anything.'

The boy nodded.

'I need you to tell me where the bees are, so I don't get stung.'

The boy opened his mouth, then closed it. 'I'm sorry, sir. I can't tell.'

Mrs. Masterson looked at him. 'Vernon, you tell that man what he wants to know.'

Vernon's skin lost color and he shook his head. 'Mama, we could all get hurt if I tell about the place.'

'How would you get hurt?' Sam said. 'Did Mr. Caplan threaten you?'

'No, no, he's my friend, he takes care of me. He promised, he would never let the brown-faced man come and get me. If it wasn't for Mr. Caplan, the brown-faced man could come to my house. He does bad things to women. I don't want to say with Mama in the room. But Mr. Caplan told me all about it. And he said the brown-faced man saw me, and might find out where I live, 'cause this is such a small town. But Mr. Caplan told him he better leave me alone. So long as I don't go back out there, I should be safe. So I never go back there. Plus, that's where the bees are. You won't want to go out there either.'

'What kind of a place is it?' Sam asked.

Vernon shook his head.

'Will you tell me if I guess?' Sonora asked him.

His mother smiled at him. 'You could do that, Vernon. If she guessed.'

'It's a railroad car, isn't it, Vernon?'

Vernon looked at the floor. 'You're a good guesser ma'am.'

'Thank you.'

Chapter Seventy

The train was on a siding. Judging by the growth of weeds and scrub through the tracks, it had been there for years. It was an old coal engine, black, three wood boxcars behind. Sonora squinted. Looked like a caboose at the end, but the track curved and she could not be sure – the tree line had grown up, encroaching the siding. A car was parked back behind the weeds, around the hidden side of the train. Sonora could see a hint of chrome bumper.

She tugged at Sam's sleeve. 'Is that Caplan's car?'

'Hard to tell. Could be.'

The tracks were rusted. The engine black. Bits of coal were scattered in around the gravel.

The crickets were loud here. Sonora heard music, faint, but close. A thick orange extension cord, the outdoor utility kind, snaked from beneath the railroad cars. It ran across the tracks, and into a utility pole and box that was fenced in with chain-link.

So he had electricity.

It was gloomy out, not totally dark, plenty of moon. Sonora hoped Caplan was listening to the music, and not the sound of their footsteps in the gravel.

Vernon pointed, hand shaking. 'It's the brown-faced man.'

'Where?' Sam said. 'You see him?'

'No. But he lives in the other car. The one after this. He looks out the window.' Tears slid down Vernon's cheeks.

'We'll take care of your mom,' Smallwood said.

Sam shushed him. 'Listen. You hear that?'

Sonora heard sobs. 'You think it's Caplan, or Collie?'

'Can't tell.'

'We better move.'

Smallwood pointed. 'If you go through that car there, it looks empty, and it should connect. Come in on him through the train. I'll head around through the woods, and go up the back way. But I'll wait and give you guys some time. That sound okay?'

Sam nodded at him. They all looked at Vernon.

'You be all right, Vernon?' Sonora asked.

The boy nodded. His face was flushed and beaded with sweat. 'Be careful, ma'am.'

'We're going to get the brown-faced man, Vernon. We're going to make sure he never comes after your family. You stay here and hide. Don't come out till we come back for you.' Sonora looked at him. Would he stay put until the cavalry came?

The music got louder. 'Paint It Black' – classic Stones.

'We got to go,' Sonora said. She drew her gun, headed for the railroad car.

It had been painted red in its heyday. The metal step was well worn and so high off the ground she had to use the rail to get up. Sam's feet were noisy behind her. The music was louder here. Sonora listened, but could not hear voices or sobs.

It was dark inside, hot, the air heavy with the smell of dust and old steel. A rusty green sign lay on its side: JUNCTION CITY. The paint on the walls was coming away in curls, and lengths of lumber lay scattered all over the floor. Seats had been pulled out of their mooring, cushions shredded, tossed aside.

Sonora shone a flashlight, shielded by the top of her hand, and saw an arm beneath an overturned seat.

'*Jesus!* Sam.'

He turned and picked the arm up. 'Mannequin part.'

Sonora took a breath. She felt sweat running under her arms. They went down the center aisle to the back door.

'Boarded up.' Sam pulled at the wood. 'Recently, with good lumber. We're not getting in this way.'

They backtracked, climbed out of the car. Sonora stayed close to the train, metal against her blouse. It was full dark out now. In the next car, she could see light, and, through a window, a silhouette.

She moved closer. Her hand was shaking.

'The brown-faced man,' Sam said, in her ear.

The man was clearly visible, targeted by light from inside the car. He stood quietly, looking out the window. His face was dark and wooden looking, as if he'd been terribly scarred. He stood very still.

'You think he's seen us?' Sonora asked.

Sam tilted his head to one side. 'That sucker ain't real.'

Sonora looked back. The brown-faced man did not move or shift position. He wore a hat, a white shirt, and pants and a belt. 'Scarecrow?'

'Works. Look around, Sonora, you see any graffiti? Any beer cans or condoms? How come the local kids aren't out here, hanging out? Something is keeping them away.'

'How are we going to do this?'

'Right through the door. We got no other choice.'

The music got louder. Something about turning away from the darkness, then a driving beat. 'Paint It Black' again, playing over and over, like a CD on repeat. And, mixed in with the music, a man sobbing.

Sam looked at her. 'Let's get the hell in.'

They moved, feet noisy on the steps, Sam in front. He kicked the train door open and Sonora went in on his heels.

It took her a minute to take it all in.

She saw Caplan first, dressed for the office. He had shed the suit coat and rolled up his sleeves, but he still wore a tie, and it trailed across Collie's swollen belly as he bent over her, a firm hand on her shoulder, and looked into her face.

Collie was tied into the chair, hands behind her back. Sonora noticed her fingers, swollen and red. Her belly looked huge and she sagged against the ropes, eyes wide but unseeing, face tinged blue.

There was a plastic bag over Collie's head, pulled tight around her neck.

She wasn't struggling.

Sonora stared, hoping to make the image go away. They could not be too late. They could not just have missed her by minutes. She could not be dead.

'Watch him,' Sam yelled.

Caplan was on the move, headed her way. He shoved the scarecrow and the brown-faced man came crashing toward her. The boom box went sideways, and the music stopped.

She was aware, on some level, that Sam was with Collie, ripping the bag off her head, his mouth over hers, and one part of her mind was going *please, please, please*.

Caplan miscalculated, expecting her to dodge the scarecrow instead of run straight at it, and him. She grabbed the front of his shirt and threw her body into his. He lost his balance and his momentum and she slammed him hard into the wall. His meaty bulk cushioned Sonora from the blow. He looked surprised. She was surprised too. She pushed a hand against his chest and brought the gun up under his chin.

It was a short but oddly timeless moment when he decided whether or not to move and she decided whether or not to shoot.

'Gage Caplan . . .' she had to stop a minute, catch her breath. 'Gage Caplan, you are under arrest.'

Sweat ran in rivers down his face, mixing with tears. His shoulders shook. Laughing? Crying? Sonora could not tell. Dark rings of misery shadowed his eyes. He looked like a man in another time and another place. Sonora smelled him. She crammed him farther back to the wall and he stayed.

'You have the right to remain silent . . .'

He said the words with her, his lips barely moving, voice soft. The familiar litany had a weird calming effect on them both.

She took the plastic rings out of her pocket and fastened his hands together. He watched her, unflinching, as if he expected something, she did not know what.

He smiled at her, and the expression on his face was as hard to read as it was familiar. He raised his hands, tightly encased in the plastic rings, and dragged a finger across her cheek in a butterfly caress.

'I was just putting her back,' Caplan said, and looked down at her indulgently, almost fondly.

She studied him, watchful. 'I don't understand.'

Her own voice surprised her, so soft and so gentle while her heart pounded hard in her chest. She heard Sam, blowing air into Collie Caplan's lungs. The sound of crickets outside. Footsteps, someone moving in the next car. Smallwood on his way.

'Heartbeat,' Sam said.

More footsteps. Smallwood getting closer.

'Breathing,' Sam said. 'On her own.'

Sonora took a deep hard breath.

The expression on Caplan's face was radiant. 'I'm so glad. I don't mean to be like this.'

'I know,' Sonora said. She looked around for something he could use to wipe his tears.

Chapter Seventy-One

Smallwood put his head in the door, stopped suddenly, rocking forward on his toes. 'Everybody okay?'

'Under control,' Sonora said. It was good to see him. Sweat streaked from his temples and slicked his hair down wet. He smiled at her and came closer, close enough for her to see that his smile was shaky and he was white under the tan.

He looked down at Collie. 'How is she?'

'Breathing.'

'Is her baby okay?'

'I don't know,' Sam said. 'You want me to ask it? Where's Vernon?'

'Puking in the grass. He followed me into the car. I didn't know he was there till it was too late. You better come next door and take a look. This one's the screamer.'

Caplan chuckled softly.

Chapter Seventy-Two

Sonora sat rigid in her chair while the bailiff lowered the blinds in the courtroom. She had seen the tape more than once. She knew what to expect.

They did not turn out the lights, so she got to watch everybody's face, whether she wanted to or not.

Liza Harden and Butch Winchell sat side by side in the front of the room. Winchell had worn the same suit to court every day. Every day the suit seemed to get looser, and Winchell seemed to get smaller. They took no notice of Jeff Barber, who sat in the back right-hand corner, a small dark-haired woman by his side. She patted his shoulder at regular intervals.

The sister who cooked, Sonora thought.

The guy with the video camera had been a little shaky. The camera jigged up and down as he got used to the feel of what he was doing.

He had started with an outside shot of the railroad cars. The area was drenched in harsh, artificial light, and cordoned off with yellow police tape. The woods pressed in from all sides, shadowy, dark, echoing with the noise of disturbed insects. Background noises were muted – a humdrum mutter of men and women at work, the sound of footsteps on metal steps, people walking near the tracks, feet sliding in the gravel.

A moth darted in front of the lens, then veered out of range.

Sonora closed her eyes for just one minute and was back

in that railroad car. She glanced across the room at Caplan, every inch the pro. The look of polite interest on his face did not waver. She thought he was sweating under the weight of the expensive suit, but it might have been wishful thinking.

The camera took them up the metal steps, three of them, Sonora counted. Started with the car where Sonora and Sam had found Collie.

Caplan had given that car the VIP treatment, though Sonora hadn't noticed until she'd seen the tape for the first time. It was clean inside, no broken windows, no trash. A lamp from home, two comfortable chairs, a CD player.

The camera zoomed in on the brown-faced man, kicked into a corner. His hat had come off, revealing the tied-off opening at the top of his head. The courtroom went silent and tense. People watched and waited.

Everyone had been warned.

Sonora saw herself, just a flash, as she walked away from the camera. She looked hot on film, cheeks flushed, hair drenched with sweat. The camera caught a look of concentration on her face that could have been mistaken for anger.

Sweat lightly coated the palms of her hands. They were getting close. The camera would pan the overturned chair, the plastic bag Sam had ripped away from Collie Caplan's face. She waited for the close-up of the ropes, hanging loose from the back of the chair, severed clean by Sam's pocket knife.

A woman sobbed, then choked it back. Sonora turned and looked, like everyone else . . . Liza Harden was leaning forward in her chair, one arm wrapped around her middle as if her stomach hurt, the other entwined with Butch Winchell's elbow. They edged closer together, holding hands.

The camera moved into the next railroad car, caught a state police crime scene technician bending over the deep sink that Caplan had put in one corner. The technician looked up at the camera. He wore a jumpsuit and thick latex gloves with dark stains that were clearly blood. He stepped backward and out of the way, motioning the camera closer with the bloodstained gloves.

Caplan had no running water, just jugs of High Bridge Springs Mountain Water, stacked in a corner, so the sink was never properly cleaned.

The camera lingered over a clog in the drain. Hair and bone fragment, Sonora knew, glad that Liza Harden and Butch Winchell could see only an innocuous wad. She could not help what they might be imagining.

The camera pulled back, taking a wide view of three mannequins – two of them dressed with care and a certain expense. Wigs, shoes, makeup. One of the mannequins had short black hair and wore a skirt and a tiny pink sweater with pearl buttons that Dorrie Ainsley had positively identified as belonging to her daughter, Micah. The other had a long dark wig and wore khaki pants and a sleeveless denim shirt, thought to be the clothes Julia Winchell disappeared in. The other mannequin had not been dressed. It stood next to the others, bare and faceless.

The forensic psychologist had thought it was interesting that none of the mannequins had been made up to look pregnant.

Sonora saw a flash of movement, looked back over her shoulder. Jeff Barber was bailing out, the dark-haired girl at his heels.

She studied the jury. A woman in a black power suit looked from the screen to Caplan. He smiled at her and she looked away. The rest of them stared straight ahead. Most sat quietly in their seats. One shredded a tissue in her lap.

The camera was on the move again, swinging left to right across a table that was covered in plastic, focusing on a brand-new craftsman hacksaw that sat in the center of the table, price tag still on the handle. The camera did a swift pan, lingering a moment, as per Sonora's own instructions, on an open box of lawn and garden garbage bags that had been placed under the table. Terry had matched the garbage bag dredged up out of the Clinch River with the roll of bags in the box.

The camera veered upward suddenly, when the operator tripped, and everyone got an unexpected view of the cobwebs in the ceiling of the railroad car. The screen went fuzzy. Gradually the image sharpened as the focus was readjusted.

Gage Caplan had treated himself to a brand-new Kenmore deep freeze.

It was white. The lid was up. Water had made drip marks down the front, and there were smudges under the lip, in the center.

The camera zoomed in for a tight shot.

There was ice, bags and bags of it, lumped around the nude torso of a woman – positively identified as Julia Winchell. One slim arm, unattached and separately wrapped in clear plastic, lay beside the swell of frozen hip on the torso's left side, as if Caplan had not been able to part with it at the last minute.

Liza Harden wailed and Sonora bowed her head.

Chapter Seventy-Three

The judge had called a recess, the jury were excused. The press, excluded from the courtroom, waited in a thick writhing mass on the courthouse steps. Sonora headed for the basement niche she and Sam had discovered years ago. Not pretty, but peaceful.

They were talking death penalty. They had done it before in Cincinnati. They would do it again.

She felt a hand on her shoulder, and a force propelling her away from the crowd toward a deserted hallway.

'Molliter? What the hell do you think you're doing? Let go of my arm. I got a gun, I won't hesitate to shoot.'

'You did not get a gun past the metal detector, and even if you did, I've seen you at the shooting range, Sonora, and I'm not worried right here at point-blank range.'

He had a tight grip and it hurt. She dug in her heels and pushed him away. 'What are you going to do? Handcuff me in the men's room?'

'I've had enough bathroom conferences to last me a while, thanks just the same.'

She tried not to laugh. It was hard to hate someone when they made you laugh.

'Look, just walk up this hallway with me, okay? Nobody up there, and we can be private. I want to talk to you a minute. Come on, Sonora. Please.'

He hadn't squealed on her. 'Okay, Molliter, we can talk. But I've got some people to see so keep it short.'

He took her at her word, and she had to move to keep

up with him – he was tall and lanky and he took big steps. He turned a sharp corner.

'Here okay?'

Sonora nodded, rested her back against the wall. He turned sideways and shoved his hands in his pockets.

'How long were you stuck in the bathroom?' she asked him.

'Been dying of curiosity, haven't you?'

Sonora nodded.

Molliter rocked up and down on the balls of his feet. '*Hours.* Six, to be exact. The plumber found me.' He sighed. 'You have likely been wondering why I didn't go to Crick on this.'

'Nah, I just figured you liked it.'

'Sonora, I am trying to talk civilly to you.'

'Let's get something straight. You want to go running to Crick, you be my guest. Go now. Soon as word gets around you leaked confidential information to the DA's office, and assuming Crick doesn't kick your sorry ass out, you're going to start eating lunch alone. Better get used to it.'

'People talk back and forth all the time. This isn't a new thing.'

'It's always new when you get caught.'

His breathing picked up, quick and shallow. 'You have to understand.'

'You know what, Molliter? You couldn't have picked a poorer choice of words. Anytime anybody has ever said that to me, "you have to understand," it means they've pulled some major shit.'

'You listen to me, Sonora. I worked vice and I worked personal crime. Years of it, day in and day out, guys plea-bargaining, getting off for lack of evidence, sometimes the same guys, over and over. And then Caplan comes along. This guy is *hungry* and he likes the chase. He goes after child molesters and rapists and pimps – not the girls, Sonora, the pimps. Goes to court on a date rape, when he didn't have a prayer of getting a conviction, but he did it anyway, because he wanted to try. Do you know how rare that is? Do you know how rare it is for a man to be so committed he risks his career for the sake of doing a little good in the world?'

'He had ego, Molliter, not morals.'

'So what, if that's what it takes?'

'Well, Molliter, there's just a small problem with this guy's favorite form of recreation.'

'I'm just trying to make you understand why I did what I did.'

'Understand? Meet Collie and Mia Caplan and give me "understand." See a pregnant woman tied up in a shitty railroad car, turning blue with a plastic bag over her head. Give me "understand."'

'I'm as sorry as I know how to be. I have prayed over this, and I'm here to try and make things right. The woman is still alive.'

'No thanks to you.'

'What are you going to do, Sonora?'

'Me? Not a damn thing. I had a problem, I took care of it. Crick isn't stupid. Anything further comes from him.'

'He . . . we've had a sort of talk. I think I'm in the clear there.'

'Good for you. God looks after assholes.'

'I said I was sorry.'

'You don't get it, Molliter. Some things you don't get to do, because sometimes "sorry" doesn't cut it. Forgiveness may be divine, Molliter, but it's a separate issue.'

He took it, stared at her, hands in pockets.

Sonora was never very good at silence. 'So what now, Molliter? You holding your temper, counting to ten?'

'Let me put it to you this way. Am I going to be eating lunch alone? When I call for backup, is anybody coming? They going to drag their feet getting there?'

Sonora folded her arms. 'I see, this is all about you. You

know, Molliter, I have never been able to stand you, but you used to be a good cop.'

'I have a wife and kids and I'm still a good cop.'

'Fine. I'm not going to gossip about you at the coffee machine, and I'm still going to watch your back. Those the words you needed to hear?'

'Yes. Thank you very much.'

She didn't say anything.

'I try very hard to be a good person.'

'I've given you everything you're going to get, Molliter. There's not going to be any seal of approval.'

'I'd like to try and see if we can be friends again, sometime in the future.'

'Look, Molliter, we never were friends. I'd like to go all warm and fuzzy with you, but the truth is, it's not going to happen.'

He nodded. 'Okay. I'm sorry, but I thought I was right. Maybe someday you'll forgive me and we can be friends. I'm willing to wait for that day.'

'You still don't get it, and you never will.'

Chapter Seventy-Four

Sonora figured on a high probability that Liza Harden and Butch Winchell would be hiding out in the basement – she had shown them the spot on that first day in court. She rounded the corner, heard voices.

The basement room had been some unfortunate's office at one time or another, and there was still a metal desk, a couple of padded chairs, and a bookcase with dust-enveloped law books. A tiny grilled window at the top of the room sat at street level, emphasizing the feeling of being down in a hole.

Liza Harden was sitting on the corner of the desk, Butch Winchell looking out the window.

'How's it going?' Sonora asked, pausing in the doorway.

They turned and looked, furtive and jumpy.

Liza had been crying. Her mascara made streaks of black down her face. Someone had brought in a box of tissues, and little white clumps were scattered across the desk. Winchell had a glazed look. The skin of his face sagged with rapid weight loss. Whatever he had lost, Liza had gained. Her face looked bloated, unhealthy, neck puffy.

They would get better, Sonora thought. This was the bad time.

'I came down to check on you. Do either of you need anything? Coffee, something to eat?'

'We don't eat,' Butch said.

Sonora believed him.

Liza slid off the desk and grabbed Sonora's hand. 'How do you think it's going?'

Sonora smiled at her gently. 'It's going as well as it can.'

'Collie . . . Mrs. Caplan. She hasn't been here the last two days. Is she okay?'

'She's fine. She only comes if she has to. She's got a baby to nurse.'

Collie had delivered a seven-pound baby boy, early but healthy, several hours after Sam had brought her around. She had named him Grey, for Mia's grandfather. She and Mia were staying with Grey and Dorrie, and thinking about moving to London permanently after the trial.

'Do you think he'll get the death penalty?' Winchell asked. His voice held very little inflection. It rarely did these days – Sonora had noticed that about him.

'I have my fingers crossed, Mr. Winchell.'

Liza looked at her. 'You were there. You . . . saw it.'

'Ms. Harden, your sister, Julia, died in a matter of minutes. Anything that happened after that – she was long gone. Hold on to that.'

They seemed riveted by her words and she looked into their faces and thought, as she had before, that no one had yet come up with the right configuration of words to handle these things.

'I have something for both of you.'

She saw it in their eyes, a sort of desperate hope, as if she could give them something to make it all better, as if she could give them the only thing they wanted, which was Julia, back home again, safe and sound.

That was the problem, working homicide. Nobody came home safe and sound.

Sonora handed them each a brown envelope. 'I'm giving each of you a copy of the tape Julia made a few days before she died. They'll be playing it in court sometime this week. She's talking about the murder, getting her thoughts down. I wish it was something else, like her telling you the things she would have said if she'd known what was going to happen, but this is all I've got. Listen to it, keep it for later, throw it away. Whatever you need. Just don't tell anybody where you got it.'

'I won't be able to play it without crying,' Liza said.

Sonora nodded. 'That's allowed.'

Butch Winchell fingered the edge of the envelope, as if he couldn't wait. 'I'll play this for the girls when they grow up.'

'You do that.'

Sonora shook each of their hands and headed back to the courtroom. At the least, Julia Winchell's daughters would have the gift of their mother's voice.

It was a small thing, but it was all she had.